Tammie Rothermel

To Becky & Jim,
Dear friends from

NEVERMORE?

the early days.
My best always,

Tammie
Rothermel

Stonehome Publishing, Inc.

Requests for such permission should be addressed to:
Stonehome Publishing, Inc.
P. O. Box 117899
Fountain Hills, AZ 85269

Rothermel, Tammie
        Nevermore?

Cover Design: CatHouse Productions
Layout: J. L. Saloff
Fonts: Book Antiqua, Daddy-O Crazy

10-digit ISBN: 0-9776216-0-X
13-digit ISBN: 978-0-9776216-0-6

LCCN: 2006903628
Copyright information available upon request.

First Edition

        Printed on acid-free paper in The United States of America.

Dedicated:

To God in thanksgiving.

To my loving husband Jerry
for all his encouragement and understanding.

Extraordinary transformation

steals in on the back of small, inconsequential moments.

Chapter 1

Moments

Nestled in a wide hollow within the virgin woods of the Oley Valley, a pristine white clapboard farmhouse with forest green shutters sat insulated from the world. A herringbone redbrick drive curved through the thickets down to the seven-acre farmstead called *Creekside*. White-board paddock fencing cordoned off the property from the bluestone cindered lane out front. Amid these rolling hills, covered bridges and lush woodlands, steadfast German traditions temper every aspect of life.

Richard Moore, a precious stones merchant originally from England, and Fran, an idealistic American graduate of political science, found the rural hills of Pennsylvania a perfect compromise in which to raise their daughter. From the beginning, they raised Nicole to be a self-thinker — with beliefs grounded in God and Dutch values. They taught Nicole to examine the facts and to educate herself on her positions. Nightly they served up healthy discussions of politics, religion or ethics along with dinner. In those spirited debates, her parents forged her core beliefs. But sometimes Nicole's hot little temper, her flair for the melodramatic or her innate trusting naiveté trumped their lessons in common sense and logic.

Saturday, March 7, 1964, offered nothing special, just the portend of a bountiful spring bursting through the winter-dry brush surrounding the man-made lake where Nicole often took up sanctuary. An ordinary teen, giddy one moment, absorbed-to-the-hilt the next, Nicole often rode her horse, Thunder, down to the lake with Beau, her Golden Retriever, in tow. There she pondered life, daring to dream of turning her Sunday morning and high school choir experience into a singing career. Often she blest the shimmering water and sentinel forest with her crystal voice.

That morning vacillated between crisp sunshine and threats of rain from steel-blue clouds. The stiff wind that changed the face of the sky tangled Nicole's long, ebony hair and whistled through the empty tree limbs, obscuring the sounds of a car door slamming and a man tromping through the brittle weeds. He wore dark glasses and a hat with lures on it, pulled low on his forehead, to the top of his shades. Collar-length, brown hair hung out from underneath the hat. He kept his focus down, as he picked his way toward the lake.

Sensing impending danger, Beau grew anxious with the first sounds of the intruder. Thunder pawed and neighed. Immersed in thought,

Nicole dismissed their warnings. As the stranger neared, Beau accelerated his nervous pacing. His clatter masked the crack of the grass behind her. Finally standing up to quell her restless troops, she came face to face with the man. They startled each other. From low in his throat, Beau growled his warning. Nicole's heart pounded. She didn't shush Beau; she made the stranger disclose his intentions first.

"Oh, sorry Miss. I-I didn't mean to scare you." Obviously flustered, he picked up the rod and tackle he dropped in the commotion. "I'm just here to do a spot of fishing. Mind if I take up a seat over there?" He gestured to a place about a hundred feet away.

"No, of course not," Nicole lied. She minded. This was her lake, and she wasn't used to sharing. Returning to her spot, Nicole tried to re-capture her reverie of the day, but he continued to creep into her focus. Intense curiosity filled her bright turquoise eyes. She wondered about him.

Still intent on the interloper, Beau warily circled him, sniffing the air. No doubt the Golden's actions unnerved the man. Unwrapping a roll from his tackle box, the stranger offered peace.

Seizing the opportunity of her dog's rude behavior, Nicole advanced her investigation. "Beau, leave the man alone. He's here to fish. Come on." She tugged on his collar, but Beau strained against her, sniffing the offering. "No. That's not polite!"

"Really. He's okay. Is he friendly? I haven't been 'round a dog in so long. Can he stay, then?" An English accent crept out as the stranger's spoke.

"You're British? Your accent sounds similar to my father's. He's a Brit. Well he was a Brit. I mean he still sounds British…"

"Yeah? I'm here on business and needed a bit of time on my own. What about you?"

"Oh, we live down the road a mile or so. By the way, I'm Nicole Moore," the sixteen-year-old stuck out her hand.

"Oh, I'm a … G…G … Gordon," he lied, but what did it matter. Innocently enough, the interloper invited Nicole to sit. Over conversation, he shyly removed the hat and glasses, exposing his soft, warm, brown eyes and angular, thin face. Nicole guessed him to be in his early twenties. Her mind calculated the age difference. Summoning all the feminine wiles available to her, she monitored her speech and mannerisms to bridge the age chasm.

Each passing moment deepened Nicole's intrigue and mounting infatuation with the stranger. The attentions of an "older man," particu-larly one with an accent, easily turned her adolescent head. After the

British invasion of the Merseymen, the Beatles, the Stones, accents — anything from across the Pond — sent giggly girls into a delirium. Something about Gordon seemed familiar. But making a determination about him eluded Nicole, since he intentionally avoided all of her personal questions.

As much as Gordon set Nicole's head spinning, this quick, attractive "bird" with raven hair catching on her pert, little breasts and mesmerizing turquoise eyes, who hadn't recognized him as one of the Merseymen, arrested his attention. Had he actually managed to snag the attention of such a beauty, without her swooning at his feet because he happened to be Grant Henderson, lead guitarist of the internationally celebrated rock group? Had he found the one bird who fancied him for himself, not his fame? Definitely, this engaging chick ignited his interest.

And didn't he deserve it? He had survived the arduous, six-year, hammer and tong claw to the top of the music heap. And once on top, for these long years, he conformed to the pressurized life inside the whirl-wind of fame. Celebrity wasn't all adulation: different dollies nightly in the sack, and great, obscene gobs of money. Intense fame, such as the Merseymen had mined, exacted a price. It held them hostage inside hotel rooms — endless, faceless, same cities where nothing changed other than the names at the bottom of the ashtrays — sweltering rooms full of glaring, hot lights teemed with brash reporters who asked the same insipid questions, then expected fresh, alive answers. And where your family of band-mates, managers and roadies never went away, were always in your face day-after-day, hour-after-hour, for months on end, and no one outside that circle could be trusted.

Played out and spent after the grueling years, Grant Henderson had cracked, abandoning his bandmates in Philadelphia. Driving into the countryside, he wanted to breathe the breath of freedom. He never expected — never wanted — an entanglement. But that's exactly what he found in that small, inconsequential moment when he met Nicole Moore, and she didn't recognize him.

The interloper had penetrated the sanctity of the Moore's sheltered existence.

Chapter 2

Decisions

Grant Henderson returned to the Merseymen in time for their concert in Philadelphia. But not before promising Nicole he'd be back for another rendezvous the following day.

The idea of Nicole not recognizing him and treating him like an average person absorbed him. He wanted to explore possibilities of a relationship with her. He might actually have pulled off seeing how a relationship outside his fame worked, if he had fostered his deception over the course of a few months. But inside Grant's tornado of compressed time, he knew he felt safe with this girl; he liked her. He wanted a relationship—for him the decision was made. He returned to the lake and Nicole to confess his true identity and asked her to consider a liaison.

Picking up her hands, Grant looked straight into her heart. "I couldn't stop thinking about you last night. Hell, I couldn't remember all the words to our bleedin' songs—because I kept seeing you—yer face, yer hair, yer words—you." A curl of a smile tugged at his soft, smooth lips.

"Me?" His words danced through Nicole's heart, hanging stars in her eyes.

But in erasing Gordon and revealing himself as Grant Henderson, the superstar poisoned his entire supposition. In rushing the process, Grant succeeded in doing the opposite of what he had wanted. He enticed her with the fairytale—being carried off by a prince of the white-hot, Rock and Roll kingdom! How could she want anything else? Then he sealed their agreement with a deep, reaching-down-to-her-toes kiss—her first ever.

He left Nicole standing in the dust from his rented red sportster, holding onto his Mary Quant black leather driving cap. Grant Henderson pursued Nicole relentlessly over the next four weeks. Vases of shell-pink roses arrived weekly. An invasion of teddy bears filled her room. Nightly from the tour he phoned her for hours.

Without a boy camping on their doorstep, complacently Richard and Fran winked at the attention, reducing it to a harmless, long-distance infatuation. They might have been able to battle the intrusion—after all age was an issue—Grant was 22 and she was 16—but in trying to protect Grant's notoriety, Nicole hid his actual identity from them.

Then tickets to Los Angeles for the Merseymen's closing concert of their U.S. tour arrived. Alarmed that this had grown into more than a hormone-driven crush of some pimply-faced neighborhood kid, Richard demanded a full reckoning. Nicole confessed everything starting with their innocent meeting at the lake and concluded with an under-her-breath comment about the age difference.

The age disparity sent the Moores over the edge. They agreed to the trip only on the condition that Nicole confess her age to Henderson. After all, what would an experienced 22-year-old want with a teenager?

In her nightly conversation with him, Nicole dressed up the fatal news in high-heels and lipstick. "I'll be seventeen in four months. My birthday's in July."

Stunned silence robbed Grant of his voice. His hesitation stalled Nicole's heart. She fully expected to hear the click of his receiver.

Recovering, Grant asked, "How much of a difference does it make to you?"

"It doesn't matter to me," a startled Nicole answered.

"I know it probably looks bad, but it doesn't change my feelings for you. If I have to wait ... I will. But, I need you now. Come to L.A. an' see for yerself what all the madness is about."

Romeo and Juliet may have thrown the age issue to the wind, but it concerned Richard and Fran Moore and the Merseymen's manager, Bruce Eckstein. After talking, the adults on both sides agreed to an L.A. meeting.

Los Angeles loomed large before the family. Reluctantly the Moores boarded the plane hoping their daughter would discover only a one-sided, schoolgirl infatuation. Nicole went intent on solidifying a relationship which she believed held the answers to her future. Riding in respectful silence, each side nurtured its own expectations. A nervous Eckstein waited for them in L.A., hoping to quash the relationship before it leaked into the press and he had another mess to clean up, or before the Moores publicly filed charges for trifling with a minor.

They had no idea of the inexorable force waiting for them. The entire pop/rock scene played out in all its insane, glitzy glory before the un-indoctrinated eyes of the threesome from rural Pennsylvania. First hand they experienced the throng of hundreds choking the entrance of the hotel. From the Merseymen's penthouse suite, they heard the delirium rise up from the street whenever one of them moved a curtain at the window. They suffered through the wall-to-wall screams at the concert obliterating the group's music and singing. And because they had been sucked into the Merseymen's world, for their own safety they were subjected to the extreme cloak-and-dagger security needed to protect everyone.

Richard and Fran understood and acknowledged the negatives of celebrity. However, with her introduction to the promoter's opulent soiree, Nicole personally tasted fame's backhand. She knew about the wrap parties following a concert, where the promoters schmoozed the local dignitaries with their chance to "see and be seen." She knew the L.A. tour-closing bash would put Oscar Night to shame. And Nicole couldn't wait to experience it all from her special position on Grant's arm.

Just before leaving for the concert and its attending festivities, in the only few seconds of alone-time they had, Grant struggled with a request. "'Bout this party gig later. The record big wigs will be there an' the band has to kiss up. I need you to kind of... ah... ah...be there, but...a...stand on your own. Get it?"

"Like we don't know each other?" Nicole questioned.

"Yes. No. I mean…sort of. ... Damn, can't you just wing it?" Grant wrestled with her inexperience to his routine.

" 'member Ben, the bloke who works with sound that I introduced you to? He'll be there to take care of you." Grant tried to be patient.

Nicole nodded. "But, will I ever get to see you?"

"Sure. I promise, Babe." He flipped her his answer. "After the party…"

A roadie interrupted, dropping off a garment bag containing her cover for the evening.

Crushed by Grant's request, back in her parent's hotel suite Nicole collapsed on her bed. Tearfully, she totaled up the mounting disappointments Grant's notoriety forced her to swallow.

Her tears brought her father to her bedside. Not about to indulge her, he spoke with quiet authority. "Pretty tough welcome, huh? This is the adult world — Grant's world. He brought you here to see it. They don't do this just for a weekend, just for a lark. This is their 'butter and eggs' and it's for keeps. In asking you to be his girlfriend, Grant wants you to make a decision — an adult decision. The decisions you make on this side of the fence will have far-reaching and permanent consequences. This is all coming sooner than we wanted or envisioned for you. There may be only five years difference between your age and Grant's, but at this stage of your life, it's a world of separation. Just remember, you have a choice. You've been thrown into the deep end of the pool. You'll either sink, swim … or get out all together. It's up to you."

Wallowing in self-pity, Nicole lay there pitting Grant's request against her father's words. When, from somewhere deep inside, she felt a stirring. Grit and determination welled up, forcing her to her feet. "Enough of this!" She scolded herself. "Tears aren't going to change things. And they certainly aren't going to help me make a decision. If Grant Henderson wants an adult, then he'll get an adult." With confident defiance, Nicole marched into the bathroom to prepare.

Nicole recognized the look packaged inside the bag as that of the London model. Better-heeled Brits derided them as "dollies," one step up from hookers. Her get-up included a long, straight, pale-blond wig; black leather mini skirt; neon-yellow, blousy shirt with matching tights; knee-high, high-heeled leather boots; gaudy chunky jewelry; and huge, black plastic rimmed, saucer glasses. Nicole completed the disguise by donning Grant's leather driving cap.

The dolly bird persona also dictated a specific style of make-up. Washing her fresh face down the drain, Nicole applied the required milky foundation, then painted on the exaggerated upper and lower lashes, adding large amounts of shadow and coloring in her cheek line. Pale pink lipstick finished the package. She didn't recognize her image in the mirror. But that was the point. When the manufactured model emerged from the bath, Fran practically fell back in her chair. Weak-kneed, Richard sat down.

Sophisticated beyond her years, Nicole sauntered through the decadent party on Ben's arm. Although when a waiter pressed a champagne glass into Nicole's hand, Ben neatly replaced it with a glass of Pepsi. Ben pointed out the notables of the business. Each category of attendee had donned their appropriate uniform for the event. The all-powerful Label executives and producers wore Brooks Brother's. The movie stars, starlets, wannabes and has-beens sparkled in their evening attire, while the moths of the press milled at the door. An array of groupies and hangers-on came in various states of undress. Nicole assumed them to be the hired escorts. They draped themselves over any unaccompanied celebrity, either for the moment or the evening.

Once outside the glare of the spotlights or the view of the Label's suits, like a coach Ben sent Nicole into the action at Grant's side. Then Grant got to pick up Nicole's hand or squeeze her close. Nicole watched carefully and learned.

Finally at three in the morning, drained of the exuberance of the day, Nicole and Grant came together, alone for the first time since their encounter at the lake. Huddled in the vacant stairwell just below the Merseymen's penthouse suite, they found enough solitude for conversation. Ben stood guard. For two hours, they discussed everything Nicole had witnessed over the past eighteen hours.

"What yer saw today is our world in the extreme, all the way 'round. The concert of a 100,000 people and the fancy producer shindig aren't typical. But some version of it plays out in every city, after every gig. Yer know it. Yer read 'bout it in the rags. Yer hear it on the phone." Exhaustion permitted Grant honesty.

But Nicole's fear of challenging reality, and possibly losing her prince kept her from asking about the girls and the groupies. Instead she substituted, "What happens to me if I come along?"

"Our life—this life—becomes yours." Tenderly Grant kissed her hand. "We'll still have to keep you a secret, but I'll be there for ya. We'll be together for each other, even if it 'tis long distance. So how about it, then? Do you have my answer for me, luv?"

Nicole picked up the gauntlet Grant threw down, changing forever whatever destiny might have been hers. "You can count on me."

The Merseymen returned to London to start work on their first film as Nicole returned to her junior year at Oley Valley High School. But the solidification of their relationship only intensified Grant's focus. In June, timed to coincide with the end of her school year, first-class tickets to London arrived for Nicole and her parents. Fame had skewed his outlook of life. At 22, Grant Henderson had become accustomed to getting whatever he wanted. The two-week trip set up his actual objective; he wanted Nicole on their summer tour with them.

Loud and long protests from her parents and Bruce Eckstein followed his proposal. Grant, however, anticipated all of them. Fran would accompany Nicole. They would travel apart from the Merseymen and become their Managers of Internal Tour Relations. As such Fran and Nicole would scout out in advance the various tour venues and bring the outside world back to the group. Then employing disguises, they would either smuggle the boys out or the outside factions in. Since summer was Richard's busy traveling season anyway, he sacrificed his wife's time for his daughter's extensive geography lesson.

By rearranging some meetings, Richard intercepted the tour in Amsterdam on July 19th, Nicole's seventeenth birthday. Turning the family reunion to his advantage, Grant used the occasion to ask Nicole to marry him. Quickly, he followed his proposal with the promise they wouldn't marry until the following fall, well after Nicole had reached eighteen. Rather than a diamond, Grant slipped a ruby ring onto Nicole's right hand, because their engagement had to be a secret.

At the end of summer though, returning to the horse-and-buggy-paced life of the Oley Valley didn't hold the same excitement for Nicole it once did. High-school sock-hops and Senior sleepovers couldn't compare to riding a comet across Europe. Listening to her friends prattle and coo over the latest teen mag's accounts of the Merseymen drove Nicole insane. She hated those magazines with their pages crammed full of awful pictures — pictures of beautiful, lean-bodied models hanging all over Grant. Oh, how those hurt!

Refusing to corral her spirit with moping, Nicole's lightning-in-a-jar enthusiasm propelled her. She kept busy, kept moving, with football games, school choir and endless homework.

Half way around the world, things weren't going well for the Merseymen. Without Nicole's diversions, the tour had begun to grind. The group's press conferences lacked their spontaneous sparkle and noto-riously biting wit. Already the cancer of low morale generated havoc for the tour.

In desperation, their manager phoned Richard and Fran. Frankly, the Moores could have cared less. After the summer, they figured they had contributed quite enough to the espirit de corp of Henderson and his group. They weren't about to sacrifice Nicole's final year in school just to solve Eckstein's morale problem. While the Moores would rather not have indulged the relationship, they knew stopping it would have been as futile as halting a speeding freight train.

Bruce played his trump card by raising the specter of elopement. As he quickly reminded them, if pushed too far, it would be only a question of time before Grant seized upon that tempting solution. Both sides conceded it would be far better to control the situation rather than leave it to Grant's inevitable resourcefulness. Bruce offered Nicole a permanent position as the Merseymen's Manager of Internal Tour Relations, complete with a salary.

The Moores countered with their own rigid demands: that Nicole complete her education and that she have a chaperone to ensure Grant didn't get carried away or worse yet, their daughter wouldn't become sexual fodder for the cadre who inhabited the music industry. Bruce concurred. The arrangement between the two factions infamously became known as "The Agreement."

Accommodating the Moores' concerns, Bruce agreed to pay for a tutor/chaperone. Although the Moores were free to hire anyone, Eckstein highly recommended Ben's sister, Mary McDonough. She had grown up in the same area, knew the group and conveniently lived in Virginia at William and Mary where she taught English as a graduate assistant.

The following Wednesday a woman in her mid-twenties, of medium build, with shoulder-length, chestnut hair caught at the neck in a band, wearing comfortable shoes, arrived. Richard took time off work to interview her. Curiosity, snapping in Nicole's bright eyes, drew her to her father's study door long enough for her to check out the stranger in the house before grabbing a kiss from her mom and dad, then popping out to catch her bus to school.

Over the course of the day, Richard and Fran interviewed several other candidates but called Mary back to offer her the position. Bruce's allotted salary nearly knocked Mary out of her chair. To that, the Moores themselves added an additional five hundred dollars a month, an outstanding sum, to personally ensure Mary's adherence to their morality code and guarantee her loyalty to their daughter.

A gust of energy swept Nicole home from school slightly after three. Her innate commanding presence preceded her into the house. A flash, she dashed into the kitchen calling for her parents, happily dispensing news of her day as she hunted an audience to listen to her.

A tense, "in here," from Richard brought her to the study, where her parents' anxieties over the impending discussion deadened the air.

Reading the ominous room, Nicole instantly stilled her natural sparkle. Her clear alabaster skin paled. "What's going on, Daddy? Mommy?" she asked with trepidation. Dread kept her from asking about the woman stranger in the room.

"Have a seat, Nicole. We need to talk." Richard waved her into a chair.

Nicole slid her tall, willowy frame into one of the leather wingback chairs. Gripping the chair arms, she strapped herself in for a bumpy ride. "Did someone die?"

"No. We need to discuss some things with you. It's about your future, Nicole," her mother answered. "We're concerned because at your age, decisions you make can affect your whole life. Today, we're going to present you with one of those decisions."

Nicole's clench tightened on the chair, turning her knuckles an anxious white.

"Bruce called us several nights ago," her father began tautly. "He's offered you a position with the group performing the same type of duties you handled over the summer. If you accept, you'll have to give up your last year here in school. A tutor will be arranged for you. You'd tour with The Merseymen and would come home when they have holiday."

A wave of relief washed over her. That was the bad news? Bruce wanted her back on tour?! Only her parents' sober faces tamped down her euphoria. For their sake, she dutifully maintained a thoughtful, rational façade.

Her mom pushed her slant on the topic. "You've already done the road thing. This will be your last year in school with your friends before everyone scatters on their different paths. If you go, you'll miss the football games, the plays, the dances, everything. Those experiences will be gone forever. They will never come again. We don't want your answer right away. Think about all the consequences."

Her father interrupted, "We want you to spend some serious time weighing out this matter. Your decision will be forever. Think about it carefully. Take as long as you need." With that they dismissed Nicole.

On her way out, she turned back to them. "What does Grant say?"

"He doesn't know anything about it, so there's no pressure. This is your decision, and yours alone," her father replied.

In Nicole's absence, Mary and the Moores forced polite conversation as Nicole's parents struggled with the inevitable. Richard wasn't sure how long Nicole's decision would take. He was about to excuse Mary when Nicole reappeared in the doorway.

While her face reflected sobriety, her eyes betrayed unbridled joy. "I want to take the job."

Her dad challenged her. "And the logic behind your decision was...?"

"I'll only get one chance for a break like this. I want to take it."

"Did Grant or what he'd think influence you decision?" Fran asked.

"Well, I tried not to think about him," she answered truthfully. "It'll be great to be with him everyday. But that will happen anyway when we get married next fall. You know I've always wanted to perform. But I don't want to use my relationship with Grant to achieve that goal. With this job, if I work hard behind the scenes, maybe I'll get my chance. At least my foot will be in the door."

Dabbing her eyes with a tissue, Fran gestured toward Mary. "Then Nicole, meet Mary McDonough. She'll be your tutor and your chaperone."

Before the two could really make a connection, Richard got down to business. "Nicole, you need to notify Bruce of your decision. He'll discuss a salary with you. Your mother and I feel a salary is important. It'll keep your position on a business level and afford you independence should the personal relationship sour. Under these circumstances, we don't want you to have to depend on Grant for money. Remember, whatever happens, we are always here for you." They may have regretted the timing of this decision for Nicole, but they knew they had raised a strong, independent young woman. Picking up Fran's hand, Richard escorted his wife from the study.

A variety of emotions paraded across Nicole's face as she talked with Bruce—surprise, thoughtfulness, giddy glee. The $800 a month salary wowed her. Her part-time job at the local ice cream shop only netted her thirty a week. Finally coming up for air, one of Bruce's questions drew her up short. Surprised, she turned the phone over to Mary. "Bruce wants to talk to you! … Do you know him?"

Affirming their relationship with a smile, Mary then addressed Bruce on the phone. "Yes, Bruce, we've met. I suppose we'll go to the school tomorrow. Saturday? In Detroit? Yes, we can be there. Sure. Ta ta for now." And she rang off.

Since the pair had only five days to prepare for months on the road, by tacit mutual assent they put off further pleasantries until they accomplished the mountain of arrangements needed to meet the tour's schedule. From behind her winning smile, several times Mary caught Nicole summing her up. Would Mary be an iron-fisted warden or her ally?

The following morning after reviewing the tutor's credentials, the vice-principal withdrew Nicole from her classes. They equipped Mary with Nicole's course specifications, textbooks and reporting guidelines. By noon Nicole Moore exited the doors of the Oley Valley High School for the last time.

Mary and Nicole spent the few remaining days packing. Returning to Virginia, Mary organized everything according to seasons, packing in terms of trunks, not suitcases, then shipped them on ahead to their destination in Detroit. Meanwhile, Nicole did the same. On Saturday morning they met up in the Moores' driveway as a cool, fall wind blew into town.

Wearing cheery faces, Fran and Richard bravely dispatched their daughter, without lingering over their adieus. Just a brief hug and an "I love you," before the van ferried Nicole and Mary up and out the lane. Momentary apprehension over her monumental decision tugged at Nicole's heart as *Creekside* disappeared in the distance.

Once comfortably seated on the plane in first class, Nicole leaned over with her Pepsi for a toast. "Here's to a successful and enduring relationship, Mary." Hope radiated in her clear eyes. "Now maybe we can get acquainted."

Eagerness to make a connection arced inside her. Rather than chew up time with trivia, Nicole reversed Mary's earlier notion of the teen's self-absorption by genuinely engaging her. "So who are you, Mary

McDonough? And how does being stuck with me fit into your scheme of life?"

This glimpse of maturity both astonished and captivated Mary. She assured Nicole "stuck" wasn't the correct terminology. After answering thoroughly, Mary returned the focus to Nicole. She really wanted to get to know her charge.

Nicole exuberantly romped through her early memories of her parents, home life and school, stopping to highlight her ambitions in music. The energy in her smile reflected her jubilant embrace of life. Her relationship with Grant lit her up. In a serious moment though, she confided her reasons for joining the group. "I really tried to let the gravity of the decision control me. But no matter how hard I enhanced the arguments for staying, the scale tipped overwhelmingly towards going and being an adult. Oh Mary, this will be a real job—maybe even a stepping-stone to a singing career. This could open the door to something big. And, such an opportunity will surely disappear if I turn it down."

Unexpectedly Nicole, in a sober blink of her eyes, stopped abruptly. "Of course I realize that traveling with Grant will cement my chances of actually becoming Mrs. Grant Henderson. It will be harder for any of those flaming groupies or models to get their claws into my fiancée when I'm there to protect my territory. If I don't go, Mary, you know, I might lose him."

Whether she meant to or not, despite her exuberant exterior, in that fleeting instant Nicole exposed her vulnerable side to Mary. In addition to a chaperone, Nicole needed someone to see her through all the confusing firsts in a maturing girl's life. It was then, beyond Bruce's handsome salary, the Moore's allotment, or "The Agreement," Mary signed on in her heart to be Nicole's loyal confidant.

Chapter 3
The Road Ahead

Touching down in Detroit in the early afternoon, Ben met them at the airport.

Nicole leapt off the air-stairs into his arms. "Ben! How great to see you. Did you hear the news? I'm here for good. C'mon there's someone I want you to meet."

Oblivious to their sibling relationship, Nicole led him over to Mary. "I want you to meet my ol' bud Ben. He kept me company at that big promoter party in L.A. and gave me the low down on everybody there. Then he helped mom and me pull off some great escapades over the summer."

"Hey, Sis," Ben enfolded Mary in a brotherly hug. "Congrats on the job," he said as he jerked a familiar nod in Nicole's direction.

Amazement dropped Nicole's jaw. "You're...

"...brother and sister. Sorry, we never got 'round to it. Do you mind terribly?" Mary inserted.

Nicole welcomed the relationship. "Cool! My new roommate is my pal's sister."

The three of them set to scheming how to pull off Nicole's surprise arrival. A first-class instigator in her own right, Nicole dreamed up an outrageous plan. To carry out the scheme Ben secured a pair of roadie coveralls and hat for her. Once dressed, Nicole tucked her hair up inside the hat. During the Merseymen's afternoon sound check in front of Bruce and a full crew, she bumbled her way onto stage. Keeping her face hidden by pulling the cap down low, she fixed her eyes on the floor.

Wham! She backed into Richie's drums.

Bang! She struck the strings on Pete's guitar.

Crash! A few guitar stands went flying.

Still focused on practice, the Merseymen muttered their complaints. But the more Nicole bungled, the louder and ruder their complaints grew.

Their increased complaining only worsened her fumbling. Finally, she got physical with them. Ricocheting off Jack, she careened into Pete. Backing up, she slammed into Grant.

Grabbing the errant roadie, Grant spun him around, giving him a good shake. "You bleeding loon, stop that! Get the hell off the stage!"

His forceful wrenching shook off Nicole's cap, releasing her hair.

Swinging her head around, coming up face-to-face with Grant. Nicole beamed at him. "Surprise!"

From their seats in the audience, Bruce and his assistants rocked with laughter. The realization finally dawned on Grant and his bandmates.

Grinning, Grant grabbed up Nicole in his arms. The others rushed over to congratulate her on the good joke. Never ones to miss a chance to party, Nicole's arrival demanded a celebration.

Settling back into their dressing rooms, Pete pried, "So you missed us, eh?"

"Come for a bit of a visit, did ya?" from Jack.

"Actually I'm here for good," Nicole bubbled.

Incredulous, Grant asked, "What do you mean for good?"

Bruce stepped in with the explanation, "You blokes were so down in the mouth, I figured we could all use a good giggle. We had a great go this summer, so I brought her back."

In a boisterous hoot, the group made themselves a party. Pete called for food. Jack played bartender. Cheerfully pulling Nicole onto his lap, Richie hauled out a pair of sticks and set the beat on the coffee table to Nicole's scat singing. Picking up his guitar, Grant pulled out the melody. Pete plinked harmonizing chords on the piano, while Jack noodled around on his harmonica. The world erupted into a spur-of-the-moment Merseymen plus one concert! What incredible chemistry between these seasoned rock stars and this fresh-from-the-farm girl of Pennsylvania!

The inevitability of the evening concert broke the party apart. Grant slid his arm about Nicole's waist. Pulling her tight to him, he leered, "Cor! I can't believe you're here. Bet on it, we've more celebratin' to do later."

Not wishing to dampen spirits, Bruce suggested Nicole stay, rather than hiding out in the hotel room as she had done over the summer during the show. "No reason you shouldn't nip into the blonde wig again and participate in the festivities this evening. The gear is waiting for you in the next room." Smugly the manager chortled, clearly heartened by the abrupt change in attitudes of his lads.

Briefly slipping out of the room Nicole returned wearing the long, straight pale-blond wig and one of the "dolly" get-ups from the summer. Kicking out her long-booted leg, the alter-ego of Nicole Moore performed a modeling spin. "What do you think? Pretty fab, huh?"

"Oh, that is positively awful, isn't it?" Grant groaned. "But unfortunately necessary if you want to be with us in public at the concert." Once again he lustily grabbed her up, his brown eyes flashing. "Oh, I can't wait to get you out of that crap!"

Grant's comment clanged the chaperone's ears. In the early days, before leaving Liverpool for school, Mary had also hung around the cellar clubs with Ben. Familiar with these cheeky lads from Mersey Town, she recognized some of their risqué chatter as an affect—some wasn't. Not sure how to take it, Grant's remarks chaffed her.

As concert time neared, Nicole noted the familiar routine endured: pre-show interviews, pictures and autographs, the concert, post-show audiences and finally the promoters' wrap party. As always, excessive knots of groupies clogged up everything.

But afterward in the Hotel Pontchartrain, Bruce reserved the entire top-floor restaurant, complete with a lavish buffet, unlimited supply of bubbly and the hotel's band for their private party. An assistant let in the few lucky beauties culled from the day's pack to act as "escorts." Popping the first cork on the champagne, Jack proposed a toast. Lifting their glasses, they toasted the new team and the road ahead, as the welcome back party shifted into high gear.

In her first time out as a chaperone, Mary managed her position from a distance. From her conversations with Bruce and Ben, she kept Nicole in sight throughout the whirl of the evening.

Once away from the prying eyes of the press, Grant very quickly stripped Nicole of the blond wig. Running his fingers through her dark tresses, he teased them back to life. Grant also ignored all intrusion from any outsiders. Incredibly enough, the other girls seemed deflected from sidling up to wheedle autographs or conversation. Even Pete, Jack and Richie, who practiced the one-for-all philosophy, kept their distance.

Grant proficiently executed the duties of escort. Realizing champagne was a new experience for her, he encouraged Nicole to nurse glasses of water along with sips of bubbly. He paced her alcohol consumption by sensually feeding her tastes of food — interspersing the hors d'oeuvres with kisses. Watch-dog Mary suspicioned his motives. It raised her hackles as he slow-danced with Nicole with his hands clasped at the small of her back, their hips locked together while he nuzzled her neck with kisses.

Around three, all the rest paired off and began to disappear. Only Jack and two members of the hotel's band remained, heads together, drinking and dueling away.

With an iced bottle of champagne and Nicole in tow, Grant headed toward Mary. "Mary dear, Nicole is beginning to look a little under the weather—first time with champagne and all. So she won't suffer in the morning, would you be a dear and find her some bicarbonate?"

Nicole's swimming eyes told Mary Grant was right. "Why don't *you* get the bicarb? And *I'll* take Nicole back to her room," Mary countered.

"And where do you expect me to come up with the seltzer? You know I can't go mucking about the hotel," Grant whined. "No, *I'll* take her to the room. *You* get the seltzer."

Heading off in different directions, Mary felt uneasy about separating herself from them, but of course she realized Grant couldn't be seen wandering about the hotel.

Mary's absence freed Grant to implement his personal agenda. As the elevator endlessly clicked off the floors, Nicole and Grant shared sweet, sloppy kisses. Arriving at the room, Nicole's heart thumped feverishly as Grant slipped the key from his pocket to open the door.

Confused she looked at him. "Grant, this isn't my room."

"I know, luv." He kissed her once, then again. "I can't be seen down on your level. So I got the key to Jack's room. He's busy now and won't need it. You can rest here until Mary gets back with the seltzer."

With her head buzzing, Nicole swallowed his story.

Shutting the door behind them, the tiny bathroom nightlight faintly illuminated the hotel room's entryway, creating light-edged shadows. Grant fumbled to put down the champagne, then drew Nicole tightly to him. His building passion of the evening exploded. He deluged her with kisses. For Nicole, the evening's champagne had weakened her moral resolve and spawned an unfamiliar appetite. Hungry for him, she returned every one of his kisses. Their breaths came in feverish pants as they tried to devour each other. Nicole clawed his back trying to get closer although he already had her locked to him. Grant's hands moved from her hips up her torso toward her breasts. All new to her, she continued to cover him with kisses. With mouths wedded together, he massaged then kneaded her breast. Drawing away slightly, he held her in his eyes, ablaze with desire. Innocent with trust, Nicole stared back at him. His hands moved to the top button of her blouse. One button slipped through the hole and opened. She let out a slight gasp; he tenderly kissed it off her lips—their eyes riveted on each other. His fingers, with sight of their own, deliberately moved down to the next button in line and released it. Silently he checked her resolve with another kiss, then proceeded. The next button fell to his fingers, and the next, the next and the final one.

With her blouse gaping open, in one seamless movement he pulled off his turtleneck baring his chest. Grant returned to her mouth kissing her tenderly, still testing her intention then pressed in closer. His hot flesh next to hers burned. His kisses grew longer and deeper, increasing in intensity and fervor. A tinge of alarm crept inside of Nicole. Sensing her change, Grant lightened up and returned to sweet, lingering kisses to ease her edginess. Slowly his hand worked its way up to her breast. Nicole felt the heat of his hand through her bra, then on her skin. Again she gasped, stepped back and landed, thud up against the door. His determination steeled. Gathering her up in his arms, Grant suffocated her with kisses trying to stifle any thoughts of rejection. His caresses erased her apprehension. They panted and moaned as the fever again overwhelmed them.

A distant noise broke through the fog of passion.

"Nicole. Nicole. Are you in there?" Mary's panicked knock pleaded. Realizing she had been hoodwinked, frantically the chaperone knocked on door after door along the corridor of their suites, until sounds of little bumps and thuds brought her to Jack's door.

Shushed silence greeted her raps.

"What the bloody hell?" Grant demanded in a whisper.

"It's Mary!" Nicole blurted.

"How in the freakin' hell did she find..."

"Mary?" Nicole answered as frenzied scrambling by the pair ensued. "Just a minute."

Wondering how late she'd been, Mary scolded herself for letting Grant dupe her.

"We're coming!" Grant growled. "What the f..."

Nicole opened the door as quickly as possible to ease Mary's suspicions.

Stepping past her innocent charge Mary came up in Grant's face. Fire shot from her eyes, even as she kept her tone level. "Don't ever try a stunt like that again. In the future you will respect me, my position and Nicole—Mister Henderson. I expect you to live up to your portion of 'The Agreement.' Do I make myself clear?"

Then she stepped into the hallway. "Come on Nicole, let's find our room."

With his turtleneck back on and the champagne bottle in hand, Grant cursed bitterly as he slid by them. "I'll see you tomorrow!" he threatened. Heatedly he foisted the key into Mary's hand. "Here, you lock up."

Embarrassed, crushed by being manipulated into the middle of an awkward situation she really didn't understand, Nicole sputtered a few apologetic explanations.

Mary knew how she handled the situation would set the timbre of their relationship. Rather than using lectures or disapproving looks, once in their room she fixed Nicole the bicarbonate along with aspirin, then settled her down with a quiet discussion about the womanly stirrings inside her. Drawing from personal experience, Mary explained those feelings and what had happened, how Nicole got tangled up in a situation pitting Grant against her. From their conversation, she could tell Nicole desperately cared about her opinion and wanted Mary as her ally. Although they never mentioned the incident again, Mary knew Nicole understood her parameters.

Turning out the light, staring up at the ceiling, Mary berated herself for losing control of the situation. Nicole broke the silence with a soft, quavering voice. "Mary, is it normal that every time I think about Grant I feel prickly hot and have trouble catching my breath?"

"Yes, that's normal."

"Do you think Grant feels the same way?"

"I don't know, Nicole," she answered. But Mary did know.

Up at eight getting their things together, Mary let Nicole sleep until the phone jangled her awake at nine. The group had to be in Chicago by noon. Going up to the suite for breakfast, everyone there looked like hell. Recognition came through slits of barely-opened, blood-shot eyes. Nicole couldn't tell if Grant resented her for last night or suffered from too much party like everyone else. Mary nursed Nicole along with water, orange juice and aspirin.

By the time Mary and Nicole boarded the plane, everyone else seemed remarkably recovered and energetic. Thanks, no doubt, to the multi-colored "vities" the rest popped at breakfast. Tamely, Grant held the seat next to him open for Nicole. Sliding the armrest out of sight, he nestled her in the crook of his arm. "Go ahead and doze if you can," he comforted. Nicole had only an hour more to recuperate before Chicago appeared and the fray began again, with no time for hangovers.

Coming to grips with the situation, Mary realized that Grant was basically still a hormone-driven kid whose sexual fantasies had been satisfied beyond most men's wildest dreams. With all those groupies hanging around, the group didn't exactly live like monks. She understood how it genuinely impressed Grant that Nicole didn't recognize him at first, and later she didn't hang on him because of his name. Grant, at that stage of his life, was very much a little boy lost. He found himself uprooted from home, cut off from people and family he could trust, adrift in a rapidly spinning whirlpool without a secure port. In the immediate, his drive for security surpassed his sexual appetite. He had latched onto Nicole because she captured his interest by being a rock, not a leech. Only after a few months on the tour did he grow comfortable enough to take the security she offered for granted. Then, she became a challenge. Short of attaching herself to Nicole at the wrist, Mary had to create ways to intrude without being a warden. She worked at building a bond of trust with Nicole. In the process, they became best friends.

When the guys left for the concert site, Mary and Nicole cracked the books, which usually afforded them about six hours of class time. Mary enhanced her tutoring by using Nicole's forays into the different towns for the Merseymen as fact-gathering scavenger hunts. In addition to bringing the city back to the group, her assignments included researching the particulars about each locale's history.

Sure, Nicole studied, but she worked at her position with the Merseymen in one mode—flat out. Although she possessed an innate business sense, Nicole pursued her own agenda. Desperately she knew she wanted to sing, but trading on her insider connection to get it distressed her. She found it difficult to even mention it to Grant or anyone else in the group, lest they see her as using them just to advance her personal agenda. To gain her own toehold in the business, she constantly pestered Bruce over subtleties of the business, always wanting to grasp more.

In mid-October, the tour headed to Mexico City, Guadalajara, and Acapulco, continuing down into South America and into their springtime. Hop-scotching across the continent, places like Rio with their nude beaches and hot Latin attitudes only increased carnal frustration between Grant and Nicole. Maturing, Nicole learned the joke about cold showers.

The last week of November, the tour wrapped and flew to Miami. From there the Merseymen would head back to Britain and into the recording studio until Christmas. Nicole would rejoin them for the opening of their winter tour in Paris on New Year's Eve.

A miserable Grant approached Nicole on their last night together in Miami. Under the night's cloak, they walked the hotel's private beach with the waves quietly lapping against the sand. Peering out over the white foam into the inky blackness stretching to infinity, Grant moaned, "It's almost four weeks until I see you again. How can I live without you? I can't do this."

"You'll be just across these waves. It's like being just across my lake," Nicole stated bravely.

"Yeh, right! Do you know how far 'just across' is? It's four thousand bloody miles, five time zones and an eternity away!"

Hoping to brighten his mood, Nicole asked Grant what he wanted for Christmas.

"You know what I want," he retorted, his eyes burning.

Unconsciously he fiddled with the ruby engagement ring on her hand, then looked up into her eyes. "Marry me!"

"I'm going to."

"No, not someday. Now! Over the holiday. Let's get married Christmas Eve."

"Oh that's such a wonderful idea. Yes! Yes, let's do it." But a thought halted Nicole's fantasy. "What about my age, Bruce and my parents? Can we do it?"

"I dunno. Let's go ask." Grabbing her hand they sprinted for Bruce's room.

Grant paused before knocking. "You know, we don't have to ask."

"How's that?" Nicole didn't catch his meaning.

"Vegas! It's only six hours away." Grant returned bursting with his discovery.

"Elope? I can't." She couldn't believe he offered it. She saw her dream of a fairytale wedding vaporize before her eyes.

"Why not?"

"Grant, my parents! It would devastate them," Nicole protested.

"Okay, so we'll ask." He rapped at Bruce's door.

Bruce met their request cautiously. "I had hoped that the careers of the group would be more entrenched before we throw another wife at the public. You know we started this ride with Jack being married. ... Well, I guess we're as solid as we can be. Now is as good a time as any. ... Okay, as long as Nicole's parents agree." Bruce offered his hand, then clasped Grant about the shoulders. Kissing Nicole's cheeks, he blessed in his best Yiddish, "*Mazel Tov.*"

Chapter 4
The Fairytale

Home—*Creekside*—The trees stood bare against the slate November sky hung with threatening snow clouds. The house felt less familiar, like it didn't recognize her. A cool tingle of panic pinched Nicole's stomach. What if her parents said "no"?

Sensing her dread, Grant wrapped an arm around Nicole. He kissed her forehead to chase away the uneasiness. "Ready? We can do this."

Opening the door, Nicole called as they stepped inside, "Mom, Dad, we're home."

Fran greeted them in the kitchen with kisses. Putting on the kettle for tea, she urged them to sit. The aroma of sweet familiarity perfumed the kitchen. Scents of cinnamon, vanilla and ginger from Fran's Christmas baking spiced the air. She set a sample plate before them while making small talk.

Richard's steps came quickly on the stairs. "Is that Nicole's voice I hear? You're here already?"

"Hi, Daddy!" Nicole jumped up to give him a hug and a kiss, like in the past.

Rising to his feet, Grant extended his hand.

"Well, … and Grant too." He addressed Grant with an air of surprise and caution. "I thought Nicole said you'd be heading back to England?"

"There's been a slight change in plans, Mr. Moore. I thought I'd see Nicole home and drop in for a bit of a chat."

Richard read between the lines. Seating himself at the kitchen table squarely across from Grant, he readied himself for this exchange between the men. "So, what brings you here, Grant?"

Out of control of the situation, afraid it would spiral horribly wrong, Nicole attempted to jump in, but the pressure from her mother's hands squeezing her shoulders hushed her. Fran also knew the participants of this dance.

"I've come for your permission, sir, to change the date of our wedding." Perspiration accumulated along Grant's brow.

"Any particular reason you're asking?" Nicole's dad fished, staring him down.

"Yes, sir," Grant reached for Nicole's hand. "I love Nicole, and I don't want to be apart from her anymore."

Skeptical, Richard wagged his head. "I don't understand the rush, Grant. She already travels with you. You're constantly together."

"Mr. Moore, I'm tired of not having her by my side. Tired of not being able to hold her close because someone might see. We travel separately. I can't go out with her unless one of us wears a disguise. I want to kiss her and not care if a man with a camera catches us. I want to cradle her in my arms as I fall asleep. I love her. I have since that day at the lake. And sir, ... 'The Agreement' is getting more difficult to live with." Grant lowered his voice to a man-to-man tone, "I think you know what I mean, sir."

Disturbed, Fran drew in an audible breath. "Grant, is that the only reason to move up the wedding? Please, ... the truth."

Grant's eyes sparked. "Yes Ma'am! You have my word. We've not been together."

"I believe you," Fran retreated. "I believe you."

Richard pressed his agenda. "If you get married now, what happens to Nicole's education?"

"That would continue. I wouldn't jeopardize her education. Mary will remain as her tutor."

"And college?"

"The same sir. I'd make it my personal responsibility," Grant bartered.

Persisting, Richard leaned in. "What about her job and her salary? Or since you're getting married would you dissolve that arrangement?" he accused.

Those questions stunned Grant. He never considered Nicole's employment. Bruce handled that side of the operation. "I ... I see no reason for any of that to change. I will personally guarantee her position and salary." he complied.

"A raise would be nice, too," Richard trumped.

The Christmas Eve date—a mere twenty-six days away—however, left her parents scrambling. Grant understood there would be unusual expenses attached to the wedding because of his celebrity status. He made it clear he expected to bear the entire financial obligation of the wedding. Giving Nicole carte blanche, happily he departed, leaving her in her driveway with a kiss and his parting words. "I'll be back on the twenty-third. I promise I won't think of anything else the entire time. Nicole, plan the wedding you've always dreamed of. Money is no object. I'll send someone to help."

The logistics of planning a wedding to a major rock sensation in total secrecy proved daunting. A large city, such as Philadelphia, offers anonymity among its masses. But in a rural community of thirty-five hundred, trying to mask the small army needed for lodging, catering and transportation embodied a ton of complexities. Grant's generous wallet greatly eased the process. They decided the best way to camouflage the affair was to hide it in the open. Richard suggested they explain the influx of visitors and foreigners as clients he had invited to an elaborate Christmas soiree. Because of security concerns, Nicole eliminated all of her life-long friends from the bridal party and the guest list. For added privacy, the Moores decided to host the reception at the house. However, even a pared-down guest list contained fifty invitees.

Without ever selecting her colors or choosing the first flower, the logistics of celebrity ate up five precious days of their tight timeframe. Finally Nicole got down to shaping the wedding itself. She asked Mary to be her maid of honor, Jack's wife Candy would be an attendant and Jack, Jr,. the ring bearer. Grant chose his brother Robert as his best man and Jack to escort Candy and represent the group.

In the afternoon of December sixth, Vada Knight and her assistant descended from London. Vada epitomized the personification of an eccentric designer with wild, flaming red hair and flowing layers of splashy-colored clothes. Numerous *haute couture* houses on the Continent and glitterati from all over the globe clamored for her genius. Grant had tapped her not only to design the wedding clothes, but to help fashion the entire celebration. Sweeping into the living room, sketchpad in hand, Vada trailed fabric swatches and ideas of designs with which to create the perfect fairytale wedding.

Dismissing the obvious Christmas colors, Vada selected a color pallet of deep blue with white and silver garnish. Transferring her wedding fantasy to paper, Vada rubbed her hands together. "Ah, you'll be the Perfect Princess." She created a streamlined version of the Dickens era, crafting the dresses out of moire taffeta, Nicole's in ivory, the attendants' in the rich winter blue.

Vada preached the credo of sensual experiences, believing that a memorable experience touched as many of the senses as possible. "Flowers," she exclaimed with her arms thrown open, grandly encompassing a wide swath as she walked. "We will have lots and lots of flowers—extravagant quantities! Ahh their wondrous perfume—especially in the dead of winter!"

Vada stayed only for two days, but in her wake she left reams of instructions for the floral arrangements, the church, the music and the reception.

Grant phoned daily. His calls brought news of the Merseymen's business. Ripe with ideas, they had breezed through their recording sessions. They had enough material for a new album with another under way. Bruce had approved a script and signed another movie deal—filming would begin at the end of the winter tour. Listening to Grant reduced Nicole's wedding plans to the mundane.

On their last night alone together as a family, and the first moment of peace without wedding demands intruding, a twinge of conscience poked Nicole as she finished washing the dinner dishes. Standing next to her mother at the sink, she fished for loose silverware in the dishwater. "Mom, what do you really think of my marrying Grant?"

Fran thoughtfully paused. "He's a wonderful lad, and he seems sincere. But I feel we hardly know him. I wish you could have met him about six years from now, after you finished college. That way your career would be started, and you would know what it was like to be on your own for a while. But... that never really was an option, was it? Not after Grant came along."

"Am I wrong?"

"That's not mine to say. I'm only saying that I would have preferred you wait until much later." Pausing again, this time she proceeded with great hesitancy. "No matter what happens," she threw a glance heavenward, "God forgive me for saying this—there will be enough money to provide you with a future. You will always have a means of independence now. We could have given you college, but Grant has the wherewithal to give you not only college but also contacts to connect you to your future. Only you have the power to turn those assets to your benefit, and that will come through wise choices. Your father and I support your decision."

Her mom's mercenary candor rocked Nicole. "What about love? You didn't mention Grant loving me—only money!"

Her mom patted Nicole's soapy hand. "Love—its absence or presence—is something only you can answer. Only you know how you feel about each other. Search your heart. You know the answer."

"Is this just girl talk, or can an old man get in on this conversation, too?" Richard asked, entering the kitchen.

Fran turned from the sink. "Nicole wanted my thoughts on her marrying Grant."

"Having second thoughts?" her father asked. "Of course, every father thinks his baby is too young, but I trust your decision. I hope everything turns out as you think it should. Marriage is never easy. And you are not saddling yourself with an average situation. Grant and his lifestyle bring a lot of extra baggage. This is not a 'cozy-house-with-a-white-picket-fence' relationship you are going into, is it now?"

Questions crinkled Nicole's nose. She didn't understand.

Her dad continued. "I mean, you won't have just the typical 'learning to live with someone' pressures of marriage. You will have all those, plus traveling around the world, plus life at the speed of light, compounded by the universe and the press watching, waiting—and hoping you'll fall. It's a lot to cope with, but you've always been resilient and resourceful. You have great inner strength, and when you need it, you'll find it. ... Why all the questions now anyway? Are you getting cold feet? Because up until you say 'I do,' it's never too late to call this thing off. We won't think less of you if you do."

Nicole snuggled into Dad's open arms for a hug. "No, it's just that we never really had a chance to talk. I wanted to make sure how the two of you felt."

"We love you, that's how we feel." Fran and Richard echoed, as they all retreated to the family room and watched the yard fill up with snow.

The final avalanche of details crashed in on them in the morning when Vada Knight, two of her associates and twelve massive trunks arrived. Greeting them with exuberant hugs and air kisses, Vada excitedly teased, "Oh Princess, do I have surprises for you!"

After setting up operations in the Moores' basement, Vada enlisted Fran to direct the small battalion amassed to assemble and decorate the reception tent. The huge, white canvas tent engulfed most of the manicured portion of the backyard. Tall branches, tiny white lights, flecks of silvery glitter created a winter forest fantasy inside the tent. Centerpieces lavish with white roses, blue delphinium and waxy-green holly spread their magic across the linen tablecloths and around the bone china and cut crystal.

Then Vada directed her attention to their country church. The muddle of musicians, florists, decorators and a stage manager overran the quaint stone chapel. Vada flitted here and there, her gown in a whirl to catch up, directing one operation, then interrupting herself to take up the reins on another.

Numb from the excess of morning activities, Nicole sat in the church watching the production unfold.

"Do you actually like hanging out in churches?" a warm whisper came from behind her.

Nicole turned to discover Grant's soft brown eyes. Forgetting her surroundings, she threw her arms around him. "Did you come to rescue me?"

"No luv, I came to join you. I hear we have a wedding here tomorrow."

"You're early. Are the rest of the guys and Bruce with you?"

"Yeah. The drivers took them to the house."

"Candy and Mary get in all right?"

He nodded. "They are at yer mum's house."

"What about your parents and family? I can't wait to meet them ..."

"Relax luv. Everyone is here, and we are all organized. You've hired a marvelous crew of meddlers."

On his way up the aisle to toe Vada's mark, the minister stopped long enough to address the couple. "Ah, the impetuous Romeo has joined us I see." He commented as he slipped by.

Turning his attention back to Nicole, Grant asked, "Do you need to be here? Let's face the music and get the marriage license business out of the way."

This was the only breach in their logistics of secrecy. No subterfuge could be employed here; they had to use their legal names in filing for the license. If Grant were recognized, all their careful planning would be up in smoke, and their wedding day would be lost in a world-gone-mad media frenzy. In an effort to escape detection, Grant put on his leather driving cap, letting it ride up high on his forehead, with his bangs tucked inside. Avoiding direct eye contact, they completed the forms, fearing that any moment they'd be met with the delirium that follows identification. Keeping his answers brief, Grant responded to the clerk's questions with a simple "yes" or "no" to conceal his accent. Operating in robotic, bureaucratic rote, the older clerk never looked up or attempted polite conversation. In the end, she formalized the document with a cold, silver seal.

Despite the mounting pressures of last minute details and the rehearsal, Grant requested a final ride to the lake. "It all began there. I really want to go back once more before the dream becomes reality."

Nicole couldn't refuse him. Saddling Thunder and her dad's horse, the pair rode out to the lake. A thin veil of ice covered the water's surface. Grant brushed off a log where they sat amid their remembrances of that fateful day in March.

"I wanted to give you my Christmas present before the hubbub of tomorrow swallows up the day." Grant brought forth a small box wrapped in Christmas green.

"I don't believe how our minds work together." Nicole pulled out a small package of her own and handed it to him. "You go first."

His fingers deftly opened the box, revealing a gold medallion and chain. Inscribed on the face, "I *agree* to love you forever. Nicole." Tears stood in his eyes and he embraced her. "You've changed 'The Agreement.' Oh, I definitely approve. How I love you!"

"Now, it's your turn."

Carefully untying the bow, Nicole lifted the lid of the box. The sun flashed back into her eyes. A two-carat, heart-shaped, diamond solitaire blazed in the sunlight.

"I always wanted you to have a proper diamond instead of that lame birthstone ring for our engagement. Now we don't have to be afraid of anyone seeing." Taking the ring from its bed, Grant got down on one knee. "This time with a real diamond — will you marry me?"

Nicole recovered her breath enough to whisper, "Yes." Admiring the ring, she fell into his waiting arms and met his lips.

Running slightly behind schedule, and with her bride and groom AWOL, Vada stood vigil in the driveway, arms crossed, the multiple layers of her dress fluttering in the breeze. Her glare tracked the approaching couple all the way down the drive. "Where have you been? Who gave you permission to ride off into the sunset? We have a wedding to rehearse — or weren't we going to participate?"

Smiling, Grant dismounted as he went to appease the angry goddess.

During the rehearsal party, Grant questioned Nicole about her side of the guest list. Dutifully she reported only her closest relatives would be in attendance because of the privacy considerations.

"But yer mates — er, yer friends. Did you invite any of them?"

"Of course not — security you know."

"Then, do it, luv. Do it. The three friends you were so close to, wouldn't it be gear if they could be there?" Grant prodded.

Nicole nodded hesitantly, "But the security..."

"Damn the security, Nicole. Do it! Call them now. Invite them!" Leading her to a phone, he picked up the receiver and handed it to her. "Call!" Grant urged. "And remember it's Christmas Eve. They should bring their families."

Of Leanne, Annie and Cookie, she dialed Cookie's number first, all the time considering how she would explain the situation, yet keep the secret.

Nicole's wedding day dawned with a hint of snow in the air. Slipping on her robe and climbing inside a pair of warm slippers, she proceeded to the kitchen where her mom and dad greeted her along with the aroma of fresh cinnamon rolls. She expected the household to be a hotbed of activity, but serenity reigned. As her mom poured tea, she informed Nicole of the itinerary. "The hairdresser will be here at eleven. Vada and her associates will meet us at the church at 2:30 to dress."

Folding the newspaper, Richard laid it down alongside his plate and handed his cup to Fran for a refill. "So, how's the bride this morning?"

Nicole mimicked a shiver, "A little nervous, but fine."

Her dad pushed a tiny box in her direction. "It's not a Christmas present, just something we wanted you to have." Her mother joined them at the table.

Nicole opened the box to reveal an elegant lavaliere, in a gold, turn-of-the-century setting. A pearl sat in the middle of the solid gold heart, surrounded by delicate gold filigree. "Oh, it's so beautiful. Thank you. Can I wear it today?" She kissed each of them.

"We hoped you would. I know it's not silver to match everything else, but it belonged to your grandmother Moore. It was a wedding present from your grandfather to her. She gave it to me when I married your father, and now it's your turn," her mom responded.

Several times that morning, Fran turned the nervous Nicole away from the doors overlooking the backyard preparations. By the time Nicole bent over the sink for the hairdresser to shampoo her hair, her stomach had parked itself in her throat. With her head under running water, she never heard the doorbell ring. The next thing she knew, Cookie tapped her on her arm.

"Okay Nicole, I can't stand it any longer." She huffed. "I didn't sleep a wink all night. So tell me who are you marrying?"

Begging indulgence from the hairdresser, Nicole substituted her mom getting shampooed so she could temporarily turn her attention to Cookie.

Once out of earshot Cookie burst, "It's Gordon. I'm right aren't I?"

"No Cookie. Come with me and I'll explain the entire thing." Up in Nicole's room she sat Cookie down. "I'm marrying Grant Henderson."

"Who's he? ... He's not from around here. Is he? Did you meet him over the summer?" The reality was so far outside the realm of possibility that recognition totally escaped her.

"Grant Henderson, of The Merseymen," Nicole prompted.

Cookie's eyes grew huge in surprise. She made the connection. "No! You're kidding! Not thee Grant Henderson!"

Briefly Nicole stepped Cookie through the entire story. She noticed the more she talked about the upcoming event and shrieked along with Cookie, the less nervous she was.

Finally Nicole could hear the hairdresser calling for her presence again.

"Ooo, I can't believe this," Cookie confessed as she hugged Nicole good-bye. "I'm thrilled for you. I'm so glad your mom called me to come over this morning. See you this afternoon. Ooh, Grant Henderson—Wow!" Then out she slipped.

A light snow began to fall as they arrived at the church. Garlands of white flowers outlined the entry arch and wrapped all the handrails—a hint of what waited inside. What a transformation! It stole Nicole's breath. White roses, deep blue delphinium and lush amounts of green holly leaves tumbled from every available space, saturating the chapel with their heavenly aroma. Vada had fulfilled her promise of surprise. From the decorations, to the specially designed pearl tiara for Nicole's three-yard veil, and even the horse-drawn sleigh to carry the couple off to the reception—Vada had far surpassed any fantasy Nicole could have dreamed. She created a new standard by which fairytales would forever be judged.

But the day wasn't just about fluff and frills. Nicole's most enduring memory of that day remained Grant's expression while they exchanged their vows. How Grant's eyes sparkled as the minister placed her hand in his. He emanated sober sincerity as he meaningfully repeated each phrase of their vows. Grant locked onto Nicole's heart when he said, "I do."

The reception heaped more icing onto the already incredible Christmas wedding fantasy. The servers paraded their bounty on hefty silver platters like servants of old at a king's feast. Crown roasts, flaming desserts, trays spilling fresh tropical fruit, and continually flowing champagne circled the guests to the winter garden. Sprinkled throughout the evening, a recurrent tinkle of crystal called for the bride and groom to kiss.

Grant delighted in introducing the Merseymen to awestruck Cookie, Leanne and Annie. On numerous occasions he hailed Ben and made sure the girls had every photo they wanted taken with the group.

Following the meal, Grant and the rest of the Merseymen approached the orchestra. Assuming their positions, Grant stepped to the mike. "Mr. Moore, could you please bring Nicole down front." Richard led Nicole to where the group stood, positioning her alongside Grant.

Grant began again, "I've been working on this material for awhile. I wrote this song for my beautiful wife. I'd like to sing it in public for the first time tonight. Nicole, luv, this is for you." Grant slipped the microphone from its stand and with the introductory chords began "On This Day I'm Yours Forever." Pouring out his heart, he sang his love song. Nicole could hardly see him through the pool of tears that filled her eyes. His devotion reduced her to putty.

Because it was Christmas, and because of the overwhelming British contingent, in addition to the wedding cake, the chef produced a wonderful plum pudding for dessert. The waiters wheeled the pudding to the center of the floor while the guests, arm-in-arm, sang "Good King Wenceslaus." Igniting the pudding, they closed the evening with a chorus of "We Wish You a Merry Christmas."

A final surprise waited on Nicole's bed when she changed for their departure. Vada left a divine, white velvet, going-away dress. And inside Nicole's suitcase was an elegant negligee of white silk, trimmed in satin, bordered with lace. Each creation bore the designer's label—Vada's farewell surprise.

Once Grant finished changing, he knocked at Nicole's bedroom door. "Ready luv?" he questioned opening her door.

"Do you realize," Nicole commented looking around her childhood room, "this is the last time this will be my room." With a touch of melancholy, she ran her fingers across some memories on her desk.

Fearing getting bogged down, Grant nodded. "I know. C'mon. They're waitin'."

With the toss of her bouquet, the pair headed for the honeymoon suite at The Morningside Inn in quaint, nearby Doylestown. The following morning they'd catch a flight to a deserted white-sand beach off the gulf coast of Mexico.

Arriving at the inn just before midnight, Grant gathered Nicole up in his arms, carrying her over the threshold. "Welcome, Mrs. Henderson," he said bestowing a kiss. Flowers, champagne on ice and a tray of hors d'oeuvres greeted them. The covers on the king-sized, four-poster bed were freshly turned down. Grant built a fire in the fireplace, turned out all the lights in the room and opened the champagne.

The warm glow of fire danced in Grant's eyes. He lingered over his kisses for his bride. Each one grew longer and more intense. No matter how many times they had come to the precipice of this moment, they had never crossed over. Excitement and nerves pricked at Nicole. Grant took the lead. Holding her constant in his eyes, he softly traced the features of her face with his fingers. Releasing her tresses he let them fall in a cascade down her back. Grant nuzzled the base of her ear, lightly nibbling, working his mouth back to hers. Their breaths had escalated to little gasps by the time his mouth closed over hers. Sliding down the zipper on her dress, they let it glide off onto the floor. Deftly Grant's fingers moved across Nicole's chest down her cleavage spreading a warmth and awareness through her body. Running his hand down her arm, he took her hand and pressed it to him, *there*. Her eyes grew wide. Pulling off his shirt, the fire-light flashed in the gold medallion she had given him. His mouth found hers again. Lowering her to the bed, their two feverish bodies melded together into one.

Chapter 5
On to Happily Ever After

Grant and Nicole returned from their honeymoon tanned, relaxed and ready for The Merseymen's New Year's Eve opening night concert in Paris. To their amazement, not one paper—not even the tabloids—had picked up the news of their marriage.

Nicole planned to celebrate their union by burning the wigs and dolly-clothes of her alter-ego, the model. Gathering up the infernal things, she readied them for a bonfire in the fireplace, when Grant stopped her. "Maybe we should think this one through, luv. Perhaps we're being a bit hasty."

"How do you mean?"

"Through some sort of miracle our marriage has escaped the press. We have a chance to protect our privacy if we keep this our secret. How bad can that be?"

"How good can it be? They don't know I'm your wife!" she protested. "You told my father you wanted to move the date up so we could be seen together, so we could travel together, so you could kiss me in public. Those reasons don't mean anything now? I'm your wife, and I'm proud of it. I want the world..."

Grant drew her to his side, kissing away her anxious objections. "Of course you're proud of it. But think of it luv, if the press doesn't know you are my wife, then you won't get mobbed. Believe me, I'd feel better about that. Plus, you'll still be able to roam around free and keep the world open for us like you did through the summer and fall. Now Bruce won't have to worry about breaking the news of another Merseyman's wife to the fans. Everyone wins!"

"Everyone, but me," Nicole pouted.

"Of course you win. We will still be together for all the important things. See," he pulled out his wedding medallion from underneath his turtleneck, "we're operating under your agreement now. I'll still cuddle you each night in the sack." Grant kissed her, hoping to buy her off.

"But what about all the groupies, all the real dollies that mob you? Will I still have to put up with that?"

Grant interrupted her with an aggressively passionate kiss. "You let me take care of the dollies, okay? Besides," he panted, "I have something else more pressing in mind."

Bruce squirmed at Grant's idea, but he couldn't deny the appeal of not having to wave another wife in the face of the fans. Nicole felt cheated, but in the end acquiesced for the good of the whole. At Grant's prodding, they removed their wedding rings and stored them in the bank vault. The birthstone ring went back on her right hand. To add validity to the charade, Bruce moved Nicole out of the flat she and Grant had shared for only a week and moved her into a place of her own. True, her new flat backed up to his, and they opened a secret passage between the two places, but it tweaked her nose that Grant had manipulated the situation so that publicly they lived separately.

On New Year's Eve, The Merseymen hit Paris, their second sweep through the Continent in two years. The group received a returning hero's welcome. Thousands lined the streets from the airport to kick-off their '65 tour.

Closing off the streets around the *Arc de Triomphe*, the officials transformed the plaza into a mega street party. The Merseymen performed on a stage erected underneath the Arc. In a platinum wig and a gear leather mini, Nicole joined the almost fifty thousand pulsating rockers who swelled the streets that night. The City of Light bathed them in its radiance. It emanated from everywhere. The Merseymen closed their two-hour concert at midnight as the sky erupted in a barrage of New Year's fireworks. A swell of the choruses from the *Marseillaise* spontaneously rose up as a partisan paraded a huge French flag through the crowd. Swaying, the throng sang along with the national anthem. Free-flowing wine kept the masses warm.

Hungry for more Merseymen, the crowd brought them back on stage following the midnight celebration. As the love from the audience flowed to them, the boys returned the warmth in number after number. The group played everything they knew, even resurrecting some relics from the old cellar days. Finally at about half past two, the multitude let them go. The four-hour emotional exchange both sated and depleted the group, leaving them physically drained. They had to be helped down the stage stairs. Exhausted, Grant draped his hot, sweaty body over Nicole. Ben, George, even Bruce, had to help get all of them into the waiting limousines.

Ironically, the morning following the triumph of Paris, a picture of Grant and the dolly Nicole landed on the front page of the tabloid, *The Reflection*. Under the image of Nicole helping Grant off stage, the headline splashed, "Paris Mob Mauls Merseymen in Love Fest!" The reporter relegated Nicole's role to that of a "lucky groupie destined to be the latest one-night stand."

Wounded at being lumped in with the despicable gaggle called groupies, Nicole memorized the writer's name, Karl Nielson. "They can't do this to me!" she protested.

Grant merely shrugged. "They can do anything they want."

"But I'm not a groupie."

"Now how would they know that? Since you decided not to reveal our actual relationship, if you hang around us in public, this is what they'll print. Get used to it." He dismissed her out of hand, as sharply as a slap in the face.

Likewise Nicole's appeals to Bruce fell on deaf ears. "Let me ring-up the reporter and correct the misinformation."

"And tell him what?"

"I can tell him ... I'm just a friend of the group ... in to help out ...I...I..." Nicole fumbled for a plausible explanation of her presence.

Bruce detailed for her the facts of life about the press. "Reporters are evil-minded idiots. They write whatever bloody well pleases them and sells the most papers—to hell with the truth. A star, or wife of a star, trades press, even bad press, for keeping the celebrity's name before the public. I don't like it. It stinks. But it's the system, chiseled in granite, held over from the dark ages."

"But can't we do something?" she doggedly kept up.

"Ya, drop it!" he plainly ordered.

And on and on the tour went, across the face of Europe. For The Merseymen only the decor in the hotel rooms changed. The same crowds swarmed, screamed and swooned at every venue. There was no way for them to distinguish a difference. They used their sense of humor and good-natured cheekiness to keep the routine novel.

Despite the captivity, life on tour was heady stuff within that prestigious on-the-road fraternity! Since British groups dominated the charts, while schlepping between cities their schedule frequently dovetailed with those of The Beatles, The Stones, The Animals—all the top names. Of course, everyone knew each other from the Liverpool cellar clubs which created an incredible bond. The grapevine kept everyone informed about locations and options. Other groups often caught The Merseymen's concert from backstage. Sometimes as a tension reliever, they'd steal into some out-of-the-way club to get in a few riffs with the other touring groups. Other times, they'd rendezvous in one or the other's hotel suite to swap road stories and throw down a few. The Merseymen devised a game they played during these visits—a "spitting contest" of sorts. They each tried to see how outrageous a scenario they could create for the visitors, all the time trying to act as if nothing unusual had occurred. Alcohol increased their bravado. Tall tales and legends grew out of those episodes.

Mid-March the tour wrapped, and Bruce herded the group back to their London studio to lay-down more tracks. Recording sessions for The Merseymen dragged on endlessly. Jack wasn't satisfied until every note reflected their sound. They slaved over sections in an unending string of playbacks and re-tapings. Eventually the tedious repetition wore on Nicole. After one especially grueling afternoon, the group had headed out for what she thought was a cigarette break to clear their heads.

Killing time, amusing herself Nicole picked up Jack's headset. Amazed to find it live with a playback, she stepped to the mike. In her wildest dreams she never figured the mike to be live too. Without hesitation she sang harmony to Jack's lead, coming through the headphones. Invigorated by the experience, Nicole reached back during the musical interlude for Richie's tambourine and used it to accompany the music. Resuming singing—harmonizing more with the lead—she finally concluded in a full duet with Jack's taped voice. With the fade-out she stepped back and bowed to receive her phantom applause.

In actuality the guys had filed into the booth for a conference with Ben and Bruce about a particularly rough section. With her back to the glass, she never saw them. To her horror the speaker of the intercom opened and the ovation for her singing debut was all too real. Whistles, hoots, bravos met her red-faced shame. Puddling into the nearest chair, Nicole buried her face in her hands. Excitedly the occupants of the booth poured out into the studio.

Pete reached her first, pulling the mortified Nicole to her feet. "That was bloody good! What are ya cryin' for?"

"Yeah! Fab!" Richie hugged her. "You can sing!"

"Hey yer eyes are leakin'," Jack teased. "Want to stop before yer ruin their fine carpeting in here!"

"Seriously, don't ya know, yer version worked," Pete assessed her performance.

His review caught Jack's attention. "Yeah! It was a gear way to cover the potty part we had. Let me hear it again."

Wiping away her tears, Nicole sang it again.

"Now try it like this," Pete encouraged.

"Fab!" Jack lauded, then picked up his section again forming a duet with her.

"Okay then," Pete picked up. "Nicole, get another pair of head-phones. We'll take it from…"

"Hold on! *What* are you thinking?" Bruce loudly cut in. "It sounds to me like you want Nicole to sing on the record."

"Killer idea, don't ya think!" Richie jumped in.

"No! I don't!" Bruce shouted.

"But it's good. She's good. What's the problem?" Pete lobbied.

"Okay. Show me where it says 'The Merseymen and *a bleedin' girl'*. Where in the damned press releases, the records or any of the publicity does it say that!" demanded Bruce.

"But, ... but..." Pete's protest collapsed.

"He's right, you know," Jack said defeatedly.

Bruce prevailed; the Merseymen acceded to his managerial acumen. On the final release Pete sang Nicole's version of the harmony.

Of all the guys, only Grant remained in the booth that day, stabbed in place by Nicole's undeniable talent. Her boldness embarrassed him. His gut-level resentment and jealousy of his wife confused him.

Although Mary didn't witness Nicole's little studio escapade, her student related it to her ally blow by excruciating blow when Mary showed up for studies that evening while the group was out for costume fittings. Unable to do more than listen, Mary didn't possess the magic elixir to soothe Nicole.

However, Nicole's first singing effort hadn't gone up in smoke; Ben had recorded it. Late that evening, Ben and Bruce stopped by Nicole's London flat. Still smarting from the sting of her antic at the mike, she reluctantly let them inside.

Bruce, with business on his mind, entered efficiently. "Nicole, we need to talk." he started, ushering her toward the living room couch.

Producing a portable tape player, Ben set it up on the coffeetable where Mary had cleared a spot.

Bruce slid in a tape. "Listen to this." Out came Nicole's voice. At the tape's conclusion, Bruce exclaimed. "That is marvelous! It's bleeding amazing! I love what I hear! And what I hear is worth millions." Then he looked at her directly, "but you've got to understand, even if I wanted you on the record, I can't introduce you into the group from thin air. It has to be worked in. Groundwork has to be laid before such a step can be taken. This all has possibilities, but we must proceed with caution."

Hearing her voice on the tape refreshed Nicole's embarrassment. Her revived humiliation defeated her ability to comprehend Bruce's meaning. Meekly she bowed her head. "I'm really sorry. I'll never let it happen again." Involuntarily her lip quivered.

Realizing her confusion, Bruce picked up her hands in a proprietary fashion and smoothed them in his. "I'm not sorry Nicole. If you hadn't been so bold, I might never have found such a wonderful, new talent. It's just going to take me time to figure out how I want to incorporate you." He raised his eyebrows in a smile of encouragement.

"What?" She blinked blankly back at him.

"I want to sign you. You're damn good, and I want to be your agent. You've got a future." His smile echoed encouragement.

"You want to sign me?"

"Yeah. If you say yes, I have the papers here."

Nicole looked to Ben's direction, seeking his confirmation. Proudly he beamed.

"Do any of the others know yet?" she questioned.

"No. I needed your okay first. Then I will have conversations with them. We will have to decide if we want to introduce back-up singers or another member. Since it is a decision which will materially affect all of them, the decision is theirs. It has to be unanimous and enthusiastic. Why don't you let me handle all the details? Besides, I may just want to start you out on a solo career of your own first."

"What will Grant say?"

Bruce rose to depart. "Leave Grant and the rest of 'em to me. I'll break the news to him." He paused, then closed the deal. "Then you'll sign with me?"

"Of course!" She declared, spontaneously coming to her feet. Taking his pen, her hand trembled with excitement. She signed her name where Bruce showed her.

Tucking the tape recorder under his arm, Ben patted Nicole on the back and kissed her cheek as they walked to the door.

Before opening the door, Bruce cautioned her. "Remember, not a word to anyone until I have spoken to them and to Grant."

Then uncharacteristically Bruce touched her cheek. "Be ready my dear."

Closing the door behind them, Nicole leaned up against it. "*My* career. Mary, did you hear? My *career*!" She repeated over and over. "The biggest news of my life, and I can't share it with *anyone*, especially Grant!"

Chapter 6
Nikki

Days crawled across the calendar as Nicole waited with prickly impatience. Enmeshed in pre-production details of the group's second movie, after two weeks Bruce still hadn't phoned. The Merseymen's workday stretched to eighteen hours. Routinely Grant came home far later than anticipated, sometimes he didn't make it to her apartment at all.

To keep herself occupied, Nicole pushed the length of her day to match theirs. Working ahead in her class schedule, by April first she passed all her senior year exams.

Nicole attended the first day of actual shooting on April fourth. The director, Graham Wannaker, a wiry, creative type with a short ponytail, ran the concert scenes first. Fifteen hundred lucky fan club members packed the concert hall as extras to play the role of the delirious audience. The Merseymen worked hard to lip-sync the songs exactly as on the master tape, struggling against the urge to embellish or ad-lib. They knew anything extraneous meant hours back in the studio getting the looping right. After five hours Wannaker cut the extras loose, then shot close-ups and cut-aways for an additional three hours.

Amid the remains of the set, at the wrap of the first day's shoot, cast and crew assembled around a small feast the producer, Sam Rottenberg, had catered. Sam, a small, squat Jewish man, with a tanned head crowned by a ring of white hair, loved cigars. Champagne corks popped as Sam proposed a toast to what he hoped was the start of a successful film.

Following the initial toast, Graham Wannaker stepped to the center of the gathering for announcements. "This certainly has been a productive first day."

The group sent up a round of applause.

"If everything goes this well, I predict a smashing success!" Wannaker played to his group of insiders—building morale—creating a cohesive team. Applause and whistles of enthusiasm erupted.

"Thank you. Thank you. But on a more somber note, as you know we signed Jane Asher to play the part of the Angel Pauline, who rescues the Merseymen from their date with death. Unfortunately, she's been sidelined with pneumonia and won't be available."

A small moan escaped the masse.

Standing on the outer fringe with Bruce and Ben, Nicole paid scant attention to all the hoopla. Hanging out waiting for Grant, she just wanted him to get done with work, so they could go home.

"But this won't delay production." Director Wannaker continued. "We've issued a casting call. And I am happy to announce, we found our replacement."

Immediately a hush of anticipation fell over the group.

"Nicole Moore, would you come up here. Nicole? Where's Nicole?"

A burst of applause broke out.

Nicole casually swiveled her head, thinking she heard someone calling her name.

"Nicole Moore, are you here?" Wannaker called out again.

"Ni-cole! Ni-cole!" the crowd started to chant.

Stunned, not realizing what was going on, she threw a puzzled look around the room. Bruce and Ben each grabbed an elbow and ushered her forward through the throng. As the sea parted, there stood Pete, Jack, Richie and Grant, alongside the producer and director, clapping.

With his hand outstretched to her, Graham started again. "Here's our new angel. ... Nicole Moore!"

Turning her around to face the group, Graham Wannaker raised her right arm, like a prizefighter after a victory. The applause bolstered by shouts of acclaim swelled.

As the realization dawned on Nicole, she covered her agape mouth.

"As you can see, she's a little amazed." Wannaker explained. "I'm sorry Nicole to do this to you, but the guys here wanted to surprise you. ... A toast to our new Angel Pauline! To Nicole! Here! Here!"

Glasses raised. Nicole bowed and accepted the toast.

A stagehand stuck a glass of champagne in her hand. As Nicole sipped from her glass, over the rim, her eye caught Bruce standing off to the side. Apart and alone, he quietly lifted his glass to her and mouthed, "Congratulations."

Finally in the quiet of midnight, Nicole got to discuss the prospect of her career with Grant. He overwhelmed her with his support. In fact, Grant confessed he had suggested her for the part of Pauline. "Oh luv, we can share everything together now. Pete even wrote you a song for your part in the movie. It's a love song, and you'll get to sing it to me. See, so now you'll be a part of the music, too!"

In between laying out their future, Grant meted out tender kisses.

Love warmed his soft, brown eyes. "Bruce is going to build you as an entity of your own. If the fans 'buy' you, then it will be natural to add you to our group. Pending fan approval, we'll phase you in. Bruce has it all worked out just like Cinderella. He'll tell the press he went to visit an old school mate, heard you singing in the kitchen, and bango, he had to sign you! Once the kids discover you, they'll fall in love with you. They'll feel you're a natural for the movie—then us!"

Grant paused, "There's only one hitch, luv. Since the world doesn't know we're married, and since now the plan has the fans discovering you—clamoring for you—you can't be seen as already being on the inside. For now we need to live completely apart."

"Well, here's a news flash—we already do!" Nicole dug in.

"No, I mean you'll have to move to another section of town. Once you get the part of Angel Pauline, the bastards in the press will see the set-up if you live behind me. And it will spoil the next part."

"What next part?" Nicole held her breath waiting for another bomb to drop.

"Our PR people will paint me as a lonely, eligible bachelor, desperately seeking the right bird to spend my life with. Eventually, inevitably, me and the new songbird of the movie will be drawn together. Zingo, we become Mr. and Mrs. Happily Ever After!" A huge smile of enlightenment filled Grant's face.

Nicole wasn't smiling.

"It's perfect, don't y'know," Grant pushed.

"I'm not so sure. I don't like the deception, and I don't like being separated from…"

"Hey, luvy, I'm not really going to be goin' out with all those birds. It'll only be for the cameras. When we can, you know I'll bring me home in the rack to you." A lusty leer glinted in Grant's eyes.

Nicole didn't want to get sidetracked by Grant's convenient sexual appetite. "I'm beginning to think my having a singing career now is a mistake. Let's scrap the plans, tell the world we are married and get on with our lives together."

On a dime Grant soured. "Hey lady, you're the one who *had* to pick up the mike and sing the other day. This is for you. This is what you wanted. You started this bunch of rot. You'll finish it. Understand!? This is the way it is written."

Nicole conformed, believing she only temporarily traded her marriage in the public eye for the start of her career. Other than being repugnant, the plan seemed feasible. Grant left it to Nicole to inform both sets of parents—no need to throw them into a tizzy. Bruce's sources found her another place eight miles away and moved her during the wee hours of the next morning. Nicole asked Mary to stay with her awhile to help take the edge off her separation from Grant.

Because of the tremendous success of The Merseymen, Bruce Eckstein's name commanded almost as much respect as theirs did. Any new talent of his garnered the media's maximum attention. Bruce called a press conference to introduce his latest sensation and to hype the imminent release of Nicole's song from the movie as a single. Masterfully before the press conference, Bruce crafted the rags-to-riches story of his new star. Of course the entire Cinderella saga would be played out soap-opera style, in installments before the media. If executed correctly, the outcry of the fans and the frenzy of the media would feed off each other, advancing each segment and creating the force driving the story. Bruce called this technique "no hands media manipulation." Nicole became the latest property to be engendered by his technique. Plus, her career launch became a free, pre-release teaser to spike The Merseymen's new movie.

For the press conference, Bruce down-sized everything. He and Nicole sat at a modest table in the front of a little room crowded with a limited number of chairs. He knew the chairs would fill instantly with the hounds of the media, all jockeying for position. The agitation of being sardined into the room would create the illusion of white-hot excitement.

Bruce coached Nicole thoroughly. "Project humility and surprise. Remember less is always more. Let them delight in prying it out of you. Make eye contact, but don't confront. Play to them. Be sincere. Above all, have *fun.*"

A hundred ravenous reporters showed up. The room sweltered under the bright-white lights. Popping flashbulbs blinded Nicole. Born of nerves, her reaction came from her heart. In a lightning volley the press fired their questions at her. With energy and captivating assurance, she deftly fielded every one of them.

After a half hour Bruce shut the show down, leaving the press hungry for more.

To review Nicole's press performance, Bruce had a tiny camera installed in the room to video the event. That evening a small group, including the Merseymen, came together in the screening room of the film studio, where Wannaker and Rottenberg had just finished scanning the dailies from the day's shoot. Wannaker had the tape of the press conference queued up for them. Because Bruce had arm-twisted Nicole's way into the part of Pauline, by trading on The Merseymen's fabulous appeal, Wannaker hired Nicole cold, without ever screen-testing her. Now, he wanted to see how the camera treated her and how she handled an audience, so he stayed for the screening, too. Everyone, but Nicole, sat forward with anticipation in their seats as the tape rolled.

The good-natured joking between the attendees ceased with the appearance of Bruce and Nicole on the screen. In stunned silence, everyone watched the thirty-one minutes of black and white images flicker through the projector's gate. Finally the lights came up.

Breaking the spell, Graham stopped long enough to pat Bruce's shoulder on his way to the exit. "Wow. ... What can I say, you dog? You picked yourself a natural." An envious grin crossed his face as he shook his head. "Wow!" He tossed hearty good-byes at the rest on his way out of the room.

The guys gathered 'round Nicole. Jack led off. "Hey, Bruce, can we just elect her the bleedin' queen now?"

Richie echoed, "Yeah, Grant. You can just sit back and retire. Let yer little bird bring home the bacon."

Jack chirped, "Queen of hearts, queen of hearts!"

"Might as well." Grant lobbed a friendly arm about Nicole's shoulder. "Ain't she just got it all!"

"Ya know we can't just call you Nicoooooole ... Mooooooore," Pete said obviously dragging out the o's in her name. "It doesn't fit that bird." He pointed toward the blank screen. "Ya need somethin' more, somethin' lively, somethin' kicky." Pete paused, thought, "Hey that's it! Kicky Nicky! We'll call you Nicky."

"Nicky? Nicky Moore?" The star-to-be questioned.

Bruce mouthed the name over and over to himself. "No. Nikki, N-I-K-K-I. Just Nikki. Like Elvis is just Elvis. No last name. Nikki." From that moment on, to almost everyone in the world, she became Nikki—the indomitable Nikki.

With gusto Bruce seized on launching her career. The tape of the press conference confirmed he had a money-maker. From the screening room, they raced to the recording studio. Bruce wanted a turn around of one week on her new single.

"Nikki, the clock is ticking!" Bruce exhorted her. "Every hour, of every day, of the first few weeks is the most critical. A once-and-done press conference without production accomplishes nothing, even from me. You'll have to keep up! It's the constant barrage in the media that keeps the excitement alive. Without excitement you're yesterday's news."

Pressure mounted on all of them to produce—and on schedule. Sitting with bleary eyes at four in the morning listening to final playbacks became normal for her. Studio life morphed into an infinite series of hurry-ups and waits. In between takes, Nikki dined on bites of greasy, cold, congealed fish and chips, washed down with sips of warm, flat Pepsi. But none of the inconveniences mattered when she stood in front of that microphone and recorded the music that filled her soul. Her balloon never landed. She greeted each day with a smile that started inside her heart. The "holy-gee-whiz!" feeling bursting inside her couldn't be quelled.

In conjunction with the print media, Bruce lined up three U.K. TV dance-party shows to introduce Nikki's single. By the end of the first week, a little horde of reporters camped out during the day on the street below her flat. With each passing day of the successful publicity campaign, their number grew. When the chart numbers came out, she debuted at number 25. By week two, she moved into the number nine position, within striking distance of The Merseymen's number one spot. That feat reaped considerable attention from Grant. Nikki passed from anonymity to notoriety in less than a week.

Simultaneously Nikki caught-on on the Continent. Bruce scheduled appearances for her in France, Germany, Italy and Spain over the following three weeks. Paparazzi now dogged her everywhere, reducing contact between Nicole and Grant to almost zilch. Grant complained bitterly to her over the phone. However, nightly the press snapped photos of his arm hooked around a different dolly.

Meanwhile The Merseymen continued to skyrocket off the U.S. charts. Because Bruce feared tinkering with their success in the extremely lucrative and supremely fickle American market, he limited Nikki's initial release to the European and East Asian continents.

Even though she had spent a great deal of time with the group, Nikki remained naïve about the relationship between a manager and a personality. Violating a fundamental rule, Nikki had Mary deliver a note to the reporter from *The Reflection* who had caused her so much grief. Following one of Bruce's many-choreographed photo ops with the press, Mary sought out Karl Nielson, requesting a private meeting with Nikki at the Brass Rail Café.

With only two patrons in the café, Nikki didn't have any trouble picking out the reporter. For sure he wasn't the impeccably dressed blonde. He had to be the one in the loosened tie, shirt sleeves and no jacket. She went in with her hand extended in introduction. "Mr. Nielson...?"

"Karl," he interrupted as he pulled out a chair for her.

"Thank you. I need to talk to you confidentially..."

"Off the record," he interrupted.

"Off the record?" Nikki questioned.

"Yeah. If you want to talk to a reporter confidentially, you need to say 'off the record.' Then he's ethically bound not to report it."

"Okay. I want to talk to you off the record."

Nielson shot glances around the room.

"Worried?" she quizzed him.

"No, just cautious. You're hot cargo. I wanted to make sure none of my competitors are within earshot. ... So what's so important?"

"Mr. Nielson... Karl, off the record, what do I have to do to get around the innuendo and downright lies in your paper?"

"Give us a story to print."

Ignoring his comment, Nikki continued on with her agenda. "Like in Paris this past January you referred to me merely as 'lucky groupie destined to be the latest one-night stand.' How do I stop that?"

"Give me the real story to print."

"But...that's it?" she questioned, floored by the simplicity of his request.

"Yep. In the absence of news, we make up whatever fits the picture of the day. Celebrities, and splashy headlines about them, sell papers. We have a quota of pages to fill each deadline. If my paper sells—I eat. If my paper sells really well—I eat better. If you won't talk to us, then what's left for us to write? We connect the dots the best we can. Stories have to come from somewhere. But that's off the record and you can't quote me on that." His eyes twinkled.

"But there's the press conferences and..."

"Oh, please! Those are so scripted. We show up for the gaffes." He paused, for a millisecond of thought, then pounced. "Aha! See, if you were in Paris then you *have* met The Merseymen already!"

Caught in his snare, Nikki's eyes widened in fear. Coolly she came back to cover her panic, "But this is off the record."

Karl threw his head back in laughter. "Don't worry, Princess. I won't blow your pat little PR story. I know how this game works. I know that if I let the cat out of the bag, I'll be cut off..."

Nikki interrupted. "Karl, what if I called you with stories? Or if you had my number and you called me with questions."

Karl's turn for amazement. "You mean you'd give me a lead?"

"Better than a lead, I'll give you stories, real stories. If you have a picture—call me. I'll explain it or give you the off-the-record low-down.

"You'd do this for me?" Karl asked incredulously.

"Not just for you. See Karl that's the problem. What about all the other papers? How can I handle all of them? Could you be a conduit to them too?"

"Like a press agent?"

"No. Just a well-placed leak, I mean source. You'll get all the calls first. In return for the inside scoop, you'd run interference for me—let me know about any dirt about to appear somewhere else."

"Lady, I like your style." He wagged his head in admiration.

"Maybe if you had the actual stories, we won't get smeared so much. You understand I can't speak for..." Nikki caught herself before she blurted out too much.

"Go ahead, we're off the record."

"Do you promise?" Realizing she was on shaky territory, she lowered her voice. "The stories right now are only about me. I can't speak for anyone else."

"Why? Who else would you be speaking for?"

Cornered, she stalled.

Karl leaned in. "You're in with them right now, aren't you?"

"Karl! I can't say anymore. I'm already over the line here."

"Aren't you?" he challenged, fixing her in his steely gaze.

"Karl, I'll give you an exclusive—the complete story—but it has to be on my terms, my timeline. You can't release it until I say when, no matter what. Understand?"

"Princess, you have a deal." He extended his right hand to seal the pact.

But Nikki held back her hand from wrapping up the deal. "If you get wind of something touchy and I ask, will you deep-six it for me?" She pushed a little farther.

"The truth, ... are you expecting anything?" Karl questioned.

"Honestly, no. But you never know what might pop up." Then Nikki extended her hand. "Deal?"

"Deal!" He said quickly. And they shook.

Gears turned as Karl mulled over possibilities. "You were in Germany, too. Dancing. ... And kissing."

Lowering her eyes, putting a finger to her lips Nikki nodded with a seductively beguiling smile. "Off the record."

He wagged his head with admiration. "Lady. Lady. Lady."

Nikki had no way of knowing the dramatic consequences, that meeting, in that café, on that day, would ultimately have on the rest of her life. And it had nothing to do with Karl and publicity.

Chapter 7
Riding the Whirlwind

In week three of its release, Nikki's single scored the coveted number one spot on the charts. The weeks until her call to be on the movie set flew by. While she made the rounds of the various dance-party shows, the Merseymen began their movie location work in Austria. Bruce practically moved her into the recording studio in putting together her first album. Pete and Jack supplied her with two original songs. The rest of her material Nikki selected from a clearinghouse for songwriters. Ben arranged them; she cut them. On April 28, 1965, Nikki's first album, *Nikki – On the Record* went into pressing.

Bruce pulled out all the stops to grab attention for his new star. Nikki's first album cover sent shock waves rippling. It featured her standing amid disheveled stacks of newspapers, wearing only a man's white shirt, cuffs undone, with the tails riding high on her thigh. A fedora with a press pass sticking out of the hatband sat askew on her long, very tussled tresses. Seductively the photographer posed Nikki toying with a pencil by her mouth. The flood of controversy produced Bruce's desired publicity coup. Inside a week, the album went gold.

Grant recoiled with objections to the cover, but Nikki merely pointed to his latest dolly pictures in the gossip rags, ending the discussion. Despite the setbacks living separately caused, Nikki remained thoroughly devoted to her Prince Charming Grant. And Grant jealously guarded the naiveté of his little treasure, keeping the seamier side of the business from her, such as the multitudes of "vities" that energized them through the days following their long nights. Occasionally he'd send one of his lackeys out for a stuffed animal to surprise her, or he'd arrange an intimate rendezvous for them as time and distance permitted. Within their private group, one might catch him grabbing her hand, petting her affectionately or hanging kisses on her. But just as likely, Grant's moods pivoted and he'd squander precious moments of their privacy, ignoring her.

Within the phenomenal twirl of Nikki's new life and her advancing career, she kept her recently minted relationship with Karl Neilson and the press a secret from Bruce. Primed with a draft of an exclusive of behind the scenes details she had given to Karl, Nikki presented it to Bruce as a surprise thank you present for launching her career. It surprised him—right into a conniption fit.

"Cute." Bruce cynically retorted. "But who released *this* to the night-crawlers at *The Reflection*?"

Proudly Nikki drew herself up to accept Bruce's praise. "I did! I talked to Karl, *that* reporter, about stopping any negative publicity. I gave him the *whole story* as a point of reference—of course it was all 'off the ...'"

Bruce's exploding fury squashed her. "You did *what*?!! How could you without asking me first? What have you done? How do you know he won't blow our storyline? What assurances did he give you he wouldn't embellish your story with his own brand of facts? He could turn on you and sink you. And take the rest of us down with you!"

Bruce sure twisted Nikki's good news inside-out with his sour milk of human kindness. Not ready to accept his version of press relations, she defended herself. "What's the point of killing the goose who keeps you in eggs? I'll feed him the truth to fill his pages. My system keeps my name on front page and gives us some control over the image. It could work! Armed with the straight dope he could run interference for us with the other news sources."

"Why have me as your manager? You've already taken this entirely out of my hands. No matter what, I can't undo what you've done. I hope your decision works out for you." Shaking his finger in her face, he warned. "Remember your boundaries. The stories you give concern you, and you alone. Don't drag the group into your fiasco!"

But it wasn't long before Bruce recognized the merits in Nikki's revolutionary idea of press relations and embraced them. At Nikki's suggestion, Bruce pulled Mary into the mix to become her publicist. Soon after, the three of them huddled with Karl Neilson to forge an official relationship. Karl insisted Bruce's incarnation of *Pygmalion* deserved a title, consequently he dubbed Nikki "the Princess," a moniker the press and her public adopted. In addition to exclusives, Mary provided Karl with a projected time line so he could make the scene when the big events popped.

A week later, Karl scooped the rest of the media as *The Reflection* announced, "Nikki Replaces Asher As Angel—Merseymen To Meet The Princess!"

Austria awaited Nikki's arrival with its arms outstretched and a valuable lesson to teach. Obviously by the size of the crowd at the airport, Karl's story had crossed the Channel. Several hundred eager fans with signs showed up to greet her. Bruce never anticipated such a welcome so early in her career, but there they were, standing in a roped-off area just off the tarmac.

Exhilarated, at the top of the plane stairs, Nikki enthusiastically waved hello.

A round of cheers answered her as the fans pushed through the rope barricade toward the plane stairs.

From the top of the stairs behind Nikki, Mary saw Bruce and Ben standing helplessly by the waiting limo, across the taxiway. Desperate, Ben started through the throng towards Nikki. Understanding their concern, Mary grabbed for Nikki to pull her back and give her a quick lesson in mob mentality. Too late, lithely Nikki skipped down the stairs into the waiting mass of adoring fans.

Photographers snapped her descent into the mob. Shaking hands, she autographed everything from scraps of paper to the backs of blouses. The spirited body pushed toward her. Oblivious to the danger, Nikki waded in deeper.

From the crowd a reporter shouted, "How do you like Austria?"

"Beautiful. The people are great!" Nikki threw open her arms.

An enthusiastic hometown cheer swelled up and pressed in to return the embrace.

"Are you excited to meet The Merseymen?"

"Yeah! Wouldn't you be? Don't you think they're kind of cute?" Nikki shouted.

Again the girls erupted.

Then instead of answering the reporters, now Nikki directed her remarks to the crowd. "What do ya think? Should I tell them you all say 'hello'?"

They squealed. Someone yelled back, "Are you going to go out with one of them?"

"Ooo, do you think I should?"

"Yes. Yes!" And everyone called out the name of their favorite Merseyman.

Clearly, Nikki struck a chord with her audience involvement. She found the power of being able to stir the masses exhilarating. In fact, intoxicating. So she fostered it. "Do you think they'll like me?"

"Yeah!"

"*We* love you!"

"Yeah. Yeah. Yeah!"

"Do you think they'll ask?" She cranked up the level.

"They will. They will!"

"And what should I say?" Nikki hollered.

"Yes! Tell 'em yes."

"You want me to go out with them?" She pushed.

"Do it for us!" Someone shouted back.

"Yeah. For us!" the cry went up. They chanted. "Nikki! For us! For us!"

The air sizzled with the electricity of their spontaneous rapport.

White-faced with fear, Ben finally fought his way to Mary's side near Nikki.

The mounting excitement drew the mob in tighter. Closer and closer they pressed. Ben and Mary tried to buttress the crushing tide. The air got thin. Individuals molded into a mass. The mass rose up like a tsunami. The tsunami lunged at them. Scared, Nikki's eyes doubled; now she understood what she had caused.

Like a ray of light Nikki caught sight of Karl in the morass and made eye contact with a silent, but urgent plea for help.

An earsplitting whistle rang out from Karl, momentarily silencing the throng, giving Mary time to latch onto Nikki. Darting back to the plane's stairs, the girls ran up them out of the mob's reach.

"Okay. O k a y!" Mary addressed them, her hands patting the air in a calming motion. "Nikki'll answer all your questions. One at a time. Please be calm. I promise she'll get to everyone."

The group quieted around the steps.

Lowering her voice to a leisurely tone, Nikki stopped fueling the fray as she answered the questions of reporters and populace alike.

By that time reinforcements had arrived, and together with the police, Ben organized the assemblage for Nikki's descent to the tarmac and her limousine. Waving her good-byes from the frame of the limo door, Nikki called out one last time. "Watch the papers. I'll let you know what happens!" Then she slid inside the waiting car and sped off in safety.

After thoroughly upbraiding Nikki for her actions, Bruce lightened a bit. "You know, I think you hit upon something out there today. The fans and the press together, what a combination! You connected out there with the people."

"Yeah. It was like I'm doing this for them," Nikki inserted.

"No doubt about it, they view you as one of them, almost as a surrogate," Karl acknowledged Nikki. "Truly incredible! And they really want you to do this for them."

"Aside from the mob thing — which I understand now — it felt so right. What if I had more talks with the fans?" Nikki nurtured the seeds of an idea.

Bruce tapped his fingers in concentration. "We could arrange 'chats' with small groups of fans and the press, seemingly impromptu. Nikki could ask their opinion—consult with them—seek their advice, and they'd respond for the 'whole.'"

"Then the press would feed her answers to the world! Oh, I like it!" Mary summed up.

"And my paper would *love* it!" Karl added his enthusiasm. "You know Bruce, the mob at the airport this morning was good news. It means you've hit the mother lode. Nikki already generates interest on her own." Then Karl directed his attention toward Nikki and smiled. "Face it Princess, your life is no longer your own."

"These little chat sessions with the fans sound great." Nikki hesitated. "I love them, and I treasure their devotion, but I'm not sure I want them deciding the course of my life. Minor decisions that we can manipulate are okay. But after that I want to live my own life."

Karl laughed, "Your own life, Princess? Then you're in the wrong business."

Bruce shrugged. "I don't picture this format for the long-term. But it should serve everyone involved nicely through the next few weeks as Nikki meets The Merseymen."

"Quite right," Karl concurred. "Well, Nikki started the ball rolling this morning by inventing the groupie chat. Now I suggest you schedule another one tomorrow after the big meeting between Nikki and The Merseymen. I'm sure the kids will have lots to say!"

The historic event of Nikki meeting The Merseymen unfolded according to Bruce's script. As she exited the hotel that morning, an encampment of media pounced on her.

"Nikki how do you feel?"

"Are you excited?"

"Did you sleep last night?"

"What will you say to them?"

"Who will you pick?"

That question stopped her. "Pick for what?"

"Which of the Merseymen will you go out with?"

Nikki laughed, "That's assuming anyone asks!" Ducking into her car, the media cortège, like eager puppies, followed them to the studio.

The Merseymen were shooting on Soundstage D. At Bruce's request, Wannaker had issued passes for Karl and a small contingent of the media's upper echelon to get the actual photos and story of the meeting. The rest of the pack would be kept at bay by the front gate and summoned for the press conference following the meeting.

Nearing the scene, Nikki began to perspire. "Geez, I think I've got a case of nerves over this thing today."

"Nerves, I like nerves. It adds a touch of realism." Bruce smiled as he led her through the hangar-sized building to the sound stage where the guys were running a scene.

Waiting until the director yelled "cut," Bruce led Nikki past the press, creating a stir. "There's Bruce. That's Nikki. Get ready. This is it." A slight clatter ensued as the press cadre got up and fell in behind the duo.

While make-up and hair people attended to The Merseymen, they clowned on the set, waiting for the next take. How strange it felt for Nikki to be separated from them.

Following Bruce across the line, Nikki glanced back at the press before crossing over. Suspended in time, they hung there, cameras poised. Overwhelmed by the building anticipation, she kicked out her leg in an excited little "here-goes-nothing" jig. Crazily they ate it up, shutters up and down the line clicked a thousand times in rapid succession. Karl secretly flashed her a wink.

Stepping Nikki from the shadows into the light of the set, Graham Wannaker made the introductions. "Guys, I'd like you to meet Nikki— our new Angel Pauline." Passing a few words around, they mugged for the cameras as shutters snapped in deafening proportions. The Merseymen's energy turned the photographers' film. Ceremonially they reviewed the script and blocked Nikki's first scene. While Jack made cheeky remarks, the three single Merseymen pretended to flirt with her. Finally they adjourned to the room set up for the press conference as Bruce admitted the pack at the front gate.

"Well, what do you think of her?"

"Fantastic." Richie.

"Cute." Grant.

"Groooovy." Pete.

"Reminds me a bit of me sister." Jack.

"Will you enjoy working with Nikki?"

"I dunno. Can she sing?" Pete.

"Does she act, too?" Grant.

"Just as long as she doesn't upstage us." Jack.

The guys dominated—after all, this was their domain. Eventually Nikki elbowed her way in too.

Finally the inevitable question, "Nikki, would you go out with any of them?"

"I don't know. I haven't even been asked yet."

Pete headed off the next question, "We have to ask our keeper first."

"Yeah. We don't normally do this datin' stuff on our own," Grant quipped.

"You know we turn in early so we can get our beauty sleep," Richie yawned.

While the insanity of the press conference continued, Mary went out to the small band of fans milling around studio's front gate and selected twenty to come back for a chat with Nikki. Fresh-faced and ready, they bounded into Nikki's private chat, brimming with questions.

"So how'd it go?"

"Great. Really fantastic," Nikki answered.

"What are they like?"

"They're kind of like us, only really witty. ... What do you think about them?"

The chatters soon grew oblivious of the journalistic intruders. Their arcing enthusiasm infected everyone in the room.

"So, do you like them?"

"How could I do anything else?"

"Would you go out with them?"

"Do you think I should?" Nikki handed it back to them.

"Oh, yes! Make it Richie, he's sweet."

"No, Pete is the cutest. You should go out with him."

"Maybe Pete is the cutest, but Grant is sincere. He'd treat you the best."

Eventually the idea surfaced that she should date all three! Their consensus ruled. Concluding with autographs and pictures, Nikki promised to try their suggestion, telling them to watch the papers to see the progress.

The following day, outside the glare of the press, they got on with the business of shooting the movie. Learning lines, exchanging roguish barbs, murdering scenes, mucking up, Nikki adapted readily. Now as part of the group, Nikki introduced a fresh element to the game.

When they weren't filming, Nikki with the guys sampled the town's nightlife, in front of the press. They photographed her discoing with Richie, singing with Pete and slow dancing with Grant. Bruce brought Candy over for Jack so the four boys could be on the town together. They rode the thrill rides at amusement parks, cut up at fests and danced till dawn at the trendiest nightspots. When Nikki's presence wasn't required on the set, she and Candy shopped the chic boutiques with the press along for the ride.

The fans soon recognized that Grant emerged as the main suitor for Nikki's affections. Pressure from the chatters mounted for them to declare their love. Readily the "M" word—marriage—surfaced. Letting the sexual tension build, Bruce delayed their declaration. He wanted Grant to publicly propose to Nikki from atop the surge of fan enthusiasm the night before their walk down the red carpet at the movie's premiere.

Meanwhile Nikki's presence with The Merseymen became generally accepted. To get reaction to the plan of Nikki singing with the band, Bruce tested its impact on the chat groups. Emphatically the fans wanted Nikki to sing with The Merseymen. Together they cut a single—overnight "My Side of Heaven" went platinum.

Bruce grew nervous, very nervous. He had never really planned to cross the two careers. The stratospheric recognition of the pairing of The Merseymen and Nikki panicked Bruce. Just the thought of America getting wind of Nikki desperately frightened him. He feared her presence might dampen the "available-male" magnetism the three singles in the group exuded. That charisma supported the group's Stateside popularity, and Bruce didn't want anything to queer that supremely valuable and lucrative prize. But, Graham Wannaker wanted to work another song into the movie to cash in on the rising tide of *their* popularity. Bruce refused. In a compromise Wannaker agreed to release two cuts of the movie; the uncut version for world consumption and the North American version, which didn't include Nikki singing with the guys.

Still Bruce continued to shore up the dike only he perceived as leaking by booking separate summer tours for them. Bruce scheduled a solo European tour for Nikki while The Merseymen did America.

The separate bookings enraged Grant. He walked off the set, then came looking for Nikki. Pulling her out from in front of a live mike at a recording session, he dragged her to the waiting limo. "C'mon," he growled. "If Bruce thinks he can run my life, then let him deal with this!"

"Driver! Take us to the airport!" Grant snapped.

Punching the gas, the chauffeur squealed away from the curb, sending the limo's occupants sprawling.

Grant's abrupt intrusion both angered Nikki and scared her. She preferred to make herself scarce when one of his "moods" erupted. "Where in the hell do you think we're going?" Nikki yelled at him.

"Back to London! I'll be goddamned if Bruce thinks he's gonna run my life! We're going to the public Registry Office, and we're going to get married. Before God and *The London Times!* That should put the cat among the pigeons! Let him stop *that* news from going around the world!" Picking up the car phone, Grant foisted it on Nikki. "Here! Call your reporter friend Karl. Tell him what we're doing."

Nikki hung up the phone. "What's that going to solve? We're still bound to his commitments for us and those stupid concerts. We'll be apart anyway!"

"He can't run our lives! I want him to stop! I want to be with you!" Grant whimpered.

"I want to be with you, too, and he *can* run our lives. He's our manager. I won't have our marriage used as a weapon — one minute you want to follow the plan. The next minute you want to beat Bruce over the head with it. I'll go with you to the Registry Office for love, not out of spite."

Breaking down, Grant's lips quivered. "I want to be with you. Make him stop. Make him stop." He wept into Nikki's arms, eventually collapsing into her lap.

Being incorporated into Grant's dilemma — once again his inability to handle their highly pressurized life — forced Nikki into action. Operating from her gut, she rang up Jack to get a bead on what really happened. Jack could tell by her tone, she wasn't in the mood for cheeky.

"That was some show yer boy put on here today. We were damn proud of him. I throttled Bruce after Grant left and demanded to know what kind of crap he pulled on you two." Jack lowered his voice, "Is Grant coming back?"

"In a day or two. He's pretty upset and needs some time."

"Take all you need. We've tied 'im up and stuffed 'im in a closet. Don't worry."

"Jack, do me a favor? Untie the bastard long enough to arrange for two tickets to London immediately, on the next flight — even if it's a puddle-jumper. Don't bother with any explanation; just have him do it. Then, let the limo driver know."

Next Nikki gave Karl a "head's up." "This is one of those times we discussed back in the café. Remember? I need you to deep-six anything you hear on this."

Karl promised.

After a long weekend, she returned to Austria with a refreshed and renewed Grant. That Sunday night, a fortified Nikki knocked on Bruce's door.

Their business genius stood before her, a shaken man. His private hell of personal culpability ate him alive. His condition shocked Nikki. The nurturing side of her wanted to reach out to him, but she knew she had to handle business first.

"These are our lives and feelings you are playing with, Bruce. This can't go on." Then Nikki laid out some new ground rules of her own, calmly, coolly. "First, from now on I will have a suite adjoining the guys'. Disguise it anyway you like, starting tonight. Second, the concert schedule will need to be re-arranged to provide for a four-day visitation between Grant and me every two weeks. We'll do all the concerts; just shift the schedule to accommodate our rendezvous. And finally, the film opens on November second. On November first, we will be 'engaged' and 'married' before the month is out. From this, there will be no deviation."

Nikki's ultimatum dissipated the tension for a while. Unity returned to the team.

Two days later the producer, Sam Rottenberg, threw a dinner party for the director, Bruce, The Merseymen and Nikki. He billed it as a farewell to Austria, but clearly Graham, Bruce and Sam had another item on the agenda. Towards the end of dinner, at Sam's urging, Bruce stood to suggest that The Merseymen and Nikki do a joint concert as a farewell to Austria and another as a welcome concert in England.

Rising in unanimous assent of the idea, with wild enthusiasm the guys and Nikki abandoned the party to assemble the roster of songs, write a few new ones and plan for the inevitable accompanying album.

Despite Nikki's records and her lip-syncing dance-party entertaining, this combination concert would be her first performance in front of a screaming, paying mob of fans. The guys rehearsed her for three days to acquaint her with her parts, the gear and the stage.

On stage the night of the performance, nervous anticipation tightened in Nikki's stomach. With the audience before her, shielded from them by only the common, anxiously quiet, cool blackness — her imagination ran rampant. Even though Grant stood next to her, squeezing her hand, Nikki thought she'd throw up!

Then the introduction, "Ladies and Gentlemen THE MERSEYMEN *AND* NIKKI!!" Gulping her final breath, Nikki held it. The heat of the spotlights hit her. When the wave of screams and cheers crashed over her, all her jitters vaporized.

Richie counted them down with his sticks and off they flew. Nikki's confidence surged as she took turns harmonizing with Pete, Grant and Jack. Stimulated, she boldly removed the mike from the stand, and the guys encouraged her. Dragging the cord behind her, going to the front of the stage they urged her on. She danced at the edge of the stage, working the crowd, clapping with them. Like proud papas The Merseymen reveled in her stage presence, grinning from ear to ear. Pete stuck a tambourine in her hands.

When the first of her two solos came around, Nikki took center stage from Jack, belting out her song. Through cavorting with the Merseymen, Nikki discovered the audience's hot-buttons which triggered their participation and emotional oneness. Playing to them, she made as much eye contact as possible, and they lapped up her attention. All too soon the end of the concert came, and nobody wanted to leave. Taking their bows to a thunderous tumult of applause, the audience demanded three encores — the group gave them two. The sweet rush of euphoria after the concert engulfed Nikki, spinning her head. She basked in the concert's afterglow for hours.

Crossing the Channel, landing back on their home turf, the London concert crowd went ballistic for the combined effort. Cashing in on their smashing success, Bruce booked them for three additional U.K. concerts and swung his fabulous music machine into high gear. A lightning round with the cover photographer placed the Merseymen in cardboard cutouts of train cars — Jack in the engine, the rest of the guys spilling out of other cars — with Nikki in a funky chugging-to-keep-up caboose. Within two weeks their collaborative album *The Merseymen with Nikki on Board* hit the streets. It went platinum within days.

Nikki's success didn't eclipse the boys'. Her star soared in conjunction with theirs. The exhilaration of the magic comet ride escalated. The crowds, the glitter, the lights, the applause, all fed the incessant ecstasy. Nikki heard the seductive song of the siren, and her name was Adulation. What a mesmerizing aphrodisiac!

Chapter 8
Destiny

Bruce brought Nikki's parents over to do a taped interview for Nikki's first TV special and to witness her performance in the last of the combination concerts. Grant couldn't resist introducing her parents to the audience. He drew the crowd's wild and frenzied reaction by kissing his "babe" on stage. Richard and Fran beamed from the front row. Because they lived outside the hype of the European press, the extent of Nikki's popularity and the magnitude of her career blindsided them. Several times during the concert, both of them remarked, "Wow, they really like her," or, "They're going crazy for our daughter."

Afterwards an "old home week" reunion of sorts took place back-stage as the band welcomed Fran and Richard. After all Fran, with Nikki, had spent the previous summer touring with the group. To celebrate properly, Bruce suggested they move the party to the film studio since he wanted to review the movie's dailies anyway.

Piling into limousines, Fran and Richard rode with Grant and Nikki. Never shy about things on his mind, Richard promptly addressed his issues. "I don't mind telling you both that this business of the two of you living separately distresses us."

In an amazing turn, Grant jumped on his comment. "We're not too terribly fond of it either, thank you. This was not what I had in mind when I asked Nikki to marry me. In fact, her career came as a bit of a bolt from the blue. Heh? Didn't it, *luvy?*" With his mockingly saccharine tone, Grant manufactured and opened a can of worms.

Tossing the responsibility of their separation back on Nikki startled her. What did he mean by it? And where had it come from? With a shrug of her shoulders and a half smile to her parents, she tried to hide her embarrassment. She knew this brush of friction sliced to the quick of their hearts and would precipitate a serious conversation with them later. But long before that, Nikki determined she would have her own tete-a-tete with Grant Henderson. His remarks aggravated her.

The group arrived just as Graham and Sam had set up the dailies from the movie shoot in the screening room. In between clips, Sam nattered on about his prize production from inside his cloud of blue cigar smoke. By the time they finished in the projection room, a spread of delicacies and a full bar had materialized on the sound stage. Delighted in playing to his intimate audience, Sam kicked off the impromptu party.

After an hour or so, Grant swaggered up to Nikki, his love of gin and tonic in clear display. A cigar in one hand, his drink in the other, he playfully growled, "C'mere, luv." With his gin-saturated breath, he whispered in her ear. "I know a lonely lil' couch in a dressing room that's lookin' for company." And he slopped a kiss on her neck.

"You do, huh? Well, why don't you show me?" Nikki cajoled, wanting to get him alone for the answers to the salvos he launched in the limo.

Carelessly he lobbed his hand with the cigar on her shoulder; its smoke wafted up into her face. His drink sloshed in the glass as he guided Nikki toward his dressing room.

Anger mixed with disgust backed up in her throat.

Closing the door, he locked it behind them. Putting his drink and cigar down on the make-up counter, he wrapped his paws around Nikki planting a sopping wet kiss on her mouth.

Nikki wiggled free. "Grant, please wait. We need to talk. I have to ask you something."

"Sure, luv, anything." He leaned against the counter, full of himself, self-assured, swaggering. "Then I have something for you." Crudely he tugged at his crotch.

Nikki ignored his boast. "I thought you wanted me to have this career. I thought you wanted me to be in the business with you."

He winced slightly in a small effort to recall the conversation. "Ya, so?"

"Then what was that attitude you pulled in the limo with my parents? You didn't sound so gear about this anymore."

Grant snickered disdain. "Well, well, *Princess*, did I embarrass you? Maybe things aren't so perfect in yer lil' world?" He picked up his drink and scowled, raising his voice, "Well look around ya, luv! Ain't this a sight! When's the last you've been with me in the rack?"

Incredulous she fought back. "If you remember, I wasn't the one who came home with the damned idea of separating. Seems like you proposed it!"

He swigged from his glass. "Yea, well no one expected you to take over! No one thought you'd amount to anything. We all thought you'd just stand in the back and hum a lil' bit!"

His comment stung, as if the back of his hand had slapped her across her face. Tears welled up inside. But she'd be damned if he'd see her cry! Pulling herself up, her eyes narrowed. Words came from deep within her throat. "Then why didn't you say so? Why didn't you find your own stupid voice and say so?"

"Well damn ya to bleedin' hell, Nicole! I thought ya could have at least serviced yer man better!" Grant took his drink, cocked his arm back and hurled it.

The glass hurtled past her ear and shattered on the brick wall behind her. Ricocheted drops of gin and tonic pricked the back of her legs.

She stepped towards him. "Then I suppose my standing up to Bruce and setting some ground rules for our tour meant nothing! You know what you need to do? You need to decide what the hell you want, Grant Henderson! And maybe we can settle on that! In the meantime sober up." Turning deliberately, Nikki walked to the door, opened it and paused. "You're right Grant, your couch does look lonely. Maybe *you* should keep it company!"

Outside the dressing room the hot sting of tears bit her eyes, then cut rivulets down her cheek. Grant's words sliced deep. Was she taking over? Did the rest of the guys expect her to just stand in the back and hum? Nikki needed answers and fast! Running to the wash room, she splashed cold water on her face to hide the puffy traces of tears, then dabbed on some more make-up so she could rejoin the party. Nikki wasn't about to let tears betray her or provoke sympathy for her. Walking fast, she picked up a rum and Pepsi from the bar for courage, then politely pulled Jack out of his conversation.

"Well Princess, what have you and your boy really been up to?" Jack raised his eyebrows in a brazen leer.

"Jack, please! It's serious."

Instantly he dropped the pretense. "What's wrong? Is Grant okay?"

"Yeah. Grant's fine. We ... we had a fight."

"Is that all?..."

"No, Jack, that's not all. Grant said some things I need honest answers to. ... We fought about my career and my singing with The Merseymen."

"I never would have guessed," Jack retorted sarcastically.

"What do you mean?"

"Just that I saw that coming after Grant's row with Bruce. He won't stand up to Bruce; I figured sooner or later you'd get it. And..."

"Did you and the rest of the guys really think I would just stand in the background and hum a little bit? Have I taken this career thing too far? Do you want me to go away or fade into the background?"

Jack's anger drew him up. "Grant said that? What a loon! What a lolly bleedin' loon!"

Nikki drank in his bitterness.

"That thick son-of-a-bitch! No. Hell no, Nikki. The night Bruce proposed a career for you to us, we ran the entire gamut of possibilities. We each had a voice in the decision—one negative and you'd still be a step-n-fetch-it today. It was very clear that you could either go on yer own or eventually be teamed with us. We wanted you with us. The vote was four to one. Bruce wanted to keep you solo, but his vote didn't really count. Why do you think Pete and I wrote you those songs? We wanted to cement our partnership and bring you luck. That's why I tore Bruce apart when Grant collapsed a couple of weeks ago. What's he so afraid of in America? We all assumed you'd be coming on the North American tour. Pete and I started workin' up new routines for you."

"Then you're not threatened by my popularity?"

"Are you kidding? To put it bluntly, the ten thousand who came to see you perform in Vienna wasn't exactly the fifty thousand we get. Besides, wouldn't yer success be good for us, too? Wouldn't we be sharing the gate? I don't see yer name solo on that marquee—or even first!"

Jack had been serious about all he could stand, "Hey, you're not part of some eeevil plot to take over The Merseymen are you?"

"Yes!" Nikki prophetically joked. "And you'd better lock up your gold."

With nothing to hide, Nikki rode back to her parents' hotel where they talked into the wee hours over tea. At four in the morning, Nikki knew the groupies had long ago given up and gone home. But instead of an empty street, the group's limo sat parked in front of her flat. Nikki tapped on the window. The driver lowered the glass; it was none other than Jarred, head of the tour's security, at the wheel.

"What's up?" Nikki quizzed.

"He wants to speak to you," Jarred motioned with his thumb. Grant laid sprawled, unconscious in the back seat.

"Okay," Nikki sighed. She thought she'd had enough for one night.

With a deep breath of resolve, Nikki slid in. Grant stirred to life, reeking of stale gin. "Oh, Nikki. Dear Nikki." Ham-handedly he patted her hair, whining, "Are ya leavin' me?"

"Good-night no, Grant. Can't we talk about this later? Why don't you go home and sleep this off?"

His stupor answered as he slumped back in the seat. Nikki had Jarred drive to an obscure hotel outside the city and check the "Smiths" into adjoining rooms. Then he helped her get Grant into bed.

Grant awoke with seismic activity in his head at noon. After throwing down a few pills, he recovered enough for a quiet supper together.

Facing each other over dinner in the room, Grant apologized for his behavior, blaming it on the gin. He wished to sweep the entire matter under the rug.

Nikki pushed for settling it. "Grant, why didn't you ever tell me that you didn't want me in the business with you? Why didn't you confide in me that it bothered you?"

He propped up his head on his hand. "I never thought it did. I'm lonely. I thought you'd be around all the time if you sang with us. But it's not workin' that way."

"It will. We'll be together until July. America is only six weeks, then we're back together. November we announce our 'engagement' and get married. But I need to know right now if you have a problem with my career. Whether solo or with the guys ... is there a problem with me having a singing career? Tell me. I have to know."

He averted his eyes. "No, ... you're not going to leave me, are you?"

"No, of course not. I made a promise to you. I'm not going anywhere." Walking around behind him, she massaged his neck, then bent down to kiss him. "You know, if you said the word, I'd give it all up tomorrow and just be your wife."

"I know, luv," he answered under his breath. "I know."

The five weeks before their separate tours drove Nikki and The Merseymen hard. Bad weather and Grant's mood swings put the movie behind schedule. Meanwhile in addition to her numerous chat sessions, Nikki cut her second solo album, *Simply Nikki*. Karl's photographer Jimmy captured a stunning solitary portrait of the Princess on stage before the microphone in a rainbow of stage light for the album cover.

Of course through it all, Grant and Nikki managed time in front of the media acting out their courtship charade.

Before Nikki knew it, the day arrived when a jet waited to whisk her off to Germany for the first of her solo appearances. Looking into her make-up mirror that morning, the realization dawned on her for the first time that she would be doing the concerts alone! No matter how many times everyone tossed around the words "solo" or "on your own," Nikki never really thought about the fact that "they" wouldn't be along side her. In the non-stop pandemonium of the previous five weeks, she lost the stark reality of those words. Now it all came down to her. For the first time, the responsibility for the entire show rode on her shoulders. Exhaling, she nodded to her image, "Here's to you, kid."

Bruce, Grant and the rest of The Merseymen congregated at the airport's gate for the final farewell scene. Desperately Nikki wanted a private moment with Grant. She needed to share a few personal words with him, to look into his soft brown eyes and have them assure her. But once again what should have been private time became fodder for the public press. From behind barricades a thousand fans waved their good-byes to her, while trying to catch the attention of The Merseymen.

Likewise Bruce also hurtled startling changes in Mary's direction. Because Bruce wouldn't divide himself between the Merseymen and Nikki, he deputized Mary to handle the managerial chores of Nikki's first tour—a mere six weeks after he had installed her as Nikki's publicist! So, as Bruce winged his way to America with The Merseymen, Nikki and Mary settled into their hotel rooms before rehearsals in Hamburg, confessing their apprehensions to each other in one massive, cathartic rant session. Over glasses of sparkling white wine, they decided if Nikki were honest with her fans, they would support her—and all the rest they'd improvise—as they had up to that point.

In the cool blackness before the lights came up, rather than tasting the dread of stage fright, Nikki united herself with the audience, feeling the energy of their anticipation, waiting, building to be spent. Touching their excitement fueled her own. She could hardly wait for the announcer's introduction.

"Ladies and gentlemen, in her first solo performance, ...the indomitable NIKKI!!

Delirious cheers of their resounding exuberance swamped Nikki. The spotlights ignited her.

"HELLO!" She hailed them. "Thank you for being here! I LOVE YOU!" Then stepping to the mike, she delivered everything they came to hear, and more. Along with Nikki they clapped, they danced, and they sang along. The audience stretched her hour-and-a-half-long gig to over two hours! Nikki finished to a standing ovation.

She planned for one encore; they demanded more.

Coming back for her second encore, out of the corner of her eye, Nikki spotted a stool. Grabbing it, she brought it onstage with her. Walking to center stage with a mike, she sat down on the stool, then turned her attention to the stage manager behind the wing curtain. "Could you kill all the lights, and could I have just a single spot on me?"

A hush of high-expectation fell over the audience. Mary watched the entire staff behind the scenes go into cardiac arrest over Nikki's request. The band threw nervous looks at each other and at Mary.

Calmly, Nikki repeated her request. "Please, just a single spot. I'll find it. Okay?"

Silence riveted the audience. In a lone spot, from atop a humble stool, Nikki offered them an unvarnished version of herself and in the process, struck for herself an enduring trademark.

"I can't thank you enough for taking me into your hearts. You'll never know how much your love tonight means to me. I will carry you and this performance with me always. But in your graciousness, you've run me out of songs. If you'd allow me, I'd like to do a couple of love songs for you. I hope their powerful emotions convey the depth of love I feel for you tonight." Bowing her head, without musical accompaniment, Nikki started a cappella, "P.S. I Love You", picked up "Grateful For You", then concluded with a heart-filled rendition of "Take My Heart". Raw emotion fortified her voice. The audience exploded in a tremendous ovation, holding her transfixed with their applause. Bowing and thanking them, she inched her way off stage.

The band, stagehands and crew swept Nikki up with their enthusiasm. Delirious, the Label's promoters filled the halls. Baskets upon baskets of pink roses overflowed her dressing room—from Bruce, The Merseymen and all avenues of the trade. Sam Rottenburg showed up to celebrate.

The heady froth of success carried Nikki across Europe. City after city fell before her wave. Reviewers raved. Every show sold out. Even SRO tickets vanished practically before the ink dried. Television and radio stations vied for interview time. Like The Merseymen, she held press conferences before every performance and continued with her informal chat sessions, usually after a concert.

Nikki found that the bi-monthly, four-day meetings with Grant interrupted the momentum of her concert series. But she considered them necessary for the health of their marriage and wouldn't curtail them. The romance of stolen moments in a steamy seaside paradise partially compensated for their separation.

July 19th—her eighteenth birthday—found Nikki in Naples. Following yet another triumphant exit from the stage, a group of promoters and elite press corps congregated around Nikki outside her dressing room door. Momentarily distracted, something drew her attention from the surrounding horde. Like a lone shaft of light piercing a cloudy gray sky, there stood a man, the likes of which Nikki had never seen before. In his early thirties, he emanated conservative class, borne of either nobility or old money. Tall—a little over six feet—he swept his sandy blond hair off to the right at a rakish angle. A roguish twinkle sparked in his incredibly blue eyes. Exceedingly comfortable in his white dinner jacket and satin-stripped trousers, his clothes distinguished him as they stood in stark contrast to the trendy-chic get-ups of the others. Nonchalantly he leaned one shoulder against the corridor wall, taking in the scene, casting a bemused smile in Nikki's direction. His intense attention penetrated her.

Slightly intimidated by his direct gaze, Nikki cast her eyes down, looking away for a moment. When she looked back up, he had disappeared, as mysteriously as he appeared. Such profound scrutiny baffled her. Who was he? What did he want?

Chapter 9
Humpty Dumpty

November second, premiere day, dawned clear and extraordinarily sunny. Successfully Bruce had convened the three corners of his publicity triangle creating a superb confluence. He built the sexual tension between Grant and Nikki to a feverish pitch, swelled the rising tide of The Merseymen and Nikki's ever-expanding popularity, and intensified the anticipation for the movie.

Vada Knight costumed them for the gala. She clothed the Merseymen in long, black velvet Edwardian cut tuxes with over-sized four-in-hand ties. Nikki glowed in her golden satin gown with natural waist and demure décolletage. Grecian curls cascaded down the nape of Nikki's neck with a string of gold sequins entwined through them. For the crowning touch, on her left hand, Grant had borrowed a five-carat diamond solitaire for Nikki to wear. Her two-carat engagement ring would be rescued from the bank vault outside the glare of the cameras.

Five limos snaked their way through the crowded streets to the theatre. Precise pacing of the cars gave the press at least five minutes solo face-time with each Merseyman on the red carpet.

Grant exited his car to questions about an "impending" engagement. Playing coy, he shyly received his accolade, biding his time waiting for Nikki's limo. When it arrived, he opened the door and offered his hand to assist her. As planned, the diamond ring emerged first, tarrying for a moment in full view of the press. Flashbulbs popped profusely, setting fire to its brilliance. Then Grant pulled Nikki up and beside him. Wrapping his right arm about her shoulder, he waved with his left. They posed together, displaying the ring.

"Congratulations! When's the big day?" the press called out.

"Thanks! What day is that?" Grant impishly threw back.

"When are you getting married?"

"I don't know yet. I have to ask her father," Grant teased.

"When did you ask her?"

"Last night. Got down on me knees and everythin'. What do ya know? She said yes!" Grant raised Nikki's left hand in triumph then drew her into a kiss. The throng erupted in wild cheers.

Inside, red velvet ropes lined off rows for their party. From their special section, Sam and Graham fraternized with assorted studio dignitaries who came to be seen at the premiere.

Taking in the action, Nikki noted a man in a serious black business suit smoothly slipped his way through the mass to Sam, Graham and Bruce, garnering their collective ear. They all nodded, smiled, tossed a look at the group, then back to the man.

"Ah, ha, somethin's afoot." Grant whispered into Nikki's ear. The others also noticed and gathered their heads together to figure out the news.

Beside himself in jubilation, Bruce strode up the aisle to the group. "That was Her Majesty's secretary. The royal family *will* attend the premiere. They've dusted out the royal box and all! Afterwards Her Majesty desires an audience with you backstage. Her footman will be 'round to instruct us in the correct behavior." Bruce grimaced at the thought of Jack receiving instructions of proper protocol.

For Nikki the excitement of meeting the Royals drowned out the film and even the wild ovation at its conclusion. Over and over in her mind she practiced her curtsey, hoping she wouldn't trip when she executed it.

Uniformed guards escorted them to a secure room backstage where the Royal Family waited. They stood in a formal reception line, and the honorees queued up in another line to be presented. Jack, Candy and Jack Jr,. stood first for introductions. Three-year old Jack, Jr., breached the walls of formality, charming everyone with his version of royal etiquette. Bowing deeply from the waist before the Queen, from his bent-over position he looked up at Her Majesty and said, "Am I doin' this right, ma'am?" Laughter from everyone cut the tension.

"You are doing just fine, young man," replied the Queen as she took his little hand and raised his position to normal stance. She bent over slightly so they could speak on more direct terms. "So how old are you, young man?" she queried him.

Jack intervened, "If I might, Your Majesty," picking Jack, Jr. up in his arms he relieved the Queen of her uncomfortable stance and allowed them to communicate at eye level.

A House of Windsor photographer snapped pictures of everyone as they met Her Royal Highness—a personal memento of the occasion.

Dashingly, Prince Charles took time for a personal aside to Nikki. "You know, normally I detest pop music, but I find your voice intriguing. I should like to attend one of your concerts."

"I would be deeply honored by your presence, your majesty," Nikki responded with a curtsey.

Talk of the royal audience followed them to the hotel ballroom where

Sam Rottenburg hosted a lavish premiere party. A larger-than-life size ice sculpture of the four Merseymen with the title of the film, *Trapped!*, etched in huge letters below greeted the guests as they entered. Champagne flowed over the base of the sculpture forming a fountain of the bubbly. Behind that, sumptuous food heaped to overflowing, spilled across a runway of tables. A full-service bar lined one wall, and waiters passed through the partygoers exchanging half-full glasses for brimming ones. The room teemed with power brokers and movie aristocracy. Sam kept the magic and glitter sparkling through the night with a planet-sized mirrored ball turning above their heads.

A bit shy to go wandering, Nikki stood at Grant's side as he led her in and out of conversations from one luminary to another, feeling free for the first time publicly to have his arm about her waist. To her utter amazement, again and again legends of the business took their time to compliment her on her performance.

In the course of the evening, Nikki returned to the champagne fountain for a bit more bubbly. Holding her glass under the flow, another glass joined hers. She cast a customary, polite glance up at her fountain companion, only to come face to face with that mysterious man she had seen in Naples. His blue eyes danced. The spotlights coaxed strands of rich gold from his perfectly styled hair. His designer tuxedo accentuated his robust frame.

Raising his glass as if in a toast to her he said, "It would have been a better sculpture had the sculptor carved your figure. But I doubt an earthly artist could capture such perfection." Then turning with a wink, the crowd swallowed him up.

Dawn's first light brought a sampling of the reviews to their hotel suite. Some version of "Mersey Man Engages Princess" captured all the bold type. In paper after paper, the picture of Nikki's rock eclipsed the premiere story, relegating it to "below the fold" position.

As time for their official marriage neared, Grant hunted a place for them to live. He eventually settled on a white Georgian manor with black mansard roof in Surrey. Willows wept gracefully over a gentle stream which burbled through its manicured gardens. A grand, curved staircase of rich mahogany swept up from the black and white marble foyer, stunning the entrants. The well-equipped kitchen, with its banks of painted white wood and leaded-glass cabinets, opened onto a garden room eating area. Walls of French doors lined the room, providing a commanding view of the grounds.

To privately commemorate their first anniversary, on December 24th, 1965, Grant and Nikki made it official for the world. In the company of Bruce, The Merseymen, and with Mary and Candy again at her side, they stood before the public registry in London and said their "I do's." This time news of their marriage flashed across the front page of every major newspaper in the world, including those in America!

Grant carried Nikki across the threshold of the Surrey house where they celebrated their first real Christmas together in the new house with his family and a catered Christmas feast.

Judging by overwhelming fan support for the union of Grant and Nikki, they had no reason to believe that either their relationship or anyone else could torpedo the Merseymen's success. In their naiveté, they scoffed at the fear of change. In his vigilant watch for the enemy from without, Bruce had forgotten about the enemy within.

Chapter 10
Sitting on a Wall

On January 6th, 1966, when they assembled to prepare for their winter tour of South America and the Near East, Richie greeted them with his big news: he and Doreen would be getting married prior to the tour, to be followed by the arrival of their blessed event in June.

Years of being on the merry-go-round of fame began to exact its price from The Merseymen. For eleven years they had consumed the dream; now it began to consume them. One of the first symptoms of the internal cracking had manifested itself that March of '64 when Grant had walked away from the group, when he first met Nikki at the lake. The guys handled the mounting repression from years of success's pressure cooker in a variety of ways. Their acid-witted humor lightened the mood, their "vities" kept them on pace and alcohol relieved the tension of being cooped up. A willing beauty culled from the daily pack of groupies also provided distraction.

No one knew when it happened or the precise cause, but the internal disposition of The Merseymen had changed dramatically by the start of their '66 winter tour. The new mood fermenting beneath the surface was so palpable, one could have used the proverbial knife on it. Yet, it was invisible, creating the false illusion of normalcy. Restlessness could have been the name of the culprit; that edgy, excitable, jumping-out-of-your-skin, something's-gotta-go-pop feeling.

Of course evolution produces growth, stagnation, death. But the pendulum of change seemed to swing out of sync from its expected course. Both Jack and Pete began introducing more complex sounds into the music, experimenting with new rhythms and instruments. Their production decreased as they spent time re-tooling the structure of the music. Because of her proximity to the group, Nikki didn't recognize her introduction into their mix as part of this process. She constituted yet another tree in their forest of change.

Grant didn't escape unscathed from this strange itchiness either. Taking Nikki's presence for granted once they became "legal," he left her in charge of their public persona to turn inside himself, spending hours alone with his new sitar creating his own sound, writing out his lyrics. He gave birth to disjointed, jangled sounds with nonsensical words. Nikki thought of them as themes in search of a topic. Seeking to understand what obviously meant so much to her husband, she engaged him about his themes. Icily he met her queries with, "If you don't get it, I won't waste my time explaining it to you." On his days off, he'd seal himself off for hours companioned only by a vacant stare and the strains of middle-eastern music saturating the room. He excused his behavior as getting in tune with the new stop on the tour, India. Nikki didn't realize he had dived headlong into the world of "mind expansion" and dropping acid.

In her innocence, Nikki also failed to recognize the recent sweet smell of pot floating through the hotel rooms. Alcohol no longer stilled the restless beast. Narcotics became the logical next step to quell the anxiety from induced captivity. Hiding their use from her, the group retreated for vast periods of time and disguised its smell with incense. Compelled, Mary pulled her aside and enlightened her. Nikki felt violated. She didn't know whether they kept her on the outside for protection or paranoia, but their banishment stung. Their drug use, compounded by their secrecy, chafed relations.

The group always enjoyed touring the Southern Hemisphere in January and February. The Southern summertime weather offered a welcome respite from the frigid North. But more changes loomed on the horizon. On the permissive beaches of South America, the group caught glimpses of Jack with a naked, dark-haired beauty. Her almost Godiva-length hair barely covered her charms. Later Solana clung on his arm through parties absent the press. Continually she joined him as they crossed the Southern Continent. With her obvious presence, the group grew nervously restive. Nikki struggled between protecting Candy from the news and revealing it to her. Her kinship with Jack dissolved into a gnawing, internal loathing. And Grant dodged all her overtures on the subject.

Each day the intolerability built. Jack now brought Solana to every performance, every recording session. The mounting tension pressurized them. Nikki couldn't let her personal feelings toward Jack affect her performance on stage, so she focused on her fans. In so many ways, they became her saving grace.

After four weeks of her protracted tolerance, Nikki resolved to tell Candy. She determined it had to be done in person, not over the phone. Grant exploded with a round of viperous expletives at her plan. He accused her of trying to break up the group. She misread Grant's hostility as weakness. His denial of the facts she interpreted as lack of knowledge. Since Solana's presence also angered Pete and Richie, she wanted their endorsement of her plan—but drew up short. Involving Pete and Richie constituted drawing a line in the sand and asking the four to choose up sides. Nikki knew if she forced them to chose, then *she'd* be responsible for the demise of The Merseymen, not Jack, not Solana. Pulled apart on the inside, she walked out of the hotel, into the night, looking for answers.

Operating on autopilot, as if invisible, Nikki didn't bother to look before entering the street to scout for fans, media or the like. Her plan only included walking until she found her answers.

Preoccupied by her dilemma, she failed to notice the two dark figures approaching fast from behind. As they closed in, their scuffling, quickening footsteps and furtive whispers woke her to imminent danger, sadly too late for evasive action. Suddenly, vice-like hands gripped both her arms, arresting Nikki in her tracks. Her captors read the fear in her startled eyes. Her fright enticed them, feeding their depraved hunger. They shoved her against a brick building. Its uneven surface dug into Nikki's back. Streetlights flashed across their swarthy faces, gnarled with several days' growth of beard. Lust from heathen red eyes leered at her. Their filthy fingers lifted bits of her clothing as they examined the merchandise. Hissing, they threw barbs and taunting jeers through their missing and jagged teeth. The exhaust of raw hooch reeked from their pores.

They infused her with their venom of panic. Nikki struggled, reflexively trying to kick her way free. Instantly their legs spread and pinned hers, splaying her spread eagle against the wall. Desperately she tried to wipe away her panic. They took turns grinding their mouths against her lips, tasting the promise of the sweet fruit of conquest. Their sandpaper stubble burned Nikki's lips and face. She pitched her head side to side to avoid contact. With a free hand, one captor grabbed a thatch of hair yanking her head back with a sharp rap against the bricks. The other unleashed the back of his hand against her cheek. Nikki closed her eyes. The slap echoed in her ears, snapping her head from the other's hold, sending her cheekbone—whack—into the wall. The energy of the violence charged his spirit. He centered her head on the stone surface and swung again. Smack! Her lips parted and she tasted the brick. Something warm ran into Nikki's mouth. His hand moved to the collar of her blouse. He loaded his fist with a hefty helping of material and ripped—exposing her.

Dazed, Nikki heard the urgent, swift footfalls of others approaching. Were these two merely advance men for a descending swarm? She heard the shattering of glass. Broken glass terrified her. Were the new recruits armed with those razor-sharp shards? Her mind raced to find escape before their reinforcements arrived.

In one fell movement, white flesh of forearms straddled her captors' throats, their eyes bulged out. Hands seized their wrists, wrenching them up along their backs. In pain they writhed face down to the ground, their arms thrust back, way above their heads. A boot to the ass sent them in a crawling slither along the sidewalk. They scuttled off into the blackness.

Unsupported, Nikki collapsed, shuddering to the ground. She tried to gather her legs under her for a retreat from the new vanquishers, but couldn't locate any power. Strong hands under her arms lifted her up. Nikki sobbed at the inevitability of impending doom.

"My God! It is her!" said one voice.

"Here, give her to me," another whispered. Nikki felt herself being laid into someone's chest. His arms encompassed her, his hands smoothed her hair. He spoke in consoling tones. "It's okay. It's okay. You're with friends."

"Get a cab," the man quietly commanded. Fearing more faces of the beast, Nikki finally summoned the nerve to look at the person—and into the face of Karl.

Gently the reporter smiled at her, "It's okay. You're okay now." He continued to smooth her hair and dab at the warm fluid from near her eye. She clutched tighter into his chest, unable to say anything; an irrepressible whimper emanated from deep inside of her. Gradually shaking off the trauma, reality came in incoherent, halting waves. Nikki tried to sit on her own, but her strength didn't follow. A taxi screeched to a stop at the curb and Karl's friend came around to help scoop her up into the waiting car.

Karl draped her arms around his neck. Nikki willed them to grab on, but they fell back limp on her. Her shoe dragged across some glass. It tinkled on the sidewalk as they loaded her into the taxi.

Karl spoke softly, "Nikki. I'm going to have the driver take us back to your hotel. Don't worry. I'll get you back to Grant."

Instantly her eyes widened in dread. She thrashed back and forth. A rush of breath escaped from her swollen lips. "No. No!"

Karl calmed her. "Okay. Okay, we'll do something else. Shh, don't worry." He muttered as he thought. "Nikki, I'm going to take you to my hotel, is that all right?" Quietly she settled back into his arms.

Karl had the cabbie park in the hotel's underground garage. He sent his friend in to retrieve a hat, sunglasses, his topcoat and a wheelchair from the hotel. He intended to pass Nikki off as an eccentric pal who consumed a little too much nightlife. Using the topcoat to cover her torn clothes, Karl pulled the hat down to the bridge of the glasses to hide most of the contusions. As anticipated, the wheelchair raised red flags with the night manager. He insisted on sending up the hotel's doctor-on-call.

Karl laid Nikki on his bed, standing at her side during the doctor's examination. The doctor concluded that probably nothing was broken; however, she had likely suffered a concussion. With his penlight he searched for signs of bleeding behind her eyes and warned of the dangers of swelling brain tissue. Adeptly the physician butterflied pieces of tape and placed them above Nikki's left eye to close the wound. Adamantly he recommended the hospital for x-rays and extensive examination. He left, prescribing ice for the swelling, aspirin for the pain, and constant supervision in case the concussion took a turn for the worse. The doctor never recognized the identity of his patient.

Drawing up a chair alongside the bed, Karl dialed the phone.

"Hello Bruce? Karl Nielson here. There's been a bit of an accident. ... No. No, nothing serious, but I'd like you to come over to my hotel directly. I'm at the Hilton. ... No, it's best not to discuss it over the phone. I'll explain when I see you. Don't worry, just please hurry." He hung up.

In the meantime, Karl and his friend fluffed a considerable stack of pillows to prop Nikki up into a semi-sitting position. Knowing she had to remain conscious for twenty-four hours, he sent down for carafe of strong coffee for his vigil and a pitcher of fruit juice for her. Nikki hardly possessed enough energy to draw the fluid up through the straw. When she did, the juice's mild acid stung her lips. In her detached state she wondered about the red splotches on Karl's shirt. Gradually biting pain replaced the fuzziness. She couldn't control an internal trembling.

Panicked by Karl's call, Bruce grabbed Mary to go with him. On the ride over Mary prepared herself for all the ghastly possibilities so she could stem any emotional outburst. But Bruce's horrified reaction as he stood in the doorway telegraphed to Nikki the grim reality of her condition.

"Cor, Karl! What happened?" Bruce gasped as he rushed in.

"A couple of street thugs jumped her."

"Where in the hell was Jarred's security?" demanded Bruce.

"I don't know. She probably ditched him. We were on our way to clear up some of the scheduling conflicts when we saw Nikki slip out of a side exit of the hotel. On a whim we followed her, just to see what she was up to. I guess we gave her too much lead. Within about ten blocks from the hotel, two thugs cut into her from an alleyway. My photographer Jimmy and I ran up the street as fast as possible, but unfortunately they got their hooks into her before we could get there. This is how we found her. They roughed her up pretty good."

Remotely, Nikki heard all their words, but nothing registered.

Bruce turned to Nikki, "Nicole, are you all right? Do you need anything?"

Vacantly she blinked at him.

Wrinkling his face in distress, he revolved back to Karl, "Why in the bloody hell didn't you bring her back to our hotel and Grant?"

At that, Nikki fussed profusely under the covers.

Karl sternly put his finger to his lips, directing the gesture towards Bruce. Soothingly he patted Nikki's arm. "It's okay. You're fine here. Don't worry."

Then Karl directed his attention back to Bruce, "I don't understand it. Of course, that's the first place I tried to take her. But any mention of Grant and she reacts that way. She hasn't spoken except to say 'no' when I asked her about going to him. It's almost like she connects him with the attack. Has something happened?"

"I dunno. But she's his wife. I can't hide this from him. He has to be told."

"Of course. ... The doctor examined her just before you came. He wanted to admit her to the hospital immediately, but that's your call. He said she probably suffered a concussion; nothing appears broken."

While the two men discussed options, Mary administered sips of juice along with applying cold compresses. After listening to the men's fruitless conjecture, Mary offered an idea of her own. "How about if we tell Grant about the scuffle, that the doctors don't want her moved and that I am sitting up with her? Grant should buy that. If she's scared of Grant, you could send her into a delirium by introducing him now. We have to buy her some time until she's out of the woods and you have all the facts."

The two accepted her plan. As it turned out, Bruce couldn't find Grant anyway until the following midday when he showed up for the concert.

By mid-morning Nikki had recovered enough to take light toast and tea for breakfast. Mary helped her shower and gently washed and fixed her hair. Bruce sent over a change of clothes. Under her own power, Nikki faced the inevitable—her image in the mirror. White butterfly bandages closing the cut above her left eye stood in stark contrast against the swelling and the iridescent purple of the bruises. The right side of her lip ballooned to double its normal size. A bluish pallor clung to Nikki's cheeks. Assorted bruises, including her assailants' handprints on Nikki's wrists, peppered her entire body. The trembling remained.

Bruce canceled her afternoon concert appearance with the excuse of stomach flu.

Following the concert, Grant summoned an adequate amount of concern and rushed to Nikki's bedside. She stiffened when she woke, and his frame filled the doorway. Mary squeezed her hand in support. Sitting up tall in the chair beside the bed, with terrier zeal Mary fiercely guarded her charge.

Grant approached slowly, gallantly, practically dropping to one knee, ignoring Nikki's protector. Taking her hand, he kissed it. "Oh luv, are you all right? I came as soon as I could. How do you feel?" He lavished her fingertips with kisses.

"I'm getting better. Oh, Grant, it was so …"

Tenderly he interrupted, "Mary, you can leave us now. I'll take it from here."

Coldly she held her ground, "It's okay Grant. I don't mind."

Resolutely, Grant insisted, "Mary, I'd like some time alone with my wife."

Nikki smiled limply, ceding Mary permission to depart. She blamed her apprehension of her husband on the concussion. Desperately she needed her prince now to sweep her up in his arms and gently kiss away all the fears and the ugliness of the previous night. Grant ushered Mary out, closing the door on the heels of her exit.

Assuming his position at the foot of her bed, Grant snapped, "Well ain't you a sight! Do we need to buy you an attack dog to take along now?"

Confused by the brusque change, Nikki weakly smiled at him, "I suppose so."

"So Nik, how did this happen?" He abandoned all concern, scolding her like an impatient father.

Taken aback she mumbled, "These guys grabbed me."

"And what in the bleedin' hell were you doin' out walkin' after dark? Have all yer senses left ya?"

"I needed some time to think things through."

"Think? About what? … Oh, so this is how you punish me for our lil' row!" Grant turned it all around, victimizing himself, erasing her attackers.

"You?"

"Yea, me. Furthermore, you missed the concert this afternoon. Or do ya care? The career you wanted so badly? Now ya can't bother to show up to play the gig! We had to cover for ya. And all the blokes askin' about ya! What did the Princess need — more attention?"

Nikki couldn't believe her ears. She felt disconnected, like she failed to track the conversation. "No, really, these guys jumped out…"

"Did you set this whole thing up so you could spend time with yer lil' reporter boyfriend? Gettin' 'im to feel sorry for ya. Grabbin' a lil' more free press! And God knows what else!" His acid words scalded her.

Advancing, Grant stripped the covers from her, grabbing for her arm.

Nikki cowered.

"Get up, bitch! Get your hussy lil' ass together. Yer goin' home with me!" Grant clenched her right forearm. With his entire force, he yanked her up out of bed.

White-hot searing pain coursed through her shoulder. A cry of pain involuntarily escaped from the depth of her soul.

In a flash Karl burst through the doors. Mary came on his heels.

Grant froze, his hand still wrenching Nikki's arm.

Nikki crumpled.

Grant dropped her arm.

Mary rushed to catch her.

Grant squared off with Karl.

Karl answered him with a resounding blow to the jaw, sending Grant reeling backwards, careening into a chair then to the floor.

He struggled to get his feet under him.

Karl grabbed the throat of his shirt, lifting him from the ground, and met Grant's face with a roundhouse punch sending him sprawling to the floor. Karl went for Grant again when Jimmy tackled him, grabbing his arms to break up the fight. Jimmy yelled Karl's name to jolt him back to reality. Finally Karl shook himself free of the bloodlust and returned to rationality, sinking into a chair. Jimmy offered Grant a hand up.

Grant staggered to a sofa in the anteroom under his own power.

Wrapping some ice in a towel, Mary presented it to Grant for his eye. "Here! Use this. Grant, you need to get back to your hotel. I'll bring Nikki around in a bit. Now get." Opening the door, she prompted his exit.

Karl held his head, sitting in the chair. He knew he'd crossed the line. A reporter doesn't beat up the hottest tabloid property in the world. "Oh, I'm sorry Nikki. I overheard. He made me crazy; I couldn't believe it. When you screamed, I just erupted. I'm sorry." He went over to the bed and picked up her hand, "but you know, I'd do it all again. I'm so glad we were around last night."

Nikki winced through the pain burning in her right shoulder. "I might not be alive today if it weren't for you. Karl, I can never thank you enough for saving me last night."

"I didn't rescue you last night, so he could beat you up today. What's going on with you and Grant? Is he abusing you? Every time I mentioned his name last night you cringed."

In denial Nikki excused, "No! No, I'm not sure why. Maybe it's because we had an argument just before I left the hotel. Then the mugging, perhaps I associated Grant with the attack."

"Well, what in the hell got into him? His wife has just been beaten, nearly killed, and he's making up stories of affairs and blaming you? Nikki, I just don't get it. But you know, I'll always be here for you—on or off the record. If you're up to it, we should get you back to your hotel now."

Mercifully when they reached Nikki's hotel suite, Grant was nowhere to be found. Mary helped Nikki change, doled out more aspirin and saw her back into bed.

Nikki woke sometime in the middle of the night to a man's hushed voice. The whisper called, "Nikki, are you asleep? Nikki. Nikki, wake up." Fighting to pull herself from sleep, she opened her eyes to see Grant sitting on the bed, his bloodshot brown eyes pleading her to consciousness.

"Wake up Nikki. I need you. I've been such a bloody fool," Grant sputtered tears. "I nearly lost you. How could I have said those awful things? What would I do without you? They almost killed you." Gaining in emotional volume, his sobs racked his body. His movement on the bed refreshed the pain in her shoulder, but Nikki willed the pain into the background. Grant needed her.

Crawling in next to her, once again he reeked of gin and incense. "I can't lose you. I can't lose you," he repeated through gasps for breath. "I don't know what came over me. Maybe I just got scared. Can you forgive me? Please? Please forgive me."

She hushed him with comforting succor.

By morning her shoulder raged with pain, stabbing her awake. Nikki got up before she disturbed Grant and shuffled into the living room of the suite. Twisting her into knots, the pain drove her into a chair, making her sick to her stomach. To quiet the nausea, she pulled her legs to her chest. She phoned Mary. Without asking permission, Mary brought Bruce and the hotel doctor.

Bruce never questioned Nikki's shoulder injury, he assumed it to be a latent consequence of the mugging. Everyone agreed Nikki needed to be seen immediately at the hospital. Bruce and Mary hastily assembled a cover story for her hospital visit.

All the commotion in the suite brought Grant out of the bedroom. His face, with a shiner below his left eye, begged the question.

"What the hell happened to you?" Bruce asked in shock.

In unison the room's attention swung to Grant, waiting for his explanation. Karl, Nikki and Mary knew his reply would set the parameters of Nikki's future business relationship with Karl. Did Grant hate Karl enough to cough up his vicious accusations from the night before, thereby forever poisoning the water between Karl and Nikki? Or did his manhandling of Nikki disturb him enough to lie?

Armed with the truth and not afraid to use it, Mary shot Grant an admonishing look, warning him not to interfere.

Carefully Grant considered the double-edged possibilities of his answer. "I ... I did a stupid thing. Last night I went looking for the bastards who knocked Nikki about. Of course I didn't find them, but I stumbled into a bar long enough to get into a row of my own." Guilt forced Grant's hand. He lied with stone-cold abandon!

Then he turned his attention to Nikki. "What do you think, luv? Shall we be photographed with our matching shiners? Bravely together even to the end!" Threateningly he narrowed his eyes. In other words, he expected her silence in return for his lie.

Nikki didn't realize that in the bargain her silence tacitly granted permission for further abuse. Involuntarily a gasp escaped from Mary when Nikki demurred, "Sure."

Jarred, Nikki's head of security, assisted her to the limo. Mildly, he rebuked her. "Nikki please, you really have to let me do my job. If you want to go out again, let me go with you or send someone. Okay? I don't ever want to see something like this happen again to you. This really tears me up."

Nikki met his caring eyes, "I promise, Jarred. From now on, I'll let you know."

Chapter 11
Teetering

After the required x-rays, poking and probing, the hospital's medical team assessed Nikki's condition as a dislocated right shoulder and immediately sedated her to realign the joint. When Nikki emerged from the drugs, Grant recited the litany of dreadful news: twelve weeks of complete rest followed by four weeks of therapy. It meant canceling Nikki's part of the tour and sending her home. Uncharacteristically, Grant assumed the reins of authority. Tenaciously he denied Nikki's pleas to stay, insisting she recuperate under her mother's care in Pennsylvania. Mary would accompany her. Grant ended the discussion by presenting her next dosage of painkillers, which returned her to unconsciousness.

A sense of finality—an end to her days with The Merseymen—brushed across Nikki's mind, insinuating itself into her departure. In a stupor of prescribed medications, Nikki didn't remember anything about the flight. Mary helped her stumble through customs and into her parents' welcoming arms before Mary changed planes to go to her home in Virginia.

For the next two days, dreams of evil, twisted, taunting faces with searing red eyes tortured Nikki's sleep. Having enough of their daughter's drug-induced coma, Fran called their family physician to see if he concurred with doctors in Argentina.

"Heavens, Frances, why would they keep her in a coma? If the shoulder is aligned properly, the pain should be gone. Stop the pain pills! And bring her in when she's conscious," Dr. Hess ordered.

After his examination, Dr. Hess shook his head in disbelief, "I don't understand. The shoulder's been correctly placed. Why prescribe immobilization for twelve weeks? In addition, there's no sign of any lingering effects from the head trauma. Why dope her up like this? Maybe I'm missing something that doctor saw in his examination. Could you get me his name, Nicole? I'd like to get in touch with him."

Her mother assured her Grant had called each evening since she arrived home. Nikki waited for Grant's nightly call so she could get the information for Dr. Hess.

Over the dinner table that evening, her mom couldn't restrain herself anymore, "Nikki, what happened to you in Buenos Aires?"

Nikki furnished all the details of the attack and Karl's life saving rescue, but omitted Grant's violent mood swing.

"So, your shoulder was dislocated during the attack?" her dad questioned.

"I suppose so," Nikki fudged, not wishing to cast Grant in the light he deserved.

"I don't understand how the doctor could have missed that on the first go round. It must have hurt you terribly?" Richard fished on.

"I had so much pain, I guess I couldn't tell one from the other." There did he buy that?

The phone interrupted their dance. Fran answered Grant's call.

Taking the phone from her mother, in the background Nikki heard the strains of Middle-Eastern music. "Hi, Grant. I miss you. What's going on?"

"So you're up. The doctor wanted you medicated for at least a week. And what do you mean seeing another doctor? What's the matter? Don't you trust me?"

"What's trust got to do with it? Mom and Dad weren't too sure about the doctors down there. Dr. Hess is confused by their diagnosis. He needs to talk to the doctor from the hospital. Do you have his name?"

"I dunno. Maybe Bruce has it. Well, gotta go."

"Wait Grant. I need..."

The connection went dead. Grant never called again.

The next day Nikki tried Bruce, but the harried manager didn't have the details from the doctor. Instead he carped about deteriorating conditions of the tour before cutting Nikki short.

Tears pooled in Nikki's eyes as she turned to her parents. "I don't understand. What's happening? No one can talk."

"Try Mary down in Virginia. Maybe she's heard something." Richard suggested.

Fortuitously, a call from Mary interrupted them. "Nikki? You're not going to believe this! Ben called today. Seems everything has fallen apart on the tour. Rumors about you are rampant. They say you're near death, you're paralyzed, even insane and committed to an asylum. It's causing hysteria. Everyday the headlines get worse. And it's spreading to Europe. Grant has told them you're in a coma, and your parents are near mental collapse. Bruce can't control what's going on."

"Mary, I don't understand Grant's lies. None of that rubbish is true. My parents are here with me. We've got to put an end to the rumors. Where's Karl? Can he help?"

"Ben told me that Grant banished Karl yesterday. He accused him of arranging your mugging just to sell papers. He's threatened to file a lawsuit, claiming Karl's presence compromises his ability to perform. He demanded Karl's touring pass."

"Mary, that's all a lie! Can't someone say anything?"

"Go against Grant Henderson? Not likely, especially since he's your husband."

"Can you catch a flight up here to Pennsylvania, Mary? We need to talk!"

"Sure. I'll be there tomorrow morning. Besides, there's something else we have to discuss." She hated to leave Nikki hanging, but she wasn't about to lay her next bit of news on Nikki over the phone. Saturated already by Grant's antics, Nikki didn't press her further. Before ringing off, Nikki asked Mary to get the attending physician's report from the Buenos Aires hospital.

Unsuccessfully Nikki tried to reach Karl at his London flat so the three of them could work on a plan.

At nine, headlights crawled down the driveway. Richard admitted the caller. "Look, Nikki, Karl stopped by on his way back to London," her father called up the stairs to her.

Her parents stayed only long enough to express their gratitude for his heroics, then suggested she and Karl might talk in comfort in the study.

Exhausted, Karl peeled off his winter topcoat, draping it over one of the leather wingback chairs. Nikki invited him to sit. Overriding concern muted her delight at seeing her friend. "Karl, what's going on? Mary said Grant expelled you."

"My questions first—what about you? I called your parents a couple of days after you left to check on you. They told me about your doctor's assessment. That didn't square with all the press's hand-wringing. Ace reporter that I am, I went directly to Grant and questioned him. He had me thrown out on my ear. The bugger seems to be hatching some sort of scheme. Do you know what he's after?"

"No. But evidently it includes cutting me out of the picture. He's upset that I'm conscious and ambulatory. Then he hung up on me and won't take any of my calls."

For the next three hours, Karl and Nikki tried to piece together the puzzle of Grant's off-beat, uncharacteristic movements. Nikki even confessed Grant's flip-flop on her career, his drug use, his mood swings and his mysterious disappearances. The lateness of the hour finally shut them down, and Nikki invited Karl to stay in the guest bedroom.

Mary arrived the following day bringing the remaining two puzzle pieces. She had spoken to the attending emergency room physician. Recalling the case vividly, he remembered he had recommended two weeks in the sling, without calling for bed rest. He only prescribed the narcotics under duress. Grant had begged for them fearing Nikki's pain might become debilitating, and then being hundreds of miles away, they wouldn't be able to get the medication. Under Grant's resolute persistence, the doctor acquiesced.

Mary swallowed hard to bolster her determination before delivering the last resounding bit of information. "Jack isn't the only one with a bird on the side. Grant has been keeping company outside your bed, too."

Genuinely overcome, Nikki sank back into her chair. "Are you sure?"

"Yes. God have mercy, yes. In fact, that's why Bruce couldn't find Grant the night of the mugging."

"Who, Mary? Who is it?" Nikki wanted to know.

"Evidently, there have been many, but recurrently it's been a model from their first movie, Bridget. This isn't idle speculation. Ben told me the other night. He found out when he and Richie got 'in their cups.' Since Richie's marriage, Grant's behavior really bothers him. With courage from a bottle of scotch, he confessed all the sordid details to Ben." Mary paused. "Nikki, I'm so sorry."

"No, it's okay. This clears up a whole lot. Is Grant planning on a divorce?"

"I don't know. Ben says he still pretends to be devastated by your absence."

"How long has it been going on?"

"Evidently since their first movie."

The longevity of his infidelity left Nikki reeling. "Does everyone know?"

"Probably. Bridget does drugs with Grant. He's planning on taking her on the tour to India, since you won't be along."

At that point Nikki's parents wandered into the kitchen, and Nikki invited them into the conversation. In utter honesty, she broke the entire story to them, including Grant's violence.

In Nikki's recounting for her parents, a light dawned on Karl. "No wonder he cooked up that cock-and-bull story about me before he sacked me! I had enough information to be considered dangerous and with my investigative background, I might have stumbled onto the rest of this entire bloody mess."

"Then his guilt drove him to fire you?" Nikki interrupted.

"Maybe." Karl tossed back.

"Or the acid? Or..." Nicole continued to sort out excuses.

Impatiently her father jumped in. "Or a thousand things! Maybe *you'll* never know. That's spilt milk. Right now you have to ask yourself some tough questions."

"Like?" Nikki led, although her heart already knew those questions.

"Will you stay with him? Can you trust him? Where does this leave your career? You get my drift and can probably come up with a few yourself." Frustrated, unable to take the retaliatory action his male instinct demanded, the entire recital boiled beneath her father's skin. Aggravated, Richard exited the room.

Karl understood the potent, masculine emotional quagmire arresting Richard. He recognized it from his own primal, male response in the hotel that night. Likewise he joined Richard outside for a breath of air.

Meanwhile Nikki struggled with the implications of the assembled puzzle. Thoughts and flashbacks vacillating between the past to the present overwhelmed her. She recalled the nights early in their marriage—his late comings from costume fittings, the gin on his breath. Was that one of his trysts? Skipping ahead, the pictures of all the dollies on his arm. Was it really just for publicity? Back to the fight in his dressing room when Nikki condemned him to a night on his couch. Did Bridget share it, too? Fast forward again to last summer and the tabloid accounts of affairs with hot models during their separate summer tours. Was that the American press run amok or reality? The night of Nikki's attack, was Grant wrestling Bridget under the covers in the hours when he couldn't be found? "What a fool I've been!" Nikki lamented, tasting self-pity. "What did I do to cause him to do this?"

"Nothing," Fran answered frostily, annoyed by a situation over which she had no control and her daughter's turn to self sympathy.

"Could it have been my career? Was it the separation? Was it the road?"

"Stop it Nicole!" Fran's sharp tone demanded Nikki's attention. "Yes, all those things might have strained your relationship. A mature person talks about the pressures and finds solutions. You grow together that way. Everything you mentioned might have fueled Grant's alienation, but he should have talked to you. Nothing justifies his actions. And nothing warrants his abuse of you."

Drawing herself alongside Nikki's chair, she cast a judicious eye at her. "So Nicole, how long are you going to wallow in self pity?" more between-the-eyes parenting. "What are *you* going to *do* about this?"

Nikki rose to meet her mother's tough-love standards. "I guess I had better talk to Grant about us. I have to find out what drove him to do this and what we can do to fix it. But I won't compromise my principles. I won't share him. I won't do drugs."

Her mom patted her hand. "There you go. That's the woman I raised. That's all you can do Nikki. And then be prepared to back up his answers with action."

To clear her head and get a fresh perspective, that afternoon Nikki rode Thunder down the dirt road to her old haunt at the lake. The weather had brightened that first of February, melting all the snow, leaving in its wake the musty sweet smell of moist, promising earth. Approaching in the distance, coming around a curve in the road, another horse and rider caught Nikki's attention.

The horse, of jumping stock, stood tall, with exquisitely etched features born of well-chosen bloodlines. His finely maintained coat radiated in the sun. The nobility of the steed perfectly matched his rider, who sported tall riding boots, jodhpurs, suede blazer and an ascot. The sun warmed the gold of his sandy-colored hair. Perfectly seated, he cantered toward Nikki. An unusual pair, their stylish presentation reaped her fascination. Nikki prepared a customary greeting as their paths by-passed.

However in the final seconds, horse and rider moved to intersect her path, pulling up to face Nikki and Thunder. Instantly she recognized the rider as the mysterious man from Naples. He nodded his head in a greeting. "Good morning. It's certainly good to see you recovering and on your feet again. I hope you are feeling well?"

"Yes, I am. Thank you for asking." His presence and knowledge of her convalescence muted her response.

"You have my fervent prayers for a complete recovery. It warms my soul to see you looking so fit. No wonder the sun is smiling today. It's trying to match your radiance. *Vaya con Dios.*" He clucked to his horse. In a striking manner, the steed reared up, and the pair left in a dashing gallop. Thunder swung around so they could watch them disappear down the road.

The stranger's appearance on the road both enchanted and unnerved Nikki. Was he following her? How was it he kept turning up—and now at her home? Who exactly was he? He always had the most charming air to him, but could he be stalking her? He ruined her contemplative morning at the lake. The more Nikki tried to concentrate on the matter at hand—the more his image, rising up on the road, captured her imagination.

Back at the house, Karl, Mary and Nikki again gathered around the table to come up with a plan for combating the awful rumors about Nikki. Mary detailed the Merseymen's latest itinerary. "They'll leave South America in three days. Rather than head off directly to India, the entourage will go back to London for a week before their two-week run at India and Pakistan."

"We have to get the good news out about Nikki's condition," Karl added. "Let's hire a camera crew from here to film Nikki's recovery story and apology for worrying her fans. I'll do the interview."

"And I can have it on the air in four days in Nikki's markets. The gossip circuit will suck up the piece immediately," Mary countered. "Then the news outlets will incorporate it into their information stream."

Following the interview, the three left for London. While Karl and Mary attended to the piece's final details, Nikki would have her little tête-à-tête with Grant.

Laying low at Mary's London flat, Nikki prepared for Grant's return from South America. She grew nervous over her impending showdown. How she despised confrontation; she wished she could put it off forever. Yet, she wanted to confront him now, to get the matter behind her.

Nikki knew her early return from her convalescence would shock everyone. Since Grant hadn't been congenial on the phone, Nikki wondered how the rest of the guys felt about her now. Not wanting to meet him alone, Nikki decided it would be best to expose her presence to Grant in public, at the recording studio. That way afforded Grant time to mask his probable apoplectic outrage at her presence. Hopefully, the others would surround her with their support for her early return. Given time, Grant may even compose himself enough to feign a tender hug and kiss. With the tension diffused, later Nikki and Grant could have a non-confrontational discussion. Her entire plan would be out the window, however, if Grant had contaminated the group to her return and they greeted her with embarrassed silence. Then divvying up the spoils of a career and a ruined marriage would be her legacy. Dismissing such thoughts as negative energy, she refused them credence.

Nikki assembled her costume for the encounter—an essay of health and desire. She chose a deep-cut, vee-neck, form fitting, red body suit with a micro-mini black leather skirt and red sheer stockings to display her lengthy legs. Seductively, she unleashed her hair.

At two, Nikki waltzed into the control booth to the delighted amazement of Bruce and Ben. Abandoning their positions at the controls, they grabbed her up in their enthusiasm and burst through the door into the studio itself.

"Hey lads!" Bruce crowed. "Look who's here!"

Beaming, Nikki threw open her arms in a "ta-da" pose. Instinctively her eyes searched out Grant. As expected, staggering shock engulfed him. Quickly she ceded him the privacy to collect himself.

The Merseymen surrounded her with their welcoming acclamation until Nikki became lost in their hugs and kisses. Finally one elated reveler spun her around and encompassed her in his arms. "Oh luv! I can't believe you're home!" She found her lips locked to Grant's who seemed earnestly euphoric at her homecoming. Nikki's heart wondered if their encounter would be easier than she had expected? Her father's phrase "trust, but verify" flashed to mind. Nikki vowed she wouldn't be swept up in the moment and dissuaded from her mission. Grant glued Nikki to his side as the recording session wrapped for the day in a delirious celebratory conclusion.

They partied like the good old days rocking on until the guys packed Grant and Nikki into a limo with lusty slaps on the back and knowing winks. Seizing the moment, Grant, ran his fingers down Nikki's long, stockinged legs, then up, up underneath her skirt. His mouth kissing hers deeply. Nikki matched his passion, tearing off his turtleneck.

Wickedly Grant growled into her ear, "Cor! how I want you. But I'll take you at home. I want you in our bed."

Nikki grabbed him *there*, purring, "I can hold on as long as you. And I promise, you won't be disappointed."

Nikki ran ahead of Grant into the house, laughing, teasing him. Grabbing a bottle of champagne, she bolted up the stairs to their bedroom. She sat on the bed with the bottle wedged between her thighs; Grant swaggered in, leaned against the jamb and watched. Slowly she worked the cork back and forth, easing it out with her thumb and forefinger, releasing it with a plump pop. Holding his eyes in a kittenish tease, Nikki raised the bottle to her moist mouth, running her tongue around the contours of its lip. Swigging from the bottle, she never released Grant's eyes. Rushing the bed, he grabbed the bottle. Covering the hole with his thumb, he shook it vigorously. The effervescent liquid erupted, drenching Nikki in its spray. Giggling she dared him—taunted him. Descending on her, he grabbed the vee of her bodysuit, tearing it open.

Her breasts spilled out. He feasted, licking off the champagne. Pushing up her skirt, he hung above Nikki, contemplating his next move. With reckless abandon he gathered the flimsy stocking mesh in both hands and ripped a gaping hole. He fulfilled his wish and reclaimed his wife in their marital bed.

Before closing her eyes in sleep, a thought crept in and gnawed at Nikki. Was that fabulous lovemaking session just Grant's way of using Nikki to erase *her* memory? Nikki pushed the thought aside—morning would be soon enough to sort it all out.

With mixed feelings Nikki rose to meet the morning, long before Grant stirred. Sitting with a steaming cup of tea, her knees drawn to her chest, Nikki watched the morning drizzle spot and trickle down the glass of the French doors. She knew last night's passion was a mistake. But maybe by giving in to the savage beast she might win his confidence, break down his walls and establish a lasting relationship. Because she didn't want their important discussion derailed like last night, Nikki dressed conservatively that morning in jeans and a turtleneck.

Finally Grant's slippered feet shuffled across the green slate of the kitchen floor. He enclosed her in his arms from behind. "Mmm ' mornin', luv," he purred in her ear, nuzzling a kiss on her neck.

Rising to meet him, Nikki returned his embrace. "Good morning, my love." She kissed him then slipped out of his arms to get him his morning cup of tea.

Nerves dried out Nikki's throat—with a dryness no amount of tea could wash away. Her words stuck in her throat, but she summoned the courage. "Grant, we need to clear up some things. We need to talk."

"About what, luv?" He blithely maintained the charade.

"Dr. Hess called the physician in Buenos Aires. He said he never prescribed bed rest. And the drugs he prescribed were at your insistence. Did you lie to me? Were you trying to get rid of me?"

Grant hedged, "No. I was only thinking of you. I didn't want you to have any pain. I truly wanted you to get all the rest you needed, so you could get better and we could enjoy our time together."

His explanation sounded so plausible. Had she blown this whole thing up out of context? Oh how she wanted to lose herself in his explanation, to wrap herself in his arms and buy the fairy tale again! Nikki could have so easily let everything else go, but Grant needed to answer one more question. Nikki swallowed, "What about Bridget?"

Grant's eyes widened at her knowledge. He leveled his gaze to meet hers. Caught, which way would he go? Nikki braced herself for his inevitable eruption of anger. Instead, puddles of tears formed in his soft brown eyes and leaked down his face. Gathering up her hands, he pressed them to his lips. His tears slid down Nikki's fingers. "How could I have been so stupid? She means nothing to me. You're everything I ever wanted. I missed you so much when you weren't by my side. I guess I just got lost. I don't know what happened."

His tears cut inlets into her heart. But she went for broke anyway. "And the drugs? What about the drugs?"

Grant drew her in with his eye contact. The film of tears magnified the size of his eyes turning them into large, heart-melting, watery pools. "You know she gave them to me. They made me crazy. I was high that night I hurt you. I didn't mean to. That's why I sent you away. I wanted to get straight for you. I couldn't hurt you again. I need you too much." Dropping off his chair, he fell to his knees, weeping into Nikki's lap. "I love you. I love you," he mumbled through his sobbing. "Please forgive me! Please!"

Nikki crumbled. Drawing him to her, she sealed the apology on his lips with a kiss. "Yes, Grant, I forgive you." Her eyes met his. "But this can never happen again. I can't do this again. Do you understand?" And her tears mingled with his in a compact of renewed love.

The rest of the day they refused to let go of each other. Grant cancelled his appearance at the recording session. Nikki postponed her luncheon with Karl and Mary until the following afternoon. Instead, they drove to Cartier of London. Grant bought Nikki a symbol of their renewed love—entwined hearts of diamonds. Ordering a gourmet catered supper, they dined at home in front of their own blazing fireplace. A light snow fell outside. Bundling up, they walked the grounds of their estate in snow's frozen peace. On a stone bench by the cold, black stream, Nikki broached one more subject with Grant—that of Jack and Candy.

Grant's answer amazed Nikki. "Talk to Candy. I'm sure she knows by now, but she could probably use some comforting. The two of you can commiserate over the unfaithful louts you married."

Nikki blanched at Grant's all-too-real reference to himself.

"It's true, you know. Face the fact, I broke our vows. But it will never happen again. On my soul I promise."

The next afternoon Grant drove Nikki to her favorite out-of-the-way bistro for lunch with Karl and Mary. He stunned everyone when he accompanied her to the table. Karl rose with uneasiness to meet Grant's extended hand.

Grasping Karl's hand, Grant spoke first, "What an appalling lout I've been. First, thank you for saving the life of my dear, sweet Nikki. Second, I apologize for my bloody awful behavior. You were completely justified in belting me when I was crackers. Of course, you'll continue on with Nikki's publicity. Can't we just forget about this whole nasty episode?" He clasped Karl about the shoulders.

Stunned, Karl sputtered his acceptance.

"Well, I really must be running. ... Mary dear, good to see you." Turning, Grant passionately kissed Nikki good-bye, "See you at home, my love. Have a great afternoon." Then out he strode, the conquering hero.

Karl waited until Grant cleared the doorway. "Would someone mind telling me who in the hell was that? Nikki, what happened yesterday?"

Karl and Mary greeted Nikki's tale of the reformed Grant with guarded capitulation, urging caution.

Following lunch, Mary dropped Nikki at Candy's house. Candy met her with reddened eyes and a tear-swollen face. She already knew about Jack's unfaithfulness. Throwing her arms around her, Nikki entered. Candy's mother was keeping Jack, Jr,. for a few days. The good friends cried together as Nikki recounted the entire saga about her decision to tell Candy about Jack and Solana, including the part about Grant's behavior and how they had just put their marriage back on track.

Candy hugged Nikki. "I know that you think the same thing can happen for us too. But it's too late," Candy's lip quivered. "Jack has asked me..." She took a deep breath to forestall another round of tears. "He wants to move Solana in with us! He wants a *ménage a' trois*! But that's not all. He's brought home pot and acid. He says if I do these with them it will open my eyes. I'll see he's right. I tried the pot. I won't do acid. Who'd take care of Jack, Jr.?" Candy erupted in a full-fledged wail.

"Oh Candy, I couldn't stay under those conditions. I'd have to leave," Nikki consoled.

"That's what I want to do. But, where will I go?"

"Go back to your parent's house. Get your own house. Better still, pack Jack's bags and toss the lout out. A proper attorney would tell you to do that."

Candy weighed the options as they discussed the consequences. Before Nikki left, Candy placed a phone call to a reputable attorney for advice.

Grant understood. "What else can she do?" he lamented. "Jack brags about Solana and the drugs. Jack would like to see me so enlightened."

Nikki's blood boiled at the hint of Jack soliciting Grant's collusion. "Of course he would, it spreads the guilt. Then he's not the only lunatic. Grant, I can't pretend any longer everything's all right. You know how I feel about Solana and the drugs. I can't face Jack. I can't tell Candy to leave him and then stick around him because I'm making money with the group. That's hypocritical. What if I bow out of the group?"

Grant concurred, "You have to do what you have to do. But understand, I have a commitment I must fulfill, no matter my personal feelings."

"I understand," Nikki said as she cuddled into Grant's arms. "I won't leave your side though. I'll still travel with you, just limit my exposure to Jack."

Grant enfolded her, "That's good because I want you with me." He kissed her. "You know you could still continue on your own from the recording studio."

"Anything, as long as we can be together. Then you agree about my leaving the group?"

Grant nodded, "I think it's best, although you may be committed for the India and Pakistan tour."

"I know. I'll talk to Bruce in the morning."

Nikki's meeting with Bruce conflicted him. While he had wanted to separate the two careers from the beginning, things were really clicking for the combination act. And Bruce desperately wanted to avoid a confrontation with Jack at all costs. "Do us all a favor, don't use the Solana thing as your reason for leaving. And please don't go toe-to-toe with Jack. If you take a stand against him, he'll bloody well turn it into a war! Damn, he'd leave bodies all over the landscape!"

The tour of India and Pakistan devolved into a full-blown disaster for Nikki. By the second day, she came down with a torturous case of stomach flu, replete with nausea and vomiting. With heroic effort, Nikki held herself together for the concerts and press conferences. Likewise, Richie also suffered a severe reaction to the spicy Indian food.

The group as a whole, however, developed an affinity for the eastern culture and its sounds. Pete and Jack incorporated the Indian rhythms and musical phrasing into their work. Grant especially dove into every nuance of the near-eastern culture. While Nikki hung over the toilet, he explored all the facets of their dynamism, occupying his time with side trips from the cities into the countryside. After a week and a half, when they reached Bombay, both Grant and Bruce insisted Nikki visit the British hospital there.

Following one of his little forays into the Indian civilization, Grant returned quite late to their hotel room. Nikki waited up for him with the physician's results.

Chapter 12
Falling

Almost three months pregnant. Nikki's news caught Grant off guard. Since their reconciliation, she had grown accustomed to the caring side of Grant. Reveling in the news, Nikki embraced the incarnation of their love. Now she wanted Grant to share her joy—no matter how unexpected—a baby!

Mustering courage from his second gin and tonic, a hint of a smile pursed his lips. "Well then, we'll have a baby. I guess Richie and Doreen's baby will be only three months older than ours," Grant mused.

Five days later, following their last concert in Pakistan, Grant sent Nikki home to Pennsylvania to deliver the news to her parents in person. He wanted to stay on with Pete and Jack to do more exploring in his newfound promised land of India. He vowed to return to their Surrey home by March first. Then they'd fill the nursery full of soft and cuddly baby things and await their new arrival.

Richard and Fran's suspicions about the viability of Nikki's marriage, at first, muted their response to her news about the baby. But the inevitability of the event and the intriguing prospect of being grandparents won them over. Within days, Fran dragged Nikki through shopping malls in a buying spree of infant outfits in noncommittal yellows and greens.

The days flew by. Before Nikki knew it, her March first departure date was two days away when Grant called. With sitar music echoing in the background, he explained how he had gotten a lot of good material and he wanted to stay another week. They agreed to meet back in the Surrey house then.

But rather than rebook her flight to London, Nikki decided to catch her scheduled flight and get the house opened up properly to meet her arriving husband. At this point, Nikki's gushing maternal hormones drove a desire to feather her nest.

Despite the security, the large, empty house scared Nikki at night, so Mary suggested Nikki bunk at her flat. By now her nausea had faded, but she couldn't shake being tired. The second day, they went over to the house and left the packages her mom bought for the baby, then hit the stores in a baby-shopping frenzy.

To work on her retirement from the combination act, launch her solo career and announce the baby's arrival, Nikki scheduled a working lunch at Mary's flat. Karl joined them at ten; by eleven, Ben dropped by and stayed to participate.

They decided to minimize her departure from the guys by playing up the positive angles of a solo career. The baby, however, presented a whole other set of questions—like how long would she continue to perform? Would she tour again? And what about the American music scene? They thrashed out all those questions, and more, until three in the afternoon.

Karl ended their work session bemoaning the fact he hadn't had a tour of Nikki's house. "Here it is, March, and I haven't been asked to see it yet! I guess you have to be someone *really* special to be invited."

Immediately Ben and Mary jumped on the bandwagon, and quicker than lickity-split, the four of them sardined themselves into Karl's mini Aston, heading out to Surrey.

Wanting to welcome her friends from inside, Nikki left the three of them standing on the front entry stoop while she ran around to the kitchen side door. On her hasty dash through the kitchen to the foyer, she noticed an empty gin bottle on the kitchen counter. She excused it as the maid forgot to pitch it out in the rubbish.

With lavish flourish, Nikki swung the massive door open. Curtseying deeply, she bid them enter. The stunning entry with its magnificent mahogany staircase, elegantly turned newels and raised panels elicited gasps of awe from them. Both Ben and Karl rotated in place, drinking in the bravura of the entire foyer.

Suddenly, from the second floor, giggles floated down to them. Expecting the house to be empty, everyone exchanged inquiring glances. "The maid must be all atwitter over something," Nikki excused, as she started up the staircase to investigate.

More laughter met Nikki on the stairs. Leaping ahead, her mind attempted to prepare her for a variety of deeds that might be engaging the maid. It all could be completely innocent, then they would all have a good chuckle about it. Although, Nikki expected to find the worst. She wondered, never having fired anyone before, would a romp while on duty constitute grounds for the maid's dismissal? At the landing of the second floor, she paused to determine the exact direction of the noise.

This time Nikki heard male undertones prompting what seemed to be sexually charged tittering, and they came from her bedroom! Once up the stairs, she listened at the door to solidify her suspicions before catching them in the act. Incensed, that they were in her bed, on her time, she determined dismissal to be the exact remedy. Again Nikki heard the high-pitched laughter of the coy feminine voice, and a man teasing her.

It was Grant's voice! Quickly Nikki reassessed the circumstances. Was Grant entertaining in *their* bed? He wouldn't do that! He promised! Not wanting to burst in with guns blazing to be wrong about it, Nikki listened again. Without question, the cooing and accompanying lusty chortles smacked of sexual foreplay. Nikki recognized Grant's line of patter. How should she handle this? She'd meet the situation squarely, head-on, that's how. Shelving the instinctive, injured ego reaction to scream and rave, she replaced it with a cool, controlled air of authority. Snapping the handle, Nikki boldly pushed the door open.

There she sat—naked, astraddle Grant. Her long, strawberry blonde hair swung around through the air as she spun her head toward the noise of Nikki barging in the door. Her pert nipples stood erect on the firm breasts of her model-perfect, nubile body. Nikki recognized Bridget. Surprisingly, no one moved or dove for covers. The sweet odor of pot pervaded the room.

From flat on his back, Grant spouted protests.

Without spending time focusing on them, instead pasting a convincing smile on her face, Nikki marched to the closet and returned with jeans and a pullover for Grant.

"Here, luv, put these on," she said in an everyday tone as if laying out clothes for a morning walk, then dropped his clothes in an unaffected manner next to him on the bed. "I'm afraid your afternoon festivities have come to an end. Your little friend will have to run on now. We are going to have some fun of our own."

Wrapping the sheet about her, Bridget ungracefully dismounted. Determined to make the two of them wallow in their discomfort, Nikki refused them quarter. Instead she leaned against the dresser, challenging Grant.

Red-faced, he angrily grabbed his pants and pulled them on his naked body, then his sweater. His nostrils flared under the heat of his embarrassment and growing temper. Rising up, he approached Nikki.

Standing her ground, erect, away from the dresser, they faced off forgetting about the wench in the bed.

Grant beat Nikki to the first word, pushing his fingers into her chest. "What in the bleedin' hell are you doing here?" His eyes on fire—his breath saturated with gin.

Nikki stepped back. "I came home to get things ready for you!"

"I didn't ask ya to, now did I?"

"I thought it would be the 'good wife' thing to do. Obviously you don't want a good wife!" she spit.

"Well, Princess, as you can see, you should stick to the schedule. See, you get yourself in trouble when ... you ... don't ... stick ... to ... the ... schedule." His fingers poked her after each word, driving home the point.

Nikki backed up each time with his jabs.

Pulling herself up to make a stand, her eyes narrowed. "Grant you promised your affair with her was over."

"Maybe it was. Maybe I could handle having you tied around my neck until you came up bleedin' pregnant!" No need for him to push that time. His words rocked her back on her heels.

Nikki used the jamb of the doorway to steady herself and come back at him. "So I was the millstone around your neck! Then why your tears? Why the apology? Why not just leave?"

Grant sneered contemptuously, "Just look around you, Nikki. Take a good, long, last look. You don't think I'd sacrifice all this for you, do you?" This time he shoved her with both hands into the hallway.

Anger and hostility swelled in her. "How long has it been going on this time?"

Grant laughed arrogantly. "This time? Why not just ask if it ever stopped! I just needed time" he jabbed her again. "Time to get all my things together."

"Oh! So you're leaving!"

He roared, "Leaving? I don't think so. You haven't been listening, Nikki dear." Bitterly he used her name, like a weapon against her, aggressively backing her farther and farther down the hall. "I'm getting things in order to get rid of *you*. The baby just delayed things a little, made the situation stickier. You're the one who's going. You didn't think for a moment that you'd get my career, my money, my house. No bleeding way! I'm going to leave you like I found you, a poor twit from the country." He backed Nikki to within a few feet of the top of the stairs.

Enraged, rising up on her haunches she fought back, "You can keep your precious money. And trust me I don't need *your* career. I've got one of my own that's going rather nicely. But Grant, I *will* keep the house to raise our child in. He at least deserves that out of the drunken bastard he has for a father. So if you'll excuse me...I'm going to pack your things. Your little trollop can help you carry them on your way out!" With a mighty shove, Nikki walked past him on her way to the bedroom.

Wrapped in the sheet, Bridget watched, blinking her vacuous, green eyes.

Half way down the hall, Grant chased Nikki until he latched onto her wrist, pulling her back to him. With a twisting wrench he spun her around. Hate sparked in his eyes. "Come back here, you lil' bitch! You're not going anywhere. I'm not through with you yet." He landed a wallop with the back of his hand against her face.

Momentarily she fell back in shock. Grant read her body language as she reflexively shrank. Then he raised his hand to land another blow.

Something visceral from deep within Nikki cried out, "Enough!" Pulling up from her cower, she met his swing, blocking it with her fore-arm. Their arms clashed like swords in a duel. Steely-eyed, she defied him across their clenched stance. "So, Grant … hitting me makes you a big man? Then go ahead hit me again. Here you haven't smacked me on this cheek." Boldly she turned the opposite cheek toward him. "Hit me here. Go ahead big man! Come on!"

Nikki's newfound aggression baffled him.

He dropped his cocked arm as she backed him down the hall. "What's the matter Grant, no guts to beat up a woman? Come on big man! Come on." She bullied him farther, then pushed past him again on her way to pack his belongings.

Nikki almost made it to their bedroom door before he recovered from his amazement. He lunged at her — an uncontrollable juggernaut. From deep within him, a guttural growl grew, "Oh no you don't! Come back here, you bloody bitch!"

His iron paws clamped onto her shoulders, heaving her into the hall-way wall. Before Nikki could recover, he threw her into the opposite wall. She caromed off one wall to another, down the hall reeling, fighting to regain her balance before he threw her again. Nikki hit the banister rail-ing. It stood her upright. She pushed off to bounce back and take another run at him.

Grant met her at the landing. Cocking his arm back, he loaded it up for another swing. He launched it. It came at her in slow motion. Desperately, frantically, Nikki searched for a way to escape the resound-ing blow. Even Grant's words reached her ears in the deep, halting bari-tone of slow motion, "Here…bitch…take…this."

The closed-fist blow connected with Nikki's right temple, propelling her off the top step, catapulting her in a lateral free fall. Instinctively she threw out her arms and legs to break her fall. Screaming, falling, the carpeted stairs rose up to meet Nikki as she hurtled towards them. Her eyes briefly snagged her horrified friends watching at the bottom of the steps. Bracing for impact, Nikki scrunched into a ball. Wham! Her right arm crashed into the baseboard and tread with a shattering crunch. The momentum of the collision angled her towards the banister and opened her tuck. Whack! Nikki took another tread, and another, and another. Upended, she plunged end over end, in a series of thuds and smacks until she landed crumpled, then sprawled out on her back on the entry marble floor at the base of the staircase. Nikki remained conscious.

Ben ran to call for the rescue squad as Mary knelt at her side, trying to assess her physical condition, afraid to move her.

The momentum of his fateful blow had pulled Grant down the top part of the stairs. Karl leapt over Nikki's body onto the third step to defend her from further attack.

No need, Grant crumpled into a sitting stupor on the steps, dazed by the magnitude of his anger, hunched forward, rung out, cupping his knees. Nikki's eyes caught the sun glinting on the wedding medallion swinging outside his sweater. Past him, at the top of the landing, a pallid Bridget matched the white sheet she clutched.

Absolute pain utterly racked Nikki. She tried to pick herself up, but Mary discouraged it. Like statues frozen in place, everyone maintained their positions, with the exception of Bridget. She disappeared to dress.

Soon the "ee-oo-ee-oo" of the sirens wailed up the driveway. Their lights flashed against the gray of the sky and intruded into the house. The police accompanied the rescue squad. Shortly thereafter, Bruce came. Ben had called him, too. Shocked and overwhelmed at the gruesome scene, Bruce sank speechless to the marble. The police collected everybody and separated them for questioning. Loudly letting their bags of paraphernalia plop down on the marble, the medics began attending Nikki. Their touch sent blinding pain coursing through her body. She closed her eyes.

Nikki drifted in and out of consciousness over the next few days. Along with another concussion and multiple scalp wounds, the fall broke her right arm, cracked three ribs—and aborted the baby. Her mom and dad flew in to spend the endless hours sitting at her bedside waiting for her eyes to flutter open so they could coax her back to consciousness.

Mary and Karl wrote an ambiguous "accident-around-the-house" press release for public consumption in an attempt to stem the hot-bed of speculation which swirled around the Surrey house after the police investigation.

In their investigation of the violence, the police found pot, acid and a plethora of other illegal substances, including cocaine, in the house. They hauled everyone present at the scene in for questioning. In deference to his notoriety, the court quietly placed Grant under house arrest and exacted an exorbitant fine for the drugs. Battery charges remained pending with the court, waiting for Nikki to be able to sign a complaint.

The incident tore poor Bruce apart. As a pacifist, he desperately wanted to be able to sweep the event under the rug and return to an idyllic life, but every fiber in his body detested Grant's actions and wanted justice to prevail. He freed Nikki, with his blessings, to exact whatever price she deemed appropriate, including ruining the career of Grant Henderson.

Almost two weeks elapsed before Nikki began to put together all the pieces and function again. Mary helped Fran find a private flat for Nikki to move into following her release from the hospital. Armfuls of flowers from her fans accompanied her home. Even after a week or two, a particularly nice bouquet of gardenias continued to arrive every Friday, just as it had while she had been hospitalized.

Nikki didn't agonize over whether to continue the marriage. Even before reading the police report, she understood that the drugs and alcohol exacerbated his behavior, but she refused to dignify those facts with any consideration. Grant had broken his commitments to her. She wouldn't set herself up to be shredded by his Jekyll-and-Hyde personality again, or to be his patsy while he played with his paramours. Grant literally had killed the only reason Nikki might have to work things out.

As much as her ribs hurt, the physical pain paled in comparison to her loss of the baby. It devastated Nikki. Even at the tender age of 19, her heart had already made the leap to motherhood. Tears and grief overwhelmed her even at the most innocuous of times. Fears of collapsing from the weight of the emotional turmoil kept her from disclosing the pregnancy or miscarriage to her fans.

Nikki contacted an astute divorce attorney, adept in handling high profile cases. In exchange for her not pressing battery charges and keeping the story of the violence out of the press, Grant agreed to buy Nikki another home in Surrey, provide her with a million pound allotment and restrain from maligning her in public.

Despite Fran and Mary's advice against it, Nikki wanted to go back to that house in Surrey, to clean out her things. More than collecting her possessions though, Nikki wanted to face down her demon there, rather than have it haunt her throughout all time. But Fran and Mary weren't about to let her go alone. Ironically, it was April first when they pulled up to the gate. A fine mist drizzled down the windshield of Mary's car. The trees, pregnant with springtime buds, prepared to burst forth in their glorious color riot of rebirth. That day the grass reflected its already lush emerald color upon the wet, brown trunks of the trees, enticing them to re-awaken to life.

The three of them stood on the front stoop. No one, not even the maid, had re-entered the house since the police finished their investigation. They didn't have to worry about Grant either, for he had already fled back to India following his release. Mary unlocked the door, swung it open and stepped back to let her friend enter. Mentally preparing, Nikki told herself, "It's only your emotions playing on your mind. Everything will be the same as always. Inside the house it will feel normal."

Once again the grand staircase commanded their attention, but this time by emanating the depravity of evil instead of the elegance of grandeur. A pool of crusted, dried blood—Nikki's blood—lay at the base of the stairs on the marble floor. Bloody footprints trailed off from it where careless personnel had crossed. The cold horror of that day flooded the three. Scuffs, scratches and gouges disfigured the mahogany panels. Fingering the panels on her way up the stairs, Nikki relived the pain anew as she visualized slamming into the walls again. A few strands of her bloodied hair remained embedded in the wood. At the top of the landing, she turned around and looked down the winding case. The emotional gravity of the scene threatened to physically pull her back down the staircase. Grabbing the banister for balance, Nikki slapped herself back to reality, then turned and headed down the hallway to the bedroom. Scrapes and dents pockmarked the hallway where her body had smashed into the walls.

Opening the door of the bedroom, Fran gasped at the chaos of the devastated room, all residue from the police search. Empty drawers hung out of the dresser's carcass, trailing remains of their contents, spilling the rest onto the floor. The dismembered bed sat torn completely asunder, its mattress and box spring carelessly tossed against a window and wall. Lampshades and pictures tilted askew.

Wading through the jumble to the closet, Nikki's foot ran up against something embedded in the carpet. It was Grant's wedding medallion ground into the floor under a pile of debris. Picking it up, she turned it over and read the sappy message she had inscribed to him. It elicited a bitter chuckle. Shoving it into her pocket, she proceeded to the closet. Stripped from their hangers, all their clothes lay heaped in a pile in the middle of the floor. Nikki picked a few of her favorites from the mess, leaving the rest.

They made their way back down the stairs, past the scene and deposited the rescued articles by the door, then headed towards the kitchen to sort through things there. It, along with the rest of the house, was in similar state of dishevelment. Amusingly, the empty gin bottle Nikki had found on her way through the kitchen on that fateful day, still maintained its original position on the counter, but now a host of other wreckage joined it. Nikki wasn't prepared for the mess left in the wake of the investigation. It sapped her strength. In the end, she took nothing. She didn't want anything badly enough to slog through the emotional battle of straightening out a war zone.

Physically they supported Nikki on her way back to the entry and out, but the feeling of forgetting something gnawed at her before Mary locked the front door. Finally Nikki remembered — the baby clothes. Mary ran back up the stairs and returned with the still neatly packed boxes. The police had left them untouched.

Sunshine parted the rain clouds by the time Mary locked the door.

But Nikki couldn't return to the rented flat just yet, so her friend drove meandering roads into the countryside. Along the way they passed a plain country church. Drawn to it, Nikki asked Mary pull over.

Inside the vestibule, before entering the sanctuary, her gaze fell on the poor box. Compelled by involuntarily forces, Nikki's fingers found the gold piece in her slacks. Pulling the chain and wedding medallion out of her pocket, she read it for the last time. Then she deposited the medallion like a coin through the slot. The gold disc dragged the chain along behind it as it disappeared down the hole of the box. A metallic clink gurgled up as it joined the coins at the bottom. "Good riddance. Let them melt down the gold to help some poor soul." She pushed open the chapel door with her left hand, when her gold wedding band and diamond engagement ring caught her eye. Immediately Nikki stripped them from her finger and returned to the box. "So long Grant," she said beneath her breath and let them fall through the open slot into the box.

Entering the church, Nikki slipped into a back pew and tried to pray. From her Christian childhood, she knew she was supposed to forgive Grant, but she couldn't erase the crazed wildness in his eyes that day. Her wounds were too fresh to pray for forgiveness. She thought about her baby, and her mind wandered to what might have been as she struggled with the loss. Nikki wanted to pray for God's guidance in her life, but worried she had abused His gifts too much already to ask for anything else. Her prayers continually got tangled up with her thoughts. In the end, all she could do was to ask God to hold her.

Chapter 13

On Her Own

Mending her bones and ending her marriage exacted less of a toll on Nikki than the healing of her spirit. In the countless hours of bed rest, self-doubt monopolized her. She had made a bad choice for a life's partner. Where had she gone wrong? Would she ever be able to trust another man again? Would she want to?

Nikki wanted to hide. And hiding included leaving the business. Even though she had never wanted a career handed to her because of Grant, in her heart she believed that was exactly what had happened. Nikki felt she had never earned her career—luck handed it to her. Without Grant and The Merseymen, would her fans want her? Even though Nikki had started out solo, since she performed with The Merseymen, in the minds of her fans, was she permanently attached to them? Did she in fact have any real talent or did the fans embrace her because of the famous four? Nikki was afraid to ask them—she worried she might not like their answer.

She called Bruce, and without confessing her misgivings, she quit. Having been thrown off, she refused to get up out of the mud. Employing a mixture of empathy and sweet talk, Bruce tried to get Nikki back on her horse. She refused. As a last resort, he promised he'd release her from her contract if she'd do just one more chat session.

So the second week of April, Nikki gathered her nerves and sat down with a large group of fans for a chat.

Immediately a girl from in front asked, "Are you okay now?"

"My ribs are still sore from the tumble, and I'll have my arm in the cast for another month. But other than that I'm perfectly fit."

Another enthusiastic hand shot up, "What about singing? Will you sing again?"

"In a few weeks, when it doesn't hurt to take a breath, I promise I'll be back in front of a microphone again."

"Why didn't you go home to America to be with your parents after this accident?"

"Because this is my home. I didn't want to leave you all."

The room erupted with cheers and applause.

"Will you do concerts?"

"Will you tour?"

"You'll do England first, won't you?"

From the back of the room, a young male stood up and shouted, "What about the freakin' bastard?"

Silence.

"Excuse me?" Nikki questioned. "Whom might that be?"

"You know," another stood up.

"Yeah. Henderson ... the lout," another launched to his feet.

"Yea, Grant!" More stood, adding their voices—building an undercurrent.

The room began to writhe. Bruce's eyes widened. Just what he needed—one of his pop vocalists cannibalizing the other. Doggedly loyal, the chatters wanted blood.

Slapping her knee with her left hand, Nikki pretended to be sincerely caught up in laughter. "Oh, that bastard!" She sprang back. "What's the big deal?" She held up her left hand, wiggling her naked ring finger. "He's gone. Hey, he preferred someone else. And I've got all of you!"

The chatters cheered.

Seizing control, becoming "one" with them again, Nikki moved into their midst. "But seriously, can we talk? I've always been able to come to you with problems. Can we do that now? I need to let you in on a little something."

Instinctively they drew near.

"Would you all mind if I tried this singing thing on my own for awhile? I love The Merseymen dearly just like you do. Right?"

A hesitant nod spread through the crowd.

"Great! ... See I knew that! ... I thought I'd like to try to sing now, just for you. Maybe it's time for me to test my wings all on my own. What do you think? ... Yeah?"

The eager male from the back piped up again, "Yeah! Show the lousy creep you don't need him!"

Oh how Nikki wanted to jump on the bandwagon of that emotion! But she knew better. "No. No, you don't understand. See, I've been working on this idea even before Grant and I split. I want to do some things differently—special for you. I want to be able to get more intimate with you. It's hard to do that dragging a band along behind. That doesn't mean you can't enjoy them too. Sometimes you want a party, sometimes you want a romantic evening alone. Get it?"

Enthusiasm bubbled up from the group. The idea of Nikki again as a solo act ignited their interest. They bombarded her with ideas and directions.

The hiccup in her performance schedule and hiatus from the public eye in actuality lasted only two months—still, an eternity to be out of the limelight. Encouraged by her return chat session, as Bruce knew she would be, Nikki worked the "grass roots" to build a solid foundation of support for her solo career. Over those next four weeks, until her ribs finished healing and she could stand in front of a mike again, Nikki toured throughout London, meeting fans, mixing with them on their turf. She kept Jarred and his security staff busy full time so she could be out and about with the people who put her on top. Nikki didn't limit herself to the cities either, but also ventured out into the countryside. Her excursion to meet the fans on their terms amazed and pleased Bruce because she wasn't just skimming off the cream of fame, she was cultivating life-long kinship with the people. Karl's photographer, Jimmy, shot her entire road tour of Britain. Karl expertly timed its release. Nikki's appeal peaked. The kids rabidly devoured everything put before them.

Feeling well enough to move out of the temporary rented flat, Nikki decided to look for her own place. She pooled her house-hunting efforts with Candy, fresh from her divorce from Jack. Within a week, they found a large, six-acre estate with a caretaker's cottage. Too immense for their single families, Candy and Nikki drew up the contract to divide the property. Candy and the baby would have the manor house and half the land while Nikki took the cottage and the remaining land. They'd share a groundskeeper, and the two could always keep an eye on each other, if need be.

By no means was this caretaker's cottage a shack. The two-story stucco-over-stone structure, with its push-out casement windows of diamond-shaped, leaded panes of glass, afforded Nikki a large, open-beamed kitchen with ample adjoining dining space. The extremely generous living room supported a massive floor to ceiling fieldstone fireplace at one end. Three bedrooms and a bath sprawled across the upstairs, and the surrounding gardens ran on forever.

Nikki wanted her home to envelop her in an ambiance of warmth—a kick-off-your-shoes-you're-home-now feeling. She chose a honey maple, farm style table with captain's chairs for the dining room and a welcoming, traditional overstuffed sofa and chairs with wood plank tables for the living room. To keep an air of rusticity, Nikki spiced up the décor with a few antiques. She splashed her bedroom in soothing pink and white, from the pink over white wainscoted and papered walls to the white eyelet curtains and rose-toned English floral comforter.

Despite her move from the rented London flat back to Surrey, the gardenias continued to arrive every Friday, with one change. Now two bouquets were delivered along with cards labeling them "downstairs" and "upstairs." The fact that the flowers followed her unpublicized move led Nikki to suspect they weren't from an ordinary fan wishing her a speedy recovery. Who had that much access to her personal life? Who got close enough to know that she now had two floors? Still absent a sender's signature, Nikki had Jarred check with the florist.

The florist could offer no clues as to the sender's identity. His floral arranger had discovered an envelope full of pound notes with instructions left on the arranging table one day. After Nikki's move, another envelope of cash containing her new address and more instructions appeared in the same place. Fearing a stalker, Jarred initiated a sweep of Nikki's security system and beefed up the provisions around the property. But nothing alarming developed.

In late May when her ribs had almost completely healed, Nikki tore back into the recording studio with a renewed vigor. Fresh and ready, she recorded her third solo album, *Nikki Off On Her Own*. Jimmy shot a natural cover photo of Nikki in boots and jeans, suede jacket slung over shoulder, looking back at the camera while embarking down a groomed dirt road into the country. In two short weeks, it went platinum. Bruce booked Nikki in a series of concerts opening the second week in June at the London Palladium. Within hours the tickets sold out. For the first time since Bruce launched Nikki, he devoted the majority of his efforts to her career, probably because her sales numbers vaulted her into the number one position in his stable. Truly, Nikki had progressed from the enthusiastic, naïve schoolgirl who almost incited a riot, to a seasoned veteran, able to read her crowd and direct them along a calculated path.

Her old studio band toured with her, providing back up. Sure, the butterflies of old also returned, but Nikki drew her energy from that marvelous pre-concert dynamism, sucking up all she could get. She leapt out of the box. Nikki had returned! The unconditional, loving spirit of the audience swelled over the footlights, blanketing her with their strident affection. Answering their energy, she gave them all she had.

As she performed, she tried to make personal eye contact with every section of the audience. Crossing the first loge box, her eyes stopped on a seemingly familiar figure of great aplomb who, in a show of respect, doffed his imaginary hat to her. The bright spotlights obscured any further recognition.

Her wave of ever-mounting popularity swept Nikki from her British concerts onto the Continent. All her free time she spent in the recording studio creating more product; she squeezed in at least two chat sessions a week. With The Merseymen, Nikki had participated only on the fringes of this life. Now it swallowed her whole, pulling her into its eye. Time no longer permitted Bruce to jump on all the requests for the television shows, interviews and performances. Nikki's career finally arrived at the place where they selected the shows and interviews designed to benefit her the most. Despite stepped up security, a bouquet of gardenias mysteriously greeted her in each new city.

Hot commitments across the Continent ate up the summer. Pressure from Asia, Japan and Hong Kong mounted. Bruce planned to open those markets near the end of the year. If all went well, they'd do the United States in a winter tour, hopefully in February like The Merseymen—for luck.

Before long, a common theme of "suitors" for Nikki emerged in the chat sessions. The press wildly speculated about her love life. Nikki tried the old saw, "I have all of you." While the fans at the sessions swallowed it, the press nagged. Gun-shy, Nikki had relegated men and dating to the basement of her priorities. In reality, her line about the fans proved to be more truth than poetry.

While Bruce appreciated her relentless dedication to her career, part of a luminary's success centers around the ability to exude a sexual presence—the sizzle that sells by teasing availability. Begrudgingly, Nikki complied and before long, this sensational pop artist made the scene with her at a disco, and that hot rising star dined with her at the restaurant du jour. Cameras caught them, the tabloids tattled on them and once again, the entertainment world blissfully rotated on its own axis. Nikki discovered "seen dating"—exclusive of romantic entanglements, each person uses the other to be "seen with," thereby enhancing his/her own status. Unwilling to risk emotional involvement, the practice provided a totally benign way to date, unless someone believed the press being generated. Rigidly she avoided dating anyone outside the business. They proved to be too vulnerable to the siren of celebrity, easily mistaking their fantasies for love. An expert on this subject, Nikki had gained her experience at Grant's invitation.

Nikki kept up the grueling concert/recording pace through the summer into fall. In between the Australian tour and the Asian trip, Bruce carved out two weeks away from the road for Nikki, then just as craftily encumbered them. "How about doing a Christmas special! I snagged a deal for a seventeen-country special to air the third week in December. The producers want a typical Christmas on the farm in America. Think your parents would open up *Creekside*? We'll give 'em the whole squishy production—snow, carolers, decorations up the … well you know. What ya say, luv? Ya up for it?"

After being with Bruce for over three years, Nikki knew he had already inked the deal. "Asking" was just his way of breaking the news to her. If Fran and Richard refused their farm, Bruce would rent one!

As Christmas specials go, the November shoot sliced production time to the bone. Consequently Nikki cut the accompanying Christmas soundtrack album at Reading's Kutztown Road recording studio with hired musicians and vocalists. Meanwhile, set decorators blanketed everything at *Creekside* with swaths of red and green, twinkle lights and fake snow! For the album cover and exteriors on the special, they "borrowed" another farm in a neighboring county to keep fans from invading the Moore's privacy.

As the last plastic flake disappeared into the production cleanup's vacuum, Nikki departed for her tour of Asia. Eighteen hours later, she deplaned to greet a crowd of over twenty thousand! Stepping out onto a platform equipped with microphones and Japanese dignitaries, a roar rose up when she bowed to the welcoming party. Pulling out her small vocabulary of Japanese from a previous visit, she called out to the thousands hanging off the rails of the airport, "*Konechiwa*!" A thunderous cheer returned her greeting. The city ambassadors presented her with the equivalent of the key to the city. "*Arigato, arigato*!" Nikki thanked them in Japanese.

The insatiable Japanese devoured all of her waking moments from her shopping excursions to her learning to skillfully operate the tricky chopsticks. She dined sitting on the floor and never squirmed when served plates of raw fish so fresh it flopped on the plate before her. Accelerating into hyper-drive, Nikki's troupe used the energy of that trip to psych themselves up for the approaching tour of the States in February.

By the first week of December, they were within hours of releasing their initial barrage of records and media hype onto the American market. Bruce picked December twelfth as Nikki's Debut Day. All of them felt the tension rising as they stared into the abyss—"The American Market." The capricious taste of the States could put Nikki literally on top of the world or break her in two. A single hit on the charts there didn't assure success. "One-hit wonders" bought nothing. Failure in the States could poison every other market Nikki had previously conquered. But the allure of the golden Promised Land shimmered and danced too seductively to be ignored.

On December seventh Nikki returned to her hotel suite to find a dour Bruce and Karl with a nearly empty bottle of scotch on the coffee table. *The Ed Sullivan Show* had postponed Nikki's appearance in February till the following September. It wasn't a fatal blow, but close. Hundreds of thousands of dollars tied up in promotion packages sat in warehouses in the States, now without a vehicle to launch them. The duo feared the impression this would make, since in the entertainment business perception *is* reality. Sitting down with Nikki, they put their heads together. Finally it was decided that they'd spin a tale that Nikki's career was too hot to take time to do America just then. Bruce would overbook her and make it look like *they* put the Sullivan people off until fall. Footage of exuberant Japan and a movie deal or two would certainly back up the premise. This approach doubled Nikki's already hectic schedule, but neatly solved the situation. They packed for two days in Seoul with a final week in Hong Kong.

East quite literally meets West, in the British colony of Hong Kong on the other side of the world. On any given corner, one could routinely pause for tea at four while looking over a stock of Chinese chickens hanging upside down. Almost everyone spoke British-accented English. Familiar red double-decker busses lumbered up and down the streets just as in London. Even the round postboxes and square, red phone booths mimicked those in the U.K. But a person could never mistake the colony for the motherland. Hong Kong moved with people. People who choked the thoroughfares then spilled out onto the water. Locked in by water, with Communist China breathing down the throat of the adjoining Kowloon Peninsula, buildings had no place to go other than up. Ever-increasing tall fingers of concrete, steel and glass stretched toward the sky.

Nikki's Hong Kong schedule included one concert, two televised interviews and three chat sessions. And the British Governor to Hong Kong invited her to the government compound for dinner one evening. These gatherings hosted by local dignitaries, while a privilege, really offered up the guest of honor as the entertainment. The host expected the honoree to meet and greet the prominent guests he hoped to impress. Protocol dictated glitzy eveningwear, yet modest enough to be worn around the diplomats' children.

A duty-free port, ships from all over the world off-loaded in Hong Kong, serving up a virtual shopper's paradise. All countries traded in this marketplace of the world. It wasn't unusual for a Soviet ship flying the Hammer and Sickle to pull into port. With Communism being the "Red Menace," this pariah so blatantly sitting in the harbor only increased the intrigue and mystery Nikki felt pulsing through its veins. It seemed as if everyone was engaged in some form of free enterprise. Both on the island of Hong Kong and the peninsula of Kowloon, stores of every kind crawled up into the skyscrapers' vast towers of merchandise. Independent vendors filled the sidewalks in front of the stores, up stairways and along back alleys, peddling their goods from pushcarts, portable display cases or even simple cloths. Local merchants constantly bombarded people in the street with their sales pitches to lure them to their merchandise. Vendors expected customers to haggle. The streets of Hong Kong offered everything imaginable, legal as well as illegal.

On Sunday, the eighteenth of December, as Nikki walked along the shops on the island of Hong Kong, she had no idea her life was about to change forever. The winter sun shone brilliantly as it played in the sapphire sky among the white puffy clouds—a perfect day to be out. Nikki tapped Jarred for a security detail for her shopping trip. Since the incident in Buenos Aires, a team of at least two always followed her at a reasonable distance.

On a whim that day, Nikki decided she wanted to purchase a ruby which she'd have made into a pendent. Nikki couldn't get over the amount of jewelry for sale in Hong Kong. A profusion of precious stones glutted the marketplace—loose stones, mounted stones, stones the size of a speck, stones larger than marbles, stones in stores, stones on the street—stones by the handful. After a while they lost their meaning and became "red ones, blue ones, green ones or white ones."

While she hovered over the display cases at Kwan's Wholesale Gems, discussing his wares with Mr. Kwan himself, a prying jewelry shop merchant from next door stood listening at Kwan's door. Eavesdropping on her conversation with Kwan, the meddling merchant ran next door into his store, then returned clutching a small velvet bag.

Loudly he called to Nikki from the sidewalk just outside the door, "No good quality here! No good! I have better. Lower overhead. Lower prices. Me, Missy. Me. I have it. I have what you want…at cheaper price. Come see! Come see!"

Mr. Kwan cut loose with a tirade in Chinese to dismiss the meddling merchant.

But the merchant insisted harder, "Poor quality. Here, I have better. I have *a deal for you!*"

His persistence lured Nikki out of the Kwan's and into the adjoining store. Behind her, Nikki heard Kwan cussing out the merchant. Intent on the thrill of the hunt, "better for cheaper" pulled her out of the store.

Leading her into his store, the merchant huddled together with her, their backs to the teaming masses outside on the sidewalk. Ceremoniously he brought forth the velvet sack again and opened it.

Carefully, as if its magnificence could only be grasped in increments, he slowly revealed a dazzling red stone. Its rich color rivaled that of a fine vintage wine. The intense spotlights in his shop set fire to its facets, releasing its deep smoldering fire.

Nikki felt the breath catch in her throat.

"You like it?" He wheedled.

Mesmerized, she nodded.

"Missy want to buy it?" He prompted, moving it slowly in his hand, letting the light dance across each facet, drawing her in, seducing her.

Entranced by its beauty, again Nikki nodded. "How much?" she asked like an addict seeking a fix, too captivated to really care what price he named.

At that precise moment, a hand reached in between the two of them and plucked the stone from the merchant's hands. Horrified that someone stole her stone from in front of her, Nikki's eyes immediately followed the arm up to the man's face. The sun beaming through the window behind him obscured his identity as his hand held her stone in front of him. He studied the stone in the sun's light.

Both the merchant and Nikki stood aghast at the intruder's boldness.

Finished, he dropped the stone back into the merchant's hand. "Go ahead tell the lady how much you're going to charge her for that worthless piece of glass," the stranger chided.

The Chinese merchant sputtered protests. "This stone priceless..."

"Worthless is more like it!" the stranger whispered in an aside to Nikki, then came back in a clear voice. "Ah, but for you, Princess, you can have it for a mere..." He paused to let the vendor name his price.

Purposely the stranger shifted his position letting the sun highlight his features, revealing his identity.

Amazement popped her eyes open. "It's you," she breathed.

Chapter 14
Alexander

Nikki's eyes locked on the stranger's eyes. A hint of merriment danced in his profound, blue pools. He met her gaze and held her there for a moment. "If you would permit me," he gestured toward the stone, "I have more than a nodding acquaintance with gems. Might I be of some assistance?"

Thwarted by his surprise intrusion, Nikki nodded.

"Now, my good man," he started by putting his hand on the merchant's back, indicating to the vendor that the players in the game had changed.

The Chinese merchant continued spewing his testimonials about the quality and the incredible deal.

Finally the stranger interrupted the merchant's endless discourse. "How much were you going to charge this lovely lady, whose own fire far outstrips your poor piece?"

Nikki acknowledged the compliment with an arch of her eyebrows.

Realizing further huckstering to be overkill, the vendor moved to close the deal, "Seven hundred dollars—U.S."

"What? You're insane! For this piece of paste! You'll take seven Hong Kong dollars, and I won't call the police," the intruder scoffed.

Clearly insulted, the merchant faced off with the intruder, braying at the top of his voice and rising up on his toes in an effort to negate the accusations.

Maintaining his cool demeanor, the stranger put up his hands to calm the angry merchant, "Okay. Okay. I'll settle this once and for all. You swear your stone is genuine. And I know it's worthless. I propose a small wager. If it's real, I'll pay you twice your asking price."

"In cash? U.S.? O.K.! I make bet," The merchant's eyes gleamed.

"But if it's a fake..." The stranger's words dangled in the air as he placed the stone on the shop floor. Nikki's eyes widened as she watched him put the heel of his leather loafer over the stone. Amazed, the merchant also stood frozen. The heel went up slightly and came down with a shatter. Only shards of red and white powder remained where moments earlier the faceted jewel winked up at them from the floor.

"Get out, get out!" The merchant screeched, disappearing into his back room.

"How, how did you know?" Nikki questioned as they left the shop.

"It's my business. That was an exceptional piece of paste, but paste nonetheless." His eyes sparkled as he indulged himself for a moment to observe her. "Where are my manners? Please allow me to introduce myself. I am Alexander Vincente ... Alex."

Nikki immediately extended her right hand, "IIi. I'm ..."

"An angel from heaven ... Miss Nicole Moore ... Nikki." He finished for her, taking her hand in his. "I know who you are. I confess to being a fan," he said as he looked up from a bow, hovering over her hand which he prepared to kiss. "Enchanté, Mademoiselle," he purred smoothly as he again met her gaze.

An embarrassed hint of a twitter escaped from her. Nikki had only witnessed such gallantry on the silver screen. Acknowledging his chivalry with a slight curtsey, Nikki hoped to cover up any residual clumsiness on her part.

Nikki got the distinct impression the inveterate gentleman saw through her masquerade, and it amused him. Alex lingered over her hand for a moment more.

"We've met before, if I'm not mistaken, Mr. Vincente. I believe I saw you for the first time in Naples."

"I'm honored," he bowed slightly from the waist. "You were paying attention after all. Please call me Alex. So, are you really shopping for a ruby or merely toying with the local merchants?" he asked, initiating a stroll down the sidewalk.

Nikki didn't want to admit that she used her gem shopping as an excuse for adventure. "No. No, I'd really like to find a ruby to have made into a necklace."

"Then may I offer my assistance in pursuit of your quest? I know a few places."

"I'd be delighted." Nikki found his debonair sophistication engaging. Taking a moment, she filled in her security team on the details. Amid their protests, she dismissed them for the afternoon.

Alexander crooked his arm, offering it to her. Slipping her hand through his arm, she followed his lead. "There are a few good shops on the Kowloon side. Let's catch the Star Ferry." They swung onto a double-decker for the ride to the ferry tie-up. Securing a seat for her, Alex stood alongside as her protector and guide.

Aboard the ferry Nikki leaned against the rail, letting the breeze comb through her hair, while Alex chose a closed-back bench backed into a corner. In doing so, he tossed a mild caution towards her, "If you have anything of value, the warning stenciled on the pillars about pickpockets isn't just for decoration."

On his caveat, she joined him in his seat.

He smiled, "Besides, since you dismissed your security, I am responsible for you." His eyes danced as he changed the subject, "Now, Nicole, what kind of stone did you have in mind?"

"Actually, Alex, I must confess, I was chasing a bargain—the thrill of the hunt—you know—plucking a gem from the shysters of Hong Kong's back alleys. Although my father deals in precious gems, I wanted to do this on my own. But I really would like a nice ruby, deep red, about the size of my fingernail."

"How unlucky for you, you ran into the tag team of the Kwan brothers. I'm afraid they set you up. The brother in one storefront hooks your attention with some nice quality, but relatively expensive stones. If he feels he's losing the sale, he signals his brother in the adjoining store. His brother lures the pigeon out of the store with a 'steal' of a deal. A near riot ensues and unfortunately in the confusion and haste to get the steal, the buyer assumes the substitute stone is of the same quality. The pigeon never really gets a good look at his wares."

"I'm surprised the second merchant let you get involved," Nikki commented.

"What choice did he have? He could either go along and hope my bravado was more ego than knowledge or close down the sting. This time he lost. You see, Hong Kong's alleys can pluck back.

"You're familiar with the Kwan brothers?"

"When you play in a sandbox long enough, you remember the players. Despite its multitudes, Hong Kong is a small island. If you want to survive, you learn. In Kowloon I have a long-time business associate named Charlie Soo. He owes me several favors. I thought we would pay him a visit."

Nikki figured they'd find Mr. Soo ensconced in a jewelry store of some repute. Imagine her surprise when they walked into an upscale porcelain emporium just off the main thoroughfare. Alexander left her to browse among the large Chinese urns while he sought out his friend. The time afforded Nikki the opportunity to visually sum him up. Obviously he had availed himself of that privilege with her on several occasions. She watched him greet his friend. She assumed Alex to be in his mid-thirties, at least six-foot, two. The store spotlights highlighted the gold streaks in his sandy, precisely trimmed hair. And what a tan he had, even in mid-December! Impeccably dressed, his customed-tailored clothes hugged his taut contours. Wrinkles didn't dare mar his attire. But the aura he exuded transcended his physical attributes. She had never met a man who wore self-assurance so nobly or so comfortably, like a pair of fine leather loafers.

While Alex and Charlie caught up on old times, Nikki pretended interest in the brightly colored vases and figurines. Not being at all familiar with the Chinese culture, she couldn't fully appreciate the priceless art surrounding her. Eventually the two found her. Alex made the introductions.

Mr. Soo, dressed in a cosmopolitan gray suit with thin black tie, shook her hand with a cool politeness, then made a slight bow and bade them to follow him into the back room. They edged past stacks of wooden packing crates to a secluded table with chairs. Soo pulled the chain switching on the hanging lamp above the table. The metal lampshade funneled all the light directly onto the table. Alex and Nikki sat while the porcelain dealer disappeared. Alex easily draped his arm over the back of his chair. To thwart her internal nerves, Nikki reverted to her proper upbringing. Sitting up correctly; she neatly folded her hands in her lap. In Soo's absence, they didn't speak.

Soon Charlie Soo re-emerged and drew a small, pearl gray velvet cloth from the breast pocket of his suit. He laid it in the palm of his hand, peeled back the folds of the cloth and exposed five large, deeply colored rubies of various shapes. Their fire ignited in the light of the lone bulb. Laying the cloth with stones on it before Alexander, he offered him a jeweler's loupe then took his seat at the table.

Alexander inspected each ruby. "Charlie, these are all great specimens," he said after he finished his examination, putting the loupe to rest on the velvet. Then he slid the entire package in front of Nikki.

Carefully she considered her actions before making a move. Her surroundings intimidated her. Acutely aware of the age difference between Alex and her, Nikki didn't want appear to be a juvenile or a flighty female devoid of class. Refraining from any emotional exclamations, she kept a business sense about her. Individually she moved each gem into the light to get an idea of color and fire, then returned each to its place as she finished with it. Finally she addressed the gentlemen, "Yes, Mr. Soo, I agree these stones are exquisite. However, I am particularly fond of this one." Nikki singled out the pear shaped ruby and let the light play on its facets.

"Perhaps you would like to examine it with the loupe?" Alex prompted.

Assured, she politely smiled, "There's really no need. Mr. Soo is a trusted friend. He wouldn't dream of trespassing on your relationship with inferior quality. And you have inspected them and given your seal of approval. I presume on your expertise."

Then Nikki addressed the Chinese shop owner, "Mr. Soo, if you're willing to part with this ruby, I would be delighted to buy it."

Smiling, Charlie Soo nodded, "Please come with me, while I prepare the stone for you." Nikki followed the two gentlemen out of the storeroom. At the front counter Charlie folded the ruby up in its own square piece of velvet and placed it in an embroidered satin bag, which he slid towards her.

Nikki halted its progress, "Mr. Soo, I haven't paid for it yet."

Using his eyes Soo motioned toward his friend with a confirming smile, "Mr. Alexander has taken care of it."

Nikki smile politely then lowered her voice, to elicit confidentiality, "Mr. Soo, I only just met Mr. Vincente this afternoon. I could not accept such an extravagant gift from him at this time. I'm sure you understand."

Returning her confidence with a nod and a smile, he never sought Alexander's consent, "Of course. I will prepare the bill for you."

Nikki's attention shifted back to Alexander. He stood back, arms folded, regarding her with bemusement, shaking his head, "You never even asked the price. How do you know you can afford it?"

"With three platinum singles and a platinum album if I can't afford it, I'd better change managers. Besides, when you brought me here to deal with your friend, what was I going to do, haggle over the price? The sale was consummated the moment my foot crossed the threshold. The only questions to be answered were: Did I like what I saw? And which one would I pick?"

Alex smilingly picked up her hand and kissed it. "Amazing! Just amazing! Will you at least allow me to have the ruby mounted in a pendant setting for you?"

"Nothing extravagant," she admonished.

He acquiesced, "Simple, elegant, I promise. Something to compliment your style." He kissed her hand again and took the satin sac from her.

Mr. Soo returned with the bill of sale, and Nikki counted out seven one hundred-dollar bills to him. With business concluded, he engagingly offered her his arm for a tour of his shop. As they strolled among the porcelain, he described the history and value of his most prized pieces. Contentedly Alexander tagged along behind. Upon completion of the tour, Mr. Soo turned to her. "My dear Miss Nicole, you would honor me if you would choose something from my humble collection. My gift to you."

In a blush, Nikki thanked him for his kindness. Thoughtfully she considered her selection. Certainly she didn't want to be greedy, stripping him of one of his priceless pieces, but she knew her choice had to demonstrate the appropriate appreciation and not insult his time or his offer by choosing something insignificant. Nikki decided on a medium-sized, blue and white ginger jar, then silently checked her choice with Alex. Surreptitiously he nodded his concurrence. Mr. Soo made arrangements to send it directly to Nikki's home.

Departing his shop, Nikki offered Mr. Soo her hand to shake. Once again he bowed. Nikki returned his bow. "Thank you so very much, Mr. Soo."

"Please," he said with a wink, "call me Charlie. All my friends do."

Once out on the street and well on their way from Soo's shop, Alex exclaimed, "You really impressed ol' Charlie. I have never seen him fuss over anyone so."

Nikki met his compliment with a self-conscious shrug of her shoulders.

"And me too, I might add," Alex continued. "I find myself captivated by your savoir-vivre, enrapt and under your spell. I would be delighted if you would do me the distinct honor of letting me take you to dinner." With his Continental flair, he turned foreign phrases as easily as some people turned pages.

Instinctively Nikki glanced at her watch, then hedged, "It's four now, I had better head back to the hotel. I really have a lot to do. Tomorrow..."

"...is another day," he persisted. "May I pick you up tonight for dinner? I know a charming little place..."

Nikki's mind raced. What was she getting in for? She certainly didn't want any entanglements. But this man intrigued her. Before she knew it, "I'll be ready at eight," slipped out.

Alex escorted her to her hotel's elevator. Waiting for the car, Nikki casually asked, "What should I wear?"

Alex stalled his answer until she stepped inside. Then, as the doors slid shut, his answer came. "You will be beautiful in whatever you choose."

What kind of answer was that, she wondered? In her room Nikki agonized over the proper attire for the proper place. Alex lent no hint where they would be going. Nikki couldn't imagine a man of Alexander's refinement taking her to any place jean-casual. After laying out her entire closet, she decided on a blue-green, polished silk, strapless sheath and matching Chinese jacket with satin frog closures at the throat. For a touch of class she added matching satin gloves.

As Nikki prepared for the evening, her mind retraced the day. Continually momentary gestures and phrases of Alex's invaded her thoughts. His dancing eyes flirted with her reflection in the mirror as she swept her hair up into a bouquet of curls.

Jarred knocked on Nikki's door. Nikki's going out again with a man she had met only that afternoon disturbed him. He plied her with questions, none of which she could answer. Since Nikki refused to ice her plans and dismissed the need for his security services that evening, Jarred departed an unhappy person.

At eight Nikki rode the elevator down to the second floor. She decided she'd descend the grand staircase to make an entrance. A cursory scan of the lobby, from atop the stairs, didn't turn up anyone who remotely resembled Alexander. As she began her descent, a tuxedo-attired gentleman stepped from the staircase's shadows and slowly turned towards her. There stood the appraising Mr. Vincente.

Alexander drank her in, lapping up every nuance, every step of her grand entrance. Extending his hand, he took her gloved hand to assist her down the last two steps.

From behind his back he produced a single flower nosegay. With a twinkle in his eye, he said, "I understand you like gardenias."

Utter surprise flashed across her face. Instantly she understood. "You! All these months! It's been you!"

His impish blues danced. "I think they fit your style—delicate elegance and sophistication in a simple package. Shall we go?" With his hand lightly on her back, he guided her to his waiting limousine.

Getting into the car, a few pops and blinding flashes greeted them. Nothing unusual—just the tabloid photographers catching Nikki in the company of someone new. Nikki apologized once they settled into their seats. "That's a hazard of my profession. In truth, I'm surprised they didn't nail us while we were shopping."

They dined at an intimate restaurant called The Pearl, nestled into Hong Kong's Causeway Bay. The staff referred to Alexander by name and seated them at the best table by the window. The busy causeway provided a kaleidoscope of the seaport cosmos as the little junks migrated back and forth over the water. Their winking lanterns resembled diamonds twinkling against the velvet backdrop of night. They supped slowly, first champagne, then oysters, followed by seafood bisque. Engaging banter accompanied each course.

Conversation flowed easily with Alex. He steered the topic back to their shopping that afternoon. "This afternoon when you recognized Charlie Soo for his integrity and value of friendship, you paid him the highest compliment possible. Charlie is a hard-bitten businessman who scratched his way up from those back alleys of Hong Kong which you find so charming. He doesn't give anything away and doesn't make friends easily."

"I was honored by the offer of his friendship. How long have you known him?"

"Fifteen years. We've been in some tight spots together. I've trusted him with my life."

Alex's admission of tight spots surprised Nikki and served to point up how much she didn't know about him. Over the Cantonese lobster curry, she commented, "Trusted friends are indeed a rarity. But I must admit I can't imagine you being caught off-guard by anything, let alone being in a 'tight spot.'"

Alex cautiously smiled across the lip of his wineglass. "That's in the past. I'd rather deal with the present. Your savoir-faire fascinates me. I find your uncanny ability to relate to people refreshing."

Despite the compliment, his move to redirect her attention caught an edge with her. Resting her fork on her plate, Nikki asked, "How long have you been watching me anyway? The first time I recall seeing you was in Naples on my eighteenth birthday."

Holding his wineglass, Alexander relaxed into the back of his chair. "It was spring of 1965 in the Brass Rail Café, not far from the 'Circus' in London. You met a reporter there. I didn't catch much, but I remember you totally disarmed him. He wound up practically groveling at your feet. He called you 'Princess' — so fitting!"

Nikki searched her memory. "You mean Karl?"

"Okay, Karl. … You fascinated me the moment you walked in the door. I would have introduced myself then, but you left with the guy. Before long, 'Nikki' began to pop up all over the place. I followed your career in the press. Naples was your first concert I caught. You enchanted me."

"Heavens Alex, that was almost two years ago. I remember you kept showing up — at the premiere party, then outside the farm in Pennsylvania. That scared me."

"Understandable, but I needed to make sure you were all right," he ceded apologetically.

The uneasiness from the encounter on the farm filtered into Nikki's memory. Was this man just a charming eccentric? A celebrity stalker? A con artist? What? Suddenly feeling ill-at-ease, she wished she had taken Jarred's protestations to heart.

Alexander read her fear. Honestly smiling, he leaned forward, "You see, Nicole, since that day in the café I have been totally captivated by your charm. Not by Nikki, but by you. In fact, your public persona complicated the possibility of an introduction."

Nikki lamely smiled.

Dismayed, Alex sat back, "I am terribly sorry. I have frightened you. That was never my intent. If you like, I will call in your security team, and they can take you back to your hotel." He readied his hand to motion.

Nikki arrested his signal. "Security?" If only they were there, she wished.

Placating her, Alex smiled. "You don't think your head of security would let you out with a stranger without sending someone along to keep an eye on him, do you?"

"Jarred stopped by earlier in the evening and, I dismissed him. You must be paranoid if you think we're being followed," Nikki laughed accusingly.

The possibility of a challenge excited Alex; he smiled raising his glass. "Princess, how much would you like to bet?"

Cock-sure of herself, she met his challenge. "Name your poison," she dared him with her raised glass. She knew Jarred and his regard for orders.

"If security is present, then you will know you are in good hands, and we shall continue our date in their presence. If no one is there, then you will immediately call Jarred to come and rescue you. And I promise I will never show up on your doorstep or bother you again. Deal?" His glass waited for hers to commence the bet.

In the exhilaration of the moment, Nikki picked up the gauntlet Alex tossed down. "Deal," she clinked his glass.

Alexander tapped his chin in thought, "Now, how to prove this?"

"We could always go out into the street. You would hold my arm and I'd call for help," Nikki volunteered.

"Great plan! And risk getting shot?" Alex chortled at the absurdity.

"Shot? Guns? Ooo, Mr. Vincente, you watch too many movies."

"My dear, how green are you?" Their game of wits electrified him. "You do not think your security is toothless? Do you? I am not about to risk my hide on your naiveté. No, there has to be another way."

"Then I'll go out by myself and call for help. When no one comes, I'll come back into the restaurant and call Jarred."

"I'm not sure I like it. It smacks of crying wolf, but if done well, it should be rather effective. But do me a slight favor. Please warn the maitre d' before you pull this thing off. We do not want the police showing up, too."

The moment of truth had arrived. Nikki gathered her things. Once she walked out, she didn't plan on coming back. She knew she was right. Jarred wouldn't dare trespass on her privacy against her order. Yet, Nikki felt a twinge; maybe she had carried this bet thing a bit too far. She didn't really want the evening to end, especially in a silly challenge of egos. She wanted to get to know this gentleman. But she had painted herself into a corner, so her feelings were water under the bridge now.

Alex stood up when she rose to leave. "If you are right, you realize this is good-bye," he lamented with a sigh. "I want you to know this has been the most marvelous night of my life, for which I do sincerely thank you. I will treasure it always. May I, one last time?" He reached for her hand.

Raising her hand to his lips, he simulated a slight snap to attention, then he clicked his heels, "Good-bye, my dear Nicole. Thank you again." He kissed her hand and, as a gentleman, maintained his position until she left the room.

Nikki didn't turn around lest she give him quarter or grant herself a chance to renege on the bet. Drawing up to her full height, she walked out proudly. Nikki was sure as soon as she left, he blithely returned to his seat to plan his next conquest of some other unsuspecting damsel in the city.

In keeping with her promise, she stopped by the maitre d's stand and briefly explained the wager. Not wishing to impugn the reputation of the fine establishment, Nikki walked to mid- block before beginning her call for help.

Almost from the moment her foot stepped out of range of the building's light into the darkness of the deserted sidewalk, Nikki heard a slight scuffling. Memories of Buenos Aires poured over her. She froze. Her mind launched into hyper drive. What if she was right and there was no security out there? Oh, those footsteps! What had she set herself up for? The maitre d' would assume her cries were just the bet. Panic reared its head. Summoning anything that remotely resembled courage, Nikki shook off the fear, determined to carry out the silly bet.

She raised her voice into the night air, "Help! Oh please someone help me!" It didn't take but a second or two—the footfalls came fast and furious. Almost instantly two figures flashed from the shadows and rushed at her. In the ambient light from the street, to her relief Nikki saw it was Edward, and Jarred himself, flying to her side brandishing firearms. Her jaw dropped visibly. Contritely, Nikki profusely apologized for her careless disregard of their jobs. To her surprise, Jarred dismissed her attempts at repentance. He apologized for his covert actions and for not disclosing his presence to her.

Turning around to go back to the restaurant and eat her double-serving of crow, to her surprise Alex waited, leaning up against his limousine, smiling.

"You win!" Nikki admitted throwing up her hands. Then she introduced Jarred and Edward.

Pulling himself up for the introductions, Alexander warmly greeted them, "Gentlemen, I do sincerely apologize for sending you on this little exercise. I am afraid I put her up to this. Please feel welcome to accompany us for the rest of the evening. I have a cab waiting so you can follow along."

He turned to her, "I thought we might catch dessert somewhere else." Once inside the car, Alex addressed her with sincerity. "Nicole, if you are not comfortable with me, I will release you from the wager and take you back to the hotel. I would never do anything to make you uncomfortable. What is your pleasure?" Then he added with a hopeful twinkle in his eyes, "Or, shall we continue?"

"Yes. I'm fine. Please." Nikki studied his suave self-assurance for a moment. "How long were you standing there?"

"For pretty much all of it. I couldn't let you walk out into the night alone. What if you had been right? Who would have been there to protect you?"

"How did you know they would be there?"

"It was really—as you say—a sure thing. I know that if I had such a precious jewel to protect, I'd never let it out of my sight. Like all good security, they are devoted to their mission."

"And the guns?"

"It's just part of the job, especially after Buenos Aires. Jarred knows the business and his subject. He knew a gun would frighten you. There was really no need for you to know."

"You know about Buenos Aires?"

"Nicole, I told you that I have been interested in you since that day in the café. You are important to me. I travel a lot in my job. Our paths intersected when I could arrange it."

"Then you knew I was married."

"I discovered that after the premiere. I did not show up after that."

"Except for the farm incident."

"After the roughing up Grant gave you, I figured he must be out of your life. Besides, I was concerned."

"Grant? How could you have known about that?"

"I have connections." Alexander wrapped his hands around both of hers. "But that is all in the past. Please just take it that I cared and let us not drag up all the details. I want you to be at ease with me. Do you still feel comfortable here?"

"Yes. It's just that I'm amazed at how much you know. It's a little disconcerting." Then a thought struck her, "You know for such a sucker's bet that was some farewell scene you put on back there at the restaurant."

Devilish amusement sparkled in his eyes. He picked up her gloved hand, raised it to his lips, with a cock of his head and a glint in his eye said, "*Carpe diem*"!

The limo drew to a stop in front of the Furama Hotel. "I thought some dessert and coffee in the dining room at the top of the hotel. Next to you, it is the best view in town."

Alexander was right. The Furama offered a stunning view of the entire harbor. They finished their decadent chocolate torte and relaxed over coffees as the entire seaport revolved below them. Alex brought out the little satin sac from Mr. Soo's shop. "See what you think of this. I had it done this afternoon." He opened the sac to reveal an exquisite setting. A triangular cluster of three small diamonds gathered around the top point of the pear to perfectly accent the ruby.

"Oh, Alexander, it's elegant! You do have good taste."

"May I put it on you?" As Alex leaned in to her, his masculine fragrance filled her nose. Opening the clasp, he gently placed it around her throat, letting it come to rest perfectly on her breastbone, tantalizingly above her cleavage. "Beautiful," he whispered admiringly.

"Oh, it is. Thank you."

"I wasn't speaking about the jewelry." Alexander fixed his eyes directly on her.

The directness of his compliment caught Nikki's breath. Unable to respond, she changed the subject, "You must let me know what I owe you for it."

"I thought we agreed this afternoon that I would get the setting."

"I only meant you could select one. I never presumed you'd buy it."

"Nicole, it is an innocent bauble. Think of it as a souvenir from our day together." Brandies with Alex quieted any further discussion of the matter. The nightcaps and conversation carried them to three in the morning, when they climbed back into the limo for the ride back to Nikki's hotel.

Parked in front of the hotel, they had trouble bringing the evening to an end. "May I see you again today?" Alex asked.

"I wish I could," Nikki fumbled. "We leave in the late afternoon. I have a thousand things to do before the plane, including my final chat session at three."

"What about breakfast?"

"Like in four or five more hours?" Nikki looked at her watch.

"Why not take care of your obligations, and I will see you at seven for breakfast."

Not really wanting their date to end, Nikki capitulated, "Okay, seven it is."

Nikki tried to organize herself for departure, but the evening crept into every deliberation. Visions of Alexander's tanned physique, so elegantly accentuated in his crisp formal wear, usurped all other thought. She took the necklace off and displayed it so she could delight in it. Then, she put the pendant back on, to have him near her. Emptying her closet to sort out her short-trip bag to go home, again she revisited how the candle-light kissed the gold from his hair and smoldered in his eyes, those blue eyes. What time was it?

At six-thirty, she woke Mary. "Mare, I'm really sorry, but this time I'm going to dump all the prep for leaving on you. Something's come up and I made plans for this morning and afternoon."

Finally able to focus, her friend's gaze fell with incriminating curios-ity on the green silk dress that she still had on. "I guess you do have plans! What's going on? What about the chat session? Do you want me to cancel that?"

"No. I wouldn't miss it for the world. I've got to change now. I met someone. I'll be at the chat session in the hotel conference room at three." On her way out she stopped. "You're really a friend. Thanks so very much." Never once in their over two years together had Nikki ever presumed or trespassed on her best friend. Mary knew this had to be something really big.

In anticipation of a time crunch at the end, Nicole settled on the typi-cal Nikki dress for the day: a black and white hound's-tooth mini skirt, an electric yellow poet's blouse and matching tights. It wasn't how she wanted to meet Alexander, but she doubted she'd have time to change before the chat session. Not wanting to give up the ruby pendant, she slipped it underneath her blouse and threw on a strand of "kicky" plastic beads with matching hoop earrings, then tossed makeup in her purse for touch-ups.

The doors to the elevator opened to the lobby shortly after seven. Alexander waited with the *Asian Wall Street Journal* tucked beneath his arm. He appeared fresh and dashing in a blue and white pinstriped oxford shirt and a navy blazer. He greeted her with a peck to the cheek and a smile. "I hoped you would keep our date. It was rather rude of me to suggest you give up your sleep to spend some time with me."

"And who's to say I didn't catch a few winks?" Nikki jibed. She didn't want him to think she had actually dropped everything for him.

Catching a double-decker, they rode uptown to the Prestige de Ville. "They have the best Eggs Benedict this side of Brennan's in New Orleans," Alex extolled. Over breakfast he commented on her attire, "My you do look incredibly 'Nikki' today."

"I know. But since I'll be 'on' this afternoon, I had to dress the part."

"And speaking of the day, what did you have on the agenda for us today?" he asked with great interest.

"Alex, you asked me. I thought you had something in mind."

"I only wanted to be in the presence of your company. The day is yours. Seize it. I am but your humble servant."

"Okay, Christmas is less than a week away. I really planned to do some shopping for gifts yesterday, but I kind of got sidetracked." She shot him a coy smile.

Finishing breakfast they headed to the ferry for the shopping mecca of Kowloon.

Shopping with Alexander wasn't like crawling through the boutiques on Carnaby Street with Candy, or even stuffy browsing at Harrods with Mary. No, Alexander elevated shopping to an aristocratic art form. They shopped from atop gilt chairs of silk brocade, with their feet propped up on little footstools, sipping Jasmine-infused tea, while attentive staff paraded and demonstrated their wares before them. At one boutique their selection of pearl-beaded angora sweaters so delighted Nikki, she not only bought one for her mom, but a couple for herself, too. On their way out of the shop, she stopped to admire a pale-blue silk business suit with pearl buttons.

"It would be exquisite on you," Alex encouraged.

"I know," Nikki sighed a lament, "But when would I wear it? It's not 'Nikki.'"

"Surely, Nicole Moore ventures out every now and again."

"Maybe, sometime," she half-considered it as she continued toward the exit.

Alex nodded.

They swam their way through the people-choked sidewalks from one shopping tower to the next when Alex abruptly stopped. A tilt of his head drew Nikki's attention to the merchandise in the store window. Sleek feminine forms displayed an eclectic array of high-fashion lingerie—bras, panties, filmy peignoirs.

"Shall we?" Alex dared with a saucy wink.

Embarrassed, but not about to display it for him, Nikki burst out laughing and kept walking.

Their arms would have been full from shopping, but Alex hired runners to periodically dispatch the treasures back to the hotel.

Occasionally someone on the street recognized Nikki and stopped her for an autograph or a picture. Over lunch she apologized after one rather drawn-out encounter.

Alex stopped her mid-sentence, "This is not something new that you invented. It is your job. Besides," he teased, "better you working, than me."

His reference to their meeting the day before afforded Nikki another opportunity to delve into his pursuit of her. "Yesterday, when you stepped into the Kwan scam, your presence there, at that precise moment, didn't just happen by accident, did it?"

Straightforwardly Alex answered, "No."

"How long were you following me?"

"Nicole," he temporarily shelved his natural amusement, "I would not call it following you. When I discovered that my business trip coincided with your tour, I made sure that our paths crossed. I just had to wait for the right opportunity for my introduction to present itself."

Nikki laughed, "Thank God for the Kwan Brothers, huh?"

He returned the smile. "I am sorry it took so long for them to appear on the scene. If they had been more on target, I wouldn't be fighting for precious minutes of your time at the end of you visit. Perhaps I should put them on my payroll."

"Speaking of payroll, Alex, what exactly do you do?"

As if he totally missed her question he asked, "What are you doing for New Year's Eve?"

"Why, I don't know. Probably spending it on the farm with my parents before heading back to London."

"Spend it here with me. The city really celebrates—fireworks, parades, dancing in the streets," he pushed to make the spontaneous sale.

"You mean come back here in two weeks?" Nikki cringed at the thought of another eighteen hour flight.

"No. Don't go home today. Stay! Have Christmas here with me. Then we will do New Years!"

"But I promised my parents I'd be home for Christmas."

Alex interrupted, "Bring them here. We can celebrate together in Hong Kong. It's not snow and sleigh rides, but then again is Pennsylvania really? It will be different, and I promise I will make it exciting!"

More than anything Nikki wanted to throw caution to the wind, to jump on the idea. But she didn't want to have her parents rearrange their plans again on the whim of someone she had just met—talk about irresponsibility!

As the minutes ticked away on the clock, Nikki grew anxious. She wished the afternoon would stretch on for an eternity, but her commitment to the fans followed by her departure pressed in on her. She didn't even need to ask. Almost before she thought it, Alex whisked her back to the hotel in plenty of time. Alexander consented to staying for the chat session, taking a chair in the far rear. As the session drew to a close, her eyes sought out Alex. At some point he must have quietly slipped out. Nikki had hoped for a good-bye, obviously he didn't do them. Or maybe in declining his invitation, she had trampled on his ego.

The usual manila envelope already occupied Nikki's seat in the first class section of the aircraft, no doubt housing details of last minute items. However, instead of itinerary changes, this one contained several eight by ten glossies of her and Alex from their date. Nikki tarried over the sweetness of the memory as Karl slid into the vacant seat next to her.

"Know who he is?" Karl asked sarcastically while tightening his seatbelt.

Taken aback by the tonal inference of his question, uncharacteristically she bristled. "You intend on staying? ... Yes, that's Alexander Vincente. ... Why? Do you know where these came from?"

"Yeah, Jimmy took them last night when the two of you stepped out."

"Karl, are you spying on me? I thought we were friends?"

"Calm down, Nikki. We are friends. I wasn't spying either. I figured I had better get those first rather than someone else. We've always worked like that. ... Wow, are we a bit touchy today!"

"I'm sorry. I'm a little tired. I didn't get any sleep last night."

"I'm not casting aspersions. But what do you know about this guy?" Karl asked, still actively concerned.

"Sorry. You hit a nerve. I'm a little angry with myself because in truth, I don't know too much about him." Nikki tossed the photos back into the envelope. "I realize it's stupid. I'm already beating myself up over that. On the other hand Karl, I find him ... interesting. ... All I know is that he was in the Brass Rail Café the day you and I hammered out our publicity deal. He's had a thing for me ever since. He travels a lot, and he showed up in Hong Kong to introduce himself. I tried to find out what exactly he does, but he avoided the question. With the hectic pace of the day though, I don't know if it was intentional or it slipped through the cracks."

"My guess would be intentional," Karl pulled the photos back out of the envelope. "That's Alexander Vincente, international playboy. A *bon vivant* employed by whatever breeze is blowing today." Then Karl produced another envelope with several grainy black and white photos of Alex. "I had my editor telex me these this afternoon. I wanted to be sure I was right."

The plane started to roll down the runway.

"Karl, the last time I looked it wasn't a crime to be rich, good looking or at your leisure."

"Wouldn't we all like to be!? But there have been some questionable occurrences surrounding him." Determined, Karl refused to drop the topic.

"Such as?"

"Some times things are found missing and people have disappeared."

"You have got to be kidding!" Incredulity crept into Nikki's voice. "Doesn't that smack of spy hooey to you?"

The plane lifted off and the seaport with Alexander Vincente shrank, then disappeared.

"When did you put this all together?" Nikki returned her attention to her friend.

"Not until Jimmy showed me the pictures this morning. I admit most of what I told you is rumor and innuendo."

"Does Jarred know? Shouldn't I be hearing this from him?" Nikki tried to shove the bird-dogging off onto someone else, figuring if Jarred had concerns, he would have already done some investigating of his own.

Karl continued, "I gave it to him as soon as I got confirmation on the pictures. I'd tread lightly with Jarred if I was you. He's a bit sensitive over last night. You know the two of you scared the hell out of him."

"I know. I apologized. But, I'll talk to him again."

"I'll leave you alone for now, Nikki. Just be careful, okay? I know I don't have a right. It's just that I don't want to see you hurt." Karl unbuckled his seatbelt to make his exit, leaving the envelope with the black and whites behind.

Nikki watched the sky transform itself into night. The twinkling stars reminded her of Alexander's eyes and their night at The Pearl. Karl's ominous warnings didn't faze her. The description of a playboy squared perfectly with the polished manners accompanied by Alex's devil-may-care attitude. Nikki wondered if she'd see him again. As much as she hoped for another rendezvous, she expected nothing. After all, she had turned him down. She suspected men like him were accustomed to having their own way. With plenty of fish in the sea, Nikki assumed he would move on to the next flounder, so she wrote off Mr. Vincente.

Homey family traditions, swirling with the aromas of cinnamon, pine and bayberry, ushered in Christmas in Pennsylvania. The Moore's celebration deliberately lacked the showbiz glitz that so inundated the house just a month before. Mom loved her sweater, and Dad tinkered all day with the super-miniaturized radio Nikki gave him.

A messenger arrived just before dinner with a package for Nikki. She unwrapped the blue silk suit she had admired in Hong Kong. The card simply read "For Nicole Moore — Merry Christmas." Nikki knew immediately who sent it. But since the card wasn't signed, for her parents' benefit she speculated about who on her staff might have been so generous.

Cookie, Annie and Leanne swung by for New Year's Eve. Realizing it could be the last time the four of them might be together unencumbered by partners, they spent a quiet evening at Nikki's parent's house. Their plans only included ordering cheese-steaks from V&S. At eleven Nikki answered the knock at the front door. It wasn't the sandwiches, but a delivery of another sort.

Beneath all the special packaging, the box contained a bottle of Cristal champagne and a card. "I'm watching the fireworks explode over Hong Kong harbor, missing you. Share a drink with me at midnight. Here's to 1967! ... Alexander."

To say the least, the delivery enlivened the house. Since Nikki hadn't mentioned Alex to anyone — now there were questions to be answered. Nikki's mom, dad and the three girls grilled her. Pulling the ruby pendant out from underneath her sweater, Nikki started with the Kwan brothers and deliberately omitted Karl's vague allegations.

Later on New Year's Day, her father borrowed the pendant to put it under his scope. "Nikki, your gentleman friend really knows his business. The diamonds he had set for you aren't throw-aways. They may be small, but they are blue-white, flawless. Normally you would never set such stones as accent pieces. I would say the diamonds out value the center stone except, ... how much did you say you paid for the ruby?"

"Seven hundred dollars. Why?" she asked, unaffected by her father's appraisal. Knowing even what little she did about Alex, her father's assessment didn't surprise her.

"You stole it! If I bought it, *wholesale* I'd have paid at least seven thousand for it. Rarely have I seen a ruby of such quality. Make sure you insure it well." This bit of news both delighted and angered Nikki.

Obviously she had been made a fool! She fumed. The diamonds he had set, the value of the ruby, the deal for the stone she supposedly made with Charlie Soo … all of it was as arranged by Alexander Vincente! He knew all along. He set it up! So it wasn't mere coincidence that the ruby's price was exactly the same as the Kwan fake! Did he play her for a reaction to further amuse himself? Was it a test? A game? Nikki resolved with their next meeting he would hear from her. And after the suit and the champagne, she knew there would be a next meeting. The only question that remained was when?

Chapter 15

Transitions

Eagerly Nikki anticipated contact from the infamous Alexander Vincente—even as she prepared a litany of questions for him. But he failed to materialize. Likewise the regular Friday deliveries of gardenias also dried up. Nikki didn't permit herself to moon over the loss. She merely noted it and moved on.

After *The Ed Sullivan Show* snafu, Bruce mapped out an aggressive year for Nikki. A close-up of a seductive Nikki bathed solely in the light from a lone candle graced the cover of her fourth solo album *Alone at Last*. Released in December, it owned the top spot on all the charts across the Continent as Nikki fever raged on.

In addition to her recordings, concerts and TV shows, Bruce landed Nikki one of the leads in the movie *Runway Breakouts*. The plot centered on three runway models who leave the image and the catwalk behind for other careers. Nikki's character, Rikki, played a model sucked into the world of espionage. Nikki sang the film's title song, "Danger Us," which became a signature hit for her. Location filming for the movie began in February all across Europe's hotbeds of *haute couture*, and Bruce conveniently scheduled concerts in the venues of the shoot.

Nikki's last concert tied to a movie location fell in Florence in early June. To liven up her stage presence, Nikki wanted to incorporate go-go dancing and flashing-to-the-beat lights into her concert routine. Eager to preview the changes before her coming concert tour, she trotted them out on the final evening.

The new details of the show absorbed her totally that night. The style changes wowed the crowd. Nikki returned to her dressing room riding atop the heady tide of exultation to find lighted candles, champagne on ice, gardenias and a note. "Bravo! Dinner at eleven? Alex." Well, well, after six months the sleeping serpent awoke!

Nikki bristled. Evidently he hadn't forgotten her. Was he keeping her in reserve for a slow night? She weighed whether or not to accept his invitation. She didn't want to appear to be at his beck and call. In the end she decided to take the meeting, at least then she could finish the business he started back in December. Backing down from the high of her performance and out of the customary promoter's soiree, Nikki prepared for her late supper with Mr. Vincente. Since she intended to make an issue of the pendant, she sent Edward to retrieve it from the hotel vault. Then Nikki combed through her wardrobe for the perfect dress. Alexander valued elegance, so she wanted something conservative, yet eat-your-heart-out gorgeous. She chose a white linen, tailored tuxedo coat, trimmed in white satin with matching mini skirt. Without a blouse underneath, the pendant dangled oh, so provocatively in the vee-cut of the coat.

To give Nikki the opportunity of making an entrance, Mary agreed to receive Alexander. Pouring herself a glass of champagne, Mary waited for him in Nikki's dressing room. He arrived promptly at eleven, rakishly well-dressed and while they waited for Nikki, he involved her in courteous conversation. Experiencing him first hand, Mary understood his mesmerizing effect on Nikki.

Fashionably late, Nikki stepped through the door at eleven-ten. Smoothly Alexander excused himself from Mary's company. By his expression, her outfit had accomplished its goal.

"Enchanté, *mon ami*," he intoned from his slight bow, as he kissed her hand. "How delightful to see you again. I'm so glad that you accepted my dinner proposal."

Nikki murmured in her best *femme fatale*. "Alex, it has been so long. I thought you had forgotten me, since I didn't take you up on your Hong Kong offer."

"My dear, far from it. But we'll discuss that later. Shall we be off?" Sliding his hand along her back, Alexander ushered her to his waiting Mercedes.

Bypassing all the notable restaurants, they pulled up at the freight entrance of Galleria degli Uffizi, one of Florence's most famous art museums. To Nikki's obvious surprise Alex explained, "I wanted wherever we went to be special—equal to your beauty. Uffizi, with its priceless masterpieces, pales in comparison, but was the closest I could come."

Alex caught the slight roll of her eyes, even as his eyes twinkled, "I knew our dinner had to be somewhere special, since I have some serious groveling to do." He guided her inside through the shadow-filled halls lit only by small footlights.

Nikki felt peculiar, nervous, about being inside the museum, so obviously after hours. Karl's admonitions of suspicious activities connected to Alexander crowded her memory. She stopped.

"I am assuming, since I didn't hear any alarms or police sirens, we have permission to be in here," Nikki tossed off, careful not to reveal her apprehension.

"Of course. I would never put you in jeopardy. Come on. It's not much farther."

Although Alex's assurance didn't quell her edginess, she disguised it with a sniff of brassiness, "Another one of your extraordinary friends, I suppose?"

Finally they entered a dimly lit exhibit room. In the middle of the room sat a small table, glinting with silver and crystal for an intimate supper, accompanied by a bottle of fine wine resting in a wine bucket. Only the individual gallery light above each painting illuminated the room. For his backdrop, Alexander had chosen the watery shades of Claude Monet. Pulling out a chair for her, he whispered in Nikki's ear, "I would have washed the room with candlelight, but unfortunately the soot plays havoc with the masterpieces."

"This is just fine," she coolly assured him as he glided her chair into place. From the shadows a man emerged long enough to pour the wine.

Alexander raised his glass in a toast, "To a wonderful evening and a forgiving companion." Their glasses met with a delicate ring to finalize the toast.

But Nikki wasn't about to allow his polish and charm to melt her resolve.

"I am sure by now Jarred or Karl has informed you as to my identity," Alex rocked her cool aplomb.

Nikki squirmed a bit in her seat; she hadn't planned to launch into her little speech quite so early on in the evening. She at least wanted to finish the meal before jumping in with both feet. Alex's comment flushed the blood to her face, as he must have known it would—playing her for her reaction again, no doubt. Nikki iced her indignation with a sip of wine, then slowly and so very deliberately looked up, "You could have spared me the embarrassment of my publicist springing your identity on me. Or, did you consider that charming, too?"

"That is another indulgence I must ask of you. I was hoping to dazzle you with my boyish charisma, not a title or bankbook," his eyes sparkled with a note of self-deprecation. "Did I succeed?"

Nikki let his words hang in the air. Not wanting to further inflate his ego, she merely raised an eyebrow and her glass.

Her subterfuge didn't put Alex off, "I see I did not succeed. Something is still bothering you. Please do not hold back."

Nikki's blood rose again. If he wanted an abrupt end to the evening, then so be it. She squared him in her sight. Her words tumbled out, all at once, non-stop. "I didn't mind your little charade as much as I minded being toyed with for my reaction. Don't you have anything better to do than to amuse yourself at the expense of an innocent girl's self respect? Is that why an investment-grade ruby at pauper's prices? ... the Cristal on

New Years? ... bundles of out-of-season gardenias? ... an after-hours dinner inside a closed-to-the-public museum? Is this merely a game to impress yourself? Flash the cash, dazzle the chick? How much did you expect to buy? No one-night tumble between the sheets is worth all this. No. All this had to be so you could watch the naïve country girl fall prostrate in wonderment on the altar of your ego. I caught your amusement in those sidelong glances you exchanged with Charlie Soo. Was it worth it? I don't know, Alexander. What do you think? Did you impress me?" The stone floor objected loudly to her chair grating against it, as she pushed back and rose to leave.

The force of Nikki's ire impaled Alexander on the back of his chair. He shook off the effect of her words long enough to lunge forward and grab her wrist. "Wait!"

"I think I'd rather go back to my hotel now." With a forceful twist, she wrested her wrist from his grasp and turned to walk off.

"Wait. You have had your say. Am I allowed a rebuttal?"

Nikki didn't stop; she merely continued her solitary exit, walking briskly.

"Okay!" He conceded abruptly. "I will take you back to your hotel. But you will have to let me lead you out of here. If you continue in that direction, you will set off every alarm in the place."

Leading the way out, Alex stayed two steps ahead of Nikki. At the car, he hesitated before issuing instructions to the driver. "Now may we please talk? You pick the place, anywhere you say."

The walk had cooled her temper a bit. Begrudgingly she agreed, but selected a place she could walk out of, if she chose. "Okay, we can talk in my hotel's café." They rode in silence, sitting separately.

Settling into a private booth, Nikki ordered a Pellegrino. Alexander left his coffee untouched.

He leaned forward and opened with sincerity, "First, I want you to know—never in my entire time with you did I use you for my personal entertainment. I deeply regret that you feel that way. What you took for trifling was actually admiration. I have never met a woman who could cast such a spell on the people around her. No one is unimportant to you. You share yourself with everyone. I have never witnessed this rare quality before. And how you discern precisely the absolute, most appropriate response at a moment's notice astounds me."

"About the ruby, I sincerely wanted to help you find a special stone. I never meant the experience to belittle you. Your insight into Charlie Soo overwhelmed me. I still marvel at how you finessed that situation with the skill of a maestro on a Stradivarius. And here is the amazing part ... I believe it was sincere.

"Your actions communicated to Mr. Soo the depth of my respect for him. Maybe it was shrewdness on your part. I prefer to call it grace. My dear, what you saw in my actions and mannerisms was pride, amazement and sheer delight. And, I humbly assure you, it was never at your expense. You take my breath away. I love to stand back and bask in the eternal sunshine that is you."

Touché, Nikki's turn to be pinned to her seat. She couldn't find the words to answer.

Alexander reached his hands across the table beckoning for hers. She slid them toward his and he enfolded them, picked them up and kissed them. "Can you possibly in the tiniest corner of your heart find room to forgive me?"

Involuntarily, without warning, silent tears of embarrassment formed in her eyes. Nikki nodded and felt them softly fall onto her cheek. Alexander brushed them away, "Do you want to get out of here?"

Slipping a few bills onto the table, wrapping his arm about her shoulders, he guided them out into the Florentine night. They walked without words. The night enveloped them. If there were other people on the street, Nikki wasn't aware of them. Stopping by a bench near the fountain, they sat facing each other. Alex held both of her hands. "I must admit to feeling somewhat unbalanced. There are so many things I wanted to say to you tonight, but after the museum I'm afraid of the reaction they might cause. This is so awkward for me."

Nikki picked up his eyes in hers, "Alex, I'm the one who must apologize..."

Putting his fingers to her lips, "No don't. You should never..."

She removed his objections, "Let me continue. You shouldn't feel muzzled because I misread you. I've never met anyone like you either ... someone who pampered me with chivalry while showering me with compliments. I've only known men who tossed out a few lines to see what they could hook. After Grant, I stopped listening. I didn't know how to take you. I was still trying to figure you out when, wham! Karl hit me with your name and your legend. I made the mistake of assuming you fit the stereotype. Of course, your six-month absence only confirmed those suspicions."

"The responsibility for the misunderstanding is mine. First, I scared you, then I made you angry enough to spit daggers. I have never bungled a relationship with a woman so badly. But then, none of them were as important to me. I didn't want to frighten you off with my name or my reputation, and in keeping secrets, I almost lost you. How incredibly stupid!"

Reversing his hold, Nikki laid a kiss on his fingers, "Only one self-recrimination allowed. Okay? Maybe tonight was exactly what we needed. We cleared the air."

"At least we have started. I have a feeling there are more questions you still have to ask me. We may as well get everything out on the table right now." Alexander put her hands down, giving her free rein to go wherever she chose.

Nikki really didn't want to get into it then, but she knew he was right. "How come I didn't hear from you in the last six months? Where were you?"

The smile returned to Alex's eyes. "So we have finally arrived at the topic I figured we would have started with tonight. I have been on assignment and unfortunately quite incommunicado with the entire world."

"You have a job?" she asked in amazement. "But Alexander, I was led to believe that as a man of independent means, at your leisure if you will, work is optional."

"It may be optional, yet unfortunately I find my skills are very much in demand. My assignments, because they take me around the world, often keep me out of touch."

"What in the world do you do?" Her mind tried to fathom it.

A somberness replaced the twinkle in his eyes. "Nicole, you must trust me on this. I cannot talk about my work. I will answer all your other questions. Everything else is open to you. I will even show you my bankbooks and the family vault, but discussion of my work is off limits."

Nikki tried to imagine an occupation they couldn't discuss.

"Nicole. You will have to get beyond this if we are going to have a relationship."

What was he proposing? "A relationship?"

"Yes. I would like to pursue a relationship with you. I am sorry, that sounds prep-schoolish, like exchanging class pins or something. I would like to become romantically involved with you." An almost boyish shyness overcame him. "But can you get over the hurdle of my work and extended periods of time without being able to communicate?"

At first blush Nikki wanted to say yes. Alex seemed perfect—too good to be true. But falling into a prince's arms was how she got involved with Grant. Ooo, Grant! The rancor of that relationship still tasted bitter on her palate. Nikki shook her head to rid herself of the sensation and image. "Oh, Alexander. It's not you. It's not even the job. I can get over that. It is just that the word relationship stirs up so many awful memories."

"I understand," he smoothed her fingertips. "My heart ached for you that night in Buenos Aires. After he pushed you, grief nearly cut me in two while you laid in the hospital. No one knew it, but I stopped in everyday to check on you. Then, the baby…"

Nikki shot him a glance.

"Yes. I know about the baby, too. You must believe me. I struggled to contain my rage, to keep from doing something I would regret later. And that was only me, as a bystander. I cannot imagine the hell you endured." He looked past her heart, down into her soul. "I hoped you might see that with me it would be different. I am not even remotely like Grant. I am not asking you to marry me. Just risk a little involvement. But I will give you all the time you need. I can wait. I want you to see that I am not some cad trying to get you into bed. I will never force anything on you."

Nikki's entire heart and soul wanted to leap at his proposal. At that moment she couldn't think of another human being with whom she would rather be involved. But any kind of affirmation stuck in her throat. She couldn't force it out. "Thank you for being patient with me. I just need some time."

"The next move will be yours," he said rising. "I will let you contact me. May I take you back to your hotel now?"

"No! No, I'm fine here. And I don't see any reason why you shouldn't call me. After all, you're the one with the strange schedule. Besides, I want to see you, too." Desperately Nikki didn't want the night to end.

"Then, are you up for some food? I am famished."

Linking arms, off they ambled in search of food at two in the morning. Somewhere in the city, over biscotti and espresso, near daybreak, an actualization dawned on Nikki. "Alex, this is really all semantics isn't? My agreeing to see you and having you call me, already means we are involved in a relationship, doesn't it?"

He smiled over his coffee, "The label was not important to me."

"Then yes, Alexander Vincente. I would like to become involved with you," Nikki announced, reaching her hand across the table for his.

He enfolded hers gently inside his. Glowing, he kissed her fingertips. "Wonderful! Because, Nicole Moore, I would like to become involved with you, too." That engrossing twinkle again danced in his eyes.

Alex summoned his driver to pick them up. In the car he opened his arms for her to crawl into and closed them around her. Several times he kissed the top of her head. For Nikki it felt good being inside the fortress of his unwavering arms. From inside his arms, she looked up at him, when a force more powerful than the rushing wind drew them together in a thunderously passionate kiss. His lips were soft, but fervent against hers. After a year and a half, Nikki finally felt ready to open up to the possibility of love. Inside the hotel's garage, the driver courteously stepped away from the car leaving them, like two nervous school kids on a first date, alone in the back seat.

Alex started first, "What are your plans?"

"I leave today for a week in London to get things together for my summer tour."

"How much time will it take for you to get ready?"

"Two to three days, if I throw myself into the exercise. Why? What did you have in mind?" she asked, hoping he foresaw more time for them in the near future.

"We are so close to my home city of Naples. I thought maybe, if you had time, I could show you my family's estate."

"I'm sure if I touched base with Bruce and made some arrangements with Mary, I could manage maybe three days. When would you like to go?"

"My thought was either this afternoon or tomorrow. I am flexible."

"Then I should make tracks. Their flights leave early."

Alex walked Nikki to her hotel door, "Call me as soon as you have cleared it with your people."

Mary met Nikki's news with skepticism, "What happened? Last night you set the stage to lower the boom. Now you're going away with him?"

"I know it seems like I'm thinking with my heart again, but his extended absence may have skewed my assessment of him. He intrigues me. Besides I can't get to know him better if I don't spend time with him."

Likewise Bruce tried to nix Nikki's plans. He had counted on her spending the seven-day holiday in the recording studio. But when she promised him a concentrated effort upon her return, he granted her the three days.

Repacking a bag for her side trip, Nikki put on casual slacks with a knit top, then met Alex in the lobby. Dressed for traveling too, Alex plopped her bag into the backseat of his black Carrera convertible. "I thought something more in tune with the road might be better than the stuffy old Mercedes. What do you think?"

"Perfect, once I corral my hair," Nikki smiled, giving her long tresses a twist.

Chapter 16

Napoli

Weaving in and out of the foothills along the western coast of Italy, they skirted past Rome. Along their route Alexander took pride in pointing out special places that held exceptionally sweet memories for him. In no particular hurry, they didn't arrive at the Vincente estate, called *Napoli*, until a little after six.

As they approached, Alexander pointed out his estate, visible for miles in the distance. Nestled on a bluff, from a spectacular vantage point above the Tyrrhenian Sea, the massive limestone mansion loomed ahead of them. More than a mere house, *Napoli's* enormity dominated the landscape. Cyprus trees lined the cut-stone driveway from the cutoff on the road all the way to the top. The same cream-colored stone used in the construction of the house also formed the winding drive which opened into a walled-courtyard entry.

A small, compact woman with thick gray streaks woven through her once black hair anxiously bustled into the stone courtyard to meet them. Alexander popped up onto the back of the seat, then vaulted himself over the side of the car.

"Zia!" he cried and ran up to embrace her, kissing each cheek. He greeted her in endearing phrases of Italian which easily rolled off his tongue. She returned the warm salutations mixing in a few well chosen chides that seemed so typically Italian.

"Zia, I want you to meet someone," Alexander said taking her hand, escorting her to the car. The little woman came along as fast as her short legs would carry her.

In anticipation, Nikki exited the Porsche and stood along side.

"Zia, this is Nicole. You remember, the one I told you all about."

"*Buona sera!*—I mean welcome," her brown eyes sparkled as she kissed both of Nikki's cheeks.

Then Alex completed his formal introductions. "Nicole, this is Maria Vivendi, but I call her Zia which is…"

"Italian for aunt," Nikki happily inserted. "I am delighted to meet you," she returned with a little bow.

Maria clasped her hands to her chest and shook them back and forth walking in a circle around Nikki, taking her in, muttering in a mixture of Italian and English. "So this is the famous singer! So this is Nikki!" She walked up to Alexander, reached up and lightly smacked his cheek. "Treat her right," she admonished. Then put her arm around Nikki and personally ushered her into the house, leaving Alexander to schlep the bags.

Alex didn't have far to carry them though. A robust man, strikingly Italian, about Alex's age swung open the massive wooden door before Zia and Nikki reached the house. He called past them to Alexander. "You must have taken the scenic route. We were about to launch a search party."

"Well, I hope you would at least have the sense to send a St. Bernard with brandy," Alex called back.

The man hurried out the door and past the women to take the bags from Alex. But Alex waved him off. "It's okay. I've got it." Drawing up to the door, they all waited for Alex to go through the introductions again.

"Nicole, this is my very good friend—my brother—Lorenzo Vivendi."

Nikki offered her hand.

With a nod from Alex, Lorenzo greeted Nikki in the traditional Italian way, with a kiss to each cheek, "*Buona sera, Signorina* Nikki."

"*Buona sera*," Nikki returned.

The doorway into the foyer towered over them by at least ten feet. Big blocks of the creamy limestone ran inside from the courtyard and up the walls. The floors were marble from the region, honed to a satin smooth finish. Giant timbers supported the vast ceiling that soared overhead, reminding Nikki of the castles in England and Germany.

In deference to their long night, Alexander postponed the tour of his home. Instead he walked Nikki directly to her room. "I am sure you are as exhausted as I am, since we were up all night. How about if we adjourn for a small nap and I'll come back for you in a few hours? Then we'll have a late supper." Shuffling her things into the room, Alex demonstrated the facilities and threw open the window, bringing in a breathtaking view of the sea.

"Thank you for coming to my home. I know you will like it here," he hugged her deeply to his chest, then brushed a kiss across her forehead. Within seconds of crawling into the down featherbed, Nikki surrendered to sleep.

Either Alex failed to wake her, or she slept through his call, but the next voice Nikki heard was Maria's announcing morning. She left a pot of tea on a small table outside her door. Bringing the carafe inside the room, Nikki poured a cup while watching a small vibrant armada of fishing boats pound the waves as they began their day. Putting on a loose white T-shirt shift and sandals, Nikki waited for Alexander to stop by her door.

On their way to the kitchen, Alexander provided an abbreviated tour of his home. Perched on the cliffs overlooking the Tyrrhenian Sea, the entire orientation of the house focused on access to the sea. The country kitchen opened to the dining area, which in turn lead to an immense terrace overlooking the water. With a grand sweeping gesture Alexander took in the vast expanse of the patio. "Almost the entire house opens onto this terrace. As you can see, here we live outside. And everything is made either of white marble or golden limestone, from the balustrades that frame the patio, to the cut wall blocks, to the floors. The Italians in this part of the country use it for everything."

"And why not?" added Maria as she brought breakfast out to them. "It is everywhere in the ground. The people add the color."

Nikki absorbed the idyllic view. A few cottonball clouds textured the otherwise smooth, azure sky. Below, small sprays of whitecaps scooted across the cerulean sea; boats dotted the sea with tiny specks of color. Along the green and brown of the cliff's crags, colorful houses cut into the landscape. Farther down the coast, the city of Naples crawled up into the hills. "I call this area Naples, although we are actually just a small town on the outskirts," Alex explained.

On an extended tour after the morning meal, Alex took Nikki to the quiet side of the house—the part away from the sea—the library. Mahogany paneling and bookcases bordered this serene, windowless room. The solid scent from the leather-bound tomes and traditionally-styled cognac leather furniture permeated the air. Over the emerald Italian marble fireplace hung a life-size oil painting that dominated the study. Alexander pointed to the portrait, "Nicole, I'd like you to meet my grandfather Antony Vincente—patriarch of the Vincente family. In our family he was larger than life itself, so it is only fitting his portrait is, too.

"Ah, the stories! It was my grandfather who founded the legendary five-star Vincente Hotels. That is the origin of the family fortune."

"And the rest?"

"Rum. Lusting for fresh adventure, grandfather turned his attention toward America. At that time the temperance leagues had gained control. Grandfather found the abolition of alcohol so horrifying that he used some of his means to smuggle rum into the southern states of America," Alex laughed. "That is the source of our real fortune. My grandfather was a rum runner!"

Continuing his narration about the family, Alexander carried the tour outside to the vast land resources of the estate. Holding Nikki's hand, he walked her through *Napoli's* cool olive groves. Eventually the topic of conversation turned to Zia and Lorenzo. "Zia likes you. I can tell by the way she teases me about you," Alex lightheartedly swung her hand.

Nikki tweaked him with the reminder of Zia's little slap, "She warned you to treat me right. Why, do you have a history of treating women badly?"

"I suppose I have a reputation for leaving a trail of broken hearts in my wake."

With merriment in her eyes, Nikki pulled up in front of him, "Well, I don't intend to be just another one in your long string."

Gathering her up, full in his arms, he raised her to his eye level, "My darling, that will never happen." He declared it with the solemnity of a vow, then sealed it with a kiss. They continued their walk through the grove, swinging their joined hands. "Oh, I cannot believe how good you make me feel!" he exclaimed.

"So finish telling me about Zia. Is she really your aunt?"

"No, not really. During those feisty rum-running days of the twenties, a sassy little blue-eyed, blonde named Sophie caught Grandfather's eye. This American bombshell from Key West really spun his head. Within two weeks he married her. Employing her charms, Grandma used to create diversions so he could pull off his rum deliveries. Eventually my father, Phillip, came along and the dear old patriarch heeded the call of his homeland. He moved the family back to *Napoli*. Shortly after that Grandma Sophie died during an outbreak of influenza.

"My father met my mother, Julia, here. She died giving birth to me. Needing a woman to care for me, father hired a widow from the village, Maria Vivendi. She brought her three-year old son Lorenzo and came to help raise me. And they stayed.

"My grandfather and father endowed a trust for me before they passed on. Although I was raised here, since my father and grandmother were Americans, I hold dual citizenship."

"Evidently you got your blonde hair and incredible blue eyes from your grandma Sophie," Nikki added as she ran her fingers through his sandy crop, then let them slide down to caress his cheek. His hypnotic blue pools twinkled with admiration as they beheld her.

"So that's why you refer to Lorenzo as your brother?"

"Sure. He has been here for me, all my life. He is my best friend." Foreboding, serious clouds crossed Alex's face. "Nicole, remember this. If ever you need me, for any reason, Lorenzo will always know how to reach me. I trust him unto death itself. You can rely on Lorenzo for everything."

His tone chilled Nikki. Alexander spoke like he had more than a nodding acquaintance with the Grim Reaper himself. Her feet rooted to the ground. Her eyes widened, "Alex, what are you saying?"

Amazed by her fear, the realization that he might have gone too far dawned on Alexander. Although he tossed off the mood with a cavalier shrug, Nikki never forgot his words. He had made his point.

That was the last time Alexander let blackness cross their paths during their holiday together. Alexander and Nikki spent hours chasing the horizon on his sailboat. The sunshine played on his chest, defining his taut muscles as he lay out over the water suspended by the tension from the sail's ropes. Nikki drank in the silhouette of his incredible body against the sea, with the breeze riffling through his golden hair. Alexander's expertise flew them over the sapphire surface, spraying white foam when they touched down. And opportunely Alex only touched down long enough to catch her with sea spray. "Oh, excuse me, *mon ami!*" he snickered through a non-repentant grin.

A moment or two later a swing of Nikki's hips sent him sprawling overboard. "Oh! Pardon me, *mon ami!*" she tossed at him from her dry perch.

Through a smile, he vowed revenge.

The next two days, they packed lunches of cheeses, meats and bread fresh from Zia's kitchen to eat in the shade of the cedar trees on various remote islands. Nikki couldn't tell which sparkled brighter—Alex's eyes or the sun dancing on the face of the sea. She'd sit for hours with Alex's head in her lap playing with the amber strands of his hair as they plumbed each other's souls.

Their last evening found them once again on the terrace, dancing beneath a seductive canopy of starlight and laughing at old romantic clichés, clinging to the moments because in the morning, Nikki had to return to work.

From the small grass-field airport where Alex hangared his plane, to London's Heathrow and then finally to the studio, Alex escorted Nikki back to her routine. She hung on his parting kiss because she understood that many long, silent months might pass before being in his company again. But Nikki accepted the price. She realized that miracles come with an enormous price tag—dear things always cost dearly.

Once home, Nikki rang up Mary to spend a girl's night together.

With the concern of a true ally Mary probed, "So is there more than smooth debonair charm to Mr. Vincente?"

Hiding nothing, Nikki confessed her heart, "I've never experienced anyone like Alexander. He's so self-assured, so mature. He loves with the passion of a man. Gone is that adolescent groping, fondling, trying to push one more limit like with Grant. While Alex's kisses are tender, they have such an assertive depth to them. And Mary, he promised he will never force himself on me. I know that if, or when, we finally make love, I'll be the one who initiates it."

"And what about his extended absences? Will he be around?"

"He works! Can you believe it? His assignments take him from one end of the earth to the other—into places where communication is impossible. But then again, my career doesn't exactly permit 'Friday night, date night' either, does it?"

"Have you considered," Mary pensively paused, "that he's thirty-two, you're twenty and he's watched you for the last two years. Why you?"

"Why not me!" Nikki returned with pluck. "Twelve years isn't such a stretch. He's not some Svengali who wants to separate me from who I am. Alex celebrates me. He encourages me. Besides, there's a mysterious side to him that makes him oh, so tantalizing."

Renewed, Nikki threw magic into her four days in the studio. Choosing a bevy of "pub-crawlin' torch songs" to bleed into the session, she blessed each of them with the depth of feeling that sprang from her core. Nikki was in love.

Quite unexpectedly, for the inaugural night of Nikki's summer tour at the Palladium, Alexander sat front row, center. Nikki was going on the road, and he had received an assignment. Alexander wanted to make the evening a farewell. He requested Nikki wear the ruby.

Impatient with expectation, Nikki pulled on a strapless red satin number for their date. The pendant set it off like never before. Mentally she thumbed through the possible places they might go. Alex would pick her up following the obligatory promoter's party.

"It's late, and I really would rather not go out to any public place tonight," Alex said as he slipped into the Bentley beside Nikki. "I'd rather spend this time completely with you and not have to share you, so I took the liberty of having an intimate supper set for us in my suite at the hotel. I hope you're not disappointed. If you are, just name the place and we'll go there instead." A dashing sparkle tickled the corners of his eyes. "Besides I think you know me well enough to know that I will be on my best behavior."

Nikki couldn't have agreed more. She didn't want to share a minute of their time together either. Alexander occupied a suite of rooms on the top level of the Savoy. London waited at their feet; an intimate dining table waited in front of the balcony view, with freshly-lighted candles, chilled champagne and iced lobster appetizers, all as soft mood music wafted through the room. Two gardenias floating in a Baccarat bowl perfumed the night.

Dexterously Alexander finessed the champagne cork and filled their glasses. Walking Nikki to the balcony doors, he threw them open. "Darling, look. All the stars have disappeared," he noted with feigned wonderment. Alex, of course, was right. The lights of London ate up their brilliance. "You know," he purred as he slid his free hand about her, "they couldn't stand the competition from you."

"Alex!" Nikki tried to diffuse his premise.

"Shh. Don't destroy my truth. Look at the city. Even at midnight people are still bustling about. They don't realize what a gem is in their midst tonight." He centered his glass for a toast, holding her fast in his dancing blue eyes. "Salute. To a long lasting relationship, full of romance and love with the most captivating woman in the world. To you, my darling."

Nikki's glass met his; it answered in a crystal voice. They sealed the toast with sips of champagne and a passionate kiss. She could have lived in his eyes and survived forever on his kiss. Rendered speechless, they retreated into the abiding joy of each other's embrace. Alex laid delicate kisses along the nape of her neck. Nikki returned to the bounty of his lips.

Breaking off before she got carried away, Nikki walked to the railing of the balcony. "Oh Alex, if only we could stay up here forever. I wish that this night would never end!"

"Nicole, I would actually give my fortune for that to be true." Alex pressed a small gray velvet box into her hand, closing her fingers around it. "I have a little something for you to remember the evening by. I thought you might like them."

Fumbling past the ribbon, Nikki flipped up the lid to reveal a pair of pear-shaped ruby earrings dangling from three small diamonds set on the post at the top. "Oh Alex! You had them designed to match my necklace."

"I could not have you walking around with naked ears, could I?"

"No wonder you wanted me to wear the necklace."

"Stunning! ... And the jewelry is okay, too," he palmed off a swagger.

Intentionally, they kept the conversation light over dinner. But with dessert Alex approached the subject neither of them wanted to recognize — their separation.

"As it happens, my next assignment is on the Continent. I will keep your itinerary with me. Whenever our schedules cross, you can count on the fact that I will be there. You will know how to recognize when I am around," he winked. "Unfortunately, I probably won't be able to give you much advance warning. Like a bad magician, I will just appear. If we can make a connection, wonderful. If not, I will be devastated. But I will understand if you happen to be unavailable, just like I will ask your forbearance if I can't make a rendezvous." Wrestling with something, Alex played with her fingers. "I don't know how to say this." His eyes sobered.

"Just say it," Nikki urged.

"Okay, here it goes. I would like to make an exclusive commitment to you."

His words stopped her heart. At that precise moment, everything she wanted in the world hung in those words.

"But?" Nikki picked up for him.

"Unfortunately, neither of our careers will permit it. From time to time, I have to squire different women around. It is part of the business. And you ..."

"I don't have a problem with narrowing my field to a team of just one," she moved to defuse his argument.

"Yes. But right now I do."

Searing embarrassment stung her, flushing her cheeks. Had she pushed too far? Nikki swallowed hard to force back any emotional response.

"Oh, dear Nicole, please don't take that the wrong way. I only mean that right now your star is too high above the horizon for me. I have to operate well below your stratospheric profile. My business associates would not be pleased if I turned up as your arm ornament. Unfortunately anyone you date creates rumors of marriage and a tail of reporters. That kind of publicity would be death in my business."

"I understand." She recouped. "And right now I need to 'sizzle' in public. If that sizzle can't be you, then I will revert back to the mindless 'seen dating.'"

Alex picked up her hands. Sincerity sparkled in his eyes. "Please understand, what I do and whomever I date is purely business. My heart I have committed to you. In my soul, I belong to you. From the moment you disappear from my sight until we are together again, you are the horizon of my life."

"Alexander, you have to know that the men with me in the magazines and the tabloids are merely placeholders. And there certainly isn't any physical exchange between us—perhaps a kiss or two for the camera, but nothing else. I'm committed to being involved with you. It's you I hold in my heart. I can't even imagine any man as a part of my life other than you."

He drew her from her chair up into his arms, so strong, so capable, so safe, holding on to both of them. "For now in our hearts, we are one."

Locking onto his eyes, "For now in our hearts, we are one," Nikki vowed.

He covered her lips with his. His energy, his passion there for the taking, how could Nikki partake of enough to last her until she saw him again? She buried her head in his powerful chest and drank in his scent, memorizing it.

They held on to each other until the last possible moment at Nikki's hotel room door. Kissing her a final time, before departing he breathed into her ear, "*Te amo*, Nicole." Then binding his declaration with an ethereal kiss as light as the wind, he withdrew.

Te amo—I love you—he never waited to hear her say it back. He left, like a knight off to the Crusades, wearing her kiss as his colors, leaving his pronouncement of love in Italian, as a precious gift. And Nicole vowed to carry it everywhere.

Chapter 17

High Tea and Espionage

Nikki's summer tour landed in Vienna the first week of July, 1967. Her stop happened to coincide with the world-class weightlifting trials being held there. Lifters from all over the globe converged in the capital of Austria for the competition.

Shortly after Nikki's arrival, the junior ambassador from the United States to Austria, Howard Bates, sent a telegram seeking an audience with her. Finding nothing unusual about the inquiry, Nikki carved out an hour from her schedule as requested.

Bates received her in one of the salons off the main reception area of the embassy. After a terse introduction, this short man, of wiry build with glasses and a mustache, got directly down to business. "I am sure you are aware of the weightlifting trials taking place in our city at this time."

Nikki nodded.

"We would be very obliged if you could do us a favor. We'd like it if you would publicly attend the competition tomorrow. Of course, I imagine the usual attending retinue of photographers and reporters will accompany you. Following the awards ceremony, naturally you would sign autographs. I understand the top heavyweight Russian competitor will ask you for an autograph. He will hand you a red pen to use. Rather than returning the pen, we'd like you to absent-mindedly keep it after writing out his autograph, and in fact, you should continue to use it as you sign others. In all the surrounding hubbub, it wouldn't be anything out of the ordinary for you to stash the pen in your pocket, purse, whatever." Proud of himself for spitting all that out at once, Howard Bates came up for a breath.

This wasn't a joke. Bates, even for a junior diplomat, was too wordy and far too serious for this to be a joke. "Once I take the pen, what do you want me to do with it?" an incredulous Nikki asked.

"Later in the evening, as you know, both the U.S. and British embassies will host a joint reception for you. Even among our ranks you have many fans and undoubtedly will be asked to sign autographs. You should use the same pen that you took from the Russian. Ultimately Ambassador Junger's daughter will ask for an autograph. At that point, simply hand the pen from the Russian to her along with your autograph.

I will see to it that the next person to request an autograph will hand you another pen.

"Of course, I can do it. But why not get the pen from the Russian yourself?"

Bates responded indignantly, "We aren't at liberty to discuss the particulars."

At that moment a sophisticated man of regular stature, in his mid-fifties with ample amounts of salt and pepper mottling in his hair, joined them. "You see, Miss Moore," he advanced, his hand outstretched in welcome, "there are some international protocol matters here that concern us. Allow me to introduce myself. I'm the Ambassador, Michael Junger."

Nikki shook his hand. Ambassador Junger continued as they all sat, "Mr. Bates and I operate in official capacities. In our roles as public servants, if either of us were to have contact with any person from an Eastern Bloc country without going through appropriate channels ... well ... it could create an international incident with a lot of fuss over such an insignificant matter as a gift. But as an international celebrity, your fame makes you a citizen of the world. For you to absent-mindedly keep a pen from a Russian weightlifter in the middle of a media frenzy wouldn't raise a single eyebrow."

"Then it's a gift from the weightlifter?" Nikki tried to follow his logic.

The ambassador nodded, "Yes, for my daughter. That's right. It's just a gift. She really likes him. It will be something that she will treasure forever."

"What if someone asks for the pen back?" she questioned.

"We hope that won't happen," Bates jumped in.

Junger cut him off, "Yes, that would be a shame. My daughter is an ardent fan of weightlifter Yuri's, and she is really looking forward to having that pen from him."

As Ambassador Junger courteously escorted Nikki to the door, he whispered in her ear, "Let's keep this pen thing just between us. People could get the wrong idea about an ambassador's daughter receiving a gift from a Russian." He clucked, "Tsk, tsk, such big deals over little things."

The next afternoon came off without a hitch. Edward from security accompanied Nikki to the trials which she even found compelling. Afterwards she gladly signed autographs and posed for pictures with the athletes and audience members. Neither Karl nor Nikki could believe the unusually large amount of press in attendance at a sporting event, all of whom seemed so enamored with Nikki's appearance.

Face to face with the Russian weightlifter, his size amazed Nikki. She hardly came to his shoulders. Her hips were the size of just one of his thighs. But she found him the quintessential cliché of a cuddly teddy bear—soft-spoken and gentle. In heavily accented English he said, "I am big fan of yours," as he handed her a piece of paper and the red pen.

"Really! Where do you hear my music?"

"My girlfriend is skater. She uses your music for skating. I don't understand all words, but I like your voice," he pushed out an embarrassed smile as he lowered his head. "*Das vadanya,*" he said humbly, before others shoved in front of him for a turn.

As instructed, Nikki finished out the session using the red pen then dropped it into her purse and headed to the hotel to prepare for the evening's festivities. With children in attendance, she chose a high-necked, sleeveless empire gown of mint pastel taffeta, trimmed with seed pearls. Piling her long tresses in curls atop her head, she finished the ensemble off with drop pearl earrings.

Floating through the party, Nikki mingled with the various dignitaries, the captains of industry and their wives. The room smelled of expensive perfume, roses and power. Despite having to work, she loved these white-tie galas. It touched her that the British ambassador and his charming wife remembered her from another ball at the Foreign Secretary's office in London.

Eventually the time came for Nikki to get out the pen to sign autographs and pose for pictures. Ambassador Junger brought his daughter Kari forward. Proudly she presented her autograph book. They chatted for a few moments then Nikki signed between the pages where Elvis in '65 and John Lennon in '66 had signed. Handing Kari the pen along with her book, Nikki smiled. She knew what a special feeling it must be to get such a long-awaited souvenir. Nikki's eyes followed her as she stepped back amongst the crowd to her father's side. Nikki continued to watch her. She wanted to see Kari's excitement and gratitude. No doubt her reaction would please her father, after all the silly nonsense he went through to get her that souvenir.

Mechanically Nikki accepted another book to sign, but something seemed off as she continued to observe those two. Kari never acknowledged the pen. And she didn't keep it! Passing it to her father, she shuffled off. She never reveled in possessing the anticipated treasured writing instrument, even for a brief moment.

Insistence of the next-in-line snapped Nikki back to reality. With a boy's book in hand to sign, now she needed a pen.

True to the ambassador's word, a pen materialized before her—gold, shining in the evening's light. Nikki looked up to thank the bearer, right into Alexander's dancing eyes. "The lovely lady seems to be without a pen. May I offer mine?"

Nikki signed, then handed the book back to the young lad.

Alex slid up to her, exquisite in his white-tie, wearing a smile, "Some coincidence meeting you here."

"I could say the same to you. If you'd have let me know you were in town, I'd have reserved some room on my dance card," Nikki teasingly reproved.

"How much longer do you have to stay here?"

"I only have a few more then I can say my good-byes and disappear."

"Good. Lorenzo will pick you up. I am leaving now."

"I'll tell Edward I'm catching a ride with you."

Alex mingled his way out through the crowd.

Lorenzo drove Nikki to a park along the Danube. From the backseat she chatted with him about trivial topics. An enveloping mist rolled off the river engulfing the park, making soft halos of the light from the street lamps, concealing other visitors to the grounds, creating a surreal atmosphere.

Lorenzo pulled to a stop along the curb of the park, "Alexander will be here directly." Then he exited the car leaving her alone.

Within seconds of Lorenzo's departure, Alex, still in his tuxedo, opened the door and extended his hand for her to alight. Maybe it had happened before, but it was the first time she noticed Alex anxiously looking around, checking out the entire scene.

"Is anything wrong?"

"No. Just old habits. Once again I find myself responsible for your safety. And I don't want to let ol' Jarred down." Not waiting for an invitation, Alexander enfolded her in his arms, "Oh, how I have missed you! I have been too long without your sunshine."

"I missed you too. Six weeks without seeing you—or a word from you is an eternity." Sharing a kiss, Nikki pulled back to look at him, "You surprised me tonight at the embassy. How did you know I was going to be there?"

"I didn't. I only just received an invitation to the party. Junger literally reeled me in from a fly-over for this get-together. Imagine my shock to find you there. But no matter how it happened, I am delighted to be in your company again."

Wrapping his arm about her shoulders, they casually strolled through the dewy lawn. "You look incredible in your pearls. But personally I prefer your red satin."

"That's a little racy for a gig with children." Fishing for details, Nikki redirected the conversation, "Where are you staying? Will you be at my concert tomorrow night?"

"Unfortunately Nicole, I am just passing through. There is no hotel room and sadly no time." He checked his watch. "My ride will be here in a few minutes. So my dear, what's new? Anything interesting happen today?"

Nikki glossed over the weightlifter trials, deliberately omitting the details about the pen. Something, however, distracted Alexander. She only engaged a corner of his interest.

Then came his probing—through a forced smile. "I had no idea you followed sports, especially weightlifting. Maybe I should work out."

Teasingly she tried flattering him into involvement. "I thought you lifted weights by the figure you cut on the boat." Her mind flashed back to those sunny days in Naples.

Alex ignored her cleverness. "Have you ever met Junger before tonight?"

"Yesterday, when we went over the details for tonight's party."

Alex lifted an eyebrow, "Mike did that himself?"

"Well actually, he had a man named Bates handle those details." It seemed like Alex was digging for something. Remembering Junger's admonition, Nikki veered away from the details, "I think he showed up more as a courtesy to meet the 'guest of honor' before he actually opened the ceremony for me tonight."

Without warning, Alex gathered her up again in his arms. "Oh, Nicole," he met her surprise with his warm, sensual lips, consuming hers in a kiss so intense it felt like he needed to draw her life to sustain his.

When Nikki opened her eyes, his were burning. He hugged her deeply into the very fiber of him, then held her away, almost at arm's length. "Nicole, I love you. Please, be careful. Do you understand? You should not trust everyone. Be safe." Quickly, he scanned the surrounding area. "I have to go. Remember, I love you."

From out of nowhere, Lorenzo stepped into her field of vision. Momentarily distracted, Nikki turned back to vapors where Alex had once stood. As quickly as he had appeared, he was gone, swallowed up in the fog. Their entire encounter lasted ten minutes at the most.

Lorenzo presented his arm, "May I escort you back to the car?"

A combination of fear and shock stole her voice, "Lorenzo, is Alex all right? I know I'm never supposed to ask questions, but..."

"He will be fine when he is back in your company again," he responded with a nice, but hollow answer.

Lorenzo read Nikki's concerns, but being true to Alex, he didn't address them. They walked back to the car across the wet grass in silence. In the distance, in addition to all the other night sounds muffled by the fog, a strange noise like a whooping chopped the night air.

Nikki lost the oddities of the day in a muddle of worry over Alex's strange behavior, then hasty departure. Spiraling into the mix was the nagging realization that by omission she had lied to Alexander. How could she have done that—over a stranger's urging? Her conscience slammed her hard. And nothing relieved her torment, not even a numbing shot of brandy. She called down to her security team for two guards to go walking with her. At three in the morning, Nikki beat herself into the pavement of old Vienna looking for answers. What did Alex mean about trust? To whom was he referring? Was he involved in the incident with the pen? What was with the pen anyway? Why had she lied to Alex? Had she put him in danger?

At the beginning of August, her tour headed from Europe to Asia. Hong Kong greeted them with the warmth of an old friend. For Nikki though, every street corner conjured up visions of Alex. After her concert in Hong Kong, eight days had been lined-out to give the staff a short respite. Not so secretly, she hoped to connect with *him*.

She arrived at the hotel to find an invitation to the Governor's mansion for a private audience at High Tea the next day.

The conservative tradition of High Tea at four in the afternoon demanded appropriate attire. Nothing "Nikki" would do. She chose the pale blue linen suit Alex had given her for Christmas, with short white gloves. A fashionable twist got her hair up off her shoulders. Nikki knew Governor Albert Brown and his wife, Ruth, from the Foreign Minister's office. They had hosted a reception for her on her last trip through Hong Kong. Usually High Tea with the Governor, despite the wording "private audience," meant other notables would be in attendance. Nikki supposed, since Governor Brown would be retiring at the end of the month, his replacement might be also present.

Arriving several minutes prior to the hour, Mrs. Brown greeted Nikki, then graciously ushered her into the parlor. The gentlemen were yet to arrive. Soon a reserved woman in her forties joined them. Mrs. Brown introduced her as Mary James—wife of the in-coming Governor. Mrs. Brown poured. It seemed only the women would partake of tea. They chatted quite politely over finger sandwiches and tea for more than a half-hour. Both quizzed Nikki about the hectic pace the tabloids painted of her life and wanted to know the latest about the pop idols she had been seen dating.

At quarter to the hour, the doors to the parlor parted and the Governor walked in accompanied by two other men. Abruptly the women terminated their conversations with regrets and left. A servant cleared, while the Governor introduced Nikki to his replacement, Nigel James, a man in his mid-forties and quite buttoned-down to business. Neither, however, moved to introduce a third, rather rumpled gentleman. Before departing, the butler decanted a bottle of sherry, pouring four glasses. With an underscoring finality, he slid the doors shut behind him.

Governor Brown made a few pleasant remarks as he distributed the sherry. He still made no attempt to introduce the stranger. Quite traditionally, they raised their glasses in a toast to the Queen. Following that the Governor began with a sputter. "Miss Moore, we would like you to know how grateful we are for the service you provided..."

Nikki used his hesitation as an opportunity to put him at ease, "Please, call me Nikki. And sir, to what service are you referring?"

Then Mr. James interrupted, stabbing at conversation, "Miss Moore, your career seems to be going rather nicely right now, doesn't it?"

Letting them lead, Nikki smiled hesitantly at the dubious direction of their discourse.

James continued, "Yes, well my point is that you have made a comfortable living from the British populace and..."

The rumpled stranger with close cropped dark brown hair and brown eyes noticeably shifted his position in his chair.

James fumbled on, "I suppose you enjoy the work. You do, don't you? Meeting all the people, traveling all over the world?"

The stranger mumbled some disgruntlement, drawing their attention. He pulled a cigarette case from the breast pocket of his brown suit. "Mind if I smoke?" he asked in his gravelly voice.

"Care to join me, Miss Moore?" he emphasized her name.

Politely she refused.

His voice betrayed his Bronx lineage.

The Governor scurried to find an ashtray while James tried to find his place.

"For cris' sakes! You guys are pussyfooting all around the issue." The American bolted from his chair, paced the room, then pulled up a seat directly across from the singer, "Miss Moore, let's talk." He stuck his cigarette in his lips. It bobbed up and down while he spoke. "Oh, by the way, I'm Bob Mann." He put his hand out for her to shake and shook hers generously. "Now here's the deal. Remember in Vienna you met a guy named Junger?"

"Yes, the ambassador," Nikki added.

"Okay. And he asked you to get a pen from a Russian weightlifter."

"Yes. For his daughter."

"Yea, whatever. Well, that wasn't just any pen."

"Ahem!" The Governor obviously cleared his throat.

"Okay!" Mann threw back at him. "Okay."

Then back to Nikki, "Anyway, you helped us out."

"And you are?" she led.

"We are a conglomeration from the CIA, the NSA, along with NATO, SEATO and a few other alphabet soup organizations."

Nikki almost fell over. She looked to the Governor and James for confirmation.

Stoically British, their poker faces offered no clues.

"The point is, you helped us out in a big way. And because you are this tremendous rock star and travel all over the world and meet everybody, we could really use your services."

Wanting to make sure she grasped his meaning, she started, "You mean..."

Mann jumped back in, "You can go places without question that would take us weeks of maneuvering to accomplish, not to mention the risk to lives and drain on manpower."

"Mr. Mann, I find it impossible to believe that I can do things your organization can't."

"Your notoriety together with your celebrity status essentially makes you a citizen of the world. That gives you unlimited access to a vast amount of different people, locations around the globe and all sorts of contacts."

Again the term "citizen of the world," but she saw his point.

"You're a smart chick. In the back of your mind you must be putting together that pen scheme. Yea, we used you as a courier."

He was right. Nikki was piecing it together.

"The Ruskie passed you some vital information, and neither you nor the world were any the wiser. Your security guy never even picked up on it! We probably could pull this pen thing off a couple dozen times. In fact, even when you aren't working for us, you should make a habit of stashing a few pens, just to establish a pattern."

"Wait a minute, Mr. Mann. What do you mean work for you?"

"Oh, wasn't I clear? I'm here to recruit you for service to your country."

Again Nikki looked to the Governor or James for verification or rescue. Silently they had disappeared from the room.

Several emotions washed over her in rapid succession. First came disbelief; it couldn't be they wanted her. Then ego inflation combined with a momentary delusion of grandeur; wow, they wanted her! Mann's pitch obliterated Alexander's parting words of caution.

Catching Nikki eyeing the bait, Mann set the hook, "This is something only you can do for us. Your country would be indebted to you for your service. Right now we are waging two costly wars on diverse fronts. Obviously the one in Vietnam, but just as crucial, the Cold War for supremacy in the West."

Fidgeting with her glass of sherry, Nikki mulled it over. His flattering flag-waving preempted her own logical dissemination of his proposal.

Mann played his lure, "It won't require anything extra of you. We'll have you attending some first class parties to pass on the little trinkets you collect for us." He made it all sound so innocuous.

At that point, for the drama of it, Nikki almost considered asking for a cigarette while she pondered his proposition. It fit the character of the moment.

"What do you think, Miss Moore?" Mann pressured. "Are you in?"

Although in a state of shock she managed a few questions. "What about danger? Is this going to put either my people or me in harm's way?"

"Were you in any danger at the weightlifting trials? Did anyone throw a pass you couldn't handle?" he cracked.

She rebuked him for his smart aleck answer, "What if I want out? Is this like the military where I'm locked in? What if I refuse a request?"

"If you refuse, you refuse. It's no big deal. If we really need your services, we'll try to persuade you, but ultimately the final decision always rests with you. You're never under any obligation. We're not the military. You're a civilian, at liberty to participate or not. So, will you do it?"

"Can I take some time to think this over?"

"Sure. Take a few minutes. But the sooner we have your answer, the sooner we can proceed. We have a job waiting for you." Mann tightened the screws.

In the abbreviated time given her, Nikki failed to notice how cleverly Mann had skirted the issue of danger. Chalk another one up to being a virgin in the woods.

Prodded by Mann's fingers impatiently drumming on the chair, she said, "Yes."

"Great!"

"Do I have to sign anything or take an oath?" She imagined some sort of initiation was needed to bring her into their service.

"Nope. Just express a willingness to help, which you did." Mann glossed it over.

"I guess now you will run a security check on me for..." there had to be more to it than this, she thought.

"Schweetie," Mann replied sarcastically with yet another cigarette dangling from his lip. "We already did that, way before we ever contacted you in Austria. Initially I'll be your contact. Now," Mann rubbed his hands together, "how about going shopping?"

"Sure. That sounds great," she answered, eager to explore the possibilities.

"In between your shows tomorrow," he pulled an envelope out of his breast pocket revealing some U.S. dollars and tossed it across the table to her, "we want you to go shopping. Use the envelope. Go to the Mao shops, I mean The Chinese Crafts Store in Kowloon. Shop all you want. Your contact will be an older Chinese woman with glasses on a chain around her neck in the fur department. You'll be looking for a blue fox coat. Pick any coat that you like. But be sure to remark to the woman that you want it to wear to go skiing in St. Moritz this winter. Leave it there to have your initials embroidered into the lining. You'll go back the next day for a final fitting and to inspect the embroidery. Then have it shipped to your home in Surrey. See, simple! Nothing out of the ordinary and you get a free fox coat in the deal! You can even keep the change."

"I assume there will be something in the coat."

"Why not let us worry about that."

"If it's shipped to Surrey, how will you get it? Are you going to send an agent to break into my house and steal it?" Nikki started to balk.

"Lady, you watch too many movies. When it arrives, have your maid take it to Harrods for cold storage until winter arrives. Once again, nothing out of the ordinary."

"Should she see anyone in particular?"

"Nope. But to protect the fur against theft from an overzealous fan what name would you leave it under? Obviously you wouldn't leave a ticket with 'NIKKI' splashed all over it."

"No, I'd use my middle and last names as a disguise, 'Verna Moore.'"

"Then use it here. When she picks it up in the fall for you, the exact same coat will be waiting." He threw back a swallow of sherry, then exhaled a cloud of smoke. "Hey, just be natural with this thing. If you shop alone, fine. If you want to take a friend or a party of people, fine. Photographers, great! Just relax. Be yourself. You can't screw this thing up."

Nikki picked up the envelope and repeated, "Older woman, glasses on a chain, skiing in St. Moritz."

"You got it!" Mann said with a click of his tongue and a wink.

"Then I guess I'll be seeing you around," she snapped the envelope in a self-assured way, stuffed it in her purse and turned to leave.

"Hey, Miss Moore!" Mann snagged her. "I don't have to remind ya that this is all top secret, and you can't tell anyone about this. Not Bruce, not Mary, not your mom or dad. Right?"

"That, Mr. Mann, goes without saying," With a wink she slid out the door.

As Nikki's limo pulled away from the compound, a strange feeling came over her. She felt cocky, yet uneasy, like maybe she had just been conned. "But what could it hurt?" she argued with herself. "I'll be in control. And I can call it off at any time." Still, it bothered her that the Agency ran a security check on her without her knowledge. And she noticed how freely Mr. Mann listed the people closest to her. Why hadn't she asked to see his credentials? She didn't even know exactly whether she'd be working for the U.S. or the U.K. Throwing caution to the wind, Nikki decided to push those naggy feelings out of her mind with a visit to Charlie Soo.

Genuinely delighted to see her, Charlie insisted on pouring her a sherry and catching up on things in the back room. "What a shame, you just missed our friend Mr. Alexander. He stopped in only a few days ago."

"Did he really?" She registered true surprise and disappointment.

"Oh, yes. He mentioned how much you loved the pendent and the ruby earrings."

"So Charlie, you had something to do with the earrings, too?"

"Of course. Mr. Alexander bought those the same day you were in,"

Charlie virtually grinned at the secret. "But you won't tell Mr. Alexander I told you?"

"Never. It will remain our little secret."

"I have something to show you. Wait here. Excuse please," Charlie scurried off and returned with a velvet pouch. "You like beautiful stones. Look at these!" He spilled several emeralds into his hand, then displayed them on top of the pouch.

"Oh Charlie! They're gorgeous!" Nikki sorted through the stones, letting the light release their seductive powers. Silently she wondered if she was expected to make a selection. Amongst the stones, a traditional cut of eight to nine carats stood out. "This really is something!" Nikki oohed.

"Here, try the loupe. Nice huh? Please not to get attached. These are already sold. I just wanted you to see my good fortune. Anymore, quality emeralds are more difficult to find than comparable diamonds."

They talked for a while, then Nikki pulled two concert passes from her purse and laid them on the table. "Charlie, I would be thrilled if you would come to my concert tomorrow night. Do you think you can make it?"

"Oh, Miss Nikki, it would be an honor to be there. Thank you. Thank you for thinking of Charlie," he kissed her hand.

"No, Charlie, really, you honor me. Thank you."

To repay her kindness, Charlie Soo leaned over in confidence to her, "You know your friend, Mr. Alexander? Well, he really has it bad."

Concern crossed her face, "What do you mean?"

"No. No. Not to worry. I mean love. Love. He has it real bad for you! Yes. ... Oh, Mr. Alexander wouldn't like me telling you. But you should know."

"Thank you Charlie. I will keep this our secret, too."

A message along with a bottle of champagne waited for Nikki in her room back at the hotel. "Hear you're free for five days. Meet me at the Royal Resort in Kaanapali, Maui? Confirm reservation if you're coming. Love, A." A plane ticket tumbled out of the envelope. Nikki couldn't wait.

In a window of four hours between shows, Nikki took Mary shopping with her when she made her contact the next day. To throw off suspicion, Nikki stopped at several other stores in Kowloon before entering the Mao shop. Together the pair ogled the jewelry downstairs—Mary bought a ring. Upstairs Nikki purchased some embroidered table linens for her mother and some vibrant cerise Thai silk to take back to Vada. Eventually, with her heart in her throat, Nikki, with Mary in tow, wandered over to the fur department. The older woman with her glasses on a chain indeed stepped up to wait on them.

Mary chided Nikki for looking at furs in July—a perfect setup.

"I'm taking time to go skiing this winter. And I don't have an evening coat."

Enlisting the advice of the Chinese sales clerk, Nikki asked, "wouldn't this be perfect to wear after skiing, when I go to St. Moritz this winter?"

Of course she agreed. With the salesclerk/contact's help, Nikki hunted for the right style of blue fox. Selecting block style letters to be embroidered inside, she completed the sale.

Nikki had to hand it to Mann, it was incredibly simple. But she wouldn't totally breathe a sigh of relief until the coat hung in her closet that winter. Of course, everything came off without a hitch. Empowered, during the chat session, just for kicks Nikki snagged two pens. Following the wrap at eight, she caught the flight to Hawaii and Alexander.

Chapter 18

Maui

Flying east against the International Date Line put Nikki in Honolulu at nine in the morning of the same day. Picking up an island-hopper to Maui, she deplaned at noon to a personal lei greeting from the man she had waited so terribly long to see.

Alex appeared different from their last stolen moments together. Rested and refreshed, his eyes were alive and vibrant. Carefree island clothes displayed his taut masculine physique. Nikki flung herself into Alex's waiting arms. His kiss said hello for all the time they'd been apart.

The resort sat outside the heavier-trafficked sections of Maui. Rather than book them in the tower, Alex had reserved two bungalows which opened onto adjoining lanais just off the beach. The ocean breeze stirred up the plumeria and stephanotis, so they richly perfumed the air. Alex realized that although the clock read noon, for Nikki's body it was two in the morning. That first day they lazed under the waving palms and in the shade of the lanai, relaxing in each other's company, reading, napping, sharing bits of conversation. As they sipped on Mai Tais, Alex pampered Nikki by feeding her fruit and playing with her hair. Later they drove to the Hilton for dinner and dancing. Upon their return, they walked at length along the ocean's edge.

In the morning they hopped another island charter for shopping in Honolulu. Alex complained that Nikki's clothes were totally inappropriate for the islands. Pulling her in and out of the shops, he outfitted her with a wardrobe of sarongs, bikinis, dresses, blouses and of course the accompanying jewels—pearls. At his insistence she changed into a Hawaiian ensemble before going any farther. Snipping a red hibiscus as they walked, he slipped it over her left ear. They never let go of each other, walking hand-in-hand or arm-in-arm everywhere they went.

In a sporty convertible with a throaty purr, Alex sped along the highway to a restaurant renowned for seafood, well off the beaten path. A veteran of the islands, Alex played tour guide showing her all the preeminent hideaways. Nikki didn't realize it, but her education at Alexander's hands had begun. Indirectly, not even intentionally, he taught her the ins and outs of exquisite, unerring taste. Nikki drew the lessons from subtleties in those incredible dancing eyes and teasing smile. More than a willing pupil, she eagerly snatched up all the wisdom he offered, questioning him on everything from wine vintages to distinguishing fine pearls. Alex taught her not to slavishly follow *haute couture*, but to pay attention to lasting trends, because true elegance endures. He echoed the words of her mother. "Class has nothing to do with money and in the end, high or low, it always shows."

Alexander enjoyed art, all forms, with a passion. Whenever they had time, he sought a museum or exhibit. Nikki developed an eye to discern quality from kitsch. Alex treated jewelry as candy for the spirit, and he loved to indulge his habit, although he never wore any himself.

Over appetizers at dinner Alex asked, "Have you noticed anything different while we have been together here?"

Nikki thought for a moment, "No, other than we are both relaxed and have all the time in the world, I can't think of anything."

"Remember my words to you in London about your profile and being seen on your arm?"

"Of course."

"Have you noticed the absence of fans, photographers and reporters?"

It never dawned on her; she had enjoyed Alex's companionship to the exclusion of all else. "I didn't even notice. It must have been the company." Then it hit her. "It has to be because this is America. They don't know me over here."

"That is why I suggested Hawaii. Close to Hong Kong, but still the States. At least for now, we can travel anywhere here and be relatively free of prying reporters."

"For now?"

"After November and *The Ed Sullivan Show*, this will all change," Alexander added a wry smile. "Do not get me wrong. There is nothing I love more than to see you interact with people. It is just the firm I work for hates publicity."

Instinctively, they saved the rest of that conversation for a midnight walk on the beach when, enveloped by the solitude of the night's blackness and enticed by the ocean's murmur, they spoke more freely. Facing Nikki, with his hands clasped at the small of her back, Alex nestled her into his chest. He kissed her hair while the ocean pulled at the sand around their feet. Between kisses he spoke into her ear, "I have missed you so much. Our rendezvous in Austria practically defeated me. I got to see you, but it was like looking at you through a store window."

"Our time was so short, almost non-existent. Alex, you acted strangely. I worried for days after our visit," Nikki pushed back a bit to look up into his eyes.

"I am sorry. Things were, umm, a little tense then. And your presence was unexpected."

"You seemed distracted. Were you working then?"

Without answering, Alexander cuddled her back into his chest. Almost before she finished the sentence, Nikki realized she had trespassed on their agreement. She floundered to change the subject, yet she wanted to test her boundaries.

"Alexander, have you had your job longer than your preoccupation with me?"

"Sure."

"Then why me? You knew all about the media glare. Why bother getting tangled up with me?" Her question rested against her heart. What if he really thought about it? What if this conversation turned his head and she left Maui without him?

Without letting a second pass, Alex lifted her chin from his chest to hold her in his eyes. "Because, my dear Nicole, from the very first moment in the café that day, without even knowing it, you drew me into your heart. No amount of time or space can erase you from me. Even before we formally met, in my most desperate of times, I just pulled out your smile, and I was reborn. Gladly I will take the stolen minutes, the hijacked days from our lives, until we can be together and I can dwell in your vitality."

He lowered his mouth to hers to share his passion in a long, fiercely torrid kiss. Pulling back with his eyes ablaze, he whispered on a breath, "For moments like this I live." He returned to her lips again.

The vigor of his passion weakened Nikki's knees. He lowered her to the sand out of the water's reach. Poised over her, the depth of his love inflamed his primal fire. He drank her in while he teased a strand of hair, then gently caressed her cheek with the back of his hand.

Nikki walked her fingers up his arms, taut and solid from bracing himself over her. She intended for her fingers to circle his shoulders then draw him to her. She wanted to taste him again. She wanted him!

But smoothly, in one motion, he drew back, caught her hands and pulled her to her feet. With his hand he sweetly brushed the sand from her back and kissed her cheek. Alex nuzzled, "Darling, we won't do this now." Sliding his hand down, he caught hers. "There is still too much unsaid between us. Let's walk."

Returned to her room, Nikki pondered his meaning of what had gone unsaid. Alexander was right. They weren't ready yet, and she wouldn't throw herself into his arms and beg. But her conscience prickled her. Did he realize in Austria that she kept a secret from him? And now she possessed an even greater secret that no matter how much she wanted to share, she couldn't. Nikki resolved somehow she would let him know she took his words in the park that night about trust to heart. After all, if she couldn't trust her government, whom could she trust?

Alexander's observation about her celebrity in the United States also plagued Nikki. At length she considered her expansion into America. The American music scene had always loomed as "the ultimate prize." But, as in all things, the bigger the prize the greater the risk. Was she prepared to suffer that risk and possibly lose the rest of the world? And how serious was she about Alex? If the U.S. offered refuge from the fans and intrusive reporters, shouldn't she keep someplace open on the globe as a retreat? But was that fair to her band and her management associates? Didn't they deserve their shot at the really big one, to see their hard work carried out to fruition? In quiet moments on the lanai, Nikki grappled with all the angles of her dilemma.

Their final night, Alex ordered an intimate dinner for them served on the lanai. Neither of them wanted to share even a minute with outsiders. In the afterglow of dinner, Nikki revisited their conversation from nights previous. "Alex, do you remember the other night, how we talked about my celebrity?"

"It is always on my mind."

"I've come to two decisions independent of each other, but you'll see them as entwined." She paused for a breath and a sip of wine. "It's no secret that the American music scene scares the hell out of me. There's so much to lose."

"Or gain," Alex's smile encouraged.

"Last year when the scheduling snafu forced us to cancel the States, I only felt relief. I know that they can chew you up and spit you out within a week and never look back. Frankly, I find my knees knocking. I know that if I fail there, I risk losing the rest of the world. I treasure my relationship with the Brits and the rest of my market. I kind of like having a secretive affair with the rest of the world, behind the back of the American music behemoth. Above all those considerations, I enjoy our intimate relationship."

Alex raced ahead, reading her mind. In a stern voice, like he was trying to avoid a tragedy he warned, "Nicole, don't! You have the charisma, the moxy it takes. You won't lose. You can't lose. Go after it!"

"Please Alex, let me finish. This isn't for you. Right now, it's for me. I also like having a refuge to go to decompress. In addition to that, yes, I like that we have a place--a whole country reserved for us, where we aren't limited to secret trysts but can walk out in public. I've decided to cancel the Sullivan gig along with the release in the States. I'll keep the rest of the world as long as they want me. The States will always be there. I can try anytime in the future, but just not right now."

Alex stared straight into her eyes, his eyes unyielding. "Do you know what you are doing? America may never extend another offer to you. You were lucky to ride this one out for a year."

"If they aren't there, then it wasn't meant to be. Besides, success in the U.S. is fleeting and fickle. Bruce taught me that. Look at how groups like The Beatles, then The Merseymen shuffled Elvis off the charts. Once you're a has-been, you spend the rest of your days trying to get back to where you were, not because you aren't any good. Hell, you're probably better! But because on a whim, the market has moved on."

"You think Europe won't hand you the same?"

"I'm prepared for it there. Besides, I've built a base with the chat sessions."

"If you do this darling, you need to know I cannot promise you anything in return. Remember what we discussed that night in London? Just because you are foregoing America will not necessarily mean I will be able to meet you there or meet you more often." Lowering his head almost apologetically, he held her hand tightly, then looked directly at her, hooking her heart with his searing blues. "I will never be able to marry."

"And I don't expect it," Nikki answered strongly, undeterred. "What I'm doing is not to get you into bed, either. Like you said, we still have mountains between us. I didn't make this decision in haste. I thought it out thoroughly. But Alexander there is one more thing. Remember I said two decisions?"

He waited.

"Independently of my first announcement, I want you to know, ... *Te amo*."

Her pronouncement brought him to her side, sweeping her into his arms, "*Te amo*, Nicole. Oh dear God, I love you. I never dared to hope to hear those words from you."

For levity in her best affected Yiddish accent, she mocked, "Vy? You tink maybe I don't know Eye-talian?" Then Nikki seriously held him in her eyes, "Alexander, please understand I expect nothing in return. I stand bound by our night in London, too."

Overwrought with emotion, Alexander enfolded her within his arms, and bestowed upon her a kiss of exquisite passion. After a small eternity he led her into the bedroom of his bungalow. He withdrew a small, gray, velvet box from the top drawer of the writing desk. "Nicole, I got this for you, so you would know my intentions are sincere and to

give you something to hold onto when months go by, and I'm not there."
He opened the lid, exposing a ring comprised of a solitary pearl set in
platinum amid a filigree circle tipped in diamonds. It reminded her of a
delicate flower.

"May I?" He slipped the ring on Nikki's right hand.

Producing a bottle of champagne, he poured two glasses. Raising his
glass while embracing Nikki in his eyes, he intoned, "To our London
covenant, with all my heart, I am forever yours. *Te amo.*"

Likewise, Nikki raised her glass, then repeated, "To our London
covenant, with all my heart, I am forever yours. *Te amo.*" They let their
glasses sing their crystal song to their proclamations and sealed them
with a kiss. Unable to do more, afraid to let go, they spent the night holding each other, eventually falling asleep in each other's arms.

No matter the sun's bright face, in Nikki's heart the dawn heralded
a melancholy day. They flew together to the Honolulu airport wearing
brave masks. Nikki failed at focusing on the tasks ahead, instead of the
matter at hand. They held on as long as they could. Her flight departed
first. She couldn't look back as their fingers finally lost their grip on each
other. Nor could she watch to see if he waved good-bye as her plane
taxied away. Nikki still tasted Alexander's final kiss on her lips.

Chapter 19
A Javelin Thrown In Paris

Nikki's summer tour of Australia wrapped in mid-August. To Nikki's surprise, no one on her management team ventured any real protest over passing on the American music scene. Even Bruce found it easy to back away from the U.S. market. Although she never closed the door on the possibility on bringing "Nikki" to America, in the hearts of her inner circle they knew it would probably never become a reality.

On the last night in Sydney, as Nikki packed for her two-week holiday at *Creekside*, she kept trying to reach Lorenzo at *Napoli* to apprise him of her schedule in case Alexander could manage some time. But before reaching him, the bellhop delivered a large manila envelope to Nikki's room. It included two first-class airline tickets to Paris, separate hotel reservations at the Ritz penthouse suites, along with special passes to all the venues of the track and field trials in Paris. The cryptic message read, "Details to follow. Pull lead reporter to capture the story of 'Nikki at Trials.' Mann." Bob Mann left the subterfuge up to Nikki as how to coerce Karl into going to Paris with her.

Catching a taxi to Karl's hotel, Nikki interrupted him in the middle of his packing. "Hey Karl, I just scored some passes to the track and field trials in Paris. Why don't we hop on over and see what's happening? I'd really like to go. You up for it?"

"Nikki, are you serious? I've already got my tickets back to the U.K. Besides, when did you get interested in sports?" he protested.

"Hey, they're freebies. And what if I fall madly in love with one of the athletes. You'll get the exclusive! How about it? It's luxury accommodations at the Ritz and a sporting event to boot. C'mon, it'll be fun! We'll work a little and hang out."

Karl considered waging a campaign between what he should do and what he wanted to do. In truth, he really wanted to attend. Finally in mock exasperation he pretended to cave, "All right then. When do we leave?"

"Three hours. I'll meet you at the airport." Hurriedly Nikki hugged him thanks, then dashed down the hall before he could change his mind.

Karl called after her, "Hey, what do I do with my return ticket to London?"

With success and anticipated adventure tucked under her belt, Nikki tossed him a flippant remark, "Cash it in and pocket the money for all I care. See you at the airport!"

Back at the hotel, Nikki repacked for her side jaunt to France. She phoned her parents to beg off from her visit with them. Then she informed Jarred, so he could dispatch a small security contingent for her. She'd contact Alex to see if they could catch some time together once she finished her Paris assignment.

She and Karl huddled on the long flight from Sydney to Paris, mapping out a strategy to maximize her profile at the trials. Deliberately she kept the plans nebulous until she received further instructions in Paris from Mann.

Nikki honestly expected the desk clerk at the Ritz to hand her another manila envelope from Mann, but nothing out of the ordinary accompanied the normal check-in packet. Similarly, nothing waited for her in her suite, and the phone never rang. Champing at the bit to get the details, Nikki called Karl and suggested they head to the stadium to pick up a schedule of events. A small contingent of fans recognized her and swamped her there. Hauling out his Nikon, Karl snapped a few pictures of her greeting fans at the arena in Paris.

The last fan in line, a little older than most, handed Nikki a sheet of paper. "I wrote this poem about you," he said pushing the paper at her. "Could you autograph it?"

Nikki read it. "Meet Bob Mann at nine this evening in the Café Orleans—alone."

The note caught her off guard. She didn't react to the strange message, merely blinked back at him.

Fast on his feet, the man came back in a disappointed tone. "Oh, you don't understand my poem. Shall I explain it to you?" he emphasized.

The double edge of his meaning hooked Nikki. "Let me look at it again. ... Yes. ... Of course I get it. How sweet of you to write such a nice lyric. I'd be happy to autograph it." Instead of her name, she scrawled, "Mickey Mouse," then handed it back to him with a saccharine smile.

"What did that chap write for you?" Karl looked up from his viewfinder.

"Just a 'roses are red' poem. Everyone thinks they're a regular Robert Frost!" she rolled her eyes to affect a slightly mocking manner.

Nodding, Karl questioned her about her activities for the evening.

Nikki lied through a stretch and a yawn, "I'm exhausted. I'd like to catch a short nap and I'll call you later. Who knows, maybe we can go out clubbing then."

Ditching Karl, and afraid to mix her security service in Agency business, Nikki slipped out a service entrance to duck Jarred's men. A quick five minutes later she hopped a taxi to get her to the back streets that housed the Café Orleans. She scanned the small bistro for Mann as she walked to a far back booth. Nothing. A few minutes later Mann eased his eternally rumpled figure into her booth.

Trailing cigarette smoke, Mann put out the wasted butt in the ashtray and took another one from his case, tapping it on the table, preparing to light it. "You threw the courier a curve today. He came back wondering who exactly we hired for this work."

"Sorry. I wasn't expecting someone to appear out of thin air. I thought you would send another envelope to the hotel," Nikki tossed out disaffectedly.

"We're a little beyond those simplistic approaches. You'll have to learn to be on your toes from now on." His steely look pierced through the smoky blue cloud surrounding him. "You think you can manage that, schweetheart?" Mann murdered his imitation of Bogey, then turned on a dime. "By the way, very cagey of you not to sign your name to that paper. Shrewd. You've got good instincts, kid."

Short on praise, he puffed more smoke and continued, "So here's the deal. We want you to attend all the trials in the javelin competition. In particular, we want you to cozy up to the top Swiss thrower, Gunter."

"How cozy do you want me to get?" Nikki jested. "You want maybe I should roll around in the sack with him?"

Her comment missed Mann's funny bone. He raised a frosty eyebrow at her. "Whatever it takes. You're really gonna have to heat this one up and fast. We need this guy head over heels with you like yesterday. We want him gone on you enough to buy you presents."

Trading sex for secrets sobered Nikki up fast, "What kind of presents?"

"Anything. We really don't care."

Indifferently, a waitress glided up to the table. In remarkably good French, Bob Mann ordered a bottle of wine with two glasses and some bread.

Mann reached inside his jacket's breast pocket, pulling out two small color photos of Gunter the javelin thrower. "This is the guy," Mann slid them across the table to her. One photo pictured the target on the field in his competition attire; the other was his public relations headshot. As might be expected, Gunter sported the hard-etched physique of a world-class athlete. Nikki judged him to be tall, with thinning wheat blond hair and deep, glacial blue eyes. She tried to memorize his features before handing back the pictures.

"Not too hard to take, huh? He's somewhat of a ladies man and attracted to the limelight. Here's the connection. He's friends with the Hungarian javelin thrower. In fact, they are bunking together. The Hungarian has a list of code names of agents "inside" at risk that he needs to get out to us. Direct contact is too risky, but he could slip the list into a present Gunter would give to you."

"So the gift has to be rather sizeable?"

"Not really. The list is on a microchip. Anything will do. You don't have much time either. We can't leave the Hungarian and our other agents hanging out there too long. At all costs, avoid any contact with the Hungarian. We don't want anyone connecting the dots on this one!" He stubbed out his cigarette when the waitress returned with his order. Mann filled the glasses, unceremoniously tore off a chunk of bread for himself, then slid the loaf towards Nikki.

"Are you going to arrange the introductions to the Swiss?"

"Nope. That's all up to you. It seems, Miss Moore, that you have charmed the world. So, work your magic on this little javelin thrower."

"Trading sex for trinkets is a bit different from swiping pens, isn't it?" She hoped to prick Mann's conscience with her sarcasm. She should have realized she couldn't pierce stone. "What do you want me to do with the 'little javelin thrower' when I'm through with this caper?"

"Toss him back. Isn't that what your type always does?" Mann sent the barb zinging back at her, then washed some bread down with a slug of wine. "Oh, by the way, eighty-six that reporter's incessant picture taking when you're making a contact. It made our guy real nervous."

Incredulous, Nikki stared back at him. "Bob, I didn't even know I was making a contact. How could I restrain Karl from something when I wasn't aware?"

"You have to learn to expect this kind of thing from now on. Devise alibis and excuses in advance. Be prepared. Weren't you ever one of those girl-type things?"

"A Girl Scout?" she assisted.

"Yeah, one of those."

"Sure, but we didn't exactly have badges in spying and lying."

"Do you think you can handle this one?" an impatient Mann questioned. "At most, you only have a week. If you can get it done before that, all the better for the poor guys hanging out to dry in the field." Bob lit another cigarette, then fished a program out of his pocket. "See, the javelin competition opens tomorrow morning at ten."

"I'll be there."

Standing up, Mann warned, "Be vigilant. Keep on your toes."

"By the way Bob, how will I let you know when I have secured the microchip?"

"We'll contact you. Probably with a scenario similar to today. Try to stay alert. ... You realize we'll send a different person each time, right?"

Nikki nodded, even though that thought hadn't yet crossed her mind. "By the way, where are the javelin throwers staying anyway?"

"They're all at the Hilton, six blocks from the venue. Why?"

She flashed a coy smile back at him.

"Ooo, I like the way you think. This is the Nikki I expected." Mann slipped out.

The urgency of the agents' safety pressed in on her. She wanted to initiate contact immediately but knew she had to check in with Karl. Besides, if she was going hunting for javelin throwers, she had to change into an eye-popping Nikki-type fare—short and showy.

A grouchy Karl answered the phone, "Oh, I thought you might be the insurance company or the office."

"Karl? What's the matter?"

"Some son-of-a-bitch broke into my room, ransacked the place and stole my camera while I was at dinner. That's what's the matter. How was your nap?"

"I'm going over to the hotel where the athletes are staying to see the sights, if you know what I mean. Are you game?" Nikki crossed her fingers. She knew her timing was awful, but necessary.

"Sure. Why not," Karl answered, exasperated. "I'll only drive myself crazy if I stay here. Besides, then housekeeping can clean up this place."

"Did you call hotel security?"

"You bet I did. ... C'mon over. I'll wait for your knock."

In a split second Nikki pieced together the unfortunate turn of events in Karl's room. Karl had photographed her contact earlier. The courier didn't want to chance his picture being released, so he stole Karl's camera. To camouflage his mission, he ransacked the room. Nikki didn't like the Agency's treatment of Karl, but understood their concern. She played dumb as Karl walked her through the shambles of his room, fuming that this kind of thing shouldn't happen at the Ritz.

At the Hilton Nikki scanned its socially dead lobby and bar looking for action, when she noticed a pack of athletic types headed out. She tugged at Karl's sleeve. "C'mon. Let's follow these guys. I'll bet they're going where we want to be."

"Are you chasing men? Is that what's going on here?" an edgy Karl pestered.

"Only one. I've seen pictures of this really cool Swiss javelin thrower. I want to meet him. C'mon Karl, let's see if he's hanging out where these guys are headed. Grab that cab," and she gave Karl a shove toward the street.

The hotel crowd of athletes descended on the Lounge LaVoille, the hot discothèque in the core of Paris' entertainment district. Squeezing into the sweaty crowd, Nikki checked out the lay of the land from the dance floor, making Karl her less-than-willing dance accomplice. Typically, gawkers opened a spot around the floor as Nikki started dancing. Pretending not to notice, she saw people whispering among themselves as they passed the word Nikki was in attendance. The circle widened with more and more of the patrons lining the floor. Then Nikki went to work. Selecting a new dance partner, she let Karl slip back into oblivion. While dancing with her partner-of-the-moment, shrewdly she scanned the crowd, finally coming up with her javelin thrower. Smoothly Nikki slid over to the Swiss.

Indeed he was tall, towering over her by a good six to eight inches. She yelled above the music, "Hi, I'm Nikki. Want to dance?"

Gunter looked down at her with a smile, "I know who you are. You want to dance with me?" He listened as the music morphed into a ballad. "This is a slow dance."

"I know. I dance to slow music, too," Nikki innocently smiled.

Stepping forward, he offered his arms. His massive extremities engulfed her. She felt tiny. But the long flight and the dreamy music soon crashed in on her. By the end of the song, all Nikki really wanted to do was sit.

Lowering himself into the booth, he took account of Nikki and the entire scene. "I feel lucky that you would notice me. I hope my dancing wasn't too awkward."

"I really enjoyed dancing with you, Gunter. But to tell the truth, I'm exhausted. I only just arrived from Sydney today and ..."

Gunter nodded. "That's a killer flight. I'm surprised you're here."

"I'm sorry. My day has finally caught up with me," she yawned, for real.

Disappointment fell over Gunter's face.

"Please, Gunter, it's not you. In fact, I'd love to see you again. I counted on coming to the javelin preliminaries tomorrow."

"Excellent. I'd love to have you in the audience," he paused. "Might I escort you home tonight?"

Bingo, in like Flynn! "I'd like that. But please let me touch base with that photographer over there. We came together. Okay?" Nikki momentarily excused herself to wade through the patrons to Karl.

"I take it this is your javelin guy?" Karl wagged his head. "How do you know you can trust him? Jarred would have my hide for letting you out of my sight! And..."

Nikki couldn't listen to Karl's excuses. "I'll be careful. See you at eight for breakfast." Then cut him off as she hurried back to Gunter.

Nikki pushed her exhaustion to the back of her brain. With lives depending on her, she couldn't afford the luxury of being tired. Hailing a cab back to her hotel's café, she and Gunter spent time getting acquainted over espressos.

Nikki had learned the quickest way to a man's heart was to listen to him, so she engaged him, plying him with questions, insisting on knowing the ins and outs of his specialized discipline. Gunter chatted on. From his face Nikki read his intensity for the sport. With dessert, he casually reached his hand over and patted hers, testing her reception. Nikki smoothed her hand over his, commenting on its strength, greeting his small advances with a demure smile.

Walking her to the bank of hotel elevators, Gunter held on to her hand, "I hope the trials don't disappoint you tomorrow. The competition will be routine—qualifying for ranking and the right to advance. Will you wait for me after the competition?"

"Of course."

"Then I will see you tomorrow. *Adieu*," Gunter kissed Nikki's hand.

Preliminarily, Nikki congratulated herself at successfully initiating contact. She fell asleep searching their conversation for a way to complete her assignment without having to crawl into bed with Gunter. There had to be a way.

A clear, blue sky with mild temperatures blessed the trials the next day. Even without any announcement or pre-publicity, an unusually large crowd of fans and reporters gathered around her at the field. The extraordinary attention amazed Nikki, so she quizzed Karl about it.

"You're right. This hype seems unusual even to me. I'll check my sources to see if someone's running something I don't know about," Karl resumed snapping pictures of her mingling with the crowds.

Suddenly, a realization dawned on Nikki. "Karl, did you buy a new camera last night? Man, that was fast! What do you have, Superman's insurance company?"

"Are you kidding!" he retorted with disgust. "They still haven't acknowledged my first phone call. No this is the one I had with me at the arena yesterday, then threw in my pocket when I went to dinner. The bastards only managed to get away with my spare. I always keep my Nikon with me. But it made me mad just the same."

Entering the field, the Swiss javelin thrower scanned the stands, searching for Nikki. She anchored his attention by standing up, calling and waving. Symbolizing his determination, Gunter shook a clenched fist in her direction. Nikki mimicked it back to him to show her support. Karl and the rest of the reporter cadre caught it all on film.

Sitting in the stands, Nikki concentrated on the javelin trials when a girl two rows down drew her attention. The girl bounded up to her parents with a handful of lapel pins. Interested, Nikki strained to pick up their conversation. Evidently she collected the pins from various athletes representing their countries. The pins planted a seed.

Gunter emerged from the morning's competition more than half a meter better than his nearest competitor. While she waited in the stands for him, an increasing number of fans and reporters gathered around her, including television crews. Seizing on the hint of a relationship with Gunter, they shoved microphones at her to scoop the hot item of the day—the rock star and the Swiss javelin thrower. They peppered Nikki with questions from how they met, to the date of their wedding.

Gunter advanced towards her and the horde swarmed him. He never flinched. Fluent in German, French and English, he answered them all in their respective tongues, then translated for Nikki.

Afterwards the pair enjoyed a walk in the sunshine. Conversation flowed easily with Gunter. Eventually she steered the topic back to where they left off the preceding evening. Somewhere in the light summer breeze, along the Seine, Nikki noticed the sun glinting off his lapel pin.

"Is that your country's pin?" she inquired.

"Ja. Would you like it? I have about forty left."

"Yes. Yes, I would. What are you going to do with the rest of the pins?"

Gunter handed his pin to her, "Trade them. Trading gets really serious at the Olympics. Everyone comes with pins to swap—the athletes, the news people, sponsors,—everyone."

As Nikki's fingers ran over its surface, an idea came to her, "Gunter, do you think you could help me collect these pins?"

"Ja, sure. But why?"

"If I could assemble a whole collection of them, I could raffle them off to benefit the orphanage charity I sponsor, Deus Foundations. I'll bet if we blew up collecting these pins in the media, the pins would fetch a lot of money. The orphanages would benefit tremendously."

The idea caught Gunter's fancy. "I'd pass the word at least to everyone in the javelin competition. I'll collect them for you," he stopped on the sidewalk. "You know it wouldn't be hard to let the other competitions know. I'm sure they would participate," Gunter's excitement escalated.

"Karl, my friend in the press, would help us spread the word. If he leaks this the other outlets will grab it for sure!"

"Ja! Nikki, we should stop somewhere and make some notes before we forget all these crazy ideas." Half a block further, colorful sun umbrellas fluttered over tables of a street-side café. Racing with the mounting enthusiasm to a table, they began scrawling the plans over a slew of napkins.

Karl met up with them at the hotel toward dinnertime. Instantly he jumped on board with ideas for rallying press support. By evening's end the three of them had established the plan. That night Karl hit the streets, putting out the word of an important press briefing the following afternoon in the main conference room at the Ritz.

Before bidding her farewell, Gunter teased Nikki with a hint of a smile, "I will have a surprise for you at the press conference tomorrow."

At the press gathering, media savvy Gunter goosed-up the corps, whipping them into a delirium for the "Sports Pins for Foundations" cause. True to his word, Gunter presented her with over seventy pins he had collected just from his overnight word-of-mouth campaign. Many kicked in their own collections. And yes, after hurriedly sifting through them, Nikki spied a pin from Hungary.

Privately, Gunter boasted about the Herculean efforts of the Hungarian who donated over twenty pins to the cause. On the sly, Nikki separated those pins from the others.

Later that evening a singular fan patiently waited in her hotel's lobby for an autograph. "You'd better hurry," the female agent shyly mimicked a bashful fan. "Dr. Mann is expecting you in the hospitality suite at the Sheraton."

Sitting on a sofa in the small hospitality suite, cigarette in hand, Mann never rose to greet Nikki. "Do you crave attention or does it naturally follow you? That's a pretty high profile you set up to pull off this caper, isn't it?" Mann poured her a glass of red wine as she assumed her seat on an adjoining armchair.

Feeling slightly full of herself, Nikki cut him some cheek, "Well, hi to you, too, Bob. You shouldn't complain. I thought you hired me for my profile. Besides, I got the job done."

Antsy with anticipation, Mann rubbed his hands together, "Well?"

Nikki withdrew the small leather pouch from Gunter with the pins from the Hungarian wrapped in tissue. Mann carefully undid the thin paper and installed a jeweler's loupe in his eye. The first pin yielded nothing. Patiently he scanned each of them. Another, nothing. And again. Nervously Nikki squirmed in her seat. Half way through, Mann pulled out a pair of fine-line tweezers. From three separate pins he removed six spots and transferred them to a tiny, highly polished metal disc in a small box. Then he combed through the rest of the lot until each pin had been examined.

"This is better than I had even dreamed. Our man managed to attach several other files we thought almost impossible to harvest." Soberly Mann glanced down at his watch. "To think you managed it in less than forty hours *and* I assume your morals are still intact," remnants of the conceited smirk lingered in his eyes.

Nikki refused to grant him satisfaction, "So, is that it? I'm finished?"

Mann brushed the rest of the pins back into the pouch, handing it to her. "You have to maintain your cover—follow through with the subterfuge you set up. But yes, you are at your leisure now. You can kick back and relax, everything's paid for. There'll be an envelope waiting for you to cover any incidentals." He paused to study her, "Seriously kid, this was good work. I knew you'd be valuable, but you've amazed me. Now we can get all the agents who are hiding out across the globe to safety."

Emboldened by her success, unaware of the far-reaching implications of her next question, Nikki pressed Mann, "You guys just expect me to know all this covert stuff. If I am such an asset, wouldn't it make sense to get me some training, so I don't blow a cover or cross a contact?"

Bob Mann's jaw dropped, endangering the precarious balance of his cigarette. Nikki thought she just caught him off guard with her remark. However, in reality he interpreted her query as a request to be upgraded in her mission status. "Are you sure?" he staggered back.

Sublimely oblivious to assumptions being made, Nikki nodded, "Don't you think it would be better that way?"

"Ya, if you're sure. I guess it would make sense," he rescued his smoke. "Frankly, I didn't figure you'd hang around this long, and I never thought they'd ever put you in this deep. But we had our backs to the wall on this one. With the way you handled this assignment, I think we can work something out," Mann rubbed his temple. "I'll talk to my people. If you're sure, it sounds reasonable to me. You'll be contacted before you leave Paris," Mann rose, signaling her exit.

Before departing Nikki handed him something else he hadn't bargained for, "Bob, I thought you might be interested in these. They're the negatives your guy failed to get when he ransacked Karl's room. Someone should be more thorough if they're going to be breaking and entering," Nikki admonished.

"Thanks." Mann wasn't terribly appreciative since she had caught the Agency at their game. Then with the barest suggestion of a smile Mann asked, "Oh, by the way, what are you going to do with the javelin thrower now?"

"Why, toss him back of course. Isn't that what my type always does?"

Gunter took the world trials, and together they collected over a thousand pins. Nikki's Foundations would make a mint raffling them off.

Nikki focused on gently "tossing back" Gunter. Even without a match, the press couldn't shake the story. On their own they concocted wild fantasies about Nikki and Gunter. In retaliation for their mongering, the pair shamelessly tweaked the media by hamming passionate kisses before their cameras. With every story that splashed onto the headlines, they called each other to roar over the reckless narratives.

Returning to her suite from shopping the next afternoon, Nikki found a tabloid clipping proclaiming her imminent marriage to Gunter, a bouquet of gardenias and a note. "Dinner at eight? That is if you are not on your honeymoon. Love, A."

Nikki's heart almost leapt out of her chest. Alex was in Paris! Wrapped in delirious anticipation of him, she unpacked the turquoise gown she bought that afternoon. Showering, she put on her make-up, then brushed her hair up into curls, leaving her shoulders enticingly bare above the layers of chiffon plunging from the satin empire bodice. Fingering through her jewelry, she wished she could wear the rubies he had given her instead of being stranded with the pearls she held in her hand.

Quarter to eight, she answered the knock at her door. With her excitement cranked to fevered levels, she drew in a deep, calming breath before opening the door to … Jarred!

Chapter 20

Nevermore

Surprised by Jarred's presence, Nikki quickly glanced past him down the hallway checking for Alex. Nothing.

"Hi Nikki. Our mutual friend sent me. Can I come in?" Jarred imposed.

Stunned, she admitted him, "What are you doing here? What mutual friend?"

"Cor! look at you. You were expecting someone else. Who are you expecting?"

She didn't want chitchat; she wanted him gone, "Yes Jarred. I was on my way out. Please get to your point, the mutual friend is ... ?"

"Oh yes, quite right. Mr. Mann sent me."

With her mind still on Alexander, Jarred's words didn't connect.

"You know, Bob Mann. He sent me to arrange for the training you requested."

Nikki stammered, "You know Bob Mann?...You're...you're part of this thing with Mann? How long have you been with them?"

"All of my adult life. They recruited me directly out of the military," Jarred answered matter-of-factly.

"So have you been working for them, while you worked for me?"

"Yes. In fact they placed me in your service for the same reason they recruited you. Your notoriety gained access for the Agency they couldn't have developed any other way. But my access obviously isn't as far-reaching as yours."

Still amazed, she stared at him, "I think I want my money back."

Jarred laughed, "I'm sure if you submit a request they'll compensate you for the double-dipping. But ... I don't think this is the night to begin your training. Evidently you and Karl are off to some affair. Shall I call on you tomorrow?"

Letting his assumption pass, Nikki glanced at her watch, five to eight. Alex would arrive soon. She had to get rid of Jarred, before he spoiled everything. Opening the door, she prompted his exit. "Yes, please call me tomorrow, and we'll arrange it,"

Closing the door on his heels, she hoped his presence didn't dissuade Alexander. Eight o'clock. Twenty-seven times Nikki paced back into the bath to check different things, praying Alex would still come. All of a sudden it hit her. She hadn't let Karl know she was going out. He'd lose it if he called and she didn't answer. She rang him with a cover story about her and Gunter. He bought it.

Hanging up, Nikki turned around only to be met by Alexander, staggeringly handsome in his white dinner jacket. "I hope you don't mind. I let myself in," he said through an irrepressible smile.

Enfolding her into his welcoming arms, Alexander pressed his potent lips, so long absent, against hers. Nikki dallied in the strength of his embrace. Then he laid a soft kiss on her brow. "Oh, I think you've missed me as much as I missed you."

Stepping back in teasing amusement, he mocked, "I hope your newly intended is not the jealous type. I was only passing through this Continent, when I noticed the ever so subtle mention of the two of you in every newspaper, tabloid and television."

Nikki feigned indignation, "So, is that it? You came to defend your territory?"

"I'm here, aren't I?" merriment sparkled in his eyes.

"You are incorrigible!" she teased.

"I've missed you, darling," Alexander took time to admire the package. The chiffon flared dramatically as she executed a small pirouette for him.

"*Que bella*," Alex kissed his fingertips in exclamation. "I always envision you in red, but turquoise suits you. How it sets your eyes on fire, like sparkling crystal. *Magnifique*."

"Why, my dear Mr. Vincente, I do believe you are mixing your tongues this evening," she playfully chided him.

Forcefully he hooked his arm about her waist and drew her into him tightly. With almost a leer, he growled, "Let me show you how I mix my tongues … You have no idea how much I missed you this time."

Then he broke the mood, "We could stand around here all night muttering to each other, or we could go out. What's on your agenda for tomorrow?"

Nikki's head swam with his presence, "Nothing. What did you have in mind?"

"Dear Gunter wouldn't be put off if you fly to Naples with me, would he?"

"He'll cope," Nikki moved toward the bedroom. "What should I pack?"

"Only your smile in the moonlight." Alex pulled her close to him again. "I think we'll find everything you need there. Shall we go?" With his arm firmly about her, he swept them out of the room. Within an hour Naples glittered below them.

Zia left a sumptuous repast spread on the terrace, complete with rich red wine and flickering candles. They danced beneath the stars to soft music.

Tenderly Alex planted kisses along her exposed shoulders and teased a few tendrils of hair down around the nape of her neck. "You know, Nicole, these pearls are nice, but they do not flatter your sparkle. You really need something that will dance with your fire." Releasing the clasp on her string of pearls, he let them slip smoothly into his waiting hand and then his pocket. "Let's save the pearls for tea time." With silent sweetness, he gently kissed her lips, then smoothly drew a velvet box from the table behind him. "Try these." Snapping open the lid, he revealed a diamond necklace in a simple princess design, accompanied by exquisitely matched diamond drop earrings. "Now, your luminescent eyes will annihilate even hardened cynics."

"Oh my...!" Nikki started to protest.

Alexander silenced her protestations with yet another kiss. "You must accept these, if not for my sake, then for the stones' sake. How can they ever achieve their purpose without your beauty to ignite their fire? Besides, you deserve these and more. Indulge me."

A piece of yellow moon climbed over the mountain backdrop, blessing the evening, as Alexander whirled Nikki across the marble terrace. They danced and sipped champagne until she couldn't remember.

Nikki awoke in her room facing the gulf, the diamonds still about her neck and in Alex's tuxedo shirt, his smell embedded in its fibers. She buried her nose inside the collar to drink him in. She didn't know how she came to be in his shirt. At peace, Nikki stretched before rising. Looking for her dress, she checked the armoire. Along with her dress there hung an entire wardrobe of clothes—from shorts and swimsuits to dressy frocks, everything in her size. Nikki showered and over the silky undergarments from the armoire, she donned the thick white terry robe.

Alexander greeted Nikki on the patio in the radiant sunshine, wrapping his arms about her. "Good morning, darling," he supplemented his greeting with a kiss. "I see you found the things Zia bought for you. Is everything to your liking?"

· Zia emerged from the kitchen with her pot of tea, "*Buon giorno*, Miss Nikki."

"*Buon giorno*," Nikki returned. "*Grazie*, Zia. Thank you so much for the clothes and everything," she hugged her.

Mopping her eyes, Zia nodded, then bustled back to the kitchen.

"In case you are wondering, darling," Alex addressed while pulling out a chair for her, "you fell asleep in my arms last night on the terrace. I carried you into your room. Zia dressed you."

"I noticed you generously donated the shirt off your back. A night-gown must have been the one thing Zia forgot to buy," Nikki gently teased.

"No. I believe there is an assortment of nightwear in the drawers. I just wanted to leave you with something to remember me by in your dreams." He flashed her an impish grin over the rim of his coffee cup.

Nikki drank in the sea breeze while reading the paper with her cup of tea. Looking up from his paper, Alexander off-handedly mentioned, "I have never seen a terry robe dressed up quite so elegantly before."

"Excuse me?"

He mimicked fondling something at his throat.

"I wasn't ready to put them into a drawer."

Alexander leaned over and kissed her, "Oh, how I do love you." Then he handed her a section of his paper. "I see you and your betrothed are still making headlines." Spread above the fold was a large photo of Gunter and Nikki, kissing at a sidewalk café.

Nikki met the picture with laughter, "I'll have to share this with Gunter. Alex, we've gotten such a kick out of the fuss the press has been making...Oh no!..." She stopped cold, "Alex, I have to get to a phone! I have to call Karl. I've got to let him know I won't be there this morning. And Jarred is supposed to drop by!" She couldn't go any farther with that explanation. Jarred would panic to find she had vanished.

"Of course darling. Use the phone in the library for privacy."

Having already discovered her absence, Karl answered in a panic. He peppered her with rapid-fire questions, "Nikki? Where in the hell are you? Are you okay? Jarred's here looking for you too! He's really upset! What in the bloody hell is going on? Where are you?"

"Karl. Karl. Karl! It's okay. Listen, I got carried away last night. I'm sorry I forgot to call you."

"Where are you?"

She paused long enough for Karl to settle down. "Listen, you can't tell anyone." Again she waited till Karl quieted enough to comprehend her statements. "I'm with Alexander. He picked me up last night."

With relief came Karl's anger, "You scared me to death! Don't ever do that again. Let somebody know."

"I'm sorry, Karl. There was no excuse. You'd better put Jarred on. I don't think he'll believe you if he doesn't get to talk to me. You know how security men are."

Jarred answered in a frantic staccato, "Nikki! You're all right? Can you talk? Where are you?"

"Of course I can talk, Jarred," she over-played her casual air. "See, you were right. I had a hot date last night and, well, … I won't be back right away."

"Who is it? Where are you? When will you be back?" Jarred interrogated her.

"He's an old friend. And since you're not my father, no more particulars are necessary. I'll turn up when I see you, probably in London. Don't look for me before the week is out. I really don't know when it will be. *I'll* call you when I return."

"You're okay? You're sure? Nikki, give me a sign if you can't talk."

"Jarred, your obsession is upsetting. You've done your job, now drop it!" Nikki let a false bravado of her agitation carry through in her voice.

"Okay. I'm sorry. What should I tell *the man*?"

"Tell him we'll continue when I return from vacation … whenever that happens to be. Now please, put Karl back on."

"Cor! whatever you said to Jarred really jerked his chain."

"Has he calmed down?"

"Yeah. He's long gone! He sure hot-footed it out of here."

"Karl, it looks as if I am going to squeeze a little vacation in after all. Everything is paid for. Stay! Enjoy Paris. And, would you mind terribly packing my things and checking me out of my suite? You're a dear for putting up with me. I'm sorry about ducking out without letting you know. I owe you big time! I promise I won't forget."

"It's all right. Geez, Jarred really got hopped up about you disappearing again."

"You know no one lets me forget Buenos Aires. Thanks again."

She rang off and returned to Alex.

"Is everything okay?" he questioned casually.

"I just forgot to tell my babysitters I was going out," she pretended exasperation.

Nikki never asked Alexander about the duration of her visit. She only assumed that they had the rest of the week. Frankly, in Alex's company she could have stayed forever.

Saddling horses, they packed back into the countryside for a lazy afternoon. Under the cedars, Nikki nestled into his arms, spoon-style. Relaxed by the wine, Alex unburdened himself. "Nicole you have no idea how good it is to be able to let the world pass by and spend time with you in my arms. On this last assignment, for the first time, I was truly afraid I would never be with you again."

Nikki let him ramble, afraid of compromising any sensitive areas with questions, yet offering her support, "You know I'm always here for you, sweetheart."

"I know," he kissed the top of her head. "On assignment I have always called the shots for myself. But this time I had to depend on someone else. I was stuck hanging out in some backwater country, cooling my heels, waiting for a flunky to do their job, so I could come back home again. I hated it. I was trapped. All I had to cling to was your face," he turned her towards him, tracing his fingers over her facial features, imprinting them on his mind.

An icy chill pierced Nikki's heart. She disguised it as best she could as it ran through her. The description of his dilemma sounded so familiar.

"Nicole, for the first time I was staring at the end, waiting for it to come, and I was afraid…for no other reason than I would never be able to see your face again or feel your caress. Oh, I don't want to lose you!"

"I'm here," she stroked his back and kissed his lips. "I'm here."

"I want to quit. I don't want to take anymore assignments."

At that point Nikki could only hold him. Any questions would be a transgression. She did venture an offer though. "In Hawaii you gave me the pearl ring to keep you close to me. Would it be easier for you if you carried something from me with you?"

He considered it. "I would like that more than anything. But a physical object –anything that symbolizes an attachment—could be used against me in a tough situation. Proof of an attachment gives them an edge, a bargaining chip. I would hate to lose my focus because of it. No. Carrying your memory must be enough for me. They can never brutalize me over something they don't know exists." For the rest of the day, Alexander never let go of Nikki until they parted for bedtime. Dressed once again in his shirt she kissed him goodnight in it, so he'd know she'd be close all night.

Morning's sunshine washed away the darkness of his disposition. A small, velvet box tied with a white ribbon greeted her at her place on the breakfast table. Slightly embarrassed by the profusion of presents, Nikki picked up the box, toying the ribbon. "Oh, Alexander."

Quietly he smiled, "Please. It is not what you think. I hope you won't be disappointed. Go ahead, open it."

A simple key ring holding three plain brass keys rested inside. She fished them out, holding them in her hand.

Alexander delineated each with an explanation, "This one is to the house, this is to the Mercedes and this to the library."

She looked at him.

"Nicole, I want you to think of *Napoli* as your home. These are for you so you may come and go as you please, whether I am here or not. Both Lorenzo and Zia love you. They will always welcome you as I do."

Alex fingered her pearl ring, "And this one is to my heart." Engulfing emotion drew them into each other's arms.

Only Lorenzo's strong voice intruded on them, "Hey! Hey! A little bird told me there was a celebration out here. I came prepared. See? I brought the champagne for a toast." Lorenzo triumphantly raised the bottle of bubbly, as he called back to the kitchen, "Mama, are you bringing those glasses? *Today?*"

Zia scrambled as fast as her short little legs could carry her. "Such an impudent boy!" she poked in a falsetto voice. "*Are you coming today?*" Zia would have given him a good-hearted back of the hand if she weren't carrying the glasses. "Yes, Lorenzo, this morning even," she continued her muttering onto the terrace.

Alexander examined the bottle Lorenzo presented, "And just what auspicious occasion are we celebrating with one of the finest vintages from my wine cellar? Hmm?" Dancing returned to Alex's eyes.

Lorenzo politely put Alexander off until Zia joined them on the terrace. Zia and Lorenzo winked at each, signaling their duplicity in this scheme.

Lorenzo began, "Today you gave Nicole the keys to the house, did you not?"

Alex nodded affirmatively, "Indeed, I did."

"Then today, she is part of our family. We welcome her to our hearts and to her home," Zia proudly announced.

Lorenzo uncorked the champagne and filled the glasses, "To Nicole, the love of my brother, now the sister of my heart, forever in our family! Salute!"

They drank.

Zia's turn for a toast. "To my son, Alexander," she lovingly patted his cheek, "and his beautiful Nicole, may they live in eternity in their happiness together. Salute!"

A familiar Italian folk song swelling Zia's heart escaped her lips. "Ya, ya, ya," she grabbed Alex, engaging him in a spontaneous dance. Similarly Lorenzo demonstrated it to Nikki, and together the four of them danced, drank and sang away the morning in celebration. Nikki's heart made careful note of the day — August 15, 1967.

Alexander spent the next two days acquainting his beloved with the house, touring her over every inch of the estate, concentrating primarily on the library, the heart of his empire. He detailed every nuance of the operation. "I want you to be comfortable with everything at *Napoli*. Nothing should intimidate you. Now, you are *mi famiglia*."

It became evident to Nikki that in Alexander's heart and soul, the ritual they had performed on Maui was indeed their wedding and the celebration at *Napoli* their reception by his family. In her heart she adopted Alex's assumption. Now, Nikki wanted to introduce him to her family. Embracing her idea, Alex secured first-class plane tickets for the following day. Nikki phoned her parents, informing them she was bringing home that special someone she had been telling them about for so long.

In preparation for their trip, Alex assembled gifts to take to her parents. He came to her room as she finished laying her things in the suitcase. "Nicole, I want to send your mother some flowers. What are her favorites?"

"Gardenias. It's where I developed my fondness for them."

Alex's eyes twinkled, "I should have guessed. I am sure it is where your charm comes from, too. I bought your father a money clip crafted from an ancient Chinese coin. What do you think?" he opened the case for her to examine.

"Dad will really enjoy that. Did I tell you he collects coins?"

"No, but it's an affinity shared by most men. Nicole, I chose this for your mother. Do you think she will like it?" Alex opened a velvet jewelry sack, and a small pin, resembling a tree, slipped out into his hand. Hand-carved jade, ivory and coral formed the tiny leaves and flowers that sat on branches of 18-karat gold.

"It's stunning."

"I know your father deals in precious gems. I hope this won't duplicate something your mother already has."

"No, Alex, she will be very pleased. Did you pick that up from Charlie Soo?" Nikki turned her attention back to her suitcase on the bed.

"Of course, darling." Alexander surprised her as he nuzzled a familiar kiss on the nape of her neck. "I love this feeling. See, already we have a history together," but he couldn't stop there. Overwhelmed, Alex turned Nikki into his arms. Passionately he arched her over backwards, exposing her lips. The love in his deep-blue eyes flashed with the intensity of naked sunlight. Poised over her, Nikki reached her arms up and clasped the nape of his neck to draw him to her. Oh, she wanted him! Still he paused, continuing to take her in, "Oh sweet God, how I love you." Fluidly, he lowered her onto the bed, their eyes never breaking contact. He inhaled her with his kisses.

Nikki would have consummated their love, but Alex stopped. Still the time was not right for them. Cooling down, facing each other on the bed, he played with her hair and continued to caress her face with his incredibly soft touch. "Have you any idea how important history together is? It unifies us, binding us together tighter than mere love alone. It's the gateway to the future. Oh, Nicole, your mentioning old Charlie Soo brought that realization to me. We have history."

"And a future to build more history together. *Te amo!*" she whispered.

"*Te amo, mi amore. Te amo.*"

Flying a commercial carrier to Pennsylvania, Alexander ensured their complete privacy by buying out every seat in first class. For their comfort, he arranged for their food and wine to be catered by his specific epicurean chef. Lorenzo timed their arrival at the airport perfectly, so Nikki and Alex stepped directly from his car on the tarmac onto the waiting ramp up to the jet. Within minutes, they were on their way.

Once airborne, Alex posed a question she really hadn't given any thought, "Nicole, I understand what you hope to accomplish with this visit. You and I have made a commitment to each other, without benefit of clergy, but a commitment nonetheless. Have you considered what your parents will think? You want your parents to accept me—us—the same way Zia and Lorenzo have. But your parents don't have any point of reference on which to base our relationship. Have you given any thought as to how you are going to explain the status of our relationship?"

Blinded by her confidence, Nikki never saw the potential dilemma Alexander raised. "Simple, I'm going to tell them that we have dedicated ourselves to each other."

"Which means…?" Alex prompted.

"Which means … what?" Her words fell flat. In her heart she knew what it meant, but to anyone outside of Alex and her, it meant absolutely nothing. Never had she given a moment's thought as to how she might express their relationship to others, especially her parents. It never crossed Nikki's mind that Zia and Lorenzo rejoiced and understood the meaning of their relationship because they shared Alexander's secret. The more thought she gave the situation, the more perplexed she became. Nikki furrowed her brow in contemplation.

"Perhaps this will help, darling." Picking up her hand, pressing it to his lips, Alexander looked straight into her heart, "Would you do me the great honor of marrying me?"

Amazed by his words, Nikki's mind leapt through various possible scenarios to explain his action, until she came to one that fit. "Oh, now I understand. This is the cover explanation for my parents. That's good, Alex. They can comprehend this. Sure, that's fine."

"No, Nicole," Alex paused, his eyes intense in their candor, "I did not mean this as a subterfuge. My intentions are sincere. Will you marry me?"

"In Maui you said you'd never be able to marry. Alex, I don't understand. What about your assignments? When? How?"

"I confess I don't have answers for all those questions right now. I don't know when, or if ever, I will be able to answer them. But I do know that I am a man hopelessly, desperately, deeply in love with you. In London I considered your profile too great a risk. But the longer I am with you, the more I cannot imagine my life without you in it. I will risk anything just to spend the rest of my days basking in your love, whether that be until we are old and gray or until some unforeseen consequence robs me of that privilege next week. I want to be yours and yours alone." Alexander slipped from his seat and fell to his knee, "Once again, will you marry me?"

Taking the leap of faith, Nicole answered, "Yes, Alexander, I will marry you, whenever or wherever you say." Sealing their commitment with a profound kiss, Nikki helped Alexander off his knees and back into the seat next to her.

Instinctively Nikki recognized their engagement could never be a normal one—with press announcements and the like. Because of Alex's extraordinary circumstances regarding his "assignments," their betrothal would be kept within the family and within her inner business circle.

Alexander removed the pearl ring from her right hand, transferring it to her left. "Since our engagement must remain with us, will this ring suffice for now?"

"In Hawaii I took it as the symbol of our commitment. It was perfect then. It's perfect now. You really don't have to move it. Being with you is all I want." Although Alex's proposal didn't change Nikki's commitment, it granted her the privilege of dreaming past tomorrow.

Not even Alexander Vincente could dismiss the rigors of going through Customs in Philadelphia. But his charming personality assured them of treatment above the bureaucratic norm. A Mercedes convertible, black of course, waited ready for them at the curb outside the terminal. With the wind flying through their hair, they sped away from the city into the countryside to *Creekside*. From the days when he had hovered over her before they met, Alexander remembered the exact route to her parent's home. The purr of the Mercedes down the lane and onto the brick drive brought Nikki's excited parents outside into the warm August sunshine.

Always the inveterate gentleman, Alex greeted Fran first, with a European kiss on the hand, then Richard with a hearty handshake and a slight bow in his direction.

Richard sized up Alex, "It's good to finally meet you. Nikki has told us so much about you over the past few months an introduction is almost unnecessary."

Nikki watched her mother measure her against Alex, "Yes. We're delighted to make your acquaintance. Please forgive me, it's just that you look so familiar. But, you're not from here, are you?"

"No." Alex answered, then causally dropped, "but I did look in on Nicole in the hospital a few times. Maybe it was there…"

Nikki hugged him in recognition of his long-term devotion.

Retiring to the backyard patio in the cool shade from the maple trees, Fran turned to Alex, "I must thank you for the gardenias and the other bouquets. The house hasn't been so filled with flowers since the wedding." Fran's face flushed a bit at her clumsy comment.

"It's okay," Alex slipped an aside to Fran, "I know all about Grant."

Not wanting her earth-shaking news to get lost in small talk, but not really sure of how to proceed, Nikki pushed her explanation forward. "Anyway, in our travels, my schedule and Alex's have crossed several times this year. And we've been able to spend some time getting to know each other. Alexander has become very important to me. But, you must know that after *all* my phone calls. And, uh…" the newness of the words caught in her throat.

Alexander rescued her, "Actually, what Nicole is trying to say, is that I have asked her to marry me."

From her parents' satisfied glances, Nikki got the impression they had surmised the underlying reason of their visit.

Being earnest, Alexander continued, "I really must apologize for springing this announcement on you in such a manner. We began our visit here for the purpose of my making your acquaintance. Nicole is very special to me. We just spent time with my family in Italy and likewise, we wanted to spend time here with you. But on the flight over, after months of thought, I proposed marriage. I would not insult you by being so presumptuous as to ask for your blessing without giving you time to get to know me. I hope after we are acquainted, you will understand that Nicole is the axis on which my world turns. She is more important to me than air. And I will expend every ounce of my energy to ensure her happiness. Eventually your blessing of our union would greatly honor me."

The news brought Fran and Richard to their feet as Nikki produced her ring. Appreciative of the harmony they understood Alex had brought to Nikki's life, Richard roundly clasped Alexander about the shoulders in congratulations. Fran and Alex exchanged Italian hugs.

Hugging Nikki, her father peered into her eyes. "He's the one, isn't he, Nikki?" Then interjecting a bit of levity Richard cracked, "After Jim McKay's interview with Gunter, on *ABC's Wide World of Sports*, we really expected an Olympic athlete in the family."

To which Alexander raised a "see I told you so" eyebrow at her.

Nikki tweaked him with a cutesy curtsey.

Remembering the exquisite ruby necklace from last Christmas, Richard involved Alex in a session of shop talk.

While the men engaged in their form of bonding, Nikki's mom led her into the hallway by their bags. Being a simple woman about to approach a delicate subject, she hedged a bit. "I'm not quite sure how to say this ... you're a grown woman. You've been married. And ..., Ahh, we were wondering ... if you and Alexander are planning on ..."

"Sharing a room, Mom?" Nikki finished for her. "No, Mom. We're not sleeping together. Separate rooms are perfect." She hugged her for the thought.

"Dad and I talked about it. We'd be been happy to put you up at the inn if..."

"Thanks for the thought, but it's not necessary." Nikki bent down and picked up Alex's suitcase, "Do you want him in the guest room?"

Immediately, Alex relieved her of his valise, "Where should I put my bag, Mrs. Moore?"

"No need to be so formal Alex, Fran or Frances will do."

"Or Mom?" he said with a peck on her cheek.

After depositing Alex's bag in the guest room, they climbed the stairs to Nikki's old room. Nothing had changed since Grant had led her out of it a lifetime ago, except her mother had properly sanitized it of any traces of Grant.

Alex pretended awe as if entering a shrine, "So this is your room!"

"Yep, show some respect!" Nikki ribbed. Then she led Alex on an excursion around *Creekside*. Alexander punctuated the various high points of the tour with kisses. A warm, loving sparkle never left his eyes.

To appropriately mark the occasion, Richard offered dinner at The Wayside Inn. As all parents do, Nikki's father regaled Alex with colorful stories dredged up from her childhood, indoctrinating him on the "real Nicole." By the time the entrée appeared, Richard had worked his way up to Nikki's little tantrum over the ruby necklace at Christmas. Sitting back in the chair, full of himself, her dad laughed, "I'll bet you got an earful when she finally got hold of you!"

"Mr. Moore, you have no idea!" Full laugh lines crinkled around Alex's eyes as he launched into his story of that stormy night in Florence. Capping the gaiety, Alex related how they had fallen in love. And, not caring that his exaltations made Nikki blush, in rich detail he extolled his very special feelings for her.

Alex spent a great deal of the meal, as he did most of his time in Nikki's company, watching her, following her every move with a blatant twinkle of doting admiration. Often he'd underscore a story by picking up her hand to kiss her fingertips or lightly massaging her shoulders with his hand. Her parents couldn't miss Alex's unabashed devotion to their daughter.

Over liqueurs and coffee Fran asked, "Have the two of you set a date?"

Nikki fielded her question, "It all depends on our schedules. Believe it or not Alex's is more erratic than mine. With us going in different directions, it will probably be later rather than sooner."

Richard defended Alex, "I can understand that, Nicole. Alex deals in quality gems. Such stones don't just fall into your lap. They require considerable legwork to produce. I imagine you pretty much scour the globe..."

"How convenient," Nikki thought, "Dad really thinks Alex is in the gem trading business." His assumption neatly handled the awkward topic of Alex's employment.

Following their return from dinner, Alexander excused them from her parent's company so they could go for a walk. Hand-in-hand, they started up the lane, venturing their opinions of the visit thus far, each recounting from their own perspective its highs and near misses.

Nikki started, "Mom bravely offered to put us up at the inn if we wanted to share a bedroom."

"She is trying accept her little girl as a woman," Alex half-laughed, "or maybe it is just the company you keep."

"You know my dad assumes you deal in stones, too," she added.

"I know. Your father engaged me in a bit of shoptalk this afternoon. How do I tell him it is only a sideline? My contacts don't exactly have stores or even stalls at market. I just get lucky with what I am able to pick up."

"Yeah. Well, we sure dodged the bullet on that subject!" Nikki crowed.

Alex abruptly sobered. He faced her, "Nicole, I really like your parents. They are genuine people who openly display their emotions. Your folks are not superficial or hollowed-out shells like the people I encounter regularly in my business associations. Those are disposable relationships, people who will toss you off without a thought, faster than you can return the favor. Your parents are solid people with integrity, who bleed when you cut them. The fact that we can't tell them the truth bothers me." Mounting agitation forced a slight tremble.

Alex paused, building toward his crisis, "Hell, who am I kidding? *You* don't even know the whole truth! That *greatly* troubles me." His mounting tribulation forced a frenetic pace. "How can I do this? What in the name of all that is holy *am* I doing?" Alexander threw out rhetorically, then swiftly began backing away from her. "I can't. I can't."

Baffled by his 180 turn, Nikki moved to close the gap—offering comfort.

Increasing his distance, Alex rebuffed her, "Stop! No Nicole, don't. Stay where you are."

Deliberately, she stepped forward.

"No, Nicole. Don't! What are you doing?! Run! Listen to all the warnings you have had from Karl and the rest. Leave me here in the lane and run! Don't look back. Don't think. Just *run*! Go home to *Creekside*. Go back to your parents. Get as far away from me as you can."

Standing stock still, Nikki refused to move. She refused to give the man that she loved over to whatever demons possessed him.

"You won't go?" he asked, like he really expected her to leave.

"No."

Compelled, he ran back to her. Grabbing Nikki by the shoulders, his eyes nailed her heart. "Then kiss me. Kiss me and I will stay, even though I may be condemning you to a life of brutal ambiguity. Kiss me before I do you the biggest favor of your life and leave you standing here."

Nikki didn't understand the mental war roiling inside him. But she knew if she wanted him in her life, she had to let him know it now. The intensity from her eyes held tightly onto his and unleashed the fire in her heart. Positioning her hands on either side of his head, Nikki brought his lips down to hers. Summoning all the strength of her love, Nikki magnified it into a singular, concentrated effort. Within their lips the conflict for his soul raged. She reached deep. Nikki had to win this one.

When their lips finally parted, Alexander engulfed her, pressing her body into his. He covered her hair, her neck, her face with kisses. "Oh Nicole! Dear, sweet, innocent Nicole!" he breathed between his kisses. "Oh darling! Do you know what you have done? Do you have any comprehension of what you are letting yourself in for?"

"I do, Alexander. I gave my heart to a man who places his life in jeopardy everyday. How is that different from a policeman, a soldier or any of a hundred other professions? The only difference for us is the distance and time. I know I just waged a battle to hold onto the man I love. No matter what, I will be here. I promised myself to you in Florence, London, Maui and on an airplane today. I won't go back on any of it now or later." Determination burned in her eyes.

He clutched her to him. "I don't know whether you are granting me salvation or condemning yourself to hell. But whatever it is, we will be together."

The cold light from the waning moon followed them home.

In a woman's heart-to-heart, Nikki confided everything she could to her mother. She told her how Alex watched her for two and a half years before they met and how she had seen him here on the road to the lake. They discussed how, at times, Alexander seemed over the top—too good to be true. Nikki assured her mother Alexander's chivalry wasn't an act.

To Nikki, her mother confessed, "Normally I'd worry that a man like Alex might try to stifle or smother you. But the opposite seems to be true. Remember though, such intense devotion can spawn a host of other severe complications, just as intense. Don't forget the lessons your relationship with Grant taught you."

Fran's admonishment revived some of the questions teeming in the deep recesses of Nikki's heart. Why had Alex always stopped short of consummating his love with her? Was she too flamboyant? Didn't she measure up to the other women who moved in his circle? Or did he have a problem? And, what about his work, would those damned extended absences continue after they married?

Alexander unwound in *Creekside's* simplicity. They rode the horses out to the lake, which seemed more pond-like now. Nikki took him shopping and bought him his first pairs of Levi's. He lived in them.

Also at *Creekside*, they ironed out most of the complications their engagement raised. Alexander would spend the next few months freeing himself from his assignment entanglements, working himself into retirement. Accomplishing that, they would marry. Nikki would continue on with her career as long as she cared to. After their marriage, Alexander assured her, he'd blissfully follow her from venue to venue being Mr. Nikki if she so desired.

On one of their rides, Alexander and Nikki discovered an abandoned stone farmhouse in the middle of acres of overgrowth. The tangle of bush couldn't hide the shutters hanging on by a single hinge or conceal the gaps in the grouting around the large stones. Whips of vines demonstrated the structure's imperfections as the wind whistled through the broken windowpanes, skipping over them to play with the cobwebs and crispy leaves inside the house.

While they relaxed under one of the estate's shady oak trees, a huge black bird perched on the peak of the house's gable called down to them. "Look Nicole. It's a raven," Alex pointed to the shiny black bird.

"It's probably a crow. There's a ton of those around," she dismissed.

"No, he is bigger than a crow," Alex approached the bird.

Warily the bird arched his wings, as he carefully regarded Alex.

Cupping his hand around his ear, Alex pretended to listen, "Nicole, can you hear him? He talks. You can tell he is a raven by his voice. Listen."

"Excuse me, Mr. Raven, will there ever be a love as great as ours?"

"Nevermore," Alex pretended a cackle for the bird.

"Will Nicole ever love anyone else again?"

"Nevermore!"

"My turn," Nikki stepped up: "Will Alex's head ever be turned by another woman?"

"Nevermore."

"Will Zia ever stop smacking poor Alex?"

"Alas, Nevermore."

They collapsed in laughter. The bird—raven or crow—tired of their attention—departed. Appropriately, they nicknamed their special spot "Nevermore". And despite its deterioration, the place beckoned them with a mysterious charm all its own. Alex and Nikki spent hours over picnic lunches on the weedy flagstone patio, fantasizing about the restoration needed to return the dilapidated farm to a grand estate.

On their last full day at *Creekside*, Alexander and Richard headed out early in the morning on an excursion to town. The two disappeared for the better part of the day. When they returned Alexander brought souvenirs from his outing ... two gold ID bracelets, both inscribed with "Nevermore". Without ceremony, Alex put them on them at supper while explaining to Nikki's parents the meaning behind the word.

Following dinner Nikki questioned Alex about the bracelets. Recalling how he eschewed jewelry, she wondered if his would present a problem for him with his assignments.

Sweetly, he kissed her hands. "Darling, unlike a ring, an ID bracelet doesn't carry a connotation of love. The "Nevermore" inscription is innocuous. No one would connect an attachment to it. In fact, it suggests the wearer has sworn off love completely. I will be the only one who understands its meaning."

Nikki understood his explanation perfectly. Both promised to wear them forever.

Too soon the days of their week ran out as Nikki again switched her ring to her right hand. Together they climbed back into the car to catch their flight to London. Not wishing to repeat the airport separation scene like in Hawaii, Alexander stayed overnight in the guest room of Nikki's cottage before flying to the Continent in the morning.

Alexander woke his Nicole for a parting kiss. Outside in a gray, drizzling, September rain a black Mercedes waited for him.

Her brave-faced good-byes wrung every ounce of energy from Nikki, leaving her paralyzed for hours. Eventually Nikki telephoned Mary, requesting she bring Bruce and Karl and come to the cottage that afternoon.

Chapter 21

In Training

Mary arrived early to find Nikki in newly applied makeup, so uncharacteristic of her while working around the house. Immediately she knew her friend had begun another forced separation from Alexander. Nikki's depleted natural sparkle spoke volumes.

Mary urged postponing the scheduling summit until Nikki had recovered a bit. Instead, Nikki employed her typical tactic of coping through over-compensation. She attacked the session with terrier zeal, driving all of them hard, pushing their limits. Rising to Nikki's challenge, Mary laid out her full complement of ideas, including a bi-weekly, half-hour teen show to be hosted by Nikki. The TV series would include makeup and glamour tips, chat session clips and behind-the-scenes vignettes of Nikki in real life situations. Calling it *Nikki Now!*, she'd spend every spare moment in front of the cameras building up a film library for the various segments. Then they'd film topically fresh updates and insert them into the canned inventory of segments to give each show an up-to-the-minute appearance. Nikki enthusiastically signed on with Karl and Bruce's enthusiastic endorsements.

Nikki ended their session by announcing her private engagement to Alexander. While all congratulated her, Karl lingered behind, suggesting they grab a bite at the Dilly Dog. Obsessed with his thoughts, they dined in relative silence until Karl finally spit out, "Nikki, we need to talk about Paris."

Hastily Nikki apologized again for dumping the piddling details on him.

Karl blocked her apology, "I didn't mind that. But I have real problems with you getting cozy with Vincente. Have you investigated any of the allegations I showed you after Hong Kong?"

"Sure I did," Nikki stretched her white lie. She had wanted to ...

"And... What about the missing people, jewelry and money?"

Karl's mention of jewelry sent a cold twinge nipping at her stomach. Were the "innocent baubles" Alexander presented to her stolen? She faked a shrug, "My investigation made nothing of any of those things. Alexander has always proven himself to be a gentleman of grand proportions."

"Most conmen are. Tell the truth, have you looked into his reputation? Or are you letting your heart do the research for you?"

Zingo! Karl hit home with that remark. Unfortunately her distress over his accusation egged on her temper, causing her to verbally assault him, "Okay Karl, where are the definitive allegations? How did you come by them? Where is your proof? Who are your sources? Are they reliable? What exactly do you know?"

"I know that I love you and don't want to see you throw your life away again!" Karl shouted from a whisper. Shocked by his words, Karl's fork hit his plate.

Retrenching, both dug into their food.

Karl re-engaged first, "Okay, right, my feelings are on the table. After two and a half years together, I'm not just an objective, independent, detached reporter. Hell, I practically work for you! Now let's get over this awkward spot and back on track. What would it take for me to convince you not to marry Vincente?"

"Karl, is that what this is about? Are you a tiny bit jealous?"

"I dunno. But my concern is genuine. I know I must sound pathological or at the very least petty. Come back to my flat with me. I have papers there. I admit they're innuendo, but you should see them."

With Karl's "conmen" warning swimming in her head, Nikki agreed. She didn't want to know any of it, yet she wanted to know it all. Only a dozen words passed between them as Karl motored to his flat.

His apartment reflected the lifestyle of a man whose work preempts a social life. Papers, pictures, articles—tools of his trade—choked his living space. Karl proceeded directly to his desk. Giving his chair a shove backward, he pulled the center drawer completely out of its mahogany compartment. "Here. Remove the tape and pull off the envelope I've attached to the bottom," Karl held the drawer in the air for her.

"Open it. Read it." Karl disappeared into the small galley kitchen of his flat, "You want a drink? I intend on having one. Hell, I'm going to have several!"

"Sure!" She didn't care what he was pouring. While opening the manila envelope, Nikki found a seat on Karl's davenport. Haphazard dates, approximate times, doubtful inventories and unnamed sources abounded for each charge. For one item, it would have been laughable, for a handful—hearsay, but for pages upon pages, the documentation appeared disturbing. "Make mine a double," Nikki upped the ante in the face of the growing evidence.

Karl set her drink on the coffee table. The potent taste of raw whiskey seared down to the knot in her gut.

The dates started in October of '57 and ran into the summer of the current year. Nikki told herself that if the dates never intersected when she and Alex were together, she'd reduce the report to yellow journalism. Carefully she calculated dates their paths crossed, then scanned the pages to find those dates.

Karl refilled her glass as he topped off his.

Incredibly the dates tumbled into place: Hong Kong December '66, a tray of assorted gems disappeared from a shop in Kowloon. Florence May '67, a Reubens and a Van Gogh vanished from two different museums. London early June '67, the central bank found itself short two million pounds. Vienna early July '67, police discovered a cache of arms along with half of the pound notes missing from the London heist the month before. The magnitude of the innuendo punched the air out of her, collapsing her heart.

"If you find the plot gripping, you'll love the art." Karl sarcastically tossed another envelope into her lap as he refilled their glasses again.

Pictures fell out of the second envelope—pictures of Alexander with women, some of the photos old and grainy, some as recent as a month ago. Model types, all of them beautiful, wafer thin, yet voluptuous, draped on his arm, sharing intimate kisses, scantily clad in low-cut, revealing gowns or barely-there bikinis. Some of the pictures were obviously staged, others captured via telephoto lens. Alexander's warnings about other women lay submerged at the bottom of the whiskey bottle, and Nikki's insecurity over Alex's failure to consummate their love surfaced instead.

By the end of the third whiskey, the amber liquid vaporized Nikki. She wept into Karl's comforting arms. Under the booze's dizzying influence, she eventually passed out on Karl's couch.

Waking with a hangover, the gloom of guilt settled upon her. Where was her faith? She tucked her hair up inside a felt floppy-brimmed hat, then covered her face with a pair of owl-eye shades. She couldn't look in the mirror long enough to put on make-up. Before she left, Nikki promised Karl she'd examine the accusations, although she didn't want the photos.

Jarred picked her up at Karl's apartment. In deference to her train-wreck he offered from the rear-view mirror, "perhaps, tomorrow morning would be a better day to start the training you requested?"

Nikki quietly nodded.

Bright and early the next day, Jarred handed her an assignment. "For the next two days, when I drive you to your filming locations, I want you to notice everything. Look at the people, notice their clothes, the colors, their cars, the background, the noises, everything—memorize it all. Then we'll discuss it. The key to everything involved with the Agency is observation, along with a few skills. The success of a project will depend on you developing an acute sense of awareness—almost bordering on the paranormal. Your hectic schedule doesn't leave much time for lessons, but I think you'll be amazed at what you can learn just on the drive between the studios and the cottage."

So Nikki's training began as she focused on the details in the world surrounding her. Her concentration became so intense it obliterated all thoughts related to the envelope she had taped to the bottom of her desk drawer at home.

Nikki gobbled up the adventure. For the first week, Jarred never varied the route. After two days, he quizzed her about her observations. Some of the things he brought up she remembered, others Nikki missed totally, like the number and type of flowers a woman carried, the style of a man's hat. Jarred's questions honed her retention, turning it into a game. Continually she tried to best her teacher by picking up minute details he might have missed, but at every turn he trumped her.

The second week Nikki rode the route blindfolded. Jarred challenged her to detail the sights from the sounds and smells. He changed the game in the third week. She had to find the inconsistencies. "This is the secret to the puzzle," Jarred explained. "You must be able to key-in to the essential elements, then instantly sort out unusual or telltale signs."

At the studio, Jarred picked up an open book of matches on one of the music stands. "Nikki, tell me about the person who left these behind."

She read the black cover, "Golden Pole Pub," turned the book over, read the address, opened the book, some of the matches were torn out. "Not much to tell, Jarred. They probably came from a guy who plays here. Obviously he smokes and likes girlie clubs."

Jarred took the matches from her. "Not bad for starters. Hopefully by the time we're finished you'll be able to walk up to the holder of these matches and hand them to him. You're probably right. I'd say they belong to a man because of the subject matter. But here's what you missed. The user is right handed. See, the matches are missing from the right side. Notice the left corner of the cover is, shall we say, worn. The person used the cover to pick his teeth, also with his right hand." Jarred smelled the book, "I also detect a slight pipe tobacco aroma in the fiber of the paper along with a bit of smoke discoloration. He holds the book as he cups his hand around the bowl while lighting. So, who do they belong to?" He handed her back the matchbook.

Nikki turned it over in her hand, "Three of our regulars here smoke pipes, including Ben. Of course, I eliminated Ben because of the nature of the club. Conveniently, the rhythm guitarist is left handed, so they must belong to the drummer Jake who's right handed."

Jarred frowned. "Your conclusions are probably right, but for the wrong reasons. In this business, reaching a conclusion for the wrong reason can cost you success in your mission. Because you think you know Ben, you took a short cut and made an assumption. Never trust information you only believe to be true. You must know it for a cold, dead-on fact. Trust no one! Did you notice the location of the pub printed on the back? I say these matches belong to the drummer because he lives in the vicinity. Ben's flat is on the other side of town." Jarred flipped the matches over to the back cover for her to re-examine. "There are always other complications to check out, too. Where do their close friends, partners or associates live? Those kind of things. Now see if these are Jake's."

The one central phrase that Mann, and now Jarred, continually used but failed to define was "success of the mission." It didn't take a genius to derive its meaning. The opposite of success was failure and in Agency double-speak, failure equaled death. So the "success of a mission" by Agency standards euphemistically meant the agent got out alive. "Sharpening your powers of perception never ends. The greater your ability to observe, the longer your string of successes." Roughly translated—the longer you live.

Like a child's eyes opening to the reality of the adult world, so too Jarred's demonstrations expanded Nikki's vision, changing forever the way she viewed everything. Never again would she look at anything without thoroughly dissecting and assessing it.

Jarred also taught Nikki incredibly simple, pro-active approaches to surveillance like booby-trapping a room to detect an intruder with a piece of unnoticeable lint or how to protect sensitive material with everyday dust.

In one of his many lectures, Jarred contradicted an old tenet from her childhood. "Never assume the police are an ally. The politicos have them tied up in bureaucratic red-tape. In our world, this ham-handed plodding only slows down our progress. They stand as hindrances at best, lethal disasters to us at their worst. If you are forced to deal with the police, make sure you control the situation, not them."

Occasionally Nikki felt the bottom of her desk drawer at the cottage for Karl's envelope, but her heart didn't permit her to open it. She hoped

Jarred's lessons would present a plausible way to secretly check out the allegations, but nothing came to light. Conveniently, Karl didn't ask her about it again.

Ever since Nikki found out about Jarred's involvement with the Agency, for some reason she felt leery of flaunting Alex in front of Jarred. Even though she didn't know the nature of Alex's assignments, she was fairly confident he wouldn't want the Agency investigating his trail.

More than a month passed since she had heard from Alexander. Nikki assuaged her guilt connected to her reaction to Karl's envelope of innuendo by resolving to confess it to Alex at their next meeting. Weekly Lorenzo phoned, assuring her of Alexander's love and good health. Still she ached for Alex. The chill of autumn along with its intermittent rain descended on October. To comfort her, weekly deliveries of armfuls of flowers began to arrive. The first note read, "May these brighten your days and keep me in your heart. Love, A."

Her latest album *With Love from Me to You*, with a new ballad written for her by George Harrison, went into pressing. An intimate portrait of Nikki penning a love letter, washed in the homey tones from a hurricane lamp had the albums flying off the shelves. And what would October be without working on a Christmas Special? "Nikki's Holiday Home," supposedly filmed at her cottage, was shot in Scotland with the interiors done on a sound stage. To spike the hype for her film, Steve McQueen, her movie's suave, spy-guy hero cuddled with her in the special on the couch in front of a fake fireplace.

Scheduled to debut the first of November, Nikki's half-hour television shows rushed her team. Adding to their film inventory, they found taping her chat sessions dramatically increased their quality. The chatters vied to outdo each other in front of the camera by endearing themselves to Nikki. This, of course, heightened the illusion of personal closeness — the precise image Mary's PR team hoped to foster.

Bruce also began pestering Nikki about getting a highly visible escort for the movie premier of *Runway Breakouts* the day after Christmas. With fans nipping at her heels for a hot romance, he arranged for her to show up with Steve McQueen to sustain the image created in the film and Christmas special. Vada Long sauced-up the sensation with her design of a highly stylized cat-suit spy outfit for her to be seen falling out of at the premier.

One November night, a particularly nasty storm blew in off the sea with cold, driving winds and gales of rain, forcing the studio to abandon their location shoot that night. Jarred drove Nikki home. From a distance she saw a candlelight glow emanating from her cottage windows. Smoke from a cozy fire curled up the chimney. Nikki didn't need gardenias to tell her what those indicative signs meant. She knew if she had recognized the telltale signs of company, her teacher had already noted them. In a preventive strike to discourage him, Nikki tore a page from his playbook and covered with the obvious. "Oh," she purred, "I see I have a date tonight."

Jarred arched an overly protective eyebrow, "You gave someone else a key?"

"Of course not. I'm not totally daft! Hannah, my housekeeper has a list of approved guests. With proper identification they are allowed to enter."

Jarred wasn't deterred, and the last thing Nikki wanted was him intruding. To derail him, she stripped away her casualness, leveling him in a searing stare, "Jarred, I understand the gravity of my position with the Agency. However, I am insulted if you think I've learned nothing. Remember, Mister, I have a life away from the Agency. I do not need you inspecting my personal life."

Nikki had bullied him into ignoring his own supreme directive to trust no one.

Once inside, Nikki momentarily ducked out of Alex's welcoming arms, "Let me tend to business first." With mighty pulls on the portiere's wands she swooshed the yards of heavy velvet drape closed. After locking out the world, she surrendered to Alex's beckoning embrace and returned his welcoming kisses.

"I have missed you," Alex whispered in her ear, "but we must talk."

Stepping over to the stereo system, he put on some slow music. Then uncharacteristically he turned the volume up, so the music filled every square inch of the cottage. "May I, my dear? I have longed to hold you close in my arms." As they danced, Alex warned her, "Darling, please don't register any emotion. Just continue dancing with me. Keep your eyes closed and put a smile on your face so you won't react to what I am about to tell you. Remember, you must hide your reaction. Ready?"

Although totally mystified, Nikki obeyed Alexander's whispered commands.

"Nicole, did you know that your house is bugged? ... Remember no reaction."

"Bugged?" She whispered back through her smile, eyes still closed.

"Yes. There are several listening devices in your telephones. Any idea who put them there or why?"

Still dancing, "No. Unless it was Jarred, for security."

"They are relatively new. They weren't here at my last visit."

"How do you know they are here now?"

"Because darling, I swept the place when I came. I haven't had a chance to check for hidden cameras though. I will do that after Hannah has left."

"Does it matter that Jarred drove me home and saw the candlelight in the house? He knows someone other than just Hannah was waiting for me. I put him off from coming into the house, but unless I miss my guess, he's watching from somewhere."

"Why darling," Alex whispered, "how very cagey of you. Are you learning to assign ulterior motives to people's actions?"

Damn. Her newfound insight had crept out onto the surface. Nikki opened her eyes and setting them dancing said out loud, "Sweetheart, I learned from the best. I learned that from you one night in Hong Kong."

Alexander picked up on her mirth, "How could I have forgotten!" Then he drew her back to him, continuing again in whispers, "I really don't care if Jarred sees me, as long as he does not get too nosy. When does Hannah leave?"

"She should be about ready now. Why?"

"Obviously I planned a private night here together, but in light of the listening devices, I think we should go out. Why not go change. After she has gone, I will check for cameras." Kissing her, he sent Nikki on her way.

Before retreating to her bedroom, she stopped in the kitchen for a word with Hannah. She spoke to her housekeeper out loud, for the benefit of the listener, "Hannah, you know the pass-list I gave you of people permitted to enter?"

With her quick wit, Hannah instantly grasped an ulterior motive to Nikki's question. Nikki knew she could rely on Hannah not to give her away, since obviously both knew such a list didn't exist.

"Yes, ma'am."

"There is always a possibility that Jarred or another member from his security team may want to see it. Under no circumstances are you to divulge that list. It's best not to let him get too cocky. It'll be our little secret. Okay?"

"Yes, ma'am. And I will be going as soon as I gather me things."

Nikki heard the door close as she reached the top of the stairs. She didn't have to root through her closet for a gown to wear. She pulled out the new one, full length of red velvet with long sleeves and scooped neckline. Red — Alex's favorite color for her — and so appropriate for her lack-of-faith confession.

While fumbling with her ruby earrings at her dressing table, Nikki determined she would give Alex the envelope Karl had presented to her. That is, if Alexander didn't find any cameras in the living room within view of the desk.

Instantly, like a rapidly spreading cancer, the idea of bugs in her cottage poisoned Nikki's thoughts with paranoia. She began to wonder, with the bugging devices and possibility of cameras, how safe was her hiding place? How much had Jarred and his crew heard and seen? What exactly had they heard? What had they witnessed in her private moments? Nikki felt so self-conscious, so very violated. Her mounting anxiety flushed blood to her face. Silently she fumed. How dare Jarred take such liberties! How dare the Agency invade her privacy! Did they challenge her loyalty? Trembling with rage, her fingers couldn't close the clasp on her ruby pendant. Emotions flooded her. In the mirror of the vanity table she helplessly watched them march over her face. She had to get control. She couldn't let Alexander see her this way. Worse yet, she knew she shouldn't put on such a display for the *cameras*! Frustrated by her fit of anger, distraught at the thought of people listening and perhaps watching her, tears involuntarily backed up in her eyes. Their presence flustered Nikki all the more.

Then a knock came at the door, "Darling, are you all right? Nicole?"

A captive of her fear, she couldn't answer. In the mirror's reflection, she stared at the door.

"Nicole? Nicole?" The knob turned. Recognizing a brewing crisis, Alexander stepped in.

With standing pools of tears, Nikki held out her trembling hand and slowly opened it for Alexander, revealing the ruby necklace with crumpled chain.

"These clasps can be quite difficult sometimes," Alexander graciously accommodated. Carefully he draped the necklace about her and closed the clasp, lightly resting his hands on her shoulders.

She turned into his arms. Alexander quieted her, "It's okay. Your room wasn't touched, and there are no cameras downstairs. You can talk."

With relief she cuddled into his arms, then remembered her mission and ran downstairs to fetch the envelope. Nikki handed the envelope to him, "Karl gave me this. Evidently he has been collecting it since we met a year ago in Hong Kong."

Sitting, Alexander pulled the pages out, scanning as he flipped through them. "What can I say, Nicole? For the most part, it's all true. I have explanations for each of these citations, but you understand—I hope—that I cannot comment on any of it." Sliding the papers back inside their cover, gravely he looked up at her, "I'm surprised Karl didn't have pictures to accompany this package. Did he assemble these himself or did someone give them to him?"

"But Alex, he does have pictures," Nikki burst out. "I left them behind. I couldn't keep those things around here. They'd drive me crazy."

"I understand, darling. Although in the light of the contents of this little dossier, I hope you still are indeed mine." His eyes pierced her soul.

Nikki swallowed and forged ahead, "Alexander, I'm afraid I did a terrible thing. I let the contents of that envelope shake my faith in you. When Karl laid all this in my lap, it demoralized me. I had a few drinks and…"

Alexander stilled her lips, "I understand. How could I not? I am sure the pictures testified to my less than angelic behavior."

"But Alex, although I was drunk, nothing happened."

"My darling Nicole, it's all right…"

Nikki interrupted him, "I didn't completely violate our commitment. I still want to be yours if you will still have me."

"Still have you? Darling, don't you think it's the other way around?" Alexander took her in his arms, pressing her tightly against his chest, kissing her face and her hair as he continued. "You are my breath, the pulse in my veins, the reason my heart beats. You are my life. I stand here before you hoping against all hope, with every fiber of my being that you will trust me, that you will still have *me*, knowing that I can't explain the details on those sheets of paper. Can you get past what appears to be such damning evidence? As for the other women, I can only promise you that in my heart, my mind and my very soul I have remained completely faithful to you."

Hanging on to each other for dear life, finally Alex said, "We have so many things to discuss. Shall we go to where we can speak freely?"

The rain continued to beat against the black night, requiring Nikki to wear a coat. For the first time she pulled out the fox coat from the Hong Kong job. As she slid into the wrap, Nikki noticed the lining color had changed to a platinum satin. The stark reality of her little smuggling escapade slapped her in the face! Instantly she dismissed it as yesterday's news as they hurried through the rain splatters to Alex's limo. Alex engaged the soundproof shield and for the first time during his visit, they were completely at ease to speak to each other.

The headlights from oncoming traffic betrayed the depth of mental anguish which tortured Alexander. Picking up Nikki's hands, he continued their conversation from the bedroom, "You know, darling, I would rather live in your dazzling eyes and inhale your beauty than discuss the nasty particulars of my seamy profession. But I must be honest. Surely you noticed in your bedroom that I vowed my absolute loyalty of heart, mind and spirit to you, with a rather obvious and glaring exception. Unlike you, I cannot promise that nothing happened. Because of this damnable business, I cannot pledge my body just yet. I taste your readiness in your kisses. Your exquisite passion lingers on my palate and burns deep inside me. I know you are eager to consummate our commitment. And for all the world that night on the beach in Maui or that day in our house in Naples, I yearned to sweep you up and to fulfill our promise. But I will not dishonor you or our love until I can be yours, and yours alone. As much as I desire you, I will not have any part of this racket sully our bed. And we will not marry until I can make that pledge. In the face of all this, can you still hold out hope for us?"

"Oh, Alexander, saying yes to you was much easier before I saw those awful pictures. I could brush away the rumors, but now they have flesh. I believe you when you say I live in your soul, because if you weren't dedicated to me, you would have already claimed your pleasure. I am hopelessly in love with you. I'll wait for you—for your retirement. God willing, it will be soon." They shared a healing respite in each other's arms before moving on to other pressing issues.

"Nicole, darling, I need you to find out from Karl how he came to possess all this information on me. This is critical. If he culled the information himself, it bothers me. But if someone else spoon-fed him this, I need to know that person's identity. These kinds of details floating around in one neat, compact package could definitely spell failure of a mission."

Fear widened Nikki's eyes. She recognized the phrase, "What do you mean?"

Wishing to avoid panic, Alex casually shrugged off his comment, "Nothing really. Every now and again I get overly melodramatic. I just meant it would be nice to know where Karl got his information. That's all." Alex's gaze drifted beyond her, out into the rain-soaked night. The possibilities of the consequences waiting out there for him absorbed his thoughts.

Nikki didn't buy his cavalier attitude and resolved to meet Karl face-to-face the next day to discuss the contents of the envelopes. Hopefully he would mistake her interest in the source as her follow-up to his investigation, then Karl would willingly provide her with his sources.

"And, sweetheart, what should I do with the information once I've found it out?" her question brought Alex back to her.

"Telephone Lorenzo with the information. He'll notify me. But remember, your phone is tapped." Alex kissed Nikki, nestling her into his arms. The contents of the envelope still possessed him, quelling the conversation as they traveled.

Each vacant moment that passed between them compounded the sense of urgency inside Nikki. But one nagging item remained on her agenda. She wanted to finish their business so maybe they could salvage the evening. "Alex, what should I do about the bugs in the house? Should I destroy them? I'd like to give Jarred a piece of my mind."

"Right now darling, be calm, do nothing, just be aware of their presence. In fact, assume from now on that anyplace you go has an infestation problem also." Alex sighed as he again looked past her, "I hope this is only Jarred's sense of duty run amok. Eventually, when I tell you, you may have to question him about them. But for right now, leave everything alone and go on with your daily routine. I'll return shortly with a present for you that will help you identify these kinds of problems."

"If any place I frequent might be bugged, then how should I question Karl about the envelopes?"

"In the open, darling. Break your routine, go for a walk outside your normal course of travel or take a picnic lunch to the countryside with no one around for miles. I know it sounds crazy, but it is the only way to guarantee privacy." Alexander laid kisses atop her head. He moved to her face. Using his fingertips, he outlined her nose, her eyes, smoothed her cheekbones and dipped into their hollows.

For long minutes Alex held her and gently caressed her lips, then opened the privacy panel. "Driver, please be so good as to take Miss Moore back to her home." Instantly the car pulled to the curb of the street.

Astounded, Nikki looked at him, her face a question mark.

"Darling," he said kissing her fingertips, "I can't do this tonight. It has nothing to do with you. It's me. I'm so sorry. The chauffeur is completely trustworthy. He'll see you home safely. I'll be back in a few days. Save those envelopes for me. Forgive me."

Kissing her hands again, he picked up a tress of Nikki's hair bringing in to his nose. He inhaled it. "You are so beautiful. I love you with all my heart." Kissing the tress, he reverently replaced it on her shoulder. "Good-bye, darling." With that, Alexander opened the door, stepped out into the rain and disappeared into the night, as the driver sped away.

Chapter 22

On the Fly

Stunned, Nikki sat in the back of Alex's car with "no" still pursed on her lips, their final moments together racing through her mind. Talking with Karl became her top priority. She couldn't wait for a nice day and a picnic. She had to talk to him now! Engaging all her resources, Nikki reasoned if Alexander felt comfortable speaking in the limo about intensely private matters, then the car must be secure. Since Alex told her the driver was trustworthy, Nikki leaned forward for a word with the chauffeur. "Sir, am I to gather from Mr. Vincente's remarks that you are at my disposal for the rest of the evening?"

The driver considered her warily from the rear view mirror, "Yes, ma'am?"

Nikki gave him Karl's address, and immediately he maneuvered their way through the city traffic to Karl's flat. Dashing up the stairs, Nikki's fox coat overheated her, and the rain-soaked red velvet dragged on her. All the time she prayed Karl would answer the door.

"My, my, Princess look at you! Where are you off to tonight in all this rain?"

"Grab your coat, Karl. We're going on an adventure!" She heaped-on the excitement although she had no idea of what the adventure would be. She'd wing it.

"Nikki, I'm in jeans and a sweatshirt! I can't go with you looking like this, when you look like that?"

"Sure, Karl, it's a 'come as you are' party. Let's go!" she tugged at his sleeve.

"Shall I bring the Nikon? Are we meeting anyone else?"

"Nope! C'mon," Nikki pulled him outside his door, with him still trying to get his arms into his jacket, and fit the key into the lock. "Hurry up!" Urgency, she knew, enflamed a reporter's imagination. They tore down the steps to the waiting car.

Nikki whispered their destination to the driver, then engaging the soundproof shield, relaxed back into the seat with a knowing smile and her eyes glinting.

"What? What?" Karl insisted.

"You'll see," she responded with a grin big enough to cover her conniving.

"*What?*" Karl begged.

Nikki twisted the tress that only minutes earlier Alex had kissed. "You know, you're right. I really should check out this guy before I jump into marriage," Nikki purred coyly. "Karl, where did you get the information on Alexander?"

Karl's eyes lighted up triumphantly, "I knew you'd come to your senses. You wouldn't believe how I came across the information though."

"Did you research it yourself?"

"Well, sort of. That's the funny thing. Remember last year when we were in Hong Kong and Jimmy snapped the photo of you and Vincente? Because he looked familiar to me, I went to the city's central office to telex the picture back to my office. I wanted archives to run a search on him. While I was waiting, out of the blue this Chinese man hanging around there recognized the photo and started reeling off information…not about you…about Vincente. Then the Chinese man gave me his card. When my office came back with the same name as the Chinese man bandied about, I decided to call him. At first he just had a lot of fluff about a quarrel. But later he sent me a letter with a few facts, promising more details in exchange for money. Totally suspicious of Vincente and his motives, I paid him and just recently got those two envelopes full."

Nikki only knew one person in Hong Kong who knew enough about Alexander to be able to assemble such a dossier — Charlie Soo. In anticipation, she waited for Karl to disclose his name. "So, … who was it?"

"What was his name? I have it back at the flat," Karl racked his brain. "Kwan! Yep, Kwai Kwan, a real tongue twister of a name, huh?"

The curve startled her. Wondering if the informant gave Karl an alias, Nikki pressed further, "Which side of the city was he on?" She remembered Charlie's shop was on the Kowloon Peninsula.

"He was on the island. I remember being relieved the central office was only five blocks from our hotel, so I didn't have to chase all over to find a telex."

"Do you still have his card? I'd like to get in touch with him."

"Sure, back at my apartment. Want me to let him know you'll be calling?"

"No, I could probably pry more information out of him if I turn on the old feminine charm, if you get my drift."

"Okay. So where exactly did you say we are going?" Karl wheedled.

After a quiet dinner in one of the Savoy's private dining rooms, Nikki accompanied Karl back to his flat to retrieve the envelope of pictures and Kwai Kwan's business card. Securing those, she promised this time she'd really check out the information, then fled back to the patient driver.

On the ride back to the cottage, Nikki debated over what exactly to do with her information. Should she call Lorenzo or would it be better to fly there directly and take it to him? What would be best for Alexander? Since there were bugs in the phone and a call from the car could be intercepted through the air, Nikki decided to charter a flight that night to Naples. She asked the driver how best to accomplish such a feat, with the maximum amount of privacy, suggesting strongly that she wouldn't want the pilot to file a flight plan. The driver immediately grasped her meaning.

"Ma'am, I can make those arrangements for you," he responded efficiently.

Changing into jeans and a warm sweater under her coat, Nikki packed a small case including the envelopes. She woke Ben with a phone call and asked him to cancel her sessions for the next two days. Leaving Hannah a note, she posted another note for Jarred on the door although she knew the bugged line rendered her note superfluous.

The weather cleared a bit, permitting a tiny window for a gutsy pilot to take off. But the flight proved rough sledding. Residual winds from the storm buffeted the small craft and drove the air temperature down to slightly above freezing. By three in the morning, frozen and a tad green around the gills, Nikki stood outside the front door of *Napoli*. Even though she possessed a key, she thought it best, considering the lateness of the hour, to ring the bell. Lorenzo answered. Setting aside his surprise, he quickly ushered her into the house. He coaxed the fire in the kitchen hearth back to life, then put the kettle on. Huddled in front of the glowing embers to thaw out, Nikki began the explanation for her arrival, when from behind, two arms wrapped about her and soft lips laid a mantle of kisses at the nape of her neck.

"Nicole! Darling, how good to see you. Never in my wildest dreams did I expect you here tonight."

With a charitable nod, Alex dismissed Lorenzo, leaving the two of them alone in front of the fire. Enfolding her within his blanketing embrace, Alexander chased away her chills while comforting her ragged spirit with his loving caresses. Along with the tea, Alex brought out a decanter of Peppermint Schnapps to soothe her stomach and warm her bones. When she had recovered, he questioned, "Darling what are you doing here?"

"It's all right that I came, isn't it?"

"Of course. This is your home now, too, and I couldn't be more pleased, especially in light of my rude behavior a few hours ago. But you had to have a reason to make the trip in such treacherous weather. Why?"

"I brought the envelopes with the information. You strongly implied its urgency. Since my phones are tapped, I didn't want to call Lorenzo. I had no idea you'd be here."

Alexander warmly drew her to him, "Dear God in heaven, what did I ever do to deserve you?"

Nikki wiggled out of his snuggle enough to ask, "Shouldn't you make some phone calls in regard to this information?"

"I would rather bask in your smile."

"Please, I'm okay. I'll probably lie down for awhile. Do whatever you must with that information. If you need to leave, fine. I know my way around. Please!"

"Thank you, darling. I will be back shortly." He exited in gallant style, bestowing a grand kiss on her in front of the fire. But the swiftness of his fading footfalls betrayed his real emergency.

The aroma of Zia's hearty breakfast breads drew Nikki out from under the sheltering comfort of the covers in her familiar room, back to the congenial warmth of the kitchen hearth. Zia halted her bustling long enough to throw her arms around Nikki in welcome. "*Buon giorno*, Nikki. Lorenzo called to me this morning, 'Mama get up! Nikki is home!' I thought this is impossible, since Alex went just last night to see you. But with Alex and his Nikki, nothing is impossible. Here, I baked. Sit. *Mangia!*"

Obediently Nikki pulled out a chair at the table as Zia brought a steaming pot of tea with a heavenly assortment of piping fresh breads. For the first time, Nikki sat inside for breakfast since fall's arrival closed the great French doors to the terrace against the gray November cold.

Lorenzo entered with his long, brisk strides, "*Buon giorno, mama!*"

"*Buon giorno, Nikki!*" he said as he kissed each of her cheeks.

Zia scolded out loud, "So where is Alexander? I baked. He should eat."

"Mama, he is working in the library. He will be along when he's finished."

"Then here, Nikki, take Alexander some coffee. He works too much," she poured a cup and held it out to her.

Before Nikki could rise, Lorenzo seamlessly intercepted the cup of coffee, "Mama, let Nikki rest. She traveled late last night. I'll take it to him." Efficiently, before objections could be voiced, he disappeared down the corridor, while Zia continued her perpetual motion about the kitchen, muttering about Alexander's excessive work habits.

Within an hour Alexander emerged from his study with a taut smile drawn across his haggard face. By then Zia had moved on to another part of the house. Nikki waited at the hearth to share breakfast with him. Alex took up the chair next to her. Rising, she massaged his tired shoulders while he hung over his coffee cup.

Without prying, she mused, "Long night, hmm? Did you get any sleep?"

"Long, yes. Very long," he nodded doggedly.

Nikki moved her hands up to his neck.

"Oh, that's wonderful darling. I don't know which I needed more, the coffee or your great hands."

She continued kneading.

In a burst of unexpected energy, Alexander reached around and swung her onto his lap. A genuine smile broke through, and the spark returned to his incredible blue eyes. "Yes, I do! I know!"

"Know what?" Nikki giggled.

"I know that your hands and sunshine smile beat a plain old cup of coffee any day!" He smacked a big kiss on her lips. "And I know I love you with all my heart. Darling, in you I am renewed. So now, what is your pleasure?"

But Nikki knew he was still physically beat and emotionally wrung out too. She doubted he had slept. "Sweetheart, why don't you lay down for awhile? There's plenty here that can occupy my time."

"I don't want to be away from you. Besides, I have to wait for a call before I am really free."

"After that will you be able to rest for a little bit?"

"I tell you what. Why don't we go into the library and wait for the call together. I will stretch out on the sofa, and you can read. At least I would get to be with you."

With Nikki sitting at one end of the great leather couch, Alexander laid with his head in her lap. His sandy blonde hair created a study of contrast against her dark Levi's and the cognac-colored leather. Gently she combed her fingers through his golden strands. Emboldened by her role in the evening's activities, she cautiously asked, "Were you able to use the information I brought you?"

"Yes. My contacts tracked down the men and questioned them about the source of their information and the reason for amassing such a dossier on me."

"I couldn't help but notice the name Kwan. Is Kwan a common Chinese name?"

"Yes, it is. But aren't you really asking if this Kwan is related to the infamous Kwan Brothers you met in the streets of Hong Kong last year?"

"Yes."

and

"Darling, in this case they are one in the same. Kwai Kwan, whom Karl ran into in the central office, was the Kwan brother with the first jewelry shop. His brother Chi Kwan was the merchant who distracted you. Both are part of the Red Tong—the Chinese mafia."

"Why pick on you?"

"I stepped on his toes. Funny thing, this was all about my interference in their little scam on you. Kwai Kwan recognized you. Making the sale to you would have bought him bragging rights. Who knows what else he would have expected! He decided to get even with me for ruining his plans."

"I'm so sorry I caused this."

"Darling, how could you have known? I had no idea he would take my part so personally—although that would not have stopped me," Alexander's eyes sparkled. "I never could resist a damsel in distress." He kissed her hand. "Anyway, in my business I couldn't have this kind of information assembled and waiting to fall into the wrong hands. I also had to find out where else they might have peddled those papers."

"And..."

"Fortunately it seems Karl was their first target. And as far as we can tell, their only recipient. They were waiting for him to publish it and blow my cover. If they had to wait much longer, I am sure they would have begun to apply pressure."

"So, now what?"

"Hopefully by now my people are in possession of their files and notes and everything is under control," Alex quietly smiled.

"Was it the contents of those envelopes that disturbed you so last night?"

"Darling," he let a sigh escape, "it was a combination of things. First, all the listening devices at your house bothered me immensely. I am hoping that they are a result of Jarred on hyper-drive over your security, but I worry that possibly they were placed there to get at me. If they were meant for me, then you may also be in harm's way. I will not tolerate having you at risk even for a moment. Paranoia—one the hazards of my profession. And then when you introduced the news of that dossier on me, I lost control. The situation's urgency compelled me to get an immediate handle on it. Wasting time is never an option. I did not want to leave you, but if indulging my selfish appetite to stay endangered even one hair on your precious head, I would never be able to live with myself."

His recitation of the tale renewed his agitation.

Nikki soothed his forehead with her lacy fingers, closed his eyes and repeated calmingly, "Shh, shh, it's okay now. You handled everything. It's okay." Within minutes he exhaled deeply as sleep claimed him. Visibly his tense muscles relaxed. Eventually she leaned her head back against the supple leather sofa and drifted off, too.

"Brriinng. Brriinng." The library phone woke Nikki to attention. Alexander continued his sleep in her lap. The second ring didn't wake him, nor the third. Afraid he might miss his call, Nikki shook him. He merely rolled over. At the fourth ring Nikki slid out from beneath his head to answer the phone.

"*Pronto?*" she said in her humble Italian.

"'allo? Alexander?" The voice spoke English, heavily accented with Chinese.

"No. Might I take a message?" she replied.

"Is that Miss Nikki?" the voice sounded familiar.

"Who is this, please?"

"This is Charlie! You know, Charlie Soo."

"Oh, Charlie, how are you?" Nikki responded in relief.

"Fine. Fine. You are with Mr. Alexander?"

"Yes, I'm here visiting. He's sleeping at the moment."

"Will you come again to see Charlie soon?"

"Yes, in late spring," she tried to move to the meat of the conversation.

"Good. I have more beautiful things for you. Maybe we can have dinner together. Maybe we let Mr. Alexander come, too," he laughed heartily.

Politely she returned the laugh. "Can I get Alexander for you?"

"No. Please not to bother him. But give him message. Tell him most unfortunate series of events happen. Kwan Brothers' store and warehouse all destroyed by horrible fire. Two blocks gone. Poor brothers died trying to save their business. Oh, horrible news! Most unfortunate! You will tell him?" Charlie reeled off his news in an energized staccato.

"Sure, Charlie, I will tell him. I'm so sorry…"

"You come see Charlie when you come back to Hong Kong, okay?"

"Of course."

"Bye, bye. Please give my regards to Mr. Alexander. Take care of him, please. Bye. Bye." With that Charlie rang off.

Stunned by the call, Nikki returned to the couch where Alexander stirred, blinking his eyes open. "Who was that?"

"Charlie Soo," Nikki answered still in disbelief.

Alex righted himself on the couch. Not at all surprised, he nodded recognition as he combed his fingers through his hair waiting for her to continue.

"He said he had awful news. No," she corrected herself, "he said 'unfortunate news.' Seems there was a fire, and the Kwan brothers lost their store and warehouse. He said they died in the fire too."

With a slight smirk, Alexander pulled himself up off the davenport and headed towards the liquor cabinet in the corner of the room. "Well, well, can you believe that! A fire," Alexander remarked to no one in particular, "imagine that. Would you care to join me in a sherry, darling?" he asked as he poured, then handed Nikki a glass with a tiny twinkle in his eye. "To Charlie Soo. A true friend. Salute!" He clinked his glass against hers.

Standing in a state of disbelief, Nikki drank, functioning only by automatic response. A sinking feeling arrested her. She couldn't bring herself to seek verification of the truth her heart knew.

Alexander read it though. "Darling, understand this. I am not sorry about the fire. I am not sorry that all their records and files, which contained lethal information, went up in smoke. And throughout all eternity, I will refuse to be sorry that those two thugs—whom the authorities wanted gone for so long from their society—died today. You must understand, if they didn't get their desired results from their latest scam, then both you and Karl would also have been their victims."

Nikki stuttered. "Y...you mean..."

"They would never stop until they stood over the graves of the three of us and whoever else got in their way."

"Why? I don't get it. All this over bragging rights to a scam that went bad?"

"Trust me. All I can say is that the Kwans were into more than just the Tong. Theirs is quite a history. This dossier on me was an attempt to remove me without strings. They used Karl. They used you. And they would have removed both of you, if you failed to perform up to expectations. You were involved—you knew too much. See, I told you, those back-alleys have teeth."

"But won't others from the Tong want revenge?"

"The Kwans' had many enemies including rival gangs and the authorities. Any one of a number of possibilities could have set such a blaze. That is the unfortunate thing about a fire. If done correctly it destroys everything. And I am sure this was quite a conflagration."

The sequence of events over the preceding twenty-four hours swamped Nikki. Alexander understood the overwhelming nature of such rash circumstances. Like an accomplished bridegroom with his virgin bride, he tenderly coddled her through the effects of this new world. They spent the day quietly in each other's company, living with her new knowledge. Nikki didn't understand why the information unsettled her so much. Two men died, not directly by Alex's hand, but to his benefit. But those two men would have killed Alex, Karl and her. Why should it unnerve her so? Clearly it was a case of self-preservation, if not self-defense.

By evening Nikki felt like rejoining the human race again. At Alex's instruction, Zia had ventured into Naples, returning with boxes of cold weather clothes for Nikki. Zia included in the fall collection a beautiful strapless, empire gown of royal purple silk moire with a bolero jacket. Being the only long gown in the assortment, she knew Alexander meant for her to wear it to dinner. The design of the dress cried for an exposed neck. Nikki obliged by sweeping her hair up into curls. Gray velvet jewelry cases holding a carved amethyst pendant with matching earbobs, both of antique lineage, conspicuously sat out on top of the dressing table in her room. She blushed at Alex's extravagance.

Zia laid out an intimate candlelit supper for them in the dining area off the kitchen. Then she and Lorenzo quietly found activities in town that evening. Alexander's breath caught in his throat as Nikki entered, awash in the purple. "I debated a long time over that color, but it is perfect."

She pirouetted before him.

"Is there anything you don't look good in! *Tres magnifique, mon ami!*" he toasted her with champagne. "I hope you like the jewelry. They belonged to my grandmother. Other than her wedding set and a watch, they were the only pieces of jewelry my grandmother wore."

"Sophie? The American rum-runner?"

"The same. You remind me of her, both of you full of vinegar and fire. She would want someone like you to have them — someone special to me." Sweet sincerity sparkled in his eyes.

At dessert Alexander broached the subject of Christmas, wondering where Nikki would spend the holiday and if he might be included.

"I thought I'd probably stay in London since the following day is the premier of my movie," she responded dispassionately. "Bruce has lined up Steve McQueen to be my escort. Our magic is supposed to continue at the premier. I'm sure we're the dowry of some arranged marriage between the two studios."

"Oh, I was rather hoping you would be heading to Pennsylvania and might invite me along."

"Really? You'd want to do Christmas in the sticks?"

"Darling, I happen to like those sticks. I propose after you and Steve do the premier and the following party, we fly back to *Creekside* for a delayed celebration with your family. We can stay a few days, then head off to the Rockies for a little skiing. Or do you and *Bullitt*-man need more time together?"

Impudently Nikki yawned, "I guess either way I'm stuck with a blue-eyed, blonde for the holidays. Man, how's that for variety?" Abruptly Nikki changed into a smile, "Actually your plan sounds fantastic, and I don't have to be back to work until the sixth of January!"

For the remainder of the evening, they cuddled before the fireplace in Alex's library with brandy and quiet conversation.

"You know, I was wondering," Alexander began, "how exactly did you put this whole phenomenal trip together last night? When I left you, you seemed a bit paralyzed by the bugs."

"I was. I've never been faced with anything like that before. I hadn't a clue as to what was safe and what was not. But you, sweetheart, gave me a lead."

Alex raised a quizzical eyebrow.

"Yes, you. You told me the driver was trustworthy. And since you spoke so freely in the car, I concluded the car must have been secure, too. It became the most expedient place in which to question Karl. I knew you couldn't wait for an idyllic picnic in the country for the information. Once I possessed the particulars, I had to figure a way to get them to you. Since I couldn't trust the phone or the mails, I..."

"But how did you find a flight here in such awful weather?"

"Your driver again. I presumed that if he worked for you, he must know the by-pass around the established system. He found a pilot willing to risk not filing a flight plan and chartered the plane for me."

"I shudder to think how much this must have cost you," Alex shook his head.

"Pay? Of course I had to hire the plane and the pilot for fifty pounds."

"Fifty pounds! You hired a plane and the Red Baron for fifty pounds! Darling, you can handle all my travel arrangements from now on. I pay that just to gas up!"

Nikki sheepishly smiled, returning to the subject of the chauffeur.

"But I assumed you had taken care of the driver. ...Oh no! Alex, was I supposed to pay the driver?"

Alexander laughed heartily, obviously savoring her delicious quandary. "Of course darling, I took care of the driver when I hired him. But you engaged him for your own service—and quite some service I might add. I assume he held his hand out for all the arrangements he finagled."

"Oh, Alex, he never did. I'm so sorry. I've made a terrible mistake." A sinking feeling closed in on her. She had wanted to succeed at this tiny mission she undertook all on her own, on several levels. First, Nikki wanted to prove to Alexander her capability. Then, she wanted to prove to herself that she could negotiate a tough situation without flinching and succeed by her own resources. What had she done?

Thoroughly engaged in her own agenda, Nikki failed to detect Alex's fun. "Was I wrong in making the assumptions that I made?" she pressed Alex. "The chauffeur was from your company? Wasn't he?"

"Yes, and all the assumptions you made proved accurate. Darling, I must admit this is a new side of you. I have never noticed your penchant for deductive reasoning before or such resourcefulness. Please, don't misunderstand, you have always been clever and quick, but I have never noticed it before channeled in this direction."

Despite a few missteps, Nikki had dazzled Alexander with her fancy footwork. Maybe this would buy her inclusion into more of his secret life. She pretended a small blush of self-conceit. "Thank you for noticing. I've decided to try and not take so many things for granted anymore. I want to take charge of more of my life, rather than drift aimlessly amid events over which I have no control."

Alex's eyes danced with pride. "If you are ever not in control, then, darling, you are the only one who sees it. I cannot imagine a person more in charge of her destiny than you. I wish I were in control as much as you are."

Alex drew in a long, thoughtful sip of brandy, paused, then got up and crossed to his desk. Activating a button which parted some books in the library shelves, he slid open a secret panel behind them. "I have been thinking about your infestation problem. After careful consideration I think the time has come for you to find out who placed them. It would be useful to know if they are bugging you or me."

Coming back to the sofa, Alex handed her a small brown envelope, "Nicole, this should help you from now on with any bug problems you may encounter."

Gingerly she undid the tiny metal clasp and emptied the contents into her hand, "It's a duplicate of the pearl ring you gave me in Hawaii. I don't understand."

Alex took the ring and held it next to the one on her finger. "The pearl in the center is slightly bigger, but it is an effective copy. Hardly anyone will be able to tell the difference. Here is the beauty of it. It is actually a transmitter detector—it finds bugs. See, the prongs that hold the surrounding stones are actually antennae; the battery is hidden inside the pearl. Once you engage it, slowly sweep your hand across the room. When it detects a transmitter, the ring will vibrate."

Carefully he removed her original ring and slipped the new device onto her finger. "You activate it like this." Lightly he pushed on the pearl. Taking Nikki's hand he slowly moved it across the face of the room. The ring vibrated as her hand pointed to his desk. "There feel that?" Alex asked.

"It's vibrating. But you don't have any bugs in here, do you?"

"The telephone, it's signaling there is a transmitter in the telephone. We tend to forget about the common, everyday articles. Of course it will be up to you to check these average items out, because the telephone is probably the number one place to position listening devices."

Walking over to the phone and picking it up, he explained. "Nicole, the telephone is a marvelous instrument. In one complete package you have both the transmitter and a permanent power supply to it. That is important because a transmitter must have a power source, be it battery or current, to operate. Without any bothersome wires or cumbersome microphones, the telephone neatly fits the bill. But you will see that when you go home, because your bugs are all in your downstairs phones."

"So, will there be a small device in my phone for me to remove?"

"If I recall correctly, whoever placed them did so by wiring an additional transmitter in your mouthpiece. It hinges on whether the installer uses up-to-date equipment or not. If he still employs old technology, you will find a hard-wired transmitter like the ones in your phones. However, if his technology supports the latest in bugging devices, he merely opens the line like this." Demonstrating, Alex unscrewed the cover and moved a wire. "There, you have an instant transmitting microphone. Before long, installers will be able to accomplish the same thing electronically without even entering the premises."

Nikki stared at Alex, "That sounds sinister."

Alex replied with a smug grin, "My dear, that depends from which side of the equation you operate." He put the phone back together again. "I would like to replace the original ring I gave you with this one. That way you will always know exactly what your surroundings are. Okay?"

"Of course, Alex. May I keep the original?"

"Sure, but if anyone ever finds it, you will have some explaining to do. Wouldn't you like me to keep it here for you?" he gently coerced.

Nikki nodded, then Alex slipped it into the envelope, placing it in the safe. He shut the compartment's door and automatically the row of books closed over the panel.

Alex returned to her, passion gleaming in his eyes. With his hands on her hips, he doled out tiny kisses on her face. "You know darling, you will have to be careful as to how you approach the subject of the bugs." Kiss on the right cheek. "You can't just tell Jarred you have a device with the capability of detecting transmitters." Kiss on the left cheek.

"Any suggestions?" she purred.

"Sure. First, before Jarred arrives, loosen the cover of the mouth-piece." Kiss on the forehead. "Then, in front of Jarred, accidentally knock your phone to the floor." Kiss on the nose. "That should effectively break open the instrument." Kiss on the right eye. "And you will see the extra transmitter and question him." Kiss on the left eye. "Then with him in tow, check the rest of the phones in the house and remove the bugs as you go." Kiss on the earlobe. "Now that is quite enough shop talk, don't you think?"

Alexander brushed a whisper by her ear, as he proceeded to the nape of her neck. "Umm, have I commented on how exquisite you smell? Are you wearing lavender to compliment the amethysts?"

"Um hmm."

Morning brought crisp, clear skies to *Napoli*. Alexander greeted Nikki at the breakfast table with his tongue-in-cheek humor. "So, darling, have you engaged that kamikaze pilot of yours for your return today? Or shall I have my safe and sane plane readied for you?" He poured a cup of coffee, waiting for her answer, his eyes friskily dancing.

She pretended indifference from behind the newspaper. "Alas, my Red Baron is off today. I'll have to settle for boring. Could Vincente the Great arrange that?"

Alexander collapsed her newspaper barricade, his eyes brimming with high spirits. "Well, pardon me, *mon ami*! The day anyone uses the words boring and Alexander Vincente in the same sentence is the day they bury me!"

"We'll see," she goaded him. "Tell me sir, can *you* fly by the seat of your pants?" Breakfast dissolved into a playful tug of war that only ended when Nikki walked off the tarmac in England, and Alex slipped back into the air.

Chapter 23
Learning to Polka

Back on the ground in London, Jarred offered a proposal when he picked Nikki up at the airport. "Don't you think it's about time you learned to drive?"

Frankly, Nikki had never considered the subject. By the time she turned sixteen, she was being ferried about in limos with The Merseymen. After that, the world revolved in such a dizzying pace she wasn't in one spot long enough to learn the mechanics of driving.

"Not that having a license will change arrangements," Jarred heightened his sales pitch. "But it would be helpful in a pinch, wouldn't it?"

"Sure. Why not?"

"Great! If you look in the glove box, you'll see that I've already taken out the 'L-Plate'—a learner's permit—in your name. We can get started this afternoon."

"But, Jarred we are filming this afternoon. You want me to learn to drive going home in the dark!"

"Uh... not quite Nikki. See, Bruce thought it would make a grand subject for your *Nikki Now!* series. He wants to do a day-by-day report of your progress. Karl will be there, too, to capture..."

"Man! You have got to be kidding!" she good-naturedly exploded. "Won't you get a good giggle out of this! Me, flubbing around in a car, jerking gears, jamming on the brakes. Oh, I can see it now!"

"Come on. You're pretty bright. It won't be that bad," he sweet-talked her.

"I smell a conspiracy—and I suppose you're in on it," Nikki mocked.

"Actually, Bruce sent me to do the dirty work."

"Well then, Jarred my man, I hope your insurance is paid up! Because you will be right beside me in this," she playfully asserted.

Before long they arrived at an abandoned airfield outside London. A small horde of people showed up to witness Nikki's first lesson. Bruce had spared no expense. He even hired a helicopter to capture the overhead shots of her first encounter with a driving machine. Rather than starting out in an old junker, there sat a brand-new, bronze-toned Jaguar XKE convertible. Once Jarred installed the L-Plate, Nikki's nightmare began.

Lightning quick, the driving instructor sped through his instructions. "Turn the key on here. Push the clutch in, first gear is here. Push the clutch in, second gear is here. Over here, next to the clutch is the brake, and the long peddle next to it is the accelerator. Ready to start, Princess?"

No need to recite the instructions slowly. It would make a better film if Nikki resembled a total incompetent! The more she struggled, the funnier the piece of business. The helicopter buzzing in and out for shots as she whiplashed her way through the gears fried her nerves. If that wasn't enough, Bruce had anchored a camera on the hood of the car to record every agonizing detail. Since this was for the general audience, Nikki was expected to mug with good humor for the camera throughout the whole humiliating trial.

In between the filmed sessions, Nikki practiced like a lunatic. By the end of the three-week course, she actually wanted to obtain her license. Over the series, innocuous little notes of encouragement, a gardenia or two and a billboard reading, "Well, pardon me, *mon ami!*" slipped into Nikki's field of vision.

Jarred also resumed her training regimen. The success of her private mission into Naples added confidence to her moves in their training games.

Within two days of being home, Nikki shrewdly set the stage to expose the bugs and prepared to discreetly monitor Jarred's reaction to them, which would prove critical. As she had learned from her teacher, the element of surprise was one of their most valuable tools. Surprise, if played correctly, gave the person creating the surprise a precious split second in which to observe the victim, before the victim realized his vulnerability and covered his tracks.

A charge of excitement surged through her as she set the sting. Nikki loosened the normally taut phone wire from under the rug, just enough to allow her to catch her foot on it as she walked by, so it would cause her to trip, which in turn would send the phone crashing to the floor. Anticipation pricked at her. She timed the caper to coincide with Jarred's morning stop at her house.

Her execution worked flawlessly. Nikki studied Jarred's face, both when she fell and when the phone toppled. Clearly, her fall didn't initiate as much alarm as the phone hitting the floor. Immediately his face registered fear of discovery as he scrambled to retrieve the phone. Nikki caught a barely discernable flush of color as she uncovered the bug.

"What's this?" Nikki scrutinized him intensely, like a demanding spotlight.

"It's a transmitter," Jarred parsed his words, volunteering nothing.

"What's it for?" Nikki didn't flinch.

"Listening."

"To what?" holding steady.

"Conversations."

Increasing the pressure, "Who do you think put it here?"

Jarred hesitated, debating over whether or not to lie, "I did."

Maintaining eye contact, Nikki relaxed her intensity to promote explanation.

"I wanted to make sure no overzealous fans threatened you when I wasn't here."

"Are there any more of these?" she questioned him sternly.

Jarred systematically led her to each phone. Making their way through the cottage removing all the devices, he driveled his excuses. As long as he told the truth, his reasons didn't matter to her. She had the information Alexander needed. However, Nikki savored the sweet knowledge that, using all her master's methods, she had entrapped Jarred, and he failed to detect it. Finally she had scored one on the teacher although she'd never be able to lord it over him. In the process she learned that inside information and surprise are tools of impressive proportions, capable of reversing overwhelming odds.

Nikki celebrated that evening with a call to Lorenzo, in code of course, to report her success. Opening a bottle of Dom Perignon, she relaxed in front of the fire, while answering some mail.

But fate and Bob Mann intruded on her celebration. Nikki offered Bob a glass of bubbly, which he obligingly took. "Geez, this is the good stuff," he coarsely commented before continuing. "Jarred tells me you're progressing with your courses. In fact, he assures me you're ready to fly solo. So, how's your German?"

"It's a passable combination of two years in high school and six trips to Deutschland," Nikki replied, not realizing he was only making conversation.

Mann plopped his molded metal briefcase on the coffee table, opened the lid and removed an envelope. He slid out several black and white glossy photos. "We've got a mole in our operation and have narrowed the field to three potential suspects. These are the three." Mann spread out the photos and the rest of the contents of his brief case. "Their names and pertinent data are on the back of each photo. We are throwing a little party at the embassy. Separately, each of them will be informed that they will be contacted by you at this party and passed highly sensitive material. We are running a trace operation here. Each packet of information is different and, of course, bogus. Whichever packet makes it through to the other side will finger our mole. We want you to pass out the packets. However, you must be sure the right packet gets to the right man and that none of them know you slipped packets to anyone else. None of these men know the other. Do you understand?"

"Yes. So, when's the party?" Nikki asked while reviewing the photos.

"Saturday night at the British embassy in Berlin."

Nikki looked up, "That's the day after tomorrow. You move fast."

Mann looked up. "Did I mention that you're the guest of honor, and they'll probably want you to perform a song or two?" He resumed his paper shuffling.

"No, Bob, you failed to mention that minor little point. What do you propose I do for accompaniment?"

He waved off her inquiry as insignificant, "There will be an orchestra there, or maybe you will have to bring somebody, won't you?"

"Why don't you speak plainly? Tell me what you expect. How many people do you want me to bring along? Do you want me to be low-key...slip in, slip out? Or are these people expecting NIKKI In Neon?"

These people are expecting the real deal. Bring along as many as you need to be believable." Mann polished off his champagne. "Eighty-six that reporter guy though. His camera gives our people a bad case of the nerves." Closing his brief case, Mann left the three packets on her table.

"Anything else?"

"Have your people at the executive terminal by three tomorrow afternoon. We've made arrangements for a private jet in your name. You'll be back in London by Sunday night."

"What about Jarred?"

"What about him?" Mann looked at her.

"How much does he know? Can I talk to him about this or is he out of the loop?"

Bob Mann pulled up short, casting an indignant brow in her direction, "Everyone in the Agency operates independently, on a need-to-know basis. He knows nothing about this mission until, or unless, a need arises."

"A need?"

"Yea. Like we have to send in a rescue mission to save your sorry hide."

Nikki shot Mann a frozen stare, challenging his off-the-cuff remark.

Mann waved his hands back and forth to negate his last statement. "Naw, this is not one of those times. Don't worry. We wouldn't jeopardize all these innocents you will be trucking along with you. All I meant was, when you receive an assignment, always assume everyone is counter-intelligence. Assemble a force of innocents as great as you need to pull off the mission, but you'd better have a believable cover story for them and a strategy covering all contingencies, including exits. The more people you include, the more babysitting your cover requires." Mann's flustration grew as he fumbled to explain, "Look kid, can you handle this or not? Jarred said you were ready!"

Nikki held her hands up, "Calm down, Bob! I'm only trying to get a handle on the internal mechanics of this Agency. Since Jarred seems to have been assigned to me, I wanted to know how close we were supposed to work. You have pretty well answered my questions. Basically I go it alone. I can handle that, just as long as I know."

"Sorry, kid. You're my first novice. I forget you haven't come up through the ranks. Jarred is your instructor to bring you up to speed on Agency techniques, that's all. The assignments are solitary operations." Mann got up to leave, then turned back to her before he reached the door. "Hey, what motivated you to ask about how many you could bring along?" He paused, "It wasn't money was it?"

"Yeah. I kind of wanted to know how much the budget would allow. That would tell me whether I should bring an accompanist or the whole bleeding band."

Mann threw his head back in uproarious laughter, "Oh, that's rich! That's too cute! Miss Moore, this is the federal government! The check is blank! Write it for as much as you want to pull off the job. Just remember you're responsible for everyone you involve." Mann paused on the doorstep of the cottage. "That's too cute. Money! Haa, haa, haa! You really made my night. See ya, kid." He shut the door with a clap.

With only eighteen hours to prepare, Nikki flew to put things together. She decided with a whole orchestra already in place, she would only take a conductor/pianist and Ben to handle whatever aesthetics for stage presence she might need. She honored Mann's request to leave Karl behind, but tapped Mary and the three-man camera crew to film shots of "Nikki in Berlin" for her variety show. Within an hour, she had lined out the logistics. Mary called Bruce to smooth over the fact Nikki had independently booked a gig at the embassy without going through him— another lesson Nikki learned and carried with her from that moment forward. In the future if the Agency wanted to mix personal appearances with their business, Mann would have to call Bruce direct, to give the appearance of going through the proper channels.

Nikki knew her apparel for the party would have to be specially designed for the mission. She needed stage splashy, yet formal and something with discreet pockets to accommodate the packets she had to distribute. Vada Knight answered her emergency call without questions. They decided on a version of a tuxedo. The blouse would actually be a barebacked halter top of silver sequins with high throat collar, complete with black bow tie. Inside the black satin jacket she'd create three pockets of specified dimensions. Black satin palazzo pants accented with silver sequins would finish off the ensemble. When Nikki mentioned she needed the ensemble by two the next day, Vada swooned, but she delivered on time.

Then Nikki memorized the thumbnail sketches and pictures of each of the three contacts. She pinned makeshift pockets inside an ordinary blazer and positioned each packet. Charles Bradley was pocket number one, top left; then followed Henry Nelson, number two, top right; and finally Peter Schaeffer, bottom right. She practiced by mentally picturing each of them and covertly reaching into the appropriate inside pocket, pulling his packet, then palming it off to him. After mastering the process in strict one, two, three order, Nikki scrambled the sequence of their appearance to make sure she pulled the right packet. She figured she could best make the transfers while dancing with them. Dancing offered the closeness of an unquestionable nature, which she needed for her surreptitious activity. Nikki also prepared for several other scenarios in case her contacts didn't dance.

Her crew mustered at the executive terminal by two. Ben had chosen Les Chatham as her accompanist because of his directorial skills. Les selected music superbly geared to an adult recital, including two radical departures for Nikki—the cabaret crowd-working number, "Fever" and the bluesy ballad "Summertime". Both songs got her off the stage and into the crowd.

They landed in time for Nikki to rehearse with the orchestra and snag a glimpse at the setup for the next evening's intimate performance. Then, grabbing the film crew, Nikki hit the nightlife in Berlin for her *Nikki Now!* show. Purposely she wrapped the filming session early so she could practice her palm-offs wearing the actual ensemble, commandeering a coat rack as her partner.

Before leaving the room, using Jarred's techniques, Nikki secured her room. If anyone tried to tamper with her room or the packets, she'd know it. Deliberately choosing the pictures hanging tightest to the wall,

Nikki hid the packets behind them. She dusted the frames well, but not obviously, with neutral body powder. No one could access the packets without disturbing the layer of dust. Finally, Nikki booby-trapped the door with innocuous lint.

Nikki's performance came off perfectly. For her encore, she descended the stage singing the bluesy ballads, stopping at tables to run a gloved hand along the jaw line of a male dignitary or two. Teasingly Nikki dipped her jacket to expose a bare shoulder, then rotated it with a seductive wiggle, while perching herself in the laps of a few more male attendees. Like a veteran, she milked the room—cabaret style—to the hoots and boisterous laughter of the guests. As she worked, she scoped out the room for her three subjects. When the crowd honored her with a standing ovation, her eye snagged two of the three targets, Nelson and Schaeffer, standing at opposite ends of the room.

The ambassador danced the first dance with Nikki, then invited everyone to join their lead. Waltzing to classical Strauss, the patrons waited to take their turn dancing with the guest of honor. With each new partner, Nikki found an excuse to move her hands at some point during the dance from his shoulder or his grasp, giving herself cover for the actual drops.

Eventually Peter Schaeffer waltzed his way into Nikki's arms. She made polite conversation with the mid-thirties gentleman as his eyes nervously darted around the room.

"It's all right," she tried to calm him, "I really don't bite."

He flinched a tenuous smile, "You have something for me?"

As Nikki had rehearsed so many times, she slipped her hand from his shoulder to the third packet, grasped it and deftly tucked it inside his coat.

"Will you please relax before you draw all suspicion to yourself?" she coached. "Now," she whispered, "politely laugh like I just told you a joke."

He stared at her, his face frozen.

"That's right," Nikki prodded with a smile, "laugh a little." She demonstrated.

Schaeffer responded as prompted.

Nikki came to realize his obvious nervousness might jeopardize his exit. "Mr. Schaeffer, I will engage you with casual conversation. Keep looking at me and respond as if we were actually having a good time." She smiled, "So, had you been a fan of mine before tonight?"

He maintained eye contact. "No, actually I hadn't really heard of you before tonight. But I assure you after this evening, I pledge to you my undying loyalty, if I make it out of here," he answered through gritted teeth.

His candor alarmed her, "You will. Don't worry. Please, relax. More. … There you go. Now, while pretending to enjoy my company — with a smile — that's it — tell me your greatest fear about tonight."

"I'm worried that someone will figure out I am carrying papers and will grab me before I can escape," he said pasty-faced.

"No one knows you have been slipped anything. But if you like, I can stay by your side a little longer."

Schaeffer nodded gratefully, "That would be wonderful."

"Okay then, when the music ends escort me to a table. I'll sit while you go to the bar for two glasses of champagne. In your absence, someone else will ask me to dance. Once I'm on the dance floor, simply ditch the glasses of champagne and work your way toward the exit. When you're in the area of the exit, I will create a small distraction so you can slip out. How does that sound?"

"Marvelous. Thank you. This is so much more than I anticipated Miss…"

"Nikki. Call me Nikki. Now laugh."

The once jittery contact calmed under her guidance. He followed the script to the last whit. Mid-way through Nikki's dance with her next partner, she raised the back of her heel and caught it in the hem of her palazzo pants. Instantly she tumbled to the ground with a small yelp. Her dance partner called for help then fell on bended knee to assist her. Within seconds, the guests milled around and security pushed though their ranks to offer their assistance. In the ensuing hubbub Schaeffer completed his exit.

In reality, Nikki's wrist broke her fall and what shock it didn't absorb, her right knee did. Nikki apologized profusely for her clumsiness. But the stinging of severely stressed ligaments ached for real, with her right shoulder burning as well. The ambassador summoned medical attention even though Nikki stridently refused.

Two security guards, with Ben at the ready, competently lifted Nikki from the floor onto a chair.

Through the gathered crowd pushed a dark-haired man. "Excuse me. I'm a doctor. Might I be of some assistance?"

Nikki looked in his direction only to come face to face with missing candidate number one, Charles Bradley. Assuming command, he issued orders to a guard. "Please evacuate the ladies' lounge."

The attending physician turned to the remaining guards, "Can you carry her to the lounge?"

"I think I can walk," Nikki protested.

"Please Miss, I would prefer you not take any chances until I can examine you.".

Bradley turned back to Ben and the guards, "Are you gentlemen ready?"

With Bradley leading the way, the guards carried Nikki into the ladies' lounge. Once inside the lounge, they positioned her on a couch. Bradley sent the guard for a first aid kit, then asked Ben to stand watch outside.

With the room cleared, rather than attend to Nikki, Bradley pulled out a pen-shaped object, which once initiated emitted a steady hum. He pointed it toward all the walls. In amazement Nikki watched as he swept the room for bugs. "Good, all clear," Bradley replied. "Let's hurry up and get this over with. You have a packet for me?"

Reaching inside her jacket, Nikki handed off packet number one.

In one continuous motion Bradley swooped the envelope up into his jacket. Then he bent down to examine her wrist, just as the door swung open.

Carrying a large metal medical case, the guard spread it open at the doctor's side.

"Thanks. That's all," Bradley dismissed him, then began ministering to Nikki.

"So Mr. Bradley, are you a real doctor or merely taking advantage of a convenient opening?" She asked as she accommodated his general inspection.

He smiled, while his dark brown eyes kept checking out the scene. "I'm not a doctor, but I played one on TV," he cracked, flashing her an impudent smile. "No, but I did three years in Nam as a medic. Let me look at that knee now." He slid her pant leg up, bending the leg and moving the joint in several directions, "Hmm. Not too bad."

"The leg or the injury?" Nikki joked.

Looking up, he beamed a white smile at her, "The injury. But the gams ain't bad either, lady. I think it may be sore when you first put pressure on it, but it doesn't seem like you tore anything inside. Okay, now let's look at that wrist."

Nikki tried to hold out her arm for examination, but the movement caused searing pain in her right shoulder. Bradley carefully picked up her wrist; already the joint appeared visibly swollen. "Wow, you did some damage there."

She winced with pain as he moved it up and down.

"I don't think you broke anything in the wrist, but you should get an X-ray to be sure. At the very least, you severely sprained it. What concerns me though is that shoulder of yours. Let me look at it." Bradley backed her left arm out of the jacket sleeve, then slid the rest of the garment over the injured right side, letting it remain immobile. He attempted to extend her arm.

Nikki stifled a cry.

"You sure did a number on this! I think when you went down you jammed your shoulder. We should ice it and your wrist until we can get you to the hospital."

Nikki looked at him. "I dislocated that shoulder some time back. It feels like it's out again. But I can't go to the hospital. I have a gig to finish."

"You've got to be kidding! With injuries like these?"

Stubbornly she nodded.

"How determined are you to finish with this bunch?"

"Very determined. I've never walked out on a gig—and I won't start now!"

He checked his watch, then looked at her. "You know, they don't give Purple Hearts for tripping on the dance floor and returning to finish the polka! You're crazy! But, lady if you're that determined, I can fix it. I have to warn you it's going to be painful when I do it, but then it will be over. Think you can you stand it?"

Nikki had no choice. She still had one envelope to deliver. "Let's do it."

Bradley went to the door. "Can you help us?" he called to Ben.

Ben followed him in and listened to his explanation of the procedure.

Horrified, Ben looked at Nikki, "Are sure you want to go through with this? No gig is worth this. We can have you to hospital in minutes. Everyone will understand."

With the strength of her conviction, she regarded Ben seriously, "Ben, a hospital will do the exact same thing as Dr. Bradley will do, except they will administer a pain killer that won't actually work. Yes. I have to do this. Please help me."

Ben positioned himself behind Nikki as Bradley had demonstrated.

Bradley opened a roll of gauze, unrolled it, then wadded it up. He looked at Nikki with sober eyes. "Ben is going to brace you. I'm going to pull on your shoulder then pop it back in place. Are you ready? It's going to hurt like hell. Here, yell into this." Without warning, he shoved the entire roll of wadded gauze into her mouth. Ben grabbed her, and Bradley pulled.

Blinding white-hot pain scorched through Nikki's shoulder. The gauze absorbed her screams. And like that, it was over. The pain subsided. Bradley immediately pulled the gauze, while Ben fetched her a drink of water.

Bradley checked Nikki again. "Are you okay? Well, let's see what we can do with your wrist." He fished through the medical case for an elastic bandage, then proceeded to wrap it. "You are as patched up as this first aid kit will allow. Let's get you to your feet and see how you react on that knee."

It ached, but as Nikki flexed it the pain ebbed. "It's going to be okay. I can walk on it. With a little touch-up on my hair and lipstick, I'll be back in business."

Bradley eyed her while she practiced walking around the lounge area. "If you've been through this before, then you know the drill about lifting things."

Nikki didn't want to hear any of his admonitions. "Did this whole episode queer your game? Are you going to be all right?" she questioned.

He let a slight laugh escape. "You think I'm a novice! Actually this will play rather well for me. I'll conveniently duck out when you make your triumphant reentry, although I had so looked forward to dancing with the indomitable Nikki. Despite the fact that I'm *persona non grata* in these parts, I thought it well worth the risk."

Nikki shot him a questioning look.

Charles Bradley answered it with a shrug of the shoulders and another flash of his pearly whites. "I'm surprised that it's taken them this long to put together that it's me attending you, rather than one of their own physicians from their tony little group. Before too much longer they'll figure it out and come looking for me."

Involuntarily the words, "who are you" started to take shape on her lips.

Bradley held up his hand. "Hold it right there, lady. Don't want to ask, what I can't answer." Nervously, he checked his watch. "It's getting a little warm in here for me. Tell you what, I'm going to hang out in the men's room until I hear the applause for your entrance, then I'm outta here. Nikki, it's been a pleasure. Save a dance for me, huh?" Bradley tipped an imaginary hat as he slipped out the door.

With Nikki's reentry, the ambassador hurried to her side to assess her condition, then called for a microphone. "Ladies and Gentlemen, Nikki returns to us. A little worse for the wear, but bravely she has consented to continue." In a sincere ovation, the people demanded a few words from her.

"I could say that you've been so warm and wonderful you really knocked me off my feet," laughter erupted. "The ambassador has asked if I'd be available for a few more turns on the dance floor? Yes, I will be. And I promise I'll stay off my partner's toes—as well as my own." More laughter. The band struck up the maudlin "When You Walk Through A Storm", which in light of her fall, Nikki satirized to the hilt.

Nikki's accident and subsequent forays into humor created a demand for personal attention from her. From out of nowhere, the notion of dancing with the fallen princess in exchange for a small contribution to her charity sprang up. Soon a line stretched around the room.

Fortunately before too long, the very unassuming, very British person of Henry Nelson stepped into her arms for a few turns around the dance floor. "You had me worried," he said through a courteous smile. "I thought I'd have to retrieve my document from an ambulance driver or doctor. Are you quite all right now? How very courageous of you to come back to make this contact." And he metered his dance steps to match Nikki's tiring gait.

Nikki melted into bed that night, too tired to ponder the faces or events of the night. Mary cancelled Nikki's schedule for the next day, arranged for the chartered jet to fly them home early, then pampered Nikki by letting her sleep until noon.

Back on British soil and as captain of her team, the rest of her group departed the airfield before Nikki's limousine arrived. When the limo door popped open, it revealed Bob Mann in the rear. Paying heed to her injuries, Nikki gingerly slid in beside him.

"You amaze me, kid," Bob crowed. "You pulled off the caper, raised your own funds and started a new career, all within a four hour span! Some day they'll write a book about you!"

"Really?" she asked quite astonished.

"No. But it would be a blockbuster. Anyway, I just wanted to tell you, good job. Results are already beginning to pour in."

"Are they what you expected? Did you catch your counter spy?"

Bob Mann tapped a cigarette on his case. "Not yet, but it will be just a matter of days now. Anyway, here's a little present." From his pocket he pulled a small box with a wrinkled ribbon strung around it.

Nikki started to undo the ribbon.

"No. Wait until later. It's no big deal. We'll be in touch. Good job, Nikki." Patting her left hand, he slid out.

Hannah greeted Nikki at the door when the limo pulled up. She handled everything, including helping her up the stairs.

Before Nikki settled into bed with a warm snifter of brandy, she wanted to open the present from Mann. Inside the plain white box sat another box, hinged, leather-coated. Inside that box rested an actual Purple Heart medal.

Nikki burst out laughing. "I guess you do get a medal for returning to finish the polka after all."

The box slid off her bed onto the floor, disassembling. Beneath the white satin-covered cardboard which held the medal, a small book fell out. "Deustche Bank" it read. Nikki opened the small book. It was a bankbook to a Swiss bank account with fifty thousand dollars credited to it. Now, that was some polka!

Chapter 24

A Matter of Inches

In the month before Christmas, Bob Mann wore out the path to Nikki's cottage. She made five unscheduled trips to the Continent for the Agency. Despite her tutoring in enhanced techniques, nothing really altered in the status of her assignments. Either they manipulated her image to divert attention, or they employed her sleight of hand with writing instruments. Twice she delivered packets from Intel. But that was all about to change and not at the hands of the Agency!

Emerging from the marble stall in the ladies room at the British Embassy in Vienna, Nikki encountered two women watching her in the mirror above the vanity. Instantly she recognized their quizzical look as they toyed with whether or not to confront her for an autograph. She'd seen it a thousand times. Nikki played a little game with herself whenever it happened. Mentally she laid bets on how long before they moved in.

She didn't track them in the mirror as she bent over the marble vanity with its gold fixtures. She knew they'd approach—she felt it. Letting her fingers linger under the water, she pushed her cuticles back while she waited for them. Nikki figured she'd turn left, reach for a towel, dry, then receive them in one smooth scripted motion. With the door in her line-of-sight, following the encounter she'd merely waltz around them to avoid being trapped.

But the pair shifted, sidling off to Nikki's right. Their calculated movements lacked spontaneity. They felt contrived, like a game of chess. "Oh well," Nikki thought. "I'm not going to play games. I'll just take the towel on the left and whisk out the door. Phooey on them if they don't have the courage..."

"Excuse me, aren't you Nikki?" One of the ladies to her right finally cooed the eternal question.

Forcing Nikki to take the towel on the right, she turned toward them, sizing them up before speaking. Their off-the-rack dresses didn't quite mesh with the rest of the *haute couture* floating around the soiree. "Sure," Nikki answered, drying.

"I told Blanche, here, it was you. You have to use the toilet like the rest of us." She fumbled in her purse, "I'd like to get an autograph for my kid." Coming up with a pen and scrap of paper, she foisted it on Nikki.

Laying down the towel, Nikki took the pen and paper. "What's your child's name?" she engaged the woman.

"Umm, it's ... uh ..."

The hairs on the back of Nikki's neck stood up. She detected some-one behind her. Before she could spin, two jacketed arms with a white cloth in its right hand reached in front of her face.

Beyond, the women watched, unfazed, without alarm.

Nikki recognized the set-up too late. In a self-defensive reaction, she threw her right elbow back to butt her attacker's chest. But forcefully the hand with a cloth full of overpowering medicine smashed it over her nose. Nikki kicked. She flailed, trying to jerk her head away from the cloth. Instinctively she held her breath, but couldn't outlast the man's strength. Inevitably she inhaled deeply. Then blackness.

Feeling woozy and nauseous, trussed up like a turkey and covered with a harsh wool blanket, Nikki gradually awoke to nighttime darkness. She lay on her side with the feeling of being in motion. Voices of two men arguing in a guttural foreign tongue jarred her into consciousness. Ultimately Nikki's wits returned. She was in the backseat of a car careen-ing recklessly down some road. Judging from the lack of streetlights, they were carting her into the countryside.

"You! Nikki person," the passenger from the front seat barked in a voice thick with an accent. "Wake up. ... You, you work for Agency."

Still foggy from the ether, her captor's statement chilled her. Stalling to discover his intentions, she moaned.

"No! Now you wake up. We have not much time. You must listen." The passenger issued a command to the driver and the car dove off the side of the road and stopped. The passenger got out, pulled open the rear door and pushed Nikki into the upholstery. Roughly he tugged at the rope binding her upper torso, loosening and removing it. Leaving her hands and feet tied, he sat her upright. Closing her door, he returned to the passenger seat. The driver spun gravel getting back on the road.

"Now, you listen. We are members of Hungarian Resistance. We know you work for Agency. You be agent."

"I don't know what you are talking about. I'm Nikki, the singer. I don't work for any Agency," Nikki denied.

"Don't waste time! We know you carry messages for Agency. Our courier from Agency was killed this night before making contact.

Resistance information must get out of Hungary to Agency. We need agent. You must help."

Listening hard, Nikki tried to weigh all her alternatives while her captor dictated his situation to her. Evidently the Resistance had their backs against a wall. Desperate, they weren't about to listen to excuses. Still, Nikki tested her parameters. "I'm only a singer. I can't help you. Please drop me off at a phone, and I will get my own way back to Vienna."

Her captor narrowed his eyes with searing intensity. "No more games! If we stop car, we throw out your dead body."

"So, what's your plan?" Nikki sighed with resignation.

"In minutes we come to place making caskets. These caskets go to Hungary tonight on humanitarian mission."

"Ja. They bury our people in them," the driver soberly interrupted.

"You ride in casket to distribution plant near Budapest. At plant, you wait for quiet then sneak into warehouse. Use staircase nearest to overhead crane house ... um, housing. Go to employee locker room in basement. Put on uniform coveralls and cap inside locker 442. Top, left pocket will have more directions."

"I don't speak or read Hungarian."

"So, too, other agent. Instructions are in English."

"What's the exit strategy? How do I get out with your information?"

"Your contact with information also have escape route."

"And do you expect me to hide in a coffin and sneak into a warehouse dressed like this?" Nikki wiggled under the blanket to indicate her evening attire.

"Clothes for you on floor of car. Give hands. I cut rope."

Clumsily Nikki maneuvered until the man in the passenger seat could reach her hands. Feeling the cold steel of the blade, Nikki hoped the driver didn't hit any bumps. Next, her captor motioned for her feet. Allies only of the moment, not through trust, the man in the passenger seat didn't turn his back on Nikki while she struggled into the heavy wool shirt and flannel lined jeans. Clunky work boots, a size too small, replaced her silk evening slippers.

Waiting near the back fence to receive Nikki, a guard sympathetic to the Resistance exchanged words in Hungarian with her captors. Before leaving her captors Nikki turned back to them. "How did you get me out past the guards at the Embassy tonight?"

Her captor shrewdly smiled. "Resistance have many friends on both sides of Iron Curtain. Is easy to believe big star drink too much." Finally he admonished, "Be successful. Many lives depend on it—including yours."

The guard separated a piece of chain-link fencing from its post, allowing Nikki to duck through the temporary breech. In stone silence, he led her to a small store of fifty coffins waiting for shipment, then stopped and pointed to one. Walking over to it, Nikki lifted the lid of the plain wooden box, climbed inside and lowered the lid. The guard's footfalls vanished in degrees.

Totally alone, abandoned to a dicey, dire fate, Nikki's situation sucked away her oxygen. Her heart's fierce pounding filled her ears. She had to still her wild breathing—gain control. She couldn't succeed if she couldn't retrieve her control. In the black void, she contemplated her options. With no one around could she make a break for it? But she had no earthly idea where she was. Was she even in Austria? She might be inside Hungary. Nikki identified the mounting odds: her disorientation, ill-fitting boots, the night, not speaking the language. No, her only way out was to play out the string and complete the mission.

Finally Nikki heard the shuffling of feet as workers came to load the coffins. Speaking gutter German, they made vulgar jokes about a woman they had passed between them. Then the forklift engine engaged, and eventually the metal forks slid underneath the coffin she rested in, scraping the wooden bottom of the casket, making a squealing sound that resonated in Nikki's teeth. The blackness of the coffin engulfed her. The vapors of the glue and the fresh-cut pine made her woozy. The unnerving sensation of vertigo blanketed her. Nikki assumed she still lay on her back because of the rough-hewn boards poking her, but in the total darkness, she couldn't be sure. Then movement. She struggled to stay still, to fight against the free-fall feeling of no control. Nikki thought she'd vomit. She came to rest with a jerk on what could have been a loading dock. Before long she moved again. With great sliding and banging, they loaded her casket into a truck. Her head smashed against the unforgiving hard wood as the truck set off into the night.

The coffin wasn't airtight, but imagining the weight of all the other caskets around her pushed the walls in on Nikki. She fought against the feeling of not enough air. Recognizing her predicament as a mental war she must win, Nikki resisted the temptation of feeling the coffin walls and further defining the extent of her confinement.

Nikki conjured up the mental image of laying on her bed at home—the wide-open expanse of her room—the comfort of her bed—Alexander and Christmas at *Creekside*. In agonizing detail, she delineated every minute aspect of the celebration. She traced the lines in her father's face as he solemnly bowed his head to ask the blessing over supper. She focused on the sweet smile of her mother with her warm brown eyes reflecting her full heart as she doted on her brood in the twirl of the holidays. Nikki concentrated on the firelight playing with the gold in Alexander's hair as the flames danced with the sparkle of his incredible blue eyes. She pretended the bumps on the road were the thumps of the saddle as she and Alex rode through the woods. They came to the lake with its peaceful waves lapping up against the shore. The sun dazzled across the water, a light breeze caressed her face, songs of birds flying free filtered down to her.

Crash! Her head smashed against the wood coffin. They had stopped.

Plainly Nikki heard a forceful "Halt!" shouted out in a man's voice. "We must be crossing over the border," she thought. The guards' voices reported out gruff and aggressive; the driver's softly placating. Eventually, the guards escalated to angry shouts as they insisted on opening the truck and checking each coffin in the load.

Fear made Nikki swallow her breath, beating back panic.

The truck doors squawked as the guards forced them open. Amid muffled protests of the driver, they hauled out the stacked coffins, banging them down on the ground. Carelessly they threw open the lids, then slammed shut the empty boxes. Nikki had no idea where her casket rested in the scheme of fifty. But with each one, the sounds got closer and closer.

Smash! Another hit the ground, wood splintered. The driver complained. The guards answered him with the cool, smooth, slide-clink of their weapons locking and loading. Manufacturing intimidation, they toyed with the driver's fear.

Wood screeched as they unloaded the stack of coffins to her immediate right.

Nikki prayed.

Careless in pulling them out, they banged them against the side of hers. One. "Eeeech," the boards complained as they dragged out another. Two. This time she felt the vibrations in the walls of her coffin. Three. They started on her stack. One more to go, she was next.

With discovery imminent, Nikki racked her mind for an explanation. Frantically she ran over possible excuses to explain her presence in a shipment of caskets. Drawing only blanks, she willed herself past her mental roadblock, to think. She must think!

"Eeersch," the casket above her dragged across hers. Her coffin walls shuddered. Nikki tried not to think about the guards, the guns, the consequences. No, don't think about the consequences, work on that alibi.

Squealing tires accompanied by resolute slams of vehicle doors brought new voices to the night air. They barked quick demands as vigorous, deliberate footsteps approached. Nikki didn't understand the voices, but they neutralized the terrorizing rancor of the guards, who now whimpered to their commands. Within seconds came the clackity-clack clatter of weapons butting into each other, as they were thrown down into a pile on the ground. Now more sliding wood, at a faster pace, but with a gentler, smoother attitude. One after the other, the guards hastily slid the caskets back into place. Nikki drew in a breath and released a measured sigh of relief.

In minutes the gears of the truck ground to life; they were on their way down the road again. The close call drained her. Nikki relaxed inside the safety of her casket, grateful now to be there.

Fatigue from the flood of adrenaline brought on by her near-miss pushed Nikki to sleep, but she soon woke with the thud of another stop. Once again the doors of the truck squealed open, then came the sound of wood surfaces sliding, one upon the other. This time the voices came filtered through the rhythm of cooperative, energetic grunts, like a well-oiled machine. Quickly each casket slid out of place, without the whirring of a forklift. On this side of the border, workers unloaded each casket by hand. Surely when they came to hers, they'd feel the weight of her body. Again she prayed.

Once again the caskets on top of hers slid off, then hers. In unloading, they scraped her casket along the grit of the truck bed, sending jarring vibrations coursing through Nikki's body. Unable to easily slide off the cargo because of her weight, the workers called for assistance. Nikki winced in anticipation of discovery. Oh, dear God! They lifted the coffin off the truck. Despite trying to steady herself, with their steps she rocked back and forth inside as they carried the casket. Inevitably her coffin came to a rest on the ground. Holding her breath, she waited for them to open the lid and expose her. But the men simply left hers on the ground and continued on with the task of unloading the remaining coffins. Nikki stayed put until they finished their task and the night went quiet again. Either they knew about her concealed presence in the cargo, or the oppressive conditions of the country curtailed their curiosity.

Lying in place for a calculated measure of time, Nikki flexed her muscles, coaxing them back to life. Then slowly she pushed against the lid to check out her surroundings. It took a moment for her eyes to adjust to even the marginal amount of light. With the coast clear, Nikki climbed out, fleeing to the warehouse.

Minimal lighting lit the inside of the warehouse. Well past midnight, the skeleton night crew was arriving. Sticking to the small aisles in the shadows of the large steel storage racks, Nikki matched her pace to that of the other workers headed for work. Downstairs she found locker 442, slipped the canvas coveralls over her jeans and flannel shirt and tucked her hair up inside the cap. For privacy she went in the bathroom to read the note. Once inside a stall, Nikki swept the john for cameras, then she opened the paper from the breast pocket.

The note detailed the plan and translated both the sign and counter-signs then spelled them out phonetically in Hungarian. "Go to the loading dock. Begin sweeping with broom. While sweeping, hum theme from Tchaikovsky's *Sleeping Beauty.*

"A man will approach you and ask in Hungarian, 'Where did you learn that American song?'

"You answer, 'It's not American its Russian.'"

"To which he will respond, 'Of course it is.'"

"Follow him. When you finish reading note, flush it down toilet." Practicing her lines, Nikki read the note twice before tossing it in. Instantly the water washed the paper completely clean before it disappeared into the sewer system.

Nikki avoided eye contact as she encountered workers on her way to the warehouse floor. This time, in uniform, she walked the main aisles. At the loading dock, she found the broom and began her sweeping and humming. Several workers eyed her nervously.

One poked Nikki and hissed at her from under her breath. Her hollow eyes simmered with a mixture of fear and anger.

Pushing the broom to another area of the floor, Nikki stubbornly kept up her humming. Before long a finger insolently pecked her on her shoulder. Nikki turned to find a man glaring down at her, his arms crossed over his chest. Angrily he asked her the question from the paper. Nikki shook her head, quietly answering with the printed reply. Giving the counter, the man grabbed the broom from her, motioning for her to follow him. Bowing her head, she fell in behind him. The woman, who had hissed at Nikki earlier, shoved her as she walked by as if to insinuate, "see I told you so."

The embittered supervisor verbally lashed Nikki as she followed. Desperately she hoped he indeed was her contact. Flinging the door open to a sparsely furnished office, he stood back, ordering her into the room. Nikki obeyed, realizing that if she had misread the situation or if this man was the one who had uncovered and killed the other agent, this confined office space offered no mercy and no hope of escape. He followed her inside, closing the door behind him, throwing the bolt of the lock solidly in place.

For an agonizingly long moment, they stared at each other. Then in a hushed voice he started in broken English, "You took long to get here! We are worried!" With an abbreviated smile he said, "I am Yoseph. Glad you made it."

"So am I," Nikki said through a sigh of relief. "What do you have for me?"

"We have files, names and pictures of double agents. All information moles gave to other side. These files document compromised codes, agents and projects. You must get these to Michael Junger at Budapest embassy."

Then came a loud rap at the door followed by a man's gruff voice, "Yoseph! Yoseph!"

Their eyes met in terror. The wrong person on the other side of that door meant they both could be shot where they stood. Under his breath Yoseph ordered Nikki, "Quickly! Strip to yur waist!"

"Ja?" He called back.

Nikki answered Yoseph with a stare of disbelief.

"Ja! Strip! Do it! Hurry!" the veins in Yoseph's forehead bulged as he spit his deadly-serious command at her.

Immediately she obeyed, exposing herself.

"Yoseph!"

"Ja! Ja!" Yoseph answered with pretended impatience.

"Stand with your back towards door. Get rid of cap." He ripped the hat from her head unleashing the long black tresses down her back. From out of nowhere, he let his open hand fly and smacked Nikki hard against her cheek. On the back swing, he landed a blow above her left breast. "Forgive me," followed the blows that raised red welts in their wake. He undid his belt and unzipped his pants, then answered the door holding them up, barely covering his private area.

"Ja!" Yoseph's foot held the door ajar allowing the intruder a view of the situation. Instinctively Nikki knew the image she telegraphed would determine her fate. She stood taller and more focused than a victim, but not tall enough to imply she enjoyed the action and wanted more. Yoseph had slapped her for effect. Nikki turned enough for the intruder to witness the abused flesh. The two spoke the universal masculine language of virility with ribald laughs liberally punctuating their speech. Yoseph had to be convincing enough to get the man to give them their privacy, but not so good that the animal on the other side insisted on making it a threesome. Yoseph tugged at his pants in his hand, indicating that he wanted to get back to business. The man stuck his head in for a better look, then slapped Yoseph on the back on his way out the door. He departed with a carnal howl. Yoseph slid the bolt back into the lock.

"Please, fix yourself," Yoseph whispered with his back to her for privacy. As Nikki dressed, she heard the clink of his belt buckle as he fastened his pants. Next, his zipper yipped into place, but he remained with his back to her.

"It's okay, Yoseph," Nikki said when she finished. "You can turn around now."

Nikki took him for a modest family man. "I am sorry. I must convince."

"It's okay. Your fast thinking saved us. Now, where's the information?"

"Snow outside will take down swelling," he offered.

"Yes. I will try some. But first, we must get those files and get me out of here."

"Ja. Follow me to laundry. You hide in outgoing laundry cart. At bottom of the cart, I put briefcase with files. Box of laundry truck is separate from cab. Overalls are counted. You must leave yours in cart. Truck will have its journey interrupted. Get out while drivers judge situation. Run, hide in woods. In five minutes, a silver Mercedes will arrive. Driver will help the men in laundry truck. While they clear road, get into Mercedes. Lay down on backseat floor. You will be safe."

Without words, Yoseph led Nikki to the laundry where he hid her in the appropriate laundry cart. Nikki quickly squeezed his hand good-bye before hunkering down underneath a bin full of coveralls that reeked of sweat and toil. Within the half-hour, two men loaded the bins into the truck. Once again, she was cargo.

The plot unfolded just as Yoseph detailed. A fallen tree blocking the road arrived on cue. As instructed, she dashed into the woods to wait for her next ride. When the Mercedes stopped to help the truckers clear the path, Nikki scrambled from the shadows into the waiting car, pressing herself into the rear seat foot-well.

Eventually the car's driver returned to his seat, put the car in gear and started off. For safety's sake, she remained on the floorboards of the car, until a smug voice came from the front. "Are you sleeping back there or just being anti-social?"

Nikki pushed herself up, "No, just being careful."

The driver's intense brown eyes watched her in the rear view mirror.

"Maybe you are so used to being chauffeured you can't sit up in front with me?"

She wasn't sure she appreciated his tone. "No. I was just following instructions. How do you suggest I get up there? You don't want me to climb over the seat do you?"

With a small laugh he replied, "No. I guess a lady doesn't vault over the upholstery, does she?" Pulling to the side of the road, he got out and came back to open the door behind his seat.

Just to be contrary, Nikki opened the passenger side door and switched around without his help. Once settled, an astonished Nikki discovered her driver to be none other than Charles Bradley, her attending physician from the Berlin embassy. He picked up on her recognition of him. "I see you are getting around much better than when last we met. It must have been the excellent doctoring you received."

"You know what they say? *Time* is the great healer of all wounds," she sassed.

Then he exchanged his conceited attitude for one of concern, "You've had a long night. If you're hungry, there's a thermos of coffee and a bag of pastry on the seat behind you."

"Oh great!" she spiritedly chided him as she retrieved the bag. "You might have mentioned them while I was back there."

A smile returned to his voice, "Geez! I hope you didn't crush them while you were down there playing secret agent."

"Well if I did, then you get the flattest one for putting them in harm's way."

They ate while traveling through the countryside, passing the thermos between them. As dawn broke up ahead, they swapped the stories they could tell about their lives.

Besides the food, the thoughtful Mr. Bradley had included a kit with some toiletries so she might clean off some of the "dirt from the road," as he put it. Nikki brushed out her hair, but when she went to put it up in a bun, the morning light exposed the strawberry on her face. That raised Bradley's concern, so she let her hair fall back long on her shoulders and brushed off the welt with a casual dismissal, "a hazard of the trade."

Bradley's retort stunned her, "Yes, but a woman such as yourself shouldn't be in this trade and should never have to endure that." He fumed silently, centering himself on the task of driving in an effort to reduce his ire.

Nikki asked if they might stop alongside the road so she could brush her teeth using some of the now cold coffee. Instead, he gallantly pulled off at a farmhouse on the way. Using his cash he bought her some toilet time. "Take as much time as you need. They can just cool their heels in Budapest."

Waiting impatiently, Junger paced the carpeted embassy halls in anticipation of their arrival. All business, he greeted them hotly, "Where in the hell have you been, Bradley?"

Bradley refused to knuckle under, "Excuse me, sir. Didn't anyone point out that in our business the trains don't always run on time? Furthermore, this poor lady has been through hell and back, including being abducted, then being handed off no less than nine times in the past eighteen hours. With that much human contact, it's a miracle she got here before midnight tonight! And while you're at it, Mike, take a look at her face. Show a little compassion!" Charles Bradley expelled his pent-up exhaust.

Rearranging his attitude, Junger politely inquired about Nikki's injury, then substituted an excuse for an apology. "We were very worried about you, especially since you were never cleared for this duty. Then the delivery truck encountered those unforeseen problems at the border." They talked as he escorted them to a private study.

Behind the closed door, Nikki turned over the briefcase full of documents while Bradley continued with Junger, "By the way, Mike, thanks for that quick service with those secret police IDs. They turned the trick for us at the border with those goons."

Stunned, Nikki looked at him, "That was you who saved me at the border?"

A smile formed around his eyes, "A friend of mine really pulled off the caper. I just went along for the ride. But yes, after losing one agent tonight, then having you forced into this mission, we had to back you any way possible. You had important business to complete. We couldn't let some overzealous gorillas abort the plans, now could we?"

Charles Bradley secured a room for Nikki in the ambassador's residence so she could get a hot shower, a meal and a nap along with a change of clothes before they returned her to London. He escorted her to the quarters, while Junger and the staff poured over the cache of files. As Charles closed the door on the room before he rejoined the others, Nikki asked him to thank Ambassador Junger for the use of his facilities.

With that, Bradley stepped back inside, gently shutting the door behind him. He wrinkled his face, "Ambassador Junger, that's a new one. Where did you get that idea?"

"From our last meeting in Vienna over the summer. At that time he was the ambassador to Austria. I suppose the State Department's shuffled positions since then."

Bradley smiled broadly, "He must have used it as a cover. He's no ambassador. Michael Junger is the Chief Agency Administrator in Europe. He came here to check up on you. He likes your work. You've acquired quite a reputation at the Agency. I suspect after last night you'll own the number one female spot of the technical agents."

"You're kidding! There's a pecking order? I had no idea there was any… I never meant to…," Nikki stammered.

"To what? Gain a reputation? None of us do. It comes with the territory. It's called saving your own skin."

"But I'm not doing this to…"

"To go for the glory? Then why are you in it?" he stood there considering her.

"To serve my country."

"Oh, puleeze!" he derided.

But Nikki didn't acquiesce to his derision.

"Really?" Bradley arched his eyebrows in reassessment.

"Isn't that the way you got in to it?" she challenged.

Now Bradley considered his motives, "Yea, I guess in the beginning it was."

"And now?"

"Now it's the money, honey. And the exhilaration of always being on the edge. … And you? Why do you really do it?"

"I still do it because they tell me with my international profile, I am doing what no one else can. And because they still desperately need my services."

Bradley wagged his head with disappointment, "Oh, I see."

Nikki didn't know how to deal with Bradley's seeming dissatisfaction with her answer. "So, where are you in this Agency food-chain, Charles?"

"I have no idea. It doesn't really matter to me," he tossed off.

She laughed, "I don't believe that, or you wouldn't have been keeping track."

With that Bradley reached for the doorknob.

Too punch drunk to fall down, Nikki didn't want him to go yet, "Do you know who the number one male is?"

"You mean the real heavyweight? The guy who pulls off the impossible? Funny you should ask. For only a matter of inches, you could have met him tonight, if you hadn't been otherwise indisposed in a casket at the time."

"You mean he was there?" her eyes widened. "I was in that much trouble?"

Stunned by his careless revelation of the icy reality, Bradley, for a split second, made direct eye contact, then averting his eyes, he answered with a shrug, "Sometimes he just shows up for the hell of it. You know, when he has nothing better to do. On really slow nights, like last night, it's better to have him out chasing coffee than sitting around doing nothing for his extraordinarily exorbitant salary."

Nikki recognized his curve-ball distraction, "So, who is this super-man anyway?"

Charles batted a tsk, tsk, at her. "How long have you been around? You know I can't answer that. Why don't you get some sleep?" he said in hopes of extricating himself from her prying as he opened the door.

"Wait!" She called him back in her quest to verify her suspicions about Junger. "What about Junger's daughter? How's she these days?"

Charles shook his head, "Where'd you get your information? Junger, like most of us, is married to the Agency; there's no wife, no daughter. Can I go now or are you going to continue this game of twenty questions?"

"Only one more, Charles. If Junger's so high up in the Agency, how can you talk to him the way you did down there?"

"Because I don't back down from anything or anyone, especially in this business. That's my edge and why I'm the outcast. But you look at who they call when they need follow-through. Besides, if they don't like it, they can always fire me." Satisfied, a grin broke out across his face. "But as you've noticed, I'm still here."

After every assignment the balance in Nikki's little Swiss account grew, one hundred thousand, three hundred thousand, then six, always multiplying. For the Hungarian Coffin Caper the Agency handsomely endowed Nikki with "hazard pay," probably out of embarrassment because they failed to run interference for her at the Embassy in the first place. Or, maybe out of desperation, they went with whatever plan the Resistance hatched. No matter, she tossed the bankbook into the back of a drawer and stopped looking at it. The money hardly compensated.

Chapter 25

Christmas

Nikki arrived home from her Hungarian side-trip on Christmas Eve morning in time to meet the delivery man carrying a beautiful wreath of pine boughs trimmed with waxy, white gardenias, clumps of holly berries and a lush red velvet bow. Its note read: "Merry Christmas, darling. Just two more days! Love, A."

Since she'd celebrate several days later at *Creekside*, Nikki hadn't planned on any festivities in Britain. But her little business family wouldn't hear of that. All of the family-less from their group banded together for their own celebration. Capping off the holiday meal, they stood around the piano with mugs of cheer, laughing and singing lusty versions of revered old Christmas carols. The gifts Nikki received from her compatriots reflected her movie role—a bottle of invisible ink and a plastic secret de-coder ring. How ironic their gag gifts mirrored her secret life.

Scores of studio people invaded her cottage the day after Christmas to prepare her for her movie debut. Vada unpacked the costume she had dreamed up for the premiere. The neckline on the skintight, black leather cat-suit plunged practically to her navel. Vada had also prepared a sheer body stocking, with push-up cups for her breasts, since every little bump and panty line translated through the second-skin suit. A single strand of rhinestones adorned the suit as a belt slung below her waist and caught on her hipbones. Three strands of diamonds in varying lengths dripped from diamond studs for her earrings. But, the *coup de grâce* was the diamond necklace—on loan—complete with pedigree and two armed escorts from Lloyds. The forty-carat solitaire would dangle provocatively above the cleft of Nikki's bosom.

As she slipped into the suit, Vada gasped at the red welt above her breast. "I thought the one on your cheek was from walking into a door. You want to tell me about this?" she challenged her.

"No!" Nikki iced, staring her down.

"Okay dearie, it's your business. Let's just put some pancake over them so poor Bruce doesn't have a conniption." With an artist's touch she troweled the masque onto the affected areas, then feathered it into the surrounding skin. "There, this should get us past the camera and Bruce." Vada scrutinized the entire package. "Ooo, can't forget these." She pulled black leather, mid-calf, cuffed boots from a box, adorned with rhinestone anklets and shortened French heels.

Nikki surveyed them with curiosity. "I would have thought stiletto heels would have enhanced the neckline's drama. Why so short?"

"Dear Steve's not so tall, don't ya know. His studio doesn't want you towering over him," Vada tattled.

Under Vada's supervision, the hair stylist teased Nikki's hair into fits of spiraled curls. The manicurist fitted her with bright red sculptured nails, sparkling with diamonds at the tip of each index finger.

Her reflection in the hall mirror startled Nikki. She didn't recognize the image, but brushed it off with a shrug as just another of the characters to be played.

An hour before their departure, a photographer snapped publicity shots of Nikki provocatively mugging from inside the cat-suit with the diamond and a Beretta. Adding to the melee, the ever-present video crew filmed it all for *Nikki Now!* The entire show tickled Bruce. As she walked past him on the stoop, Nikki stopped, dragged a red acrylic index nail across his jaw line, then held his chin on her finger. "Only because you begged so nicely," she purred. And Nikki planted a spunky ripe kiss on his lips. Blushing, he rubbed his mouth to remove the red impression. The video crew caught it for her private collection.

Eleven blocks from the hysteria of the theatre, Steve McQueen joined the entourage. In old double-standard form, he was dressed in a regular issue tuxedo while she was stuck in the cat getup. Wearing him on her arm, they stepped out of the limo amid the searchlights to the popping flashbulbs. The media focused on Nikki. Although with his irresistible smile, Steve also charmed his share of attention from the press on the red carpet.

All in all, the film played well—not Oscar material, not a flop either. Lloyds retrieved their diamond after Nikki's mandatory appearance at the post-premiere party. Blessedly by midnight, she slid into the limousine and Alexander's arms.

Alexander chortled with unbridled amusement, "My, my, don't we look purr-fect. I am not sure whether to kiss you or scratch you behind the ears."

"Me-ow!" she playfully retaliated. "Rather than a kiss, shall I unleash these on you?" Nikki held up her red-painted daggers.

"Ye-ow! Bruce was going for a look, wasn't he?"

Once home, she peeled herself out of the leather suit, Nikki washed cat-woman down the shower drain, but then carefully re-camouflaged the welt by her eye. No need to worry the innocent. For the long plane ride to

Pennsylvania, she eased into comfortable jeans and a cuddly cable-knit
sweater. Now she could embrace her love.

"I have a bit of a surprise for you," Alexander confessed on their ride
to the airport. "You must know how much I detest the inconvenience of
commercial airlines. So I bought a jet for my travels."

Somehow the extravagance of his purchase surprised Nikki.

"This is the largest Lear they make. I want us to be comfortable."

Pulling into the expanded executive section of Heathrow, the lights
in the hangar gleamed off the sleek, white-body fuselage of Alex's acqui-
sition, making the hangar a beacon in the night. On the nose of the jet,
below the pilot's window, graceful gold script lettering read, *Wings of
Nevermore*.

Alexander introduced her to his private pilot, Reed Dawson. The
seasoned Korean War veteran presented Alexander with a bottle of champagne. After popping the cork, Alex handed the gushing bottle to Nikki.
"Darling, would you christen the craft for her maiden flight?"

Alex had designed the interior salon himself. He replaced the traditional two rows of seats with four sumptuous, cream-colored leather
recliners. A wall with a door screened off the section containing a sofa,
which unfolded into a full-sized bed across the back. Of course the jet
included a small, functional galley and a lavatory. A light meal with a
chilling bottle of Cristal waited on board.

Clearing the hangar, Reed fired up the engines, maneuvering down
the tarmac. Alex reached across the aisle to take Nikki's hand, as he
always did for all take-offs and landings. A full-throttle roar of the jets
sent them hurtling down the runway. With her nose to the wind and flaps
scooping up air, Wings proudly lifted off.

Chasing the dawn, they touched down in Reading at eight, the
morning of December 27th. As the couple swung into the driveway of
Creekside, Beau lifted his head from his spot on the stoop's sun-warmed
bricks. Let Christmas begin!

With cookies and cups of brandied eggnog, the family settled in front
of the tree and the fire to exchange presents. Alex gave Fran and Richard
the presents from him. Nikki gave her mom and dad theirs, then she
handed Alex his present, an actual sidearm used by Washington in the
Revolutionary War. Everyone opened their gifts and made the appropriate gestures of gratitude. With that, the gift exchange came to an abrupt
halt. Nikki had received nothing!

She tossed out a few hints about the lopsided exchange, but no one
noticed. Her mother droned on about the clogged stores and rude clerks
over the holiday. Her dad expounded at length about the bells and whis-

tles on the new Mercedes he had just purchased. Of course, Richard's new car piqued Alex's interest.

Nikki's dad proposed a test ride in his new wheels. Having nothing better to do—like opening presents—Nikki begrudgingly put on her coat and went along.

In the driveway, her father tossed Alex the keys, "Want to try her out?"

Without hesitation, Alexander slid behind the wheel. Richard rode shotgun while Fran and Nikki sat in the back. Adjusting the rear view mirror, Alex focused in on Nikki, snagging her with a dazzle of his blue eyes. "Ready darling?"

"You bet," she answered with a twinge of bratty sarcasm.

Alexander put the car through its paces on the valley's curvy roads, hugging the hub of the turns, then accelerating out of them. Richard approved. Eventually Alex pulled off the pavement onto a rutted, overgrown dirt path and stopped. Nikki couldn't believe he chose to stop—at *Nevermore*!

"Have you ever seen this place?" he asked Nikki's parents. "Nicole and I found it on one of our rides last summer. Come on. It is pretty run down, but it has some interesting features. Watch your step."

Everyone bailed out of the car.

Nikki shot Alexander a look. How could he bring others to their special place!

Correctly he read her glare. "I know, darling. But I am so excited, what with being here, and you, and Christmas, and all, that I am afraid I got carried away. Forgive me." He pecked a kiss on her cheek to atone for his exuberance. Throwing his arm around her shoulders in a hug of exceeding flippancy, he urged Nikki on faster to catch up with her parents.

The tall grasses and wild flowers of summer had disintegrated into the brittle brush of December. *Nevermore* sprawled from one barren tree-lined border to the other barren tree-lined border, exposing the vast amount of rolling land in her dilapidated domain. Nearly naked, the massive old stone home took center stage, the brave sentinel of the estate.

Winter changed the house at *Nevermore*. Its mouth yawned wide open; someone had ripped the front door from its hinges. As they approached, Nikki noticed a sheet of paper stabbed onto the jamb. Alexander saw it too and ran ahead. Snatching it down, he scanned the printing. "No!" Alex exclaimed. "Can you believe it! This old place has been sold!" He dropped the paper to his side in disappointment.

Running up to him, Nikki grabbed up the piece of paper. Sure enough the top line read, "Deed of Sale." Her heart sank. How could they sell *Nevermore*? She read on. Who had stolen her dream? But something wasn't right. How did her name get tangled up in all the legalese? Nikki couldn't make sense of it. What did the buyer want with her? She looked to Alexander, for an explanation.

He stood alongside her mom and dad. With everyone wearing wide smiles, they sang out, "Surprise!"

"Merry Christmas, darling!" Alex proudly proclaimed, bursting at the seams.

Nikki didn't comprehend what the Merry Christmas was all about. Not when *Nevermore* was gone!

Joyfully, Alexander took the deed and showed her the line giving her title to the property. "It is my Christmas present to you. *Nevermore* is yours! Let's take a look."

"*Nevermore...?*"

"is yours." Alex kissed Nikki and carried her over the threshold.

Nikki's eyes swept the room as she tried to let the enormity of it all sink in.

Setting her down, Alexander wrapped his arms around her. "When will this house be lonely and desolate again?" he asked.

"*Nevermore*," she answered.

He kissed her again. She looked over his shoulder at her magnificent present, from inside his hug, still trying to believe it.

Richard and Fran took off wandering through the drafty halls, then called for the couple to come on the double.

They found them in one of the back rooms. Richard started, "Alex and Nicole, this is our Christmas present to you." They stepped aside to reveal a beautiful walnut, six-panel door with an old black-iron door-knocker. "Merry Christmas!" they chimed.

Nikki's mom brought in a picnic basket she had secreted in the trunk. "I thought we might have lunch in your new home."

Over Chardonnay and sandwiches Alex explained, "Remember last summer when your father and I disappeared for a day? Well, our real mission was to execute the purchase of this property. Since then I've lined up Gus Schubert, a friend of mine, who is also employed by the same company as I am. He runs one of their reconstruction teams. Besides being a master craftsman, I trust him. Your father found a landscape architect, while your mother has hired a decorator who specializes in local history. All of whom will show up here within minutes to help you re-make *Nevermore* any way you want. It's yours, darling."

They had all conspired to set her up. How Nikki relished the love they shared.

However, Nikki's eyes glazed over with the construction details like headers and dry rot. Gladly she left the mechanics of the construction to Gus and her father's capable hands. While with the designer, Nikki and her mom selected chandeliers, wood finishes, wall colors, everything necessary to turn the house into her home.

The renovation plans ate up the daylight hours of their three days at *Creekside*, but at night everyone put away the blueprints. Hours passed as the family laughed and told stories around the table. After surviving Hungary, Nikki quietly thanked God for letting her experience this.

Most nights she and Alex stayed up late after her parents retired, sipping wine in front of the fire, planning their return trip to Pennsylvania and their move to *Nevermore*.

On their last day, thick gray clouds swallowed up the sun. Snow, in huge white fluffy feathers, blanketed the landscape. Nikki couldn't wait to see *Nevermore* under its white shawl. Alexander snuggled with her inside *Nevermore's* living room as they watched the flakes fall outside. Listening to the solitude, they swayed to the music in their hearts, then waltzed across the living room to the snow's grand harmony.

The morning of New Year's Eve, Reed Dawson charted a course for Vail. Years earlier Alex had purchased land in the fledgling ski-community, sight unseen, as a favor to a friend. Now, besides skiing, Alexander wanted to see his investment.

He secured a suite of rooms on the ground floor, mountainside, for them. They spent the remaining daylight hours acquainting themselves with the town and shopping for all the ski paraphernalia Nikki could possibly need.

Alexander ordered a candlelit supper to be served in his room. In honor of New Year's they dressed for dinner; he in black-tie, Nikki in forest-green velvet and pearls. On his private terrace, they watched flaming necklaces crisscross the face of the slope, as skiers with torches descended the hill in a magnificent pageant of light.

"I find it hard to believe it was only a year ago tonight that I stood alone on my balcony in Hong Kong watching the fireworks explode over the harbor, missing you desperately," Alexander mused.

"And what a stir you created in the Moore household that night with the bottle of champagne all the way from Hong Kong!"

"It has been quite a year for us, darling. I started 1967 thinking we had something special together. Then the next time I saw you, you let me have it with both barrels."

"I'm glad you turned out to be so persuasive, or who knows where I might be standing tonight."

"How well I know! At this very moment you could have been in the arms of that Swiss javelin thrower or maybe some gorgeous movie star."

Alex sobered. "No, Nicole. Your little temper tantrum couldn't have changed my heart. I would have been compelled to try again. And again. You are the sun in my universe. Your light is the reason I get up every day. I cannot imagine life without you. And here we stand a mere year later engaged, the rest of our lives stretching ahead of us. *Te amo*, Nicole. *Te amo!*" Then his lips consumed hers.

The next morning, invigorated by the promise of a new year, Alexander knocked on her door carrying a tray with their breakfast. Nikki couldn't cap the excitement bubbling up inside her—a new year to begin together and her first day on the slopes! Wearing her skin-tight stretch ski pants and turtleneck, she met Alex with giggles.

Proudly she pirouetted before him, demonstrating her outfit.

"Darling, I think I am going to be very sorry that I won't be the one taking advantage of this exquisite view today. You are a vision in your navy and white. Maybe I should stay with you for your lessons."

Nikki brushed his lips with a kiss. "Wait until tomorrow. You'll like that outfit better. I saved the best for when we ski together."

Nikki also spent a long moment appreciating how Alex's black ski pants detailed the musculature of his strong legs and thighs. The red and black snowflake print of his sweater across his upper torso accentuated the width of his shoulders. She found him incredibly sexy, almost too good to pass up. Their good-morning kisses could have lasted into the night, but the first day of skiing waited.

Both had agreed Nikki would spend her first day in ski school—a far better arrangement than testing the extent of Alex's patience. Once Alexander entrusted her into the care of her private instructor, he skied off towards the lift to the mountaintop with their pilot.

Endowed with handsome Nordic features, Erik, Nikki's instructor, resembled an Olympian. She listened as he patiently explained their goals for the day.

"Baby steps. Everything comes in baby steps," Erik reminded her. Nikki didn't understand how such an indistinguishable incline as that of the bunny hill, when viewed from the bottom, could rise up to rival Everest when she stood at its summit. But it did. Swallowing hard, Nikki pushed off from the summit. Her instructor's immortal words hung on the air behind her. "Wedge! Wedge!"

With all her heart and every muscle in her legs, Nikki wedged. But even from her wedged position, she flew. Down the hill she blazed in a blinding blur. Her heart raced. Her adrenaline pumped. With unbridled exhilaration, Nikki flew!

The euphoria of accomplishment engulfed her. She did it! She lived! "More!" she shouted in her frosty breath. "I want to do it again!"

Bitten by the addictive serum of the ski bug, all she wanted was more!

The afternoon brought the normal setbacks—but mightily Nikki forged ahead to the intermediate hills. By late afternoon, Nikki stood on the catwalk at the headwall above her first intermediate blue hill. The steepness of the run gripped her. The temperature outside had nothing to do with her frozen mental attitude.

Erik skied to her. "This can't be giving you pause. Not the fearless Nikki."

Her breath caught in her throat. She couldn't see the bottom. "It's so steep."

"Mental attitude is everything. If you're not ready, we can take the catwalk down to the easy portion of the hill and ski back to the lodge from there. No harm in returning tomorrow."

Tomorrow? Tomorrow, Nikki wanted to ski with Alex. Determination seized her. Her inexperience wasn't going to confine them!

Erik saw it in her eyes. "Take a deep breath and yell with me, 'Here we go! Here we go!'" He took off, his voice trailing him.

With a mighty push and a yell, Nikki too sailed over the headwall. Following in Erik's tracks, she ended the run by spraying him with snow. The hill dared her to challenge it again, and this time, Nikki didn't hesitate at the headwall.

Laughing and reliving moments of their day, Erik walked Nikki into the lodge to meet Alexander for drinks. Roses, baskets and baskets of claret-red roses, filled the lounge where Alex stood casually propped up against a booth engaged in conversation with the other patrons. Her entrance prompted their applause.

Erik leaned over to her. "Looks like someone is proud of you."

Alex met Nikki with a glass of champagne and a kiss. "To my Nicole. May your toes stay warm, may you always have fresh powder and, unlike in the theater, may you never, ever break a leg."

Alexander introduced Nikki to the roomful of his new acquaintances. The magic time of *aprés ski* lasted only about two hours before everyone disbanded to ready themselves for dinner.

Dressed in ski attire designed for nightlife, not the slopes, Alexander and Nikki walked down to the Edelweiss Haus where they joined Reed for dinner. True to old German form, singing, toasting and hearty revelry accompanied the meal.

After dinner Alex hired a horse-drawn sleigh for a starlight tour of the village of Vail beneath a waxing moon. Bundling together under the lap robe, Alex wrapped his arm around her. A light flurry of snow fell, sticking to their hair and clinging on their eyelashes. When they came to vast open spaces leading up to the base of the mountain, Alex called for the driver to stop.

"What do you think, Nicole? This is part of my holdings here." Alex spread his free arm to vaguely indicate the size of his property that they viewed.

"All this?" she asked, straining to find the boundaries.

"To the base of the mountain and more. It goes farther. I'll show you in the daylight."

"And you've never seen this before?"

"No, not until today. But I am pleased." An enthusiastic glow turned up the corners of his eyes.

"You have plans for this, don't you?" Nikki noted.

"I think we should do something with it. I am not certain what. It is too big for just a house, maybe condos, maybe a hotel." His smile broadened into a grin. "Maybe a grand Vincente Hotel, in the style of my grandfather's hotels. We would build it to harmonize with the village's Old World Bavarian theme, but equip it with the conveniences of today!"

Alexander's excitement pulled him out of the sleigh into the mounting snow in the vacant field. Using great strides he paced off tracts for this and that. Nikki joined him in the field with his dream. Even the horse watched with interest as Alexander tromped the lot expounding about the hotel. In his boundless joy, Alex picked Nikki up and swung her around full circle, closing with a kiss. "A hotel here will be perfect. It will provide a nice income in about seven years and besides it will give us a first rate place to stay during the season."

His exuberance couldn't be tamed. Impishly he reached down and brushed some snow up into her face. "Oh, pardon me, *mon ami!*"

Declaring war, Nikki hurriedly formed a snowball and launched it at him. They rolled in the snow, trying to horde enough weapons to annihilate the other. Eventually Nikki collapsed and conceded defeat. The victor exacted his price of a kiss before pulling her up to her feet and walking back to the sleigh, brushing the snow from their clothes.

Alexander and Nikki skied all the next morning. On some of the hills, Alex shushed down ahead of her, keeping his skiis perfectly parallel and feet together. On other hills, Nikki led off under Alexander's admiring gaze. At the top of one of the mountain lifts, they even posed for a ski portrait by the resort photographer. After lunch Alex enrolled Nikki in lessons with Erik while he pursued his dream. Afterwards they followed dinner with a sleigh ride to another site in the vast Vincente holdings. And so their days and nights continued for their five-day stay in Vail.

On their last morning, they drove to each of the properties with the architect Alex had hired. With executive efficiency Alexander dissected the architect's preliminary renderings. Respectfully, Nikki watched him shepherd his idea from dream status to reality.

Absorbed on the flight to New York, Alexander ran construction cost estimates and revenue stream projections, while dictating notes into a cassette recorder. Alexander embraced his future. In a matter of months his stint with his employer would be terminated, they would be married and his new career, which started at the base of the Vail slopes, would sustain them.

Chapter 26
Death on a Rooftop

Nikki returned from her hiatus in Vail invigorated, ready for her tour's return to South America, then on to the Winter Olympics in Grenoble, France. Nothing could dampen her excitement over the winter games; she counted down the days until the trip.

Grenoble promised a convergence of all three components to Nikki's personality. Her Nikki persona would perform in-concert for the athletes there, host live segments of *Nikki Now!* and provide color commentary for the European networks.

Bob Mann, no doubt, planned covert activities to test the talents of the Agency's Miss Moore. Already she anticipated the aphrodisiac of, as Bradley phrased it, "living on the edge". The more she sampled glory's exhilarating fruit, the more she wanted.

And of course, she hoped Alexander had already designed a romantic rendezvous with his Nicole.

No doubt about it, Grenoble offered to culminate in an orgasmic crescendo of all the excesses of Nikki's life. And she couldn't wait!

Bruce mobilized a small army to travel with Nikki to Grenoble, including an expanded nine-man video team with three cameras and enough gear to tape a live concert. Karl pulled two photographers and another reporter to accommodate all his angles of coverage. Meanwhile Jarred threw on beefy bouncer types to ramrod their way through the congealed masses of humanity spawned by the Games themselves.

Nikki also assembled her personal team for the assault on Grenoble. Preparing for the two-week gig proved to be no small feat. Her coat wardrobe alone called for no less than fifteen coats, since hemlines ranged from parka to full-length maxi coat.

A week prior to the Games, a cryptic note with a room reservation at the Ritz in Paris arrived by ordinary post at Nikki's Surrey cottage. "Paris, two days prior to opening ceremonies. Check in at eleven. — Mann."

According to the protocol established after Berlin, whenever the Agency needed "Nikki's" presence for a mission, Bob Mann booked her through Bruce. Since the Agency needed her for several Olympic diplomatic parties, they paid top dollar for the privilege at this in demand venue. In contacting Bruce, Mann pretended Paris was necessary to coordinate details. Still, Bruce groused vigorously at Nikki's running off prior to the Opening Ceremonies. Mann promised to have Nikki in Grenoble the morning of the day *before* the Opening.

At precisely eleven that morning, as Nikki finished checking her secure case of jewels into the vault at the Ritz, Mann appeared to escort her to his waiting limousine. Nikki hadn't even seen her room yet.

In the back seat he fidgeted, drawing in air through his teeth in a strange whistling sound. Noticing he was absent his customary cigarette, Nikki laughed. "Could it be that you have quit smoking, Bob?"

Humorless, he growled, "Yes, three days ago! Now change the subject!" Involuntarily he patted down his breast pocket then picked up his whistling again.

Mann squired Nikki into Agency headquarters in Paris and into a room with two Military Service guards posted outside the door. Michael Junger waited for them in a room paneled in rich mahogany with deep leather armchairs of oxblood. Graciously he rose, greeting her with his hand extended. "It's so good to see you again, Miss Moore, particularly under circumstances that are less taxing than those before."

Nikki realized his presence indicated the magnitude of the scope of this operation. Moving to the built-in bar, he pulled out three glasses. "May I pour you a sherry?" Filling the glasses, they toasted the success of the Games.

Bob Mann downed his in one swallow and immediately chased it with another to still his withdrawal jitters.

Junger and Nikki made small talk, trying to be oblivious to Bob's nervous pacing. Short on social graces, Bob nudged Junger. "C'mon Mike. Tell her."

"Tell her?" Nikki echoed in a question.

Mike Junger forced a smile. "We have a sizeable undertaking this time. As a result, we are calling in a lot of our agents over the course of the Games. We have it from Intelligence that Igor Makarov, Russian skating coach for their top skater, Sasha Golinka, along with two other operatives who work with the bobsled team, want to defect. They are agents for the KGB with vital information for us. The possibility exists that a few others from the Eastern Bloc nations will come over, too. It will take a lot of work to pull this off without arousing Soviet scrutiny."

Nikki nodded. "With my notoriety, there isn't much I can contribute, is there?"

Junger anticipated her. "Well, in fact, there is. We are going to need all the splash and flash you can muster at the appropriate times as a diversion. Conversely, when we are in motion, we will need you to direct attention away from our operation. And, we may need you for a reconnaissance mission before the actual defection. To pull this off we are teaming you with one of the best agents. We brought you in early to get acquainted with your new partner, so you will work smoothly together."

"A partner!" His words rankled her. Nikki's face flushed at Junger's perceived slap at her capabilities. For the last year she'd operated solo, pulling herself up from a know-nothing. How many times could she have used help from them, without receiving any! A partner! Where's the glory in that! "You're not serious! A partner?"

Mann halted his pacing. "I told you this wasn't going to go over."

Junger held up his hand to stem Mann's complaints, directing his attention back to Nikki. "Miss Moore, I'm not challenging your competence. We would never consider assigning you to a matter of such grave consequence if we didn't believe in your abilities. I understand I am trampling on egos here. Believe me, your partner also has an inflated opinion of himself. He's already adamantly lobbied against the idea. But this assignment requires two agents. These are the cards you've been dealt. Live with it," Junger's stern voice resonated.

Not only did she not like the partner idea; she didn't like his tone much either. Nikki recalled Mann's words about declining an assignment anytime she chose. If ever there was a time, this was it. They could call her the next time a solo gig came up or don't bother calling at all. Hungary, she felt, entitled her to privileges. Looking down into her sherry glass, Nikki pondered her tack. Bradley had talked straight to him. She would, too. "I guess, Mr. Junger," she paused for effect, "I am going to have to decline this assignment. In covering the Olympics, my plate is already pretty full. I don't know if I'll have time for an assignment this time around..."

Junger forced a laughing retort. "Where did you dream up such a notion? You don't just walk out. You've heard the assignment. We can't let a primed agent loose in a targeted environment. If you want to take a hike on this detail, we'll have to keep you in protective custody until the mission is complete."

His turn to pause. "But, I'm not sure how we would explain the disappearance of the world-famous Nikki."

"Maybe a kidnapping by terrorists," Mann demonically offered.

Junger feigned contemplation, hanging out, wasting time, letting the consequences of his words take hold. "Yes, terrorists would certainly explain it. We, oops, I mean they would have to hold her for at least three, maybe four weeks. Such a pity...the loss of revenue from the networks cancelled coverage, the missed concerts, the lost wages to the assembled crews," he smiled a saccharine, self-assured smile. "Yes, the financial shortfall could be devastating to so many—including the misplaced Nikki."

Junger didn't have to spell out the word "blackmail". Weak in her maneuvering position, she considered him, then tried one more challenge. Leaning back in her chair, snuggling into a comfortable position, Nikki smiled at him. "You know, a vacation would be nice. Four weeks of total privacy, no press, no fans, no cameras. I could use a good rest. They've made a mint off me. So what if they lose a little now!"

Calling her bluff, Michael Junger stepped to the doorway, beckoning the guards. "Please show Miss Moore to *secure* quarters. She will be our guest." Instantly, the Military Service deftly advanced to within inches of her. Exuding their domineering presence, the contingent waited for Nikki to fall in.

"All right, Mike! You win! Bring on this terrific partner of mine," Nikki capitulated, glowering.

With a small nod from Junger, the Service silently exited the room to resume their posts outside the door.

Nikki vetted her anger, "I hope you understand this is a one time deal. I will never work with a partner after this go 'round. Hell, I may never work for you again!"

"As you wish. We will deal with the future when it becomes the present," Junger patronized her.

Junger stopped Mann's pacing. "Tell *him* we're ready."

Mann questioned Junger's order with a look of quiet desperation. Obviously he dreaded contact with this mysterious partner of Nikki's.

They waited in silence, frozen in their places for her partner to make his entrance.

Within a few minutes, the same door latch clicked open. They heard a deep voice growl some obscenity.

In a gasp, "Alex!" slipped from Nikki's mouth as an agitated Alexander Vincente stepped through the door.

Alexander's eyes sparked in anger as they swept past Junger and landed on her. He exploded, "*Porco del Diavolo!* Junger! What is *she* doing here?" Alexander rushed to Nikki's side to defend her against the evils of the man-devil, Junger. "She's no bargaining chip! I will give you what you want, but she goes free. Do you understand!" Alexander grasped her shoulder, standing his ground next to Nikki's chair.

Michael Junger's mouth flew open in astonishment as he struggled to get up to speed on the scene playing out before him. He pointed his finger back and forth between Alex and Nikki. "You know each other?"

"Yes!" they both answered in strong defiance.

Junger digested them for a moment, then burst out in laughter. "Mann!" he called, "Get in here. You aren't going to believe this!"

Meanwhile, flatfooted, Alex and Nikki traded confused looks.

Mann stepped back through the panel door.

Over his laughter, Junger explained to Mann, "Can you believe it! They know each other! They actually know each other. He thinks we brought her here to persuade him to take a partner." Junger poured another sherry with gleeful animation.

"Oh, this is too good," Mann rubbed his hands, joining in.

Alexander wasn't about to swallow their ridicule. He flashed over, recoiling from her side, drawing his arm back, loading up his fist, lunging in Junger's direction. Bob Mann stepped in his path, blocking him. "You *really* don't want to do that, Alex!"

Mike holstered his humor, sobering immediately.

"You son-of-a-bitch!" Alexander snarled, struggling from inside Mann's lock. "You God-forsaken, son-of-a-bitch! How dare you involve her! She is an innocent!"

Alexander shook off Mann's grasp in an effort to calm himself enough to allow Junger time for as much explanation as he would stand to hear.

"It turns out, Alexander, your lady friend is not quite the innocent you imagine," the corners of Junger's mouth turned up in a villainous smile. He knew he held the trump card. "Whose skin do you think you saved back in December, when the guards were throwing coffins off that truck in Hungary?"

The blood drained from Alex's face. He spun around on his heel to Nikki. "You!?" he demanded and questioned with incredulity all at the same time.

"You!?" she matched his tone. Alexander consumed her focus.

Junger tossed out to Mann, "Looks like they could use some time to catch up on old news. Let's get some coffee." They slipped out through the door in the panel, leaving Nikki and Alex to face the truth they both had kept hidden for so long.

Rooted to her chair, the unsettling shock of Alexander walking through that door prevented Nikki from rushing into his arms.

Evidently he felt the same. For the first time, uncomfortable silence opened up between them, while they struggled to sort out the staggering reality. The enormity of the revelation and its consequences overwhelmed their senses. Their glut of emotions constricted their behavior, forcing them to prioritize to make sanity of the situation. First, they would deal with business.

Alexander stared past Nikki. The vivacious, dancing light his eyes always held for her evaporated. "So, you're involved? How long have you been with them?"

Mechanically she answered, "Since June of last year, when I copped a pen from a Russian weightlifter in Vienna with secrets inside."

Alexander dredged his memory. "That wasn't the party where we met by accident and I handed you a..." Alex's voice trailed off as the pieces fell together. "You were working then?"

"I didn't know it. It was unofficial, but yes. That was my first assignment."

"Damn it!" He crossed to the bar to pour a scotch muttering to himself. "I was right. I knew it! For days after our meeting I had the strangest feeling they might be involving you. But I dismissed it. I told myself it was just the paranoia again. Damn it! I knew I should have pursued it." With detached courtesy, he asked, "Do you want anything from here?"

Nikki crossed to him with her glass. "I'll take another sherry."

"You said you didn't know you were working." His eyes narrowed, "When did they set their hooks into you?"

More comfortable in her chair, Nikki sat again as she gathered her thoughts. "A couple weeks later, in Hong Kong right before I met you in Hawaii. Mann contacted me at the Governor's compound there."

Alex zeroed in on the date. "I remember. I just left as you arrived. I spent several days with Mann, Brown and the new guy, Nigel James. Usually they mention bringing in someone new. Okay, go on."

"Go on with what?" she tossed back. "Mann waved the Flag in front of me, told me how no one could go where I could go because of my celebrity, and there you are. I jumped on. That's all there is to it."

"That's all there is to it," he derided. "You went from boosting pens to hiding in coffins in six short months! There's been a lot of buzz about this hot new number in the Agency. Some ruthless bitch who could nuke a country by day, adios a head of state by night and never even chip her nail polish. In my wildest dreams I never thought that it would be my, my..." he couldn't say it. The adjustment to the reality thwarted him. "So you're the flavor of the month!" A decided edge invaded his tone as he paced between the chairs and the bar. He poured another double with his last pass.

Nikki didn't appreciate the words he bandied about and reversed the tide with a few questions of her own, "I assume this is the work you couldn't tell me about?"

His turn to nod.

Nikki sniffed a small laugh. "How stupid can I be? I never figured it out. Maybe because in the back of my mind I worried you would turn up in some sort of capacity in a rival agency. But I never connected you in this."

"What do you mean 'rival' agency? You don't mean the other side, do you?" Alex's eyes narrowed. Accusatory aggression coarsened the timber of his voice.

"No, never! I don't know exactly. Sort of like, maybe the CIA versus the NSA...something like that." Uneasy quiet invaded the room. Nervously, Nikki moved to dispel it. "So, you are my new partner."

Alex got up and walked to the panel door. "Well, get this straight, baby. I don't need any damned partner. For years I've worked alone. I do not need some hot-shot rookie trying to teach me new tricks at this stage of the game." He opened the door. "Junger! Mann! Let's go. Let's get this thing over."

Walking back in her direction, he looked at his watch. "Hurry up," he sputtered contemptuously under his breath. "I have a plane to catch to Grenoble," he sneered, raising a disdainful eyebrow. "I am meeting my sweetheart there. I don't want to keep her waiting. I have some flowers to buy—gardenias. Yes. Gardenias are special to her." The icy, razor's edge to his voice sliced into her. Drawing first blood with his initial reference to their personal life, he succeeded in wounding her.

Involuntarily jammed into attack mode, Nikki readied to hurt him back. But she summoned every ounce of internal fortitude to force his opening assault from her front burner. First, they'd settle business.

"Alex, understand I am just as opposed to the idea of a partner as you are. This wasn't my idea. In fact, I just tried to decline the mission because of the partner ball-and-chain business. But Junger summoned the Service to slap me in irons."

"Where did you get the idea you could decline an assignment? Is that part of their new recruiting program?"

"That's the second time today I've heard that. When Bob Mann recruited me, he made that part of the package. He said I could forgo any mission."

Alex laughed abruptly, out loud. "I bet you never tried to exercise that option before today! Bob gets carried away. The Agency doesn't keep a chokehold on us by handing out options. But it was a hell of a selling tool, wasn't it?"

Mann re-entered the room, followed by Junger.

Alex stood at Nikki's side, his hand resting on the back of her chair to impart the idea of solidarity between them. "We've had an interesting conversation. We are both of the same mind. You can shove the idea of partners. Tear the assignment in half and give each of us a segment. We'll handle it that way. Otherwise, we both walk," Alex confidently asserted authority, leaving no room for discussion.

An amused smile crossed Junger's face. "Nice try, Alex. I admire your guts. But here's how we'll play this. You and Miss Moore will work together on this assignment. Now if you need more time to adjust to each other or the idea, take another ten, fifteen minutes, then we will discuss business," Junger headed toward the door.

"Okay Mike, listen." Alexander tried another tack, gesturing with his scotch. "How about if you find something else for Miss Moore to do. If you are so damned determined I need a partner, why not bring in Bradley. I'll work with him. Why not substitute Bradley for Nicole?"

"Quite frankly, because Bradley doesn't look as good as Miss Moore does in a dress," Mike answered dryly.

"Son-of-a-bitch. You are a hard ass, Junger. Okay, let's get down to it," Alexander heatedly submitted to his superior.

They all gathered around the desk as Junger unrolled a set of blue-prints to the skating arena and analyzed the objectives for the mission, spreading out the grand scope of the multi-faceted operation. Neither administrators filled in the details. They merely sketched out the endgame. How their operatives arrived at the result rested with them. Nikki bowed to Alexander's leadership, listening, watching as the master formulated the intricate details.

After an intense two-hour session, Alex and Nikki walked out of the room past the stoic Service onto the street, where storm clouds roiled over Paris. Without a word, Alexander picked up the pace, walking briskly with bold strides. Nikki had to march in double-time to keep up. He didn't speak to her for the first four blocks. Finally he snapped, "This doesn't change anything Nicole. Or should I call you by your Agency name, Miss Moore? Despite the orders, I'm not working with a partner. You can pull off your little part on your own. Do you hear? I'll handle the rest."

Abruptly Alex turned into a building. It took Nikki two extra steps to answer the sharp change of course. He sneered, "Having trouble keeping up?"

In that instant Nikki understood Alexander's game. He wanted to prove to her, and to himself, that she wasn't fit for Agency business in general, and to be his partner, in particular. In his game of "keep-up," he ran her up stairs and down back alleys. All too quickly, Nikki lost track of her bearings in the city trying to equal him. As they ran, he berated her about the partner thing. With gumption, she returned fire. At times Nikki threw in acute turns of her own, forcing him to change his path, if he wanted to continue the contest. Their infantile game of besting the other consumed all their attentive energies.

They swung into the marbled interior of the *Tour Axa* office building and rode up the snail-paced elevator to the fifth floor. Nikki dogged Alex in and out of several offices as he deposited personal papers, sniping at each other as they proceeded.

Their war continued as they waited for an elevator. Alex rang for a "down" car. To be contrary she rang for an "up." Alex's arrived first. Temporarily they suspended their rivalry when they stepped into the elevator car going down that contained two men. Once on board, they adopted typical elevator behavior, falling silent, facing forward, their backs to the rear of the car. They scantly paid any heed to the two dark-business-suited types. Had they been children, their stubby little fingers would have continued their shoving and poking at each other. But as adults, they sustained their silent war with exchanged glances and minute head movements.

Despite the protracted personal hostility between Nikki and Alex, Nikki thought their two companions in the car rode too close to them for comfort. When one accidentally jabbed her in the back, Nikki turned around to ask them to please step back. She turned into the barrel of a snub nose .38. The shock on her face stopped Alex cold. He looked around to meet a Ruger pointed at him.

The ringleader, with the barrel of the Ruger stuck in Alex's back, maneuvered them until he could reach the elevator's control panel. Using the key to the panel, he held them with the doors closed on the third floor. "Please turn around, Mr. Vincente…and your pretty accomplice as well," the taller of the two calmly ordered with a slight motion of his Ruger.

They obeyed.

Nikki's eyes caught Alex's as they revolved again to face the front. In that split second of eye contact, she tried to convey to him her coolness under fire and unity with him.

But the intense look of gravity in his eyes pierced her. Alex let Nikki know they were in deep.

"Mr. Vincente, I must tell you, this was more than I dared to hope for, to find you so distracted. I assume you have the information we are after on you?" the man with the Ruger scoffed.

Alex answered smoothly, "You have been following us. You must know I've already passed it off. You don't think I'd hang on to it for easy picking, do you?"

With a minor amount of exasperation the Ruger-wielder returned, "Mr. Vincente, the papers you passed off today had nothing to do with what I want. But you know that. Shall we stop playing games?"

"What about the woman, boss? Do you think she's his contact?" the shorter goon asked.

The leader turned the key to release the suspended elevator and changed their direction. They went up. "We will see for ourselves, on the roof."

Alex and Nikki exchanged glances. They both knew the plans didn't include them leaving the roof alive.

The small tough confirmed their dread, "Yea, the dead can't object to searches, can they?" Ratcheting up the anxiety with another deft poke of the .38, he reminded Nikki of his control.

"That's right, my friend," the one in charge answered. "And we will be back across the border before they find their bodies and discover the data is missing," he said as they passed floor six.

Nikki watched the numbers on the elevator board increase...seven, eight, marching their way to thirty-nine. Her mind flashed across all possible scenarios to disarm the thugs and make their break. She had to find a way to communicate with Alexander. If they found Alex distracted, then they must have heard them bickering. Nikki's mind told her to go with the obvious. Hide her message in the obvious.

Nikki launched into her attack on Alexander again, "Great! You macho, son-of-a-bitch! Why don't you just give them whatever they want! Or is this your way of getting rid of me, too?" She focused on Alex with riveting intensity.

He narrowed his return gaze to her, as if to say, "Yes? I'm listening."

Nikki continued to hide her message in her attack, "I suppose you're gonna step all over me here, just like you stepped all over me with the Kwan ruby." She hoped he caught her point.

The thug jabbed Nikki again with the tip of the gun. "Shut up!"

She rolled her eyes toward the numbers...twenty, twenty-one.

Then Nikki waited, amassing all her strength for her desperate attempt to save their lives. Her plan could only succeed if Alex acted in concert with her. If not, certain death. In those last few seconds, Nikki visualized every fraction of every single move she planned against her attacker.

With a small lurch, the elevator settled as it arrived at its rooftop destination, on the thirty-ninth floor. Nikki used that lurch to throw herself backward onto the toes of her captor, hard, with her wedged heels. At the same time, with every ounce of strength, she propelled her right elbow into the arm holding the gun, deflecting it as she spun right. Bringing the heel of her right hand up sharply under his chin, Nikki forced its exposure, then smashed his windpipe with her left. He crumpled to the floor. The .38 tumbled out of his outstretched hand. She snatched it away and stood with her back against the elevator wall leveling his gun at him.

Alexander had zeroed in on her meaning and likewise dispatched his abductor. Sharply he cracked the butt of the Ruger against the assailant's head for added insurance, then thrust it into Nikki's hand. "Here, hold this," Alex commanded.

One by one he dragged the two out onto the roof while she held the guns steady on them.

"Cover them while I search them. I don't think they'll give us any trouble, but I don't want any surprises." Ripping off their ties and belts, he used them to bind their hands and feet. Deftly he stripped them of their wallets, watches, rings and all personal items. Stuffing their personal effects into his pockets, he ransacked one motionless body, then the other. Tearing into their clothes he rifled through the interior of their suits searching for smuggled items. Their linings yielded some crumpled papers. Wadding those up, he also shoved them into his pockets. Picked clean, he growled, "Come on! We have to get out of here!"

Shell shocked, Nikki desperately wanted to run, but found herself pinned to the scene. She wanted to know their exact disposition, to make certain. Their eyes still stared at her.

Alexander jerked her away.

Inside the elevator, Alexander tucked in his shirt, straightened his coat and tie and combed through his hair with his fingers trying to cover up any signs of confrontation. Nikki did the same.

Through gasps of breath, he ordered, "Give me the Ruger. Put the .38 in your pocket. Keep it ready. You may have to use it. They may have friends in the neighborhood, so be careful. Follow my lead."

The elevator stopped on the fourth floor. Before the doors opened, Alexander pulled Nikki into his arms and sucked away her breath in a fiercely passionate kiss. His hands moved all over her, as he groped her body. Nikki recognized the passion as a cover to thwart recognition and groped back. It worked. The party stepped away from the car, deciding to take one less "occupied". They broke for breath, but Alex resumed the cover when the doors opened in the lobby. They exited the elevator kissing and carrying on. But as the oblivious, busy crowd washed over them into the vacant car, they dissolved from a couple into two individuals, cleansed of their connections with the building and the roof. Although they exited separately, Nikki mirrored Alexander's movements, keeping a few steps behind him.

Outside the building, the blue-steel sky spit thick drops of rain and wind buffeted them. Once well clear of the office building, Alex reached back and grasped Nikki's hand, pulling her even with him, keeping her close. They dashed through the streets and around buildings in a crazy zigzag pattern, with an eye to their rear.

Involuntarily, Nikki retreated within herself. She had probably just killed a man. It was self-defense, but it was her hand. Initiating the action that saved their lives exhilarated her. But leaving the men on the roof, with their eyes open, felt unfinished. Were they really dead? Her moral Dutch upbringing wagged a damning finger at her. She murdered and she ran. How absurd, she beat back. What else could she do? Confess? Call the police? Not likely. But still she ran, like the guilty would run.

With every step she took, the unconventional weight of the .38 jouncing in her pocket reinforced her vulnerability. Gladly, she now surrendered control of the situation to Alexander, happy to have someone relieve her of the responsibility for action. A dozen blocks later, when Alexander felt it safe, he hailed a cab to take them back to headquarters.

Stopping just short of their destination, they walked the rest of the way. A few urgent code words from Alexander swept them past the guards. Magically the Service appeared to shield them, whisking them upstairs to Junger's private office.

Startled, Junger looked up as they burst through the door.

"We just had a go-round with some vile visitors!" Alex exclaimed. "Two men almost finished us in the *Tour Axa* downtown. Here, Mike, look at this!"

Alexander pumped the contents of his pockets onto Junger's desk. "These two guys tied into us in the *La Defense* financial district. I have never seen them before. They spoke excellent American. I assume they were double agents."

Sorting through the personal effects, Mike punctuated Alex's account with questions. Reeling their spiel, they spoke fast in encrypted Agency shorthand that she didn't follow. It didn't matter though. All virgin territory to her, Nicole Moore stood quietly by the door, preoccupied with her conscience, reeling from the entire spectrum of events that afternoon.

Adrenaline revved up both Mike and Alex. "Hopefully this provides some accurate clues to their identity. I'd like to tie this up before we launch the Grenoble mission," Mike said.

"And I would like to know who is after my skin in such a big way," Alex added.

"I assume from your loot here, you finished the job at *Tour Axa*," Mike stated matter-of-factly as he sifted through the effects.

"Yes, but they didn't tip their hand before they went out," Alex answered, just as routinely.

Mike glanced up at the unusually silent Nicole, waiting by the door. "Is she going to be okay?"

Alexander threw her a quick look. "Yes. I am going to take care of her. She will be fine."

Mike interrupted, "Isn't this her first one, Alex? The white-coats from I.A. should see her. It's S.O.P. I'll call them now."

"No! I said, *I will* handle it," Alex steadfastly maintained.

Concluding their business, Alex turned to Mike, "Have a car waiting out front for us. I need time with Nicole. We're going to disappear overnight. Maybe longer."

Immediately Mike buzzed the motor pool.

Alex continued talking over the top of Junger's call. "You will have to notify Nicole's people. Think hard, Mike. Come up with an excuse for her absence. Do not try to contact us—I will not answer. You know these next few hours are critical." Grabbing Nikki's hand, Alex wheeled them around.

Mike stood over the booty of personal effects spread out on his desk, bracing himself with his arms. "Where are they now?"

"The roof of the *Tour Axa*, in all probability on ice," Alex tossed out.

"How bad is it? Will we need to send in a cleaning crew?"

Alex answered automatically. "No one ever fired a shot. Someone may want to tidy-up a bit. But it looks like a heist. Sanitation may not be necessary."

"We'll scope it out from the air before we go in," Mike assured him.

Alex reached for the doorknob, when a thought hit him. "Nicole, give me the .38." Alexander relieved Nikki of the gun and pulled the Ruger from his pocket. "Here take care of this hardware too, will you? I will be in touch in a few days. Understand?!"

"Understood."

Chapter 27

The Aftermath

Alex opened the door of the standard-issue black Mercedes for Nikki, then slipped behind the wheel. While the gates opened, he adjusted his mirrors, and they roared off into the Parisian streets. All business, his eyes darted from mirror to mirror—every car, every person a menacing suspect. They made several sharp turns with Alex monitoring conditions around him. Satisfied, he finally asked her, "Are you at the Ritz?"

Nikki nodded.

"Well, we can't go there. I will send someone around tomorrow for your things." Alex spoke more out loud to himself than to her, "The question is where should we go? It has to be somewhere where they won't recognize you. ... I know." Pulling up to a pay phone, Alex placed a call. Nikki watched him from inside the car, in between the slashes of the wipers across the windshield. Coming down hard, the rain quickly darkened the shoulders of Alex's jacket and pasted his hair to his head.

In expedient silence, they drove to a residential section of the city. Alex parked the car along the curb, then led her through the driving rain to a brick apartment building with peeling paint. An ample housewife answered, suspiciously cracking open the door at first. After trading a few words in French, she pressed a key into Alex's hand.

Climbing three flights of stairs to the loft apartment, Alex turned the key and opened the door to a clean, commonly decorated living quarters with mustard-colored walls and moss-green rugs on the wooden floors. Nikki stood just inside the doorway dripping while he cased the digs.

"It's okay. You can come in, Nicole." Closing the door behind her, Alex stripped off his jacket, then helped her out of her soaking coat. Nikki shuddered. Alex maneuvered them over to the couch where he wrapped her up in his arms. The torrent of adrenaline, the excess of emotions ranging from shock when Alex had first stepped into Junger's office, to the desperate fear in the elevator, had caught up with Nikki and shut her down. Alex gently laid her out on the couch to rest.

White zips of lightening sliced through the apartment, jangling Nikki awake in a start. Her sudden movement brought Alex instantly to the couch, reassuring her. Rain drooled down the window. Nikki looked into Alex's face, barely illuminated by the muted light from the street. "Is it all over?" she asked, speaking her first real words.

"Yes," Alex brushed the hair away from her face.

"Are they...dead? ... Did I kill that man today?"

Alexander picked up her hands, his fingers caressed hers. "Does it matter? What really matters is that you saved our lives."

"It matters. I killed that man, didn't I?" Nikki's voice grew.

"Yes. With a solid blow to the throat." Alexander's eyes pulled at hers. "It was self-defense, Nicole."

"I know. It was our lives or theirs. It's hard to explain. I keep seeing that startled, crazed look in his still-open eyes. It doesn't feel finished. Then we ran. What about their associates? What about the police? It feels like *someone* is going to come after me."

Alex comforted her, "No one is coming. You are safe. *They* can never come after you again."

While Alexander scrambled eggs on a hotplate in the kitchenette, Nikki splashed water on her face in the bathroom. She returned to a candlelit table with two plates of eggs, fried liver, chunks of bread and healthy-sized glasses of red wine. They drank to life. Over the meal, Alex kept their conversation light and trivial.

But the past few hours had erased Nikki's will to listen. She had faced imminent death and saved their lives. She wasn't in the mood to endure pointless chatter. Seizing on the topic of their relationship, she wanted the news—good or bad—and she wanted it straight. After surviving an attempted execution, she could weather a breakup. "Alex, what's going to happen between us? Our meeting at the Agency today shocked both of us. We couldn't even touch each other! Are we finished?"

Her question pulled him up short. With a deliberate drink of wine, he changed gears. "You stunned me today, Nicole. Like most men, I assumed the flower that waited for me to be delicate, fragile and above all, innocent—someone in desperate need of my maleness. Your appearance at the Agency as my equal shattered me. I never wanted a partner. I was not going to like whomever they had waiting for me. But when they pulled you out of the hat! Then, Junger and Mann ridiculed me for my reaction! Well, rather than stepping up like a real man, I retreated to the boy they humbled me to. To say I behaved badly is an understatement of the highest magnitude."

His true confession was more than Nikki wanted to hear.

But Alexander had been through hell, too, and wouldn't be deterred. "Nicole, if you have not faced this fact yet, then it is time you did. My actions today almost got us—that is me and *you*—killed. You almost died today because of my damned ego! I don't mind for myself — I always figured I would get it in a deserted alley someday — but not you. I might just as well have held a loaded gun to your head myself! Then, you came up with the plan that saved our skins, not me, not the great protector! Face it, whether we have a relationship at all depends on you and how you deal with the outrageous lack of respect I showed for you."

"Lack of respect?" His words blew her away.

"What else would you call it? I didn't think anyone was equal to working with me. Then, when I found out you would be my partner, did I call to mind all your wonderful qualities that have so captivated me and count myself lucky to have such a savvy individual as a partner? No. I regressed to the Tarzan and Jane syndrome of a knuckle-dragging Neanderthal." Getting up abruptly from the table, Alex took his wine and tramped into the living area, with his festering rage.

Nikki followed him. "You're angry?"

"Damn right I am angry. I am a raving maniac on the inside. I am mad as hell!" He turned towards her, his eyes livid torches.

Nikki didn't cower. She didn't fear him.

For all the turmoil churning inside of him, gently he caressed her face with his fingertips. "Do not misunderstand, Nicole. I am not angry with you. Despite all my indefensible behavior perpetrated on you today, I love you. Oh, those words taste terrible in my mouth after my performance!"

Nikki moved her fingers to still his lips.

He shifted them aside. "Don't, Nicole. You must hear me out. My anger is with the fiend inside of me. Yes, I am angry, and frustrated. I want to walk out into the night, rather than face you any longer. But if I do, I will elicit sympathy from your good heart. Then I will have made this whole mess about poor me, rather than giving you the cold truth with which to make your decision. So instead, I will lay out the facts for you and talk with you at the table, like an adult."

As Alex ushered them back to the table, his words repeated in Nikki's ears as she considered them. While he accurately assessed his behavior, he failed to take into account her behavior, too. "First of all, Alex, my presence in the room, as your partner, blindsided you. Neither of us could change that, so let's grant each other some indulgences for shock value, okay?"

He conceded.

"Coming off my last success in Hungary, I confess to being drunk on the power of my own abilities. I was as opposed to a partner as you. Six months ago I accepted your proposal of marriage. You were good enough to be married to, but not qualified to be my partner. Talk about inflated ego! Your resistance to me hurt my feelings. So, I struck back at you. To make matters worse, I encouraged your silly game of cat and mouse through the streets of Paris by challenging you myself. Who endangered whom? My dear Mr. Vincente, there is plenty of blame to go around. Don't you agree? My only question is, where do we go from here? And can we salvage our relationship?"

Falling to his knees, Alexander picked up her hands. His humility caught Nikki's breath. "My only salvation is you, Nicole. Humbly I apologize for my excessive ego, for not recognizing you as my equal. But I am utterly sorry for placing your precious life, even for a single second, in jeopardy. I have no right to ask, but I pray that in the days or months that lie ahead, you can somehow forgive me."

Nikki fought her emotions that wanted to rescue Alexander from his confession and get him off his knees. But he expected a reasoned response, not carte blanche. "Oh Alexander, you can't imagine how badly I feel about the ego and the games on my part this morning. But I have something far more devastating for which I need to seek your forgiveness."

Nikki paused for courage. "I knew the day I made the pact with Bob Mann something didn't feel right. In Hawaii I lied to you. I consciously made the decision not to tell you about my involvement with the Agency. With our commitment in Hawaii, and then when I accepted your proposal of marriage, I should have told you everything. But I kept it all from you."

Alex started to protest. Nikki lifted him from his knees, asking him to sit again.

"This you can't object to, Alex. At least you were up front with me. From the beginning you removed discussions of your assignments from the table. I should have been so forthright with you. How will you forgive my deliberate lies of omission?"

None of Nikki's apology registered with him.

Instead, Alexander poured more wine in their glasses. "Secrets are an integral part of the Agency's business. Once you hired on, you could not have told me, no matter how badly you felt. That is perfectly understandable to me. But I am curious, how would you have kept your involvement in the Agency from me once we married?"

"As soon as you retired, even before we married, I planned to resign. No matter how imperative the assignment or how dire the threat; from that moment on, I would always be unavailable to them. So, my dearest Alexander, you have a monumental decision to make. A lie, even one of omission, is a violation of trust. Can you forgive me? Will you ever be able to trust me again?"

Alexander left the table to stand by the front window. Lightning sporadically ripped through the darkness in the apartment, making him a silhouette against the night. With his left arm raised above his head, he leaned it against the window casement, as he stared into the darkness. "Nicole, I can't answer you."

His hesitation stilled her heart. She prepared herself for the end.

An eternity later, still facing out the window, he continued. "Do not misread my stalled response. I cannot answer you, until you have answered me. I refuse to push you for your forgiveness. I will pray for it every day, but if it never comes, I will understand. To answer you now would be to pressure you to forgive me. I will not do that."

Nikki paced the apartment examining her heart. She found nothing in his confession unforgivable. She only withheld her response to add dignity to his request. In her heart of hearts, she desperately wanted to throw herself into his arms. But she stopped. With a few more hurdles to surmount, Nikki joined him at the window. "Alexander, is your affiliation with the Agency your only secret? Or are there others?"

"No. That's it."

"Then I'd like to talk about how our confessions will change things. Where we go from here."

Alexander continued leaning against the casement of the window, searching the future. "I hope you believe me. I have nothing else to confess. If we go forward after tonight, then I want out of this damnable business. If we split, then it won't matter. I will keep at it until someone finally finishes me and they spread my effects over some administrator's table in the Kremlin. But if we are together, we will work together until we can extricate ourselves from this devil. No more flying solo for either one of us. We will be a team until we can work ourselves out of the Agency's claws."

"And what about the...the other women?"

Revulsion threw Alex's eyes wide open. Mightily, he caught her up in his arms so she'd feel the sincerity coursing through every fiber of his body — to know it from his burning eyes. "That's in the past. The Agency will have to find another way. Never again! Do you understand? No other woman will ever come between us again. I am yours. Or I am no one's. I may live in hell, but I will never dance with Satan again!" Poised, he hovered over her. Hung on the moment, his searing desire to kiss her, tangible, palpable in the air. Hotly he held her in his arms, only a breath separated them. Just the stranglehold of her forgiveness kept him at bay.

On a flash of lightning Nikki whispered, "If you can forgive me, I forgive you."

He drew her into him. "Oh, Nicole!" With lips trembling in gratitude he kissed her…tiny kisses at first, only on her face and then her fingertips, but building. Building from the pent-up passion locked inside him. Alexander leapt from the precipice.

"Oh, my darling Nicole, I love you. How very much I love you!" His kisses stoked his passion, breathing fire. He kissed her more deeply, more ardently than Nikki thought possible. His lips moved down her neck, her throat, to the top of her cleavage. She kissed his face, his hair as he moved down her body. Nikki brought Alex's lips back to hers; she couldn't live without them.

Nikki paused long enough to take stock of his incredible eyes — those pools of liquid blue lava blazed from deep within. "Tonight, Alexander. Love me tonight," she breathed.

Sealing his lips to hers, vigorously he swept her up into his arms. With a kick he opened the bedroom door and laid her down on the fresh sheets. Nikki reached up for him, "My arms are so empty without you."

"I promise they will never be empty again. For me there is no life outside them." Stripping off his shirt, a streak of lightning clung to Alex's bare chest before he lowered himself to their destiny. "Fill my wretched life with your radiance, Nicole. *Te adoro. Te adoro,*" he whispered before his mouth again found hers, the source of his life. And the incredible miracle of intimacy carried them beyond all earthly boundaries they had known.

A giddy, whirling, lightness filled Nikki's heart. For hours afterward they lay in each other arms, sharing a thousand benedictions, greeting the new day together. No matter how dark their immediate past, their intimate pairing stripped it all away. Dressing in old clothes scrounged from the apartment, they ventured out to find breakfast in those eloquently silent hours just before dawn. Nikki shoved her hair up inside an old fedora and Alex pulled the brim of another rakishly across his forehead. Hand-in-hand, they started out into the street, keeping a wary eye peeled to activities around them, talking incessantly.

"Judging from their reactions yesterday, neither Mann nor Junger caught on to the extent of our involvement with each other," Nikki mentioned.

"I warned them after August I had become involved with someone and would be leaving the Agency. Of course I did not name names. Looking back on our conversations now, they did not believe me. But how could they believe me? I didn't believe me." Alex swung Nikki into his arms. "Well, they will have to believe it now because we are going there today to lay out the entire situation for them. And, to let them know you're okay." He kissed her, and they resumed their search for food.

Heavenly aromas from a corner bakery drew their attention. Homing-in on the divine scent, they picked up some hot-from-the-oven brioche for their meal. Alexander even finagled two mugs of the baker's own fresh brewed coffee from him. Sitting on the morning's news on the sidewalk, their legs draped over the curb, they ate as they talked.

Dawn's arrival brought a warm sun to blot up all the puddles from yesterday's torrent. Over the course of the morning, Alex and Nikki connected the dots and the missing links of their separate lives. The bugs in Nikki's house made sense to Alexander now and posed less of a threat. With Alex's explanation, Nikki understood his divided attention that night in Vienna. They discussed everything, including her career. From that day forward they planned on being an item, openly, even for the media. Alexander felt the public scrutiny would discourage the Agency from using him, thus hastening his retirement.

In the ragged clothes from the apartment, they stood before Junger and Mann, dizzy with their excitement, explaining the new order of things. Alex laid out, how from that moment on they would be a team, operating openly together, with an eye on exiting the spy game by the first of May.

Their news stupefied Mike. Bob sarcastically stabbed, "Oh great! Yeah, we're really happy for you two kids." He lit a cigarette.

Then Mike and Alex settled down to the business at hand. Mike began with news on their assailants. "The two thugs you iced yesterday turned out to be Americans alright. Americans active in the Soviet underground, who joined the KGB and were operating out of the U.S. We're trying to determine their positions in the food chain. Evidently the Reds suspect high-level activity on our part over the course of the Games. They've set their sights on you, Alex, as the man in charge. At this time though, we don't think you have been targeted for a sanction."

"Sanction?" Nikki asked.

"Kill, darling, Mike does not think killing me was their prime objective, merely a means to an end." Alexander off-handed his explanation with a cool casualness, like he might quote stock prices rather than speaking of murder—his murder.

"In any case, Alex," Mike continued, "your hiding in plain sight of Nikki's celebrity may be the ticket to a healthy life for you for awhile. But it sure as hell complicates our plans for the defection."

"Not necessarily," Mann butted in. "Nikki used her reputation to open up a virtual pipeline of information with that pin trick of hers last summer. She's an expert at manipulating her image to our advantage."

"I agree with Bob," Alex interjected. "Darling, what are your thoughts on it?"

"I think with the spotlights shining brightly enough, we could get half of the people out of the Eastern Bloc if you're up for it." Nikki's comments engaged the imagination of the three. "We won't need tunnels in the ice arena or anything so drastic. The only snag will be in communicating the specifics of our plans with the defectors to liberate them. But if worse comes to worse, we can always use the pen or the pin trick again to pass the details on to the other side."

At their request, Nikki laid out the ease of secreting the defectors out of a public gathering, while she schmoozed her way through a media circus of interviews with their hot skiers or skating stars in some glitzy nightspot. As the four of them huddled over the desk swapping details to lynchpin the operation together, a clerk entered with a message.

Junger came back to the table. "We've just intercepted a rabid call from Nikki's manager to the Ritz, questioning her whereabouts. Since she hasn't arrived in Grenoble as promised this morning, Bruce and her staff are frantically doing follow up. Of course, the Ritz reported that immediately after checking in, a man escorted Nikki from the hotel, and she hasn't been seen since. Her manager is near apoplectic."

Alex looked up. "Geez! Mike, how could you! Didn't you take care of that last night? What in the hell is the matter with you? If you don't handle this in the next thirty seconds, you will have half the known-world down our backs!"

Alexander looked at his watch, calculating a timetable. "Bob, wasn't there heavy weather down south, towards Grenoble last night?"

"Yeah. Yesterday's rain here was a blizzard in the mountains."

"Great. Nicole, get Bruce on the phone. Explain that the horrendous driving conditions last night forced you into an out of the way hostel that lacked services, etcetera, etcetera. Mike, can you have us on a jet down there in about two hours?"

Junger agreed.

"Then, gentlemen, we will finish this en route. Let us away. My lady has a plane to catch. Oh, and Mike, send someone around to pick up

Nicole's things at the Ritz, including her items in the safe. Have the courier bring them to the airport."

Within the half-hour Mann, Junger, Alexander and Nikki took off for the Winter Games in Grenoble, France. Agency business dominated the in-flight conversation. Even so, Alex enfolded her hand within his protective grasp and never permitted his eyes to wander far from hers. He meant to make it clear to the whole damn Agency his compass had finally righted itself.

Chapter 28

Grenoble

Upon their arrival in Grenoble, Bob Mann absorbed the brunt of Bruce's anxious ire. Bob gave Bruce enough time to see him completely settled out. Alex went with Junger to sort out things at operations HQ, vowing to catch up with his love later in the afternoon.

Meanwhile, Nikki trundled off to the first of numerous agenda meetings, followed by every conceivable check imaginable—sound checks, lighting checks, wardrobe checks, camera checks with and without various backgrounds and, of course, security checks.

Beyond the meetings and the checks, Nikki's constant shadows dogged her every move. Bruce, Jarred, Mary and Karl all spoke into walkie-talkies to their invisible minions. Nikki desperately tried to maneuver her main four aside to clue them in on her openly changed relationship with Alexander. Unfortunately, the avalanche of pre-Games commotion squashed that possibility.

Just as Nikki's internal batteries sputtered their last, Alexander appeared in the wings to revive her. Squiring her off the sound stage, he escorted her to a waiting limo. From behind the privacy screen Alex reviewed the intricate details of the plan for the opening gala that evening. "Everyone from sponsors, to head coaches, down to the elite stars of the winter sports themselves attend the opening ball. Nicole, you will arrive and enter alone. Your job will be to artfully enjoy the soiree in front of the cameras, gliding across the dance floor with everyone from both sides of the Iron Curtain, being chatty and witty. Without being obvious, the main target of your affections should be the Eastern Bloc 'trainers,' who we know are actually guards assigned to corral their athletes. If the Agency is to gain access to the defectors, then their 'trainers' have to be distracted. Meanwhile, I will float on the fringes, targeting decoys to throw enemy suspicion away from the real Eastern Bloc objectives. This will allow other Agency players free access to those seeking to defect. Nicole, your signal to stand down from your assignment of diversion will come when I ask you to dance. At that point, all the Agency operatives will have completed their missions."

Like so many other sporting events she attended, once again the Agency had ginned-up a media mob to fall all over Nikki. Entering in her sapphire velvet and Vincente diamonds, before a tidal wave of frenzied press, Nikki electrified the free-world attendees and generated an insatiable curiosity among the Eastern Bloc. Brazenly she sopped up every ounce of attention. With enticing teasers, Nikki created the appetite to whip the multitude into a froth. Her band struck the opening chords to "Danger Us", her signature hit from her movie. Singing a few bars, she then pumped the audience for their involvement. They rocked the arena with their clapping and singing. Everyone, including her targets, the Soviet "trainers," caught the fever. Meanwhile, the other agents tagged the candidates seeking asylum setting up communication pipelines.

Coming off stage to tumultuous applause, Nikki waltzed through the evening identifying her marks scattered throughout the throng. She interspersed her dances with them between random selections from the crowd and those bold enough to request dances on their own. After curtsying a thank-you to her latest partner, she came up into the waiting arms of Alexander. Spontaneous electricity arced in their eyes. After the previous night, denying her emotions lapsed into the realm of impossibility for Nikki.

Once in each other's arms, love's delirious vacuum enveloped them. The world disappeared. The music, the crowd, all melted into oblivion leaving only the two of them dancing to their own music, in their own private universe. Nikki couldn't detach herself from his rich, deep, cobalt orbs alive with joy. Nor did she want to.

In no time the discerning eyes of the paparazzi read the validity of their relationship. Ten thousand flash bulbs exploded in a blinding hail of white light as they danced. Alexander drew Nicole tighter into the safety of his chest. Closing their eyes to them, they continued their waltz. With the concluding notes, Alexander gallantly dipped her, then brought Nikki back up with an extravagant kiss. They met unbridled applause as they opened themselves to the world.

By now the universal press had pushed the guests to the back of the room as they closed in on the couple with their microphones and cameras, all shouting at once.

"Nikki, who's your new man?"

"Are the two of you serious?"

"What are your plans?"

Alexander and Nikki traded irrepressible smiles. They couldn't quiet the magnetism they radiated. Standing speechless before the mob, deep in jubilation, they blushed like teenagers; Alexander tenaciously held onto her hand behind her back, supporting both of them. Bruce and Karl fought their way through the press mob to the middle of the room where the couple stood. The world devolved into a blur of strobe flashes and camera auto-winders. Grabbing a microphone, Bruce achieved control that allowed for questions to be funneled to them.

Proudly Nikki introduced Alexander Vincente to them.

"When did you meet?"

"Years ago—and we just kept running in to each other here and there."

"Did you know he would be here?"

"He surprised me." She looked up into his eyes.

"Any future plans?"

"Please, you might spoil a surprise for later," Alex winked.

Eventually Nikki reminded them, "Of course we, like you, are here to watch the top athletes of winter sports and not to talk about my love life. So this will be the end of these questions during the Games."

With the evening's conclusion, the driver took a circuitous route to a chalet outside of town where Alexander was staying. They relaxed for a while in each other's company before Nikki went back to her hotel. Leaving his arms, after spending a lifetime there the night before, proved inhumanly difficult.

No matter her fatigue, her night was not yet to end. Karl, Bruce and Mary—her big three—waited for Nikki in her room. They wanted answers to her very public display with Alexander.

Thoroughly upset, Karl immediately started in on her with a sarcastic diatribe directed towards Nikki's manager. "Bruce, I really have to compliment you on your organization of that spur of the moment press conference at the Olympic gala tonight. It seemed so impromptu, so spontaneous. It appeared as if you had been caught completely unprepared, with your britches down around you ankles."

"Well, thank you," Bruce mimicked back, "it took years to prefect the technique of looking like such a daft dolt in front of the world press corps."

The two turned their gaze to Mary expecting her to throw in with them. But she passed, reserving her comments in favor of the two-man comedy team.

Bruce continued his lambasting, "I must say Karl, I have to share some of the limelight of my success with you. Tonight you appeared to be an ass caught napping in front of your colleagues, also."

"No higher praise than to have the respect of one's peers," Karl returned.

Nikki knew she deserved it and gave their anger free rein to run its course.

Finally Mary stopped them mid-sentence. "Cool it guys. Can't you see something is going on? When have you known Nikki to disappear before a contractual commitment? Or vanish from a hotel? Something's happened. So what's up Nik?"

"Leave it to you, Mary, to notice. Where should I begin? I had just checked in at the Ritz, when Mr. Mann picked me up to run over a few of the details for the embassy gigs at the Games. We decided to hone a few of the finer points over a glass of wine at a corner bistro. As we approached the bistro someone came up from behind, clunked Bob over the head, stuck a gun in my ribs and nabbed me."

"Good God!" Karl came up out of his seat.

Bruce followed, "You're kidding! Right?"

"Not really."

"So how did you get away?" Karl urged.

"My guardian angel rescued me. Alex happened to be checking into the Ritz, as Bob and I started off for the café. See, Alex and I planned a little rendezvous following my business that afternoon. But when the thug showed up, Alex came up behind him and got in a few lucky punches. So we picked up Bob and high-tailed it out of there."

"Who was the creep?" questioned Karl.

"We didn't stick around to find out. In case he was either a robber or a stalker, Alex decided I shouldn't go back to the hotel. So, he hired a car and we started driving until we got bogged down in the weather. We found this rustic hostel where we hunkered down for the night."

A faint smile of recognition crossed Mary's lips. "So that's what happened!"

Nikki shot her a look. "What do you mean?"

"That's what different about you. Your relationship with Alexander has changed. You positively lit up when he stepped into your arms. Nikki, you're really in love!" Mary hugged her with her blessing. After the nightmare with Grant Henderson, she appreciated Nikki's ability to love again.

Nikki could do little more than blush. "I wanted to tell you all ever since I arrived. After our episode in the streets of Paris, we've decided to move things up a bit and make our relationship public. I didn't think it would be tonight though. I didn't know it showed."

"Are you kidding? The two of you illuminate each other! Anyone in the same room with you needs sunglasses," Mary added.

Despite her request for restraint, news of Nikki in love grabbed front-page copy throughout Europe. She became the hot ticket in town. Every Olympic party of note included not only the top athletes, but also an appearance by Nikki and her Alexander, although they never stayed too long.

Usually they broke off early to work on their own part of the mission. The plan called for smuggling the defectors to the West at a public venue—like a nightspot frequented by the athletes. So Nikki ferreted out the places where the European and Eastern Bloc Olympians hung out. Mingling with the athletes, she flaunted her persona. Readily they seized upon Nikki's presence, making it easy for her to exploit the audience's participation in her diversions. Meanwhile, behind the scenes, Alexander arranged the intricate details to facilitate the disappearances.

Because the "in" spot occurred spontaneously on the whim of the revelers, the Agency tracked the probable places, making contingency plans for each site. Of the thirteen days of the Olympics, the Agency wanted to put off the transfer until the end to avoid as much disruption as possible to the Games, but it became evident that after the tenth day of competition, the ranks of coaches and participants would rapidly disintegrate. As individual competitions concluded, the athletes and their staff moved out. This would translate into less cover to protect the operation. Agency headquarters determined they had to remove those seeking asylum by the ninth day at the latest—before the end of the skating competition. The disappearance of the top Russian skating coach Makarov, several Russian attachés and the East German bobsled coach would create a massive upheaval at the Games, but it couldn't be avoided.

Under the ever-watchful but unsuspecting eyes of the elite "trainers," Agency operatives communicated with the defectors so by the sixth day, all of the candidates knew their escape to freedom would come on the ninth night in a popular nightspot. Alex tied the site of the transfer to Serge Golinka, the top Russian Men's skater and the defecting Russian coach's number one student. All those defecting knew to track Golinka's movements on the ninth night and that they should wind up where he partied that night.

Endearingly called Sasha, Golinka was the odds-on-favorite for the gold and consequently a hero to the Soviet regime. Golinka's elite status in the U.S.S.R. provided him an outlet for his insatiable appetite for publicity, the good life and high-profile women. Undeterred by the media splash over the love between Alexander and Nikki, Sasha set his course to conquer not just the competition, but Nikki, too. His inflated ego made him an easy mark for Nikki to play to.

Night after night, Nikki found the flamboyant Sasha partying in the sizzling nightspots surrounding the Olympic village with his court assembled from the athletic world. They danced or sang together until the Soviet coaches called "lights out." Nikki brought along her news crew to gather "up close and personal" coverage of the athletes' after-hours haunts. The television angle both stroked Sasha's psyche and increased his status, thus meriting his homeland's enthusiastic endorsement of his participation with Nikki. As a Western outsider, a relationship with her outside the cameras, even on a purely social basis, would have been forbidden. But while in the camera's eye, the elite corps surrounding Sasha relaxed their stance as far as Nikki was concerned.

While Sasha lapped up the attention, in the back of the various pubs his coach, Igor Makarov, sipped vodka and lit one cigarette off the other, nervously biding his time. Before long the sentries abandoned his table to congregate up front around the action. If they suspected anything, they suspected Nikki passing something to their star. Consequently they dropped their collective guard around the coaches as they tightened their web around Golinka.

By the fifth evening, Sasha established a pattern to his partying. Of the two possible sites, the Agency narrowed down the probable one to the Hofbrau Tavern. Sasha loved singing German drinking songs and the camaraderie they inspired. Although he only drank soda water, he heartily joined the other patrons as they belted out one rousing chorus after another. On several successive nights, as Nikki made her way into the Tavern, dragging the camera crew with her, she casually took attendance. The six defectors sat scattered throughout the room, struggling to be as inconspicuous as possible, establishing a precedent of behavior.

Even though the Agency had calculated, with reasonable certainty, that Sasha would choose the Hofbrau, there was no guarantee he wouldn't, on a whim, switch to his second favorite nightspot, The Nail Bag. "The Bag," was a raucous, exceedingly loud, glitzy discotheque. Sasha's handlers hated the place. Repeatedly they tried to steer him away from it, because the extreme decibel level rendered their communication system useless and the pulsating strobe lights played tricks on their eyes. Sasha confided to Nikki that he went there on days when he felt particularly spiteful towards his keepers to punish them because he knew it tormented them. For all the reasons that Sasha's elite cadre detested the place, the Agency also hoped Sasha wouldn't choose The Bag on night nine.

But the choosing wasn't in their hands, so both places and their adjacent buildings had to be prepared in advance. After business hours on days seven and eight, the Agency's prep team opened up passageways from adjacent buildings into the restrooms of the Hofbrau Tavern and The Nail Bag. Rigged to maintain their normal external appearances on both sides, the passages actually supported façade wall panels, which led to the passageways on the other side. On night nine, one by one, each of the defectors would step into the end stall at the nightspot and disappear. On the other side of the wall, they would don jumpsuits of the plumbing repair company working on the abutting business and depart in their panel-truck. The plan sounded so simple, but hinged on precise timing. Agency mechanics allotted twenty minutes from the moment the first defector crossed over until the last one passed through.

Earlier on day nine, while Nikki covered the ski jumping preliminaries, an agent disguised as an ordinary customer visited the neighboring businesses next to both potential nightspots. Covertly he stopped up the plumbing system and placed a router on the business's phone to the Agency's dummy plumbing company. No matter which plumbing company the shopkeeper phoned, automatically it triggered the Agency's line. "Due to heavy demand," the shopkeeper would be told, "the plumbing repair team wouldn't be able to be on site until about nine in the evening."

Everything was set. All that remained was for Sasha to decide where to party.

Night nine: Nikki's job was to keep the party ebullient and loud while the agents started the procession of defectors through the wall. The entire time Nikki knew Alexander would be on the other side of the wall handing through those fleeing. Nikki knew if she failed to control the room up front, dire consequences would follow.

The TV network Nikki was working for liked her idea of capturing the about-to-be-crowned champion the night before the biggest performance of his life. Indeed he chose the Hofbrau to make his stand. As the voltage surged through the spotlights, the self-assured Sasha sprang to life—life of the party, proving to the world *he* could do it all. The Tavern rocked as energized patrons took their turn at the microphone to lead the singing. Nikki organized sections to sing harmony, continually pumping up the volume. The windows vibrated. From her vantage-point at the front of the room, Nikki watched as Makarov made his trip to the toilet, abandoning his vodka. Within minutes his assistant similarly faded from view.

Riding high on the vivacity of the crowd, the band struck up a round of polkas. Sasha grabbed Nikki and whirled her about the room. Wildly those not dancing sang out the words, trying to be heard over the band. As they finished their round, a teenage boy waited for Nikki with pen and paper to sign an autograph—nothing unusual. She leaned down to get his request amid the boisterous background.

He demanded of her, "I know you are helping people escape tonight. I represent three other separatists, including two women, who will blow your cover if you don't take us, too. Please. We must get out. Help us!"

Startled at being picked out as an agent, in horror Nikki flashed a look up into the boy's eyes. Desperation and dread stared back at her. Immediately raising a smile for a mask, involuntarily she scanned the room for the four remaining candidates, to determine which one of them had divulged the plan. The East German sled coach's eyes locked onto hers, rife with gut-wrenching fear. Instantly Nikki had her answer, and immediately she looked away. Taking the boy's pen she started to sign the paper, stalling while she thought, when Sasha pulled her away to do the "Chicken Dance."

The fast-paced, gesture-full German folk dance didn't allow for other thought. Appearing unfazed, jovial and involved consumed all Nikki's efforts. She managed to sneak peeks at the patrons, however. She found the table where the boy and his cohorts sat, just yards from the East German's table.

Without a break, the band launched from the "Chicken Dance" to another polka. By this time Nikki needed a break, but she had to keep the party going. Another defector disappeared from his table. Three, including the bobsled coach remained. Before she could take a breath, another patron swept her into his arms and across the dance floor to the beat. It was Charles Bradley.

"What's up?" he asked through his smile, spinning her fast to avoid being tapped to change partners.

"Where did you come from?" Nikki tried not to look startled.

"This is my gig for the evening. I'm supposed to help you watch the front. I picked up some bad vibes. What's going on?" Bradley kept them moving.

"That boy who just asked me for an autograph is an attaché of the East German bobsled coach. He's one of four, and they want to go, too."

"That's going to louse up the schedule and could cost us dearly! Not to mention it could be dangerous," Bradley managed through smile-gritted teeth.

"I know, but he knows the plan. He's threatening to blow up the operation if we don't take them."

"That makes it suicidal to ignore his request, and he knows it," Bradley returned through his forced laughter, as he again changed course.

"Then what choice do we have?"

Bradley danced them into camera range for more protection. "But we have to be able to communicate with them without attracting attention."

"Can they get out the same way as the others?" Nikki asked.

"Sure, but how do we explain two females in the men's room?" Bradley thought out loud, "make your way back to their table and knock one of their drinks to the floor. As you bend down to pick it up, tell them in German we will do it, but they need to rearrange themselves to look like men. Then describe how to get out." Again he spun her.

Nikki flashed a smile at a photographer. "I'll tie up the loose ends." The song ended; she grabbed for the microphone and signaled for a waitress. "*Wunderschoen!*" Nikki said through her gasps for breath. The pub erupted in applause. "Let's try something new. We're all going to sing the 'beer song' *auf Deutsch*—in German—but, of course, we all need beers. So while you polka, Elke the waitress and I will deliver you the beers for the song. Okay?" The revelers roared back their enthusiastic approval.

Elke fed Nikki mugs of beers to distribute while the dancers packed the dance floor. As she dropped a mug off to the bobsled coach she whispered, "You go as scheduled. The others will come too, shortly after. *Verstehen sie?*"

He nodded his hesitant approval.

Again, Nikki looked up, two more assistants gone. The bobsled coach was next.

Three tables over, as she tipped over a beer, Nikki confirmed the separatists' readiness. The two females left and never came back.

Not as experienced as Elke, Nikki's back ached from manhandling the heavy mugs. The lifting, singing and dancing desperately fatigued her. Pure adrenaline pumped through her heart. Sheer will propelled her to ensure the mission's success and Alex's health.

"Okay! Everybody ready?" Nikki hefted her mug and called Sasha and the other athletes of note to the fore. Locking free arms, they lifted their mugs and began the song, swaying to the tune as they sang. Finally, the last separatist, the one who contacted Nikki on the dance floor, slipped from his spot at the table.

No time to relax though, as the clock ticked off the minutes in the recovery phase of the mission. Operations allotted the repair team a maximum window of eighteen minutes. While the first team transported the defectors to safety, the recovery team worked feverishly to remove the drain stops and phone routers, while locking the pre-built walls into place before the guards discovered the absence of the coaches and the assistants. Detection before completion would jeopardize the entire mission and the futures of not only Agency operatives, but also those fleeing the hostile regimes.

Ratcheting up the pace, Nikki involved the entire house in another go at the "Chicken Dance," this time to be danced in the round. Next, she encouraged Sasha to start the popular Russian folk dance where they all joined arms and danced in concentric circles. Employing her feminine wiles and the camaraderie already established, Nikki enticed the keepers into joining in. The band labored to keep pace.

As the dance wound down, Operations still needed two minutes—five to be safe. The guards began to cast eyes over the dancing circles, trying to track their charges. Nikki had to do something—she needed to buy two more minutes!

Ducking out of the circle, she bounded up on stage. With mike in hand, she called, "Sasha! Sasha, please come up here!"

Sasha leapt up onto the stage beside her in one step.

"Sasha, tomorrow will be your big day—the gold medal!"

A thunderous cheer broke across the room.

Sasha pretended to blush at the recognition.

The throng chanted, "Sasha! Sasha!"

Before they quieted, Nikki seized their enthusiasm. "You should practice your stance on the winner's platform." Formally she faced him, removed her chunky costume-jewelry pendant and draped it around his neck. Nikki kissed both of his cheeks as an official presenter would. "The winner! Then the band strikes up the national anthem." Nikki cued the bandleader. In an abrupt change of course, the band began playing the Soviet anthem. Sasha raised Nikki's faux gold medal in one hand, the other hand he raised as a fist in triumph. Quietly Nikki surrendered the spotlight, melting from the stage. The room swelled with Soviet pride. Poised on that solitary moment, everyone stood mesmerized at the sight of Sasha triumphantly holding her bit of kitsch in one hand to the triumphal strains of the Soviet Union national anthem—an image most assumed would be repeated the following evening for real. Cheers consumed the audience as the anthem ended.

As soon as respectability allowed, the goon squad of "trainers" lifted their eyes, scanning the momentarily stationary gathering. Taking attendance, their eyes frisked the room. When the first sweep failed to turn up their wards, panic telegraphed through the cadre. Springing into action, they rudely shoved a swath through the crowd, sending up disgruntled gasps from the patrons, as the "trainers" roughed their way through them. Frantically they searched, shifting the mood of the entire room, setting it on edge. A "trainer" nearest to one of the cameramen snapped an order to turn off the cameras. A knot of the rogues congregated in the back to hastily compare notes. Coming up empty, they dispatched contingents to investigate the lavatories and kitchen.

Surreptitiously, Nikki checked her watch. Hopefully the recovery team had an extra sixty seconds to spare!

Nikki spun to answer a tug on her arm. The field director of the network crew barked at her over the chaos. "Nikki, I don't like what's going on here. It doesn't look good. We're clearing out. These gorillas will smash our equipment if we try to shoot hard news. I gotta call the network. What are you doin'? Are you stayin'?"

Nikki protected her cover by nervously looking around and feigning confusion. "I-I don't know! What's happening?" she nervously stammered.

The director turned to issue sharp commands to the crew, then continued with his star, "Evidently some people are missing. That's trouble. I'd split if I were you!"

"Right!" she said, grabbing up a handful of equipment suitcases. "I'm right with you." But the panicked patrons had already snarled the path leading toward the door. Either by incredible coincidence or by design, Charles Bradley appeared to run interference for her exit.

"Leaving the party?" he quipped, as he pried an opening for her amid the mob.

A surge in the crowd crushed Nikki against his chest. Recovering, she searched his strong brown eyes and whispered from their close quarters. "Do you think they made it? What about Alex?"

In that instant, a cadre of goons threw Nikki and Bradley out of their way as they bulled their way out of the building, wrenching the two apart.

With the Soviets' departure, the alarm settled out of the crowd. Bradley swam his way back to Nikki and pulled her aside. "Judging by their speedy exit, I'd say we were successful. Evidently they didn't uncover the hole in the john. If they had, the police would be storming in now. We'll camp out here until the mob mentality subsides." Bradley drew out a pair of chairs at a nearby table, where they watched the rest of the patrons file past, still in a disheveled state of disarray. Distracted by their singular mission of escaping the Tavern, no one bothered to look down at Nikki and Charles. Amid the turmoil they carried on in anonymity.

"So," Bradley began, "Quite a ride you've had lately, huh? Imagine my surprise to find out that the woman I planned to put moves on, Alex had already laid claim to!" Impishly he lifted a brow as a grin spread across his face.

Remembering his words in Budapest, Nikki laughed, "You, Bradley? Oh, that's too good to be true. Seems to me you're the independent type."

Elke walked over two mugs of freshly drawn ale. "These are for you, from the manager." She shook her head at the mess and disorder the panic left behind. "Good times till *they* got crazy, ja?"

Bradley clinked his mug against Nikki's. "Here's to success. I heard you and Alex came close to biting the big one in Paris the other day. You know, that shook up a whole lot of people? Seems to me that they play fast and loose with you. I think the administration forgets you're a civilian and not a dedicated terminal agent."

"Yea, well...," Nikki discarded with a laugh.

But Charles Bradley wasn't laughing. He looked her straight in the eye.

"What can I say, Charles, we got careless. It won't happen again. Besides it will all be over when we retire."

"Retire?" Bradley studied her.

"Yes. Alexander and I have told Mike to write us out as of May. We won't be available anymore. He's finished, and I'm sure not sticking around." She laid an exaggerated, cutesy smile on him hoping to lighten things up a bit.

"Nikki, you won't have any trouble. But they'll never let Alex walk..."

"Mike's already approved it," she interrupted, "he's going to start scaling him back."

"You don't understand, Nikki. Mike can say and do whatever he wants, but he's not in control here. Hell, he can even throw Alex a wing-ding of going away party complete with a gold watch and it's not going to change things. Alexander is a terminal agent. He'll never be free." Anger or exasperation worked itself into Bradley's tone.

He stood up. "Come on. Let's get you back home."

As Nikki rose to go with him, Bradley turned back to her. "And to be perfectly blunt, I'm surprised that Alex even got involved in a real relationship—especially with you. You don't deserve what you are up against." Charles Bradley helped her into her parka, then guided her towards the exit.

Outside a light snow drifted toward earth. Out of earshot, Nikki pursued the conversation. "I don't understand. Who's in control? Who are they? And what's a terminal agent?"

As if he hadn't heard her questions, Charles turned his head a bit and spoke quietly into his lapel. In seconds a black Mercedes snapped up to the curb. Bradley opened the door for Nikki, her mouth still pursed in a question, but as she bent down to enter he said, "Alexander knows. He'll explain. Or ask Junger. He'll give you the straight goods. Better still, get Mann. He recruited you. Hold his feet to the fire."

Nikki scooted across the seat to make room for Bradley. Instead he waved, "Good night, Nikki. Good job tonight. *Danke.*" With a few words of instruction to the driver, he closed the door, leaving her alone to ponder his meaning.

She sank into the seat, physically and emotionally drained. Nikki knew Alexander would find her. And, did she want some private time with him—especially after Bradley's talk.

Tension, not festivity, charged the air in her hotel. People spoke in hushed tones, their eyes darting up and down hallways. Deviation from routine resulted in spates of nervous silence. Eavesdropping as she proceeded to her suite, Nikki didn't hear anything definitive, just a jittery presence pervaded the landscape.

For the first time since Nikki came to Grenoble, she found her room empty. Pages of notes and scheduling changes for the next day's activities waited on her desk. The emptiness felt peculiar, unsettling. Nikki drew a hot bath, then poured a sherry to take the edge off. Bradley's admonition skewered her focus; a ticking clock and no Alexander only increased the pressure.

In an effort to pass time, she decided to navigate through the pages of notes her team had left for her. Pouring another sherry, Nikki sat down at the desk. Someone had left a pack of cigarettes on the desk, which she had to move before she got down to her notes. Eventually Nikki ran out of notes before running out of time. Yet, the clock continued its hollow march—still no Alexander. Had there been complications? Did something go wrong?

She poured another sherry, and, what the hell, in her quest to quiet her uneasiness, Nikki pulled out a cigarette and lit it. Her fingers shook as she held the match to it. She eased the smoke into her lungs, carefully at first. Its fabled calming effect, however, failed to materialize. By her second cigarette, she drew the smoke in deep. Her restless fingers found the cigarette pack and Nikki carelessly flipped it around on top of the desk, when she noticed a piece of paper underneath the cellophane wrapper on the back.

In an instant, her teacher's words came back to her: "Question everything."

Unfolding the paper, Nikki read the words written there.

"Won't make it home for awhile—traveling heavy. Tell Lorenzo. After Closing Ceremonies meet me at the chateau, in front of the fireplace, at eight. Wear white. I'll bring gold. Have champagne on ice. Love, A."

It didn't take a rocket scientist to break that code.

Chapter 29
Honey and Sunshine

Nikki unearthed Alexander's cover the next morning as he turned up on the society pages of the reputable news organs. Looking extremely urbane in his Dior evening attire, Alex hosted a fund-raising ball hundreds of miles away in St. Moritz. Within his circle they raised over a million dollars for their pet wildlife foundation. Of course, reporters on the scene questioned Nikki's absence. "Unfortunately," he explained, "my intended has the commitments of a 'working woman.'"

Nikki honored those commitments, slogging on with her network coverage of the rest of the Games for the remaining three days.

By noon the next day, all ten of the defectors publicly turned up on Canadian soil. The three days following the extraction of the defectors wreaked havoc on the Games. Devastated by his coach's absence, Sasha finished well out of medal contention. Then France's charismatic skier Killy eclipsed Sasha in the popularity contest.

Nikki's presence at the Hofbrau Tavern drew questions from the authorities. Interpol conducted routine interviews with all who accompanied her. Nikki's imitation of confusion in the face of the turmoil, along with her reputation as a rock and roll performer, bought Nikki her alibi. No one in officialdom expected anyone in her profession to have two nickels worth of brains—a misconception the Agency had relied upon.

Smelling a story in the face of monumental coincidences, the worldwide media dogged Nikki for her eyewitness account of the earthshaking events. Even the American press cornered her, referring to her as "the European Singing Sensation". Duty-bound by secrecy, Nikki couldn't provide poor Karl with a heads-up on the events. Her friend found himself compelled to join the pack.

Nikki's parents, along with Zia and Lorenzo, flew in to be part of Alex's plans the evening of the Closing Ceremonies. Nikki also asked Bruce, Karl and Mary to drop by the chateau.

Fran and Zia orchestrated a lavish, private reception for the small gathering. Baskets of cream-colored white roses, and a gardenia and stephanotis bouquet arrived the morning of the eighteenth, in preparation for the rite to be performed that evening. By late in the afternoon, still no one had heard a word from Alexander. Even without contact, Nikki trusted his note as gospel.

At the appointed hour of eight, with confidence in her heart, she floated down the steps of the chalet's hand-hewn staircase from the master loft above. Floral swags wrapped the timber banisters on either side of the stairs. The hem of her long, white jersey gown softly fell from step to step as the grace of a chamber quartet greeted her entrance. The gentle off-the-shoulder folds of the scooped neckline revealed the beauty of her ruby pendant.

As the intimate group of ten watched her descent, Nikki's eyes eagerly sought out the designated rendezvous spot. There, in front of the massive fieldstone fireplace, in a winter-white tuxedo, with his incredible blue eyes snapping with joy, waited Alexander. Lorenzo, bursting with brotherly pride, stood for his best friend, as Mary did for Nikki. A chaplain from the village administered their vows. With their eyes blissfully locked together, they pledged their love and lives to each other. After all the extravagant jewelry Alex had presented to Nikki over the course of their relationship, for her wedding ring he slipped a simple, but abiding, gold band on her finger. Nikki reciprocated.

Without haste or hurry, the euphoric couple dined and danced with those in attendance, enjoying their company. At Nikki's request, Karl captured the event on film. He promised to wait two days before breaking the news of their marriage.

Slightly after one, a limousine pulled up in the fresh layer of powder to ferry the couple to another chalet Alexander had arranged for them. Alexander never let her satin-slippered feet touch the snow as he swept her up out of the car and carried her inside.

The reserved hideaway exuded warmth, with spruce logs softly crackling in the hearth. The graceful glow from a hundred candles scattered everywhere pushed back the shadowy corners of the open-beamed chalet. With snifters of brandy, they danced to the ambient music of love within the cedar walls. Whispering their hearts to each other, they spoke of the past, the depth of their commitment and the promise of their future together. Gently they nuzzled each other before finally ascending the stairs to their wedding bed. Alexander peeled the covers back between his tendersweet kisses. The scent from hundreds of gardenia petals lining the sheets perfumed their bed. Their bodies released the fragrant oils as they pressed against them. Nikki fell asleep in Alexander's arms, as she had longed to do for the last two years. She awoke there, too, as she planned to do for the rest of her life.

Slipping from her husband's side in the morning, she dressed in the silky peignoir she found carefully laid out for her. She crept downstairs so she could wake him with a cup of fresh coffee. But before Nikki finished, two arms wrapped around her from behind and soft lips caressed her neck. "Good morning, Mrs. Vincente."

She turned to meet Alex's muscular bare chest. Before their wedding, Alex, the soul of propriety, never casually exposed himself around the house to her. The sight of his exquisitely etched physique with only a towel wrapped about his waist stole her breath. His still-tanned skin provided a stark contrast against the white towel, which intensified the depth of the delight emanating from his blue eyes.

His hands rested on her hips. "Today is the first day of our honeymoon. Have you decided where we shall spend the first weeks of our lives together?"

"Where? Alex, I assumed this was it. What else do you have in mind?"

"It's up to you, my sweet Nicole. I meant this cottage only as a bridge between last night and our final destination."

Through what could only be the magic of Alexander, breakfast appeared in the kitchen. They adjourned to the farmhouse table laid out with bright silver-domed dishes holding an array of warm breads, eggs and steaming breakfast meats. "Darling, the world is indeed your oyster. Name your pleasure. Shall it be skiing in St. Moritz, a warm beach in Maui or a safari in Kenya? Name it, and we'll be there this afternoon."

Amazed, Nikki sat back considering his offers.

Her quandary amused Alexander. "Perhaps, you would like only a few days at a resort and spend the rest of our three weeks on the grand tour."

"The grand tour?"

"We can travel around the world to all my holdings—that, as of yesterday—are now half yours. In case anything should happen to me, you really should know what the estate entails."

"You've got to be kidding!" The implications of his statement flabbergasted her. "Alexander, I, ...I never married you to get... I mean...I never expected..."

"Of course you didn't, darling." He came around and massaged her alabaster shoulders, "It's not in your nature. And if it were, I guarantee you wouldn't be sitting here today as Mrs. Vincente."

Nikki turned to meet him, "I only want to be your wife...to fill up my days with you...raise a family. It never occurred to me..."

Alexander silenced her with a long passionate kiss.

When she finally drew back, his eyes sparkled with her living in them, "You want to raise a family? Are you sure? What about your career?"

"With a word from you, I'll give it up tomorrow. Of course I want to have your children."

Tenderness welled up in his eyes, "My children. Really? All these things we've never talked about. I didn't want to resurrect painful memories from before—from those days in the hospital. I wasn't sure you were past the pain yet. And then, I didn't bring them up because I didn't want to rob you of your time to shine. I wouldn't ask you to forego that. I just figured, one day you would be ready and would want them, too."

"No. I want them with you and I want them whenever you say."

Alexander kissed her fingertips, then moved to her lips. His fingers gently slipped beneath the shoulders of the filmy ensemble robe and flicked it off them. In a silent poof, it fell around Nikki's feet. Alexander slid the spaghetti strap on the gown off her shoulder, as his soft lips caressed her, working ever closer to her neck. "Maybe," he purred, "now is not too soon to start."

"Now would be the perfect time," she whispered back.

They left the eggs cooling on the table.

Ultimately, Nikki opted for Alex's grand tour, with an initial stop in St. Moritz to ski the fabled Alps. Reed Dawson had them in St. Moritz in time for *aprés ski*.

The next morning, on their way to breakfast, Nikki noticed their wedding picture plastered across the front pages of every newspaper in the rack. Bold headlines blared: "Princess says 'I do' to Groom #2!" "Nikki and Alex—Princess weds Playboy!" "Whirlwind Courtship Leads to Nuptials." Turning into the small slope-side café, a similar version of the story greeted them from every newspaper, at every table. Nikki felt so conspicuous.

With a deep breath and a smile, Nikki walked past all the suspicious eyes looking up directly from their papers at her. Disregarding the headlines, she paraded past the papers then earnestly engaged herself in conversation with the most fascinating man in the room—her husband. They had so much territory to cover. Only every now and then, did she feel the eyes of the other patrons intruding on them.

Eventually a lone brave soul ventured over to their table. "Excuse me. Aren't you Nikki, the one in today's paper?"

"I'm Nikki. Am I in today's paper?" she blotted her mouth with her napkin.

The English-accented woman unfolded the newspaper to reveal the headline and picture. "It says you got married. Is it true? Are you on your honeymoon, then?"

"Yes, we did...and we are."

The woman, too enamored with her discovery of celebrity to depart under her own power, remained at the table's edge, so Nikki introduced her to Alex.

In European chivalry, he rose, "Enchanté, madam."

The woman blushed.

To gently move her along, Nikki offered, "Did you want me to sign this for you?" She wrote across the bottom of the paper and handed it back to her.

Smiling, the woman studied the autograph as she returned to her table.

To the couple's delight, the rest of the meal passed without further interruption. The woman's boldness answered the collective questions of the room. Satisfied, the other patrons resumed their own activities. Later, Nikki commented on this to Alex.

"It's simple, Nicole," Alex educated her. "The majority of the people who frequent St. Moritz are totally unimpressed by celebrity. They would never presume to intrude on your time. They were merely curious and a bit fearful."

"Fearful?"

"Yes. They fear the intrusive press. When you frequent a place like St. Moritz, where privacy is prized, it is assumed that you wish to remain anonymous. They were waiting to see if you could be trusted or if you were actually a publicity hound."

So went Nicole's initiation into the intensely private circles in which Alexander moved. As a fairly successful rock star, she had assumed no social class to be closed to her. She was wrong. Through Alexander, Nikki discovered an entirely new stratum of people. With their tremendous wealth, these people wielded enormous power, which far surpassed the limits of normal comprehension. They were wealthy enough to consider mega-media stars such as Paul McCartney or even Elvis as mere players — people to be hired to entertain at their gatherings. Their sphere included royalty, business tycoons and those of generational means. Nikki never found them to be, as so many assumed, pretentious or haughty, with an aire of superiority. They were, simply by virtue of their extreme circumstances, removed. They lived daily with the knowledge that their situation made them walking targets: Targets for political zealots, targets as hostages, targets for extortion. Therefore they limited their contacts to people and places that protected their identities, where they felt comfortable and safe.

Nikki and Alex spent three heavenly days skimming over the Alpine slopes of St. Moritz. They laughed. They played. Nikki rubbed snow in Alex's face after one spectacular fall, and he gleefully returned the favor.

On the fourth morning, they began the grand tour. Traveling light, carrying only personal grooming bags, they bought the clothes they needed as they went along. Reed doubled as their bodyguard. Encircling the globe, they stopped at Alex's penthouses in Vienna, London and New York — the cities he frequented most on business — legitimate business. He never stayed anyplace familiar while on assignment.

Having been there just two months earlier, they skipped Vail, flying instead to a remote, private Caribbean island Alex owned, which the family aptly named *St. Vincente*. "Grandfather built the house that sits on the property," Alex explained as Reed made a pass over the island before setting down on the grassy landing strip.

Verandas and porches wrapped entirely around the big two-story white house, which sat nestled among the birds-of-paradise, a thicket of banana trees and graceful palms. Louvered, forest green hurricane shutters framed the windows and doors. Gleaming sky-blue porch ceilings reflected the light of the sky into the house. The island breeze swooshed through the windows all day and sang to them at night.

Alex and Nikki rode horses in the surf, sailed a catamaran across the ocean spray and romped free of all encumbrances in the privacy of their own secluded beach. Alexander toured her through secret caves cut into the rock, hidden behind a large waterfall at the grotto. "Grandfather used this island in his rum running trade. See, we left a few cases in the caves as a monument to his illustrious career." Alex pointed to the token bottles in wood crates caked with dust.

There he produced for her an entire ensemble of scuba gear. His unusual gift rendered her speechless. "Darling, I hope you will grow to love diving as much as I do. Shall we try out the gear in the shallow end of the grotto's waters?"

Alex instructed Nikki on the various pieces of apparatus and demonstrated them for her. As she got acquainted with heft and feel of the gear, Alex slipped into his. He fitted Nicole's diving mask to her face.

With Alexander's accommodating patience, Nikki eventually adapted to the alien devices and discovered the extraordinary world under the water. Sailing the island yacht, the *Vincente Bellissimo*, a small distance offshore, Alex gave Nikki her first taste of the Caribbean. The vivid colors of the fish, the graceful plants and the coral just below the surface amazed Nikki. Indeed, she couldn't get enough. Sometimes they dove as many as three times in a day. As the gear became second nature to her, Alexander increased the distance from shore and the depth at which they dove.

Three days before their departure, they put on wetsuits for the first time to make their deepest dive of all—seventy-five feet. Prior to the dive, Alexander explained that the deeper they went, the more they would be overcome by the effects of increased nitrogen in their systems, which induced a euphoric feeling similar to being drunk on alcohol. He referred to this state as nitrogen narcosis. Although Alexander promised to watch out for her, he warned that she also must realize the effects of being "narked" and that she must fight against it, just as vigilantly as she would try to suppress the feelings of too much alcohol. To pass off or ignore the effects of the increased nitrogen could be fatal. Alexander wanted her to let him know immediately when she felt any effects of the nitrogen, so they rehearsed their communications with each other several times before breaking water.

She watched the dial of her depth meter count down the feet of their descent. The light grew noticeably less the farther they descended. The pressure increased, but even at sixty feet, Nikki felt nothing extraordinary. By seventy feet, a small giddiness buzzed inside her head. With such a slight "feeling," she deliberated whether or not to tell Alex. For safety's sake though, she passed him the signal, quantifying it with her index finger and thumb to signify just a "tiny bit."

He nodded his understanding and signaled asking if she felt like continuing.

Nikki agreed, and they descended to the planned depth of seventy-five feet.

Without any more effect on her at that depth, they swam around a little, investigating their surroundings, then Alex motioned for her to go deeper.

Again, Nikki agreed.

They passed eighty, eighty-five, ninety feet. At a little over ninety feet, Nikki stopped to observe a passing school of fish. She couldn't believe it—as they swam past, each of the finny friends blew little fishy kisses in her direction. "How cute!" she thought as she pulled out her regulator to blow some fishy kisses of her own back to them. The sudden rush of bubbles brought Alexander immediately to her side. Gently, but forcefully, he fed the regulator back into her mouth, then shook her.

With his two fingers shaped in a vee, he pointed them at his eyes, which he exaggerated to be open largely—their signal for focus. How silly he looked—all agitated. Nikki laughed in spite of herself, while her head spun delightfully in ethereal euphoria.

Alexander shook her again, then tapped on the lens of her mask. He narrowed his eyes sternly at her, then brought his prong-fingered vee against her mask several times to get her attention and again pointed to his mask. He repeated the maneuver several times, increasing the ferocity each time. "FOCUS!" he rigorously admonished.

Reality blazed through. Nikki understood. Happily, she obeyed. Identifying being in the state of nitrogen narcosis didn't lessen its effect. She just admitted to it, then examined all further actions for their sanity before initiating any of them. Nikki definitely ruled out blowing any more fishy kisses even though it didn't stop those pesky fish from teasing her and blowing more kisses in her direction.

At Nikki's side, and stopping often to check on her, Alex continued the dive. Slowly they ascended, then swam back down to a slightly deeper depth. Up and down, around and around like dolphins playing, they swam. Eventually Alex signaled time to surface and slowly, stopping often to let their bodies adjust, they began their ascent. Back at fifty feet the effects of the nitrogen dissipated.

After a week in the tropical paradise, they flew to their final destination—Hong Kong.

"No one owns anything in Hong Kong. It's all leased from the government. But I have a penthouse there. And I'll have it until the communists take the island back in'97. That's where I want to spend the final days of our honeymoon," Alex said. "After all, it's where we really began. For that reason, Hong Kong will always be special for me."

But when the taxi driver pulled up in front of the hotel, Nikki remarked to Alexander, "Oh, the Furama, I thought we were going to your penthouse."

"Then you remember it?"

"Of course. You brought me here on our first date, right after my stupid stunt with my security."

"Well, darling, directly below the restaurant, and thoroughly sound-proofed, I might add, is my apartment. Shall we go up?" Alex offered his arm.

Inside his apartment he drew back the drapes on the floor to ceiling windows with a large wand, revealing a stunning view of the entire harbor. With Hong Kong moving below her feet, Nikki looked up into Alex's eyes. "Is it safe here for you? I mean, this being the home of the Kwan Brothers and all."

"Darling, they are dead—distant memories now." Alex kissed the top of her forehead in reassurance.

"I know. But what about the rest of the family? Aren't they waiting to avenge their brothers' deaths? Isn't there a family vendetta of some sort out for you?"

"No. That's all been taken care of. The clues in the fire pointed directly to a rival gang. Their deaths have already been avenged and re-avenged." Alexander lifted Nikki's chin until their eyes connected. "I have been here three times since the fire. Everything is fine. I would never put you in harm's way, *ever*. Now, should we pay old Charlie Soo a visit?"

Charlie almost quite literally danced to hear the news of their wedding. "I knew it!" he cried. "I knew it! I told Miss Nikki the last time I saw her—I told her—you had it bad," Charlie poked Alexander in the chest with his forefinger.

Scurrying to pour a round of sherries for them, Charlie bemoaned not having any champagne on hand. Raising his glass to them, Charlie intoned, "A long healthy life to both of you, one blessed with many babies."

"I certainly hope so!" Alex smiled. "Charlie, anything new to show us?"

Back in his private office, Charlie laid out a black velvet cloth. He produced a stunning choker necklace with three strands of pearls coming together in the center on an extraordinarily huge, traditionally cut emerald encircled with diamonds. Proudly he handed Alexander his loupe.

Alex felt the quality of the pearls first, then popped the loupe into his eye. "Ahh. Yes. You did a marvelous job, old friend. It is exquisite. Care to look Nicole?"

Even before engaging the loupe, something seemed familiar. "Charlie, isn't this that beautiful emerald you showed me last July? The one you had already sold?"

Charlie rubbed his hands together. "Miss Nikki has an excellent eye. Yes, it is! What an eye!" he confirmed Nikki's increasing prowess with gemstones.

"You certainly did do a terrific job," she looked up, to find the two of them trying to stifle their collaborative smiles.

"Okay, what's up?" she demanded.

"So you like it, Nicole?" Alex struggled to contain his bubbling mirth.

Charlie erupted. "It's yours, Miss Nikki. Happy wedding! From Mr. Alexander!"

"You're kidding! No!...Alexander! Oh sweetheart, thank you."

Catching Charlie Soo in his duplicity, Nikki shook a teasing finger at him, "You, dear friend, knew all along. You knew last year when you showed the emeralds to me!"

Charlie nodded excitedly, "Yes! Indeed! Yes! Blame Mr. Alexander though! He told me to use the stone you picked. Guilty as charged!"

Nikki reached down again to feel the strands of pearls, still stunned by the gift.

Charlie disappeared giving the newlyweds a moment of privacy, then returned with a tiny box of his own. "Miss Nikki, this is for you, with my best wishes for your marriage."

Lifting the lid, Nikki opened the box to reveal emerald earrings that perfectly complimented the style of the necklace. "Charlie Soo! They are beautiful. Such an extravagant present! You shouldn't have. But, thank you so very much."

Alex and Charlie slapped each other loudly on the backs, displaying the depth of kinship each held for the other. Outwardly an embrace of appreciation for a gift, but Nikki knew it encompassed years of their abiding friendship and gratitude for mutual acts of survival. "Thank you, dear friend. Thank you," Alex said.

"Thank you for letting Charlie be part of it."

With the men in danger of "showing too much face," Nikki moved to lighten the moment, "All these beautiful stones and no place to go."

"Well, we can't leave the lady without a venue to display your work Charlie. We should do the town tonight. Shall we generate some sparks in old Hong Kong?"

After their night on the town, Alex and Nikki spent the next two days shopping in the free-port city. Like giddy teenagers, they clung to each other, ranging in and out of shops, laughing and teasing each other. This time Alex finagled Nikki into that pricey lingerie boutique. Pouring over designs in the custom tailor shops, they ordered from the endless array of Thai silks, satins, linens and worsteds. And they bought souvenirs for everyone.

Never had their relationship been so carefree and casual. For three delicious weeks, her world consisted of Alexander's gorgeous blue eyes and his soft, sweet lips. Bradley's words about "terminal agents" had disappeared from Nikki's head.

Chapter 30
The Terminal Syndrome

Their arrival in London in early March rocketed them back to reality as they faced the consequences connected with their spontaneous marriage. Nikki's career posed the most immediate of all the questions. Would she continue? Refusing to impose his will on her, Alex left the decision entirely in Nikki's hands. Truthfully, she no longer possessed the heart to continue the mind-numbing schedule Bruce had laid out before their union. Nikki wanted a life with her new husband. So Bruce, Karl and Mary met over her kitchen table to pare down her schedule.

Nikki wouldn't give up her recording. Music reflected her soul, her voice, her method of communication. Even on their honeymoon she had found her mind cataloguing songs for albums or germinating fresh ideas for arrangements. She didn't want to abandon that. But she jettisoned all commercial endorsements and the pending movie deal. When her contract for *Nikki Now!* ran out in April, she wouldn't renew. Nikki wanted off the tour merry-go-round — yet she wanted to say good-bye. Bruce proposed a farewell tour.

He'd announce her retirement from touring in a London press conference, two days prior to Nikki's trip to Australia and New Zealand. From there, she'd sprint through Japan, fly to Hong Kong, then back to Europe, finishing up with a swing through the U.K. and closing in London at the Palladium. On May first, Nikki wanted to sip the champagne of retirement on the terrace of *Napoli*.

Where they should reside presented The Vincentes with another quandary. In the short term, Alex commuted between the Agency's headquarters in Paris and Nikki's cottage. The converted caretaker's place wasn't suitable housing for the two of them. But his *bon vivant* bachelor penthouse in London also wouldn't serve. They decided to look for something else once they understood their mood when Alex retired.

In his first couple of commutes to Paris, Junger let Alex tie up the paper loose ends other agents left dangling. Idealistically, Nikki permitted herself to be lulled into the routine. But on the Ides of March, while packing for her final sweep through Australia, she found his wedding ring secure in its ring case in her drawer. An icy chill shivered through her heart. Nikki knew it signaled his involvement in the field again, a cold reality of fact. They had talked about it. She understood it. Still, it didn't decrease the knot of fear. Like the piper who must be paid for his tune, Charles Bradley's words returned to haunt her. Prior to departing on tour, Nikki sent for Bob Mann.

Bob met her in a smoky, dark, hole-in-the-wall pub. Again off cigarettes, he responded to her with extraordinarily frosty candor.

"Bradley and I had a chance to talk at our last meeting," Nikki began. "He made some pretty damning accusations about the Agency's claim on Alexander."

Mann leveled his eyes on her, "Is that supposed to shock me? I suspect he wanted you to see what you're letting yourself in for. You evidently didn't listen. Why, what did he say?"

"He went on about things like the Agency may retire Alex, but they don't call the shots. He kept referring to *they*. *They* won't let him. *They* are in control. So who are *they* anyway?"

"You're an intelligent woman, Miss Moore. Excuse me, Mrs. Vincente. I'm surprised you haven't figured it out. Take a minute to think about it. I think you'll get it." Mann impatiently drummed his fingers on the table, "C'mon, you know the answer. Face it! Spit it out!"

"Alexander is in the field, and my heart is in my throat, Bob. I don't know. Tell me! Who are *they*?"

Bob narrowed his eyes, lowering his voice, "*They* is *them*. You know, the Chi-Coms, the Ruskies, the Reds—the bad guys we battle against on the other side.

"Just because we say it's enough, doesn't mean that a memo gets sent out to all sides, inviting them to his gold watch party. *They* don't just show up at some fancy-schmancy tea and agree its okay to take an agent out of play. Depending on how critical a player a particular agent is, *they* may never relinquish their claim to him. He may know so much that he's always a threat to *them*."

Although she tasted dread in her mouth, with resolve, Nikki met Mann's gaze and asked anyway, "How much of a threat is Alexander? How critical is he?"

"You know the answer to that," he said coldly. "Do you want me to take you by the hand and walk you through it? How much do you want me to spell out for you?"

"All of it, Bob. I want to hear all of it."

Bob Mann began to sweat. He patted his breast pocket for his reliable pack of smokes. "Son-of-a-bitch!" he cursed, stalking off to the tavernkeeper, returning with a pack.

Roughly pulling one out, he threw the rest down on the table with disgust as he lit up. "Hell, this job will kill me long before these things will!"

Keeping her hands steady so they wouldn't give her away, Nikki reached for one.

"You, too, huh? It's gettin' to you, isn't it?" Mann noted as he held out a match for her. "You know Alex is the number one agent. And if you want the awful truth, that's on three continents."

"So, *they* want him pretty bad?"

"Real bad."

"But I thought Mike said there wasn't a sanction out on him," she bargained.

"Nikki, that was that one particular time. Those goons on the roof were interested in what he was packing, not his hide in that one instance. But if they smell a rabbit, then he's fair game."

"Does Alex know all this?" she asked suspiciously.

"Bleedin' hell, woman! How dense are you? Of course he does. That's what none of us can figure out. He knows the score. How can he put *you* at such risk?"

"Me?"

"Yeah. Forget scenarios like stray bullets and the innocent bystander bit. You're a target for kidnapping, torture and all that kind of stuff, just to get at him." The heat of their discussion set in on Bob. Impatiently he waved for another round. "How could he do that to you?"

"In all fairness Bob, he tried to warn me off. I didn't buy it."

They fell silent as the waitress delivered the round.

"Besides," Nikki began again, "if you think so much of me, how could you involve me in the first place." Her question scored blood.

"Touché, my dear Mrs. Vincente. Touché."

Nikki clinked her glass against his to negate any hard feelings. "I guess we pretty well covered that subject. So now explain to me the meaning of a 'terminal agent.'"

Stunned, Bob met her eyes, "You just don't let up, do you?"

He read her determination. "Okay. There are two classes of agents, technical and terminal. We hire the technical agents for a special skill they possess, use them on a limited basis and don't really expose them to other agents—our side or theirs. They're basically couriers."

"Give me an example of a technical agent. Do I know any?"

Exasperated, he sighed, "You are a text book example of a technical agent."

"And the risk to them?"

"Relatively low. They don't know anything or anybody."

"Which is why I can walk away at any time, right?" she prodded.

"Yeah."

Nikki pulled in a breath, "And the terminal one?"

Rung out, Mann shook his head, lighting another smoke from the last. "A terminal agent is fully involved. He handles the sensitive data. He knows the players on both sides."

"And..."

"And is called terminal because in all probability he will be killed by either their side or his own."

She added, "And retirement is not an option."

Mann spit out smoke, "Sure, it's an option. It's just never been done before. Now, are you satisfied?"

Nikki stared Bob Mann down. "I promise you, if there's a way, Alexander will do it." Then she picked up herself to leave.

Bob Mann grabbed the sleeve of her coat as she passed him. His sober eyes pierced her. "Be careful, Nikki, like you've never been careful before. Your notoriety may help Alex, but it puts you square in the crosshairs." Then Bob Mann squeezed her hand.

In assessing their conversation, Nikki thought she had handled the straight-talk in a stand-up manner. But the uncharacteristic blush of humanism from Bob scared her down to her shoes, as he meant it to.

Nikki quickly discarded the hazard of her personal risk; it was the possible destruction of their new life that troubled her the most. To blot out the demons, Nikki threw herself into rehearsals. Nearly driving the band and backup beyond the breaking point, she whipped them and herself in an effort to erase her fear. As her closest friend, a few well-chosen words from Mary about the tough pace slapped her back to reality.

The news of Nikki's retirement intensified the spotlight on her, swelling her popularity. A black market in her concert tickets sprang up. Fans now offered hundreds of dollars for a spot at the chat fests. The concert crowds bordered on insatiable. At her last concert in Sydney, the fans flat out refused to leave until Nikki performed an entire additional set. Overwhelmed, Bruce turned to her. "I can't believe what retirement has done for your career! How can you walk away from this?!"

Capacity crowds met Nikki's plane in Tokyo and Osaka. An envoy bearing a gardenia greeted her in Hong Kong. Since staying with Alex at his apartment would constitute sheer folly, she sent Edward over to slip a note under his door. "Sweetheart, hopefully you are standing in our apartment reading this. Sorry this note is greeting you and not my arms. Fans are insane this time around—too risky to stay there. But I can arrange a side trip—just whistle. I know you can do that. I'm around the corner at the Hilton under the name of Raven. Your, Nicole."

And oh, could Alex whistle! Nikki received a cryptic note in return. "Pick you up at eight. You'd be a vision in emeralds and white. We'll do the town! Love, A."

Nikki's itinerary the following morning included some "public shopping" in Hong Kong. Bruce often arranged such trips to display her personal side and to demonstrate her interaction with the fans, all caught, naturally, by her camera crew. This maintained the image of Nikki as a touchable star. Since Nikki felt comfortable being in relatively familiar territory, she only tapped Edward from her security stable to accompany her. While Nikki strolled the streets for her casual shopping spree, Alex answered a summons from the new Governor, Nigel James, at the compound.

Emerging from a porcelain shop in front of the public and film crew, Nikki bowed to thank the owner for his kindness, when an eerie undercurrent sizzled through the crowd, like a premonition before lightning strikes. Then, an incredible flash of silver-white light blinded the area, immediately followed by an earth-shattering blast. The air vaporized into a choking smoky haze, robbing her of breath. A crushing weight knocked Nikki to the ground. Fast footfalls scurried all around her. Metal and glass debris rained down all around. The sidewalk ran red. The heavy air and excessive weight covering her choked off her breathing. For an eternity Nikki laid pinned to the spot. Scuffling feet dissolved into unsettled quiet, pierced with screams, shouts and the approaching wail of sirens. A wide stream of thickened blood flowed into the gutter from underneath her chin. Nikki felt warm and wet.

Struggling, she pushed against the dead weight smothering her. Wriggling, she freed herself. With a sickening thud, a body flopped off her, smacking the sidewalk. Staring face up, with the vacant eyes of the dead, covered in blood, laid Edward. A metal projectile lodged in his throat. The wound gushed a river of blood, then quickly lapsed into a miserable dribble. It bathed his entire body in clots of crimson. Nikki crawled to him, feeling for a pulse. There was none. Cradling his head in her arms, she prayed his name over and over again in mantra through her tears.

Forceful tugging pulled her away from Edward on the sidewalk. "Here! Quickly, Nikki. Come!"

Nikki looked up into the face of a Chinese man.

"Hurry. Much danger. No time! Come! Come!" he jerked her out of the scene.

Foggy with shock, stunned that he called her with familiarity, she followed.

Moving quickly, he dragged Nikki down the glass-littered sidewalk, past the skeleton of a burned out car, away from the carnage.

Suddenly from an alleyway, a pair of hands leapt out, clasping his throat. The hands pulled the Chinese man into the alley shadows.

Wrenched away, the Chinese man released his grasp on her.

The hands of a hulk from the shadows wrestled him to the ground. Within seconds, the Chinese man's thrashing feet fell motionless.

Nikki knew she should run. She scanned the streets for an escape route.

The hulk's footsteps approached. From the shadows, the hulk materialized into Jarred's face with a stream of blood trickling from his forehead. Jarred offered his hand. With a tremendous sigh of relief, Nikki collapsed into his arms. Momentarily he cradled her, then with an enabling arm, urged her forward. "C'mon Nikki! Let's go."

He helped her back to the scene where he sat her on a stoop, propping her up against a building. "You're covered with blood. Are you hurt? Are you bleeding?"

By now, hordes of police and rescue squads swarmed the scene. A yellow tarp blanketed Edward's body. Only the blood-drenched loafer from his right foot stuck out.

Cautiously Jarred proceeded with his physical evaluation of Nikki's condition.

She reached out to touch his forehead wound, "You're bleeding."

"It's just a flesh wound," he moved his head away from her prying finger.

"What happened?"

"It was a car bomb," Jarred replied. "I thought the guy leading you off was a Tong member. I know what I told you about getting involved with the police. But this time it's necessary. Besides the film crew has you on tape at the scene."

"Did you see Edward?" Tears filled Nikki's eyes.

Jarred nodded respectfully.

A clot of medics and police surrounded her. Jarred surrendered her to their care. Quickly they determined she suffered only a superficial wound on her left leg and wrapped it with a gauze bandage.

The police, however, weren't so fast to release Nikki. A car bomb outside a store where she had just finished shopping smacked of too many coincidences for them. They questioned her at length about her recollection of the scene before, during and after the blast. They interrogated her camera crew, impounding their tape. From eyewitnesses they learned of Nikki's removal from the scene. They demanded an answer for her disappearance.

She explained she was dazed, and the man leading her away told her she was in danger. Nikki pointed toward the alley, down the street, where she assumed her assailant still lay. They grilled her for what seemed like hours as she sat on the stoop. Her ears still rang from the blast. From time to time, she put her hands out in a desperate attempt to keep her balance because the shock interfered with her equilibrium. No matter, her condition didn't faze the police. They wouldn't permit Jarred to get close to her again. Stalwartly, he stood with edgy concern outside their ranks.

Soon a black Bentley with little flags on it parted the police cordon. Detached from the world, Nikki watched it pull up across the street. The driver emerged and spoke to the police captain.

Before long, the police captain approached, "Please, Miss Nikki, you are to go with this man to the Governor's compound."

Nikki revolved her head, looking to Jarred for his confirmation.

Involving himself with the official and the captain, Jarred returned to her. "It's okay, Nikki. The Governor has sent for you."

"Are you coming?"

"No. I'll stay here with Edward, then see you back at the hotel later tonight."

"Tonight? But we're supposed to leave this afternoon."

Jarred shook his head, "Not after this. Go ahead. I've got things here."

Wrapping a maroon blanket around her, the driver tucked Nikki safely inside the Bentley. Bracing herself in the corner of the car, she rode in stilted silence to the Governor's compound.

Alexander wore out the sidewalk waiting for her. Anxiously he paced under the canopied portico of the front entryway. Afraid of aggravating any possible injuries, he gently drew Nikki from the car as it pulled to a stop. With a shepherding arm, he escorted her into the foyer of the Governor's mansion where a concerned Governor James joined them in the vestibule to check on Nikki's condition.

In the ensuing commotion, the blanket covering her fell away. Alex's eyes went wide with fear, "My dear God, are you okay?"

For the first time, Nikki caught a glimpse of herself in the hallway mirror. Blood soaked her clothes, dried red rivulets stained her face, coated her arms and legs, and knotted her hair. "I believe other than being dazed, I'm okay. The medics said I only have a small cut on my leg. But Edward..." Tears filled her eyes and she trembled. Unconcerned about staining his clothes with the blood, Alexander drew her into him. The Governor dispatched a servant to escort Alex and Nikki to a quiet room in the residence where she could clean-up.

Inside the sanctuary behind the closed doors, Nikki released the terror of the day, sobbing into Alex's chest. He encircled her with his soothing comfort. Before showering, Alex had her lie down on the marble vanity top, with her head over the bowl. Gently he rinsed and combed through her hair using tweezers to remove the fine shards of glass and metal which peppered her head. Nikki looked up into his eyes, deep with concern as she lay there and he ministered to her. "How did you know to send the car?"

"You don't think such a small thing as a car bombing goes unnoticed by the local source of government, do you?" he smiled a bit.

"I guess I'm not thinking clearly yet."

"It's okay," he paused. "James and I were in conference when his Chief of Staff ran in with the bulletin. I immediately thought about your safety. When we switched on the TV though, I never imagined that *my wife, covered in blood*, would be the first image that flickered onto the screen! I could not believe it! It was like living in a never-ending nightmare. The television ran it, over and over again. Your camera crew was doing a live feed at the time and caught the entire thing. One moment you were bowing to the shopkeeper, the next the camera went out of focus. Then it came back to you—drenched in blood, pushing off Edward. Next, someone dragged you off-camera. Unfortunately for me, the film crew stayed with the scene and didn't follow you. I was frantic. James immediately ordered a car to be sent. What happened? Where did you go?"

"I don't really know. This Chinese guy said I was in danger and yanked me out of there. I realize I should have questioned him, but I didn't have my wits about me. I just followed. Thank God Jarred was there to take care of me."

Invoking the name of God brought Edward's memory back to her. "Edward saved my life, didn't he?"

Alex nodded solemnly, "Yes, I suspect he did. We will know for sure soon."

By his answer, Nikki knew as soon as she could handle being on her own, Alex would be off to police headquarters to begin his own investigation of the day's events.

"Did you see the face of the Chinese man who grabbed me? Did you recognize him?"

"Not really. But I am sure by this afternoon everything will be clear." Alex's answers shortened as his mind launched into putting together the entire scenario.

The Governor's doctor knocked at the bedroom door. Leaving Nikki in his capable hands, Alex lightly kissed her good-bye on the cheek, then departed for police headquarters. After taking a sedative, Nikki slept into the evening.

The circumstances grounded Nikki in Hong Kong for two more days. Alex and the Governor's attaché accompanied her down to the police station the next day to finish her interview. Both sat with her while a captain conducted the proceedings. In deference to Nikki's companions, this time he conducted a much more cordial interview. At its conclusion, Alex had her security escort Nikki back to her hotel. He stayed on to wrap up his own investigation.

The official police report branded the bombing as "Tong related" with Nikki's presence an "unfortunate coincidence" of poor timing. The authorities labeled Jarred's role in the death of the Chinese man "justifiable homicide". Neither Alexander nor Charlie Soo recognized the corpse of the thug who grabbed Nikki.

Edward had indeed saved Nikki's life by throwing his body on top of hers. Alex flew him home to his family in England, quietly picking up the entire funeral expense in gratitude for Edward's supreme sacrifice. Gray skies never lifted the week of Edward's funeral as rain fell continually.

During that time, a disconcerting silence grew between Alex and Nikki. Finally she confronted him. "The investigation fingered random gang violence as the cause. Was it really?"

The question caught Alex off guard. Nikki's solemn face told him she wouldn't buy sugarcoating. Alex shook his head, "Nicole, I just don't know. The police seemed genuinely convinced of Tong involvement. The shopkeeper owed them a tremendous debt. The Tong sent a warning. It appears you happened to be in the wrong place at the wrong time."

"Was the guy Jarred iced part of the Kwan family or the Tong involved with the bombing?"

"Neither."

"Then why grab me?"

"The police theorize he acted as a loner, seizing the opportunity of the moment to hustle some bucks on the back of the tragedy. He probably wanted a hostage for ransom. Being the center of media attention made you a target."

"Tell me the truth, Alex. You don't know if that's what actually happened or whether this was an elaborate plot by *them* to get me, in an attempt to get at you? Right?"

Alex's face registered shock. Nikki had struck pay dirt. "That's what has you so tied up in knots, isn't it?"

Defeated, he nodded.

Nikki went for broke. "The night of the Grenoble caper, Charles Bradley made some damning allegations. I confirmed them with Mann shortly after our honeymoon. They said you are a 'terminal agent' and that things like Hong Kong will continue to happen because *they* won't let you retire. Is that true?"

Holding his head in his hands, Alex didn't look up. "I pray to God, Nicole, they are wrong. I've invested my life and now yours, in the conviction they are wrong." His red eyes met hers. "I can't believe that if I strip myself of all my contacts and take myself out of play that *they* would still consider me a threat. If I'm no longer in the loop, why come after me? With the speed information travels these days, within a month I'm old news—within six months, a useless dinosaur. But to answer your question, yes. The terminal agent syndrome continually plays in the back of my mind."

Hong Kong simmered in the recesses of their hearts. Alex and Nikki spent long hours immersed in conversation about the incident and the syndrome. Alex couldn't dispel his feeling of utter impotence over being separated and without communication between them. "How can I ever be separated from you again, without memories of that day terrorizing me?"

The idea of remaining in constant communication with each other possessed him. He spent countless hours researching, voraciously devouring a variety of technical journals. Alex sent and received communiqués from numerous sources.

In the week before Nikki left England to begin her final sweep through the Continent, Alex proposed an idea. "The technology for incredible miniaturization of transmitters, receivers and their support power exists today. My thought is, why not permanently install such devices in people? I found a doctor in Austria who believes in the possibility of such implants. This might give us the ability to be in constant communication with each other, no matter how many miles separate us. Nicole, in three weeks your tour will stop in Vienna. Would you meet me in Dr. Hartz's office while you're in Vienna?"

His proposal astonished her. It sounded as far out as the new sci-fi TV show *Star Trek*, with its transporters and phasers. For his benefit, Nikki tried to hide her reaction, but her heart wouldn't surrender its skepticism.

Alexander anticipated her tepid response. Patiently he walked Nikki through how a transmitter could be lodged near her larynx with a receiver strategically placed near the auditory canal of her ear. The battery pack could be installed in a crown of a molar. He'd have identical equipment installed.

Nikki could see the possibilities although it still seemed so far fetched to live with these devices inside her. But Alex truly believed, and she believed in him. Upping the ante, Nikki offered, "I still have a week before I resume my farewell tour. Why wait until the tour reaches Vienna? Why not visit Dr. Hartz today?" Hartz would either answer all her questions or provide her with enough ammunition to fight Alex's plan.

Klaus Hartz typified the young, opportunistic, whiz-bang kid of that era. Like his counterparts in NASA or the geniuses fueling the computer revolution, he kept one foot grounded in basic principles and the other strapped to the silver rocket of technology. In his mid-thirties, with shining eyes, Hartz launched into a full explanation of the fundamentals of the design, the procedure and its supposed operation.

With the rest of her tour scheduled to resume in a few days, Nikki questioned him on the recuperation time and possible interference with her vocal chords.

Speaking with supreme confidence, Klaus addressed every single issue of hers. Alex also threw in a few concerns of his own which Hartz also answered efficiently. In the end, the two of them consented. Since the operation required both of them to be under anesthesia at the same time, Alex sent for Lorenzo. At six that evening, with his top three assistants, Hartz operated.

Alexander insisted on "dead on" secrecy. No one from the Agency ever knew about the operation. Only Hartz and Lorenzo knew the patients' true identities. Hartz took great pains to obscure the parts of their faces outside the operational field. Throughout the operation and in his subsequent private notes, the doctor referred to them only as "subjects male and female." Then Alex bought all the rights to Hartz's work, guaranteeing the totality of it would remain forever outside the government and private sectors.

Lorenzo never left their sides during the four-hour surgery or their night in recovery. Hartz had them on their feet at sunrise; however, to minimize swelling, he froze their throats and insisted on two days of total silence. Testing the devices, he sent soft tones resonating through them. The tones as a side effect actually promoted healing. On the third day, Nikki awoke to Alex softly bidding her "good morning". Her eyes fluttered open, with Alex nowhere in sight. From another room, through the implant, he spoke to her. Nikki, Alex and Hartz spent the rest of the day testing and fine-tuning the devices. And Alex returned Nikki with enough time for two days of rehearsal before her Hamburg opening.

Alex and Nikki worked out codes and signals for communication without words in case the need should arise and they weren't able to speak. Nikki felt as if a special guardian angel sat on her shoulder. Anywhere, at any time, they could send messages to each other. With her eyes closed, it felt as if Alex were always by her side, only a heartbeat away. In fact, the "life sounds" of the other person—their heartbeat and breathing—abided in them as a constant comforting rhythm, although Hartz had refined the devices to allow them to minimize those sounds heard by the other person. They could be dialed up if necessary or dialed down to the point of elimination. Dialing down the communicators proved a useful tool to mask private conversations like when Alex made arrangements to surprise his Nicole with flowers at all her tour stops. When in the dialed-down mode, a private code between them let them know to dial up the device to receive a communiqué.

As Nikki boarded the jet to take her across the Continent, Alexander warned her that the communication devices didn't supersede the need for security or vigilance. He cautioned Nikki, in his last kisses, to hang close to Jarred.

The three-week interruption of the tour from the car bombing and death of Edward only heightened the crowd's hunger for Nikki. The venues weren't large enough to accommodate the demand. Continually

Nikki fought off exhaustion, pushing her limits to keep going. Mary rescued her several times to keep her voice from collapsing during the lengthy interview sessions piggy-backed onto the concerts. Nikki found the adulation rush of those final days intoxicating. At times she felt like she soared over life itself. Sometimes she worried how she'd survive without fame's magic elixir. But in the quiet moments after a long day, the memory of the magnificent light from Alexander's eyes snuffed out the lure of fame's fleeting candle.

Crossing the Channel back into England, the emotional radiation electrified the air at Nikki's last show. It crackled and sizzled across the blackness before the introduction, pulsing through her body. The lights flashed on. Energized, poised on the highest pinnacle of the rollercoaster, Nikki stood up, flung her arms in the air and dared the crowd to ride with her. Together they surged over the peaks and plunged down the precipices in that delirious final ride. Her group, her backup, the audience, all refused to let go. When they came to the end, they went again. They wanted more, so they went again. And for a final time, again.

Sam Rottenburg rented an entire soundstage at Pinewood for her farewell party. He invited *everyone,* as only Sam could do. Notables from the music world, the European glitterati and of course, Hollywood, stopped by Sam's bash. Alexander declined. He wanted Nikki to enjoy the final fruits of her labor without his intrusion. He didn't want Nikki to feel obligated to attend to him and thereby miss meaningful opportunities with her colleagues. *Wings of Nevermore* waited fueled and ready to carry her off to *Napoli* whenever she decided to leave, be it in two hours or two days.

Somewhere around dawn, Karl, Bruce and Mary rode out to the airfield with Nikki. Reed Dawson waited at parade rest by the air stairs to escort her into the jet. Exhaustion blunted their emotions and spared everyone a tearful departure.

Nikki found *Napoli* strangely empty. She knew Alex wouldn't be there, but Zia and Lorenzo were gone, too. Escorting her inside, Reed conducted a security check of the empty house before taking his leave. Padding her way down to her old, familiar room, Nikki slipped into Alex's shirt—still in the armoire—and slid in between the cool sheets of her old bed. She didn't come to until the sun woke the world the next morning.

Still in the foggy fingers of sleep, Nikki put on the white terry robe over Alex's shirt and made her way to the kitchen. Zia gently drew Nikki into her arms as a mother would enfold a child fresh from sleep. "*Buon giorno*," she greeted, smoothing Nikki's cheek with her hand. "You must have slept very well." She poured Nikki a cup of tea, ushering her to a seat in the nourishing sun.

Revived once she finished her tea, Nikki returned to the kitchen to greet Zia properly. "*Buon giorno*, dear Zia."

They chatted for a moment before Zia slid a tray with a cup of coffee and a cup of tea in front of her. "Why don't you take your husband a cup of coffee?" A twinkle sparkled in her eyes, as a sly smile rested on her lips.

"Alex is here?" excitement invigorated Alex's wife.

"Sure. He arrived yesterday afternoon, in time to watch you sleep." Nikki's eyes lit up.

Zia patted her face. "Ah, it's so nice to see the joy of love. Here, wait." She stacked a tray with some of her oven-fresh breads.

Since Nikki had never been to Alex's room, Zia led the way. Holding the door open for her to pass through, she silently and definitely latched it behind Nikki. The size of Alexander's room elicited a gasp from her. A large living room would have been dwarfed inside his chamber. The centerpiece of the room—his bed—drew her eyes immediately. The immense, four-poster rosewood bed rose so high off the floor, a two-step bench assisted in access. Opposite his bed, at a comfortable distance, a bank of huge floor-to-ceiling terrace doors stood flung open. The heavy, sage-colored velvet portieres puddled inside the sash, leaving the white Belgium sheers to billow in the morning breeze. Exquisite, deep-pile silk Oriental rugs blanketed the stone floors and led into the master bath. Massive furniture, carved from the same wood as the bed, tastefully simple, yet exquisite with detail sat comfortably in the room.

In the bed, on his side, his skin bronze against the white sheets that swathed his torso, lay her husband. Nikki watched him sleep as she tiptoed to the nightstand along side the bed and set down the tray. Wisps of sunlight reflected the spun gold in his hair against the pillowcases.

Nikki sat on the bed, easing over next to him.

With her weight on the bed his eyes opened, bright, blue, alert. A smile instantly followed as he reached his arms out to enfold her. "Mmm, good morning, darling," he pulled Nikki to him and kissed her.

Wiggling closer to him, she slipped free of the robe leaving only his shirt between them. Lifting the sheet so she could climb in next to him, Nikki could see she was still overdressed, so she doffed the shirt.

The steaming beverages had cooled by the time Alexander carried them out to his terrace. "When I arrived yesterday, you were sleeping. I did not have the heart to wake you. I sat by your side for a while. The angels and I watched you sleep."

"I must have been really tired," Nikki excused.

"Incredibly so." A gentle sea breeze tempered the dazzling morning sun. Alex teased, "I suppose in your exhaustion you found your old room yesterday and collapsed there. You aren't planning on making that your permanent residence, are you?"

Creating a place for her in his lap, Nikki purred, "Of course not. I'm not about to let you rumble around in that big old room any longer by yourself."

"I hope not!" he laughed heartily. "Lorenzo can move your things over today."

"If you don't mind, sweetheart, I'd rather do it. It will feel more like coming home. Anyway, I'm part of the family now. Zia and Lorenzo aren't here to wait on me."

Alexander wrapped her in his arms, plying her with tiny kisses. "Nicole, Nicole. You do so astound me!"

Eagerly Alex helped Nikki move. Of all the armoires and assorted chests in his room, nearly two-thirds of them sat empty. He threw open their doors, exposing their cavernous vaults. "See, just waiting for you!" Her clothes from the other room didn't even fill one unit. And other than a few choice gowns, Alexander had no intentions of moving her clothes from the English cottage over either.

For two days they relaxed at *Napoli* without timetables or plans, gliding over the crystal sea in the sailboat or exploring the surrounding landscape hand-in-hand. They danced the evenings away on the terrace in their finery under the starlight. Then Alex arranged an extended shopping trip to update Nikki's wardrobe to reflect the grace of her current station. They visited all the houses of *haute couture* from Dior in Paris to Magli in Milan. Alexander aimed to fill up those armoires.

Jetting back to Nikki's cottage, they packed up sentimental items and left the rest until they decided exactly where they'd call home. Dressed in blue jeans and old shirts, they spent their last night ever in the cottage, rummaging through packing boxes and trunks, tagging furniture to be shipped to *Nevermore*. The rest of the household items and articles of "Nikki clothing" would be auctioned off to benefit her Deus Foundations.

On the first of June, Alexander popped the cork on a bottle of champagne. They drank to his official retirement from the Agency and a future full of each other.

Since the car bombing threw off Nikki's schedule, they missed the prelude to the summer social season—the festival at Cannes. But June's arrival kicked the season in the Mediterranean into high gear. By now, news of their nuptials had reached all of Alexander's set. Every day brought another round of invitations. Gladly, Nikki surrendered the social calendar into Alex's experienced hands. As he slit one envelope open after another, he whistled, "These people sure want to check you out! I don't ever remember a season with so many invitations!"

"Yeah. They want to see who removed their most eligible bachelor from the menu." Nikki walked around behind him, kissed his neck and slid her hands inside his shirt, down the front of his chest—just to establish her territory. "Hope they approve."

"Their opinions have never mattered to me, darling. I inherited these people from my grandfather. Occasionally they provide some interesting distractions." Alex pulled an engraved invitation with a nautical theme out from the pile. "This one sounds rather engaging, though. Magda always throws nice little get-togethers on her boat at the beginning of the season. Shall I tell her we are coming?"

Magda Forsburg, of the steel Forsburgs, with distant ties to the Romanovs, operated as the unofficial empress of the set. Each year she launched the social season, always timing it with the arrival of the summer's first full moon. That year it would be on June eighth.

"So what should I wear to my social unveiling?" Nikki's word choice obviously amused her husband.

"Unveiling? Hmm ... interesting. Oh, any old thing, after all, it's just on a boat. Why not go shopping? Buy something you like, and I'll supply the accessories to compliment your selection." Then Alex disengaged totally from the subject, declining even to go along shopping. Obviously in this, Nikki would sink or swim on her own.

Nikki shopped in Naples for an outfit in keeping with the fete's nautical theme. She chose a bare-midriff top of white linen-lined chiffon with long sheer sleeves and navy blue satin trim on the sailor collar and tie. Matching wide bell-bottom trousers, contoured to ride on her hips completed the ensemble.

"Perfect!" Alexander praised as she pirouetted before him. "The white is gorgeous against your beautiful tan." He added sapphire teardrops surrounded with diamonds for her neck and ear apparel.

Nikki felt special stepping into the launch carrying them out to Magda's boat. But as they rounded the rocks of the cove where the Forsburg boat was moored, Nikki found Alexander's use of words to be decidedly less than accurate. The "boat" transformed itself into a yacht of over two hundred feet, complete with a helipad. The "little gathering" meant a guest list of no less than one hundred. With their approach, Magda's yacht grew in enormity, and Nikki could see that everyone's attire was incredibly formal. Aghast, her eyes widened in anticipation of her public humiliation.

She swung around to Alexander who met her horror with amusement. "Alex! This isn't some little gathering. There are *lots* of people, and they are *all dressed!*"

"As are you!" he greeted her complaints with a damned smile!

His response infuriated her. "You knew!" she accused. "Are you trying to humiliate…"

Alex recognized the tone of her anger and its direction. "Just the opposite, darling. I wanted you to be comfortable in whatever you chose to wear. I found your selection entirely appropriate, and not a cookie-cutter replica of the others. After tonight, they will remember you, and not for being a lamebrain would-be trying to crash their circle. They will recognize your independence and remember your strength of character. Use your ability to finesse people and their opinions. Take control, like only you can, when you walk on that boat! I guarantee you, by the end of the evening, they will be rethinking *their* choice of apparel." Smiling, he kissed her hand, "You will make their night memorable."

Attentively Alexander stayed at her elbow throughout the introductions, delighting in her natural sparkle. As Nikki's comfort level increased, she wandered from his side, although Alex couldn't release her from his sight. More than once she caught his eyes hanging on her with pride as she mingled with his friends. Nikki fielded a host of compliments on her outfit, which she politely dismissed as comfortable. True to Alex's predictions, before long, quite a few disappeared below decks to slip out of their formal attire and re-emerge in their own version of comfort.

Alexander didn't bring his Nicole to the party to pretend aloofness or boredom in marriage. Without being obnoxious, he flaunted his affection for her. They danced together and, thanks to her South American dance lessons, they stopped the party with their rendition of the tango. In encouragement, the guests enthusiastically plucked roses from Magda's multi-tiered floral arrangements and threw them at the couple's feet.

On the culminating crescendo, Alexander arched her back in an overdone kiss. "Have I told you lately how much I love you?"

Through the month of June they drifted from one event to another, a weekend retreat at a Sicilian wine cave, a powerboat regatta off Majorca, surf parties on the Isle of Crete, yacht races around the Greek Isles. Routinely members of various royal families rotated in and out of the enclave. Although kept at arm's length by bodyguards, the paparazzi usually trailed along behind them. Most of the people in the group distanced themselves from the limelight that infected the royals. Following polite salutations, the majority scattered for the safety of anonymity. Not wishing to contaminate her new playground, Nikki, too, took a powder at the mere sight of anyone attached to a camera.

One night during that golden summer, Nikki dreamt of a magnificent house, high above the coastline, with waves crashing on the breakers below. Shades of cream and white washed the entire vision. So vivid was the dream that she remembered dividing up her furnishings by whether they fit in the new house or not. Cut limestone block walls supported soaring carved mahogany ceilings with long corridors of travertine marble running everywhere. Floor-to-ceiling windows welcomed in all the beauty of nature. Nikki related the peaceful and engaging dream to Alex over breakfast the next morning. Determined, he set out to find the castle of her dreams. On their Mediterranean journeys over the summer, Alexander often pulled Nikki away from the festivities for house hunting. Lorenzo traveled ahead of them, bird-dogging candidates. But nothing matched her dream. And Alex wasn't interested in almost.

Alex proposed to be in Pennsylvania for her birthday. *Nevermore* would be nearing completion and more than anything, she wanted to see it. Nikki's mom and dad insisted that Zia and Lorenzo come, too. They all flew back early in time for an old-fashioned, small-town celebration of the Fourth of July.

Even Nikki's dreams couldn't have fathomed the renaissance of the transformed estate. Their contractor, Gus Schubert, had resurrected the crumbled stone fence, enlarging it to enclose the entire estate's expanse. The stones in the house gleamed from their cleaning and new grouting. New fascia and shutters in French blue with traditional Amish heart cutouts complimented the gray hues of the stonewalls. Even electric candles, hearkening back to a centuries-old custom, lit every window. Inside, new walls with the patina of antique plaster concealed the modern wiring and new plumbing. Refined commercial appliances mingled beautifully with the honey hue of the hickory cabinetry in the country kitchen. Slabs of carrera marble covered the countertops. Gus even had uncovered the old walk-in fireplace at the far end of the room where the first lady of the house, two hundred years ago, had cooked the meals.

The antique long-trestle table and authentic Windsor chairs Nikki had selected before they left now sat in front of the hearth. Picking an armful of wildflowers, she arranged them on the table in an old Mason jar from the cellar. By the end of the first day, they had placed their smattering of furniture and officially moved into the house. Even though it was July, Nikki insisted on lighting a fire in the fireplace and sitting inside her husband's arms, reveling in their life together. Sipping summer wine, they added new dreams to their foundation of old ones.

In keeping *Nevermore* as their country retreat, they dispensed with formal dress for dinner in favor of living in jeans. They decided to furnish the entire house with period-appropriate antiques from the area.

In addition to the house, Gus had renovated the dilapidated old barn. While they were in residence at *Nevermore*, Thunder moved from *Creekside* into the refurbished barn. Nikki's father and Alex went on a buying trip to the local auction and came home with a chestnut Hunter with impressive bloodlines for Alex to ride. Unable to wait a single moment, Nikki and Alex saddled up Tomorrow's Destiny and Thunder for a turn around the countryside.

Alex planned a small open-house to show off *Nevermore's* renovations with a simple backyard cookout marking Nikki's birthday. The man-of-the-hour, their contractor Gus Schubert, arrived early. His tall stature always surprised Nikki no matter how many times they had been together. Handing Gus an iced Heineken, Alex further elaborated on his long association with him. "Nicole, remember I told you when we hired Gus that he worked for the same "company" as I did? Well, had things not been quite so hectic, you might have met him on your last assignment. Gus handled the demolition and reconstruction for the Grenoble caper."

Rolling his Germanic blue eyes, pretending exhaustion, Gus nodded, "Yes, it was the razor-thin timeline on that job that left me hankerin' for the relaxed lifestyle of the private sector. Not that seven months to rehab *Nevermore* left any time for sitting with my feet up, readin' the sports pages. But it's nice to know that if I miss a deadline now the only thing it might cost me is a few zeros in my paycheck."

The relaxed celebration at *Nevermore* centered around the picnic table filled with fresh wildflowers, under the old oak looking down the rolling yard to the stream and the woods beyond. Besides the family, Alex made a point of including Mary. She arrived with her new beau, a Navy man named Clint, whom she had met while on hiatus in Virginia.

Before sunset, Alex emerged from the house carrying a box, which he set not in front of the birthday girl, but in front of her parents. "If it hadn't been for you, such happiness would never have been possible for me. For your daughter's presence on this earth, I will be eternally grateful." Fran unwrapped a hand-carved wooden box with a small brass key to wind the music box. A gold plaque inside the lid read, "Daily I thank God for Nicole. I will treasure her forever."

Picking up Nikki's hand, Alex led her from the picnic table down to the creek as the little band of revelers scampered along behind them. At the creek, Alex moved a large plywood box that covered a hefty natural outcropping of bluestone. There in the stone Alex had hired a mason to carve, "A.V. loves N.V. Alone nevermore."

"What more could I give you, than my soul's profession forever in granite?" Alex kissed her hand entwined with his. "Happy birthday, darling."

Within the week they flew west to check the progress of Alex's hotel venture. A thick, dark-green plush covered the summertime slopes of Vail. They drove directly to the construction site where structural steel now poked up from the ground. In front of the development stood a sign with a full color rendering on it. The project resembled a storied Black Forest country home. Alex ran up to the construction trailer in search of the project's superintendent. Quickly he emerged with the super. Both wore hard hats and carried one for her. Steve Murphy led off on a tour of the site. Walking among the concrete and girder skeleton, Steve detailed different aspects of the construction. While the men spoke, Nikki snapped the project from various angles with her camera.

Steve invited them to his home for dinner, a charmingly rustic log cabin set on the edge of the national forest. Over the meal he apologized for tying Alex up with details. His wife, Linda, offered a day of antique shopping while the men worked again.

Alex cringed, "Wonderful, Linda! We just finished our home in Pennsylvania. I am sure Nicole will find your area antique stores most interesting."

"Remember darling, what you buy has to fit in the plane," he teased Nikki.

She responded by tossing him a smile, "Sweetheart, they have a wonderful new service here. It's called UPS—they even ship to the back-water hills of Pennsylvania."

"Then I suspect you will need this." Pretending resignation, Alex fished his credit card out of his wallet, grandly handing it to her.

"Ooo, plastic!" cooed Linda. "Do I know the places to use it!"

Alex appreciated the extra time on the project. In addition to spending a quiet, girls'-day-out shopping with Linda, Nikki found several nice accent pieces perfect for *Nevermore*.

Throughout the day, even though separated, Alex and Nikki tapped out little messages to each other on their communicators. "Is there room left on the card for me to buy lunch?" Alex drolly questioned. Of course, without a limit on his credit, room for everything existed.

"No!" Nikki tapped, then dialed down her communicator to taunt him.

The third day Alex and Nikki rode the lift up the mountain and picnicked along the trails inside the woods. She packed their favorite wine and cheese lunch to spread out on a blanket among the trees. As they basked in the dappled sunshine shimmering through the leaves, Alex sighed. "Never in my life have I met anyone, who understood me so thoroughly, so completely. I don't have to ask for anything. You just know. I promise you, Nicole, with every breath in my body and beyond, I shall always be there for you. I will love you forever." Overcome by the seclusion within the cathedral of trees, Alex stole a few kisses, then dared to steal more.

With the Vail project underway to Alex's satisfaction, they returned to the high life of the Mediterranean, sailing to Cyprus for the grape harvest. August and September passed in uneventful routine. Alex began to acquaint Nikki with parts of his olive oil, wine, and, yes, rum businesses.

Life for both the Vincentes slowed to a delicious crawl. Nikki hadn't exercised her voice since she left the tour. Indeed, while walking through the olive trees one day, Alex commented on their extended period of leisure. "Do you realize that four solid months have passed since I have had any contact with the Agency. I did not know life could be so peaceful." He hugged her to his side and kissed her forehead. "I should be so far out of the information loop by now that I am sure I am officially a know-nothing. So much for the terminal agent syndrome, four months and not even a single incident that could be misconstrued."

"But it's been on your mind the whole time though, hasn't it?"

"Of course it has. You don't think that everyplace we went this summer I didn't check out in advance? We never entered a room that I didn't sweep for bugs. And you never left my sight when armed security didn't accompany you." Alex let all of this fall off his tongue in matter of fact fashion.

"You're kidding?" Nikki questioned, semi-stunned.

Alex wrapped his arm about her, "Darling, I will never take a chance with your precious life ever again. But soon, hopefully, all this worrying will be in the past."

"You mean even in the States, like when Linda Murphy and I went shopping?"

"Two cars, each with two of my men, followed you everywhere. Once you even turned around too quickly and ran into one of them."

Her mind poured over that shopping trip. "I remember running into a big guy. I ran back to get something and plowed right into this hulk of a man. He was yours?"

"Yes, that was the one. Does it bother you, Nicole?"

"Of course not. How could I be bothered by my husband caring so much that he wraps his protective arms around me even when I'm miles away?"

In early October, a real lethargy fell over Nikki, and her stomach felt upset all the time. She put on a brave face, but wanted nothing more than to rest on a chaise in the sun. Alex never mentioned it, but she was sure he noticed.

October also brought a dangerous Czech uprising, as a hearty band of peasants tried to throw off the shackles of communism. An urgent communiqué requesting Alexander's intimate historical knowledge of that theater sucked him out of Nikki's arms and away from *Napoli*. Alex promised Nikki he'd be safe inside Agency headquarters, that Junger merely wanted to siphon from him his protocol knowledge. But a heart-wrenching shudder racked her when she found his wedding ring back in his ring box.

Chapter 31
Yet Another Horizon

As a distraction in his absence, Alex suggested over his communicator that a trip to Pennsylvania might be in order.

The chill of autumn permeated the air at *Nevermore*. Each morning Nikki awoke to frost covered fields. Actually she relished the nip in the air as she loved to snuggle inside her bulky, warm sweaters. To that end, she moved over a cedar chest full of sweaters from her old room at *Creekside*. But she found even that small project physically depleted her. Despite the thousand nit-picky details of decorating and arranging that cried out for attention inside her house, Nikki spent most of her time either sleeping or curled up around a hot water bottle to soothe her tummy.

A week into her stay, Alexander finally joined Nikki at *Nevermore*. Surprising her with his arrival, she woke one morning to feel his warm lips caressing her forehead and cheek. Slipping under the covers next to her, he wrapped her up in his strong, loving arms, and sought comfort from the long absence they had endured. Breathing him in, she again imprinted on his masculine scent while nestling into his chest. Nikki pulled away only momentarily to retrieve his wedding ring and to return it to its rightful place.

During a routine visit to *Creekside*, Fran drew Alex aside to share with him her concerns about Nikki's health. Accusing them of conspiring against her, Nikki dismissed her condition as a bout of Asian flu. Alex accepted her explanation and didn't pass judgment when she left her wine untouched and half her dinner on her plate. Instead, when they returned home, he stoked the fire in the fireplace, and Nikki cuddled up in his arms as they pulled out more dreams for their future.

However, following breakfast the next morning, Dr. Hess rapped on the front door, answering a request from the co-conspirators. He performed the usual rituals with his instruments, then took swabs of saliva and drew blood.

By late afternoon he returned with his diagnosis. Nikki was with child and from his questioning, he placed the approximate time of conception in early September, thus calculating her due date to be about the first of June.

Alex couldn't contain the magnitude of his happiness. Sweeping Nikki up into his arms, he swung her around and covered her with kisses.

Dr. Hess calmed him down long enough to accept payment for his services. Then he handed Alex Dr. Jeffrey Weisberg's card, a doctor considered the best OB man in the state.

Like a child on Christmas, Alexander couldn't decide which way to jump first. Reacting in typical first-time father fashion, he immediately sat Nikki down on the couch. Putting her feet up on an ottoman, he sat beside them, rubbing her ankles. "Darling, I thought I could never be happier than to have you by my side. But this! You don't know. I am just..."

"I know. I couldn't be happier either," Nikki cautioned. "But I really don't want to get too carried away. I'm...I'm so afraid that losing the first one might have damaged me. Maybe I won't be able to carry..."

Alexander quieted her, "I understand. When we see Dr. Weisberg tomorrow, we will ask him if it presents a problem. Don't worry."

Still, Nikki's admonition couldn't stifle his optimism or his attentiveness. He politely passed on her parent's invitation to dinner because he couldn't guarantee his silence about her condition in their presence. Instead Alex whipped up an omelet with home-fried potatoes for their supper. They spent the rest of the evening in the glow of the fire, discussing everything other than the obvious.

Assuring Nikki that the fall she suffered more than two years ago shouldn't present her with any consequences, Dr. Weisberg issued her a clean bill of health. Loading her down with vitamins and schedules, he sent the couple out to conquer their new world.

All the dreams with which they had filled *Nevermore* now stood on the threshold of coming true. In front of the fire that evening, in their own private celebration Nikki and Alex began the great debate of boy or girl. And, of course, they toyed with names.

Sitting next to her with their heads almost together, Alex picked up a tress of his Nicole's hair and caressed it. "You are incredible. You have no idea, how very much I love you. Never forget, my darling, no matter what may happen, I will love you beyond life itself."

Laying out concrete plans for their dreams, Alexander wanted the baby to be born in the United States, in Pennsylvania to be specific. Accordingly, they structured their schedule to be at *Nevermore* for the last trimester through the birth and recuperation period. They began redesigning the upstairs to accommodate the baby, deciding to turn the room next to theirs into the nursery. They would open up the wall between the two rooms with a double doorway. Alexander offered to have Zia and Lorenzo move in to help after they brought the baby home. Nikki gratefully accepted.

Nikki passed on the initial gratification of telling her parents to include Alex's side of the family. In time for Thanksgiving, Alex flew in Zia and Lorenzo to be part of the grand celebration. Tears and champagne flowed as the family embraced the news.

The Thanksgiving holiday almost fell by the wayside in the shopping frenzy stirred up by the grandmothers. Riding high on their excitement, Alexander egged-on their buying sprees by slipping them money to fund their extravagances. Alexander dedicated himself to carrying out his unspoken intention of spoiling Nikki in an attempt to erase the last time. Of course nothing could erase it, but Nikki loved him for trying. She cherished every smile and each self-satisfied chortle as every day they displayed the new additions to the layette. It wasn't fair, but she couldn't help but compare the two pregnancies. Reveling in the differences, she imprinted each wonder-filled experience on her heart and thanked God for another chance.

November slid into December, and a ravenous appetite replaced Nikki's queasy stomach. She begged Alex to take her for walks or to begin a project to help her stay away from food. That went against Alexander's bent of indulging her, but for her sake later, he tried to be helpful—when he remembered.

Christmas approached. Under the guise of working on the nursery, Alex secretly brought in his old friend from the Agency, Gus Schubert, to build a state-of-the-art recording studio in the cellar for Nikki. "I had rather hoped you might record some songs for the baby." Alex prodded as he walked her through the studio Christmas morning.

Alex's suggestion planted the seeds in her heart for an album of children's songs. For the first time since May, music again stirred in Nikki's soul and flowed from her onto a spinning reel of tape.

Throughout the holiday, conversation centered on a New Year's Eve celebration in Hong Kong, which Alex had promised the entire family. Two years ago, in an effort to tantalize Nikki into staying with him, Alex dangled in front of her a promise to make New Year's Eve in Hong Kong "exciting". Never in his wildest dreams could he have anticipated the level of excitement the city would serve up in the coming holiday.

Chapter 32
Cataclysm in Hong Kong

They arrived the day before New Year's Eve in the magic city, resplendent in lights, awash in fairy dust confetti and shiny metallic streamers of silver and gold. More than any other event, Hong Kong greeted the New Year with enthusiastic effervescence. The spectacle of the ornately arrayed city bent on celebration transformed their parents into kids in a grown-up's fantasyland.

Naturally, Alex and Nikki toured them through the noted landmarks of the harbor city — like the alley where they first met in the middle of the Kwan scam and the street outside The Pearl restaurant where Nikki discovered the determination of her security team — all the regular-tourist high spots. They dropped by Charlie Soo's porcelain shop for introductions, only to find it uncommonly dark. With so many sights to take in, Alex moved their little band on to other things, vowing to catch Charlie another time.

In what seemed to be a never-ending pattern of "firsts" for Alex and Nikki, as they readied for dinner, Nikki felt the unmistakable flutter of life inside her for the first time. It came as a soft brushing, like a butterfly kiss. The news brought Alexander to his emotional knees. Wanting to crow to the world, his elite civility forced him to settle for an intimate observance between the two of them to mark the occasion. Clearly Alexander relished his involvement in every aspect of his unborn child's life, beyond his participation in the conception.

Of course to do the town on New Year's Eve, their attire needed to be formal. None of Nikki's gowns fit her any longer, but being in Hong Kong with its fashion-in-a-flash tailors, Alex treated all the women to new threads in which to usher out the old and ring in the new. Early in the morning, in the shop of their favorite couturier, Jimmy Chen, the women selected their fabrics and patterns as the seamstresses fitted them. The finished garments would be ready for pickup at five that evening.

With Hong Kong waiting and the rest of the day at their leisure to drink in the magnitude of the festivities pulsating through the town, they spent the day in the streets with the crowds. The celebration began atop Victoria Peak, where the group lunched in the open-air amid dragon and lion dances, accompanied by typical Chinese music. With the advancing afternoon, they joined the revelers spilling down the mountain and back into the city. Moving with the flow, they drifted along the street, sampling from the various food carts lining the sidewalks, roaming the shops. Towards late afternoon, before stopping at the dressmaker's, Alex suggested they hop the ferry over to Kowloon and attempt to pay Charlie Soo another visit.

Anxious to show off their parents, Nikki and Alex were delighted to find his shop open. In a giddy little bumble, their troop burst through the doors eager to have their friend Mr. Soo make their acquaintance.

Charlie met them, stiff-faced, with a cool, polite bow.

Oblivious to the swirling subtleties, Nikki dropped a quickie curtsey on her way to greet Charlie with her customary overtly-familiar hug.

Alex's fingers pressed tightly into Nikki's flesh, quickly catching her and forcing her to conform by returning Charlie Soo's polite bow. In a very stern tone through his communicator, Alex issued a crisp command, "Just bow! Follow my lead."

Instantly, Nikki dropped her smile and complied.

"Good afternoon, sir," Alex said respectfully from his submissive position. "Please excuse my band of rowdy American tourists. They only wanted to check out your fine collection of porcelain."

Alex stood up and barked at them. "Please control yourselves, while I make arrangements for you to view this gentleman's fine wares."

Instinctively everyone relented to Alex's uncharacteristically brusque manner.

With eyes cold and as black as midnight to match his somber expression, Charlie bowed again. "Sir, I humbly beg your forgiveness. My shop is closing at this time. All my clerks are gone. You should bring your group back another day, when I can *send for help* to accommodate you."

Alex returned the bow, "My humble apologies for intruding. I am so sorry. We will return at a later date. Thank you, sir."

"Yes. That is the best plan," Charlie bowed stiffly for a last time.

Efficiently Alex ushered them out and with another short bow closed the door. In silence, Alex swiftly shepherded them down the street, past the corner. After a few turns, they were out of sight of the Soo's shop.

The entire time Alex communicated madly with Nikki. "Take everyone to the dress shop. Keep all of your appointments. Charlie's in trouble. I have to go back."

"Is there anything I can do?"

"Just stick to tonight's itinerary. I will catch up with you when I can."

"Should I contact the police?"

"No! Follow the plan. Have Lorenzo track me."

With that, Alex began patting down his breast pockets of his jacket and initiated audible conversation, "Damn! I think I dropped my wallet back at that man's shop. Darling, you all run on to the dressmaker's before they close. I'll have to go back." Alex brushed a hasty kiss along Nikki's cheek, turned on his heel and dashed off.

As she laughed off his behavior with light-hearted excuses, Nikki heard through her communicator. "Darling, I love you. I'll be in touch." His extreme physical exertion left heart-pounding echoes in her ear. Nikki knew it must be bad. Even she had picked up the words "send for help" from Charlie's minced conversation.

Lorenzo also read Alex's distress. As soon as they reached the dress-maker on the island and Nikki had otherwise occupied the interests of the rest of the party, Lorenzo separated her so she could clue him in. "What's going on with Charlie Soo?"

"I don't know. Normally he's so cordial. Alex wants you to track him."

"Already done." replied Lorenzo. From the neck of his sweater he pulled out a gleaming gold medallion; she could see it quiver. "I slipped in my earpiece as soon as Alex left us." He demonstrated by touching his ear. "But here in the street, it only gives me an audio signal. I need to get back to plug it in to be able to have visual contact."

Nikki listened intently on her communicator, "I'm not getting anything else on the communicator. I guess now we wait."

"By the intensity of the radar signal, he's not far," Lorenzo tried to reassure her. "I assume he's doing re-con at Soo's shop. All the same, let's get back to the apartment and plug this thing in so we can pinpoint him."

Rounding up their purchases, Nikki hurried them back to the Furama. Perhaps everyone grasped the gravity, since their once boister-ous little band grew reserved with Alex's departure.

Nikki's stomach knotted itself around her heart. Back at the apart-ment, she put on a brave game face, continuing the positive pretense even as she listened for anything from Alex. As she was about to engage Zia and her mom in the preparatory rituals for their big night on the town, her father cornered her. "Nikki, I know something is up. I picked up on Alex's abrupt change of demeanor. Shouldn't you or Lorenzo do something to help Alexander and Mr. Soo? Shouldn't you call the police?"

Nikki saw his eyes laden with concern. "Dad, I'm not sure what's happening. I need some time alone with Lorenzo to figure this thing out. Can you occupy Mom and Zia for awhile?"

"Don't worry about us. I think everyone knows something's going on."

"Thanks, Dad," Nikki kissed his cheek and headed to Lorenzo's room. "We won't be long, then we can go out for the evening," she offered in appeasement.

"Take care of business first; then we'll see about going out. We'll be fine for as long as it takes."

Lorenzo sat in front of an open case with a radar screen on it. A green blip blinked at him. "I've put an overlay of Hong Kong island and the peninsula of Kowloon on the screen. See? He's still at Soo's shop. But I don't see any movement. Do you have anything?"

"Nothing. Just normal rhythm patterns. I'll see if I can raise him again." With her heart in her throat, Nikki tried again. Nothing. Then a long click came through, like Alex had clenched his teeth. "Alex, can you click once for yes, twice for no?" she asked.

One soft tap—"yes."

Nikki knew better than to ask if he was okay, so she proceeded. "We show you near Charlie's. Are you there?"

"Yes," he answered only with taps.

Hoping she wasn't coming across too loud for his situation she asked, "Do you need me to go to code?"

"No."

"Are you inside his shop?"

"Yes."

"In the store room?"

"Yes."

"Can you see Charlie?"

"No."

"Is Charlie there?"

"Yes."

"Is he all right?"

"No."

Her heart plummeted as she relayed each message to Lorenzo.

"Should we send the police?"

"No."

"Should I call Governor James?"

One tap, hesitation, then... dead air. Maybe Nikki heard the beginning of a second tap. Maybe she didn't. After the first tap, Alex's heart rate spiked, then rapidly declined. Within seconds, it sank to sleep rhythm.

"Lorenzo, they found him! He's unconscious!" Nikki cried in terror.

"I have slight movement on the screen. They must be dragging him."

"C'mon. We've got to save him!" In a blind protective panic, Nikki raced towards the door.

Lorenzo grabbed her arm. "Hold it! You're not going anywhere. I'll go," he said with gripped determination.

Her eyes flashed, "I'm going! You'll need me for communication."

Lorenzo disconnected his medallion and picked up the tracking device that looked like a transistor radio. "He'll kill me if I bring you along!" he said as he stuffed the pockets of his coat with the tracking device and added ammunition.

"If we don't get to him soon, that may be a moot point."

Pulling a gun from a waist holster underneath his sweater, Lorenzo flipped out the cylinder, checked his rounds, then snapped it in place. "Here, take this." he slapped the gun in her hands with the precision of a surgeon. Nikki deftly slid it into her pocket. From his suitcase he removed a .357 magnum, a derringer, a long blade and a roll of tape. Pulling his right pant leg up, he asked. "Do you have anything from him yet?"

"No," Nikki tried again. Nothing. "What can I do?" she asked as he ripped tape with his teeth and strapped the derringer to his leg.

"Get cash! Cash always comes in handy. Grab everything you have!"

As she flew out of the room, he hoisted the other pant leg. She heard more tape rip from the roll.

Spinning the dial on their bedroom safe, Nikki nervously clicked through the tumblers missing the combination the first time. Bingo! On the second try the door popped open. Grabbing the entire wad of Hong Kong dollars, she reached for the epitome of all currency—U.S. dollars! But, how much was enough? With Alex's life at stake, she wanted more.

Slapping down her frenzy, she pretended an air of calm before calling her father into the hallway.

Immediately he met her in the corridor.

"Dad, I don't have time for questions. Can I borrow all the cash you and Mom have on you?"

Pulling out his wallet, he put what he had in her hands. "There's not much here. Give me a second and I'll round up the rest from your mother." Nikki knew it took great strength for him to rein in his questions. Surely he figured it for ransom—and any way you spelled ransom, it translated into danger.

From her Agency experience, Nikki knew to change into black clothes, and she needed a dark coat with pockets for the gun and the money. She had none in her closet. From Alex's side, she grabbed his dark brown bomber leather jacket, still trying the whole time to raise him on the communicator. Nothing.

Her father met her in the hallway. "Here. It's all we've got," he snapped a two-inch stack of bills into her hand.

"Thanks," she said, cramming it deeply in the inside pockets of the jacket.

Her father gripped her arm, "You're involving the police in this, aren't you?"

"This isn't a police matter. I will work through the Governor's office," she reassured him. "That will be our first stop. We'll be okay. Don't worry." Then she tore down the hall to meet Lorenzo.

Lorenzo, with a black turtleneck on over black slacks, met her halfway, his coat draped over his arm. "Ready, Nikki?"

Lorenzo noted the concern on Richard's face, "Don't worry. I won't let Nikki out of my sight for a moment. I won't let anything happen to her."

Swiftly they disappeared out the door and into the elevator.

"Are you really going to the Governor's compound?" Lorenzo asked.

"Do you speak Chinese?" Nikki queried.

Lorenzo shook his head.

"Then we'll at least need an interpreter. I'll call the Governor."

Lorenzo stopped her. "Would Alex want to involve him?"

"I don't know, but he's not available now and since he didn't want the cops, I'm guessing this isn't a simple robbery gone wrong. It also rules out the Tong. In my estimation, this has the Agency's fingerprints all over it. We have to get some help. We need someone who knows the city and who can speak the language."

From the lobby Nikki phoned the Governor's mansion. She didn't waste time hanging on the phone. Breaking common courtesy and all protocol rules, Nikki issued a command to Nigel James. Tersely she dictated her immediate need for an interpreter/guide and notified him of her imminent arrival.

Normally recriminations for such bad manners would have haunted her. Instead, she prayed James heard her urgency and duly noted that something severe must be unfolding for her to have the audacity to issue an order to a superior. She hoped he'd honor her demands, without delay or questions. In between her prayers, Nikki tried again and again to raise Alexander, unsuccessfully.

Governor James waited outside for her, nervously puffing on a cigarette. Dressed in a tux, Nikki had obviously interrupted his plans for the

New Year. As the cab pulled up to the formal front entry, James threw down his smoke, grabbed the door and jerked it open. Nikki jumped out, leaving Lorenzo sitting inside the shadows of the cab.

"What's the emergency?" James questioned with agitation.

"Alex came upon a friend in a jam and went in to save him. I'm pretty sure they have him now, too. I'm going in to get him."

"In where? And who's the friend? Someone from the city?"

"Let's just leave it at a friend, okay?" Nikki wasn't sure how much to reveal.

"Why not call the police?"

"Alex said not to."

"Where are you going?"

Fire leapt from her eyes, "Wherever I have to, to get my husband back!"

Nigel James displayed no comprehension of the extreme gravity of her plight. Hijacked by her desperation, Nikki couldn't shake the feeling of beating her head against a brick wall. "Governor, this is *Alexander* we are talking about. He's in trouble! Now, do you have someone for me or not? We're wasting time here."

"Yes! I have someone. Is there any possibility you'll be going to the Mainland?"

"I don't know. Maybe. Whatever it takes," she didn't understand his point when Alex's life clearly hung in the balance. Deliberately, Nikki kept her answers short, hoping to impress upon him the dire emergency of the situation.

"Well then, you'll need papers. Give me your passports, and I'll issue them under the cover of a trading visa."

Impatient with the delay, but glad he had thought of the angle, Nikki turned to relate the matter to Lorenzo. Already his hand met her with his passport in it. She fished out hers, then turned them over to the Governor.

Sliding back into the cab while they waited, Lorenzo whispered, "If you're bringing someone else on board, you'll have to be careful with the communicators."

"Good point. I'll tell him Alex is wearing a wire."

"That should work," Lorenzo pulled out the tracking device and opened its hinged front. Plugging in the medallion, it blinked to life. "I don't have any further movement. What about you?"

Nikki stilled herself and listened, "Nothing."

It seemed like an eternity, but within five minutes, James re-emerged with a good-sized Chinese man dressed in a black Mao-type pajama outfit. Nikki jumped out to meet them. "This is Jack Chow, one of ours.

He speaks perfect English and five dialects of Chinese. He knows you are on a rescue mission and may need cover as a delegation from this embassy researching trade routes in China. Good luck. Report in when you can."

With haste, Nikki turned back towards the cab, when the Governor halted her mid-stride. "Nikki, let the taxi go. You may need more than a poor cabby to get you through this night. Let me get you a car."

Within seconds a black Mercedes squealed to a stop out front. Jack hopped in next to the driver. Under way, the Governor's man assumed authority, personally introducing himself and the driver, Lance. By no means a small man, Lance had the heft and hulk of an American body builder.

This wasn't a tea party, and Nikki made no attempt at polite conversation. Short on details, she brought Chow up to speed on the destination and the precise nature of their mission. On her direction, they sped off towards the ferry to Kowloon and Charlie's shop. The blip on Lorenzo's monitor remained stationary.

Down at the docks, they found that the New Year's celebration clogged the harbor, with over an hour's delay at the ferry crossing. "Can't you buy us a private ride across the causeway?" Nikki questioned Lance and Jack, pulling out a wad of dollars.

Chow's eyes lit up as he reached for the bills, "Ahh, the universal language! Cash will work faster than any Governor's pass. I'll be right back."

Jack quickly returned, directing Lance out of the hopelessly mired line for public transportation across the causeway and redirecting him to the pier for private launches. Even the private boats had waiting lists, no matter how much cash they flashed, but with shorter queues than the lumbering public ones.

Frantic to get off the island and across to the peninsula to her husband, Nikki looked around. She needed an angle to get them to the head of the line. "Jack, go back down to the boats and loudly announce, so the whole lot of boat pilots can hear, that 'Nikki, yes *the* Nikki' needs a ride and she will…"

"Will what," she thought to herself, tussling her hair with her hand. Her *Nevermore* ID bracelet moved on her wrist. "I'll trade my bracelet for a ride across the channel right now. In fact, let me go with you, Jack, and I'll tell them, myself!"

Jack regarded her idea with indignant skepticism. But with nothing to lose, and keeping in mind his prime directive of her safety, he hastily escorted her to the docks.

Racing to the pier, Nikki jumped ahead of him. "Helllooo!" she called loudly in a grand manner, like she had just stepped onto a stage. "Helllooo! ... It's me—Nikki!"

People turned around and looked. Instantly recognizing her, they nudged one another and moved closer.

"How's everyone tonight?" Nikki asked loudly, as a knot of curiosity seekers accumulated.

Astounded, Jack immediately elbowed her way through to the men Nikki needed to reach.

"What a great night! Happy New Year!" she called with unbridled exuberance.

Closing in, some in the crowd waved sheets of paper for Nikki to sign.

Jack hoisted her up onto a short stack of boxes, giving her a platform.

"I really need a ride to the other side, and I'll trade my bracelet, a one-of-a-kind gift from my husband, to go right now!" Nikki took off the jewelry and dangled it above her head. "Who will take my car and me?"

Several boat pilots stepped up. Negotiating with them, Jack handled the details.

The pilot who won the right to ferry the celebrity, pocketed a stack of money along with Nikki's bracelet before ordering his seaman to maneuver her car onto his boat. The crowd parted as they directed the Governor's vehicle through the morass.

Meanwhile, continuing with her persona cover, Nikki signed autographs while waiting for the car to be secured to the boat.

Crazy with worry, she wanted to fly across the causeway. But once aboard, while Lance and Lorenzo waited in the car, she knew she had to continue being "Nikki". The boat pilot had bought the right to ferry a star across the water. Implicitly, the deal included bragging rights to "being with" Nikki. Acting as her bodyguard, Jack waited outside with her while she chatted it up with the pilot and posed for pictures. Then she sincerely thanked them for helping to get her across the bay. Having finished her business, Nikki returned to the car before they reached the other side.

Back inside the Mercedes, Jack Chow began, "That was marvelous, Ma'am. I've never seen that done before. But the rest of this trip won't work that way. The people we will be dealing with are only fans of Chairman Mao, if you get my drift. The people we are going up against are exceptionally brutal. They play rough and for keeps. I sincerely hope, Ma'am, that you're not opposed to blood. Because in all probability, this will boil down to kill or be killed. If Alex fell into a nest of the enemy from the other side, by now they know who and what they have, or he'd already be dead in some alley. The Governor made it clear to me that you are in charge of this mission, but he instructed me my prime directive is to deliver you safely back to the compound, no matter the cost."

Nikki swallowed uneasily. She knew the "cost" had nothing to do with dollars and everything to do with human life—theirs. From the corner of her eye, she noted Lorenzo nodding along in silent agreement with Jack.

"Mr. Chow, my goal is to get my husband and his friend back alive. I will do whatever it takes to make that happen."

As they neared the store, the blip on the scope slowly began to move.

"They must be traveling," Lorenzo pointed out.

Nikki urged Lance to drive faster, but pouring on speed in streets choked with revelers proved an impossibility. Sporadic fireworks burst overhead. Each boom repeated danger in her heart, feeding the festering pit in her stomach. Like a salmon swimming upstream, Lance battled against traffic that flowed down towards the causeway. Nikki directed the driver to pull up a block past the store. They'd walk down onto Charlie's shop.

As they emerged from the Mercedes, the blip leapt, blinking furiously. "That's him!" Lorenzo shouted from a whisper. "He's in that silver car that just passed us!" Jumping back into the car, Lance tailed the silver sedan, allowing two cars between the vehicles. Then Lance turned onto parallel side streets, mirroring their movements, relying on the tracking device to pace the sedan's progress.

Watching the blip move steadily north, Jack spoke up. "Without a doubt they are heading for the Chinese border. What do you want to do, Ma'am? Should we intercept them before they reach it? It could be difficult to get him back once they've crossed."

"But if we stop them, they might kill him," Nikki protested. "Besides, we have these visas to get us inside."

"Excuse, ma'am. China is a brutal communist country. You're not Chinese. You don't blend in. Movement will be impossible. If they discover you, they will kill you without asking questions. Chances of any of us coming back alive will be almost zero. But it's your call."

Again Nikki pretended to speak into her sleeve to raise Alexander. Nothing.

"Ma'am, we are nearing critical mass here. A decision must be made. Nikki still couldn't raise him.

Again he pressured her, "Ma'am, how do you know he is even alive in that car?"

Hotly, Nikki stared him down, "I know!...What is your proposal for intercepting the car?"

"We'll ram him head on," Lance said coldly.

Aghast, she stared at him, "That's it?! We couldn't have car trouble in the middle of the road? Or invent some kind of a roadblock?"

"There's no time for one. And they'd never stop for the other. They will not stop unless they are stopped," Chow said without apologies.

"Will we live through it?" Lorenzo asked. "The lady is pregnant."

"This is the Governor's car with armor plates, bulletproof glass and cross-strap restraints. The driver is a professional. We're out of time. Decide!"

"Can you do it without killing those we are trying to save?"

"I will try my best Ma'am," Lance stared her down from the rearview mirror.

"Then do it!" Nikki resolved.

Lance floored the car. It rocketed ahead, outpacing the blip of the sedan. Lorenzo made sure the straps around Nikki were secure, then he checked his own. Jack checked the driver's restraints for him, then dove into the backseat behind the driver and strapped himself in.

The plan was to hit the sedan head-on, striking the driver's side. Gaining distance on him, Lance calculated exactly how far ahead he needed to be before he spun the vehicle around and started toward them. Speed and distance constraints pushed them to within a kilometer of the border. Lance yelled at his passengers to brace for the turn. At the precise moment, he hit the brakes alternately with the accelerator and with an acute turn of the wheel, slid the car into a one-eighty. Tires squealed as they crashed through their own haze of burning rubber. Pushing the accelerator to the floor, their turn placed them on a collision course with the silver sedan — dead ahead.

Checking the screen, Lorenzo confirmed they indeed had the target vehicle in their sights. Then he pulled the medallion from the monitor and stowed it for impact.

Frantically Nikki called to her husband. "Alex! Alex, it's Nikki. We're going to ram your car. Brace yourself. Brace Charlie. Alex, do you hear me! Alex — brace yourself. Alex! Alex!" The racing engine roared in her ears.

Piercing her with mad-dog intensity, Lorenzo commanded, "Whatever happens, stay in the car!"

Chow barked, "You must do as you are told. If I say drive back to the compound, you do it!...as fast as you can, and don't stop for any of us. Do you understand?"

Automatically Nikki nodded back to them.

"We're going to try to save Alex, but if we can't, you must survive," Jack shouted.

"Understand?!" Lorenzo demanded.

The entire scene played out in surreal stop action. They hurtled towards the silver sedan at light-speed — in slow motion. Lance cloaked his intention of a collision to preclude the sedan from initiating evasive action. With the sedan in his sights, he would swerve from his lane and cross in front of the sedan at the precise moment. To keep the driver from evading them, Jack was to take him out just before they crossed into the sedan's path. To this end, Jack raised an Uzi-type weapon and opened his window. Checking the door lock, he threw his body weight against the door. Lorenzo, on the opposite side, pulled out his .357, opened his window and did the same. Lorenzo would fire only if Jack missed.

Lance signaled, "Ready. On my mark, — three — two — one!" An instant before Lance swerved into the path of the oncoming car, Jack Chow, with his profile tight against the car, leaned out and sprayed shots at the driver, then slid back down inside the car and his restraint.

Hit, the driver of the sedan actually turned into them. In a thunder-ous cacophony, brakes screamed, metal shrieked, glass sprayed and then the bone-jarring, godawful thud. The two vehicles recoiled from each other, jolting into a standstill.

Miraculously, Jack and Lorenzo sprang out of the belts. Using offen-sive moves, they charged the wreckage, guns drawn.

Commando fashion, Lorenzo threw open the driver's door, trained his weapon on the driver, then jumped back. The target was dead. Next, Lorenzo ripped open the rear door. He dragged a bleeding passenger out and threw him on the ground kicking his head into the pavement. The body fell limp, his resistance melted into the asphalt.

The rider in front on the passenger side must have been dead as Chow jumped to the back door with his weapon targeted on the unknown. From his defensive posture, Chow tore open the remaining door. He, too, pulled out a mangled human and savaged him into the ground.

After taking stock of the situation, Lance inquired about Nikki. Since their vehicle suffered only superficial damage, he backed it away from the wrecked sedan, spun it around and positioned them ready for their escape.

There was no sign of Alex or Charlie anywhere inside the car. With the interior of the silver sedan secured, Lorenzo scrambled to retrieve the keys to check the trunk.

Unable to wait in the back of the Mercedes any longer, Nikki bolted towards the wreckage. She moved faster than Lance could grab.

Bent over the trunk cavity, Lorenzo worked on two large, blood-stained canvas sacks crammed inside.

Jack frantically called for Lance to supply cover so he could help Lorenzo.

"Alex!" Nikki cried as she watched Lorenzo attempt to move the dead weight. She couldn't detect any movement from the bags. Her own heart, jumping inside her chest, covered any life rhythm sounds she might have picked up from her communicator.

"Nikki!" Lance called from the side of the sedan. "Come here!" Lance had already consolidated the scene by dragging one of the injured from the rear seat around the sedan to where the other one was sprawled out on the pavement.

Torn about leaving the trunk area, Nikki followed the command and joined him alongside the sedan.

Lance stood poised with his weapon trained on their crumpled mass. "Run over to our car. In the trunk is a roll of duct tape. Bring it!"

Obeying orders, Nikki ran full speed to the Mercedes. Sliding into the driver's seat, she shut down the ignition and grabbed the keys. Inside the trunk she found the tape, then raced back to the wreckage.

"Here! Cover them, while I tie them up." Lance slapped his gun into her hands. "Then I can lend them a hand back there."

Again she obeyed. Her heart tempted her to divide her attention between the wounded men on the pavement and the trunk. But Nikki knew better than to chance it. She forced herself to focus.

The bodies on the pavement offered Lance no resistance. Once he trussed them up, Nikki tossed him the keys and joined the operation at the trunk.

Lance brought the Mercedes around to throw light on the scene.

Using the blade he had strapped to his leg, Lorenzo carefully sliced the first sack open. Inside Alexander lay lifeless, bleeding from his head. Under the faint light from the trunk bulb, he looked incredibly pale. Lorenzo felt for a pulse and checked his breathing, "He's alive."

The three men carefully lifted the opened canvas sack containing Alex from the trunk and gently laid him on the pavement. Kneeling beside him, Nikki ran her fingers over his face as she called his name, trying to wake him. In the Mercedes' headlights, Lorenzo checked him over. "He probably has a broken bone or two along with that nasty head wound, but unless there's internal bleeding...I think he's okay."

Lorenzo left Nikki with Alex while he went to help with the other sack. They freed the sack from its wedge against the spare tire. Maneuvering it to the open area of the trunk, Lorenzo again carefully slit the canvas. The bag parted to reveal Mr. Soo in disastrous shape.

Jack Chow gasped in horror, "My God, it's Charlie!"

Nikki noted with surprise Jack's recognition of Charlie but continued ministering to her husband.

With severe bleeding from several wounds, multiple contusions, probable fractured ribs and internal bleeding from being impaled against the spare, Charlie was critical. Fearing even lifting him from the trunk, they cut away the bag to make him more comfortable until they completely checked out his condition. "He has a faint pulse," reported Lorenzo.

Chow drew a radio from inside his shirt. He radioed the compound for two military helicopters. One he wanted with medics and two stretchers on board. The other he ordered for cleanup. After Nikki's run-in with thugs in Paris, she knew what that meant. Chow cautioned the choppers to come in low and land from the south to avoid arousing suspicion from the Red Chinese border guards, a mere two kilometers away.

As he came around, Alex labored harder to breathe. Grimacing with pain, he fought to open his eyes as he grappled against unconsciousness. He smiled at recognition of Nikki's face, tried to raise up, then coughed. Unable to speak, his eyes shut again and he fell back, coughing and gasping for air. Nikki yelled for Lorenzo.

Instantly at her side, Lorenzo admonished his brother firmly, "Alexander, you were in a car crash. You must not move until the medics get here. You might make something worse. Do you understand? Don't move!"

Then Lorenzo dragged Nikki away from Alex for a moment, "This could be worse than I anticipated. Whatever you do, don't let him move. I don't like the way he's waking up." Lorenzo's caution sent chills racing up and down her spine. How critical was her husband?

Returning to his side, Nikki continued to soothe and quiet him. She filled in the missing pieces she thought he could absorb. Numerous times he asked about Charlie. To quiet Alexander, she lied about the severity of their friend's condition, by dismissing his case with "I don't know yet."

It took an eternity of seconds for the helicopters to arrive. Two teams of medics finally hit the ground running. Nikki surrendered her husband to their care. She regretted not tending to Charlie, but she couldn't detach her attention from Alexander.

When the second chopper landed, squads of men in black jumpsuits, wearing specialized headgear including night-vision, swarmed the sedan wreckage like vultures. With precision they shoveled out the two bodies from the front seat onto surgical drapes for examination. Cautiously others picked up the two from the street who had begun to squirm back to life and packed them into the helicopter. Combing through the sedan, they cleaned up any evidence of guns or secrets, sanitizing as they went. With glasscutters they removed the bullet holes from the windshield, then shattered the rest of the glass to discourage detection of weapon use. They matched the number of spent rounds from Jack's weapon to the number in the bodies and holes in the upholstery, retrieving as they went. Snapping on rubber gloves, they carved out the remaining bullets from the corpse of the driver, then returned the corpses to the front seat of the car. With some errant metal shards from the accident, they ruptured the sedan's fuel tank. After both choppers were safely in the air, Lance would ignite the wrecked sedan before driving the Governor's car back to the compound.

The helicopter with Alexander and Charlie took off well before the crew completed their cleanup tasks. The celebration's fireworks exploding over the harbor concealed the fireball that erupted at the crash site.

The longer Alexander fought off unconsciousness, the more lucid he became, although years of conditioning denied him the release of verbalizing his pain. Nikki smoothed his hand as she watched his agonizing winces escape. After the preliminary examination by the medics, Alex pleaded again for more details on the extent of Charlie's injuries. Nikki had a corpsman relay details to Alex on Charlie's critical condition. The medics confessed they held out little hope for Soo. Even with Alex strapped to the stretcher and his movement restricted, the news about Charlie's condition clearly agitated him. He demanded to see Charlie. To mollify Alex, Nikki promised that after his examination by the doctors, they would see Soo together.

Alexander narrowed his eyes to a searing pinpoint; with a death grip he seized her arm, "Get to Lorenzo. Have him come to the hospital." Exhausted, he fell back.

"He's here, sweetheart," Nikki said, motioning Lorenzo over to the stretcher.

Speaking Italian in a whisper to Lorenzo, Alex ordered, "Get Hartz."

Organized confusion reigned in the emergency room, with those in

Nikki's party no longer controlling the situation. ER staff separated the two patients.

Before leaving to handle Alexander's prime directive to call Hartz, Lorenzo warned Nikki, "No matter what, don't leave Alex's side. Do whatever you have to, even if it takes throwing your body over his. Stay in the same room with him. First, they must not discover the communicators. Second, if they want to put him under, stall them until you can get word to me. And finally, don't let them inject anything until you've seen the vial they draw it from, and you recognize the substance. You're his wife. They must listen to you. I am going to call Dr. Hartz and get him en route, then I'll stay with Charlie. Jack Chow will be outside this exam room. If you need me, send him."

Nikki didn't comprehend the "why's" behind Lorenzo's statements, but she knew they carried the same force and effect as if Alex, himself, had issued them. As the medical personnel massed around Alex, Nikki watched with vigilant eyes. Alexander's head wound turned out to be superficial, but since it had caused unconsciousness, it generated concern about brain swelling and concussion. For fear of their discovering his communicator, Nikki refused them permission to x-ray his skull. She figured Dr. Hartz could handle that aspect of Alex's treatment. A trip to radiology did, however, point up four cracked ribs, which explained Alex's difficult and painful breathing. The technicians cleaned his head wound and dressed it, then secured Alex's ribs with elastic bandages. Alexander flatly refused (the) any painkillers. Resuming control, traces of nervous anxiety crept into Alex's attitude.

With the examination finished and treatment begun, the medical aides attending Alex dispersed. Jack left his sentry post outside the door to join them.

Alex, careful of his painful ribs, extended his right hand in welcome to Chow. "Jack, so good to see you again. Thanks for the save and for getting Nicole down here so quickly."

Alex's familiarity with Jack surprised Nikki. It never crossed her mind the two would know each other.

Jack laughed as he gingerly squeezed Alex's hand in a greeting. "Hey, old man! How are you feeling? I have to confess though, I didn't get Nikki anywhere. She brought me! She's the one who mobilized us to save your sorry ass…"

Alexander interrupted him, "You mean…"

"Yeah, Alex. Your little lady here called James and told him how this thing was going to shake out. She refused to take no for an answer. Then, when we couldn't get across the bay because of the holiday traffic, she stormed the beach, auctioning off some jewelry to buy our way across."

Obviously impressed with the role Nikki played in the caper, Alexander flashed her a look of unabashed pride. "And you, Jack. What was your part? Or were you just along for the ride?"

"I pumped a few rounds into the bast... I mean, the car. But that's about it."

"They got Charlie pretty good, didn't they?" Alex commented.

Chow shook his head with dismay, "It doesn't look good for him."

Anxious to begin moving, Alex motioned for help so he could sit up.

"He pretty well had it back at the shop. They pulled out all the stops for poor old Charlie," Alex wagged his head. "Damn! Once I got inside, I thought I had all of them in my sights, but one must have slipped by me and came up from behind. Then, whamo, that's all I remember."

Alex looked away to collect his thoughts, "I understand the head wound, but how did I get broken ribs?" he asked as he continued to flex his limbs, assessing their readiness.

Jack jumped in, "That must have happened in the car crash. We had to stop them before they dragged you across the border, so we rammed your car. Lance pulled off the maneuver with surgical precision."

Alex blinked his eyes open wide, "You were in a car crash?"

"Yeah," Jack tossed off as a matter of routine.

"Then, where was Nicole?" Alex asked, still trying to piece together her role in the grand scheme.

"In the car with us, of course. She sat in the middle..."

With all of his attention riveted on her, Alex rose up, "You were in a car crash?"

Nonchalantly Nikki shrugged, trying to stave off the coming storm.

"Have they checked you out since we've gotten here?" Alex swallowed as much of his alarm as possible.

"Of course not, sweetheart. It was more important that the doctors look after you and Charlie. I'm fine," she hoped to change the subject.

Taking action, Alex rang for the nurse as he fought his way to the edge of the bed. "Where's Lorenzo?" Alex questioned.

"With Charlie," Nikki responded.

When the nurse appeared, Alex, with the air of a command, requested a wheel chair.

Dismissing his request as premature, the nurse turned heel and left.

Determined, Alex sent Jack for a chair. When he returned with one, Alex climbed into it without their aid, just to prove his ability. Then he went to Charlie Soo's side. Jack wheeled him down the hallway, but recognizing protocol, waited outside the door while Alex and Nikki entered Charlie's room, joining Lorenzo.

Lorenzo shot Alex a questioning look, "Are you supposed to be up?"

"Sure," Alex answered with a wince and a wave of his hand. "Bring me up to speed," he said, reaching for the signaling button along side Soo's bed.

Lorenzo began his de-briefing as the nurse appeared. Alex interrupted him to address her, "Please take Mrs. Vincente for a full examination, including a complete gynecological work up."

The nurse appeared stunned by Alex's nerve at issuing orders.

Comprehending, Alex responded, "She's my wife, and I understand she was in a car accident earlier this evening. She is five months pregnant. I want to make sure that both she and the baby are okay."

Immediately the nurse came to Nikki's aid to assist her to an examination room.

"Alex, are you sure you want to do this?" Nikki questioned. "Do you realize? The media...?"

Oblivious to her protests, Alex wheeled over to kiss his wife's hand, "I really don't care. We will deal with that later. Please, darling. I will see you back here when they are through. Do this for me."

Melting in the light of his concern, Nikki let the nurse lead her away when the realization dawned on her that Alexander had timed his request for her medical attention to coincide with his de-briefing of Lorenzo and probably Charlie Soo. Besides genuinely wanting an exam for her, he had found a way to politely remove Nikki from the scene, so she wouldn't be privy to whatever sensitive information he may extract from Charlie. Thinking back on it, as she walked down the hall with the nurse, Nikki remembered Alex subtly sweeping the room for bugs as they entered.

Nikki's exam took a little less than an hour and turned up only superficial bruising from the car restraints. Everything else appeared to be normal with the baby and the rest of her body. But true to her premonition, a horde of press swamped the lobby. Obviously, hospital personnel had tattled to the media, and the offending party had left nothing out, including the facts regarding her pregnancy. But the scavengers of the press weren't the only ones hoping to see her.

Looking sick with worry, huddled quietly in one corner of the lobby, just below the radar antennae of the press, Nikki's parents and Zia waited. Nikki caught sight of them while moving between exam rooms. Once the nurse installed her in a private room, she summoned them. Nikki explained to the anxious relatives how, after rescuing Alex and Charlie, they were involved in a car crash. She apologized for not being able to call them and wondered how they found out they were at the hospital.

Her mom's answer amazed her, "Karl called from London. He got the news over the wire service there. He was about to take off for Hong Kong but wanted to make sure you were all right first. He couldn't believe you were pregnant and didn't tell him. Of course I never let on that we didn't even know you were in the hospital. By the way, how are Alex, Lorenzo and Mr. Soo?"

Truly, the far-reaching tentacles of the media astounded Nikki. After updating them on everyone's condition, Nikki encouraged them to return to the apartment.

By the time Nikki got back to Alexander, he had finished his de-briefing and had already received her test results. Nikki marveled at how, even as a patient, he got the earth to revolve at his discretion. But Alex made it clear he wouldn't leave the hospital until Dr. Hartz had arrived and examined Charlie Soo. Fortunately for the hospital, their idea to monitor Alex's concussion over the next few hours coincided with Alexander's plans to stay in their facility. The hospital could do nothing about his insistence on installing himself in Charlie's room. Steadfastly, Nikki also refused to leave. Not even Alex could budge her resolve to stay.

Dr. Hartz arrived on a Vincente Industries' jet eight hours after Lorenzo's initial call. Now six hours into the morning of the year of 1969, Hartz accomplished his swift arrival due to the fact that he was actually nearby in India at a medical conference, when Lorenzo reached him.

Charlie managed to cling to a thread of life throughout the night. In and out of consciousness, Alexander spoke with him on several occasions.

After conferring with the attending physicians, Dr. Hartz completed his own examination of Charlie Soo. Concurring with hospital staff physicians, he prepared Alex and Nikki for the worst. When Mr. Soo again fluttered into consciousness, he used what strength remained to relieve the hospital's doctors of their responsibility and place himself in the care of Dr. Hartz.

Nikki stood at Alexander's side as he spoke with his dear friend Charlie Soo, for the last time. His directness chilled her down to the marrow of her bones.

"My dear friend," Alex began, "I'm afraid you are only moments away from dying. It's time to move on. There is nothing left now for you, except to leave here."

With his eyes wide open, Charlie clearly comprehended Alexander's words. In complete concordance, he nodded. "I ... sign papers ... first. I

... leave everything to you ... friend," Soo wheezed through broken breaths.

At that, Alex called in Jack, Dr. Hartz and gathered Lorenzo and Nikki around Charlie's bed. Lorenzo carefully wrote out Charlie's last wishes. With a weak hand, Mr. Soo signed it. Following his signature, the four of them, absent Alexander, signed as witnesses. With Soo's final business concluded, Jack returned to his post outside the door.

But Charlie Soo hadn't breathed his last, "... in my shop ... behind false panel ... underneath most valuable Ming vase ... is personal case ... Please, take."

As Nikki stood there, she couldn't believe a man so lucid, so disposed, could be dying. Even his speech seemed to gain momentum with each new breath. He seemed to be coming around. Given a few hours, he'd be out of the woods.

Nevertheless, Alex continued his farewell, "You have been a true friend in life and so it will continue in death. Good-bye, dearest friend, until we meet on the other side." With that, Alex folded his hands, as if praying, and reverently bowed, Asian-style, as far as his ribs and bandages would allow him. Lorenzo did the same. Nikki followed suit, but she wanted to throw in a pitch for not giving up, for not tossing in the towel — for life! Charlie seemed so close to making it.

Solemnly, Lorenzo and Nikki followed Alex out of the room. Outside Charlie's door, Alex returned to the wheelchair. Feeling famished and lightheaded from hunger, he suggested they get something to eat from the cafeteria. Nikki could hardly think about food at a time like that! And she wondered how Alex could. But for his sake, she went along.

An hour later when they returned to Charlie's room, Jack Chow stood his post with tear-reddened eyes, talking with Dr. Hartz. Within moments, Dr. Hartz accompanied orderlies as they wheeled a gurney past them with a body bag on it.

Touching the bag as he passed, a tear slid down Nikki's cheek. "Good-bye dear Charlie," she mournfully murmured, almost inaudibly.

Lorenzo accompanied poor, old Charlie Soo downstairs to the morgue as Alex's personal emissary.

Nikki couldn't comprehend Charlie's death.

Jack radioed for a car to be sent around for Alex and Nikki.

They left the hospital with Alex in a wheelchair and Nikki walking by his side. Hospital security held back the barrage of reporters and photographers, who had descended. They hailed the couple, calling out questions, madly snapping pictures. Looking grim, Nikki had been through too much to address them.

Before they could return to the Furama, they had to stop at Charlie's shop. In a race, they had to beat police and officialdom to his store before they sealed it up along with all of Charlie's possessions. To avoid governmental intrusion, they had to move fast. Alexander finessed the lock to the back door just as he had done hours earlier. A deafening silence now engulfed the shop. Walking through the warehouse, no matter how Nikki tried to muffle her footsteps, they sang out with a hollow report she had never noticed before with life in the store. Of course, Alexander knew which vase to look under. Since he couldn't bend down, Nikki retrieved the black case.

Following their stop at Charlie's porcelain shop, Alexander had the driver head to the Governor's compound. "I'm assuming, since this was your operation, Nigel is expecting a report from you. I suppose we should take care of business while we are out. Shall we, darling?" Alex said as he eased from the car then offered her his hand to alight.

Nikki attributed Alexander's callous behavior to complications from his concussion. Certainly she didn't feel like reporting to James right then, not in the light of the previous twelve hours and Charlie's death. But Alexander coolly walked her through the reporting process, embellishing the areas prior to and following his rescue with what he remembered.

James mentioned that the two survivors of the car crash were indeed Red Chinese agents. "At this very hour we have teams interrogating them to get at their mission. I don't expect to get much from them though. They've always been tough nuts to crack. But we will keep them out of circulation for awhile. I'll send their passports back today along with official apologies and the ashes of the other two who died in the unfortunate auto accident."

Alex concurred with the Governor's assessment of the situation. They chatted about appropriate arrangements for Charlie. Since there was no widow and no children, the Agency could sidestep further entanglements. Alexander knew the Hong Kong citizenry regarded most Westerners as interlopers. Not wishing to step on toes, he'd leave any tribute to Charlie Soo—businessman—to Hong Kong's commerce community. In light of his demise a mere seven hours ago, it amazed Nikki how easily the two of them put Charlie Soo away. All in all, their shallow visit lasted a little over an hour.

Finally, by noon the pair exited the elevator at the floor to their apartment. Physically spent, as well as emotionally drained by the events of the last eighteen, rollercoaster hours, Nikki retired to their bedroom and fell on the bed. But Charlie's face and words clung to her, just as he had clung to life. Nikki found she couldn't put away Alexander's cold-hearted attitude towards his friend.

Her humor grew blacker with each passing moment. After stewing for a half-hour in her venomous juices, she heard the door crack open. Alexander peeked in. She sat up.

"Oh, I'm sorry, darling. I didn't mean to disturb you. I just wanted to check on you," his voice dripped with kindness as he neared the bed.

Nikki rose up on her knees, then came to her feet.

Alexander enclosed her in his arms, tenderly cuddling her into his chest, petting her back, kissing her head. "It's okay. It's over now," he soothed.

Just like it was over for Charlie? How easy it was for him to say that! Had he no feelings? He just condemned his friend to death! He never tried to save him! The volcanic toxins boiling inside Nikki erupted in a manic display. She pushed back from inside his arms. Her hands clenched into fists. She used those fists and beat on his chest while hot tears of anxiety poured from her eyes, "How could you! How could you! Where is your heart? Do you even have one?"

Nikki checked him for a reaction. Nothing registered on Alex's face. So, she hit harder. She wanted to dent his tough-skinned armor. She spat her accusations at him, "You sent Charlie to his death! I saw him. He wasn't dying. He called you his friend. He gave you everything he had! And you let him die!" Slowly Alexander closed his arms around her again, drawing her nearer in to him.

Still no reaction. "What, did you do it for — the money! To get what Charlie gave you! What kind of a monster are you?!!"

Constrained by the tangle of their proximity, the harder Nikki tried to hit, the weaker her blows landed. Frustrated by him, his lack of emotion, his lack of reaction, and lack of pain, she threw at him the last viperous weapon she had in her arsenal, "You probably don't love me either! Are you just stringing me along until I no longer serve your purpose? Then are you going to tell me 'it's time to move on'? Huh? Is that how it works? 'Sorry, Nicole, there's nothing left for you except to leave…get the hell out — die!' Is that how it works with you, Alex? Huh? Huh?"

Smothered, now tight against Alexander's chest, Nikki cried. She cried until she had nothing left inside. She cried until she couldn't stand anymore. Carefully Alex lowered her to the bed, ministering to her, comforting her until, exhausted from her rampage, Nikki finally quieted.

Then sitting face to face, still stroking her hand, Alexander softly began, "Nicole, I hoped it wouldn't come to this. I hoped you would be able to let this go. But it was naïve of me to expect you to cope without specific knowledge. You are right. Charlie wasn't dying. With every passing moment, he grew stronger. While you were out of the room, he and I talked. The Red Chinese had cracked his cover. That is what yesterday was all about. When we came in, they had just invaded his store. If it had been anyone but us, he would have used the entrance as a diversion to skip out. But he could not leave us in their hands, so he sacrificed himself. By the time I got back there, they had already begun to torture him to get at his information. Charlie withstood it. He never gave them anything. I was in the process of formulating a plan to extract him when one of them got the drop on me. If it had not been for you, darling, both Charlie and I would have been goners," Alex paused to kiss her fingertips.

Then Alex continued, "In my conversations with Charlie in the hospital, we discussed his lack of options. They had his number. He could never go back to his life or his shop. His only chance at life, was death. But accomplishing that, when the supposed corpse is recovering, began to prove difficult. Several times Lorenzo administered the sedatives Hartz prescribed over the phone to keep Soo down until Hartz could arrive. For Charlie to 'die,' a doctor had to examine a corpse and sign the death certificate. Hartz came to replace the hospital's doctors to facilitate the process. My farewell words contained code. I had to tell Charlie that our arrangements were all in place. I meant it when I said that I would be his friend in death as in life. Charlie understood. He signed over all his possessions so I could sell them to raise the capital needed to keep him in seclusion. The black case we retrieved from the shop contained a few personal effects, jewelry he wanted and some secrets for our side.

"With all the business accomplished, Hartz injected him with an effective sedative to simulate death. We went to the cafeteria before the procedure to put distance between us and his death. We couldn't afford to arouse suspicions. Hartz performed a public examination, witnessed not by us, but by hospital doctors and staff, with their concurrence. He pronounced Charlie dead based on that examination. Even as we speak, Lorenzo and dear old Charlie are heading for his secure retreat."

"Oh, Alexander," was Nikki's only response. His explanation hit her from left field. "I had no idea procedures like this existed."

Rolling all the events around in her mind, Nikki came to focus on Lorenzo. "I never realized that Lorenzo worked for the Agency, too. You should have seen him, Alex. He was so smooth. Lorenzo really knew what he was doing."

A tiny smile pressed across Alexander's lips and he shook his head, "Lorenzo has never, nor will ever, work for the Agency. In fact, they really do not even know about him. Didn't you notice that no one at the Governor's mansion knew him?... How Lorenzo stayed in the shadows? I try to keep it that way. Please be clear on this, Nicole. He works for and is loyal to me. I trained him. Not only is he skilled in self-defense and weaponry, he also has degrees in pharmacology and human physiology. That is why he stood in during our operations and could administer drugs to Soo. He is my 'Tonto,' you might say. And now, he is yours, too. We are very lucky to have him."

"Then what about Jack?" Nikki asked, still trying to ferret out the players. "Jack has a budding career as an actor. He looked as if he'd really been crying when we came back from eating."

"Jack Chow wasn't acting, Nicole. He really believes his friend Charlie Soo is dead, as does the Governor and everyone else. Only three people in this whole world know the truth—four, now that you are included. See, I didn't want to burden you with keeping this secret. The more you know, the more they have to use against you. Once they know where you live, your life is over."

Nikki's mind ran over everything Alex laid out for her. "What will happen to those two that we pulled from the sedan? They knew Charlie, they know you, and because Lorenzo and I helped, they know us! So now what?" She envisioned an entire and very plausible lethal crisis building on the horizon for all of them.

"After we get what we can from them, it will be unfortunate, but necessary, they will succumb to their injuries sustained in the car accident. Their ashes, too, will be shipped back to their families."

"That's murder! Won't that cause an international incident? How do we explain that?"

"Officially, they have to accept whatever explanation we choose to offer them. That is the funny thing about the spy game. They know we have them. We know they have them. Both sides jump through some extensive hoops, but in the end, we just put on smiles and pretend. Absent a coerced admission or fingerprints, all one side or the other really has is conjecture."

Relaxed with her knowledge, Nikki nestled into Alex's chest when she felt the bandages through his shirt. In horror she recoiled, "Oh, Alex, I'm so sorry! I...I hit you. ...I..."

He stilled her apology, "I had it coming. Of course my attitude disturbed you. I am lucky you didn't do worse. I deserved worse! Charlie was also your friend. How could you understand without knowing the whole truth?" He kissed her, then snuggled her back into him, still soothing her, calming her, cleansing all the poison from her soul.

"But I must have hurt you? Oh, I'm so sorry," images flooded Nikki of her beating on his chest as he steeled himself, stoically accepting her blows, never even hinting at what must have been insufferable pain. He accepted it because, ... because he was Alexander, who loved her more than life itself, and once again he understood.

Chapter 33

Adam

The three weeks it took to conclude Charlie's business in Hong Kong brought Alex an uncomfortable, sustained level of visibility, particularly from the media hoopla caused by Nikki's celebrity and the fatal car accident involving the Governor's car. Impatient over the morass of media and legal entanglements, Alexander feared being bogged down long enough that the Red Chinese might get wind of him. Ultimately, Alexander decided that his profile in the port city had reached an all time critical mass. Within a week, he sold the lease on his penthouse, complete with its furniture. Before the end of January, they took final leave of Hong Kong, years before its occupation by the communists, years before Alex had planned to be finished with it.

Once back within the safe harbor behind the stone walls of *Nevermore*, Nikki and Alex hibernated for a month without leaving its protective confines, not even for doctor visits. Paid handsomely, Dr. Jeffrey Weisberg made house calls.

Within days of their return to *Nevermore*, Lorenzo arrived. The three of them pretended to spend several carefree days lounging in the glassed-in garden room nursing Alexander's ribs back to health when, in fact, they were really dissecting the minutiae of that cataclysmic night. Alexander wanted to know every single detail of how the two of them had tracked him down, along with every nuance of how Lorenzo and Nikki had worked together. At length they analyzed the effect and the performance of the communicators and tracking devices. Alex made notes for updates and improvements to the equipment.

His near-death experience shook Alexander down to his soul. Even though he genuinely encouraged Nikki to use the recording studio, she recognized it as a ploy to hide his frustration and the fathomless, worry-induced funk that plagued him. Nikki knew when he had pieced together all the different components between his heart and mind, they would talk about it.

Alex's brush with death intensified his passion for his Nicole. Although Alexander wanted Zia and Lorenzo always available, he found the closer quarters of the stone home, as compared to the ample spaces and rambling halls of *Napoli*, too confining. Privately, he groused at not feeling comfortable to share intensely romantic moments with Nikki in their presence. He thought about building a guesthouse for them, but building would take time, and Alex wanted his privacy with his wife instantly.

That same week a small gentlemen's farm next to the Moores' property came on the market. Once he learned of the offering, he toured the property and inked the deal instantly. Alexander paid a hefty premium to move the sellers out within the week so he could have the new house immediately.

Moving out Zia and Lorenzo permitted Alex to come to grips with the thoughts that had so tormented him over the past month. Coincidentally Nikki and Alex's first dinner alone also fell on their first wedding anniversary. Naturally Alexander arranged a romantic fare. Crystal and china adorned the trestle table in front of the walk-in fireplace of the dining area where Alexander built a crackling fire. The executive chef from La Baladin, their favorite French restaurant, catered the meal.

As all couples do, the Vincentes reminisced over events of a year ago as contrasted to present day. "As I held you in my arms in front of the minister and pledged my undying love to you, never did I believe we would be where we are today," Alex fondled and kissed his beloved's fingertips as he spoke.

Playfully Nikki couldn't help but interject, "Where, in Pennsylvania?"

"No, darling," Alex tenderly rebuked her, "I mean, I am retired, you have given up the 'Nikki' thing and within four months our baby will arrive."

Shelving her smart answers, Nikki opened her full heart. "You are my life. When we married a year ago, I promised myself to you without conditions. I've been fortunate, and I've managed to pack a lifetime of living and career into a few short years. At this point in my life, the only career I want is to be your wife and the mother of your children."

With his customary bemused smile, which had been missing since New Year's, Alexander pulled out a small box. "You sacrificed something precious that night you rescued me. It has bothered me that we don't match anymore."

Opening the lid, there lay another ID bracelet with "Nevermore" inscribed on it. "Oh, Alex, thank you. I've missed wearing my bracelet so much. But I didn't want to say anything," she extended her wrist for him to put it on her.

"The original price of this trinket pales in comparison to the healthy ransom I paid to retrieve it," he held her with amusement in his eyes.

His statement stunned Nicole. "You mean..." she checked the

bracelet. Sure enough, the upper right corner bore the brush marks from where she scraped it in a fall. "It's my bracelet!" Nikki exclaimed as she examined her old friend.

Alex leaned over and tenderly laid a kiss upon her cheek. Nikki looked up into standing pools of tears in his eyes.

"My dearest, darling, Nicole," brushing back the hair along her face, his fingertips caressed her skin, "How close I came to losing everything precious to me. I almost lost you, our time together and our future."

Drawing Nikki up into his arms, he locked her securely inside his heart, kissing the hair on her head. "I love you. Beyond life itself, oh my dear God! How very much I love you. I'm terrified at being separated from you. I just want to hold onto you — tight. So, tight that you could never be separated from me again. I hear you through the communicator. Your breathing, your heartbeat — the sounds of your life. But ... the thought that someone could silence that forever — could take us away from each other..." Alex struggled for control. "I want you so close that no one could rip you from my grasp." Swayed by the profundity of his love, forced by its energy, he rocked Nikki back and forth inside his arms until it grew into a lullaby.

They stayed in each other's arms for hours, talking. It comforted Alex to know that she and Lorenzo had worked so capably together. Alexander had hoped she would learn to rely on Lorenzo. He confided in her his fear that somehow the Red Chinese agents had been able to communicate with their compatriots across the border in China about his identity. He worried that *they* knew about him. If *they* knew about his activity, no matter how innocent or inadvertent, the Eastern European communists would be made aware, too. Then he would have to start over from ground zero, establishing his separation from the Agency. He viewed extended absences with no visibility as the only remedy to the Terminal Agent Syndrome. Only time would tell whether he had skirted detection by *them* on New Year's. In the meantime, using secure lines of communication, he'd put out feelers to test the climate in regard to his status.

March's breath of spring renewed the wanderlust in Nikki's husband. After obtaining Dr. Weisberg's approval for travel, Nikki and Alex struck out for *Napoli*.

Alex's itinerary included reinvesting the proceeds from the sale of his Hong Kong penthouse. Together they spent weeks shopping for property, when Alex decided on an innocuous island of several square kilometers off the mid-Italian coast. A roil of tides and surf made approach by boat impossible. As a consequence the island remained uninhabited.

Despite its lush vegetation and stands of ancient Cyprus trees, locals referred to the property as the *Isola della Morte* — Isle of Death. Because of its tumultuous water conditions, Alex viewed the property from a helicopter and bought it without ever setting foot on the island itself. Nikki didn't understand what motivated him to make such an ill-conceived purchase.

While on the Continent, Alex scheduled meetings with Hartz and Junger. Opting out of the loop, Nikki never questioned Alex about these activities. She knew he maintained a confidential, covert agenda in order to procure his freedom and their security. In the interest of keeping her occupied while away on his sojourn, Alexander suggested she drop off the master tape of songs for the baby to Bruce in London.

Bruce received her tape with enthusiastic elation and lost no time in putting the rough-cut master tape in the hands of arrangers and engineers to perfect the product. They titled the album *Baby, Baby, Songs for Babies of All Ages*. Mary suggested a pen-and-ink stylized Madonna-and-child portrait for the cover using Nikki and a sweet-cheeked anonymous child. Karl filmed a series of interviews for the work. In four days they pulled together the publicity and promotion package assembling everything to launch Nikki's first album since her final tour, almost a year ago.

Alex and Nikki played at the end of their tether as long as possible before returning home on May first to await the birth. No matter the doctor's glowing reports, Alex refused to leave her side for a second after that.

Late in the afternoon of June 7th, Nikki went into labor. The hospital in Reading, with its traditional waiting rooms for fathers, found itself ill-prepared to deal with the likes of Alexander Vincente. No one dreamed a father would want to be present for the birth. However, Alex wasn't about to leave his Nicole. His presence in the labor room sent shock waves through the hospital. But it was Alex's advance warning that he intended on being with her in the delivery room, that threatened to derail the entire system!

Protecting their sacrosanct territory, the nurses first tried to appeal to what they assumed was the squeamish, weaker side of his male character. Grimly they prophesied horrific stories of blood, guts and gory deliveries. Their tales never dented Alex's Agency-calloused shell. Next, they invoked divine ordination of their duty, which also held absolutely no sway over him.

Alex charmed, he cajoled, and finally, he downright bribed them. However, he made it eminently clear — one way or another — he intended to be at Nikki's side throughout the entire ordeal.

Dr. Weisberg broke the standoff by issuing an order for Alexander to remain. After surviving a night of bureaucratic wrangling along with Nikki's wails of pain, at four in the morning, with Alex participating actively from his position by her side, their son arrived.

Dr. Jeffrey Weisberg, in defiance of their nurses' officiousness, made the unprecedented move of asking Alex to cut the umbilical cord. Once he examined the baby, the doctor lay the boy in Nikki's arms, and, after some momentary bonding with him, Nikki handed him over to Alexander to name his son. Adam Antony Vincente debuted into the world on the morning of June 8, 1969 — just over seven pounds, with hair the color of burnished copper and eyes that would be blue. Within the hour Zia, Lorenzo and Nikki's parents got their first glimpse of their grandson.

Since Adam was so healthy and robust, both father and son moved into Nikki's private room for the customary five-day hospital stay. Once news of the birth crossed the Atlantic, her room and the adjacent one quickly filled with flowers and stuffed animals for Nikki and Adam. Mary came and made order, recording each gift. With the help of a small army of hospital volunteers she distributed for Nikki the flowers to forgotten patients and the toys to disadvantaged children in the hospital and surrounding shelters.

The night before Nikki's scheduled departure from the hospital, a contingent of maternity floor staff wheeled in a dining cart with a specially prepared gourmet meal on it, complete with linen, a candle and a single rose. "We thought," the head nurse announced, "you might like a romantic evening alone. It might be the last in a long while, now that Adam has arrived. So we brought you a special little treat."

Unceremoniously, she prepared to wheel their baby out. "I'll just take Adam down to the nursery, so the two of you can have a little peace together. I promise, he'll be in my sight every moment."

Charmingly, Lorenzo fell in step along side her, "You don't mind if I keep you company? Do you? I don't want to be a fifth wheel and ruin your generous surprise." Of course, the baby would never have been permitted out of the sight of an immediate family member, for any reason — just in case.

The first Sunday home, Nikki's family and her business inner circle all went to Nikki's country stone church to dedicate Adam. Zia had brought with her the same christening gown Alex wore at his baptism. Lorenzo stood as godfather — Mary was godmother. Zia and Fran arranged for a catered reception at *Nevermore* following the ceremony.

Because fatherhood enhances innate instincts of a man, within days of their homecoming, Alexander had Gus Schubert install a sophisticated alarm and monitoring system. Constructed from Alex's own specific knowledge, it exceeded anything available anywhere.

Alexander cherished fatherhood. Often he'd gently lay a tender "thank you" on Nikki. On many occasions, even with Adam peacefully asleep, Nikki caught Alex sitting next to the cradle just watching him. A significant sense of family enveloped them when Alex sat up with Nikki as she nursed their son. Involved in every aspect of Adam's care, Alex willingly answered their son's demands.

Even though Adam would never remember, Alex felt the pull of his paternal forebears to walk the halls of the ancestral home with his son, as generations before had done. As soon as Nikki was capable of travel, they jetted home to *Napoli*.

By now, *Napoli* felt like home to her, too. She longed to wake up with her husband and son in their masterful bedroom, bright with the July, Mediterranean sunshine and billows of sea breeze. Nikki had worked hard on losing the "baby fat", now she wanted to dress for dinner and dance again with Alex under the glittering starlight.

The height of the social season had already begun — including Magda's opening party three weeks prior to their arrival. A year ago, Alex and Nikki had romped through the social events of the register's calendar across the breadth of the Mediterranean. This year, if they participated at all, it would only be at the affairs which included children.

Summer slipped by peacefully at *Napoli*. For Nikki's birthday, they passed on an invitation from the social elite in favor of an intimate outing at sea on a private yacht. Alex was testing the craft for a friend. Zia insisted on keeping Adam at home which gave the pair a welcome romantic interlude. Lounging on the deck, they assessed the boat's performance as the captain sliced it through the azure swells. The amenities of the boat impressed Nikki; a hundred and twenty-five feet of first class luxury with three staterooms, gourmet galley, large salon with dining area, massive deck and, of course, quarters for the four-man crew. It even included a pad for the helicopter next to the bridge and a boarding launch.

Alex and Nikki used the launch to nip out to a small island with a picnic lunch. As they pushed through the sand on the shore, Alex hooked his arm around Nikki's slimming waist, "My dear Mrs. Vincente, I don't believe I have told you how ravishing you look today." Then he pulled her tight, "Good enough to eat, my dear."

"Not so fast," Nikki teased back. "What about lunch? You're not carrying that picnic basket just for exercise, you know."

Immediately Alex dropped the hamper, "Who needs the basket! I would rather have you!" Catching her up in his arms, he wrestled Nikki to the ground. "Well, pardon me, *mon ami.*"

Nikki scampered out of his grasp, grabbed the basket and ran for the cover of some cypress trees. Alex trailed at her heels. Nikki intended to be caught; she just wanted more privacy than the open beach provided.

After a satisfying lunch all the way around, they lay on the blanket and watched the breeze chase the clouds across the sky. Leaning up on one elbow, looking at her, Alex broke in on her contemplation. "You know, your bikini fits you now like it did last summer," he smiled while he traced little designs across her breastbone. "But I want you to know that you didn't have to deny yourself to please me. The only thing I want is you here, next to me. I don't care what shape that comes in, just as long as you are only an arm's length away." He slipped his mouth over hers. Nikki laced her fingers across the nape of his neck and let him pull her to a sitting position while still tasting his kisses. "Do you know that I love you, Nicole?" he affirmed, his powerful eyes dancing.

"I have a pretty good idea. But do you know how very much I love you, Alexander Vincente?"

"Darling, I am surer of that than I am of the sun rising each morning."

A change in the wind shifted the yacht's direction on its mooring, so they had to motor around the back to get to the side boarding area. Across the stern, a white banner hung. Nikki figured, at Alex's prompting, the crew had dropped a corny birthday banner over the side. But as they neared, the sign didn't read "Happy Birthday" at all. Fancy script lettering spelled out "Bella Nicole".

Questioningly she looked to Alexander, "What's that?"

Alex attempted a nonchalant shrug, but failed to pull it off, "The name of the boat, I suppose. That is, if you agree." To bail himself out, he flashed her a crisp smile.

"Why would I agree?" she quizzed, not catching his drift yet.

"Because, darling, I hoped you'd let me name the boat after you, my beautiful Nicole, Bella Nicole."

She spun around, "Alexander!...You don't mean!...You said you were..."

"...testing the boat for a friend," he finished for her. "You're certainly my lover. Adam proves that. But I always imagined you were my friend too, yes?" Amusement leapt in his eyes.

Balancing his steps, Alex carefully assisted Nikki as they maneuvered from the launch to the gang area where another crewmember extended his hand.

"Welcome aboard, madam. May I take the liberty of wishing you a happy birthday?"

The skipper came down from the bridge to greet them. Bowing diplomatically, he introduced himself, "Madam, I am your captain, Jacque Maxwell. Please call me Max. If you will permit me, I would like to familiarize you with some of the features of your new vessel." Captain Maxwell extended his arm to guide Nikki through the parts of the boat she hadn't seen yet, as Alex tagged along.

As they strolled, Nikki assessed Max, guessing him to be in his early forties by the slight graying at the temples. He still sported a rugged build and the swarthy complexion of a man of the sea. Well-spoken, with polished manners, he had received his formal training as an officer in the British Royal Navy. He concluded her tour with a click of his heels and a snap of a salute, "I am, madam, at your service."

Alexander's string of surprises continued into their stateroom where he left lying on the bed a new sea-foam green, strapless gown, with an empire waist and a full skirt of graceful chiffon. They always dressed separately for dinner because Alex delighted in the magic of her entrance and in seeing the completed package, rather than witnessing the rituals required to produce it.

Moored in a cove to block any sweep of the evening's wind, they dined on the rear deck with candlelight. Making her entrance, Nikki couldn't help but appreciate the impressive figure Alexander cut in his white dinner jacket as he leaned his back against the ship's rail, waiting for her. The last rays of sunset splashed gold and rose tones across the walls of the cove. Their reflection accentuated the gold in Alex's hair and dazzled in his eyes. As she pirouetted for him, the filmy layers of chiffon lifted to life in a willowy whirl. Alexander nodded approvingly, then threw out a wink to someone outside her field of vision.

Carrying a silver tray with two glasses of champagne and a sizeable velvet jeweler's box, a crewmember approached. Alex presented a glass to Nikki, then elegantly raised his in tribute to her birthday, sealing his toast with a kiss. Carefully, Nikki sipped the champagne, her first since her pregnancy. Romantic mood music hung on the evening's breeze.

Continually, Alexander found plenty of excuses to round out Nikki's jewelry wardrobe. This birthday was no exception. Opening the box, he revealed a decadent necklace and earring set of matched marquis emeralds, highlighted with enough diamonds to rival the Royals' collection. Amid all the excesses of the day, Nikki couldn't help but protest. Of course, Alexander wouldn't hear it. "Darling, you deserve these and so much more," he whispered in her ear as he fastened the clasp of the necklace. "My gifts pale in comparison to what you have given me. I can never thank you enough for being my wife, for our family life and now for a son." Turning her around, he offered his arms to waltz them across the deck.

Chapter 34

Consequences

At July's end, Alexander, Nikki and Lorenzo flew to Austria for a visit with Dr. Hartz. Alexander refused to take Adam on any business remotely connected to covert activities, so their son stayed with Zia within the intense security of *Napoli*.

Gathered in Hartz' office, everyone sidestepped the subject of Charlie Soo. The only reference to Hong Kong came in Nikki's debriefing as she delineated the shortcomings and positive aspects of the communicators' performance.

Using the latest miniaturization techniques and breakthroughs in battery power, Hartz had further perfected their communicators. Now advances in the stability of plastic compounds enabled Hartz to create the devices in a pliable, non-degradable soft plastic rather than in metallic alloys to lessen the possibility of the communicators leaving their footprints in x-rays or on scanners. Able to increase the clarity, pick up ambient background noise, while decreasing their size, Hartz readied the new devices for transplantation. With their reduced size, this time he performed the operation under a local anesthetic. Dispensing with outsiders, Lorenzo assisted, monitoring the drip of Pentathol and their vital signs, while Hartz operated to insert the new devices. Without having to shake off the effects of heavy anesthesia, by the following evening they completed the necessary adjustments and tests, then headed home.

Intermittently over the summer, Alex picked up several encrypted communications from the Agency since his subterranean visit there in March. From his comments, Nikki gathered things hadn't gone well in the spring. But Alex dismissed it as irrelevant and refused to "be a target" or to "muddy the waters" with another visit. Since their retirement, in matters concerning the Agency, she didn't ask about what she wasn't told. Lorenzo knew, but he kept his confidences. Besides, if Nikki wanted to know, she'd ask her husband rather than compromise Lorenzo.

As the cool breath of autumn descended over the Mediterranean, Nikki finished the master tape of torch songs she began in May. Bruce and the rest of her management team eagerly awaited her arrival in London, hoping to be able to pull off a release in time for Christmas. Fearing exposing Adam in public for an extended period of time, Alex sent Nikki on ahead for the week of foundation work with the engineers in studio. Husband and son would follow later. Although she dreaded being separated from the baby for any length of time, Nikki shared Alex's worry about baby-snatching. The child of a celebrity always presented a high profile risk.

Nikki stayed in Alex's London penthouse, putting up with its cool bachelor attitude in exchange for the security and convenience it provided. Being back in the business again, she could foresee future visits and decided when Alex arrived, they would discuss a makeover for the apartment. For now, Nikki only slept in the penthouse since she essentially lived at the studio for eighteen hours out of the day.

Jarred, a familiar old face, came with a limo every morning before dawn to pick up Nikki, and he returned her safely each night before midnight. More than a year had elapsed since she'd seen him. They caught up on old times. Naturally, she bored him with unlimited photographs and prattle about Adam. He seemed genuinely interested as he plied her with endless questions about their now private lives. Neither of them ventured a word about the Agency. Nikki found nothing unusual about that since the Agency worked on a need-to-know basis. She had no idea of his current involvement, but obviously Bruce still maintained him in his security stable.

During her week in the studio, Nikki remained extremely low-key, without makeup and only a good hair brushing before she tucked her entire length of locks up underneath a brimmed pork-pie hat. Glasses and an upturned collar against the bitter fall weather granted further protection if she chose to roam the streets around the studio.

Work for the week progressed extremely well. While desperately missing her family, Nikki relished being in the midst of artistic and inspired musicians with their collaborative juices flowing. They worked seemingly non-stop, bouncing ideas off one another in the creative give-and-take of formulation. Nearing the end of the week and tired of the studio's stale automat sandwiches, Nikki ducked out alone to a small pub for a plate of bangers and mash—one of the few dishes she missed.

In her dressed-down disguise out of public view, Nikki hovered over her lunch, soaking up the latest in a gossip rag, when a voice with an incredibly bad, affected English accent interrupted her, "Don't cha know that goes better with a pint?"

She looked up to see Bob Mann with two mugs of ale pushing one towards her as he shoved into the seat across from her. He barely got out a grimace of a smile before sticking a cigarette in his puss.

"Oh, won't you please join me?" Nikki sarcastically put in.

Typically, Mann let the point of her barb roll off his back. Nodding in a hail of sulfur and spark, he lit his smoke, "Ya, hi to you, too, Princess."

"So, how's tricks?" he offered after a slurp of ale — still a class act. "Ya know, you and that new husband of yours are real hard to get in touch with these days. You been hidin'?"

Nikki didn't appreciate his irreverence. "I wouldn't say that, I think we just move in different circles now." She wanted to add, "I try to stick to the human race," but kept her wisecrack to herself.

"Well, we've sent messages and no one seems to be picking them up. Junger is real anxious to speak with Alexander."

"Oh that's why you're here! Geez Bob, all the time I thought it was my sparkling personality that brought you out from under your rock," her agitation snuck out.

Bob smiled, "Feisty. You're getting feisty in your retirement." He pulled another cigarette from his pack, then gave it a shove in her direction — his best attempt at an offer. "No, seriously. Junger really needs to speak with Alex. Can you tell him?"

"Your last meeting in March wasn't enough for you? Bob, obviously you don't understand the meaning of retirement. It means we've had it! We are off the charts. It's been over for more than a year now. *Capisci?*"

Bob stared at his pint, drumming his stubby fingers on the table, a cloud of blue smoke circling him. Having enough of her insolence, he broke in on Nikki. "Look it here, my dear *Mrs.* Vincente, we're not playing around. You were both warned about the possible consequences of the two of you hooking up. There's serious shit on the table — and now you've got a baby involved."

The very mention of Adam aroused Nikki's indignation, she came out swinging, "You son-of-a-bitch! What the hell do you mean?" She removed her fake glasses, giving Mann the full benefit of the fiery daggers shooting from her eyes.

"Evidently your *loving* husband neglected to inform you that *they've* issued a sanction on him," Bob's verbal wallop came from left field, without warning and left Nikki reeling. She remembered "sanction" was Agency-speak for a murder contract.

Bob knew he wounded her. This time he picked up the pack of cigarettes and with a much gentler gesture shook one out, renewing his offer.

She took it and leaned over to his lit match to pull in the drug. He let her get in a drag or two before continuing.

"We told him back in March a rumor surfaced on the street that someone was willing to pay to ice him. I can't believe he never told you."

Nikki sat there sucking on the cigarette, her heart frozen in fear. Bob noticed her hand shaking, but going easy on her, he said nothing of it. He snagged a waitress's arm to bring a round of whiskey, then lit another of his own.

"Well, before it was just rumor. Probably real, but nonetheless, still rumor. It's beginning to look real credible now and—I really should be telling this to Alexander himself."

The waitress slopped the shots of whiskey on the table.

Picking up one of the glasses, Nikki raised it to her lips and downed it, then dragged deeply on the butt, leveling her eyes at him. "Finish it!" she demanded with a drop-dead glare. "I want the whole damn thing. To the bitter end!" For emphasis, Nikki spit out each of her words individually, just above a smoke-filled whisper.

Bob lowered his head delivering the tough news, "Every time the offer filters back to us, the price has increased. So far it's not serious money, just enough to bring out the riffraff—those I am assuming your own security would spot immediately. But, if it goes much higher, I don't know what will happen."

"Who, Bob? Who's named the price?"

Bob gulped his whiskey and ordered another round. Out of nervous habit, he cased the joint. "It's beginning to look awfully Red Chinese. So far intelligence hasn't dragged anything up, but it seems to be coming from that direction. You know they don't exactly publish in the *London Times*."

Stung with terror, she stammered, "Then, then you know about…"

"New Year's Eve? Yea, we heard. James called Junger and updated us when the other two bought it. It's a stinkin' shame about Soo. I never worked with him, but he was legendary for saving our guys' sorry asses when they got into deep shit."

The next round of whiskeys came. Nikki bummed another cigarette and tossed back the hit. A faint buzz danced in her head. She didn't care if she got plastered.

Bob matched her, "Those bastards got what they deserved, but it turns out they weren't just throw away street joes. Their big boys had cracked Soo's cover. So they sent in an elite torture and re-con team. Whether they made Alex that night or pieced it together later, we'll never know for sure."

"What the hell does it matter? They know," the whiskeys began to make her a little sloppy.

"So it seems. Now, would you please have Mr. Vincente contact us?"

"I'll deliver the message. More than that, I cannot do. You know Alex."

Bob slid out of the booth and pushed the half-empty pack of cigarettes along with his Zippo towards her, "Here you may need these to finish the day. Stay low, Princess. Take care." Mann sidled out.

Nikki left her partially eaten plate of food, stowed the smokes and lighter in her purse, put the glasses back on then stalked out. With the buzz from Mann and the whiskeys intensifying, Nikki was in no shape to stand in front of a microphone, but she had to go back to the recording studio to catch her limo back to the penthouse. Clearly, she couldn't let anyone inside see her in her condition—rumors would abound.

A parked Mercedes, however, sat in front of the pub. Reed Dawson, their pilot, got out of the back seat and appeared at Nikki's elbow. With a conciliatory tone he ventured, "May I offer you a ride, Mrs. Vincente?"

In gratitude, she smiled and let him escort her to the waiting car. "How nice," she thought, "Someone must have read my mind."

But they didn't go to the penthouse. Instead they turned off in the direction of the passenger airfield, where *Wings of Nevermore* sat parked.

"What's going on, Reed?" Nikki questioned, fighting against the whiskeys.

"Mr. Vincente suggested that you might like to return to *Napoli*. He sent me to escort you home," Reed smiled benevolently. "I've taken the liberty of packing your things at the apartment. You can use the phone in the car to cancel your schedule of commitments for the day."

Picking up the phone, Nikki excused her absence due to feeling ill after lunch. She promised Bruce she'd return in a day or two to finish the work. In parting, she asked him to tell Jarred that he could stand down from his ritual of picking her up and seeing her home until further notice. Bruce denied sending Jarred, but promised to pass on the message if he came around. The confusion over Jarred puzzled Nikki, but she attributed the misunderstanding to the whiskeys.

Nikki snuggled into the feeling of being taken care of. She liked someone anticipating her desires, as if they had been listening or could read her mind. Then, foggily it hit her. Someone had been listening. Alexander, through the communicators, knew everything. Nikki could have felt spied upon and sent for like an errant child. Rather, relief blanketed her. Now, she wouldn't have to try to recreate the story. He already knew it, word for word. This was yet another example of Alexander reaching out through his extensive network, covering her with his concern and always taking care of her. On board, Nikki gave in to the liquor, falling asleep on the bed in back.

Alex met her at the door with a welcoming kiss on his lips, however, the seriousness in his eyes betrayed the turmoil seething inside.

Nikki shelved her maternal longing to cuddle Adam to deal with the immediate situation. Tension twitched in Alex's hand as they walked to the library.

Drawing the massive solid doors closed, he poured himself a sherry. Nikki only wanted a tall water. Smoldering disgust replaced the natural ebullient light in Alex's eyes as he fumed. She'd never seen him in such a state. Not even the partner snafu had enraged him so. He positioned them on the leather sofa facing each other.

"Darling," taking a deep breath, he steadied himself, "I almost do not know where to start. Today distressed me on so many levels. I flew into a purple rage when I heard Mann's voice coming over the communicator. I would have torn him apart had I been there." His speech escalated as his anxiety spewed out, "He never should have approached you! And he never should have been able to get to you in the first place!"

Alex's anger forced him to his feet. He paced. "I still have not decided what to do about the security detail I assigned to protect you. They have all been put on notice!"

Nikki didn't offer any defense for them, rather she let him continue.

"In a big way this is my fault. Had I acknowledged Junger's communiqués, at least he wouldn't have found the need to bother you. But I didn't want to worry you, especially with the baby coming. I never could have forgiven myself if you lost...If there's a price on my head, there's really very little I can do about it, other than take out the person who put it there. Back in March, that was not possible. We only had rumors to run on. So I fortified the house security and stepped up the detail. It really doesn't matter how Mann got to you. The point is, he should not have been able to. No one should be able to get to you! See why I am questioning our security's ability?"

Nikki nodded to his mostly rhetorical question.

"Anyway, I have known about the sanction rumors since February, through my own grapevine. Now it seems that the rumors are intensifying. I already knew the gist of Junger's messages. I hoped that if I stayed submerged long enough, my contacts would finger the source of the sanction, and I could have the entire mess cleaned up. Then, I would never have to worry you about any of it. Damn the Red Chinese!"

"So, what are we going to do about this now?" she asked, throwing herself into the equation. "I've always assumed I was a target, too, but today Mann pulled our son into the scenario. Is that true? Is Adam in danger?"

Alex didn't fly to Nikki's side to comfort her, as she expected, as she wanted. That in itself frightened her. Instead he walked over to his desk. Considering the question, he fiddled with a book. Picking up the book, he thumbed through it. Snapping, with tremendous force he closed the book and hurled it. The book slammed into the bookcase with a thunderous crack. "Damn it, Nicole! I can't answer that. I don't know! None of this was supposed to play out this way! None of it! And it would not have if it hadn't been for Charlie Soo."

"And what were you supposed to do? Leave your friend to be tortured and killed? You had no idea this would come of it. Besides, didn't Charlie save your life on several occasions?" Nikki challenged him.

"You are right. He saved me so many times, he took to calling me 'the cat' because of all my lives. But now I may have traded his life for my family's."

"Then we'll just have to lay low until your contacts identify *the source* and he can be dealt with."

"Darling," a weary smile crossed Alex's lips, "you said 'we.' Don't imagine for a moment that I would..."

She cut Alex off, "Remember, we're a team. And of the two of us, I'm the one most visible."

"You are right. I guess we had better make a trip to Paris to meet with Junger so we can keep the lines of communication open.

Rising, Nikki went to Alex and held her arms open for him. She knew he felt defeated by the forces beyond his control. Maneuvering him into a chair, she massaged his back. While working on his knot of muscles, Nikki dropped kisses along his neck, "If you could hear everything on your communicator, then you also know that I bummed a few cigarettes from Mann during our conversation. I don't do it very often," she added with a half laugh. "It seems only when Mann comes around. Anyway, he left me the rest of his pack. I'll have to remember to throw them out."

Alex moved his shoulders to maximize the effect of her hands. "An occasional cigarette hardly bothers me. We have all done it. They certainly come in handy on occasion. But Mann left you something else."

Nikki tried to recall. "Only his lighter. I guess he thought I was too desperate to find a pack of matches on my own."

Alex pulled Nikki around and into his lap. "Do not be so willing to assign such benign motives to Bob Mann. You can check your purse, but I assure you the lighter is not there. After you got on the jet, Reed conducted a routine sweep of the aircraft before taking off—a normal precaution. He found transmitter signals coming from the lighter in your purse. It seems that Mr. Mann would like to know where we live. Reed disposed of it. His lighter now swims with the fishes in the Channel."

Aghast at Mann's nerve, Nikki could do little more than sputter at his audacity.

"Which brings me to my second topic of concern, Nicole. You are going to have to be more careful from now on. Every minute of every day, when you are away from the compound, you must be on alert." Even though Alex avoided scolding, his serious intent came through clearly.

"I know you have not given any thought to our security detail assigned to you in months. That is my fault. I kept them at arm's length to allow you a feeling of autonomy. I indulged your illusion of immunity from danger. I didn't want to see you living in fear. But starting this afternoon, you will know all the members of our security force as well as they know you. You will not go anywhere without acknowledging them and making sure the entire complement is in place. Rest assured that anyone I have allowed to have access to us, like the captain or crew of the boat, the chef, Reed, anyone, has been thoroughly checked out before I hired them. Each of them is a trained specialist in anti-terrorist tactics and is armed at all times. They are there not only to serve, but also to protect. You can call on any one of them should the need ever arise. This is serious business, darling. I can no longer allow you to be blasé about your protection now that we have Adam.

Fear puddled in Nikki's eyes at the thought of the insidious threat possibly touching their son.

Alexander meant to summon her to action, not to terrorize her. He laid kisses on her forehead and cheeks to ease her anxiety. "I know Jarred did a wonderful job of training you. Look at the missions you pulled off on your own. But maybe some refresher courses might be helpful. What if I supplemented your training? Besides, I am sure you could probably teach me a trick or two."

Nikki didn't take offense at his olive branch diplomacy, nor the insinuation that her haphazard training might be lacking. No doubt, it had gaping holes in it.

True to his word, they started that very afternoon. Alex provided her with dossiers on their entire security staff, so Nikki could learn each member's area of expertise. Every morning Dirk, the head of the detail, apprised her as to how many and whom she should expect to see in her company that day. It seemed petty to keep track of how many in the day's complement, but as Dirk pointed out, "If you know how many are around you, then you can recognize if any disappear and react accordingly."

Alexander taught her to read eyes—the window to a person's conscious mind. "The eyes will always give away the petty and inexperienced." He taught her how to concentrate on one thought, while carrying out a totally unrelated task. "Only the best can redirect their focus and maintain their true purpose."

Alex re-emphasized the need for Nikki to mentally record every single detail around her. They drilled, using the unsuspecting staff or even people on the street as their foils. Again teacher and student challenged each other in an eternal competition of accelerating intensity. She enjoyed trying to best Alexander. His rewards or retributions proved more frisky and gratifying than those of old Jarred.

Within a week Lorenzo, Alexander and Nikki sailed the yacht to a remote island location. Leaving the staff on board, the trio motored to shore.

Alexander placed a .22 pistol in Nikki's hand, "We'll start with something small. Because when we are finished, I want your weapon to be a part of you."

Lorenzo set up target after target for Nikki while Alex stood by her side, patiently instructing. Having mastered the rudiments of aiming the .22 from a wide variety of positions, Alex handed her the more substantial, short barrel .357 magnum. Nikki hated it. Even with plugs, the concussion rang through her body, and the recoil required all her strength to control it. But Alex refused to revert to a smaller caliber.

Training Nikki army style, Alex and Lorenzo focused not only on shooting, but also on dismantling and reassembling the gun, all without benefit of sight. The exhaustive drills lasted for hours, and they timed the exercises.

Alexander lectured her on the drill's purpose. "In all the times I have had to draw my weapon, I cannot recall a single incident where I had either the light or the time to check its status. I relied on a series of detailed procedures to know its state of readiness. I also knew it by its feel. By the end of our lessons, you will depend on the feel of your weapon to know whether it is loaded, if the safety is on, or any number of things, without ever physically seeing it. I want the weapon to feel absolutely natural. If you should ever need it, you must be able to rely on it." After a month, Nikki could draw into a drop-dead aim in the blink of an eye, from any position.

Before completion of her refresher courses, she and Alexander flew to Paris for their one-on-one with Mann and Junger. Prior to entering the complex, Alex reminded her that despite whatever theories may be espoused behind closed doors, she still remained one of four who knew the actual fate of Charlie Soo. Nikki would have to monitor not only her speech, but also her mannerisms to act accordingly.

Mike and Bob greeted them with great congeniality.

Not a patient man when his family's lives hung in the balance, Alex cut to the chase, a frank discussion of the facts.

"It's definitely the Red Chinese," Mike Junger started. "Our connections are absolutely clear on that. You broke up their operation before they got what they wanted from Charlie Soo. That really angered them."

"I'm pretty sure it put a crimp in Charlie's day, too," Alex grimly retorted.

"Now it seems they want revenge. To make matters worse, since New Year's they've also learned your true identity. Your scalp would make a nice trophy to hang on their wall of honor."

"What about my scalp?" Nikki questioned. "I'm the one directly responsible for the rescue and the car crash that killed their people. Do they want me, too?"

"That's a good question, Mrs. Vincente," Mike picked up, "One I don't have the answer to either. So far your name hasn't surfaced in the rumor mill."

Quickly Alex turned back to Junger, "What does intelligence say? Could this thing bleed over to the Soviets or the Eastern Bloc?"

Junger shrugged, "It's hard to say Alex. You've been out of that theater for over a year now. If I were to hazard a guess, I'd have to say you have zero value to them now. I can't see them getting involved."

Mann chipped in, "Yea, well, the Red Chinese are supporting a rapidly expanding war across Southeast Asia now, which pretty much ties up their resources. I can't imagine you are a big fish over there either with Soo gone."

Alex tried to get the pieces to fit, "I know. With Charlie gone, it closes down our pipeline over there. Common sense tells me they should be more obsessed with where we'll open up a new pipeline, not with a has-been who stumbled in on their operation."

Nikki interrupted, "Isn't this all academic now anyway? We aren't talking about if there is a sanction, are we? Isn't the status of the sanction definite? So why waste time talking about if and protesting their logic, when we should really be talking about who and how to neutralize it?"

Alex smiled with broad admiration, "Good call, Nicole!"

Mike addressed Nikki, "Of course, you're right. The sanction is the one known quantity in this whole equation."

She came back, "Then isn't it possible that the operatives didn't know Alex wasn't working when he hid out in Charlie's warehouse to help him. Charlie may have been tied into something with tentacles. They may think Alex is walking around with that information, and it could still hurt them."

"She's right you know. You could be 'hot' as an active agent, even though in this case, you were just an innocent Good Samaritan," Junger quickly picked up.

But Nikki wasn't so quick to bet the farm on just a single theory — any single theory, even hers. "But then again it may be a case of simple revenge. If one is bent on reprisal, being spread thin only increases the challenge, it doesn't deter it. Bloodlust, the ultimate catalyst, accomplishes its goal, no matter the cost."

"Personally, I would like to concentrate on the active agent theory Nicole advanced," Alex pitched. "Somehow we need to find whoever holds that misguided notion and change it. I can't do a damn thing about someone holding a grudge against me, except identify and eliminate him."

"Yea," Mann jumped in. "If we can work the active agent angle, we might be able to follow it up the entire chain of command and take out a whole operation."

"Easy, Bob. Easy," Alex added. "I am not looking to bring down any dynasties. I just want to erase the threat to my family and me."

"Alex makes a good point," Nikki butted in. "Please, don't entice more people to paint us as targets."

Junger denigrated Mann with a lethal sidelong glance, "Don't worry, Alex. I respect what you've accomplished. We won't compromise it."

"So, if it is a case of my being mistaken as an active agent, who do you have over there that you can send in to get answers?" Alex asked.

"Would you use Jack Chow who helped me in Hong Kong?" Nikki inserted.

"Probably not. I think he's the only one left outside of Soo's network that James can count on," Mike responded. "Charlie had a whole organization in place over there. Their discovery of Charlie taints everyone else in his operation. You can count on this fact: by now they are either dead or useless because they have already gone over to the other side as double agents. We'll have to work through Nigel James on this one. He must have somebody inside who can find out what Soo was into, which put a price on your head." Junger turned to Alex, "You played in that sandbox. Don't you know anyone who could be trusted over there to sniff out the rat?"

Shaking his head Alex lamented, "Unfortunately, I worked completely inside Soo's operation. I am an Anglo. Charlie always interfaced for me. Without Charlie's support, I am so recognizable I am radioactive. That's why I got out of there p.d.q."

"But if James came up with some leads on Charlie's last operation, could you piece it together from that?" Junger asked Alex.

"Mike," Alex responded, "I have not been on a mission there in over two years." Alex tossed a fond smile in Nikki's direction. "That is an eternity in our business. My relationship with Charlie Soo, of late, was purely personal."

"Then we'll have to leave the active agent scenario in James' hands," Junger concluded.

"But in case the other scenario proves true and if their motive is revenge, where do we go with that?" Nikki queried. She could tell Alex knew the answer, but he joined her in waiting for Mike Junger's response.

"We have a few trusted people," Mike began, "that we can encourage to nose around and try to pick up the offer. Hopefully if one of ours offers to fulfill the sanction, they will come up with its source. Although, picking up a sanction doesn't always give you a roadmap to its source. It all depends on how deep his cover is."

Then Mike riveted his attention on Alex, "You realize, though, because this isn't a national security matter, this assignment is strictly voluntary. Any trusted operatives you'd like us to contact? What do you think? Should we give it a try?"

Alex agreed, "I will try and come up with some names. I thought that was the course you would follow. I just wanted to hear it from you."

Alex rose, extending his hand, "Thanks, Mike. It is all I could ask for. Hopefully we can nail this…this… source… before he nails me. Oh, and I promise I will not be so incommunicado in the future. I will contact you if I hear anything at all."

As Nikki thanked Mike for his cooperation, Alex shared a not-so-quiet word with Mann. Going toe-to-toe, Alex dressed him down, "If you ever try to intimidate my wife again, so help me God, you will have to deal with me. Do you understand my meaning?" Alex deliberately enunciated each word to emphasize his message. Reaching into his pocket, he pulled out a duplicate Zippo lighter. "Here is your lighter back—sans the bug. Never try a trick like that on me again. *Comprende*?" Alex turned on his heel.

Preoccupied with the meeting and its implications, Alex sped silently through the streets of Paris on their way to the airfield. Finally he shared his thoughts, "Nicole, did you understand the implications in Mike's statement that the assignment to send in an agent to smoke out the source would be voluntary."

"I heard the words. But since I took them at face value, obviously I didn't comprehend the double-speak."

"If the service of an agent is 'voluntary' then there is no Agency weight behind his actions. In other words, he would be freelancing. In effect, he would become a soldier of fortune which means he could very well play the source of the sanction against me. The side that offers the most money wins. The more agents who try to pick up the sanction, the more agents you stand to lose to the highest bidder, which might be to the other side. The whole process builds risk, not only for the targeted agent, but for the entire operation. That is why Mike asked me for names of agents I can trust. They will only ask someone to volunteer who they are pretty sure can be trusted dead-on to stand for me and not be tempted by the money."

Encouraged, Nikki added, "That should be a slam dunk. After all your years in the Agency, you must have a ton of names!"

Alex's laugh unnerved her, "Darling, I wish it were so. The more time you spend 'inside,' the less you trust anyone. The truth is, I cannot come up with a single name. I have such a bad feeling about the whole endeavor. Any time you roll the dice in the vengeance game, danger is always the winner."

Reed and Lorenzo met them on the tarmac at the airfield. Grim-faced, Alex boarded the jet. Dutifully each man carried out his assigned tasks to get the craft in the air. Reed came back to check on their destination.

Alex considered his options, "Head north till we clear the U.K. With that as our radius, turn left and make a circle. I want some breathing room. And Reed, I see no reason to file a flight plan."

Reed Larsen understood perfectly.

Once airborne, Nikki sliced some cheese and opened a bottle of wine.

"You don't mind if Lorenzo joins our discussion, do you?" Alex asked before buzzing Lorenzo out of the cockpit.

Lorenzo took his seat, "Things stacked up about as you expected?"

Obviously Alex and Lorenzo had talked prior to the little summit with Junger. Nikki took no offense at being left out of their private confab.

"Nicole brought up the active agent scenario. Which, by their posture, I gathered they never considered." Alex proudly turned to her, "You see, darling, that is one of the reasons I hashed things out with Lorenzo before involving you. I wanted your fresh perspective on the situation."

"So where do we go from here?" Lorenzo asked.

"I am torn" Alex picked up his glass of wine. "I can't ask anyone to front for the sanction. I know the risks if I turn loose a set of agents. The Agency could wind up with another bloodbath like they had three years ago. I have half a mind to go under myself and find the source."

Responding, Nikki set her glass down rather loudly, "Pardon me, *mon ami!*"

"I knew *that* would go over well. But darling, if I go in, it will be one-on-one. Either I get him, or he gets me. That way you and Adam are safe, no matter the outcome. The Agency is spared, too."

"Like I care what happens to that blood-thirsty lot when it comes to the life of my husband. I'd much rather Adam grows up with a father, and I have you by my side, thank you very much."

Realizing she came on rather strong, Nikki lightened her tone, "Unless, you indeed live up to your vaunted reputation as super-agent. In that case have at it! And while you're at it, bring me back some jade," she impertinently winked, raising her glass.

Alex clinked his glass against hers and stole a kiss. With a lift of an eyebrow and a tiny glint in his eye he added, "I am even better than that!"

Putting away the fun, he sobered, "But facing facts, since the sanction is East Asian, my chances for survival without Soo's network are almost zero."

"It would truly be a suicide mission then," Lorenzo noted. "Too bad we can't ask Charlie what he was working on."

"Why can't we?" Nikki asked.

Stunned, Lorenzo shot her a look, which Alex answered, "It's okay, Lorenzo. Nicole knows. I told her that afternoon."

Then Nikki continued, "Since Charlie is the one who knows exactly what business he had on the table and its possible connections, maybe you should ask him."

"Before I do that, I want to thoroughly examine all the other options," Alexander squashed the idea.

"I don't see very many other avenues open," Lorenzo iced. "Either you hide out in America, go under to find the source, unleash hell or see Charlie."

"Some choices!" Nikki exclaimed. "Before you try the first three, I think you should start out with a visit to the grave."

Somewhere over the North Sea, it was decided Alex would go alone to see Soo. Lorenzo would stay behind with the family. It wouldn't happen immediately in case the Agency had incorporated a tail on them. Alex would wait for an opportunity at an undisclosed time, then simply disappear for a day or two.

Nikki arrived home at *Napoli* to urgent messages from Bruce inquiring about the state of her health and the date of her return to London. Alex didn't have to ask her to stall. Nikki knew travel at that time would be foolish at best. Bruce would have to accept disappointment, temporarily.

But temporarily grew into forever. Nikki never finished the album or shot the promotion package, including the cover. While her excuses covered up the real reason she couldn't come back to London, Nikki always meant to finish the album. Finally after two weeks of broken promises, she bluntly told her manager she doubted her ability to deliver a finished product in the foreseeable future. Desperate for a new release, he sought Nikki's permission to release the record "as is." Nikki agreed. Bruce titled the album *Love – Nikki's Unfinished Symphony*. He used pages of sheet music with scrawled notes trailing off the page for the album cover—the first ever without a picture of Nikki on it.

The publicity never gave a reason for her public disappearance or why the album remained unfinished, but it built a mystique. The disc went platinum in days. The tabloid press wildly speculated about why she dropped from sight. The more outlandish their hypotheses, the closer they came to the actual truth. Half-seriously, Alexander and Nicole joked that they hoped spies didn't read the gossip rags!

Chapter 35

Confirmation

As it had to be, Nikki woke one morning to find a note on her pillow. "Off on my hunting expedition. Didn't have the heart to wake you for a farewell. I leave you all my love, even as I take yours with me. Love, A."

Worry pounded inside Nikki's heart. What if someone tracked him? What if he decided, against better judgment, to go into China by himself and take out the source? What if he never came back? Clearly, driven by the preservation instinct to save his family, Alex might bolt after his conversation with Charlie and hurtle off in one of many available courses. She spent the entire week of his absence clutching Adam to her chest, keeping busy, trying try to still her roiling maternal hormones to protect her own.

The risky rendezvous with Charlie Soo confirmed their worst fears. The sanction emanated from high up in the Red Chinese command. Soo had been working on choking off the direct link between the Chinese and the North Vietnamese. Soo was within two days of severing the connection that fed the communist war effort in Vietnam with both human fodder for the battlefield and millions in financial aid. The four upper echelon Supreme Guard sent to Hong Kong to take out Soo reported directly to Cho Lin Cao, the Chinese Minister of Defense. Losing Soo, before the Guard could extract the information Cao needed, created a huge disruption for him since he had no way to accurately assess the extent to which Soo had compromised their vital links. It would take months to ferret out the moles inside their ranks. The Minister's loss of his four Supreme Guards and Charlie Soo along with his information really enraged Cao. But having Alex, the number one European Agent, also slip through his fingers caused him to lose face. So, the Minister avowed the sanction. Without hesitation Charlie Soo declared the sanction's impetus to be revenge.

Revenge, the word terrorized Nicole. Alex, however, faced down the threat with his usual casual coolness, although she knew it consumed him. Routinely he disappeared for hours, then days at a time. Sometimes he took the *Bella Nicole*, other times the jet. Sweetly, but decisively, he dismissed her attempts to accompany him.

One day out of the blue, Alex sloughed off the comment, "Good old Charlie complains about 'retirement,' as he calls life underground.

Although he has all the creature comforts he desires, he misses his shop. He tires of living long days without a purpose. And without a purpose or family and friends, life feels like prison."

Eventually November's slate gray skies and chilly breezes chased the Vincentes' out of *Napoli*. Although the weather was the same at *Nevermore*, the approaching holidays warmed their spirits there. On the crisp autumn days, radiant with sunshine yet vivid in contrasts, they'd take the horses for a walk through the countryside. Alex carefully seated Adam in front of him on his saddle. The cool wind polished Adam's apple-dumpling cheeks to a stunning crimson, igniting the rich sapphire of his eyes and exciting the copper glow in his hair. How Adam laughed—a contagious, effervescent giggle bubbled out of him. The more they rode, the more he giggled, almost to hiccuping. When Alex stopped, Adam bounced up and down in the saddle, urging them to go again. Alexander vowed that by two, Adam would have a pony of his own.

They had only been back at *Nevermore* two weeks when Junger summoned them back to Paris. Alex's situation and the possible impending harm it could bring to the Agency occupied Junger's mind. After lengthy consideration, Mike Junger had conceived a plan. As usual, they met in the richly paneled room at the Embassy, this time without Mann's presence. Mike poured sherry while they sat in the conversationally arranged leather armchairs.

"We've made progress in tracking down the source of the sanction," Mike began. "That's the good news. But it gets worse. It appears that the source of the sanction emanates from one of the military types inside the Prime Minister's Cabinet. They assumed Alex to be an agent actively involved in the mission."

The source of the sanction matched Soo's opinion, even if the ideas on the motive clashed. Nikki monitored her reactions, being careful not to hint at her inside knowledge.

Alexander cocked a smile, "Oh, then if I lay low for a period of time, my supposed information should cool off enough to relegate the sanction useless. So, I will be home free then, right?"

"I'm afraid not in this case, my friend," Mike shook his head. "The scope of Charlie's mission was incredible. The information they assume you have will be sensitive for many years to come. I don't think you can hibernate long enough."

Cautiously, Nikki stepped in, "You really aren't leaving us very much wiggle room, Mike. With the official so highly placed, we can't take him out, can we?"

"No. That would be impossible. But I thought the opportunity might be ripe to 'lawyer' your way out of this situation."

With unabashed perplexity Alex passed, "Come again, Mike?"

"I assume you follow U.S. politics. You must know that President Nixon and his State Department are in the process of making friendly gestures towards China. I suggest you cozy up to the Administration— make yourself indispensable to them. Maybe the diplomats can straighten out the error in your mistaken participation that night."

"I don't know, Mike. It seems we are constantly cleaning up the messes the diplomats leave. They continually dig holes for our guys to crawl out."

"I know. But sometimes they also ride in like cavalry and pull our sorry souls out of the fire."

Alex laughed, "I know they do. With their polite words, quiet little voices and briefcases full of papers, I know they have saved us on several occasions. It is just that I hate to leave something as big as my family's welfare in some diplomat's lap. I feel so … so …"

"Out of control?" Nikki interjected.

"Precisely. Out of control," Alex concurred.

"Sometimes," Mike smiled shrewdly, "*you* aren't in control."

Mike's idea of opening up diplomatic channels as a viable remedy for the sanction gnawed at Alex all the way home. Nikki gave him his head to explore the field of possibilities. But half way over the Atlantic, she decided to test the waters. Bringing over a bottle of red wine, she poured him a glass and sat across from him at the table where he struggled with his options. "So, have you figured out the best way to worm your way into the heart of the Nixon Administration?"

Surprised from his preoccupation, he smiled a welcome at her, "Darling, how did you know what I was thinking about?"

"It's rather obvious, sweetheart. You haven't thought about much else since we left Mike's. You think there might be merit in Mike's suggestion, right?"

Alexander nodded, "His scenario could work. I have been trying to find an edge that would put me in essential proximity with the White House or the Foreign Service."

"To me, your strength lies in your aptitude with security. Look at the tremendous system you instituted at *Nevermore*. You designed a system with technology superior to anything the government has. I think your connections with the cutting edge inventors of these gadgets would be enticing to the government."

"Sure, I could put together a business peddling those devices to the

Administration. We would have to move to D.C.," he challenged obliquely.

Nikki picked up the gauntlet, "Great! you can't beat the cultural opportunities. Why don't we nose around down there this week and see what we find?"

In the capital gripped by post-election flux they found a red-brick, Georgian style townhouse in a neighborhood richly peppered with enough dignitaries to be considered less of a security risk.

A disaster on the inside, "Look beyond the mess," Alex counseled. "Is this enough room for us? I intended on gutting the entire place anyway to add the security web we need. We will bring our old friend Gus Schubert down for the remodeling."

Nikki tried to visualize the townhouse's potential. Once she agreed the four stories provided adequate space, Alex closed the deal and called Gus.

Nikki and Alexander spent at least five days of every week in the Washington area. A suite of rooms at the Hilton became their temporary lodging as Alex's technicians installed the security web to his exacting specifications. The excessive demands on their time and lack of a controlled secure environment forced them to leave Adam at *Creekside* in Fran's care.

Alex also decided on a storefront for the business across the Potomac. While Alex feverishly worked to open his business, Nikki met daily with interior design consultants or shopped in marathon sprees to stock the townhouse. The cosmopolitan flavor of the capital required Nikki to re-configure her wardrobe with mandatory suits, career dresses and an extensive collection of conservative formal wear.

To Nikki's amazement, Alexander already knew a preponderance of the major players in the State and Defense departments. Nightly they hosted the departments' loftier stratum for dinner at a spectrum of five-star restaurants surrounding the city. While slipping his business cards into their pockets, Alex whetted their appetites for his talents and toys. As he won their business, Nikki engaged their wives, entertaining them. Absorbing everything, instinctively she knew the value of keeping an accurate mental record and a closed mouth. Alex profoundly apologized for subjugating her to the role of corporate wife.

Alex worked his way through the Pentagon, Langley and Quantico.

He paid an unheard of premium for the most sophisticated and innovative ideas in surveillance gadgetry, communications and personal weaponry. Alex's infusion of serious dollars into the marketplace siphoned off the inventions of the best and the brightest from the world market, leaving government espionage agencies sucking dust. Using his ability to mastermind the grand scheme of things, Alex bundled several analogous inventions together, producing an enhanced end product. Then he dazzled the politicos with the extent of technology available to him. Quickly, he moved into a position of indispensability.

On Tuesday, December 22, with the recommendation of Secretary of Defense Laird preceding him, Alexander received a summons to the White House to meet with H.R. Haldeman, Nixon's Chief of Staff.

In the middle of planning the finishing design touches for their townhome, Nikki never knew anything special transpired until a bouquet of three-dozen red roses arrived via messenger, along with a small package.

The enclosed note read: "Let's have champagne! Just you and me tonight. Take the afternoon off. Surprise me. I will pick you up at 8. Love, A. P.S. I thought you might find these interesting."

In Tiffany's distinctive box, Nikki found a stunning sapphire pendant and earrings. A gentle "S" of diamonds looped from the stud to cradle a pear-shaped sapphire drop. She had nothing in their temporary quarters to wear with them. Alex knew it. He challenged her with the phrase, "surprise me".

Alexander's message tantalized Nikki. He wanted a date. Just the thought of a rendezvous accelerated her breathing to racy little pants as a warm tingly feeling pulsed through her. Surprise him indeed! She'd peel his precisely pleated, tuxedo shirt right off his magnificent body.

Rubbing elbows with Christmas clientele, Nikki shopped until she found a Prussian blue velvet gown with a plunging empire bodice that allowed the pendant to seek its own level deep in the cleft of her bosom. From a local florist, she ordered six miniature gardenias, wired on individual stems. Pinning her tresses up in large looping curls, she strategically positioned each of the blooms among the curls.

Promptly at eight, Nikki rode the express elevator to the Mezzanine Level at the top of the grand staircase. Alex wanted a reprise of her entrance from their first date—and would she give it to him! Wearing a smile that started from the glow in her heart, regally she descended the stairs into the lobby. The heavy velvet of her gown softly lapped on the steps behind her. Nikki felt the collective gaze of the populace, but she played to her audience of one.

Extending his hand to help her from the last step, his scintillating blue eyes danced their approval. "Darling," he looked up with an amused smile, "I may have to rethink my fondness of rubies. The sapphires toy so delightfully with your eyes. Enchanting!" Tucking her arm into his, he led her to the door where their limo driver met them with Nikki's white mink and a formal cloak for Alexander.

Downy soft flakes of snow fluttered down, landing on them. A web of Christmas lights spun over the street transformed the night's harsh darkness into a soft velveteen glow. Their route took them down Pennsylvania Avenue. Nikki's heart stopped at the sight of the White House in the feathery snowfall; its portico bathed in lights with the national tree ablaze out front. By her side, Alex made any place heaven. But Washington, Nikki thought after seeing it decked out in holiday glitter, might prove to be extremely intriguing.

As they passed, Alex interrupted her thoughts, "I was *there* today." He surprised her.

"Really?" Nikki cast another glance at the magnificent manse, then checked Alex to see if he was merely teasing her.

With assurance, Alex confirmed it, "Really."

"Oh! What was it like? Is that why we are celebrating?" Nikki gushed.

"Darling, we are celebrating because you are so beautiful, and I am the luckiest man on earth to be in your presence. But, if later on you care to raise a glass to Bob Haldeman and the relationship we struck up today, I would be inclined to join you," a smile teased at the corners of Alex's eyes.

They dined at the Robespierre, opening the evening with champagne and an eclectic selection of French delicacies. As dinner progressed, Alex detailed his meeting at the White House with H.R. Haldeman—"Bob" as his intimates called him. Interested in installing some elaborate devices outside the purview of the FBI, Haldeman was anxious to do business. As added incentive to assure Alex's cooperation, he promised a joint meeting after the holidays with Defense's Mel Laird, along with the new rising star within Nixon's inner circle and on the international scene, Dr. Kissinger.

Alex effervesced, "I thought Mike Junger fell off the turnip truck when he proposed the diplomatic route for our immunization against the sanction. But Nicole, after today, I have the feeling this might actually work. If Dr. Kissinger can really pull off half of what Bob told me today, we are definitely on the right path."

With their last course, Alex put away his recitation of his meeting. For dessert and coffee, they retreated to a cozy room within the restaurant, lit entirely by candlelight. Fronting on a terrace, they watched the snow twirl and eddy outside just beyond the parquet dance floor. Rich strains of chamber music sweetened the finale of their meal. Dancing close, Alex nuzzled Nicole's neck while whispering his love in impassioned tidbits. He wondered if they shouldn't cut short their dancing in public for some more intimate contact in private. With pretended indifference, Nikki teased him just long enough to fan the flames of his desire into a blistering swelter.

The mirage of the sanction being lifted purged the dark specter that had clung to the recesses of their daily lives and had hovered in their bedroom over the last few months. Alex's self-assured air of devil-may-care charm returned. Once again, only his passion for Nikki possessed him. His kisses sucked away her strength, as she surrendered to his scorching tenderness. Unfettered, they made love into the early hours of the morning, like new lovers unable to get enough of each other. Afterward they prowled the streets, scuffling through patches of deeply-drifted snow to find a just-opened bakery with steamy, freshly baked bread. The palpable feeling tasted like Paris after their first time. They couldn't see past each other.

Their afterglow spilled over into the daylight. Alex alerted Reed, before dawn, of their intentions to fly home before noon. Christmas was coming! Giddy with their new hope tucked securely in their pockets, the Vincentes' raced to get back to their son and *Nevermore*. In a hurry to wrap themselves in the holidays and the warmth of home, they abandoned Washington without even packing.

An exceptional seasonal splendor descended on the holiday, the likes of which Nikki had never experienced. All the dreams for the future holiday that she and Alexander had spun the year before, crystallized into reality. Each moment became the very quintessence, of the perfect holiday. They arrived home to a new mantle of snow covering the ground, just enough to freshen the landscape, but not enough to snarl traffic. Lorenzo had set up a seven-foot tree in the house while Zia and Nikki's parents had festooned the staircase and outer window sills with evergreen boughs. The tree, the mantle and the wreath at the front door waited for Alex and Nikki to imprint with their own style.

Perfumed with fresh cut pine and Fran's German cinnamon waffle cookies, their home welcomed them back within its comforting confines.

Alex brought the decorations down from the attic and lavished the dainty, multicolored lights on the tree branches. Nikki bounced Adam on her hip while "supervising" Alex and the family as they hung the ornaments. As they decorated, Fran's chicken potpie slowly simmered on the stove.

The village planned a carol sing around the community Christmas tree in the town square. Alexander arranged for a large, horse-drawn sleigh to take the seven of them to the celebration. The sleigh's runners glided easily through the daylong accumulation of snow. The horses' clip-clop cadence lulled Adam to sleep before they ever reached the festivities. His parents snuggled him under the generous lap robe as Fran passed out the hot-buttered rum she had packed. A gentle dusting of snow blessed them from the heavens.

What a wonderful feeling at the conclusion of the evening, when they turned the horses back up the lane, to see *Nevermore* sitting all aglow in the holiday with smoke curling lazily out of the chimney. Peace on Earth for the holidays waited for them.

On Christmas Eve, the family assembled at *Nevermore* in the rose of the afternoon to dine on a traditional Christmas Eve fare of seafood and fish before going to evening worship at the old stone church. Following the service, Alexander and Nikki settled down on the sofa in the soft glow of the firelight and the tree lights. The elaborate gifts of last year gave way to smaller, more meaningful tokens. Alexander gave Nikki an English walnut jewelry box with the hand-carved image of *Nevermore* on it. She gave Alex a gold pocket watch inscribed, "For all time, all my love".

Cuddling into each other's arms, they shared tiny kisses in the ambient glow in the room. A gentle snow started again, layering its peaceful freshness over the landscape. The entire scene generated such an enchantment Nikki didn't want to leave the snow, the fire, the tree or Alex's arms to go up to bed. So, Alex made a pallet of sofa cushions for them on the floor so they could bask all night long in the soft crescendo of Christmas splendor.

Christmas morning, as normal for any six and a half-month-old, Adam enjoyed the sparkle of the tree and the brightly colored paper of the presents more than anything else. Staying quietly connected, they relaxed in each other, realizing that all too soon their focus would shift from the rural hills of Pennsylvania back to the high tension environs of the Beltway.

On New Year's Eve with the inauguration of the new members of Congress only four days away, Washington unfurled in a celebration of conducting out the old and ushering in the new. For the last time from their suite at the Hilton, Nikki and Alex prepared to party hop. Privately Nikki contrasted the present evening against the mad terror of the year before when she and Lorenzo flew through the streets of Hong Kong in a desperate attempt to save the lives of Alex and Charlie. She gave thanks for the brief respite they enjoyed from the anxiety-fraught days created by the sanction. Nikki also prayed for the day when the insanity created a year ago would end.

While Nikki adjusted the lines of her sedate, off-one-shoulder, black crepe dress, Alex received a phone call from Mike Junger, notifying them of the crash of the plane carrying Hong Kong's Governor James and his wife. Junger didn't draw any inferences about the deaths of Nigel and Mary James, but silently Nikki totaled up the carnage in the past year of everyone connected with last year's rescue. First, a car bomb had taken out Lance, then Jack Chow was killed when his boat capsized on a calm, sunny day, and now the Jameses. It struck her as more than coincidence that the Governor's plane crashed into Hong Kong's Victoria Peak on its approach to the causeway airport—territory intensely familiar to the Governor's pilot. Although he didn't speak it out loud, Alexander's sudden ashen tone told Nikki he added up the coincidental deaths the same way she did. Thus, the sanction's specter returned to their lives.

"Perhaps," Nikki gamely smiled at Alex, "you'd like to stay in this evening. I have no objections to a quiet supper in our suite in light of the recent developments."

"Darling, there is nothing I would rather do than be anywhere on Earth alone with you." Alex kissed the nape of her neck as he closed the clasp on her opera length pearl necklace, studying her reflection in the mirror, "But we can't. Tonight, *because* of the recent developments, it is more important than ever that we hob-knob with our contacts. We cannot get weak-kneed in the face of adversity. If we are going to pull this thing off, we have to continue the game. You will be as enchanting as ever tonight. We will mingle with Haldeman and all his pals in this town, and no one will ever know we aren't celebrating right along with them."

Momentarily they paused in front of the mirror to reassess themselves when impetuously, Alex swept Nikki into his arms, bending her over in a passionate embrace. With his eyes on fire, he vowed, "I love you more than life itself. I always will. And this I promise you, we will succeed. They will never have you!"

They were scheduled to fly home the next day to pick up the baby and fly back on the following day to begin their life in Washington, D.C. However, before leaving for the evening's festivities, Nikki came upon Alex engaged in a private phone conversation with their pilot. Quite by accident, she overheard Alex instructing Reed to call in all of his backup. Alex wanted a stem-to-stern, inside and out, physical check of the aircraft. "Take as long as you need to do a thorough job. If it takes an extra day or two to get us in the air that is fine with me." He also ordered the security detail around their jet increased. Alex closed his conversation by saying, "From this point forward, consider this standard operating procedure. It should be easier to gain access to Air Force One than our aircraft. I will check in with you later this evening."

Startled by her presence, Alex looked up at Nikki as he smoothly slipped the receiver back into the cradle, "Just in case, darling. One can never be too careful, right?"

It wasn't until after the congressional investiture that they finally returned to D.C. to take up residence. White drywall dust from Gus Schubert's reconstruction team permeated everything. Nikki stationed Adam permanently on her hip rather than let him down in the chalky residue. Although being carried infinitely pleased Adam, it severely hampered Nikki's ability to get things sorted out in their townhome.

During construction, the Vincentes' lives developed a routine around their friend and contractor. Usually in the early morning, Alex and Nikki finished their last bit of morning together, then Nikki put on the coffeepot for Gus. Over coffee, the three of them discussed the plans, interspersed with small talk. After Alex departed for the office, Nikki woke Adam as Gus started his crew on their project of the day.

At the noon-time meal, while Gus's crew huddled around their lunch pails, Nikki and Gus kept up to date at the kitchen counter. Either she recounted Adam's latest feats, or Gus expounded on the nature of one new girlfriend or another. Adam often insisted on sitting in Gus's lap so his fingers could explore the fascinating world of Gus's tool belt, while the adults talked.

Inside a month, Gus's men completed the work on the main floor just as Adam began experimenting with becoming stable on his knees.

At least once a week in the beginning, then two or three times a week as the relationship progressed, the Vincentes' made evening plans with

Gus. Either he would come for dinner, or they would meet him, with his date, to try a new restaurant or engage in some other diversion.

Life in the D.C. meat grinder menaced Alexander. He spent his days with people consumed by their own devious agendas and hidden motives, who carved up their own to feed their jaded personal intrigues. Alexander played the game, too—well...very, *very* well, but it revolted him, as did the accompanying artificial lifestyle. He encouraged their association with Gus. Gus's presence reminded him that people had successfully retired from the Agency. Even though Gus had been a "technical" agent as opposed to a "terminal" one, it permitted Alex to dream about the possibility a normal life.

By mid-February, it became evident Haldeman was stalling on his promise to hook-up Alexander with Dr. Kissinger. Despite Alex's repeated references, Bob Haldeman politely skirted the issue, even as he pressed for more "goodies." Accustomed to performance and response, not political impotence, despondency descended on Alex. The quagmire of paralysis only confirmed Alex's initial feelings about Junger's idea of a diplomatic solution to the sanction.

Several times a month, Alex disappeared. He always wrote notes explaining these "business" absences and included an accurate prediction of his expected return. Nonetheless, fear chilled Nikki's heart whenever these trips came up. Nikki trusted Alex. The thought of infidelity never crossed her mind. But as the incidences increased, she feared he might be carrying water for Junger again. With each absence, she checked his ring box, which he kept in the third-from-the-top, middle dresser drawer. To her relief, she found it empty. Certainly it wasn't an acid-test guarantee, but Nikki felt as long as his ring remained on his finger, he wasn't being extorted by the Agency.

Upon his return, Alex never offered any details. Truthfully though, since that fateful New Year's Day a year ago, Nikki didn't want details. But with the threat of the sanction looming over her husband and son, forces inside her demanded to know.

Following his latest return, Nikki anxiously confronted her husband, "Are all these business trips necessary, Alex? Every time you disappear, worry eats me alive. I'm marking time swimming in a whirlpool in the middle of this sanction, clawing to keep our heads above water. You and our son are my life. I lost my first chance at having a family. I can't lose this one!"

Alex brushed her cheek with a kiss of appeasement. "I know," he said, "I know."

Chapter 36

Hiding Out

Despite his former connections with the Agency, Gus knew nothing about the actual tenor of Nikki and Alex's lives. But he took it upon himself to watch over Nikki and Adam whenever Alex left on business. On those days, Gus called several times and stopped by at least once to make sure they were okay. Nikki always assumed Alex had requested the service. Later, she discovered Gus had assumed the responsibility on his own.

One of Alex's business trips fell over their second wedding anniversary. His absence crushed Nikki. She cried into her pillow the morning she found Alex's note on the nightstand. Feeling scared, disappointed and pouty the little brat inside taunted her with, "If he *really* loved you!" Unable to stand wallowing in self-pity, Nikki banished the brat and resolved to count her blessings instead of toying with the ridiculous.

Her day hadn't progressed very far when Reed Dawson appeared at their front door, "Good morning, Mrs. Vincente." He bowed slightly before entering, "Mr. Vincente suggested I pick up the baby and you. He thought you might enjoy an outing." Reed lifted up Adam from the floor and flew his hand-turned-airplane into her son's chest, forcing a squeal of delight from him. "Might I be of some assistance in assembling some of your things?"

Knowing Alex's affinity for spur-of-the-moment diversion, Nikki excused herself only long enough to throw together a diaper bag for Adam. Alex hated waiting. Nikki knew in his own inimitable fashion, as he did with everything connected to her, he would take care of all the other details he deemed essential. Within minutes, with Adam in her arms and Reed toting their two bags, they skimmed down the townhome's frozen steps to a waiting limousine.

The slightest prickle of conscience poked at Nikki as she strapped Adam into his seat on their jet. How could she entertain, even for a moment, the thought of Alexander forgetting their anniversary? After breaking free of Washington air space, Reed swung the craft onto a southerly course, following the coastline of the eastern seaboard. Nikki spread a few toys on the carpeted floor of the cabin and let Adam explore, while she relaxed with a gourmet brew of *kaffee mit chocolade*. Unwinding, her mind wandered through the possibilities in store for them.

By early afternoon they touched down on *St. Vincente*. What a perfect haven away from the bitterness of D.C.! A tremendous bouquet of tropical flowers laced with gardenias greeted Nikki in the foyer of the manor house. Alex's message read: "My Darling, Nicole, I am only a few islands away in the Caymans. Cursed business will deprive me of dancing with you in the moonlight tonight. But I promise to make it up to you tomorrow. I can't wait to see Adam encounter the sea. Do you think you can find that red bikini again? The very thought of you is air to me. Love, A."

Nikki threw open the house, letting the island breezes tease the gauze curtains at the windows and fill the rooms. She inhaled deeply down into her soul.

From a hallway closet of miscellany, she dug out wide-brimmed beach hats, sand toys and sunscreen. Slathering the lotion all over Adam, Nikki then carried his precious, bare little body down to the shore for his first encounter with the ocean.

Tilde and Pierre, their native caretakers on the island, followed Nikki down to the beach with an array of creature comforts including sling back chairs, an assortment of blankets, towels, toys and an umbrella.

To Nikki's amazement, Reed and his co-pilot joined them at their little encampment on the shore soon after they set up. Stationing themselves under a few lanky palms, they never relaxed. Nikki noticed their eyes continuously scanned the extensive horizon. Their vigilance, no matter how well masked, set her own antennae on edge. From behind her sunglasses, she also covertly scanned that infinite line of blue, moving closer to Adam so she could scoop him up at a moment's notice.

Nikki halfway expected Alexander to show up at nightfall. Such a move would be so typical of him—emerging from the shadows with a broad smile, his eyes alive in the moonlight and his arms hungry to hold her. Nikki fell asleep with the dream of her prince discovering her within the confines of her gauze-shrouded bed, but she awoke alone, the drone of an engine whirring in the background. Shaking off morning's cobwebs, she realized the invading machine brought her husband. Quickly Nikki scurried to wash away the taste of sleep and brush out her hair.

Alexander approached with the long strides of a returning hero to gather Nikki up in his loving embrace. Laying tiny kisses along the nape of her neck, he whispered, "Darling, it was such a long two days. Can we take a walk, or will Adam be up soon?"

Quickly she arranged for Tilde to sit in the room with Adam as Alexander squired her at his will. Trussed up with tension, they walked separately, in silence. Nikki found with every step toward the horizon of trees, more of his cares fell away. He opened his collar and soon lost his loafers. Barefoot, finally grasping at her fingertips, they crossed the dazzling sand, making their way to the thick tangle of tropical vegetation and waterfall that cloaked the rum-runner's caves.

Within the confines of the cave, Alex drew Nikki to him, wrapping her in his arms. "Oh, let me just hold you. I need to bask in your sunshine. Let me lose my fingers in your rich, black tresses. Oh, dear God, you smell so good!"

Purring in his ear, she smoothed his back with her fingertips, "It must have been a rough trip for you to 'need' me so badly after only two days."

"I assure you, I wasn't on a picnic in the Caymans."

His next statement seared a hole through her, "I've been with Junger and Mann. They brought me the grim news. There is a cavalier on the Continent now."

"A cavalier?"

"A soldier of fortune, a black-knight—a shooter looking for me. Someone has picked up the sanction and is actively pursuing me. We spent these two days combing over the leads." Stress squashed his natural spark, "I am so afraid time is running out."

"Between the three of you, none of you could come up with a name?"

"Worse yet, the news of the sanction has broken wide open inside the Agency. It has already polarized our people. Whether or not I ask for volunteers to help me smoke out the rat, a bloodbath will probably ensue." Alex clutched her tighter to him. "Oh, Nicole, a whole lot of people could lose their lives over me."

"So now what?" a tinge of fear raised her voice a bit.

"I don't know, darling. That is why we are here. I needed a place to hide out and think. This place is pretty bulletproof."

"Is that why Adam and I are here?"

"No. Since I was down here out of the blustery Eastern shore winter, I figured you would appreciate a reprieve, too." He kissed the top of her head.

Mentally Nikki debated whether she wanted to challenge his explanation. Sure, she appreciated the sunshine, but Alex had to understand she had signed on to be a partner in their life together. While she doted on his devotion and his role as her protector, Nikki didn't want to be kept in the dark either. She needed answers—answers to help her protect her family. "Sweetheart, were Adam and I in danger in D.C.?"

Dropping the façade of a carefree existence, Alex picked up her hands. Brushing kisses across her fingertips, he looked into Nikki's heart.

"It concerned me that a mad man is scouring the Continent for me. It's only a matter of time before he traces me to the States. I didn't like leaving you unprotected."

"But I have your security..."

"I know. But it's not *me*. I just feel better at this time having you close. Besides, darling, yesterday was our anniversary. I really thought I'd make it home in time for a moonlight dance with you on the terrace. And isn't it better to dance in the sea breezes than the arctic gales of Washington?" Alex nibbled her ear, then moved his mouth down her neckline.

"I fell asleep expecting you," she whispered just before his hands loosened the closure at the back of her dress. It fell down around her feet on the cave's sand floor.

Of course Alexander brought Nicole's anniversary present with him. Besides jewelry, he updated their scuba ensemble with the latest advancements. But because it would be impossible to guarantee their security in the ocean, they tried out their new toys in the secure confines of the island's crystal, grotto pools.

In between dives, they spent the rest of the week on St. Vincente in the sand at the surf's edge, under the vigilant gaze of a half-dozen from their personal security team along with Reed. As Alex pointed out, in the past, the sentries had always been present, but never so openly. Even now they didn't sling their weapons outwardly in plain view, but they visibly maintained a safe perimeter even if they dressed casually. Never far from their minds, Nikki and Alex often talked about the looming sanction. To their daily routine, they now included a review of survival and escape routes should the worst come to pass. Nikki embraced the security rituals with the vigor of a lioness protecting her pride.

In mid-March, they slid over to *Napoli* for a week or two. Even with the cool, changeable springtime weather, it felt good to come home. Life at *Napoli* moved slower, at a take-life-as-it-comes pace—a reprieve from their beleaguered existence in D.C. They relaxed on the leisurely European timetable. Somehow, even though on the Continent and physically closer to the threat, at *Napoli*, the sanction seemed further removed.

Although it had been less than a month since Alex last huddled with Junger, the pair made the trip to Agency headquarters, hoping for more encouraging news this time around. A steady, warm springtime drizzle drenched Paris.

Drastic changes surrounded their visit. This time they didn't convene within the inner sanctum of the library. Wearing dark, hooded rain ponchos under the cover of night, Junger met them a distance from the rear gate and escorted them himself. They slipped past the cameras, skirting the view of the sentries, as they descended into the bowels of the building.

Once inside the spartan bunker-type room of naked concrete with four chairs, one table and a bare bulb, Mike encouraged Alex to check out the room for electronic surveillance equipment, "Sweep it yourself, for your own peace of mind. I know I sure as hell would if I were you."

Mike turned to offer Nikki his apology, "I can't tell you, Nicole, how I hate having to go through the cloak and dagger crap; but unfortunately, right now you two are almost radioactive."

Completing his sweep, Alex clasped Junger in an embrace, "It is better for you this way and definitely better for me, just the price of doing business these days. Shall we get down to it?" Alex pulled out the old, gray Steelcase rolling desk chair for Nikki.

"So tell me, Mike, how bad has it gotten?"

Mike shook his head, "Everyone is looking over his own shoulder."

"I couldn't help but notice," Alex hesitated cautiously, "Bob is not here."

Mike waved the comment away, "Mann? No. He's okay. Really. He's out on assignment. It's just that with this offer on the table, everyone wants to fly solo. No one will team up, so Mann's been playing pickup."

Alex laughed, "Mann? Oh, I can just see that happening! He must be livid. He has been out of field service for over a decade. I will bet he is smoking again!"

Junger lightheartedly joined with Alex, "Did he ever really stop?"

Then Alex sobered, "So when will you initiate the ID program?"

"We've pulled in all the stringers, ceased maneuvers and started the imprinting."

For Nikki, they might as well have been speaking Greek, "Imprinting?"

A slight smile crossed Alex's face, "Sorry, darling. Imprinting. An ID program. It's when the Agency closes down a section, sends out erroneous information, then waits to see who carries the bogus news to the other side."

"Like the mission you ran for us in Berlin, remember?" Mike inserted. "That was on a much smaller scale than this ID program. For this one we will go through the entire European operation and imprint every agent."

"Are you going visual? Using standard issue?" obviously Alex understood.

"Yes, lapel pins. They're an easy graphic," Mike answered.

"What's your system and time frame?"

"We want to push through this one, so we're on main street, daily, with an ascending/descending auto-spectrum," Mike finished the code.

"Where are you in the rotation now?"

"Tomorrow is black, ascending."

A sharp creek of the steel bunker door followed by Mann's muddy shoes on the concrete steps interrupted the conversation.

"Alex, Mrs. Vincente, how good of you to show up!" Mann addressed them with more surliness than usual.

"Bob," Alex nodded his greeting. "What's with the six days of stubble? Mike said you were in the field. I thought field agents dressed…"

"Yea, save it! You could look like this, too, if you were the one slogging through all this shit!" Mann dragged out a smoke. Scratching a match on the concrete wall, he lit it, then plopped himself down at the table. "After tonight, I probably added another five percent to the pass list." Mann coldly eyed Junger. "The worst of it is, all this crap we're going through probably isn't necessary!"

"Then why the long face? I don't get it?" Alex asked.

Bob Mann raised up from his chair, getting into Alex's face. "We're burning the midnight oil, doing a lot of unnecessary work at a huge risk to operations just to protect your ungrateful ass. When all the time, the deeper we dig, the more the answer comes up her!" his accusatory finger landed on Nikki.

Instantly Alex leapt to his feet, "You can't be serious! My wife is not involved!"

"Yeh, Yeh!" Mann flung back at him.

Hot herself, Nikki cut him off, "Don't use that tone with me, Mister Mann! Do you understand? How dare you make it sound like everything would be fine if it weren't for that dumb broad over there that is jinxing the place. Don't forget it was you, Mister, who came looking for me! I wouldn't even be connected to this bleedin' organization if it weren't for you!"

Mann's affront and Nikki's rage ratcheted Alex's temper, winding him up. The mood in the room rapidly deteriorated to a barroom brawl mentality.

Instantly Junger jumped in the middle of the bad blood, coming down hard and loud with his fist to the table, trying to halt the erupting hostility, "All right, Bob, sit down! Come on Alex! We are all on the same team. Save your schoolyard feud for someone who cares!"

Retrenching, he continued once the rest returned to their seats, "I think Bob was making the point that, no matter which way we turn this riddle, we seem to keep getting a link to Nicole."

Junger questioned her, "You have any ideas where this might be coming from?"

Nikki shrugged, "I haven't had contact with anyone since our last meeting."

"Well, I don't know what to say. The chatter on the street has it that the cavalier is looking for you, Nicole. The word is, 'find Nikki and the shooter will have a highway to the target,'" Mike declared with glacial sobriety.

Alex and Nikki exchanged horrified glances. "Are you saying that their real target is Nicole?"

"No. That's the strange twist to this. As far as we can tell, Nicole isn't the target. She is merely the conduit, although connected this closely she may well become collateral damage. But she is not the primary objective. In our checking, we determined the order of the sanction hasn't changed either. It's still against you, Alex. Only the cavalier's directions point from Nicole."

Fallout from the shock silenced the room.

Mann stubbed out his cigarette and cleared his throat, "Mike, don't you think you'd better get them on the program. They shouldn't be walking around on the street dressed like this."

"That's right," Junger agreed. "Being unidentified on the street now is dangerous. Since we're using midnight for the change and it's after the witching hour, these will get you started." Mike pulled four pins from his jacket pocket and distributed them.

Alex attached his to the right lapel of his jacket, as did Junger and Mann. Bluffing her way through, Nikki followed suit.

"Not to be smart about it, just so we are all on the same page, the next is red," Bob added in an assuaging tone.

Alex picked up on Mann's concession to him, "Thanks. It always helps to have a little extra clarification." Alex threw him a conciliatory half smile.

"I guess I don't quite understand why you can't peg the most loyal agents right now?" Nikki broke in.

No one comprehended her meaning.

"You know," she continued, "take Charles Bradley for instance. He's one I'm sure you could automatically count on our side."

Knotting his brows together, Mike winced. Mann exhausted a heavy sigh. Evidently Nikki jumped smack in the middle of an extremely sore subject.

Alex attempted to run interference, "Nicole, darling, that's just the point. We can't be sure of *anyone*."

"But Charles..." she protested.

"Charles Bradley," Junger sternly stopped her, "is a prime suspect. If you remember, he was one of the three targets you ran that mission on in Berlin."

"Of course I remember, Mike," she insisted, "but he helped me with that mission. He also showed up during the casket caper in Hungary, then at the defector melee in Grenoble."

Junger leveled her in his dead-on gaze, "I know you have strong feelings for someone who helped you out of several tight spots, but are you willing to risk your husband's life, or your son's, out of some misplaced loyalty?"

Still young enough to see things in a black or white perspective, Nikki didn't understand how someone who risked his life for her on several occasions could turn and switch sides. She looked to Alexander for help in making Junger see the truth.

Alex put a pacifying arm around her inexperienced shoulders, "Darling, remember how I tried to tell you what a dirty, despicable, vile business this was? How you can't trust anyone? Even though you and Bradley made a connection, you have no way of knowing his sincerity. He may have been using you. Charles Bradley has always been somewhat of a free lancer—a rogue, if you will. What better way to strike at the heart of the Agency than to cultivate a relationship with the wife of a top agent?"

Nikki recalled Bradley proudly admitting his renegade status to her.

Alex went on, "The Agency, with good reason at times, has regarded him, at best, as a loose cannon. Some of the information that Mike and Bob brought to me in the Caymans smacked of a connection to you."

Junger injected himself into their conversation, "Bradley's the one who's had the most contact with you—more than any other agent. The sophistication of the cavalier's tracking suggests an intimate connection somewhere between the contacts you and Alex have made."

Trying to make sense of it all, first she studied Mike's face, then Alex's.

"Nicole," Alex spoke softly, "people sell out all the time. It happens. Sometimes it's for a king's ransom; other times it's simple revenge. It's just part of the business." Alex's eyes pleaded for her understanding.

"I'm sorry," Nikki apologized to her husband, then turned to Mike. "I'm sorry. It just never occurred to me. Of course I believe what you are saying." Deliberately she made her voice stronger to convey her conversion and impart her unity in the effort, "Please continue. You can count on me. I'm on board."

But in her heart, Nikki still didn't understand how she could have read him so very wrong. Over the course of her instruction in Agency ways, both Jarred and Alex taught her the importance of instinct for survival in the business. And her instinct had trusted Charles Bradley.

Alex slid his chair back from the table, "Well, Mike, Bob, I guess we'll be on our way. I'm not sure we will get back in here before this thing comes to a head. You know how to reach me, if you need me."

To Nikki's surprise, Bob Mann approached her with his hand extended, "I hope to see you on the other side of this fiasco, Mrs. Vincente. I apologize for ever calling on you in Hong Kong. Your recruitment has always given me heartburn. Take care of yourself, Nikki. Watch your back. Okay?"

Likewise, Mike Junger dropped kind words along with a warning for her safety in his farewell.

Both men clasped Alex about the shoulders. Their actions clung eerily to Nikki as they walked the deserted alleyways away from the compound.

The humidity from the rain ripened the night air, closing in on Nikki with its oppressive weight like an overly-warm blanket or smothering perfume. Needing to sniff out fresh air, she suggested they turn up a few streets until they reached some of the life pulsating on the streets of Paris.

In agreement, Alex cut towards center city. As they walked, he briefed her about the string of code Mike had thrown at them. "During an imprint process, it is necessary to identify the agents tested and determined to be loyal. In simple cases, usually the process is visual, like the lapel pins Mike gave us. Because anyone could easily duplicate the pins and pretend to be a loyalist, they switch pins at different intervals. This time they chose daily, with each day starting at midnight. Loyal agents track the pin changes. Because the targeted area in this case spans the entire continent, there needs to be a central communication point in each major city. These are usually pre-determined. For this program, ours is 'main street'. In every city there is a main street. So, after midnight on the main street, we look for the sign to tell us which lapel pin is in for the day. Mike declared the 'system' of recognizing change to be the 'auto-spectrum' system. This is not as complicated as it sounds. Auto means vehicle, as in car. The spectrum relates to the rainbow spectrum. So tomorrow, after midnight, we look on main street, for a red car, with its visor down on the passenger side and a lapel pin on it, the next day an orange car, then a yellow one, and so on. It's pretty simple really."

"Too easy for me. How do you keep the bad agents from catching on?"

"An agent is only given the code after they are confirmed as 'loyal.' The point is, no one knows an imprint program is running until they have been cleared and branded as 'in' or loyal to the Agency."

"Couldn't someone just catch on to the system and duplicate it?"

"It would seem so, but there are probably over a hundred different systems, many complicated enough to need a score card to follow. Besides, unless you are on the inside, you don't know the timeframe. Not all of them involve a twenty-four hour clock. Some time schemes are multiples of hours; still others have a reversing pattern. You have to be in to know. But for this operation, they used something easy."

"And inside agents won't divulge the code because an agent on the outside, pretending to be on the inside…"

"A mole," Alex supplied.

"Right, a mole, is a danger to everyone."

"Darling, you've got it! It's all in the manual, you know," he cracked off-handedly.

The muggy spring night brought the city to its feet. People spilled out of bistros, stood in doorways and packed the jazz clubs. Paris had rejuvenated itself to a city in motion, in this portend of summer. Alex selected a side-street café where they ordered espressos and cake.

Wrapped in the quiet of a dark corner of the café, Nikki still couldn't dispel the strange feeling their departure from the Agency left on her. "Evidently something happened back at the Agency that went over my head. I got the distinct feeling we said goodbye to Mike and Bob for the last time."

"Hmm, that's always a possibility."

"But, Alex, their good-byes carried the finality of the grave. Those were our final farewells, weren't they?"

Alex replied relatively free of concern, "The threat is close enough now, that they thought this could be the last time they might see us alive."

Nikki blinked her astonishment at him, "You're very casual about their attitude. Have you heard it before?"

"A time or two. Look darling, any time an agent goes on assignment, everyone accepts the risk to life as routine. We all whistle going past graveyards. Every now and then though, the severity of a situation forces your immediate circle to recognize the transitory nature of life. So, you lay aside differences and dance the dance, in case you don't come back. That's life."

Taking his hand, Nikki looked into his palm, "You've really built up a layer of calluses over the years in the Agency."

"It's just one of the hazards of our profession," he tossed off. Then he gently closed his hand around hers, brought it to his lips and kissed it. "Let's finish here and join the rest of the lovers walking along the Champs E´lyssés."

Nikki found Alex's answers too off-the-cuff to accurately read him. Something at that meeting absorbed him though. Not even the romantic mood along that famous thoroughfare dented Alex's preoccupation.

They strolled the avenue, hardly making small talk with each other. Alex walked Nikki down one stretch of boulevard, then turned and walked them back over the same path. Nikki knew retracing their steps had nothing to do with his mental fixation. Alex never did anything extraneous. He wanted her to notice something...something she missed the first time through. Rapidly playing catch-up, Nikki cleaned and stripped the street of every available sight and sound, processing it for some sort of clue, when it smacked her in the face. There sat a black Porsche, parked along the curb, its passenger visor down and a small silver pin attached to it. She knew it instantly.

Never breaking her stride, she merely whispered as they passed, "Son-of-a-gun if that one doesn't match ours."

Alex squeezed her hand, "Very good, darling. I hoped you would have noticed it on our first pass, but you really had nothing to go on. I'm betting that you won't miss the one tomorrow."

"I guess it'll do, since I didn't know *which* street was considered 'main' in Paris."

"Right you are. We have a lot of territory to cover for your survival over these next few weeks."

Chapter 37
Eternity

Alexander and Nicole flew home to *Napoli* under an oppressive cloud of introspective silence. If Alex had realized how much his deepening quiet frightened her, he'd have done his best to entertain her. Surreptitiously upon their return, he slipped away again for three long days.

However, within hours of receiving an urgent communiqué from Washington, Alexander returned to *Napoli*. Haldeman had finally come through; Dr. Kissinger would see him. Alexander groused about dancing at the end of Bob Haldeman's string; nonetheless, they immediately lifted off from their Italian strip, bound for D.C.

Edgy like a cat, like Nikki had never seen him before, Alex paced aboard the jet.

Finally he poured cognacs for them and approached the table where she sat. Contemplatively, he swirled the liquid in the snifters, washing the chiseled veins of the Baccarat crystal with its rich amber color before presenting one to her.

Taking the seat opposite Nikki, he produced a gold cigarette case from the breast pocket of his blazer. He opened the case before her, offering her one. Nikki had never seen him smoke. In the past, she had smoked only in desperate times. Secretly she wondered if they were smoking the last cigarettes of the condemned. Withdrawing one, Nikki held it between her index and middle finger, waiting for a light. Then Alex pulled one from the case. Shutting the gold-hinged lid, he tapped his on the case before placing it between his lips. Indeed, as he deliberately flicked the lighter into life, Nikki got the uncanny sensation they were about to seal some sort of pact together. The flame burned forever in his hand between them, before he offered it to her. Nikki put the cigarette to her lips, then leaned in slightly to the lighter. She inhaled the smoke into her lungs, only to discover it wasn't an American cigarette.

"It's Turkish," Alex explained. Then he lit his own. "Their depth enhances the essence of the cognac," he said through a cloud of blue haze.

His eyes gleamed with a lustful fire as he looked up at her, pricking her soul, "Try it, you'll see." Enticing her, he picked up his glass and raised it for a toast.

Nikki raised her glass to meet his, but he baited her, pausing mid-way. "Here's to Turkish cigarettes with cognac," he said with a sneer, "and hell."

Then the chime of their Baccarats meeting each other sang out.

The smooth fire from the cognac smoldered every inch of the way, as the liquid traveled down, down to the very seat of her.

Transfixed, Alex's hot cobalt spheres seared wherever they rested. And they rested first intently on her eyes, then her lips, down her throat, to her breasts.

Alex breathed in another drag, and Nikki matched him. Something animalistic, crazed and illicit, seethed between them.

With her eyes, Nikki dared him to an unnervingly long sip of the fiery liquor.

Locked on her, exhibiting a hint of a licentiously menacing leer, he met her taunt.

On a corrosive, collision course, Nikki inhaled deeply again on her Turkish smoke, her desire as red-hot as the burning cherry at the end of her cigarette. Her fingertips yearned to rip through his fine-tailored linen shirt to get at that panther-like physique! Instead, she coyly dragged her nails across the tabletop.

Alex tossed her an amused smile, teasing her, keeping his hand just out of reach.

Nikki dipped her fingertip into his glass, then sucked his liquor from her finger.

Insane, his eyes leapt for her.

She snuggled into the back of her chair and laughed.

He took a final drag from his cigarette, then stubbed it out. Presenting his hand, he wickedly beckoned, "Shall we, darling?"

Placing her hand in his, she rose to meet him.

His hand slid smoothly from hers to around her waist, drawing her in tightly. Resting his hand on her hips, he guided her toward their private compartment.

Under the spell of the Turkish smokes, the cognac and her roguish husband, Nikki's head spun slightly in a delightful whirl. She ached for him, but moved slowly, deliberately, daring him.

Recklessly, he pulled her into his arms, arched her backward and bared her throat, priming her lips for his. Then he devoured her with ferocity. His hands moved from her neck down to her blouse. He gathered the silk in his fists.

Narrowing her eyes to intense slits, she provoked him.

Mightily he ripped, sending the pearl buttons popping, exposing her. "Pardon me, *mon ami*! But no apologies tonight," he growled. "It's time to unleash the animal!" And all the ancient elements of the universe crystallized in their blistering lovemaking.

Even in the afterglow, while she lay surrendered inside his arms, his kisses throbbed with intensity. His hands never stopped moving up and down her body, tugging at her flesh, caressing her. At one point, he hovered over her, his blue eyes still arcing sparks as he purred, "You are the passion of my life. I don't know how we will come out of this, but I want you to remember one night between us that makes you weak in the knees, elevates your heart rate and brings a flush to your graceful face. I had to quench the savage fire that has burned inside me since I first saw you. No one has ever so possessed the heart, mind and soul of anyone as you have of me. I know my love is so strong that, while my enemies may kill me, they will never extinguish my passion for you that will burn for as long as time runs. *Te adoro, mi Nicole. Te adoro!*"

Alexander didn't realize his profession of love, coming in the midst his passion, revealed another facet of his mindset. For the first time, he acknowledged to her that he might not be able to immunize himself against the sanction. Such talk seeded terror in Nikki's heart. In desperation, she pinned her hopes on the meeting with Dr. Kissinger.

Bob Haldeman arranged the thirty-minute meeting for two in the afternoon at the Pentagon. When his absence grew to more than two hours, Nikki paced the floor. At six, a secretary phoned Alex's apologies; he would not be able to join her for dinner. So mother and son dined alone while Nikki employed any technique she could think of to keep from watching the clock. She prayed the extra time meant progress for Alex. When the phone rang and it was Gus, she rushed him off the line just to keep it open.

Shortly after nine, she heard Alex's key turn in the lock. His face gave nothing away when she kissed him in the vestibule. Desperately she wanted to see that characteristic light from his eyes smile at her again. Nikki did not get her wish.

Alex decanted a bottle of Bordeaux. They settled into the sofa for their discussion. Earnestly Alexander confessed, "I really like Dr. Kissinger. He is a fascinating man with an uncommon understanding of the mindset behind the various civilizations. We talked for hours about Russia, China, communism and the values driving those cultures. He is laying the groundwork for the government's policy towards these nations. He actually foresees a visit by Nixon to initiate a neutralization of hostilities. He referred to it as *détente*. I admire him. He is truly a visionary, but unfortunately for us, he is about two years behind where we need him to be."

"I don't understand. What does that mean in real terms for us?"

"It means," Alex shook his head, "that when you open a dialogue between two nations which you hope will eventually support reciprocal goals, you don't initiate the discussion with demands, or by requesting favors, unless they will be mutually beneficial. Openly admitting to spies in their theater would effectively squelch all subsequent talk." Alex moved closer to Nikki on the couch, taking her hands in his. "I am afraid, darling, we are on our own on this one. We will have to solve this dilemma ourselves," apologetically he kissed her fingertips.

The dismal news disheartened her husband. He had stretched himself out on a limb in hopes of neutralizing the sanction through diplomacy. But Nikki would not let this meeting-gone-awry sound their death knell. Gut-level determination swelled inside her. Physically she drew herself up tall in the sofa before her husband. With righteous resolution of the joined battle, Nikki declared, "Then we fight it. You and me. First we do whatever it takes to secure safe haven for Adam. Then we turn and fight this evil."

Her reaction caught Alex off guard. He stared back at her, amazed.

Nikki persisted, "In our hearts, we always knew diplomacy was a long shot. You doubted Mike's recommendation from the beginning. Alex, if you are really honest with yourself, you'd have to admit you only tried this round-about way for my sake. So now it's back to the fight we always knew we would have—us against them."

"Yes, but, all this time, all this money, all wasted for nothing."

"Let's be honest here, money isn't really the issue, is it sweetheart?"

Alex half laughed, "Darling, how wise you are. Of course it's not about money. We've spent four precious months flailing around with all sorts of machinations, which got us nowhere. We wasted a far more valuable commodity than money. We wasted time. Time we could have used to hunt this thing down and chop it off at the roots."

"That's really spilt milk, isn't it? Now we know where we stand. Now we fight. Lay out the plan. Do we tell Junger? Is this something we carry off on our own? Use me in whatever capacity. I am in this with you, to save our family."

Nikki's final comment struck a chord in Alexander. "Hold on, darling. There is no doubt I will put together a plan. In fact, all along, I have been formulating a parallel course of action. But that plan will *not* include you! I *will* have you and Adam, the two most precious people in my life, safe. From the very beginning, when I determined I couldn't live without you in my life, I knew the risks. I knew I might not be around to live in your magnificent light for more than a few days. God knows, I never dreamt of the possibility of children! How blest I have been! If I must pay the ultimate price for my privilege, I am ready. But I will have both of you safe. On that there will be no equivocation, no negotiation."

Alexander made plans to carry out his course of action. Curtailing his government projects, he separated himself from his business to devote his total effort to neutralize the sanction. Behind the closed doors of his storefront, Alex prepared to go underground as a guerilla. In an all-out effort, Lorenzo trained him daily to return him to peak physical condition.

Now relegated to the sidelines, the situation compelled Nikki to also maintain appearances. She followed the customary rituals of a suburban housewife, taking Adam for outings in various parks, but always making sure she shuffled her routine. Sometimes after Gus's usual morning check-in, he would accompany them on one of their jaunts.

Outwardly, life droned on in monotonous daily detail, while exquisite terror built on the inside. Nikki couldn't endure lying next to Alex in the early morning, watching him sleep. It simulated death too much.

The second week of May, they flew to *Napoli*. On the first morning, she woke early. Creeping from their bed, Nikki slipped down the long corridor into the guestroom. Throwing open the shutters, she watched the colorful fishing boats bob up and down on the crystal sea. Curling up in the bed, in her mind she reversed the clock, pretending it was two years ago when she had first visited *Napoli*. Gradually the hypnotic little boats lulled her off to sleep in a precarious sort of peace.

On his rounds Lorenzo, noticing the door ajar, peeked inside. With polite hesitation, he approached. "Is everything okay, Nikki?"

"Hmm? ...ah, yes," she answered pushing out of her nap and up in bed. "I just wanted to remember the magic I felt on that first morning here."

Lorenzo motioned towards a chair, an unspoken request to sit, "That seems like a million years ago, doesn't it? I'm sure you could use some of that carefree serenity about now."

"Why, does it show?"

"No. Of course not. I just know what you must be going through."

Not wishing to spoil her reverie, he returned to the former subject with a beaming smile, "I remember Alex during that visit. He nearly wore out the stone floor waiting with the patience of a child anticipating

Christmas. Never had I seen anyone capture him so! And, Nikki, I've known him since his first infatuation in primary school."

Nikki smiled at the thought of Alex upside-down over some school-girl filly.

"Did you know you were the first woman that Alex ever brought here?"

"No!" Nikki declared in genuine amazement.

"You are. From the moment Alex told us he was bringing you, we knew. And long before your visit, Alex treated me to constant updates about you and your career, ever since that fateful day in the café."

To stem Lorenzo's gush, Nikki switched the path of their conversation, "What about you, Lorenzo? Hasn't there ever been a unique someone to set your heart on fire?"

"Oh, I've had a few relationships. Certainly nothing special—no one I'd bring home," Lorenzo remarked without regret. "Alex required my full attention. Living and working with him has never been dull. We've been from literally one corner of this Earth to the other, in and out of some tight scrapes, with enough female talent along the way. Alexander pursued life with a vigorous appetite, creating an intoxicating recipe for existence, to say the least. But, that all changed, when you burst upon the scene."

"Trust me," Lorenzo hastened to add, "the change was for the better. Alexander deserved his reputation as an international playboy. The family business, while it afforded him a sumptuous lifestyle, bored him. He got involved with the Agency for the adrenaline rushes. Frankly, Alex didn't care if the games he played carried lethal consequences. But you, you ignited a fire in his soul."

"And Alexander is like no one I've ever met. At first, his self-confident air disarmed me. I mistook his admiration of me as a belittlement. Oh, that infuriated me!"

"How you mystified him! It took him nearly two years to set up the perfect scenario so he could approach you. He wanted to smoothly swoop in and sweep you off your feet. Then it seemed that the more he polished his approach, the less of an impression he made. Alex almost convinced himself to give up on you. But he needed you more than he needed air."

"I thank God he didn't give up on me. I wouldn't trade my life…" Nikki's voice trailed off, "well, maybe some parts of it…"

"You must know that part drives him insane! Like I said, when Alex was unattached, the consequences of his actions actually fed his enthusiasm for living. After you came along, he thought he had devised a plan to leave the Agency. It probably would have worked, if it hadn't been for

Charlie Soo in Hong Kong. How many times he's mentioned to me his willingness to lay down his life for you and the baby, except Soo confirmed to him the inherited legacy of a Chinese vendetta."

"Inherited legacy?" Nikki echoed aghast.

Amazed by her reaction, Lorenzo murmured, "I thought you knew."

"No, I don't. Please explain."

Now the messenger of bad news, Lorenzo lowered his head in shame, "The Chinese will bequeath or pass down a vendetta on the male heirs in a family. Even if Alex sacrificed himself, eventually they would visit their revenge on Adam. And you might very well become an extenuating casualty. By wiping out the entire lineage of their enemies, they eliminate problems for future generations of their own."

Lorenzo's words brought new, more terrifying consequences to her, which froze Nikki's soul with fear and stole her breath.

"Obviously, Alexander knows that self-sacrifice is *not* an option! You pretty well understand the rest. Except, I don't know if you know the emotional turmoil this has created inside him. He deeply regrets the position he has put you in. Alexander only wanted to wrap you and the baby inside his love forever. It tortures him to think that he is responsible for all this chaos and threats of death to a wife he cherishes beyond life itself and a family he loves so desperately."

"But this isn't Alex's fault, or even the Agency's. The fault lies in the fact that we—the three of us—cared enough to come to the rescue of a friend. However, I can't even comment on your news, Lorenzo, that the monster who called the price on my husband won't be happy until my innocent and so precious son is also destroyed. That I can't comprehend!"

Deeply saddened Lorenzo apologized again, "I never would have broken that news to you. It's just that I … I thought Alex had told you."

"He's known since his meeting with Charlie, hasn't he?"

Lorenzo confirmed it with a sad nod.

"Don't worry. I won't let on that you told me. Alex tries to protect me so I won't worry. But this is something I needed to know."

Lorenzo pushed out an unconvincing smile. Accidentally betraying his lifelong brother and being the bearer of ill tidings troubled him deeply.

Outside the door footsteps approached. "Well, I wondered where you wandered off to this morning," Alex remarked as he stepped inside the doorway. "Is this a private party or is anyone invited?"

Nikki rose up on her knees in the bed and stretched out her arms to him, "Of course you are invited, sweetheart." Even mired in gloom, her heart still leapt for him as he entered a room, and her eyes reflected a warm welcome inspired by his presence.

Preparing to exit, Lorenzo offered his seat to Alex.

"No, don't be silly Lorenzo. I am the one intruding. Please don't let me chase you away. Besides, I will take *this* seat, if the lady of the manor doesn't mind?" Alex gestured toward the spot next to her on the bed.

Nikki patted the place Alex had eyed. "I didn't want to disturb you, so I came down here. Lorenzo noticed the door ajar and popped in to check it out. We were just recalling my first visit to *Napoli*, eons ago."

Before long, they heard the rambunctious, uneven footsteps of a toddler thumping down the corridor, followed by the protestations of a grandmother forced to play keep-up. "Adam! Adam, come here."

Adam answered by only pushing on faster and trailing giggly squeals of delight. Ducking into the open doorway, high on his victory of speed, he stopped in surprise to find a room full of people.

Caught in one of those precious dichotomies of parenthood, Nikki wanted to burst out laughing and scoop him up in her arms. But, she knew she should reward his errant behavior with a firm dose of scolding.

Extending his arms, Adam scampered to Nikki. still giggling.

With a face as stern as Nikki could masquerade, she addressed him, "Adam, didn't you hear Noni calling you? When Noni calls, you must listen. Now tell her you are sorry. And I want you to mind Noni. Do you hear?" Then Nikki handed him into Zia's capable arms. Lorenzo and Alex only half-successfully hid their smiles.

"You must not do that again," Zia sweetly chided him, melting under the charisma of her grandson's charm.

Needing to take her frustrations out on someone, she turned on them, "The three of you must think I have nothing better to do than to cart breakfast all the way down here to you! You'll eat in the kitchen or go hungry…unless you need to run the legs off a poor old, crippled woman!"

Obediently, they fell in line behind the satisfied little Italian general and her accomplice, the toddler terrorist.

As customary, Alex and Nikki took their meal out on the terrace in the glorious morning sunshine. Finishing his last sip of coffee, he joined Nikki at the terrace balustrades overlooking the sea. "You know what I'd like to do today? I'd like to take out the *Bella Nicole* for a little while. Are you game?"

Leaning out over the bowsprit, Nikki let the snappy sea breeze, warmed by the intensifying May sun, buff her cheeks and slide through her hair. Still too cool for a swimsuit, she wore shorts and a light wind-breaker as they sliced across the blue-green swells. Eventually Alex joined her at her perch.

Before long an island came into view. As they neared, it looked famil-iar. Alexander confirmed it as *Isola della Morte*—the Isle of Death. To Nikki's surprise, they swung around to the lea, or calm side, of the island and anchored. The term "calm" being relative, however, for even a thou-sand yards offshore, the waters roiled and churned enough to smash any craft to smithereens upon the jagged crags encircling it.

Alex helped Nikki down from the bowsprit, leading her to the aft deck. There, carefully placed for each of them, lay their diving gear, including full wet suits. The light of recognition dawned on Nikki, "So this was your game all along. You brought me sailing so we could try out our gear here."

Readily Alex declared, "guilty." Two members of the crew assisted them into the gear. Lorenzo, of course, would remain topside to monitor their dive. After a check of all systems, as they sat on the platform getting ready to fall back into the water, Alex leaned over and whispered, "Do you trust me?"

"Of course I do," Nikki answered automatically.

"Good. Because we are going to swim over to the island." He flashed a smile at her, but his eyes held steady, indicating he was serious about their destination.

An initial reaction of fear betrayed Nikki, "You can't mean in this water? Won't it throw us up on the rocks?"

"Remember, you trust me," Alex said through a calming smile. "Just follow me. I promise you, we will be all right. Come on, I have something amazing to show you." With that he put the regulator into his mouth and broke water.

Taking a deep breath for courage, Nikki did the same.

She found the Mediterranean murkier than the crystal waters off *St. Vincente*, but then, what wasn't? Although in the lead, Alex stayed close by her side. Below the first twenty-five feet, the agitation of the surface water ceased to affect them. They swam ahead through placid halls of underwater beauty.

As their depth meters clicked off every foot of their descent, Alex checked her repeatedly at major levels. Nikki easily crossed fifty feet, then seventy-five feet. Instinctively she understood that all their deep dives in the Caribbean had been in practice for this dive. Alexander had taken her to one hundred feet for a reason. Anticipating the greater depth, Nikki mentally prepared herself for it. Nitrogen narcosis noticeably set in just prior to hitting ninety feet. Nikki tapped Alex to let him know she felt its effects and indicated to him her ability to focus with her fingers pointed in a vee at herself. He answered with a nod and flashed her a "thumbs up".

At close to a hundred feet, they reached an unusual outcropping of rock which formed an arch. Swimming through it and into a narrow corridor formed by a cleft in a rock wall, Alex switched on his underwater light. Nikki did the same. The confinement forced her to recall all the warnings she had read about diving into restricted spaces. But she couldn't help notice the walls of the rock canyon had been scraped free of barnacles and were relatively smooth—completely uncharacteristic of anything underwater. That told Nikki this was a heavily trafficked area. Obviously someone had been through here many times. The passageway widened out the farther they swam, and, despite the gloom, Nikki noticed they slowly started ascending. Only the depth meters registered their ascent, as somehow the light from the nearing surface wasn't reaching them. Eventually they surfaced into a pool of water inside a cove, under a dome of rock. Two lanterns lit the area. Alex scrambled up onto the surrounding ledge, then reached down for his wife.

Helping Nikki out of all the gear with the exception of their wetsuits, he stalled the explanation of their whereabouts. He led Nikki up some steps hewn out of the rock to where a heavy steel door barred their way. Alex pushed against it, and it easily pivoted open. Inside the utilitarian room, dry clothes for them hung from pegs. They left their wetsuits on another set of pegs positioned over a drain. Once again, Alex silenced Nikki's questions with a finger to his lips. Then he opened the door.

Nikki couldn't believe her eyes! The door opened into a magnificent mansion! Twenty-five foot limestone arches supported timber beams and richly paneled tray ceilings of inlaid mahogany. Satin-finished sheets of ivory travertine ran the length of the hallways and into the rooms. The immense rooms fit the dimensions dictated by the height of the ceilings. Banks of tall French doors bathed the rooms with light and decorated them with their scenery. Nikki stared at everything with wide-eyed, schoolgirl amazement as Alex shepherded her from room to room. Their footsteps echoed down the hallways. Finally they arrived at the heart of the home, the kitchen. Arches of cream-colored limestone flanked the walls and formed carved-out niches for the appliances, with great runs of granite slabs for countertops. A wall-sized fireplace and hearth dominated the far end of the room. Vases of red roses sitting on the countertops perfumed the air, while a single gardenia floated in a crystal bowl in the middle of a cypress-planked table, the only piece of furniture in the entire manse.

Alexander cuddled Nikki in his arms, "Does this place remind you of anything?"

"Of course. This is the house from my dream, the dream I had right after we married." She continued to look around at it from inside the sanctuary of her husband's arms. "I can't believe you found it. But even more, I can't believe it was on the *Isola della Morte*, which is where I assume we are."

"Yes, darling. That is precisely where we are." With a gentle brush of his hand he redirected her attention back to him, where he held her in his thoughtful blue eyes. "This is where I have been coming on my 'business trips' when I would disappear for days at a time. I built this for you—for us."

Nikki's eyes broke away from him again to wander through his magnificent creation. "Oh, sweetheart, this is truly fabulous! It's exactly like my dream. I can't imagine how you accomplished it. I can't believe you would do this for me."

Again Alexander directed her attention back to him, "I wanted it to be everything you desired in a home, since it may well become your prison, too."

His words startled her to attention. Involuntarily, she checked his eyes for his typical bemused look that signaled his playful intentions. Gravity snuffed out any merriment.

Aghast she bleated, "I don't understand."

Alexander kissed her cheek, drawing her to him. Distressed, his chest heaved heavy sighs. He hugged Nicole to him long enough to gain his composure before he again held her in his eyes. "If I am not success-ful in taking out the author of the sanction, then you and the baby may have to disappear. This will be your safe haven."

"And what about *you*?"

"If I am still alive, then I will live here, too, with you."

Full of nauseating shock, his words clanged in her ears. Nikki ducked out of his arms. In desperation she ran to one of the sets of French doors. Focusing outside, frantically she searched the grounds for some-thing, anything, that could help her come to grips with Alex's words. "Won't they eventually find us? I mean a house this size, alone on an island in the Mediterranean?" panic usurped her voice.

"I don't think so. The house is perfectly camouflaged from the air by the trees and the exterior is constructed of the stone naturally exposed in the area. The windows have a reflective coating that mirrors its surroundings." With masterful serenity, Alex walked her through all the security precautions he included in the structure and the perimeter of the island.

Every obstacle Nikki threw up to him, Alex answered perfectly, in the extreme. The windows contained bulletproof glass with shields that automatically deployed for added protection. The thick stonewalls kept them safe from bombs. As a last resort, he had outfitted the room off the dive dome as a safe room. An encrypting communication system, secretly piggy-backed from a government spy satellite, blanketed the island in security and provided a communications link to the outside world. Other than air-drop, the only way on, or off, the island was via the water tunnel. In time, Alex would add more foliage so not even a helicopter would be able to land. Everything and everybody needed to build the fortress had to either swim in or be dropped by chopper. Hordes of sophisticated technology and weaponry, which Alex had purchased over the last few months, he either employed or stored for future use within these walls. Even outside, standing close to the structure, the house transitioned seamlessly into the landscape of the hillside. Yet, for all of its futuristic gadgetry, the house exuded old world elegance inside.

Nausea swelled in the pit of Nikki's stomach. Here, she confronted the cold, hard reality of their situation. She stood in the bricks and mortar manifestation of not only the possibility of their future, but the probability of it. How she wanted to turn heel and run—run far away from that awful place! The Isle of Death, what a fitting name! In an instant, the vast expanses shrank to the size of a tiny cell, threatening to smother her. Internally, she gasped for air. The color drained from her face. Nikki lost her smile.

Surely Alex noticed, but he continued on with the details. Details she should have been listening to but the rush of fear had obliterated.

Reality stripped away the rose-colored tint of her world. As her husband spoke, Nikki studied his face, analyzing it for the first time in months. Worry had carved deep trenches across his noble, aristocratic face. Distress replaced the sparkle that once naturally danced in his eyes. Despite the excellent condition of his physique, he appeared older than his chronological years actually numbered him. Lorenzo had correctly assessed the debilitating effects from stress that the sanction had caused Alexander. What turmoil must be boiling inside to have wrought such external physical changes! It couldn't have been easy to build such an extreme habitat knowing its use meant the world for your family would be unobtainable. No matter how glibly Alex seemed to toss off the value of his own life, this habitat displayed how desperately he wanted to continue to participate in their lives.

Again, Nikki looked at the fortress Alex referred to as her prison. However, this time she measured the house against the price the sanction exacted from her husband. Her attitude and her breathing relaxed. What an incredible act of courage, to admit in such concrete terms the likelihood of what life held for him and his family. What a tremendous act of love! Mentally Nikki slapped herself back to attention. As an adult, she could no longer afford the luxury of running away from her problems. Her courageous words demanded the strength of her conviction and actions to match.

A smile, reflecting the love she held for her valiant husband, built from her soul until it overcame her face. Instead of walking behind him on his demonstration discourse, Nikki now walked with him, slipping her arm through his. Gratefully, he smiled back. Overwhelmed by her rising tide of emotion, Nikki reined him into her embrace, "Oh, dear God, thank you. And thank you, Alex, for loving me this much. Thank you for building all of this for us. How can I ever tell you how much I love you?" Tears slid down her cheek.

Her contagious tears infected him. His own tears now streamed down his cheeks as he wept into her hair. "Oh, darling. I'm sorry! I'm so very, very sorry that this place is even necessary. How could I have done this to you?! How could I have condemned you to this kind of life?"

Sinking to the floor, they melted into each other's arms, awash in tears. Only God knows how long they sat in the hallway there. They cried once, then cried again. They kissed desperate, passionate, life-sucking kisses. And they kissed gentle, tender, breath-of-life kisses.

They spent the night on their island of life, without furniture or cover, in their fortress against the world. Alex laid a fire in the kitchen hearth to chase away the chill. They made love in front of it and snuggled in each other's arms all night long.

Over the course of the next several days, Alexander and Nicole discussed all the pertinent facts regarding *Eternity*, their code name for the fortress on *Isola della Morte*. Inside the room, off the rock dome, water conversion facilities, air compressors to re-fill their dive tanks and power generation equipment already existed. They purchased furniture, linens and domestic goods, down to the most trivial of items needed to operate a household, then assembled everything to be airlifted to the island. Books, records and school supplies for teaching Adam had to be included.

While they came and went either on the *Bella Nicole* or with Reed Dawson at the controls of the helicopter, no one outside of Alex, Lorenzo or Nikki ever set foot on the island or were given knowledge of the purpose of the preparations. In building their refuge, Alex fanatically parceled out the various efforts of the procedure in piecemeal fashion so no outsider could garner a complete picture of the operation. Alexander employed, and handsomely paid, workers from remote, third-world countries to build the fortress. He flew them out of their country by night, importing them directly to the island, then returned them the same way. Flying them in "blind," in windowless cargo helicopter transports, they would never be able to disclose the location of the island.

The couple's discussions also included the specific sign and counter sign of "eternity" for each of them to use to indicate their intention of retreating there. From that moment forward, they struck the word "eternity" from their vocabulary unless they were making a specific reference to the fortress. Lorenzo was the only other living soul to possess, with full knowledge, the code sign of *Eternity*.

As preparations advanced each day, Nikki never looked back. The only lamentable aspect of their possible confinement required that until the threat subsided, if ever, they would lose all contact with their families. Depending on the situation and the timing of when the order to *Eternity* came, it may or may not include the families. If the families were to be included then Alex had made sure there was adequate space and provisions to include Fran, Richard, Zia and Lorenzo. If, however, the order did not include their families, then they would be notified of the tragic deaths of Alex, Nikki and Adam, which of course, the families would probably follow with memorial services for them. Alex and Nicole could not spare them in any way. The agents of the author of the sanction would be watching. Their grief had to be positively genuine. For all intents and purposes, their deaths to the families had to be very real. The families' lives would be endangered otherwise. Lorenzo would be their only contact with the outside world. And their communication with him would be limited, always encrypted and non-existent for several years. Escape from the island might come after years in hiding and then only after considerable reconstructive surgery. Nikki lived in the moment, trying not to think too far in the future. She tried to imprint all her favorite sights and sounds from *Nevermore*, *Creekside* and *Napoli* to carry with her into their secluded safe-haven.

Predicting if or when the retreat to *Eternity* would come was impossible. If Alex succeeded in taking out the author of the sanction, then all their preparations would be unnecessary. Realistically though, they realized his chance of that would be slim. Without guarantees, their lives' timetable turned upon the cavalier's whim. As Alex accurately assessed, they couldn't even be sure they would all be together when the moment arrived. But he promised Nikki would know it when it came.

Chapter 38
Closing In

Feeling the acute pinch of time, Alex intensified Nikki's training course. Worried he might be taken out and she would have to survive "on the street" alone long enough to get to safety, he schooled her in the most advanced techniques of the business. Possessed by their dwindling number of days, sleep for them came only in stolen catnaps. Each day's instruction primed Nikki for action.

With her daily lessons, Nikki understood that Junger and Manns' departing words troubled Alex more than he admitted. But rather than hashing them to death with discussion, he dealt with them in concrete terms.

Crisscrossing Europe over the next ten days accomplished two purposes. First, it gave Alex a classroom for her training, and second, they finished accumulating items destined for the fortress. Placing the furniture and household goods on the island the last week of May provided them a refuge from the Continent, which had become a minefield of treachery. The longer they remained in the open, the greater the odds increased of the shooter finding them. To make matters worse, Nikki's two-year hiatus from the spotlight only increased the press's ravenous appetite. Despite the sometimes-elaborate disguises, the media corps sniffed out her whereabouts and dutifully reported it. City-hopping kept her two steps ahead of them.

Adam's first birthday on the eighth of June neared. Alex intended to remain in Europe through the second week of June to settle family business. Not wanting Nikki's parents to miss the milestone celebration, Alex sent for them. He scheduled their arrival on the fifth and planned that he and Nikki would return with the rest of her clan.

On June second, the couple concluded stocking their fortress, and Nicole and Alexander walked out of their citadel with all preparations complete. The stress from the sanction, her training and preparing for possible exile exhausted Nikki. After Adam's birthday, while Alexander tended to the Vincente empire, Nikki hoped to curl up on a chaise in the terrace sunshine. In addition to the mental exercises, Nikki now worked out with Alex in his sessions with Lorenzo. The physical strain gave Nikki a queasy stomach; food held no appeal for her.

They were about to turn their attention to preparing for the festivities surrounding their son's birthday when an urgent communiqué from Junger reached them on the morning of the third. Succinct and cryptic, Junger sent: "Get in now. News on shooter—Bradley."

Alex printed the message and shared it with Nikki at breakfast. She read it twice, then a third time trying to make sense of those seven words. "Does this mean Bradley is the shooter?" she asked Alex, with her heart in her throat.

"I don't know. Damn Junger! The message isn't clear. But it would seem so. One thing for sure, we are on our way to Paris as soon as we get ready."

Retreating to their bedroom, they dressed for their rendezvous with Junger. Alex began by throwing open the doors to Nikki's wardrobes. Sliding hangers across the rods, he assessed each article of clothing in his search for appropriate attire for her. While paging through her closet, he itemized his desires out loud, "I am looking for neutral colored slacks and matching jacket, something that allows you a full range of motion, but nothing so baggy it gets in the way."

Nikki directed him to several options. Alex chose a navy ensemble with deep pockets. "Okay Nicole, now find a blouse."

She pulled out the accompanying white middy shirt with navy blue trim on the sailor collar and tie.

"Absolutely not," Alex nixed. "First of all, white is a target. And the collar and tie might become a distraction, resulting in lethal consequences. Darling, show me short sleeves, dark and non-restrictive."

Obeying, she produced a navy and maroon Madras plaid shirt. He concurred.

After a final appraisal of the choices made for her, Alex added a final touch, "We need a way to at least attempt to disguise that famous face of yours." Once again, Alex went to her closet. "A hat, Nicole. We need something for you to tuck your hair inside. Something that fits well. Something with a slight brim. And of course, you will wear your shades...that should help to make you less obvious." They settled on a smart, business-style pork-pie hat in navy.

From his closet, Alex pulled a copper-brown casual suit and a black knit shirt. His robing procedure reminded Nikki of Lorenzo's that night in Hong Kong. Before donning his trousers, Alex carefully taped a derringer in a nylon holster to the inside of his upper thigh, near his groin. Next he slit the stitching in his pocket of the same leg. Alex caught Nikki's dubious expression. "This is the weapon of last resort. Sometimes when they pat you down they miss this one. Or, if I am hit and if I am lucky, I can finagle it through my pant's pocket. Without going into too many details, let's just say I would rather have it than be without it." Then, with a wink of playful mischief, he dryly remarked, "I'll let you remove it when we get back home." Pulling on his trousers, he checked the drape of his pants in the mirror. Next, he hoisted up his left pant leg. The adhesive tape complained loudly as he stripped it off the metal spool, taping a scabbard with a blade to his calf. He bit through the tape with his teeth, slicing it off the reel. On the right leg he secured a small-caliber pistol. His shoulder holster completed the arsenal before he slipped on his jacket.

"This is it, isn't it? I mean, you're expecting to meet *him* today, aren't you?" Nikki's question smacked of stupidity, considering she had just watched her husband pack on a weapons depot under his clothes, but she wanted verbal confirmation.

"Junger's message was not clear, but it was to the point. He would not risk having us come in, if he didn't have critical information. No doubt the cavalier is in the vicinity. I assume Mike has a line on his whereabouts, and now is the time for confrontation. Believe me," Alex squared Nicole directly in front of him for emphasis, "you would not be coming along if you weren't so crucially involved."

Alex embraced her, holding her in his eyes of cool, blue steel. "With my whole heart and soul, I would much rather have you here safe, than a possible target on the street." He laid a kiss upon her lips. "Come on now, let's get you dressed."

Nikki's armaments weren't nearly as involved. She wore a shoulder holster along with a smaller caliber weapon near the small of her back in her waistband. Alex gave her a lightweight knife with a retractable blade to carry in her slacks' pocket. Before they left, Alex produced their lapel pins for the day. Standing back, he assessed her and laughed in spite of the situation. "I cannot believe it, you are stunning, no matter what you wear. But with that hat and tailored suit, you look, so ... so stereotypically like a spy. Unfortunately, it can't be helped. Here, these should complete the picture." Alex slipped her sunglasses on her, with a kiss on the cheek.

They covered all possible contingencies on the short hop to Paris. They'd travel by car to within a kilometer of the Agency. From there, they'd be on foot through the back alleyways to the bunker-type facility. Their meeting with Junger would determine their course of action and probably the timing of their confrontation with the cavalier. If at all possible, they hoped to lead the shooter away from the city into the countryside, where they would have more room to maneuver and less possibility of innocents being involved. Lorenzo, while equally armed, would not be with them on the street. Instead he would be in a car, with Reed driving, shadowing them, providing backup or rescue should they need it.

Anxious determination built inside of Nikki. She wanted this to be finished. Driving all negative consequences from her mind, she recalled Jarred's words, "the element of surprise always tips the scales over-whelmingly in favor of the party doing the surprising." Mike's note, for all intents and purposes, labeled Charles Bradley as the shooter. In their meeting with Junger, hopefully, he'd finger his location. Then they'd pop in unannounced, catch him off guard and drop him before he ever got off a shot. Killing someone Nikki considered a friend left an acid taste in her mouth. But when a friend turns, there's no other choice. And, by God, Nikki's family would survive! Triumph would be theirs.

Walking crisply down the back cobblestone alleyways to the bunker, their senses honed to razor precision, they each scrutinized the surround-ings as they advanced. Purposefully, Alex and Nicole proceeded inde-pendently of each other, neither speaking nor holding hands. The alley seemed uncharacteristically vacant to Nikki. She wondered if Alex noticed. Continually her mind raced ahead to the bunker and beyond. She tried to keep alert and scan the streets. Still, her heart leaped two hours into the future, focusing on their victory.

Suddenly a voice behind her breached the stillness of the alley, "Nikki!"

Her mind screamed, "No, not a fan now! Of all the times!" Instinctively, she spun around to check it out.

In her communicator she heard Alex. "What the hell! Be *careful*!" he warned.

But the deserted alley gave up no one.

"Nikki! Nikki!" again split the air. She had to locate this threat to their mission and eliminate it! Now was not the time for the nonsense of idol-worship. They had hotter pokers in the fire. Nikki advanced toward the direction of the voice. It seemed to come from inside an adjoining café—getting closer.

All her senses felt Alex moving in concert with her, his adrenaline-hyped breathing on the communicator close in her ear. His presence kept her on point—alert.

"My God it *is you*! Oh, Nikki! Wait! Please! *Nikki*!!" the voice from the alleyway now rang with familiarity.

From the blindside of the café, Jarred stepped out and started running up to her, arms outstretched in greeting.

"Son-of-a-bitch! Of all things! Not now!" Alex cursed in the commu-nicator.

Jarred's timing couldn't have been worse. Relaxing, Nikki briskly walked to meet and get rid of Jarred's unwelcome intrusion.

Now waiting for her, Jarred stopped. His hands dropped to his side, his welcoming smile increased. His eyes enticed her to hurry. Something wasn't right.

Nikki's senses set off alarms, her eyes covered every inch of him as she neared. Then she remembered Alex's warning that the eyes give away the soul. Too late, her eyes fell on the lapels of his jacket and discovered them both naked.

Nikki looked up to find Jarred's burning eyes riveted on hers. Instantly he recognized she had found the mistake.

In the infinity of a shattering second, the world erupted.

Without a blink of an eye or a flinch of conscience, Jarred's hand smoothly reached inside his jacket. Nikki knew he was going for his gun.

The advantage of surprise belonged to him. Reaching for hers, she knew she was a split second behind him.

Surreal slow motion reduced the sights and sounds of the alley to a sluggish crawl. From behind her in time-lagged speech, Alex shouted, "No! Gun! Look out!!"

Suddenly the distinctive "thwp, thwp" of two silenced bullets zipped through the air, accompanied by the bizarre, heart-stopping vacuum of waiting to discover their target.

Jarred's eyes bugged-out, wide with shock. He arched backwards. The force drew him up on his toes. His chest bulged outward, red spots appeared on his shirt, then spurted blood. His drawn weapon spun limp in his hand, clattering to the ground.

With gun drawn, Alex rushed the scene. He stepped in front of Nikki, shielding her from further gunfire with his body.

From behind Alex, Nikki watched Jarred teeter on his toes, then topple forward, exposing the figure of Charles Bradley, still crouched in his shooter's position, behind Jarred in the alleyway.

Immediately Alex targeted Bradley.

By reflex, Nikki stepped out of Alex's shadow and into stance, leveling Bradley in her sights.

Alex gutturally commanded Bradley, "Drop it! Drop it! Or I will drop you! Drop it! Now!"

Slowly, painstakingly slowly, Charles released the grip of his hand on the gun and lowered his weapon to the pavement, all the time bargaining with reason. "Don't shoot, Alex. I saved your life! I saved Nikki's life. Don't shoot!"

Assessing the scene, Nikki dressed down Bradley with her eyes. He worked his way back up to a standing position, hands extended, when the sun glinted off something on his jacket.

"Alex!" She yelled, her weapon still trained on him. "Don't shoot! Look! He's one of us. He has the pin! He's one of us!" Throwing caution to the wind, Nikki did the reckless thing. Holstering her weapon, she ran past Alex.

"No! Nicole! Stop!" Alex shouted. "Don't!"

With temporary wits of an emotional fool, she failed to heed his warnings.

But Nikki pulled up short of Bradley, stopping where Jarred writhed in the alley trying to get a foothold so he could clamber to his feet. Soaked in desperation, he reached his hand out in appeal to her. "Nikki. Help. Please. Help," he gasped, extending his bloody left hand towards her.

Nikki now stood directly in Alex's line of fire. He gave up his draw-down stance on Bradley, while all the time he cagily closed the gap between them — both hands precisely clenched on his weapon, still at the ready.

"Stop right there," he ordered Bradley.

"Stay back Nicole," Alex ordered his wife.

With Alex's attention divided between Nicole and the scene, Charles Bradley neatly sucked up his gun off the street and also closed in on the scene, commando style.

Now Bradley joined Alex in shouting warnings to her. "Nikki. Stay away. He still might be armed. Nikki!" Bradley barked at her, holding Jarred in his sights.

Severely wounded, Nikki couldn't see how Jarred offered any kind of a threat. Still, she heeded her husband's command and waited for him.

Alex's and Charles' eyes met in an implicit truce. With Alex's weapon firmly trained on the downed man, Bradley approached Jarred. With his own gun in a dead-on aim, Bradley used his foot to roll Jarred over.

Jarred flopped over on his back. His wilting body slapped the hardness of the pavement. His right hand remained crammed in the pocket of his pants.

Bradley circled to the other side of Jarred. With his foot he crushed Jarred's left wrist into the street. "Pull your hand out of your pocket, slowly. And it better come out empty. Do you understand, slime?"

Jarred nodded weakly, following Bradley's commands, though his eyes remained glued on her. "Please, Nikki. Please," he pleaded in a whisper.

Out-gunned and out-numbered, Nikki felt safe to kneel beside him, "I'm here, Jarred. What is it?"

"I ... I'm sorry. I never wanted to kill you," he fought to keep his eyes from rolling back into his head.

"Then why, Jarred?"

"You. ...You changed things. You left me ... for him," Jarred gasped. "But ... but," he struggled to go on, "I'm only the first. They're coming. There's more. ... An army ... Oh, I'm so sorry..." Death choked off further clarification.

"Well, ain't that a kick in the head!" said Charles Bradley as he crouched over the body, feeling for a pulse, making sure Jarred was dead.

Holstering his gun, Bradley looked up into Alex's face, "What army?"

"We'll cover that later," Alex threw back.

Rashly, Bradley patted down Jarred's corpse. "Look at this!" Bradley sneered. "He was going for it! Breathing his last, the bastard was *still* trying to take you out." Bradley displayed the small caliber pistol he produced from Jarred's pocket where his right hand had been.

Casting quick glances around, Charles cased the alley for an errant witness. "So far we're clear," he announced. "But we gotta give this body a reason for being here." Bradley quickly rifled Jarred's pockets, grabbed his wallet and tucked it inside his own jacket, then left Jarred's pocket lining hanging out. "There, now it's a robbery. Let's get the hell out of here. See you at the bunker as soon as you can get in, okay?"

Sheathing his weapon, Alex nodded. "We are out of here, too!"

In a heartbeat, Bradley fled down a side street. Alex and Nikki slipped into another adjacent alley and disappeared.

Bradley, Mann, and Junger paced nervously inside the concrete bunker as Nikki and Alex descended the stairs. In a flash, Alex swept the room, then joined the group where all traded congratulatory hugs.

Bradley rushed Nikki with a celebratory embrace. "Son-of-a-gun, Nikki, I thought you were going to drop me back there! Great acting! ... Then you, Alex..."

Alex clasped his comrade in sobering relief. "There was no acting. I had every intention of taking you out, especially after Mike's message this morning! If it hadn't been for Nicole spotting your lapel pin, you would be keeping company with Jarred right now in the alley."

Instantly the euphoria in the room evaporated. "What message?" an amazed Mike Junger questioned, jumping in ahead of Charles Bradley.

"The one that brought us here in the first place. The one you sent this morning identifying the cavalier as Bradley and ordering us in," Alex answered.

Alex's answer impaled Junger, "But, I...I ... never sent you a message this morning, let alone one naming Bradley as anything. That had to be..."

"I damn well hope it was Jarred that got that off!" Mann bellowed.

Alex went white. "Well, if it was, that means that he mimicked perfectly your frequency, then succeeded in copying your field and path to me. That makes me feel real secure! Son-of-a-bitch!" Alex exclaimed with a deft fist to the table.

Then Alex cross-examined Bradley, "I assume it wasn't coincidence that put you in the same alley with us this afternoon, Charles."

Alarmed, Bradley came back emphatically. "By no means was it coincidence, Alex. I have been dogging Jarred for six days now, trying to close him out of the imprint program. About two weeks ago, I began to believe he went sideways on us. I was tailing him to his contact for confirmation. But, when the two of you appeared in the alley and I heard him calling Nikki's name, well, something didn't smell right."

Out of patience, Alex replied in disgust, "No doubt. It was a perfect setup—narrow alleyway, closed-in, no traffic, no witnesses, no mess. Detecting you on his trail, he lured us both there, figuring to take us all out at once."

"It would seem so. Evidently he wasn't counting on his former student, Nikki, being on top of her game. If she hadn't noticed my pin, he might have succeeded—at least halfway," Bradley laughed off his comment.

"How can we be sure that it was Jarred who sent the message and that he wasn't being set up too?" Nikki innocently threw into the conversation. An astounded room turned to her.

Charles Bradley broke the silence first, "Damn it, Nikki, you could be right. I never got to trace the roots of his contacts before he went ballistic this afternoon. What if Jarred wasn't independent? What if that bastard was just the shooter?"

Junger leapt back into the fray, "Damn it! Who else could he be connected to? Bob, we need history on him—from recruitment through today. Run *everything*!"

In a flash, Bob Mann vanished up the steps and out.

"Mike, it is critical that we get a look inside Jarred's Paris hide-out. How about some sort of documentation for Bradley and me so we can pay the morgue, police HQ and his residence a visit?"

Concurring, Junger set the wheels in motion to cook up official bureau investigator credentials for both Charles and Alex.

"I don't want to throw a monkey wrench into your plan, sweetheart," Nikki interrupted. "But since I had a working relationship with Jarred, wouldn't I be valuable in identifying items and connections you might find in his apartment?"

Alexander kissed her hand. "Darling, you would provide infinitely better insight than perhaps anyone else. But how would we justify your knowledge of the situation? Or your famous presence to whatever gendarmes that might be assembled there?" Alexander made excellent sense. "But I will photograph everything, and you can count on sitting down with those photos and a fine-toothed comb."

While Bradley and Junger finalized plans, Alex escorted Nikki from the bunker. "Have Reed fly you over to London. Wait for me at the penthouse. After going through the morgue and Jarred's latest haunt here, Charles and I will finish up at Jarred's London residence, then I will meet you at the penthouse."

As they surfaced onto a major thoroughfare, Reed and Lorenzo pulled to the curb. "Be careful," Nikki cautioned Alex before they set out on their separate paths.

"Always, darling." Almost an afterthought he threw in, "You will probably want to lose those clothes before you go much further." Then Alex turned back into the maze of alleys that swallowed him up.

Once on board their jet, Nikki set about pulling down her knot of hair and changing into a fresh outfit, but a wave of exhaustion defeated her. So she simply tucked herself into a pair of jeans and a raglan sweater, then collapsed on the bed for the short hop to London. Her sudden fatigue surprised her, but she assigned it to adrenaline depletion from the skirmish in the alley.

Cold, empty sheets on Alex's side of the bed greeted Nikki in the morning. With trepidation born of fear of the worst, she dialed up her communicator to listen for his life sounds. A sigh of relief escaped when she found them.

Within the hour, Alexander and Bradley came through the door carrying sheaves of pictures covering everything from Jarred's corpse in the morgue to the dingy dive he occupied the morning before their confrontation in the alley. The photographs from Jarred's apartment produced no other clues. But Alex and Bradley drew plenty of conclusions on their fact-finding mission, including the definition of the "army" that Jarred alluded to with his dying breath. Evidently cabinet minister Cho Lin Cao's pockets ran deep, deep enough to launch an entire army, if needed, to rid the world of Alexander's presence.

Bradley rose to the occasion, "So what's next, *mein freund*? The two of us could mount a mission to China to take out that Red bastard."

Alex laughed at the insanity, "Into China? You do have a screw loose! With our round eyes and white skin, we would never make it any farther than the cover of one night could take us. And in case you haven't heard, there is a war on over there, which kind of makes the Chi-Coms a little jumpy."

Nikki listened intently as the men mined the possibilities. She knew Alexander had already explored some sort of plan like Bradley espoused, since he put himself on his rigorous training regimen. Alex's hedging on the topic let him pick Charles's brain for a fresh slant on the situation.

Eager to take the bit in his teeth and run for the thrill of it, Bradley answered, "Maybe you're right about only having the cover of one night within which to operate—but we could do it! We'd catch a ride into Peking and then use the darkness."

"Using what for transportation—the Orient Express?" Alex needled.

"Yea, right. We'd use troop transport through South Korea," Bradley answered.

"And..." From Alex's comeback, Nikki knew Charles had snagged his interest.

"From the Korean DMZ, we'd catch a ride with the Seals across the Yellow Sea. Once we swim the Gulf and make landfall, it's no more than a hundred miles to Peking."

"You *are* crazy!" Alex chided him. "The Gulf of Chihli is a closed body. Since it is the gateway to Peking, their holy city and their capital, I imagine they have it pretty well wired. With the war raging in Nam, all their antenna are up. What cruise ship were you planning on sailing into their harbor?"

Bradley sprang back, "Come on Alex! Remember the impenetrable Iron Curtain? How many times did we walk in past the sentries, the walls, the barbed wire and everything? Hell, it's practically a revolving door to us now." The enticement of the hunt sparkled in Bradley's eyes. "We may have to do some jungle crawling to get to Peking, but one night should provide plenty of time and cover to pull this thing off. Besides, look at you. You're in tremendous physical condition. You're familiar with Asia. And with your passable command of Mandarin, you won't be operating totally in the blind. I know Charlie Soo is gone, but you must have some other contacts left."

Nikki knew Charles Bradley's eagerness left Alex considering the possibilities of an actual assault on Cho in Peking. Only they understood the extent of the forces available to them in the form of Special Ops. She wondered if Alex could swap some of his high-level technology in return for Haldeman urging his Boss for special support from the tactical teams. The possibilities existed, and grew, as they plotted around the table into the late afternoon.

Without a doubt, taking out Cho provided the only total solution to the sanction. Removing Jarred had only eliminated the first of many cavaliers to come. His death solved nothing and left so many questions unanswered. Was Jarred working alone? How far had Alexander's communication system been compromised? Did anyone else have access to that information? Was she still considered a conduit to Alex?

As Nikki listened, she couldn't help but weigh the risk versus the reward. No matter how many times she stacked up the chips on each side of the wager, life as they had known it in the past, came up the loser.

Chapter 39
The Rub

In total, their pivotal journey to Paris kept Nikki and Alex away from *Napoli* for only thirty-six hours. By six that evening, they boarded their jet back to Italy. Nikki's parents were due to arrive at ten the next morning, on June fifth. Another emotion-packed day had taken its toll on Nikki. Sitting upright in her seat, she fell asleep shortly after take-off. Her fatigue permitted Alexander to yield to his preoccupation.

From the moment Nikki's eyes opened on the morning of the fifth, she had the answer to her unusual need for sleep. Deep-seated nausea engulfed her. As Nikki hung over the toilet bowl, she embraced another possibility — she was pregnant. Normally Alexander would celebrate such news with grand style, but within the dire throes of their dilemma she couldn't be sure of the effect such life-altering news would have. Not wanting to either alarm Alex or build unnecessary hopes, she decided to keep her secret until she could confirm it with a visit to the doctor when they got back to the States. Until Nikki had a definite conclusion to report to him, her husband certainly didn't need the added pressure of an expanding family. So before the house awoke, she rose and munched on the crusts of day-old bread in an attempt to stave off the bouts of morning sickness — if that was indeed what it was.

Alex considered it safer for everyone concerned if Zia and Lorenzo met Nikki's parents' plane at the airport, while they stayed at home to put the final touches on a special welcoming party aboard the *Bella Nicole*.

Lazily that afternoon, the seven of them sailed south to an enchanting winery encased in a cave called the *Legato Grotto*. A raucous place, it burst forth with good-natured native exuberance, salty jazz and a bounty in Neapolitan cuisine and fruits of the vine. Adam drank grape juice until his lips turned purple. Before departing for home, Alexander arranged for a lavish fireworks display as a perfect end to their evening.

For the next three days, even in their private moments, Alex and Nikki put away any discussion of the sanction and its complications. Life spun with selfish conceit on its axis around their son's milestone and the attending family. Steeped in excess, Alexander hosted three days of spectacular events guaranteed to delight everyone from Adam to Zia.

Wishing to spare Zia the headaches of being hostess, Alex imported a chef and staff to prepare and serve all the meals along with maintaining the household. He wanted his entire family to enjoy the occasion.

Alex declared the night before Adam's birthday to be a special holiday requiring white tie attire. A string quartet entertained on the terrace, which Alex had transformed into a magical garden of cooing white doves, radiant candlelight and latticed tiers of baskets dripping fragrant flowers. The chef prepared a fresh seafood feast plucked from the waters only hours before. Following Alex's instructions, the wine steward selected only the finest vintages from the wine cellar to pour. The superlative of epitome kissed everything that evening.

Catering to her husband's penchant for her in rubies, Nikki wore a provocatively simple strapless red taffeta moiré gown, with a natural waist, letting her new diamond and oval rubies illuminate her. Alex's latest Dior dinner jacket emphasized his newly toned musculature. Like always, his striking appearance stole Nicole's breath.

The family laughed. They feasted. They sang. And they danced. Dancing with Alexander carried the promise of forever. Nikki reveled in the strength of his magnificent arms and the encasing steel of his devotion. She loved witnessing from close quarters how the candlelight caught the sparkle of adoration emanating from his eyes.

"I have longed to have our families together, sharing a delightful evening." Alex confided to Nicole as they floated over the terrace marble. "It almost happened in Hong Kong. But we…" Alex came dangerously close to crossing their invisible line. Clearing his throat slightly, he saved himself, "But we were unexpectedly sidelined. We had so much to rejoice over that night too, just like tonight." Alex teased with a discerning wink then availed himself of her lips. "So tonight, my darling, better late than never, our families are together, we are with them, and I intend to celebrate until dawn if the mood strikes us!" His hold tightened around Nikki's waist, as he exuberantly swept her away on the music's crescendo.

When the chill of the deepening night herded them into the library to warm themselves, they shared family stories over snifters of brandy. Discretely, just in case, as she had all evening long, Nikki opted for fruit juice instead of alcohol. Sitting in a circle, the family resurrected tales from the early days about Alex and Nikki. Taking turns, each side recounted their child's misdeeds, eliciting shrieks of laughter from the gathering at Nikki and Alex's expense. Not minding in the least, Alex even prompted Zia's memory with some hints about his own rascally past.

At three, Alexander stood up with a slight yawn, "Please excuse us. I know my son's mother will have to answer his call in the early morning, so we will toddle off to bed now. But please, no one else should hurry off on our account." Alex presented his hand to escort his beloved from the room, as the rest of the family declined to break. Their ringing laughter followed the couple down the hallway to their bedroom.

A silver tray of crackers, grapes and cheeses, ringed with plumeria, along with a decanter of sparkling apple juice, waited for them in their room. "It's been a long time since dessert," Alex considerately explained. "I thought you might like a snack before falling into bed."

Slipping off the red moiré, Nikki stood, clad only in her silky under-things as she undid the white tie from around her husband's throat, then slid each white pearl stud through its hole, exposing his chiseled chest. "If you don't mind, I'd like to borrow the shirt off your back. A girl could catch a nasty draft, you know." With a coquettish smile, Nikki relieved him of his shirt, wrapping it around her.

Sitting cross-legged on the deep Oriental silk carpet at the foot of their bed, with Alex still in his satin striped trousers and Nikki in his shirt, they picnicked on the snack tray. So reminiscent of the days from their courtship, they filled up the final hours of the waning night with intimate conversation, living in each other's smile.

Eager to start his big day, Adam scampered away from Zia and into his parent's arms at about eight. The leisurely breakfast on the terrace was the only deference shown to the adults on Adam's birthday. The energy and vigor of the one-year-old dictated the fast-paced schedule for the day's remainder. Beginning with a romp on horseback, they continued into the mid-day meal with a sail to a small island for a picnic lunch and plenty of sun, sand and water for Adam. His giggles filled the day. Gratefully, all the adults collapsed for a nap when he laid down for one, too.

Of course they finished with a dinner at home. For Adam, the chef prepared the child's favorite dish of macaroni and cheese while the adults dined on a fare of *foie gras* infused pheasant. Both Zia and Fran cooperated in baking Adam's birthday cake. The pair of grandmothers chased the chef from the kitchen so they could personally bake the required amount of love into the traditional dessert for their grandson.

How the wonderment reflected up on his face! His blue eyes stood wide-open and his mouth formed an involuntary circle O, as the one candle burned brightly before him. Nikki helped him blow out the candle on his cake while Alex, in classic daddy fashion, photographed the entire event. As is typical of most one-year-olds, Adam reached both hands into the icing, then slathered it all over his face in an effort to get its sweet gooeyness into his mouth.

Over cappuccinos in the library, Alex surprised the group with his proposal of an early departure for them. "I received several messages from the D.C. office this morning. Seems they have found a couple of stumbling blocks in service to our number one client. I guess I will have to abandon the bit of family business I had here and, if no one minds too much, I would like for us to leave at first light."

Recognizing his explanation as pure fabrication, Nikki left discussion of the true urgent matter for the privacy of their bedroom.

Alex saved her the time of asking for clarification. He spilled it all, once he shut their door. "Darling, I hope you weren't counting too heavily on another two weeks here." Alex let his words trail him as he walked into the bathroom. Nikki picked them up, following in behind him. "I would have discussed it sooner with you, but I know that over the last few days we tried to breathe the air of a normal life without all this Agency nonsense. The truth is that Bradley and I planned to meet with Haldeman as soon as possible to explore the accessibility of Special Ops." Standing in front of the gilt-framed wall-to-wall mirror over the vanity, he began undressing, loosening his tie. Without turning around, he spoke to her image in the mirror.

Nikki's heart sank. She tried to masque her emotions by also performing usual nighttime rituals. But she knew deep down inside, this conversation had always been coming. "I take it that you have decided to run with Bradley's suggestion of going to get Cho yourselves," she said flatly.

"We are considering it," Alex tossed back just as flat.

"But you'll weigh all the options before *we* make a decision, won't you?"

"You don't have to plead your case with me, Nicole. I know you have no taste for what you consider to be cowboy heroics. But I have to evaluate every option. Without question, the only way to remove the continued threat of the sanction is to remove the person authorizing it."

Facing him in the mirror, Nicole listened.

"I am not like Bradley—free, single, skating on the edge, desperately seeking my next adrenaline fix. He has nothing to lose but his life. Don't confuse me with Bradley."

"Have you abandoned the idea of *Eternity*?"

"I have not abandoned anything. Nicole, I told you I am looking at every facet of this situation. I hope you realize that *Eternity* is not a perfect solution. Do you understand the consequences of being forced into solitude? Do you understand the daunting development problems for Adam growing up without outside stimulation? We may well be alive. But what will our quality of life be? I am also looking for a resolution to that problem."

"There has always been a tiny piece of our life together, even after marriage, that has been separated by a wall of secrecy because of the Agency. And I've been careful not to interfere. I just want a chance to voice my opinion on this."

Alexander's eyes seared through the glass, penetrating her conscience in their first mutually heated exchange. "Even in our recent past, *we* have not always been completely forthcoming with each other, now have we?" Alex accused.

Pangs of guilt attacked her. Color flushed to Nikki's cheeks. Desperately she tried to stifle her reaction scored by his direct hit. Was he referring to her efforts to camouflage her possible pregnancy? Did Alex suspect her news about a prospective baby? Instantly, Nikki assuaged her guilt with a re-enforcing dose of rationalization about the "greater good." Besides, he would know as soon as she had a definite answer. Seeking refuge, Nikki bent over her washbasin to rinse her face in cool water.

She surfaced to find Alex standing close, offering her a towel. "Oh my darling, what are we doing to each other?" he asked as she dried off. "Nicole, we can't let this damnable thing divide us." He enfolded her into his arms, "I am where I want to be—forever in your arms—married— with responsibilities. And those responsibilities of a family weigh heavily on me. My commitment means nothing if you and the baby aren't safe. That is my primary concern; even if I have to exchange my life to make it happen, I will. You know that I would be out that door with Bradley in a heartbeat if I was assured of success in removing Cho, no matter the price. Since this mission doesn't carry guarantees, I at least want favorable odds. If I lose my life and Cho continues, only to visit the legacy of his sanction on Adam and you, what have I gained? What sense does it make to have risked it all and lost, and leave you unprotected in the bargain?" He hugged her deeply into his chest and kissed the top of her head, "Darling, you must always remember that I love you beyond life itself. Please remember that."

"First light" was not just an expression with Alexander. Reed worked his team through the night to prepare for their dawn departure. Expecting that they would all be back in a matter of weeks to spend the summer, Zia stayed behind at *Napoli* to tend to the preparations for the season.

Delivering her parents to *Creekside*, they flew on to D.C. Upon touchdown Alexander headed out to pick up Bradley at his hotel, then swung over to the White House for their emergency sit-down with Bob Haldeman and Mel Laird.

While Alex and Bradley huddled at the White House with Nixon's Chief of Staff, the Secretary of Defense and others, Nikki proceeded with her day. First, she secured an appointment with a local doctor for a pregnancy test in two days. Then she plowed through her long-neglected personal correspondence. Deliberately, Nikki left dinner unplanned since she figured they'd dine out that night with Charles Bradley. But she had figured wrong. Mid-afternoon Alex phoned to request that they have dinner at home with Gus and his date of the evening.

To Nikki's mind, nothing eventful happened that evening. Proudly they passed around the pictures from Adam's birthday celebration. Once Adam opened the bright yellow Tonka truck from Gus, the adults could no longer compete for his attention. Happily he putt-putted his prized new toy all over the floor. While the men made their customary small talk, Gus's date and Nikki cleared the table and prepared the dessert. The swinging door between the kitchen and dining room kept Alex's discussion with Gus private.

The morning of June eleventh broke without clear direction. Alternately, banks of threatening clouds dominated the peaceful, warm June sky only to be scotched by a dose of brilliant sunshine. Nikki let the ominous weather intimidate her into spending the morning inside. By afternoon though, she decided to brave the capricious clouds for an outing in the park with Adam. Pushing her son on the tot swing in the park, she obsessed over thoughts of Alexander and his recourse to the sanction. Adam squealed happily as the swing soared, when a voice from behind startled Nikki back into reality.

"Now I can see why Alex guards his life so vigorously."

Turning, she found a smiling Charles Bradley leaning up against one of the brace supports of the swing set.

"Geez, Charles, you scared me out of half of my life coming up like that!"

"Sorry," he straightened a bit, but didn't move any closer. "Don't you know you're supposed to have eyes in the back of your head? Would Alex be pleased if he knew that I just walked up on you like this?"

"Well, to walk up on me like this, as you put it, you had to either kill or buy off my guards," Nikki handed back to him as she took attendance of her retinue. Dirk signaled her that they had indeed handed Mr. Bradley a pass. "So what can I do for you, Charles? How goes the war?"

"There's progress. I know we could pull off this operation. It's being passed under the noses of the bigwigs now. Alex will spell it all out for you. But that's not why I stopped by. I felt that I owed you a thank you and an apology for my behavior following our last mission together."

"A thank you? For what?"

Bradley edged a bit closer, "I understand from Junger that you were the only one who believed in me at the start of the imprint program. Evidently you pleaded my case before the almighty himself. Junger was right, by the way, in telling you that you could never trust anyone, but I thank you for your vote of confidence anyway."

"Well, you see how far that vote of confidence got you the other day with me. I had you lined up in my sights to take you out — only that lapel pin saved your life."

"You acted very professionally — like the trained agent you are. But none of this is what brings me here today. Do you remember our last conversation?"

"Do you mean the one right before you dumped me in a cab in Grenoble?"

"That would be the one. I really came because I wanted to tell you I was wrong." Charles kicked at a clod of grass and continued, "I ... I can only chalk up my rude behavior to a fit of jealousy."

"Jealousy?" That word was too delicious to pass up.

"I'm afraid so. I was quite jealous of Alexander. First of all, because he snagged the only woman I had come across in all my wanderings that turned my head enough to make me think twice about my line of work..."

"I really don't think we should be talking about this."

"Please Nikki, let me finish. Second, was my envy and resentment, which came from my realization that Alex might pull off his retirement idea. No Terminal Agent's ever done that before. I envied him. And now I hope the Agency actually has to put together a bleeding retirement plan for you. Of course, we have this immediate dilemma to solve first. Anyway, I just wanted to let you know I was way off base that night. Alex indeed has the world by the tail. Look at this — a wonderful wife, beautiful son — happily ever after in suburbia! What a life!"

"I didn't think that was even in your field of vision, Charles. What happened to living in the moment, risk, danger and all that adrenalin rushing?"

"I'm plenty happy, Nikki. However, being on the outside doesn't hold too many warm and fuzzy times. Sometimes it would be nice to know where you will rest your head from one night to the next."

She couldn't believe Charles Bradley's seeming change of heart.

"Well," he said, rearranging his position, "we'll get Alex over this rough period, then I'll be the one to deliver his first Agency-be-damned pension check. Would you cook for me when I bring it?" Bradley ribbed, with raised eyebrows and an impish grin.

"Of course, Charles."

"Okay, well, I'm headed out." With that, Charles brushed the top of Adam's copper locks and planted a peck of a kiss on her cheek before ducking through some bushes. He left Nikki twisting with her reconciliation of the Bradley of the past versus the Bradley she had just talked to.

To Nikki's surprise, Alex met Adam and her at the door when they returned from the park. She expected him to still be involved at the White House, Pentagon or some similar place. Before becoming distracted by cocktails and dinner, she wanted answers to the questions posed by the sanction. She turned Adam over to Lorenzo so she and Alex might talk.

"Did Bradley find you at the park today?" Alex opened the conversation, handing Nikki a glass of apple juice, while he poured a sherry for himself. They settled-in across from each other on the living room sofa. "I gave him the location of several parks where he might find you. He wanted to say thank you for not plugging him the other day."

"He gave me quite a start. I probably wasn't as alert as I should have been, but this thing has really consumed me, and I knew the service was around us. Man, old Charles was in rare form."

"He asked me how much he had to worry about with you in the alley. Basically he wanted to know if you could actually shoot that thing or if you just looked good holding it. I assured him that you would have only needed one shot to drop him where he stood. I must say, that impressed him. I think after Hungary and Grenoble, he has a lot of respect for you. I only wish I could have seen you in action as he did."

Anxious, Nikki pushed to the meat of the matter, "He made it sound like everything is set for an operation into China to get Cho. So are Haldeman and Laird putting the Special Ops teams at your disposal?"

Alexander laughed out loud at her question. "Darling, I am afraid the government doesn't quite work that way. Oh, how I wish they did! But unfortunately they have a different view of the world. The best we could hope for is that they have some teams in the area we might be able to fall in with or that they would look the other way while we cross their path. That would be the height and breadth of their cooperation."

"When you and Charles talked the other day about getting the cooperation of the Seals, you made it sound like they would be under your direction."

"I am afraid that was another case of Agency-speak. To the un-indoc-trinated ear I can understand how it sounded like we would command the troops."

"Then, you won't be able to use them. So, I assume the mission is off?"

"Actually, the talks went surprisingly well. Just a word from me and the operation is a go."

"Do you stand a good chance of getting to Cho?"

"That's the unknown. Basically the answer to your question comes down to what we—you and I—want to do. This is the conversation you asked to be a part of, Nicole. So what say you now, my darling?"

Nikki had no answers, only questions. Of course she didn't want him risking his life half way around the world, where he might be killed or maimed and she couldn't get to him. How would she ever know if some-one was coming for Adam or not? On the other hand, the sanction would never be canceled unless Cho disappeared. "Alex, in all the played-out situations and conversations that I ran over and over in my head, I never dreamed that I wouldn't have an answer for you. I hoped that by the time we actually had this talk, everything would be academic. My imagination always included a defining moment or a solution. So far nothing has turned up. Never have I been in so much turmoil and without a resolu-tion."

Nikki expected a cool, reasoned response from Alex. She expected him to lead her through whatever scenario he had elected, argue its merits and convince her of its wisdom.

She didn't expect his reply. "I understand. I, too, kept hoping that the perfect solution to the sanction would present itself. It hasn't. Bradley worked a sweet deal with Laird in Defense, but Intelligence can't confirm Cho's exact whereabouts. He hides in secret bunkers all over the Chinese landscape. Since he is not on Defense's hot list, they don't have an exact bead on him. We can get inside, but it will be without assurances that he will be where we surface. Of course we can try to bait him. But it is all so imprecise. I am so emotionally involved, it is interfering with my intuitive insight. Failure to achieve our goal is not an option. I can't leave you and Adam unprotected if the mission falls short. Yet, if I do nothing, Cho eventually will satisfy the sanction." Abruptly Alex turned to her, "You understand now that satisfaction of the sanction includes taking out Adam, too, don't you?"

"Yes, Lorenzo spelled out the meaning of the 'legacy' of a Chinese vendetta."

"I know. He told me. That devastated him. I should have told you myself rather than putting either of you in that position. It is just that I didn't want any more pressure on you than already existed."

"So where does this leave us?"

"To be brutally honest, I don't know. I received a communiqué from Paris early this morning. They are tracking several cavaliers on the Continent. At least one of them isn't sticking anywhere. He is traveling and might be headed this way."

"Then it will be the back alley of Paris over and over, won't it?"

"We shouldn't be surprised. It is a fulfillment of Jarred's dying words, 'an army is coming.' And they will keep coming. Obviously we can't keep plinking off these shooters as they cross the horizon. They are not unsophisticated ducks in a shooting gallery. Eventually one will slip through our security web."

"Then we are back to eradicating the sanction at its root."

"And all the problems it creates."

"It would seem that the only other alternative left to us is *Eternity* and all its consequences."

A curl of resolution turned up on Alex's lips. "So it would seem. But that will be so devastating to everyone — your parents, Zia, Lorenzo, Adam and not to mention — us." Then Alex shifted gears. "Why not wait. Let's see what tomorrow brings. We don't have to make a decision right this minute. We have tonight."

Alexander came around behind the sofa and kneaded Nikki's worry-weary shoulders. "Come on, darling, let us put this away for tonight."

In the blink of an eye, Nikki let it go. Wrapped up inside his loving arms, his tender, smooth lips met hers, and the world melted away. "So what is your pleasure this evening, my darling? Shall we dine in or go out on the town? Do we dress to the nines or kick back in our comfy clothes? We could even run up to *Nevermore* if you desire. You name the tune. Tonight is your night."

More than anything, Nikki wanted her family around her. So, she opted for a casual dinner in their townhome. The clouds dissipated late in the afternoon, and an even-tempered breeze ushered in an idyllic June evening. Assuming the role of master chef, Alex grilled steaks out on the walled-in terrace. While he conducted the valiant struggle to obtain the perfect temperature for the briquettes, Nikki tossed a salad and heated some rolls in the oven. In addition to their steaks, Alex made sure Adam's hot dogs were done to a turn. Meanwhile, Adam enjoyed running between the two work areas, playing his version of peek-a-boo. His calling "Mommy — Mommy", "Daddy — Daddy" punctuated with giggles echoed throughout the townhouse.

After dinner, they sat on the glider positioned at the far end of the bricked terrace and rocked. Nested together, in lazy motion they glided back and forth, watching the fireflies hop-skip their way across the yard. It wasn't long before Adam drifted off to sleep in her arms. Rather than hurrying him off to bed, Nikki let him doze there. His precious baby face and little, rounded milk lips heaved heavy sighs of contentment. An end-of-the-world peace settled upon the three of them that night in the garden.

Quietly, Alex and Nicole whispered to each other their prayers and dreams for their son and family, just as they had a year and a half ago when they first discovered her pregnancy. With an ethereal, feather-light touch, Alex traced long lines up and down her forearms, stopping every now and then to kiss the side of her head.

With evening's encroaching chill, they lay their son in his crib. He breathed a tremendous sigh, then easily turned into his teddy bear and resumed his sleep with the angels.

Without the intrusion of electric lights, they strolled down the hallway to their room, opened the window to let the breeze in, then slipped into bed. Ever so gently, Alex continued caressing her arms, her back and eventually her body with his mesmerizing touch. Exquisite relaxation washed over Nicole. She melted into him until in thundering silence, they became one. Never in all the times that they made love had they shared such deep, abiding intimacy as that night. Its resonating afterglow lingered in Nicole's heart.

Morning broke radiantly, with a smile on her face. For the first time in months, a song replaced the anxious pit in Nikki's heart. Everything seemed so fresh and new; she would remember even the tiniest detail of that day. June twelfth—what a magnificent day to be alive! Alex greeted her with a kiss and an aromatic cup of herbal tea.

"Darling, I have a wonderful idea. Why not take the morning and go shopping. You haven't pampered yourself in quite a while. I can take Adam with me down to the store. Between Lorenzo and me, we can show him quite a time."

Nikki couldn't even pretend to protest, his idea played perfectly into her scheduled visit to the doctor. "It would be nice to pick up a few summer outfits for Adam," she excused.

"Nonsense, Adam has enough outfits. Surprise me with something new for you! Then join Adam and me for lunch at Café Italiano at one-thirty." Alex's eyes danced.

How could she refuse such an offer? Dressed in creased, white linen slacks with a blue oxford button-down shirt, he tied his pale yellow cashmere sweater about his shoulders to ward off a morning chill. His attire accented his bronze skin and brought out the brilliant blue in his eyes. Out the door with a jaunty whistle, he went to the office to accomplish some paperwork before returning home to pick up Adam.

No sooner had Alex stepped out, than Gus arrived for morning coffee with fresh *Apfel Kugel* from the bakery. Adam played on the floor with his toys while Nikki shared with Gus her exciting news about the possible pregnancy and her mission to have the test done that morning. He rejoiced at the prospect, promising a grand celebration that evening should the results come back positive. Before leaving, Gus promised he'd wait to hear from her as to whether to plan the party.

Sweeping Adam up off the floor, Nikki waltzed him up the staircase to the tub for his morning bath. They dawdled over the tub longer than usual as he enjoyed sinking his yellow ducky with some powerful blasts from his fists. Then Nikki dressed him in his little white sailor outfit trimmed in navy. Since his daddy was wearing blue and white, why shouldn't his son compliment him?

They came down the stairs singing "Three Little Duckies" just as Alex walked in the door. "It is beginning to warm up out there," he remarked, neatly draping his sweater over a kitchen chair. "Are you ready for a day out with Daddy?" Alex asked Adam.

Adam answered by running full speed at Alex and throwing himself into Alex's open arms, giggling the whole time. Maternal pride almost burst Nikki's heart.

Alex hoisted Adam up into his arms. "Give Mommy a big hug and kiss. Tell her 'we'll see you later'."

" 'ater Mommy. See oo 'ater," Adam cooed, then laid a wet slobbery kiss on her cheek.

Nikki gathered a nose full of the aroma of baby sweetness as she kissed his rosy cheek good-bye and combed her fingers through his copper-colored hair.

Giving her a playful nudge, Alex cleverly turned their private little cliché, "Hey, remember me, *mon ami!*"

"I'll see my two men for lunch," Nikki said as she put Adam's little sailor's cap on his head and turned to her husband.

Still holding Adam, Alex embraced his Nicole and laid upon her a very meaningful kiss. "Wow, residual afterglow from last night," Nikki thought.

For a long moment, Alex held Nicole close before they separated. With sincere eyes he whispered, "Remember, I love you beyond life itself." Then he kissed her again and stepped out into the sunshine. The rays lit up the copper in Adam's locks and the gold in Alex's.

Nikki called down the steps to them as they got into the car, "Have fun. See you at one-thirty at Café Italiano." In a flash the gleaming black Mercedes purred out the drive and down the street. Adam, sitting in his car seat, held up his tiny hand, opening it and closing it in delightful succession, which was his cute little way of waving bye-bye.

Singing, she showered in preparation for her doctor's appointment. In her heart she knew she was pregnant. For the first time, Nikki let herself embrace the possibility. No matter what the conflict in their lives, it couldn't change what was happening inside her. Convenient or not, they would be parents again. It was time to accept it and rejoice in it. As the water splashed off her skin, she toyed with the eternal question—boy or girl—conjuring up family scenes for each of the possibilities.

Nikki could barely contain herself for the rest of the morning. Over their communicators Alex sent her little love messages. She answered them. But just before walking into the doctor's office she sent him an excuse, then dialed down her communicator, so her conversation with the doctor wouldn't give away the surprise.

Back out on the street before eleven, Nikki drove to the mall to oblige her husband and shop for herself. Suddenly a panicked restlessness flooded her, obliterating her focus. She found it impossible to decide what to shop for—casual clothes, daytime suits, formal wear—nothing struck a chord. She couldn't shake her ominous nervousness. With forced concentration, the idea of maternity clothes came to her. Although it would be months before she needed them, Nikki decided it would be a perfect way to break the news. She'd come down the stairs modeling her new look.

Nikki didn't want to tote her news-breaking wardrobe to lunch with her, so at close to one she hurried home to drop off her packages. As she turned the key in the lock, from the corner of her eye she picked up two men in suits approaching her. Inside the phone rang off the hook. Instinctively Nikki raised her defenses. Throwing questioning glances at her security team, they merely took a step backward. This wasn't good. Why were they backing away? Had they been bought off? The suits got dangerously closer. Pretending to drop her bags at the door gave Nikki cover to reach inside her purse and ready her weapon. With her security backing away, she wondered how many of them she'd have to take out?

Before Nikki could come up with her gun drawn, one of the men stopped her by calling her name, "Mrs. Vincente? Excuse me, are you Mrs. Alexander Vincente?" Keeping her gun concealed inside her purse with her finger on the trigger, the safety off and a round in the chamber, Nikki rose cautiously to meet the men face to face. Every nerve in her body readied to its highest alert.

Chapter 40

The Greater Good

"Mrs. Alexander Vincente?" the man questioned again.

"Yes," she answered guardedly. His use of her husband's first name struck her as odd. Intuition told her this man was not the expected shooter, but Nikki refused to give up her defensive posture.

In that instant, her eye zeroed-in on the second man, standing behind the first, reaching inside his suit. Now the first man did the same. Shoving aside her intuition, Nikki readied herself to fire the moment she saw a weapon emerge from their coats. Acutely she focused her concentration on their hands inside their suit coats.

"Nicole! Stop!" called Dirk of her security team, now closing on the scene. "It's okay."

On security's say so alone, she halted raising her gun from her purse.

Both men produced badges with ID's instead of weapons. Instantly Nikki released the trigger, backed down the action and snapped the safety back in place.

"Mrs. Vincente, we are detectives from the Montgomery County Police. Might we come in for a moment?"

Dirk, her senior guard, nodded his consent.

"Sure," she responded hesitantly, fumbling now for her keys to unlock the door.

Being more than helpful, the men picked up her dropped packages while she let them follow her inside. Immediately Nikki's mind shifted from alert status to sickening dread. An uncanny foreboding told her they didn't have good news. Nikki made the conscious decision to remain standing.

Each detective introduced himself, presenting her with his business card. The lead man continued, "Mrs. Vincente, do you have a black Mercedes with license plate 218 DHJ?"

"Yes, we do. That's my husband's car."

"Then I regret to inform you that there's been a traffic accident."

The word accident didn't compute. Nikki expected him to say a shooting. What did he mean an accident? "What?" she didn't understand. "What kind of accident?"

In the next instant, her world slammed to a stop.

"Your car was involved in an accident on the American Legion Bridge late this morning," The detective remained monotone.

"Are they okay? What happened to my husband and my baby?" Nikki broke in on them as they just stood there looking at her. This was like pulling teeth. What weren't they telling her?

"My husband? My baby? What happened to my husband and my baby?!" she precisely delineated, hoping they would understand her.

"Their car was forced off the bridge into the Potomac. By the time we got to the car, their bodies were no longer inside. They may have escaped and swum to shore. We don't know. Or they could have been washed down stream by the current. We have divers about to go..."

"They might be alive?" Nikki repeated as she immediately dialed up her communicator. Listening intently for Alex's life sound, her mind blotted out whatever the two detectives were saying. She strained to hear. Turning the volume all the way up, Nikki heard nothing. She got up to get a tissue to both wipe her eyes and use for cover as she called to Alex. But she got back only dead air. She stretched her mind, frantically searching for a clue as to what to do next.

Lorenzo—did Lorenzo know? The two detectives stood before her, their mouths moving. Nikki pushed past them to get to a phone. She had to call Lorenzo. God, she wished those two monkeys would go away. Her security detail closed in. Nikki hoped they would read her body language and get rid of the detectives so she could handle the situation. This felt like a quagmire of nightmarish proportions. Hindered by the presence of the detectives, she couldn't escape from them to save her husband.

Then all of a sudden a thought washed over her, spreading its warmth like a comforting blanket. *Eternity*! Alexander said they probably wouldn't be together when it came...that she would know it when it arrived. This had to be her call to *Eternity*. Now Nikki *had* to get to Lorenzo! He would know how to get her there. But how could she make that call with these two jokers standing here in her face? Nikki motioned to Dirk. Her security detail also appeared shaken.

"Dirk, you have got to get rid of these guys. I need some space and time to think. Can you help me out here?" Nikki pleaded.

He looked at her. "Nicole, don't you understand? There's been an accident involving Alexander and Adam. These men are here to take you to the scene. Don't you want to be there when they find them?" he insisted, almost making her out to seem off balance.

"Dirk, *you* don't understand. I have to call Lorenzo. I need some privacy! Can you do that for me?" She couldn't believe the denseness of everyone surrounding her!

"Nicole, Lorenzo is there! Didn't you hear the detectives? They told us he's already at the shore supervising the rescue. He's waiting for you." Dirk's eyes bulged out for emphasis. Nikki knew this wasn't the way it was supposed to be. Again she listened for Alex's sounds. Now Dirk's lips moved, and nothing came out. Still Nikki heard nothing.

She had to call her husband! How could she call her husband on her communicator with all these people around! Why wouldn't they leave her alone! "*ALEX!!!*" Nikki finally screamed out in shear desperation. Immediately the swirling sounds surrounding her crashed into silence. Thank goodness, now she could hear. ... Hear... nothing.

My God, Alex! Adam! Was everyone right? Were Adam and Alex really gone? With fright in her eyes, Nikki searched Dirk's eyes. She needed answers, "Dirk, are they really gone?"

Gravely, he nodded.

"Lorenzo. Yes, I must get to Lorenzo. Please tell me how to get to Lorenzo. How do I get there? I must get there." Nikki pulled out her keys, ready to drive to wherever she had to go.

Dirk politely took her keys. "That's not necessary, Nicole. These men know right where to go. They will take us." Then he signaled to the detectives her acquiescence of going with them. With a shepherding arm around her, Dirk guided Nikki to the detective's car. Numb to everything, Nikki kept trying to reach Alex on her communicator and got nothing. Her head spun, and she felt dizzily detached from reality. Her salvation lay with Lorenzo. He would know exactly what she should do. What was taking them so long to get there?

By the time they arrived, a sizeable throng had amassed along the riverbank. Two news helicopters hovered overhead. The detectives employed uniformed officers to battle their way through the swarm of assembled news people. Bulbs flashed and the elbowing hounds of the press shoved microphones in Nikki's face. "How do you feel?"

Reducing them to a vulgar annoyance, Nikki ignored them.

Focusing on the figures beyond the yellow police tape, she tried to pick out Lorenzo. Helicopters beat the river to a froth, making it appear choppy, cold and inhospitable. Frogmen dotted the surface of the water. Nikki couldn't imagine her baby in there. She wanted to rush headlong down to the shore. Dirk attentively helped her maneuver the bank's rough terrain to get down to the scene.

Once over the rocky crags, Nikki broke free of Dirk and the detectives and ran to the familiar figure pacing the shore. "Lorenzo! Lorenzo!" she yelled, racing to him.

He turned around and, with relief on his drawn face, ran to meet her.

As if one in thought, they both glanced over their shoulders to be sure they had absolute privacy. Once clear of all eyes and ears, Nikki searched his face, "Tell me, Lorenzo. Tell me what happened? I can't hear Alex's life sounds on my communicator. Where are they? Do we go now?"

Lorenzo studied her intently, "Go? Go where?"

"To *Eternity*," Nikki insisted in a hush. "I know this is it. I know I have to have an accident, too. And I can wait. Just tell me they are safely on their way."

Lorenzo's brown eyes never relented, "Nikki, I have nothing to tell you other than the awful truth. Alex's car was rammed while he crossed the bridge. I don't know if it was an accident or the cavalier carrying out the sanction. But they went over the side."

"Lorenzo, its okay, you can let me in on it. I can act. No one will ever know."

Tears swelled in his eyes, "Nikki, you have to believe me. I was right behind them. I saw the whole awful thing. They never had a chance. If they survived the impact, there's a slight possibility that they might be alive, washed up on some bank around here. The good news is they didn't find their bodies in the car. There's still a small shred of hope, but not much." Lorenzo pierced her with his sincerity.

Nikki read his face again and again. She only found genuine grief— no hint of an alternative agenda. "Lorenzo, oh please, please, tell me that they're not in there."

Profoundly wounded, he nodded.

"No. They can't be! No! Not my baby!" The impact of what every-one had been trying to tell her finally sank in. "NO!!" she screamed, "Not my baby! Not my Alex!"

Lorenzo tried to console her. Nikki wouldn't have it. She broke from him and ran to the water screaming. "No! No!" Before anyone could catch her, she threw herself into the water. Her baby! She had to find him. He couldn't be in there.

Nikki never knew how far she got or who pulled her out and wrapped her in blankets. At dark, the police called off the search until first light. However, Alex's entire cadre of security came down to the river to conduct their own search of the shoreline. Setting up powerful lights, working in relay teams, they combed the banks and inlets around the clock.

Lorenzo sent the jet for Nikki's parents. A panicked Fran then called Mary, who had been visiting her fiancé in Virginia—an hour away. Driving like a madwoman in the night, Mary rushed to her friend's side. She found Nikki, crazed with grief, withdrawn from everyone, a silhouette against the blazing lights. Nikki refused to leave the shore. Staring into the black water, she spent the night. Mary, Nikki's parents and Lorenzo stayed with her. She wouldn't leave the water's edge for the thought of her baby and her husband in that cold, dark water.

Hour after hour, they sat with Nikki as she kept her vigil. Nikki functioned only on the simplest life-sustaining levels. Gus arrived after seeing the news and told Fran about Nikki's suspected pregnancy. For preservation of the possible life within, Fran coerced Nikki into eating the food she carried down to the water's edge.

Nikki refused to go back to the townhouse. When fatigue knocked her down, she slept in a heap in the sand. She wouldn't leave her baby and her husband. At least once a day, Mary or Fran coaxed her away from the riverbank long enough for a hot shower at a nearby hotel. Afterward, she returned to her post.

Three days later law enforcement changed from a "search and rescue" to a "search and recovery" operation. Someone courteously made sure Nikki understood the difference. On the fourth day, they successfully dragged the hulk of Alex's Mercedes from the depths of the river—hardly recognizable as the sleek black machine that pulled out of their driveway only a few days earlier with Nikki's son waving bye-bye to her. In addition to the water damage with silt and muck deposits caked in it, the Mercedes revealed the substantial damage it sustained in the crash, first from the impact with the other car and then on the other side where it careened through the bridge's guardrail. With the exception of the car seat, the Potomac had washed away any evidence that Nikki's husband and her son had ever been in that car.

After ten days, the police called off the search. They attributed the disappearance of the bodies to them being washed too far downstream. For closure, Richard proposed holding a memorial service for Alex and Adam at their stone church in Pennsylvania. Surrendering, Nikki allowed herself to be led away to return to *Creekside* to make preparations for their services.

The tragedy devastated everyone. So disturbed by the deaths of Alexander and Adam, Zia couldn't even make the trip over to the States to attend the services. Zia's state of mind worried Lorenzo to the point that he stayed only long enough to see Nikki back to D.C. before leaving to tend to his mother.

Detached from time, a depressing fog enveloped Nikki. Her shell functioned without recollection or consequence of circumstances as they played out before her. Numb, she couldn't cry, yet graciously, she received everyone. Outsiders noted how well she carried herself. But her vacant eyes, reflecting her hollowed-out soul, disturbed those closest to her.

Hundreds of people attended the memorial service. Later Nikki recalled them as faces passing by her like slides in a picture show. She remembered the ones who seemed out of place, like Junger, Mann and Bradley from the Agency. Funny, she remembered Bob Mann being presentably dressed with red eyes. Bradley hugged her with tears in his eyes. "I'm so sorry," he whispered to her. "We could have made it. I know it."

Junger, wearing a brave front, delivered the standard "grateful nation" speech as he presented her a folded American flag. Unable to sustain the front any longer, he broke down, "Alex always gave more of himself than anyone ever expected. He was revered. I can't tell you how very much I will miss him." A 21-gun salute followed.

Nikki's friends from the entertainment world also came. Among the many, Pete and Richie of the Merseymen showed up.

Following the reception after the services, Nikki went back to *Nevermore*. She intended only to take inventory of what she needed to bring from D.C. for her eventual move back to *Nevermore*. After just ten minutes in the house though, her fog began to subside. She found the memory ghosts inhabiting *Nevermore* comforting and familiar. She touched their things, and they reassured her. Immediately Nikki recognized that *Nevermore* held the hope for her survival. She could live out her days within the walls of the home where wonderful memories of her son and husband still resided.

While going through things in their bedroom, out of old habits, Nikki found Alexander's ring box in their dresser drawers. Musingly she opened it, fully expecting it to be empty, because she remembered seeing his wedding band on his finger when he neatly hung his sweater on the back of the kitchen chair. To her surprise, inside the box sat a beautiful pear-shaped ruby ring with three diamonds clustered at the top. The mounting exactly duplicated the setting Alex had created for the ruby she had bought from Charlie Soo. A rolled up piece of paper peeked out from inside the finger loop. Her heart skipped a beat. Nikki unrolled the note.

"My dearest, darling Nicole,
If you are reading this note, then the worst possible thing has happened. I know you have spent many discon-

solate, lonely days. I am truly sorry for them. Whether heaven or hell has been chosen for me as my final resting place, every minute of separation from you is torture of unspeakable magnitude. How I will miss your loving ways with the baby. Know that our son continues on in heaven, basking in the radiance that your presence in his life gave him. I know that every day the angels will sing songs about you to him.

I leave you this ruby to brighten your dark days.
Remember, I love you beyond life itself.
Love, A."

Alexander's last words to her, she clung to them, even though they sucked her back into the black spiral of desolation and her private hell. Holding the box for an eternity, she vacantly stared at the ruby. Until, a shaft of light streaming in through the window ignited the ruby's facets and a ray of hope. Could Alex have hidden a coded message in his final note to her?

Alex wrote most of his notes to her in code. She wanted this note not to be an exception. The language seemed to indicate that the missive teemed with underlying meaning. But at that moment its precise meaning was lost to her. No doubt he meant to reassure her, but of what—her life would go on—his existence? What? Did he mean that he and the baby were alive somewhere? He never used the signature word *Eternity* as they had promised each other. Maybe the note, precipitated by the increasing desperation of the situation, was nothing more than a final farewell. Nikki poured over the note again and again trying to divine his intent. She felt that the significance of the ruby contained the key, since Alexander punctuated his statement with an actual stone in a reproduction of the Soo setting. And Alexander never did anything extraneous. Was she supposed to glean from it a reference to Charlie Soo and his life underground? Did this mean Alex and the baby were still alive? Why wasn't he more specific?!!

Committing the note to memory she burned it. Then pulverizing the ashes, she scattered them so if Alex and Adam were still alive, no physical clue, no matter how encrypted, would be found to give them away. Yet his clues seemed so obscure. With every fiber of her being, Nikki wanted to believe Alex had taken the baby to *Eternity* and would send for her. But Lorenzo's eyes had told a drastically different story. She recalled that fateful New Year's Eve, the furtive glances flashing between Alex and Lorenzo, when Charlie Soo left for the underground. Nothing now seemed as concrete as that had seemed. And if Alex were alive in *Eternity*, why not use the communicators?

Flinging herself on their bed, Nikki flailed about in a flood of tears—tears of cautious hope—polluted by the bitter agony of the probable truth. She thanked him. She cursed him.

"Alex!" she bleated through her tears, "Where are you? Are you really gone? How could you leave me? You took my baby away from me. Grant killed my first child, and you've robbed me of my son. My precious son, and now I am alone. I don't have you. I don't have h-iii-mmm." Tears stanched her tongue.

"Damn you! Damn you for leaving. For taking my son away from me. How will I live? I loved you. I'll always love you. How can I live without you? How do I go on? Do you hear me? How do I go on?" plaintively she wept.

In the end, her tears bought her the sweet release from her prison of detachment.

Nikki pushed her common sense into the deep recesses of her being. In her heart, she decided that he was alive because her heart willed him to be alive, despite all evidence to the contrary. Unreasonably she hoped that he would come back from time to time to *Nevermore*.

She must allow him unrestricted privacy for that possibility. It was then she decided, when she left, to seal up *Nevermore* and never go back. And since she chose to believe in Alexander and Adam's continuance underground, she couldn't go back to their familiar haunts only to find them as deserted as she had left them and the door to their communication—the ring box—undisturbed. Nikki didn't want to face irrefutable truth.

Finally collecting herself, Nikki sat down to write her husband a final note.

> "To my eternal sweetheart, Alexander,
>
> I know we share the profound sorrow that our separation in death brings us. But you have left me a treasure beyond earthly riches, which are the jewels of memory of each of our days together. How I will go on without you and our son confounds me.
>
> The places we shared are lost to me forever. I will never step foot inside *Napoli*, *St. Vincente* or *Nevermore* again, as they belong to your memory, and they only rekindle the tragedy. Nor can I claim any part of the estate that would have been for our son.

My dearest Alexander, I know you are in heaven with our son. Kiss him for me. Tell him that I love him, and he lives always in my heart. Remember, I, too, love you beyond life itself.

Forever yours, Nicole."

Impossibly Nikki hoped he would find her note to him although her mind admitted the reality, then scolded her for giving credence to such frivolity of the heart—an exercise in the folly of denial. But the luxury of her folly cost her nothing and allowed her to feel better. So Nikki folded the note just like the one she found. Slipping it inside the ruby ring, she replaced the case in the same place within the drawer.

As she stood before their dresser, a distinct feeling of "presence" came over her, the feeling of someone standing behind her. The thought occurred to her as she closed the drawer that *he* might be inside *Nevermore* even as she stood there. Briefly Nikki considered searching the house to find him; maybe he was watching her from their bedroom closet, perhaps he was in the basement. Could she get one last kiss good-bye? But she thought better of it. No, she couldn't endure the pain of leaving him knowing it might be the last time forever that she would ever see him. How he did it that morning when he walked out the door with the baby, she didn't know.

Of course, she couldn't explain the real reason behind her decision to close *Nevermore*. Everyone assumed her overwhelming grief drove her to it. Her father's lawyer, after strenuously protesting her action, helped Nikki draft her rescission to what was rightfully hers—the Vincente family holdings. But, if her fantasy proved true and Alex and Adam were still alive, they would need the fortune more than she would.

The nagging possibility still remained that Nikki had read too much into the note. Alexander was supposed to have used the code word "eternity" concerning any matter of a life underground. He should have used the code. He could have used it to tell her *not* to go to their hiding place. Nikki couldn't understand why he didn't.

Between dusk and dawn, in those black hours of despondency, such cancerous thoughts gnawed at her. Sometimes they grew to oppressive proportions, resulting in a misery that brought on endless crying jags. In truth, Nikki didn't know for sure whether they had perished or survived the accident. Living with her fantasy, however, proved far sweeter than finding out for sure.

Chapter 41

The Ultimate Decision

Nikki's grief drove her to consider suicide. However, her trip to *Nevermore* and the possibility of Alex and Adam actually being alive forced her to the decision for life. Her probable pregnancy and their possible continuance left her no choice. Having chosen life, an overwhelming urgency possessed her to put away the tragedy and get beyond it.

Worried that the new resonance in her outlook may be an aberrant manifestation of grief, her mom and dad tried to get Nikki to remain at *Creekside* for a few more days of recuperation. But Nikki needed to get moving. She felt that the only way to regain control was to face down the gaping loss. Realizing the longer she put off the confrontation with the raw components of her grief, the more difficult the healing process would be. Swallowing hard, she went to embrace her bitter pill. Besides, she knew verification of her pregnancy waited in D.C.

Lorenzo accompanied her back to D.C., making sure she was safely situated in the townhouse before flying Alex's jet back to Italy. It would be Nikki's last opportunity to talk face-to-face with him. Alone and absolutely sure of their freedom from bugs in the townhouse, Nikki knew she could ask him anything. She also knew, however, of his unquestioning loyalty to Alexander, to the point of blatant lying if necessary. Carefully she weighed the information she hoped to extract against the probability of its adulteration. Nikki knew if Alex couldn't leave her the outright truth in his final note to her, then Lorenzo's answers, though well intended, would be just as empty. So, rather than questioning Lorenzo, she used him to send a message to Alexander.

Always a caretaker, Lorenzo tested her emotional stability, while putting on the kettle. "How does it feel being back here? Do you think you'll be able to deal with it?"

"Strange. It really feels strange. If there were a way to have avoided coming back here and still being able to recover, I would have taken it. Everywhere there are last minute reminders of both of them. But I won't ever be able to cope with the loss if I don't face it head on. My biggest hurdle will be to try to forget how they went. I can't dwell on that, or I'll go crazy."

Tears stood in Lorenzo's eyes. He patted her hand, "I know. That awful thought plagues me, too. Continually I see his Mercedes crashing through the guardrail, hanging in mid-air, then plunging nose first into the river. It seemed so surreal when it happened. I couldn't believe it was unfolding right before my eyes. The only way I can erase that horrible vision is to think of where they are now instead."

Nikki couldn't help but wonder, if they were still alive, how Lorenzo told the tale about the accident with such incredible emotion and believability. "Yes, I prefer to think of them as being in heaven."

Lorenzo sipped his tea. For a tiny moment Nikki imagined she detected a prick of conscience. But she was sure she only manufactured it. Then Lorenzo changed the course of their conversation. "I suppose you will be moving back to *Nevermore* once you've finished here. I am sure it will feel good to be close to your family."

Reflectively, Nikki shook her head, "No. I don't know where I'll go, but it won't be back to *Nevermore*. Actually I said my good-byes to *Nevermore* yesterday."

"Really?" She caught him by surprise.

"Yes. It felt so familiar, so peaceful. I imagined I felt Alexander there with me. For the first time since the tragedy, I felt connected again. I was getting a few things together to bring back to D.C. to tide me over until I could move back. In going through our dresser, I found Alex's ring box from his wedding ring. We used to leave messages to each other in it whenever he'd go out of town. For old time's sake, I opened it and found a note, which I committed to memory." Nikki recited the note to Lorenzo, carefully monitoring his response to it.

Lorenzo listened intently, without any detectable reaction. Then taking in a huge breath, he exhaled loudly, "Mother of God! That's intense." To avoid responding, he turned it around on her, "What do you think it means?"

Nikki looked into Lorenzo's eyes, without accusation, but with unwavering strength. "Lorenzo, let me be clear about this. I'm not looking for an answer from you. I would never compromise your devotion to Alex. What I believe it means is that Alex and Adam are alive and if they aren't at *Eternity* now, they soon will be. Just as Charlie Soo exists under some other name in a secret location, I think Alex used the ruby to convey that idea. I am hoping it means that he has met the same fate as Charlie Soo."

Lorenzo stared at Nikki, like he was humoring her, as if not to do so would risk pushing this distraught woman over the edge.

But Nikki wouldn't be dissuaded. She didn't take his reaction as an insult or to have any significance at all. In fact, it bolstered her assumption. Forthrightly she continued, "If I am correct, and Alex and Adam are still alive, then it will take considerable funds for them to continue their life underground. To that end I have had papers drawn up renouncing my claim to the Vincente family fortune, returning all funds, property and entitlements to the estate itself."

Lorenzo's jaw dropped, "How do you propose to explain your actions?"

"I incorporated language into those papers that referred to a Prenuptial Agreement between Alex and me," Nikki hinted.

"But such an agreement never existed. You know Alexander would never ... He never meant ..." Lorenzo protested.

"I know. I know," she assured him. Then gently she prodded him. "But if you look around, I think you might be able to find such Agreement lying around *Napoli*."

Amazement stymied Lorenzo, "I ... I ... guess we can. I mean I guess we will."

"Furthermore, from yesterday forward, I will never step foot inside either *Napoli*, *St. Vincente* or *Nevermore* again. If things cool off for Alex and Adam and they need to travel, these will always be available to them. No one will ever know, including my parents, that my extreme grief hasn't kept me at bay. I tried to put all of this in a note to Alex that I left inside the ruby ring in the ring box."

"With both of them dead, none of this is warranted or necessary. Are you sure you really want to do this?"

"Trust me, Lorenzo, I made these decisions freely and with full knowledge of what I was doing. I don't know why Alexander didn't take me with him...or why he didn't include the code sign *Eternity* in his note to me. Maybe he and the baby really are dead. In that case, profiting from their deaths is abhorrent to me. But I don't think they are gone. Alex has given up so much for me. This is the very least I can give in return for his success in his final mission."

Tears trickled from Lorenzo's eyes. "Alex truly found a one of a kind gem when he found you. Since you won't visit *Napoli*, it may be a long time until I see you again."

Nikki nodded.

"May I visit you in the States from time to time? I would hate to lose contact with someone I have come to regard as much more than a mere sister-in-law."

"Of course, I'd really like that. My life would be so empty without you and Zia. I know my parents would like that, too." Tears now flowed between the two of them. Even as they embraced and swore their commitment to a continued relationship, in her heart Nikki knew decades would pass before she'd see him again. As a practical matter, for the welfare of the mission, they couldn't have any contact with each other. Both of them lied to each other—it was easier than saying good-bye.

When Lorenzo walked down the steps—the same steps Alex carried Adam down just two weeks earlier—Nikki knew she lost her final link to Alexander and the world she cherished so dearly. Closing the door, she fell into gut-wrenching sobs. Every corner of that cursed townhouse taunted her with what was, and never would be again. No place offered her refuge from the yawning misery. Awash in heartache and tears, it took hours before she struggled to the surface for a breath. When she did, the letter from the lab with her test results stared back at her.

Nikki's mind carried her back to that fateful morning and her conversation with Gus. She had fully intended to share the news with him back then. Why not now? God knows she needed some strength. Sensitive to her pain, Gus dropped everything to come over. Nikki splashed water on her face, then tidied her hair, trying to hide her festering despondency.

Gus's discomfort showed when Nikki opened the door. Would she break down? Would he know how to comfort her? Setting aside his apprehension with the valor of a true friend, he entered. Nikki's mood drained her of social graces. Sparing them the uneasiness of small talk, directly Nikki handed him the letter. In a gentlemanly fashion he escorted her to the kitchen table where they sat. Using his index finger he sliced through the top of the envelope, leaving saw-tooth edges of paper sticking up unevenly.

Nikki readied herself, for until the words were actually read, they weren't real. But once pronounced, her fate became inescapable.

Gus had no earthly idea of how to break the news. So, he spoke quickly and plainly, "The results are positive."

Nikki knew it! Oh, how she wanted to tell Alex the good news. With that, the cavernous hole in her life opened up all over again. She fought back another deluge of tears. With a trembling lip, she told Gus that babies were happy news, and she refused to cry about the circumstances. But unable to hold back the flood much longer, she excused herself from the rest of the evening. It had taken all her strength to sit up straight and face the news. Nikki didn't have the legs to walk Gus to the door, stare down those steps one more time and say good-bye to someone else.

Dragging her exhausted body upstairs, she thought of their bed with Alex's scent still in the sheets. She wanted to cuddle up to it. But his trailing scent only twisted the red-hot poker of anguish deeper inside of her. Nikki needed to share this news with him. She wanted to nestle up to him and delight in the dream of new life with him again.

The overriding silence of the townhouse pierced her, interrupting her bouts of crying. In those respites, she found herself instinctively listening for her son's breathing. Those simple reflexes of motherhood ripped fresh holes in her heart. Finding herself in the stilled nursery, she gathered his little blanket in her arms. Rocking with it, she filled her nose with his lingering baby sweetness—an empty blanket, an excruciatingly empty heart.

After thrashing about the house for half the night, she finally crashed, falling asleep in the incomplete guest bedroom.

A nagging doorbell brought morning abruptly. Still trying to focus, Nikki staggered to the door, only to find Gus standing there. With a box of fresh pastry and hot coffee, he all but burst through the entry. Nikki knew she looked a fright with puffy red eyes and hair askew. Pulling closed her cotton housecoat, she tried to dismiss him, but Gus cut her off.

"I've got to apologize for my awful behavior last night," he said, sitting her down at the counter, busily unpacking breakfast. "I was so afraid I'd say something wrong and make you sad." He sniffed at his statement, "Can you believe that! Like you weren't in the dumps already. I guess I was really thinking, 'Gee I hope I can skate in and out of there without her making *me* feel uncomfortable.' Imagine that! How insensitive can one stupid guy be? What would it hurt if I saw you cry and maybe shed a few tears myself? After all, Alex was my friend, too!"

By now Gus had Nikki's tea uncapped and a fresh cherry danish on a plate before her. "I haven't been to sleep," he continued. "Can you tell? I've been up torturing myself over leaving you last night. But I've had a revelation, and I'm here to talk about it." Gus took his customary seat across the breakfast counter from her. His presence that morning, like so many mornings before, smacked of sweet familiarity, bringing Nikki comfort and new strength.

Gus didn't broach the main topic of his conversation right away. Nonchalantly he walked around picking up the baby's toys while he diverted her attention with small talk.

Revived enough after breakfast and a healthy dose of conversation, Nikki excused herself to get dressed and take care of the usual morning maintenance. She returned to find the reminders of a horrific day gently put away and Gus with the morning paper spread out on the counter, pouring over the sports section.

"Does the day look a little brighter now?" Gus asked full of hope.

Nikki nodded, "At least I feel human. After last night, that's a tremendous improvement."

"Good. Because if you feel up to it, I have something I'd like to discuss with you. So many things went around in my head last night. As I closed your front door behind me, I looked back at you one last time. There you sat, a resolute soldier on a wooden chair in the kitchen, the blackness of night pouring in the window at your back, the letter with the test results open on the table. Something forced me to focus on the totality of the scene. Its magnitude smacked me squarely between the eyes. I left a distressed woman, alone in the huge townhouse with her dead baby's toys strewn all about her on the floor, the sweater of her beloved Alex still hanging neatly across the back of his chair. The scene dwarfed you, reducing you to a casualty of horrendous circumstances.

"I couldn't purge that scene from my head, or the fact I had walked out on someone so fragile. I wondered how you kept the enormity of it from crushing you — alone, yet living in the company of your dead husband and dead son. How long could you last?

"First, I beat myself up over what a heel I had been, then I examined what I could have done. Your being alone with a baby on the way bothered me. We've been friends for quite awhile. I wanted to help you. I need to help. I decided to get more involved in your life, visit you, make sure you had the things you need, when a conversation I had with Alex two days before his accident knocked me flat. Do you remember the night I came over and brought Adam his Tonka truck?"

"Sure. You brought a date, and we had dinner. What was her name?"

"That doesn't matter," Gus brushed away. "While the two of you were in the kitchen, Alex and I sat shooting the breeze. And this is the part that knocked my socks off. He asked me if anything ever happened to him, would I look after you and the baby."

Nikki's teacup hitting its saucer loudly punctuated Gus's recollection, "What?!"

"I know. Astounding, isn't it? Alex must have had some sort of premonition or something. I can't believe that it took me two weeks to remember that conversation. But then I couldn't get it out of my mind. Of course I promised him I would. All night I thought about the commitment I made to Alex. I'd never let him down in the past. And I wasn't going to welsh on this promise. I started thinking of all the ways I could keep my promise to Alex. Then it all fit. I wanted to get involved and help. I promised to do it. Then my idea came to me."

Gus paused long enough to clear his throat and summon his courage, "I thought ... that we should ... get married."

His proposal hit her broadside. "Excuse me?" Nikki blurted.

"I think we should get married," he re-affirmed. "You really should-n't be alone now with the baby coming and all. The little guy needs a father. I know I could never compare to Alex, but I'd do a good job. You saw how I helped with Adam. The brightest spot in my day was coming over here to see you and the little one. And I promise I'd take really good care of you."

Floundering, she still couldn't believe her ears, "Gus, I'm touched that you want to be involved. But marriage? That's such a big step — for both of us. I ... I ..."

"Don't worry. I don't expect you to love me. You just lost the love of your life. I know you can't fall in love with me after losing someone like Alexander. But I will always treat you with respect and great care. Maybe someday we can both grow into the love part. And I won't push you for the marriage bed deal either. We'll start off with separate bedrooms." Reaching for more ammunition to cinch the deal, Gus rambled.

Nikki threw up her hands, "Hold it! Gus, hold it. I see your point. But I don't know what I want right now. I just spent the worst night of my entire life! I have to get my feet under me, give myself some time. You're a wonderful person. Maybe someday. But right now, I can't make such a life-changing commitment." Her sentences came out disjointed. She didn't want to hurt sweet Gus's feelings, but...

Gus's eyes mirrored rejection as he listened, without saying a word.

Feeling compelled to justify herself, Nikki kept on, "You don't want to rush into this just because you feel sorry for me. I'm not some stray on the street, you take into your house, feed and give a warm bed. You are volunteering to live with someone who's far from perfect. And in about eight months another little person will come along who will demand far more attention than a new truck and a cookie. It won't just be a couple mornings during the week. We'd be a full-time package, twenty-four hours a day. You've never done the marriage bit before. Don't cut yourself short in life. You deserve to find a woman you're crazy in love with, and she with you — just like Alex and me. You deserve that kind of love. When Alex asked you to take care of us, I'm sure he never envisioned you marrying me. I'm sure he only expected you to look in on us every now and then like you did previously with Adam and me." Liking her argu-ment, Nikki paused to see how Gus reacted to it.

Gus waited for her to finish, "It's okay, Nikki. I understand your hesitation. But my offer wasn't out of pity — well maybe in the beginning.

But I've really grown with my decision. Believe me, I understand the commitment marriage requires. Why do you think I'm thirty-three and still single? Over the course of last night and this morning I've given this a lot of thought. I can see us growing old together."

With a glance at his watch, Gus changed gears, "I've got some running to do this morning. I have concrete guys waiting on a job in Bethesda for a truck of mud. Let me run take care of business. How about we talk over dinner this evening? Six okay?"

Gus left Nikki little choice but to take him up on his offer of further discussion and dinner. Immediately her mind set to work on developing an argument to squelch his idea of marriage. With pencil and paper she worked on logical lists of pro and con. She created the "pro" side to throw him a bone and let him down easily. With vigor, Nikki concentrated on the "con" side.

Gus's proposal forced Nikki to focus on her future—her survival, the future of the coming arrival. She didn't want to have to think about those things. She wasn't ready to think about them—getting through life in the interminable hours ahead hammered her. Just breathing required work.

Throughout the morning, she labored over her arguments against marriage, taking a break from time to time to look about in thought, gathering insight. Again Nikki noticed how much easier she breathed without the obvious reminders of that awful morning calling out to her. How thoughtful of Gus to recognize those and temporarily set them aside. Again, pain and guilt smothered her. "Am I setting aside Adam by setting aside his toys? Adam, where are you? How can I put you away? What right do I have to feel better when you should be here? Why should I feel better when I'll never hear your footsteps or your sweet little voice..." Her guilt fed her sequence of sorrow. Her heart dragged her heavy head down. She collapsed on the desk, awash in anguish.

Eventually, something Gus mentioned tugged at her attention. Alex had asked him to watch out for her and *the baby.* "The baby." "The baby." Through her grief the phrase repeated. He could have been talking about Adam. Gus supposed he was referring to Adam. But instinct told Nikki that Alex actually meant the baby on the way. Thinking back on that day, she recalled how she expected they'd have dinner with Bradley that evening. Instead Alex had her invite Gus. Evidently at that juncture, Alex had already planned out his conversation with Gus. And if he had planned his talk with Gus, then he already knew exactly all the details of his disappearance including the fact that Adam would be going too. So the baby he referred to in his conversation and in his letter was the little one on the way. Alex knew Nikki was carrying his child! Alex knew!

Pieces of the puzzle tumbled into place. Now she understood why there was no call to *Eternity*. He couldn't cart her off to a deserted island while she was pregnant. He wouldn't risk endangering the new baby's life and hers in childbirth without care or facilities on the island. The next cavalier must have been at hand, and there was no time to make other preparations. Alex must have carefully set up the entire episode. Was this proof that Alex and Adam still lived?

Nikki's mind wandered back to Alex asking Gus to look after them. Maybe Alex really meant for Gus to marry her. Knowing this was all coming down, she knew he had given the situation an inordinate amount of thought. Alex would never have casually asked someone—anyone—to care for her unless he deemed them to be the best possible available. And she knew Alex could arrange for *anything*. If he believed there was someone better suited for the task, then they would have magically appeared on Nikki's doorstep to see her through. No, Alex picked Gus to care for them. They had been friends in the Agency, well before Alex contracted with Gus for construction work. Alex trusted Gus. Tearing up her lists, Nikki decided she'd be bound by her husband's choice.

Briefly, Nikki's human side rebutted her decision. She didn't love Gus. She couldn't imagine being sexual with anyone other than Alex. Nikki wondered how Alex could give her away to someone else, knowing that eventually she would have to share a marriage bed with him. How could he do that?! Was that the "torture of unspeakable magnitude"?

Impossibly cornered with the lives of his wife and now two children in the balance, Alex had surrendered Nikki in the name of life for all. Oh dear God!

Chapter 42
Another Chance?

Gus returned that evening with a bouquet of sweetheart roses. More charming than she had known him before, clearly with each passing moment, he had grown into the idea. Nikki recognized his behavior as courting. He no longer viewed her as a friend, or an obligation, but his future mate to be accorded all the refined attention such a state included. The epiphany, from just twenty-fours earlier, astounded her.

Prepared to convince Nikki of the merits of his proposal, a relieved Gus listened as she revealed her conclusion to him. "I feel badly about the circumstances surrounding my decision," Nikki started their dinner discussion. "Normally after accepting a marriage proposal, we should kiss. But I can't. Only two weeks ago I buried my love. Even though I believe I'm following his wishes, and we will marry, I can't turn him off and turn you on. The idea of romantically kissing another man at this time is offensive to me. Gus, you deserve so much more than I can give you right now. I know you said we could start out in separate bedrooms. I can't promise you when we will actually move in together as husband and wife. This arrangement will take a lot of patience, understanding and time. Are you sure you want to begin a marriage traveling with so much baggage?"

"Nikki, please understand, parts of this still seem wrong to me too — like being intimate. For ten years, Alex has been my friend. I would never put the moves on a friend's widow, especially so soon after his death. I'd never have come up with this idea if Alex hadn't asked me to look after you. Romantically, you're right, marriage at this time stinks, but it makes practical sense. You shouldn't be alone with the baby coming."

Both played with their food while considering their commitment to Alex.

"Alex's request is what sealed my decision. I actually prepared lists for my argument against your proposal. But when I thought about how Alex accomplished things he deemed important, especially in regards to my life, I knew I had to do this."

The dual-edged sword of awkwardness periodically intruded on their conversation: while silence sharpened it, laughter usually dulled its uncomfortable edge. Agreeing to set the date sooner rather than later, they picked the next available Saturday, which by coincidence fell on July

4th. The week gave Nikki the chance to make a few meager arrangements—like breaking the news to their families and planning a quiet, simple affair, with the guest list limited to the immediate family and some of Nikki and Gus's closest friends. They decided to leave first thing in the morning to head back to Pennsylvania.

Bright and early, Gus appeared on her doorstep. Under the daze of her catastrophic loss and the heavy burden of their huge news, Nikki climbed into Gus's reliable Chevy pickup.

Both Fran and Richard remembered Gus from his work at *Nevermore*. Sitting her parents down, Nikki took the "good news—bad news" approach in unveiling their startling announcement. First, she confirmed her pregnancy. The baby would be born mid-January, and Nikki would be moving out of the townhouse. On the heels of her joyous news, she sprang on them her intention to marry Gus.

Shock dissolved their smiles as they collectively objected. "We don't understand. What about Alex? How can you?"

For the better part of the afternoon, Gus and Nikki answered her parents' questions, reassuring them and coincidentally beginning to forge a bond. Eventually, Richard recognized Alex's intent to endow his Nicole with continuity of sustenance for body and soul. As a provider, he understood the inherent wisdom of their plans.

Fran, though, wasn't ready to put Alex away. The absence of love bothered her. Privately, Nikki shared with her mother all her misgivings of disloyalty and fears of intimacy. Walking her mother through Alexander's particular proclivity of providing for her down to the last detail, Fran finally accepted the practical reality of the plan deigned by Alexander himself.

Since Gus was an only child, they only had to break the news to his mom and dad. Unfortunately, his parents had never met Nikki, so in his course of introduction Gus also had to explain the surrounding circumstances. Stunned, they listened as their only son announced to them his plans to marry to a newly-widowed woman, who was carrying another man's child. Surely they wished their son had found someone else—anyone else. Graciously, however, they welcomed Nikki to their family, even as they also doled out their condolences over her recent loss.

Next, Nikki phoned her ever-faithful musketeers: Bruce, Karl and Mary. Stifling her surprise, Mary reassured Nikki. "I haven't missed one of your weddings yet. And sure as heck, I will be at this one, when you may need me the most."

The night before the ceremony, sequestered in her bedroom at *Creekside*, Nikki called Mary to join her. Crying her eyes out, desperately she wailed over how much she missed Alex and Adam! Over and over again she scolded herself that Gus deserved better than a weepy woman condemned to a marriage of convenience.

Common sense berated her with the deaths of her beloved and their son. Marrying Gus would fulfill the deathbed plans Alex seemingly had made for her. But she couldn't shake the dreadful feeling she was cheating on Alex. What if they were alive? After the baby was born, would Alex then summon her to *Eternity*? Nikki wanted a sign telling her whether Alex really intended her to marry Gus or was her call to *Eternity* coming? Something subtle—really anything would do.

"Gardenias," she announced aloud, "would be the perfect sign."

Alex always used gardenias to announce his arrival. An arrangement of gardenias would confirm her suspicions—Alex and Adam were alive—and that *he* would return for her.

Knowing Nikki to be devout in her Christian belief, Mary assumed in Nikki's verbalization she had issued a challenge to God. Not knowing about their communicators, Mary never dreamed Nikki's message was actually a plea to Alex, himself, just in case he still had his communicator switched on...in case he could hear her...and above all, in case he was alive.

Emotionally spent, Nikki softly sobbed into her pillow, "Do you really want me to do this? Do you really want me to abandon the hope of you and our family in *Eternity*? Are you coming back or will it be—nevermore?"

Acknowledgments

Thank you to Rita Cobain Brown—the toughest editor and best friend a book ever had. Without her focus, this book would not have been possible. My friend always.

To Jerry Lee Rothermel whose love and confidence in my abilities saw me through the tough times, I thank you for backing me in all those important ways.

Thank you also to the many who have had profound influence:

My mother and father, Mary and Richard Rairigh, for their wisdom, leadership and guidance;

My daughters, Kristina, Victoria, Jacki and Jodi, for their support;

My family, David Rairigh, Donald & Laura Rairigh, Richard & Bobbie Rairigh, and Anthony Hood, for their interest;

Dr. Herbert Robinson, who helped me refine my writing ability with the valuable editing experience of his two books;

My teachers, Fay Gridley, June McKnight, Michael Rasmussen and Robert Arner,

fer larning me good;

My test readers whose lush praise and earnest criticism motivated me—Kristina Bulmahn, Sharon Yourk, Brenda Joshlin, Lynnette Good, Pam Bates, Ramona Yoder, Kathy Shumski, Paul Kadavy, and Fay Gridley. Your belief in me and in *Nevermore?* carried me when doubts would have spelled defeat;

My friend and best wielder of a red pen ever, Lynnette Good;

Jamie Saloff of Saloff Enterprises, who was instrumental throughout the entire book birthing process;

Tom Bird and his "Get Published Now" seminars for helping me navigate through the publishing world maze;

My Italian expert Lorenzo Giuliani;

PIO Chris Vassall and Chief Rodbell at the Scottsdale Police Department for their professional help through their excellent Citizen's Academy;

The design artists at CatHouse Productions, R.C. Brown and Peter

Brown, for employing their many diverse talents to produce the great cover and the all the additional graphics needed;

My web gurus, Ian and Lela McFarland, for creating my vision for my web site www.TammieRothermel.com and www.Nevermore.BZ ;

My friends Earlene "Cookie" Smith, Linda Standridge, Judy Yoder, and Annie and Lee Ann wherever you may be;

And to John for inspiring me.

Printed in the United States
49511LVS00004B/64-204